She had been madly in love with him for years, although it had been some time until she could admit to herself that her interest in him was more complex than guilt over his imprisonment. Now, as Princess Sylvia waited on the dock at Gaeta for the prison boat, she told herself she must treat Franco carefully. She was still beautiful and, as the widow of the Prince dell'Acqua, one of the richest women in Italy. That she was in love with a former convict she had not even touched for twelve years struck her as wildly improbable, but the fact remained that she was.

The first thing he did after getting off the boat was to kneel down and kiss the dock. The next thing was to come up to her. He was wearing the same cheap suit he had worn twelve years before at his trial, except now it was too big for him. They looked at each other. Then he said, simply, 'Grazie.'

'You owe me no thanks,' she said. 'I owe you twelve years ...'

Also by Fred Mustard Stewart
THE MEPHISTO WALTZ
THE METHUSELAH ENZYME
STAR CHILD
SIX WEEKS
and published by Corgi Books

Fred Mustard Stewart

Century

CORGI BOOKS
A DIVISION OF TRANSWORLD PUBLISHERS LTD

CENTURY
A CORGI BOOK 0 552 12060 X

Originally published in Great Britain by
Hamish Hamilton Ltd.

PRINTING HISTORY
Hamish Hamilton edition published 1981
Corgi edition published 1982
Corgi edition re-issued 1982

Corgi Books are published by
Transworld Publishers Ltd,
Century House, 61–63 Uxbridge Road,
Ealing, London W5 5SA
Printed and bound in Great Britain by
Cox & Wyman Ltd, Reading

"The Italians have a big appetite,
 but such poor teeth."

> —OTTO VON BISMARCK

"Cu e surdu, orbu e taci
 campa cen'anni 'impaci."

("He who is deaf, blind and silent
 lives a hundred years in peace.")

> —Sicilian proverb

"On or about December, 1910,
 human nature changed."

> —VIRGINIA WOOLF

"Che lascia la via vecchia per la nuova,
 so quel che perde e non sa quel che trova."

("Whoever forsakes the old way for the new
 knows what he is losing, but not
 what he will find.")

> —Italian proverb

INTRODUCTION

The seven-year-old girl had no idea why she was being summoned to the office of the Mother Superior. Princess Sylvia Maria Pia Angelica Toscanelli was known in the convent as a troublemaker—when she wasn't falling asleep at Vespers or drawing hilarious cartoon sketches of the nuns, she was stealing cookies from the kitchen—but for the past few days she had been surprisingly good and attentive. There was a reason for her good behavior: It was the end of June and in less than a week her father would be coming to St. Ursula's to take her home for the summer recess, and Sylvia didn't want a bad report from Mother Umbertina to cast a shadow on her long-awaited holiday. Thus, when Sister Giovanna had removed her from geography class to take her to Mother Umbertina's office, Sylvia wracked her brain trying to think what the summons could mean.

St. Ursula's had been founded and endowed by the Medici in the sixteenth century. It was situated in the hills south of Florence, and its lovely buildings and beautiful gardens had come to be a second home to Sylvia since her father had sent her there the previous year, 1858. The nuns were, for the most part, kind. And although the convent was strict, Sylvia and the other girls found ample opportunity for fun and mischief. The girls were from the most distinguished families of Florence, but few of them had a better pedigree than Sylvia, whoses family could trace its origins to the eleventh century and included a pope and a score of cardinals. All the Toscanellis lacked was money, but in the Florence of the day, money was considered rather suspect —something for the *borghesi*, or middle class. Certainly Sylvia never thought about it. Life at the Palazzo Toscanelli on the via di San Gallo or at the summer villa in the beautiful hills near Fiesole, northeast of Florence, was comfortable, if not luxurious. The Toscanellis might have been strapped for cash, but somehow there were plenty of servants and food and wine and fresh fruit. Prince Filiberto, Sylvia's father, might have only one carriage—and that with frayed upholstery—but he was still the best-dressed man in Florence, and his general's uniform was, many said, the best-cut uniform in the army of the Piedmont king, Victor Emmanuel II.

Besides pedigree, the Toscanellis had something else money can't buy: looks. Prince Filiberto was the very *beau idéal* of an officer—tall and dashing—and his wife, Princess Caroline, had been one of the great beauties of Milan. Sylvia only dimly remembered her mother, who had been killed in a railroad accident when she was only five. But she had studied the portraits in the palazzo and marveled at her mother's fair hair and blue eyes. Sylvia had inherited her father's dark hair and green eyes, but she was already at seven such a beauty that some of the sisters worried for her immortal soul: Such good looks could only mean trouble. But they consoled themselves with the thought that, despite her mischief-making and occasional displays of temper, Sylvia seemed to have a good disposition in general. She was also highly intelligent, and few doubted that one day she would make a brilliant marriage.

When Sister Giovanna showed her into Mother Umbertina's spartan office, Sylvia was surprised to see her aunt Mathilda. Fat 'Aunt' Mathilda was really a cousin, but after Princess Caroline's death, Prince Filiberto had brought his spinster relative into the household to run things and 'look after' Sylvia.

'Aunt Mathilda!' exclaimed Sylvia, wondering why she was wearing a black veil.

'Sylvia, dear child.'

Sylvia ran into her arms to be hugged and kissed. Aunt Mathilda usually smelled of good things—cologne water or verbena—but right now she smelled of brandy. And she was crying.

'What is it? What's wrong?'

'My darling, there was a battle—two days ago, on the twenty-fourth, at Solferino. It was a great victory for us and the French, but there were many wounded . . . terrible casualties . . .'

Sylvia was vaguely aware of Mother Umbertina coming around her desk and taking her hand.

'Your father, dear child,' said the Mother Superior. 'He was a great hero. When Italy is finally united into one nation, your father will be remembered as a martyr to the motherland.'

It took a few moments for it to sink into her young mind. She was aware that the emperor of the French, Louis Napoleon, was

8

helping the King of Sardinia in his attempt to oust the Austrians from northern Italy. It was all part of something her father had been keenly enthusiastic about: the drive to unite the various kingdoms, duchies and papal territories of the boot of Italy into a single modern nation.

But her beloved, wonderful, handsome, impecunious father . . . dead?

She was so stunned, she didn't cry. She stared at her Aunt Mathilda, then at Mother Umbertina. Then she whispered, 'You're lying.'

It was the first—and one of the few—times in her long life that Princess Sylvia Toscanelli refused to face the truth.

'Massa give Ole Jeb fifty dollah Federal,' said the ragged slave with the frizzy white beard, 'an' Ole Jeb show him de buried treasure.'

Private Augustus Dexter of the Third New York Volunteers thought the ancient darky must be simple-minded or drunk. Or both.

'What buried treasure?' he said, lighting the cigar he had found in the desk drawer in the library of the gutted plantation house outside Savannah. It was December 23, 1864, and General Sherman's troops, after devastating Georgia, had 'marched to the sea,' taking Savannah two days previously. Gus Dexter, a stockily built son of a schoolteacher from Elmira, New York, had been made a courier by dint of his expert horsemanship. He was returning to Savannah from Atlanta, where he had been sent with some confidential papers from General Sherman himself. Being tired and in no great hurry to return to Savannah before morning, he had decided to spend the night on the porch of the burned plantation house. Burned plantations were a common enough sight in those days, and Gus, like many other Yankee soldiers, wasn't averse to a little looting. It was surprising what you could find, although so far this place had yielded nothing but the stale Havana. Still, buried treasure? The old darky must be crazy. Gus put his hand on his holster. You never knew with these slaves.

'Dey's a diamond necklace an' two ruby earbobs an' a diamond pin big as a hen's egg,' said Ole Jeb. 'Miz Annabel done buried 'em in de garden in a crockery jar last month, jes before she an' de Massa went down to Florida. She didn't think no one seen her, but Ole Jeb don't sleep so good, an' Ah heard her spade hit a rock. Clang! Like dat. An' Ah peek out de window an' see her.' The old man crackled, reinforcing Gus's conviction he was a loony. Might as well jolly him along, he thought. Nothing else to do.

'I suppose Miss Annabel buried her jewels because she was afraid of us Yankees?' he said.

'Oh, she feared of more dan you Yankees! She feared of banks and Injuns in Florida and robbers . . . She de *fraidest* lady in all Georgia!'

'Uh huh. So you saw her bury the jar in the garden. How do you know what's in it?'

The old man looked surprised.

'I dug it up to peek!' he said, as if the answer were obvious. 'After dey go.'

'You dug it up to peek,' repeated Gus. 'All right, then why don't *you* take this fabulous buried treasure? Why sell it to me for fifty dollars? Or are they paste?'

'What dat?'

'Paste. Fake.'

'Oh no, dey's genuine! Yessuh! Miz Annabel's got some de finest jools in Georgia. She famous for her jools.'

'Then I repeat, why don't *you* take them?'

The slave looked astounded.

'*Me?* Ah take dem jools, when Massa come home he find out 'bout it an' give Ole Jeb de whupping of his life. No, suh. Wouldn't *touch* dat jar. 'Sides, what would Ole Jeb do wif jools? *Wear* 'em? Couldn't sell 'em. Dey puts me in de jailhouse for sure. Lock me up an' trow 'way de key. But you? Nothin' stoppin' a Yankee from takin' 'em. Everybody knows Yankees is teeves.'

Gus Dexter grinned.

'Glad to hear we have such an excellent reputation. Well, I tell you, Jeb: I think you're a lying rascal, but you've got a good imagination.'

'Not makin' it up! No suh! Ah *prove* it to you. You wait here. Ole Jeb be back in ten minute.'

And he hobbled off the porch to head around the house. It was getting dark. Gus went inside the house, found two candles and brought them out, lighting them. Then he sat down on the steps to watch the moon rise. Jewels. Buried treasure. What a laugh. Still, you never know. Stranger things could happen in this crazy war.

Gus Dexter was a literal-minded man without much sense of humor or fantasy, but he was human enough to toy with the thought of finding a buried treasure. What would he do with it? he mused. Well, he sure as hell wouldn't take it back to Elmira.

10

Oh no. He'd had enough of that hick town. Take it to New York, he would. Sell it and set himself up in a fine business. Stockbroker, maybe—he loved reading about the crooks making and losing fortunes on Wall Street. Or perhaps a bank. Yes, a bank. All that money . . . Gus Dexter loved the feel, the smell, the idea of money. Yes, maybe a bank. Small at first, of course, but it could grow . . .

'Here! Look. See? Ole Jeb don't lie.'

Gus jumped at the sound of the darky's voice. The old idiot had crept up on him. Now he was holding out his hand.

'Look! It's de pin Ah tol' you 'bout.'

Gus took the piece of jewelry from the gnarled black hand and held it up before the candlelight. His eyes widened. The schoolteacher's son from Elmira had had little opportunity to see diamonds, but even his untutored eye could tell the big, clear stone was at least ten carats.

'Didn't believe me, did you?' Ole Jeb was cackling. 'De whole jar's yours for fifty dollah Federal. Den Ole Jeb gwine into town an' buy hisself a fine meal an' a piece of poontang.'

Gus Dexter was too smart to fight destiny when it had showered him with luck. He only had thirty dollars, but he gave them to the slave along with the gold watch his father had given him when he was drafted into the Army. Then he followed Jeb around the house to the garden.

In his excitement it never occurred to Gus Dexter that he was, in fact, a thief.

PART I

FRANCO AND VITTORIO

1880

CHAPTER 1

Alice Fairchild Dexter stood at a window of her bedroom in the Villa dell'Acqua and watched the huge orange moon rise over the hills of Monreale. There was magic in that moon, or at least Alice's vivid imagination liked to think there was magic. Did its orange tint suggest the bloody history of Sicily, the two-thousand-year record of successive conquerors—Greeks, Romans, Arabs, Normans, Spaniards and, just twenty years before, Garibaldi and his famous Thousand Red Shirts—who had drenched the Sicilian earth with blood? Or was the orange tint merely a local phenomenon of the atmosphere? Alice preferred the former interpretation—it was much more romantic—and certainly there was romance in the beauty of the scene below her. The formal gardens of the villa, its tall cypresses elegant silhouettes against the moon, its baroque statues pale figures set amid pools and fountains. The villa itself was magnificent, having been built in the 1790s by the present Prince dell'Acqua's great-grandfather. For a New Yorker like Alice, the setting was wonderfully exotic, particularly against the background of violent Sicilian history. The violence to Alice was, of course, all in history books: she had only recently heard the word 'Mafia,' and to her it conjured up visions of operatic brigands. It was all very exciting. But there were no brigands in the gardens of the Villa dell'Acqua, and for the hundredth time she thanked her lucky stars for having met the Princess dell'Acqua the previous month in Paris.

The two women had much in common, despite the vast difference in their background. Both were young: Alice twenty-six, Princess dell'Acqua—the former Princess Sylvia Toscanelli —twenty-eight. Both were married to older men: Augustus Dexter was forty-one, while Prince Giancarlo dell'Acqua was well into his fifties, Sylvia being his second wife. Both were attractive. Alice was a charming blonde who had married

15

Augustus—no one had called him Gus for years—six years before. Princess Sylvia had blossomed into a willowy beauty whose looks and magnificent jewels and clothes were famous throughout Europe. Both desperately wanted children, but whereas Alice would never bear a child because of physiological difficulties, the Princess had failed to conceive apparently only because of bad luck. Both had active minds with similar interests in art, fashion and travel. They had met at a dinner party in Paris and hit it off immediately. The Dexters were on a combination business and pleasure trip to the Continent, though to Augustus it was mostly business—banking—while to his young wife it was mostly pleasure. The Princess was on her way to Sicily from St. Petersburg, where her husband represented the new Italian king, Umberto I, at the court of Tsar Alexander II.

They had lunched together the next day while Augustus talked to Paris bankers. They had shopped together, gone to the Louvre together, perused the bookstalls along the Seine . . . within three days they had become inseparable. Was it because they were both basically lonely? Alice had wondered. Whatever the reason, the American had been delighted when Sylvia invited her to spend a month at her husband's villa outside Palermo. Alice had long been interested in Sicily and had always wanted to see it. Besides, the promise of spending the heart of the winter in a balmy Mediterranean climate rather than returning to snowbound Madison Avenue held obvious attractions. Not unexpectedly, Augustus gave his ready consent. Augustus could hardly wait to return to Wall Street. Besides, the company of his young wife was always something of a strain to him: Alice knew he wouldn't object to a month of bachelor freedom eating at his club, droning endlessly with his friends about interest rates and the bond market. Thus, two weeks before, Augustus had left on the boat train for Le Havre, and Alice and Sylvia had taken the train to Nice, where they boarded the Prince dell'Acqua's yacht for a leisurely, if windy, sail to Palermo. That afternoon they had been driven in one of the Prince's carriages up to the hill town of Monreale, then a few kilometers beyond to the Villa dell'Acqua in the tiny village of San Sebastiano. They arrived at the villa shortly after four. Alice had been conducted to a guest suite by the portly butler, Cesare. She had bathed and napped, and now had just finished dressing for dinner. So far, her impressions of the villa and Sicily were more than favorable.

There was a knock on the door. Alice turned away from the tall window with its exquisite lace curtains and said, in Italian, 'Come in.'

16

The door opened, and the most beautiful child she had ever seen entered.

Was he a child? No, a youth, perhaps twelve or thirteen, tall for his age. He was dressed in the blue-and-green livery of the villa, in which he looked rather uncomfortable, Alice thought. Though he had dark curly hair, his skin was fair, unlike many of the olive-skinned Sicilians who, particularly in the west of the island, had Saracen blood in their veins. His face was the face of an angel: rather thin, with delicate features and enormous brown eyes that looked a bit frightened.

'The Princess,' he said, hesitantly, 'says the guests are arriving.'

Alice had an ear for languages and spoke excellent French and Italian. But this boy's Italian was so heavily accented by the Sicilian dialect, she had trouble understanding him. She came across the spacious room toward him: He looked ready to bolt. She smiled at him, and he relaxed a little.

'What's your name?' she asked.

'Vittorio.' It came out 'Vitturiu,' since Sicilians replaced the Italian o's with u's.

He was staring at her with those big eyes, and Alice found herself entranced.

'You are a very handsome young man, Vittorio.'

He said nothing, continuing to stare. She laughed.

'I'll bet you've never met an American before, have you?'

'No, Signora.'

'Well, what do you think?'

'I . . . I think the Signora is very beautiful.' He gulped.

'Thank you, Vittorio! I can see you have that famous Sicilian gallantry. Now, will you take me downstairs?'

'Yes, Signora.'

He looked almost relieved at being released from the conversation, which amused Alice further. There was something irresistible about him. Good heavens, she thought, what a lady-killer he'll be in a few years! He held the door as she left the room and went out into the upstairs hall. Her room was opposite the marble stair that led down to the entrance hall, and dozens of candles illuminated the enormous space designed with baroque theatricality by the architect Forzini. On the ceiling high above, a pupil of Tiepolo had painted a florid allegory representing the apotheosis of one of the Prince's ancestors who had bribed his way to the papacy: Dozens of plump *putti* gamboled in swirling clouds as angels elevated the Pope—who looked, in Alice's opinion, capable of murder—to a starry firmament. It was second-rate art, Alice knew; but in the candlelight, with the imposing dimensions of the stair and the hall below, it was nonetheless effective. The Italians were excellent at stage setting.

'The Princess tells me,' said Alice as she followed the page down the stairs, 'that we are being honored at dinner by the Archbishop of Palermo?' Alice knew that Europeans frowned on making conversation with servants, but with all her love of continental pomp and display, she was very much an American. She would talk with whomever she pleased.

'Yes, Signora. Cardinal dell'Acqua.'

'And he is the younger brother of the Prince?'

Vittorio looked blank, as if thinking about this.

'Yes, I think so,' he finally said.

'And you, Vittorio: do you live in San Sebastiano?'

'I live here, in the servants' quarters, with my brother.'

'And what does your brother do?'

'He's a gardener, Signora.'

'And your parents?'

They were almost at the bottom of the stairs. Now Vittorio looked at her.

'They are dead, Signora.'

She felt embarrassed at asking the question and, at the same time, a pang of pity for this angelic child. No, not a child: a young man. But yes, a child, too.

'I'm sorry, Vittorio,' she said, softly.

Cesare, the butler, came up and bowed.

'The Princess is in the grand salon,' he said, shooting Vittorio a cold look. It occurred to Alice she might have gotten the page in trouble by talking to him, so she smiled at Cesare.

'Thank you, Cesare. And may I compliment you on this young man? You have trained him beautifully.'

The butler's fat face melted into a buttery smile, and he led the pretty young American in the yellow silk dress across the hall to the tall doors of the grand salon. Opening them, he announced, 'La Signora Dexter,' and Alice walked into a room that Mrs. Astor or Mrs. Vanderbilt would have paid a fortune to install in one of the Italianate mansions that were beginning their inexorable crawl up Fifth Avenue. Except this room was no import—or at least it had been imported only from nearby Naples, the home of the architect. Its swirling gilt walls and heavy chandeliers seemed not excessive but, somehow, right. Candlelight from the half-dozen torchères between the tall windows reflected on gleaming parquet. Princess Sylvia stood up and came to embrace her American house-guest.

'My dear, how beautiful you look!' she exclaimed, but Alice thought, with a twinge of envy, that her friend looked more beautiful. The Princess was almost five feet ten, slim, with translucent skin and green eyes the Roman gossip columnist-poet, Gabriele D'Annunzio, had floridly described as 'limpid pools of mystery and intelligence.' Her dark-brown hair had been piled in a crown of curls on top of her head, the front half of which was corraled by a delicate diamond tiara. She wore a smoky-rose dinner gown she had bought in Paris. Monsieur Worth's décolletage would shock no one in France, but in more conservative Sicily it might raise eyebrows. However, its daringness had been somewhat subdued by a swirl of tulle secured to her left shoulder by a diamond star. The Princess looked shimmering and radiant.

She kissed Alice, then led her to the tall, macaroni-thin man in the red moiré soutane who had risen from his gilt armchair.

'Alcide,' said the Princess, 'may I present my dear friend from New York, Mrs. Dexter? Alice, His Eminence, Alcide, Cardinal dell'Acqua.'

The cold brown eyes of the Prince of the Church took in the American. Cardinal dell'Acqua was, Alice judged, in his mid-forties, but his skull-like face could have belonged to a man twenty years older. Alice thought the Cardinal must have been born middle-aged. She looked at the ruby ring on his extended hand, then said, 'Your Eminence, since I'm an Episcopalian, I'm not quite sure how I should greet you.'

The Cardinal smiled a cool smile.

'Would it not perhaps ease the torments of the soul of Martin Luther if one of his followers kissed the ring of a Prince of the Church?'

Alice didn't like this, nor did she like this chilly aristocrat. But when in Rome . . . Wondering what Reverend Compton would think if he saw his parishioner giving in to Papist ritual, she knelt and kissed the ruby ring.

The man on the terrace watched through the window, his young face a mask. He was standing in the shadows, but the tall windows afforded him an excellent view. He watched as the Princess introduced the American woman to the fat Mayor of Palermo, Count Sclafani, and his fatter wife. He watched as the Princess led the party into the adjacent dining room. Then, moving down the long terrace with its stone balustrade, he took up a new position to watch the party being seated at the table. He had seen this dining room many times: its tall walls lined with green silk and hung with gold-framed portraits of members of the dell'Acqua family, who stared down at the party with varying degrees of beauty and intelligence. The heavily carved mantel of Carrara marble. The high-backed chairs, behind each of which stood a footman. The long buffet groaning with silver. The gleaming table with its two magnificent candelabra, their tall tapers shielded by graceful shades. If the young man had had any schooling, he would have regarded this scene as an almost pluperfect symbol of the feudal class that had oppressed his family for centuries. But Franco Spada had never heard of Marx or Engels, nor did he regard the Princess dell'Acqua as an oppressor. To the nineteen-year-old gardener, the Princess was a key to the prison of his life.

For the moment he was content merely to watch.

'And how did my brother take your refusal to spend another winter in St. Petersburg?' asked the Cardinal, who was sitting at the right of the Princess.

'Giancarlo suggested I leave,' replied Sylvia. 'I was so sick last winter . . . You can't imagine how terrible St. Petersburg is in the winter! The sun doesn't come up till almost ten, and the cold and the snow . . . it's torture. Poor Giancarlo. What a martyr he is to take that wretched post. But the King has promised him Paris next. Needless to say, Paris should be an improvement.'

'But the Tsar's entertainments are spectacular, aren't they?' asked Count Sclafani, who was seated at the Princess's left and was eyeing the turtle soup with disappointment. The Princess preferred French cuisine, and the Mayor of Palermo missed his beloved pasta.

'Yes, of course. The Tsar's the richest man in the world—his entertainments *should* be spectacular. And the Zeemnee Dvoretz —the Winter Palace—is one of the sights of the world. But St. Petersburg is so tense . . .'

'Because of the Nihilists?' interrupted Alice, who sat next to Count Sclafani.

'Yes. The Tsar lives in constant terror, and terror can be contagious. All of St. Petersburg is waiting for something to happen, but no one's quite sure what it will be.'

'I understand,' said Countess Sclafani, who wore a black plume in her hair that was echoed by her faint moustache, 'that the Tsar has a mistress.' She looked disapproving, though her eyes sparkled with curiosity.

'A mistress?' laughed Sylvia. 'She's practically his wife! Princess Dolgoruky's the most powerful woman in Russia.'

'Shocking.' The Countess's lips pursed. 'How can one expect the morals of the lower classes to improve when the rulers of the world behave so sordidly?'

'Perhaps,' said His Eminence, sipping the Dom Perignon the Princess adored, 'no one should expect the morals of the lower class to improve.'

The cynicism of the remark grated on Alice.

'In America,' she said, 'our working people have excellent morals.'

'*All* of them?'

'Perhaps not all, but the vast majority are decent, God-fearing and hard-working.'

'My dear Mrs. Dexter,' said His Eminence, touching his coronet-embroidered linen napkin to his thin lips, 'America leads the world in productivity. I am sure that—given time —America will lead the world in decadence as well.'

Franco Spada had seen enough. Now he left the terrace and walked through the moonlit garden. He had made up his mind.

Tomorrow, he would do it.

Padre Nardo—or Don Giammaria as he was known to the villagers—was the parish priest of San Sebastiano. His church was small, a whitewashed stucco edifice that had been rebuilt on its Norman foundations after an earthquake in the seventeenth century. But there was no need for a large church in San Sebastiano. Not only was the town tiny, but it was close to the imposing twelfth-century cathedral in Monreale, the gorgeous cathedral with its famous mosaics, Byzantine interior and Norman exterior. Monreale was the seat of a bishop almost as powerful as the Archbishop of Palermo. Monreale was not much of a town, though there was a Sicilian saying—*Cu va a Palermu e 'un viri Muriali, si vinni sceccu sinni torna argnali*—which roughly translates as 'he who goes to Palermo and doesn't see Monreal is an ass.' Still, small or no, Monreale was a Goliath compared with the David of San Sebastiano. So Don Giammaria's church was small.

Nevertheless, every town had to have its church, and Don Giammaria in his fifteen years as priest had faithfully kept the records of the town, the births, confirmations, marriages and deaths that were the only local history. Don Giammaria was respected, even though everyone in the town knew he was overly fond of wine and often could barely make it through Mass. Not the rich, red-brown Marsala wine, which he found too sweet, but the dry, greenish-yellow Alcamo wine that came from the hills behind Trapani. Don Giammaria loved his Alcamo, and his broad belly and double-chinned face bore testimony to his affair with the grape.

On this late January evening, he was sitting in front of the fire sipping his Alcamo and trying to focus his fuzzy attention on a week-old newspaper from Naples when he heard a knock at the door. He looked at the ornate clock on the mantel which had been a gift from the Bishop of Monreale on his fortieth birthday. Eleven-thirty. San Sebastiano consisted of one street and a piazza, and the villagers went to bed early to conserve candles and kerosene: who could be out this late? Don Giammaria shoved himself out of his chair with difficulty, placed his glass and the wine decanter out of sight behind a fat Bible, then aimed for the wooden door of the parish house.

A strong winter wind had sprung up: the southwest *libeccio scirocco* that sometimes blew a fine, high haze of sand from Africa, which created the orange moon Alice Dexter had noticed earlier in the evening. Now, as Don Giammaria opened his door, he braced himself against the wind that swept in, flapping his soutane. When the priest saw who was standing outside, he thought it must be an ill wind.

'Father, may I see you a moment?' said the young man in the cheap boots, the battered brown pants, the gray shirt under the leather vest. Yes, he's handsome, thought Don Giammaria. Handsome as the Devil. And why not? Wasn't his mother a witch?

'Since when have you taken to visiting priests?' said Don Giammaria.

'Since tonight. May I come in?'

The priest stood aside. Franco Spada came into the stone-floored room. As Don Giammaria closed the door, Franco looked around. He had never been in the parish house before. It was spotlessly clean. Most of the houses in San Sebastiano were clean because Sicilians, contrary to their reputation abroad, were immaculate people. But old Donna Bellonia, who lived next door and cleaned the church and parish house, took special care of her charge, for Donna Bellonia was scrubbing herself into a special niche in heaven.

Franco looked at the faded photograph of Pope Pius IX on the wall.

'Is that the Holy Father?' he asked in his soft voice. Don Gammaria didn't like Franco's soft voice, his quiet way of expressing himself. It wasn't Sicilian. But then, *he* wasn't Sicilian, was he? Oh yes, his father was, but the mother—the *strega*—she had come from the hated north. Some village in Tuscany, it was rumored, though the witch never spoke about her origins. Her caution was understandable: the story he had been told was that her villagers had almost stoned the woman to death for casting the evil eye on her cousin. And now the *strega*'s illegitimate son was casting *his* eye on the former Pope! Of course, Don Giammaria didn't exactly believe in such supersititions as the evil eye, nor was he irrational enough to think that just because Franco Spada's mother had been a witch, a whore and a northerner, it *necessarily* followed that her son was evil, too. Still, he didn't like Franco staring at Pius IX.

'That's the former Pope,' he said, testily. 'The new Holy Father is Leo the Thirteenth—which you'd know if you ever went to church. What do you want?'

Franco turned to the fat priest, a slight smile on his clean-shaven face. That skin! thought Don Giammaria. No Sicilian has skin like that! That's northern skin, whore skin . . .

'I want to give the Church a present.'

Franco pulled a gold watch from his pocket and held it up by its chain, twisting it slowly. The firelight made the filigreed cover gleam. Don Giammaria came over and held out his hand. Franco dropped the watch into his palm. The priest inspected it a moment, then looked up suspiciously.

'Where did you get this?' he whispered.

Franco shrugged, said nothing.

'You stole it!' continued the priest. 'This is worth at least a thousand lire—you must have stolen it! The Church doesn't accept stolen property.'

'Then *you* keep it.'

The priest thought a moment, then walked over to a table and put the watch in a drawer. Shutting the drawer, he looked back at Franco.

'What do you want?' he said for the second time, although this time his voice was more friendly.

'I want you to look after my brother if something happens to me.'

'Vittorio? He has a job, doesn't he? Isn't he a page at the villa?'

'Yes, if you can call that a job. But Vittorio is young. He and I are hated here . . .'

'That's not true, my son.' Don Giammaria became unctuous.

'Bullshit,' replied the nineteen-year-old gardener. He said it quietly, without emotion. 'We're hated because our mother was a whore, and because these cretins in San Sebastiano think she was a witch.'

'Let's face facts, Franco,' said the priest, removing the glass and the decanter from behind the Bible. 'I personally don't believe the stories about her supposed witchcraft, but on the other hand she certainly bewitched your father. A glass of wine?'

Franco was amused by the mellowing of Don Giammaria's attitude after his 'donation.' Everyone in Sicily knew the Church was corrupt—some priests were so brazen as to refuse to perform the sacraments unless they first received a 'donation.' But Don Giammaria's lack of even a flicker of guilt about the watch had its funny side, as it also had its tragic one.

'No thank you, Father. And yes, my father was bewitched by my mother. She was a beautiful woman, after all. But the point is, they're both dead, and the villagers have passed on to my brother and me the hatred they felt against our parents. I've fought it all my life. Now, I don't give a damn for myself. But for Vittorio . . . Well, if something happened to me, he'd need someone to help him. And who could be better than our beloved parish priest?'

Don Giammaria didn't fail to catch the note of sarcasm. He filled his glass with Alcamo, stoppered the decanter, then raised the glass and took a sip.

'Of course, I will look after Vittorio, my son. But what is going to happen to you? You're young and strong . . .' He hesitated. 'Are you in trouble?'

'No. But I may be soon.'

And with that he turned and walked out of the house.

Don Giammaria stood by the fire, watching Franco as he closed the door. A strange bird, he thought. Very strange. But that's a beautiful watch . . .

He finished the wine, refilled his glass, then went over to the drawer. Opening it, he took out the watch, held it up and admired its gold case.

'Beautiful,' he said to himself.

He wondered what it was Franco was planning to do.

Prince dell'Acqua was the richest man in Sicily. He owned the town of San Sebastiano. He owned the lemon, orange and olive groves that surrounded the town and provided work for most of the townspeople. He owned a palace on the Piazza Marina in Palermo, and a summer villa in nearby Bagheria. He owned a palace in Rome. During the 1850s, when he had represented the Bourbon King of the Two Sicilies in Paris, he had gambled on the Paris exchange and made a fortune in railroad stocks. The Bourbons had been thrown out of Palermo and Naples by Garibaldi in 1860, and Italy had been united under the crown of the Piedmont monarch, Victor Emmanuel II. The Prince had at first been against the Risorgimento—he was a cautious man who instinctively disliked change—but he had been quick to support the new order of things when it became apparent it was here to stay. And the new King of Italy, eager for support from the Sicilian nobility—particularly from such a powerful man as the Prince dell'Acqua, whose brother was a cardinal—had rewarded Giancarlo with a number of important diplomatic posts.

Two years before, in 1878, the first King of Italy had died. Some thought it ironic that in the same year, Victor Emmanuel's bitter enemy, Pope Pius IX, had also died, a self-imposed prisoner of the Vatican, his 'captivity' caused by the Italian conquest of Rome eight years before. The temporal power of the popes had been reduced in a few years from the Papal States that had once sprawled across the middle of Italy to the 104 acres of the Vatican. Even the Quirinal Palace, once the home of the popes, had been taken over by the House of Savoy when the capital was moved from Turin to Rome. The Quirinal was now the royal palace, the home of the new king, Umberto I—whose white-moustached face would some day adorn a million olive oil cans—and his beautiful, bigoted queen, Margherita.

It had been at the Quirinal that Giancarlo first met Sylvia Toscanelli. The first Princess dell'Acqua had died in 1870. She had mothered two children: the young Duke of Marsala, who was sowing wild oats in Paris, and a daughter, Felicia, who had married a Neapolitan count. It was said in court circles that the Prince would never remarry. Not that he mourned his wife that much, but the Prince seemed a cold man, lacking, in a very un-Sicilian fashion, much interest in the opposite sex. The gossip was proved sensationally wrong when the Prince was introduced to Sylvia at a ball at the Quirinal. Since the death of her beloved father in 1859, the orphaned Sylvia had led a miserable existence. Her father's estate amounted to nothing but debts. To pay them off, the palazzo in Florence and the villa in Fiesole had had to be sold. Homeless, parentless, Sylvia had returned to the convent, where Mother Umbertina and the other nuns became her entire world. In 1871, when she was almost nineteen, she was taken from St. Ursula's to the home of her mother's sister in Milan, where her relatives began scheming to find the beautiful girl a suitable husband. It was on a visit to Rome that Sylvia met the man her relatives thought was ideal.

Giancarlo fell in love almost at first sight; Sylvia didn't know what love meant. He courted her avidly for a month, then proposed. Sylvia was anything but in love with this tall, rather chilly man who was old enough to be her father. She didn't even particularly like him. On the other hand, he was intelligent, well-read, worldly and rich. He could trace his family back to the Roman Empire, to a certain Gaius Publius Seleucus who was awarded a *latifundium* in Sicily by the emperor Trajan as a reward for his military victories in Parthia. Such exalted lineage, not uncommon in the Sicilian nobility, made even the Toscanellis seem like *arrivistes* by comparison. Sylvia's relatives pressed her to accept his proposal. She sensed she was making a mistake, but being literally penniless, she couldn't resist her family's pressure.

.They were married in the fall of 1872. Sylvia spent her wedding night in tears, but she resolved to make the best of a bad, if familiar, situation. And there was, after all, all that money to be spent.

Sylvia counted the day spoiled that she could not have her morning ride. And so, the morning after she arrived at the Villa dell'Acqua, as was her custom she came downstairs at eight dressed in her English riding habit with its veiled silk hat, and walked to the stables behind the villa. There she was helped on to her saddle. Then, seated sidesaddle, she cantered out of the stableyard and on to the dirt road that led out through the orange groves to the west of the village. It was a superb day. The *scirroco* of the night before had abated, leaving a sky swept clean. The temperature was briskly cool, the sun wonderfully warm, and the snows of St. Petersburg were so far away as to be forgotten.

She had ridden ten minutes when she saw someone lying on the road in front of her. She reined in her horse. When she was next to the man, she stared down at Franco, her gardener. She knew the story of the Spada brothers. How their father, one of Giancarlo's tenants, had fallen madly in love with a Palermo prostitute. How she had bedeviled him for years, squeezing the little money the man had out of him, driving him insane with jealousy, bearing him two illegitimate sons but refusing to have anything to do with the raising of them. It was a wonderfully Sicilian story, she thought: full of operatic emotions, love, jealousy . . . and even ending operatically. For when the prostitute died, Angelo Spada was so crazed with grief, he shot himself in the head. Suicide had crowned a lifetime of wrongdoing by local standards, and the two children of this tempestuous love match had been made pariahs by the village. But Giancarlo had taken pity on them and hired them at the villa—happily, as far as Sylvia was concerned, because she adored her beautiful page, Vittorio. Franco she saw less of, not only because he worked outside the villa, but because he was so disturbingly handsome. Sylvia didn't love her husband, but she respected him and had remained faithful to him. Franco tempted her, and she was afraid of temptation.

Now, as she stared down at the apparently unconscious man sprawled on his back below her, she couldn't help but marvel at his looks. Franco's face was not as refined as his younger brother's. It was slightly coarser, though the difference might be attributed to age, but it was still the face of a god. And his body . . . she had seen him working in the villa's gardens barechested and knew that his body was smooth and muscled. It was the body of a god. A pagan god, she thought. So appropriate for Sicily, which teemed with the ghosts of pagan Greek and Roman gods still haunting their beautiful ruined temples at Segesta and Agrigento. Looking at Franco, Sylvia felt something pagan inside her stirring.

'Franco,' she said.

He moaned.

'What happened?' She dismounted and knelt beside him. Removing her glove, she put her hand on his forehead. 'Was it bandits?'

She hardly believed what happened next. His right hand was behind his back, as if he had fallen on it. Now the hand was brought out and up, and Sylvia was staring into the barrel of a pistol.

'Don't move,' he said, thinking to himself thank God he had given the watch to Don Giammaria because if this didn't work, he'd get ten years at least. Quickly he got to his feet. 'I don't intend to hurt you, Principessa,' he said, almost apologetically. 'But this gun is loaded. Now, please . . .' he gestured to her horse. 'Get back on your horse.'

'What *are* you doing?' Her voice was incredulous.

'I'm kidnapping you, Principessa.'

Her eyebrows soared with surprise. Then she burst into laughter.

'Oh, really . . . This is fantastic!'

It was his turn to look surprised. Then angry.

'What's so funny?'

'You! You're not *serious?*'

'Why wouldn't I be serious?'

'Really, Franco, put that silly gun away, and we'll forget this happened. I don't have to remind you that kidnapping is a crime —even here in Sicily—and there *are* law courts—even here in Sicily.'

She didn't have to remind him. Ten years . . . he was frightened, but he told himself not to let her see it.

'Get on your horse.'

'What ransom are you asking?'

'Enough money to send me and my brother to America. They tell me in Palermo it will take eight thousand lire.'

'Well, that sounds cheap enough. I'm not sure I shouldn't be insulted. And what happens when you and Vittorio get to America? Neither of you can read or write. What kind of jobs will you get? You may think America is paradise, but I hear it's not very pleasant for immigrants. Particularly Italians. They call us Wops, you know.'

His face looked puzzled.

'Wops? What does "Wops" mean?'

'It's not flattering. Now put that gun down before it goes off by accident. And you're *not* kidnapping me.'

'Why?' He sounded belligerent.

'Because in the first place, you're much more frightened than I am.'

'That's not true!' he lied.

'And in the second place, I refuse to be kidnapped. Help me on my horse. I intend to finish my ride—alone, thank you.'

She walked to her horse, and Franco knew he was defeated. It had taken all his courage to go this far, but her queenly composure—not to mention her laughter—was too much for him. Suddenly he was Franco the gardener again. Franco the ignorant peasant. Franco the pariah, the bastard, the son of a whore and a love-crazed orange picker. She was looking at him, waiting for him to help her up. He put the pistol he had stolen in Palermo in his pocket, came over and cupped his hands for her foot.

Once mounted, Sylvia looked down at him as he looked up at her. Damn her, he thought. Goddam her! She's so beautiful, so damned aloof . . . The thought occurred to him he might be able to get the watch back from Don Giammaria. He had stolen it along with the pistol, and the two of them might bring fifteen hundred lire at a pawnshop.

'We'll pretend this didn't happen,' said Sylvia. 'It was a stupid idea of yours. Are you stupid?'

'No.' He sounded defensive. He didn't *think* he was stupid.

'Come to my library after lunch, and we'll see if you are.'

She switched her horse's haunch with her crop and galloped away. Franco Spada watched her recede in the distance, her horse's hooves kicking up puffs of dust. He felt like a fool and an ass. Where was his courage, his manliness? Why hadn't he gone through with it? She was nothing: a woman! He should have beaten her! And she had stopped him with a laugh and a look.

He started the long walk back to the Villa dell'Acqua, hating himself and wondering why she wanted to see him after lunch. It also occurred to him that of all the women he had wanted, and had, none was more desirable than the Princess. But he had about as much chance of making love to her as he had of getting to America.

Which, right now, was none.

'He tried to *kidnap* you?' exclaimed Alice Dexter. They were in the library of the villa, a room with high walls filled with hundreds of leather volumes. 'Were you afraid?'

'No,' said the Princess, who was standing at a window. She wasn't entirely truthful: She had been a little afraid at first. Though she sensed his nervousness, there had been determination in his eyes and the sulfurous suggestion of not-so-latent violence. Was there something else she had sensed? Something within herself as she confronted this superb man? Something erotic? The idea was disturbing. In fact, it was almost irresistible.

'But why did he do it?' Alice continued.

'For money, of course. And I can't say I blame him. He has nothing. He's desperate. They're all desperate, all the Sicilians. At least he showed a little gumption: at least he *tried*.'

Erotic. Why had she gone to lengths—not great lengths, but lengths—to avoid the gardener in her walks through the villa's grounds? Sylvia's sexuality had never been aroused by Giancarlo's cold lovemaking, but the sight of Franco Spada was prodding it out of its sleep. She turned to look at Alice.

'We haven't known each other too long,' she said, 'and I imagine you think of me as rather shallow woman. I suppose I am, in a way. But one thing I'm not shallow about is Italy. I'm a very patriotic woman.'

'So am I about America.'

'But your country is young. Italy is old, even though

politically we're the newest nation in Europe. Don't think I don't know what foreigners think of us. We're a country of pasta and pizza, operas and vendettas—not that there isn't some truth to that. Clichés are always founded on truth. Europe laughs at us —why shouldn't it? We're laughable. We're trying to be a Great Power with capital letters when we've only been a country twenty years. But my father gave his life for what he dreamed Italy could be, and maybe *I* should do something for it, too.'

'Like what?'

Sylvia went behind the Prince's heavily carved desk and tugged at a bell cord. Then she returned to the attack—and Alice began to realize that was precisely what it was: an attack. Or, perhaps, a defense. Behind her calm exterior, the Princess was going through a mental struggle of sorts, as if trying to rationalize to herself something she was planning to do.

'Sicily's been losing hundreds of young men for years now because they know there's no hope for them here, so they go to America. Why shouldn't they? I would, if I were in their shoes. Somebody has to start doing something for people like Franco, or there won't be any Italians left in Italy. They'll all be in New York.'

'You still haven't told me what you're going to do.'

The Princess went to one of the bookshelves and examined the leather spines of a row of thick tomes.

'If this Franco has any brains, I'm going to teach him to read.'

Alice thought about that.

'Well, I suppose that's not exactly revolutionary.'

'Around here it is.' She pulled out a book and flipped through its pages. 'Giancarlo will probably be furious, but that can't be helped . . . Good Lord, doesn't he have anything *readable* here? *A History of the Church in the Tenth Century*—who'd want to learn to read just to read that?' She replaced the book and continued her search. The door opened and the butler came in. 'Cesare,' said Sylvia, 'send in Franco.'

Cesare nodded and left.

'Are there no schools?' asked Alice.

'There are a few in Palermo, but none here. And the Church doesn't care. Mind you, I'm a good Catholic, but I have nothing but contempt for the Vatican's policies, and I don't care if my brother-in-law *is* a cardinal. Less than five percent of the country is literate, and since you can't vote unless you can read and write there are obvious advantages to the government to keep things as they are . . . Here's something. *I Promessi Sposi*. A novel might interest him . . .'

30

The door opened, and Alice turned to see the gardener-cum-kidnapper enter the room. When she saw how handsome he was, she wondered if there might not be another motive to the Princess's decision besides social uplift.

'Ah, Franco,' said Sylvia, bringing the novel to the desk. 'Here: sit down.'

She pointed to her husband's chair. Franco looked bewildered.

'Hurry up. I haven't all day.'

He walked across the room and sat behind the desk. Sylvia opened the book to the title page. Then she pulled a sheet of paper from one of the drawers. Placing the paper next to *I Promessi Sposi*, she took the plumed pen from the elaborate silver inkwell, dipped its point in ink and handed it to him.

'All right: I want you to copy these three words on the paper.'

'Why?'

'I want to see how bright you are. If you can copy words quickly, you should be able to learn to read quickly. You *would* like to learn to read?'

He nodded.

'Good. All right: start.'

The gardener stared at the page a moment. Then, gripping the pen tightly, vaguely realizing that something momentous was happening in his life, he began scratching:

I   P-R-O-M-E-S-S-I   S-P-O-S-I

Despite Alice's remark, the education of Franco Spada did constitute a revolution of sorts in the tight little world of the Villa dell'Acqua. Word spread like wildfire that the Princess was teaching Franco to read, and the shock was evenly divided between amazement that the Princess would do such a thing in the first place and bewilderment that she would pick the unliked —and unlikely—gardener to do it to. Alice, too, felt mixed emotions. She had known Sylvia was intelligent, but there had been nothing in the fun-loving, worldly companion she had met in Paris to suggest that the Florentine beauty felt anything but a passing interest in current politics or the problems of the Italian poor. And yet, out of the blue, Sylvia had committed herself to a considerable, time-consuming project. Was it merely the whim of a rich woman, a new weapon to use against the eternal enemy of the privileged, boredom? Or had the Princess been galvanized into a genuine compassion for her would-be kidnapper? Or—and Alice didn't like to think this because she truly liked the Princess

—was there something else in the equation? The gardener was, after all, *so* attractive . . .

On the other hand, Alice couldn't help but admire her friend. Whatever Sylvia's motives, she was throwing herself into the project with gusto. Convinced Franco was bright, the next day she converted a small room on the ground floor of the villa into a makeshift schoolroom. Releasing Franco from his gardening duties, she sequestered herself with him for two hours each morning and two in the afternoon. The villa buzzed with rumor, but Sylvia either didn't hear or didn't care. At dinner the third evening after beginning the project, she glowingly reported to Alice that Franco was making 'remarkable progress,' that he had already learned the alphabet and was tackling simple sentences, and that she was not only delighted but 'thrilled.'

'I can see you are,' said Alice, 'and far be it from me to throw cold water on your enthusiasm, but . . . have you thought of the consequences?'

'What consequences?'

'To Franco, for one. I mean, you've taken him out of the garden into the schoolroom. All right, so you teach him to read —then what?'

Sylvia sipped her champagne.

'Then at least he knows how to read. That's something, and a good deal more than he knows now.'

'But will he go back to being a gardener again? I'd doubt he'd want to. And from what you've told me, he's already a sort of pariah around here. What will he be after graduating from the dell'Acqua Elementary School?'

The Princess smiled.

'I like that. Perhaps I'll have a sign painted and hang it on the schoolroom door.'

'You're not answering my question.'

'Only because I don't have an answer to it. I don't know what will happen to Franco, but right now I don't care. I'm having the time of my life teaching him, and he's having the opportunity of his life learning—and he knows it, too. He's far from being a fool. Who knows what will happen later? At least he's been given a hand up. If people thought out all the consequences of doing things, I doubt anything would ever get done at all. Half the worthwhile things in life are started on impulse.'

'But what about the consequences to yourself?' Alice persisted. 'I know this is probably none of my business, but . . .'

She hesitated. Sylvia looked at her.

'Are people talking?' she asked. 'Is that what you're trying to say?'

'I have no idea. But certainly people *might* talk.'

'Let them. There's nothing to talk about.'

'Your husband might think differently.'

'He might.'

Her tone had become chilly, and Alice realized she had gone too far. But she couldn't help feeling that a Pandora's box was being pried open.

The next morning she was walking near the stable when she saw Vittorio come out. The boy was not in his page's livery, but wore a tattered shirt and dirty trousers. He was carrying a bucket. When he saw the American woman coming toward him, he froze.

'Good morning,' said Alice, lowering her white parasol.

'Good morning, Signora.'

She stood under a tree and smiled at him, thinking that of all the people connected with the little drama unfolding in the villa, Franco's younger brother must be one of the most concerned.

'And what have you been doing, Vittorio?'

The boy looked down at the bucket and gulped.

'Uh . . . cleaning the stable, Signora.'

It was then Alice realized what was in the bucket.

'Oh. Well, why don't you empty that, then come back and chat with me a moment?'

He hurried away behind the stable. Alice sat on a wrought-iron bench under the tree and admired the garden. It was a beautiful morning, almost unreal in its tranquility. How different this Sicilian garden was from the New York City she had grown up in, the New York City she loved. Alice's father was a prominent lawyer who later became a judge, and her childhood had been nothing if not conventional by the standards of her time and class: a French governess who had taught her the language of Voltaire and made her a lifelong Francophile. Then classes at the exclusive Miss Dobsen's School on East Thirty-first Street. Sylvan summers in the Catskills, cozy winters at the family brownstone near Madison Square, a wide circle of relatives and friends. An adolescence that would have seemed confining to later generations but one that to Alice seemed pleasant. Loving parents, two beloved older brothers. Servants, plenty of money, security. The only drawback—the only irony, in fact—was that, having been raised to become a wife and mother and having submitted to an arranged marriage which while comfortable, was anything but passionate, she had found out she would never bear

33

children. The fault was, her doctors had vaguely explained, a malfunction in her fallopian tubes. Alice's knowledge of the female anatomy was even skimpier than her knowledge of the male anatomy: She had no idea what the fallopian tubes were. But the realization she was barren had been the greatest blow of her sheltered life. She had survived it, for Alice was strong. But there was an emptiness in her existence.

'Signora?'

She turned to see Vittorio. He had put the empty bucket back in the stable and was standing a few feet away, as always looking rather uncertain, rather frightened of this foreign woman.

'So,' she smiled, folding her hands over the ivory handle of her parasol, 'what do you think of your brother going to school?'

'I think . . .' How shy he is, she thought. I suppose I can't blame him. 'I think it's good.'

' "Good." Yes, I suppose it's that. And how about you, Vittorio? Would you like to learn to read and write?'

He nodded solemnly. Good lord, she thought, how adorable he is!

'And if you could read and write,' she went on, 'what would you like to be?'

'An American.'

He said it so simply, but it produced a complex emotion in Alice. How lucky she had been being born where she was, what she was. And how unlucky this beautiful boy was, being born in Sicily . . .

It was then, she realized later, that the seed became planted in her mind.

CHAPTER 2

On the night of February 17, 1880, the Tsar of All the Russias gave a banquet for the Prince of Bulgaria. Among the guests standing in the Malachite Room of the Winter Palace before dinner was the Italian Ambassador, Prince Giancarlo dell'Acqua. Giancarlo was a naturally distinguished-looking man, but his distinction was reinforced by his beautifully cut suit of tails, his Collar of the Annunziata (awarded to him the year before by the King of Italy thus making him an honorary 'cousin' to the royal family), and the diamond-studded star of the Order of Orlov (given him by the Tsar) pinned to his chest. Giancarlo was talking to one of the Grand Duchesses when dinner was announced. The crowd started through the endless halls of the gigantic palace overlooking the frozen River Neva toward the state dining room.

The Tsar was about to enter the dining room when the French Ambassador asked him a question. The crowd waited as the two men talked in low tones for a few minutes.

Then a furious blast tore the two doors of the dining room off their hinges. As the guests of the Tsar screamed and ran for cover, black smoke roiled out of the room.

When the smoke cleared, nothing was left: The room was a void. Forty Finnish guards who had been in the room below were blasted to eternity, as were a number of footmen. A carpenter named Khalturin, one of the founders of the Moscow Workers' Union, had smuggled a huge amount of explosives into the basement of the palace with the intention of annihilating the imperial family. Only the chance remark of the French Ambassador prevented him from accomplishing his mission.

The next morning Giancarlo decided he had had enough of St. Petersburg for a while. He informed his wife and his king—not in that order—that he was returning to Sicily for a month 'for reasons of health.' Not only had his near brush with an explosive death shaken the Sicilian nobleman, but he missed his beautiful wife more than he had thought possible.

Also, certain remarks she had made in her letters had begun to bother Giancarlo.

The Prince dell'Acqua did not like to be bothered.

Don Pasquale Barraba was the *capo* of the Monreale Mafia and, as such, was one of the most powerful men in Sicily. Monreale being situated above Palermo, Don Pasquale controlled the all-important mountain streams. He could literally shut off the water to the *fruttéti* below Monreale if the orchard owners refused to pay him an annual 'fee.' Furthermore, since the roads to the interior passed through Monreale, if the Mayor of Palermo—Count Sclafani—did not pass a certain percentage of the city's revenues on to Don Pasquale, all the farm produce coming into Palermo would be stopped at Monreale. Of course, Count Sclafani would never dream of not cooperating with Don Pasquale. Cooperation with the Mafia—the individual gangs of which were known in Sicily as *cosche*—was a way of life, and the percentage handed to the *cosche*—the percentage known as the *pizzo*, which is the dialect for the beak of a bird, and to wet the beak was called *fari vagnari u pizzu*—was the grease that enabled the machinery of Sicilian society to function smoothly. The alternative was violence, either to a person or to a community. For centuries Sicilians had resorted to violence as the most practical method of redressing wrongs. Some said it was a result of the Arab Conquest. Others blamed it on the centuries of successive waves of foreigners, the conquerors failing to establish any truly effective police system. Still others blamed Sicily's extreme poverty, which led to banditry and, ultimately, to violence. Whatever the reason, violence was accepted and respected in Sicily, and *uomini di rispettu*—'men of respect'—commanded their respect by terror and murder.

Don Pasquale was respected, but a stranger would never have guessed why by looking at him. With his white beard, kindly face and rumpled black suit, he looked more like an out-of-season Father Christmas than a *capocosca*. His office was a small room behind Monreale's only barbershop. There he spent most of his day receiving visitors and clients, quietly issuing orders that often terminated someone's life, calmly picking his teeth and sipping lemonade. It was relaxed and yet, at the same time, formal. Like most things in Sicily, it was a ritual.

Since all classes of society at one time or another passed through Don Pasquale's office, he was not too surprised when, on the morning of March 17, 1880, his assistant, Nani, a swaggering *picciuottu*, or young Mafioso, came into his room and announced that Prince dell'Acqua was outside wishing to see him. Don Pasquale was not surprised, but he was curious. The Prince—powerful, rich, close to the royal family—made it a point of keeping the local Mafia at a respectable distance. Not that he hadn't called on Don Pasquale for favors before: he had, twice. Moreover, his estate manager, Don Fortunato Burgio, was, like almost all estate managers in western Sicily, a Mafioso. Still, the Prince kept his distance.

'Show him in,' said Don Pasquale, running his hands over his thick white hair to smooth it. Don Pasquale was powerful, but even he felt a certain awe of the island's nobility. To demonstrate it further, he stood up when the Prince came through the door. Don Pasquale *never* stood up.

'Your Excellency,' said Don Pasquale, thereby acknowledging a certain social inferiority, for only the nobility could address the Prince as 'Prince.' 'It has been a long time.'

'It has indeed, Don Pasquale,' replied the Prince, shaking the man's hand.

'Would you like a coffee?'

'Yes, thank you.'

'Nani, a coffee for His Excellency.'

Nani, who wore several thick gold rings to flaunt his importance, hurried out into the barber shop as Don Pasquale gestured to a chair before his plain desk.

'Please.'

As the Prince seated himself, Don Pasquale returned to his own chair. After he had sat down, he remarked, 'You are looking in good health, Excellency. I of course read of the tragedy in St. Petersburg.'

'Ah yes, the explosion at the palace.'

'A terrible thing! Terrible! I am amazed the Tsar has such little control over his people.'

'Perhaps he needs *you,* Don Pasquale.'

And the old Mafioso smiled, showing two gold front teeth. He had hoped the Prince would say that.

Nani came in with the coffee, which he handed the Prince, then hurried out, quietly closing the door. The Prince stirred his coffee, looking around the small room. Even though it was a cool day, the iron shutters had been closed over the two windows: Don Pasquale did not like the world to see what went on in his office. The slats of sunlight striped the wooden floor. Next to the door, an ugly glass-door cabinet stood, its shelves empty. Behind Don Pasquale hung a photograph of Garibaldi: twenty years before the Don had fought with the great man when he landed on Sicily.

Otherwise, the room was bare except for a torn leather sofa behind the Prince.

Giancarlo smiled cooly at Don Pasquale, who was waiting for his visitor to speak.

'Do you know one of my gardeners named Franco Spada?' asked the nobleman.

Don Pascale frowned.

'Yes, I know him.'

'You frown, Don Pasquale. Don't you like him?'

'With all respect to Your Exelllency, I must say no, I don't like him.'

'Why?'

'He is not . . .' The Don made a slight gesture with his right hand, '. . . trustworthy. He came to me a year ago wanting to work for me, but I told him I didn't want the son of a whore.'

'Your judgment is sounder than mine. As you know, I did hire him.' He paused. 'I have come to regret it.'

'Has he stolen from you, Excellency?'

'No. But I want to get rid of him. Not . . . you know . . . not to harm him. That would be . . . indelicate, and the situation is . . . delicate.'

Don Pasquale knew what he meant. He had heard the rumors about the Princess and the handsome young gardener.

'I understand, Excellency.'

'But perhaps something along the line of what happened to Brasi Camorro five years ago, if you recall.'

'Ah yes, of course. I remember.'

'Good. I would appreciate it, Don Pasquale. You know how high I hold you in my esteem and respect.'

'Your Excellency is too kind.'

The Prince set the coffee cup on Don Pasquale's desk, then pulled a black leather wallet from the beautifully tailored frock coat he had bought in London. One by one, he took out forty one-hundred lire notes, which he handed across the desk to the *capocosca*.

'I trust,' said the Prince, 'that is satisfactory?'

'Most satisfactory, Excellency. Is there any particular time you wish us to do this?'

The Prince stood up.

'As soon as possible. I think perhaps it would be better if it happens on a day that my wife and I are out of town. For instance, next Wednesday we are going to Palermo for the day.'

'Next Wednesday should be satisfactory. That will give us time to . . . plan.'

Don Pasquale accompanied the Prince to the door. There, the nobleman said, softly, 'I want Franco Spada never to return to Sicily.'

'It shall be done, Excellency.'

Don Pasquale opened the door, and the Prince walked into the barber shop.

Carla Sganci was known, with unconscious cruelty, as the 'halfwit' of San Sebastiano.

She had been born eighteen years before, the fifth child of a farmer named Ugo Sganci. When it became apparent 'Carluschia,' as she was called, was not 'all there,' the other villagers clucked sympathetically. They might have blamed her affliction on the punishment of God for some sin of her parents, but Carluschia's parents were so poor, so hardworking, so decent that in this instance her defective brain was shrugged off as an accident of Fate. Carluschia was tolerated with sympathy. During the summer, she worked in the fields along with the other women. But in the winter she was left to herself, the unspoken consensus being that the poor girl deserved some compensation for her misfortune. When the weather was bad, she would sit by the fire and hum to herself, or play with her doll or the crude toys her brothers made for her. When the weather was decent, she loved to take long walks by herself in the surrounding hills, particularly to a rock on the top of one hill. No one thought of accompanying her. Who would hurt Carluschia? Besides, God looked after 'half-wits,' didn't He?

On the morning of March 21, 1880, Carluschia set out from her parents' house, walked through San Sebastiano, then headed for the hills. She carried a rag doll with her which she had named Theresa, after the saint. She wore a heavy wool shawl to protect her from the wind. She was a dumpy girl, but her face might have been attractive if her eyes hadn't had that sad, vacant stare. Villagers seeing her pass, nodded and said, 'Good day, Carluschia.' She smiled back at them, but didn't answer. Carluschia rarely spoke to anyone but Theresa.

An hour later she sat down on her favorite rock on top of her favorite hill. The wind was strong, but Carluschia loved this rock and didn't mind the gusts from the west. Here she was

alone with Theresa and the sky and God and—in the far distance
—the sea. It was beautiful here. Carluschia was happy.

She saw the man on the horse riding toward her and wondered
who it was. Few people ever came to her rock, which was one
reason she loved it.

'Who is it, Theresa?' she whispered to her rag doll. Theresa's
face smiled happily. Theresa always smiled.

The man came up to the rock and dismounted. He was tall,
about thirty, with a black beard. Carluschia recognized him as
Santo Matta, who sometimes came to San Sebastiano from
Monreale. She didn't know what he did.

Santo walked up to her and smiled.

'Hello, Carluschia,' he said.

She smiled back at him. Theresa smiled.

Santo Matta began unbuckling his thick leather belt.

Vittorio and Franco shared a tiny, one-window room on the
top floor of the Villa dell'Acqua. In the winter they could use it,
but in the summer it became so hot they slept outdoors.
Although the Prince had installed plumbing in the villa five years
before, it was an indication of his attitude toward his dozens of
servants that no plumbing had been installed for them, though
the additional expense would have been insignificant. The
servants used the outhouses.

At eleven-thirty on the night of March 21, 1880, the door to
the room burst open. Franco sat up in bed, shielding his eyes
from the glare of a bull's eye lantern. He saw three figures
squeeze into the room and heard one of them say, 'Franco
Spada?'

'Yes . . .'

'I have an order for your arrest.'

Franco, still groggy from sleep, wondered if he were dreaming. He saw one of the *carabinieri*—or *sbirri* as the police were
called—come to his bed.

'Hold out your hands.'

When he saw the iron cuffs, Franco woke up.

'Under arrest for *what*?'

'For the rape and murder of one Carla Sganci.'

Murder? Carluschia? He thought of the poor, dim-witted
girl . . .

'I didn't murder Carluschia . . .'

'You'll get a fair trial.'

' "Fair" shit! This is crazy—'

The policeman grabbed his left wrist and clapped the hand-cuffs on it.

'NO!'

He was roaring now, panicked. He slugged the *carabiniere* in the face with his right fist, then tried to bolt through the others to get to the door. He was grabbed by the two *sbirri*. As he raged and struggled, they shoved him against the wall, then attached the cuffs to his other wrist. The captain of the *carabinieri,* a young man with a black moustache, was panting from the exertion. Now he said: 'Will you come peaceably?'

Franco simmered down. He didn't understand what was happening to him, but his common sense told him that to fight was useless. He nodded.

The captain signaled his men, who pushed Franco through the door. He turned to look back at his younger brother, who had watched this with silent terror.

'Vito,' he called, 'whatever they say, I didn't do it. You understand? I didn't do it.'

Vittorio nodded numbly. But he didn't understand. He didn't understand at all.

The Princess dell'Acqua was reading in her bedroom when she heard the shouts. Then, silence. Getting out of bed, she threw on a robe and hurried to the door of her bedroom. She let herself out into the hall and listened a moment. Voices from downstairs. She walked quickly to the head of the staircase, then started down. She saw her husband in a wine-colored velvet smoking jacket. He was closing the front door.

'Giancarlo, what is it?'

Her husband looked at her.

'It was Captain Antonetti of the *carabinieri*. He came to arrest your pupil. It seems he raped a girl in San Sebastiano, then strangled her to death.'

Sylvia was standing on the bottom step, her hand on the smooth marble balustrade.

'I don't believe it,' she said, amazed at the calm she managed to convey. 'What proof do they have?'

Giancarlo was puffing his pipe to life.

'When they found her body this afternoon, she had a piece of paper in her hand. Apparently in the struggle she tore it away from the murderer. The paper was a page from one of Franco's copybooks. He had been practicing writing his name. Franco Spada, Franco Spada . . . over and over. Your Franco may be a bright student, but it would seem he's a stupid murderer.'

41

He exhaled a cloud of pipe smoke, which whirled like Sylvia's brain.

'Why would Franco rape anyone?'

Her husband smiled.

'My dear, that's a rather stupid question.'

He started toward the library. She followed him.

'It's not stupid! Franco would never do such a horrible thing . . . Good Lord, he could have any woman he wanted . . .'

'Could he?'

He stood aside to let his wife enter before him. She stopped in front of him.

'I hope you're not implying he made love to me?' she said.

'Of course not. I have perfect faith in you. Have I made any remark that would indicate I suspected something immoral was going on between you two?'

'No. And there wasn't.'

'I'm sure.'

She went into the library and sat in a leather fauteuil.

'We'll hire a lawyer for him, of course,' said her husband, going to a butler's tray which held a cut-glass decanter. 'Whether he's innocent or guilty, I want him to have legal representation. A Cognac?'

'Please.'

'I think probably Professore Bonfante in Palermo would be best for the case. He has an excellent reputation for defending criminals . . .'

'Franco's not a criminal!'

'The police seem to think otherwise. I'll go into Palermo in the morning and talk to Bonfante. I've met him several times. He's a pleasant man, though his table manners leave something to be desired.'

He brought the Cognac to his wife, then went behind his desk and sat down. The green-globed desk lamp cast its rather bilious light on his long face.

'Giancarlo,' she said, softly, 'swear to me you had nothing to do with this.'

'I beg your pardon?'

'Don't pretend you don't understand. If I know anything, I know Franco would never commit violence . . .'

'You told me he tried to kidnap you.'

She bit her lip.

'That was different.'

'How?'

'It just was. I *still* say he would never murder anyone. I *know* it. I've worked with him for seven weeks now, and I've gotten to know him. He's a fine, intelligent young man. If nothing else, he had no *reason* to do this! So if Franco didn't do it, who did? And who made it look as if Franco was the murderer?'

The Prince warmed his Cognac.

'I see. You think I arranged this, presumably because I don't like the idea of being considered a cuckold by my servants and by my tenants.'

'Exactly. You have a motive to get rid of him.'

'That's excellent reasoning, my dear, and Arsène Lupin would be proud of you. But there are a few holes in your argument. (A), I didn't do it. (B), I have never objected to your little social experiment with Franco. I think it's a waste of time, admittedly, but I've never objected. So I think that your accusation is not only rather foolish but, um . . . shall we say not very flattering to your husband?'

She sipped her Cognac, eyeing him. She knew he was lying.

'What will happen to him?' she asked.

'He may not be guilty.'

'But if they say he is?'

The Prince inhaled the aroma of the Cognac, then took a satisfying sip.

'Well, since the government has foolishly made capital punishment illegal, I suppose he'll get life imprisonment.'

He looked at her across the desk. She came very close to vomiting. Instead, she stood up. Placing her snifter on the desk, she looked at her husband. Her beautiful face was chalky, her eyes even larger than usual.

'If that happens,' she whispered, 'if his life is thrown away and you caused it, may you rot in hell.'

And she walked out of the room.

CHAPTER 3

A letter from Princess Sylvia dell'Acqua to Alice Dexter, dated May 24, 1880.

My dearest Alice:

As I predicted in my last letter, Franco has been convicted of the murder and sentenced to life imprisonment. The trial was a farce, in my opinion. Professor Bonfante's defense was lukewarm. The judge obviously was convinced of Franco's guilt at the start (or else he was paid for his bias; it wouldn't surprise me). The prosecution was vicious, and with that scrap of paper which was found in the girl's hand, Franco didn't have a chance. As luck would have it (if it was 'luck') he had no witness who could vouch for his whereabouts on the day of the murder. Giancarlo had driven me into Palermo for a luncheon party, so my regular classes with Franco had been cancelled. He spent most of the day by himself, studying first in his room, then, later on, in one of the orchards. So neither I nor anyone else could help him by testifying he had been seen. This, with the page from his notebook, finished him.

Of course, there is another explanation of what happened. Someone stole the page from Franco's notebook and stuck it in the girl's hand after she was killed. This would have been easy enough, since Franco kept the book in his room, which is never locked. Then the murder might have been arranged for a day when I would be away, thus denying Franco his most obvious alibi and character witness—me. Of course, the murderer would have to take the chance the girl would walk to her favorite rock so she would be *available* (a cold-blooded choice of words, but you know what I mean). But since the girl went there regularly, the murderer must have assumed—correctly—that the odds were in his favor. And this is what I think actually happened.

Because, dearest Alice, I know in my heart Franco did not commit this disgusting crime. He simply had no reason. And to leave something as damning as a page from his notebook in his victim's hand? Impossible. Oh, I know: it's possible it was a crime of passion, that he went temporarily insane or something. It's possible, but hardly likely. No, no, I don't believe it. I'll never believe it.

No, the truth is that this murder was *arranged*. And who arranged it? Dear friend, it kills me to write this down, but I am convinced it was my husband. It would be so simple here in Sicily with the Mafia for hire to do one's dirty work. Make the proper payment and presto! An enemy is killed—or, as in Franco's case, stuck in a prison for the rest of his life, which may be worse than killing. You ask me why I don't go to the police and tell them my suspicions? Dear God, if only I could. But I don't have one shred of evidence. The police (and the courts, for that matter) are infiltrated by either Mafia members or supporters or informers. So even if I *had* any evidence, they would either bury it or—and this is a real possibility—bury *me*. I swear to you that in Sicily what the Mafia wishes is *done*. The only possibility I can think of to free Franco is for *me* to hire the Mafia (they could easily arrange his escape if they wanted. The prison guards respect Mafia wishes. I know you must think I am fantasizing the power of this evil organization, but I swear to you what I say is true). But I know they would never take my money. One of the few people they respect in Sicily is my husband. It would not be politic for them to cross him.

So where does that leave us? It leaves Franco in the Ucciardone Prison—a pesthole built in the 1830s by King Ferdinand II. It leaves Giancarlo smiling smugly at having gotten rid of a man he obviously assumed was, or would become, my lover. And I swear to you, Alice, our relationship was pure.

And it leaves me crushed with guilt at being the ultimate cause for this gross injustice. Yes, it was *I* who charged blindly in, making Franco my pupil, assuming no one would ever suspect *my* motives, assuming I could handle Giancarlo. Oh God, of all the stupid, interfering women on this planet, I must be the worst! And yet I swear I only wanted to help Franco! I suppose the unpleasant truth in this corrupt world is that people trying to do good often create misfortune. And what a horrible misfortune I have created for Franco! I will never forget the look he gave me in the courtroom as the judge sentenced him. He turned and stared at me, and it was a look of unqualified hatred. Sweet Jesus, will I have to live with the memory of that look the rest of my life?

I *loathe* Giancarlo. The night they arrested Franco, I accused my husband of having engineered the whole thing. He blandly denied it, but I know—and he knows I know. How I misjudged the man I married! Life is cheap in Sicily, but I had no idea he would go to the horrible lengths of destroying two lives merely to protect his 'honor'—and I'm sure that is how he thinks of it. The only revenge I have is to turn to ice, and I have. This is indelicate, but I can assure you his nocturnal visits to my room have given him anything but satisfaction. This naturally aggravates the situation. Our marriage has become an unrelenting, silent duel to the death.

And Vittorio! He is so crushed by what has happened to the brother he worshipped that for a time I was worried for his sanity. Giancarlo wanted to dismiss him after Franco's arrest—out of sheer viciousness, though he made some lame excuse about the possibility of Vittorio harboring his brother's 'criminal' tendencies—but when I threatened to cause a storm, he relented. If he had been kicked out of the villa, the boy would probably have starved to death. The villagers are delighted Franco has been convicted—such ghouls!—and they would have liked nothing better than to watch his brother die.

I wish I had some cheery note to relieve this picture of unrelieved gloom, but I don't. I am miserable, dear Alice. Miserable. If there were only something I could *do* . . . but the deadly beauty of the Mafia is that it works so secretly, one doesn't know how to strike back. There is nothing I can do, no one to turn to. If there were something I could do, I'm not sure I'd have the courage to do it.

Please write to me. I need the support of *someone*. But for God's sake, don't mention my suspicions of Giancarlo! He's not above reading my mail.

Your despairing friend,
Sylvia

The jewels Gus Dexter had bought from the old slave outside Savannah he sold six months later in New York for $40,000, a fortune in 1865. Gus determined to use his grubstake as a springboard to millions. Renting a furnished room near Wall Street, he began studying the market. The schoolteacher's son from Elmira had a knack for figures and a gambler's instinct. He entered the market, cautiously at first. He was badly stung a few times, but learned from his mistakes. By 1868 he was considered a force to be reckoned with. In the spring of 1869, after making a killing in gold stocks, Augustus realized with considerable glee that he was a bona-fide millionaire.

He got out of the market and opened a small banking house on Pine Street. He had enough connections on Wall Street to attract business. He was shrewd enough to prosper from the difficulties of other, bigger banks. When Jay Cooke and Company failed in the Panic of 1873, Augustus managed to attract many of his customers to his own business. By 1876, as the economy boomed, the Dexter Bank was a thriving institution. In that year Augustus bought property at 25 Pine Street and built a graceful, neoclassic edifice that was as distinguished, conservative and solid as the former soldier had become himself. Like many self-made men, Augustus, after making his pile by speculation using funds received from looted jewels, became more established than the Establishment.

On a warm June day in 1880, Augustus emerged from the bank at five o'clock, as was his custom, climbed into his waiting carriage and was driven uptown to Thirty-ninth Street and Madison Avenue, where he had bought a four-story brownstone two years before. Prosperity had added sixty pounds to his frame, which, with the heat and his frock coat, made life uncomfortable in summer. So the first thing he did after coming into the cool, if rather gloomy, entrance hall of the house was to go upstairs to take a bath. Augustus and Alice had separate bedrooms; his overlooked Madison Avenue and was dominated by a big brass bed. Now he removed his clothes and went into the tiled bathroom to fill his gargantuan, claw-foot tub. As the tub filled, he opened his medicine chest above the porcelain washbasin and surveyed its astonishing contents. Augustus was something of a hypochondriac, so the chest was crammed with Dalby's Carminative, Lee's Antibilious Pills, White's Gout Pills, Thomas's Colocynth and Mandrake Pills, Bateman's Pectoral Drops, Eau Médicinale d'Husson, Ward's Essence for the Headache, Griffin's Tincture for Coughs, Bailey's Itch

Ointment, Ditchett's Remedy for Piles, Coxe's Hive Syrup, Berthold's Chilblain Wash, and a host of other ointments and elixirs. He pulled a bottle of Balm of Thousand Flowers mouthwash off the bottom shelf (where it reposed between a tube of Dr. King's Tooth Paste and a bottle of Erasmus Wilson's Hair Wash for the Prevention of Baldness) and gargled—for Augustus was fastidious and not a little vain. This completed, he eased his bulk into the tub and sighed with contentment.

For the moment all was right with Augustus Dexter's over-stuffed world.

When he came downstairs, dressed for dinner, Alice was waiting for him in the darkly paneled drawing room.

'You read Princess Sylvia's letter I received last week,' she began, after her husband kissed her cheek. 'I've been giving it a lot of thought, and I want to discuss something with you.'

Augustus took his favorite Charles II brocade chair in front of the green marble mantel, aware that his normally calm wife seemed strangely tense.

'What's that, Alice?'

She sat on an ottoman beside him.

'Augustus, it's my fault we can never have children, which has caused me great anguish . . .'

'Alice,' he interrupted, 'it's not *your* fault. It's a fault of nature.'

Augustus was overly proud, domineering, stubborn and a bit of a pompous snob. But for all his faults, and for all his intense disappointment at his wife's failure to produce an heir, he had never blamed Alice. In his undemonstrative way, he loved and respected her.

'That's kind of you to say, Augustus, but the fact remains we have no children. I know it's as great a disappointment to you as it is to me. It's particularly galling when your sister has had *five* . . .'

'What does Virginia have to do with it?'

'Only that it seems unfair that they've been so blessed, and we haven't.'

'We have a great deal to be thankful for.'

'Oh, I know, but we have no children. And Augustus, I have the answer!'

He looked at her.

'What?'

She swallowed hard.

'I want to adopt Vittorio.'

'You . . . want to adopt . . . an *Italian?*'

He blurted the words out with almost comic dismay.

'Yes. Oh Augustus, he's the most adorable child, and so handsome and bright . . . He has nothing, and there's so much we could give him . . .'

'Preposterous. Absurd! I won't have a filthy Italian in my family . . .'

'He's not filthy! And he wants to be an American more than anything else . . .'

'They all do! Every ragtag Polack and coolie . . . They all want to come here! America's turning into a slum! Look at the Irish, the Jews . . . they're *pouring* in! It's a disgrace, a national disgrace! And if you think I'm going to add to that disgrace by importing a greasy Dago . . .'

'He's *not* greasy!' exclaimed Alice, telling herself not to become angry. 'And I *want* him!'

'It's out of the question. I want to hear no more about it. What's for dinner?'

Alice Fairchild Dexter had never fought for anything in her life, but she was determined to fight for Vittorio.

'I sent him the passage money this morning,' she said, quietly. 'Vittorio will arrive in New York on the seventh of July aboard the *Servia*.'

Augustus stared incredulously at his wife.

'He is coming,' she added with a slight smile of defiance, 'first-class.'

Vittorio had never traveled farther from San Sebastiano than Palermo, so the trip to Rome and thence to Paris, London and Liverpool was something akin to a dream. Accompanied by Princess Sylvia, which in itself was close to the miraculous, he stared at the passing countryside from the windows of the trains, eyes agog, barely listening to his former employer as she repeated over and over again the instructions Alice had written her. 'If you have difficulties on the ship,' said Sylvia, 'you must go to the purser . . . say "purser." '

'Pur . . . ser,' said Vittorio, sidling up to the English language with caution.

'That's good. His name is Mr. McGillicudy. Say "McGillicudy." '

Vittorio took a deep breath.

'Mc . . . Gillicoody.'

'Well, that's close enough, Mr. McGillicudy speaks some Italian, so you'll be able to talk with him. Now, Mrs. Dexter has sent you three hundred dollars cash—that's four thousand five hundred lire.'

Vittorio looked at her uncomprehendingly, as if such a vast sum were beyond reality.

'Even though everything is paid for on the ship, there may be some emergency, so she wanted you to have extra money . . . Oh, look, Vittorio: there's the border! We're in France now. Say good-bye to Italy. . . .'

Vittorio stared at the two passing flagpoles, one bearing the tri-color of the Third Republic, the other the royal arms of the House of Savoy, but leaving Italy meant little to him because 'Italia' was still a vague concept in his mind. Home was San Sebastiano. Home was his beloved brother, Franco. The tears that welled in his eyes were not tears for Italy: They were for Franco.

'Principessa,' he said, softly, 'will you tell Franco what has happened to me?'

The Princess reached her gloved hand over and took the hand of her former page. She saw his tears. She knew.

'Yes, Vittorio,' she whispered. 'I'll tell Franco.'

She didn't have the heart to tell him what she had learned three days previously: that Franco had been transferred from the Ucciardone Prison to the tiny island of San Stefano, thirty miles off the east coast of Italy in the Tyrrhenian Sea, there to spend the rest of his life at hard labor. Her already crushing guilt and despair had, if possible, increased at the thought of him on the notorious island-prison, leading a bestial existence at the mercy of undoubtedly bestial guards. The letters from Alice had at least given her the distraction of action, of preparing Vittorio for his new life, buying him a suit, shoes, a valise, making the travel plans, buying the tickets, accompanying him to Liverpool . . . In her activity she found a momentary release from the guilt that was already transforming her life. Like all crimes, the murder of Carla Sganci had had ripple effects, changing the lives of not only the alleged murderer—Franco—but his brother, Princess Sylvia and the Dexter family as well.

'I swear to you, Vittorio,' she said, still squeezing his slim hand, 'I will never stop trying to free Franco. Never. And some day, God willing, you'll see your brother again.'

This unlikely couple looked at each other, the twelve-year-old peasant and one of the most noble and beautiful women in Italy. Vittorio knew in his heart she meant what she said.

The Cunard liner *Servia*, the biggest ship to be built since the ill-fated *Great Eastern*, was the first big, steel-hulled ship on the Atlantic, and the first to be lighted by incandescent lamps. She had five decks, the grandest staircase of any ship on the Atlantic, and some of her staterooms were even fitted with Broadwood's patent lavatories. She carried 480 first-class and 750 third-class passengers, and was the first Cunard liner to emphasize the comfort of trans-atlantic travel, thereby answering the challenge of the newer Inman and White Star Lines whose comfort-oriented floating palaces had taken away much of Cunard's business in recent years.

The other first-class passengers wondered who the shy, handsome boy in Cabin 112 was. He stayed by himself, appearing infrequently at meals in the first-class dining room where even the few Italians aboard were unable to get more than guarded sentences out of him. However, the purser, Mr. McGillicudy, knew some of the story, having been contacted by both Alice in New York and Princess Sylvia when she brought Vittorio aboard at Liverpool. And before lunch the second day out, when a certain Mrs. Andrews from Albany sniffed that 'Prince Del Corso told her that the boy spoke like a Sicilian peasant and should be in steerage,' Mr. McGillicudy said quietly, 'The boy is a ward of Princess Sylvia dell'Acqua.' The purser had the pleasure of seeing Mrs. Andrews almost choke on her chicken.

For Vittorio the luxurious ship with its pleasant attendants was an unparalleled joy; and even though he was frightened of the other passengers, he found the experience of ocean travel exhilarating. He had some idea of how incredibly lucky he was: letters from Palermitans and Monrealeans who had emigrated to America in steerage had spread word around San Sebastiano of the horrendous conditions they suffered crossing the Atlantic. Cramped, ill-ventilated spaces jammed with men, women and children. Rotten food, filthy water, people reduced to eating rats they trapped in the hold . . . Only the fierce dream of the promised land, of America *La mecca del dollaro*, sustained them in their wretchedness. He, on the other hand, was living a miracle. He didn't understand why the American Signora was bringing him to New York. The Princess had told him Mrs. Dexter was going to adopt him, but he didn't understand what that really meant. Would he become one of her family? Was that possible? He didn't know the Cinderella story, but if he had, he would have been skeptical of the glass slipper that was being

51

squeezed on his foot. Rich Signoras—even rich American ones —weren't so *pazza* as to bring ragamuffins like himself across the ocean in princely style and take him into their family.

And yet, it was happening.

On the morning of the tenth day, after going through quarantine, the *Servia* entered New York Harbor and sailed slowly past Bedloe's Island, which was being considered as a possible site for the colossal Statue of Liberty then being constructed in Paris. It was a hot July day, and Vittorio stood at the rail watching the wondrous towers of the half-finished Brooklyn Bridge soaring over the river to the right; he gawked at the enormous Hudson River to the left, so huge as to make the Tiber or the Seine, which he had seen on his way to Liverpool, seem like streams in comparison. He gazed in awe at the spire of Trinity Church, the tallest structure in the city. The Golden Door was opening before him. Gripping the rail tightly, the sun beating on the right side of his face, his eyes wide, Vittorio realized he was being born again.

If he had been in steerage, he would have had to go through Castle Garden, the fortress at the tip of Manhattan that had been converted into a music hall—Jenny Lind had made her sensational appearance there in 1850—and then, in 1855, as the swell of emigrants from Ireland, England and Germany necessitated more space to handle them, reconverted into an immigration depot. He would have lined up with hundreds of other ragged Europeans; been given a perfunctory medical exam, been asked if he could read or write (to which, like the vast majority of immigrants, he would have answered no), then been sent into a separate room where he would have stripped and taken a communal bath with fifty other males. After this degrading ritual, he would have been turned loose in the streets of New York, probably to make his way into the swelling mass of Italians who were already turning the area around Mulberry Street into Little Italy. He would probably have ended up operating a pushcart, or becoming a barber, or—most likely —becoming a shoveler, using his muscles the rest of his life doing construction work. Bleak as this prospect was, it was infinitely better than the future offered him in Sicily.

But Vittorio's destiny was different. When the *Servia* docked, he walked down the gangway with the other first-class passengers. No passports were required, and there were rudimentary customs checks, so he quickly passed through the officials. He was being yelled at by a hoard of 'runners,' or porters, who surrounded him babbling in heavily accented English to carry his single suitcase, when he spotted the woman in white. Alice, on tiptoes to see over the heads of the crowd, at the same time spotted the young man in the brown suit and wide-brimmed brown hat, clutching the leather suitcase.

'Vittorio!'

She made her way through the crowd and moments later was hugging him.

'Welcome to America!' she exclaimed in Italian, beaming at his face, then hugging him again. Vittorio, overwhelmed by the effusiveness of this woman he barely knew, said between hugs, 'The Signora has been very kind . . .'

'No—no thanks! I wanted to do it. Was your trip all right?'

'Oh yes, Signora. It is a beautiful ship.'

'And the Princess? She's fine?'

'Yes, and she sends her love. I have a letter for you in the suitcase . . .'

'Good. But first, let's get in the carriage.'

And, chattering excitedly, she took his hand and led him through the crowd to the street where a handsome varnished victoria was waiting, pulled by two matched bays. As the coachman held the door, Alice climbed in, followed by Vittorio. Moments later, they were heading up Broadway, which was choked with traffic. Above them the hot sun was partially obscured by thousands of telegraph wires, strung in a maze from wooden poles, some bearing as many as a dozen crossties. The iron wheels of carts and delivery wagons clanked against the cobblestones, sending up a din that almost drowned out the furious shouts of the drivers, cursing each other in the uncontrolled traffic. On the sidewalks, derby-hatted stockbrokers lurched through crowds of young messenger boys hurrying through the financial district to deliver their messages. Other boys, ragged and dirty, hawked the city's numerous newspapers: the morning *Times, Herald, Sun, World, Tribune*; the early editions of the afternoon *Express, Post, Brooklyn Eagle, Staats Zeitung*. With all the noise and movement, the scene was electrifying compared to the languid Rome and Paris Vittorio had glimpsed.

'There's the Western Union Building,' exclaimed Alice, who had been delivering an almost unheard tourist-guide spiel to her newly arrived Sicilian. She pointed to an ornate domed building across from Trinity Church. 'See the flagpole on top of the dome? And that round, red ball at the top of it?'

'Yes . . .'

'Every day, at noon exactly, they drop the ball to the base of the pole. That way, everyone can check the accuracy of their watches. Isn't that clever?'

Vittorio agreed that it was wondrously clever. By now they had been in the carriage almost twenty minutes, making their way slowly uptown through the massed traffic. Vittorio turned to his companion and said, 'Where are we going, Signora?'

Alice's pretty face never changed its smiling expression, but the boy thought he saw a certain tension come over it.

'We're going to meet my husband at his bank, Vittorio. He especially wanted to meet you as soon as you disembarked.'

Vittorio studied his benefactress a moment.

'Is the Signor Dexter . . .' he began. 'I mean, did he want to bring me over from Sicily?'

She marveled at his perspicacity. How could he guess that Augustus had raged when presented with her *fait accompli* the previous month? And then, the even more ominous and disturbing silence that he had sunk into on the subject of Vittorio. As often as she had tried to discuss the boy's future with him, her husband had refused to talk about it, merely saying he would meet the boy first before making any decisions. And now, the —to her—dreaded interview was about to take place. As much as she didn't want to frighten Vittorio, she felt she had to warn him that her husband in all probability would be something less than gushing in his welcome.

'To tell you the truth, Vittorio, my husband was against it. I made the arrangements on my own . . . bought your ticket with my own money. But I know that once he meets you, he'll come to love you as I do.'

Vittorio thought about this, watching Alice's face. Then:

'Do you love me, Signora?'

Suddenly, impulsively, in full view of the crowd, she took the boy into her arms and squeezed him against her.

'Very much,' she whispered. 'You are going to be my son, no matter what Augustus says.'

After a moment, her Victorian sense of decorum reasserted itself, and she released Vittorio. For the first time, the boy began to understand the American Signora's need for him.

A few minutes later, the carriage pulled up in front of the Dexter Bank at 25 Pine Street, and a top-hatted doorman held the door for Mrs. Dexter and her young charge. Alice led him inside the bank. The main banking room had a dark, wood-coffered ceiling, ornate marble columns and elaborate wrought-iron grilles protecting the tellers' cages. They crossed the marble floor to the door leading to the executive offices. A few moments later, Mr. Grimsby, Augustus's private secretary, admitted them to the office of the president, a paneled room hung with large views of New York and a big-gold-framed portrait of the bank's founder, Augustus. Behind a heavily carved desk, the subject of the portrait rose to his feet. Vittorio looked at the imposing man with his bushy sideburns and cold eyes.

'Augustus,' said Alice, 'this is Vittorio.' Then, switching to Italian, she added, 'This is my husband.'

For a long moment, Augustus inspected the Sicilian, his face impassive. Vittorio returned his look with equal impassivity. Then Augustus gestured to two chairs and said to his wife, 'You will translate for me, please.'

'Of course.'

They sat down, as did Augustus. Another long moment. Then the banker spoke.

'Tell him he was brought here against my wishes.'

'I already have. But I think you might make some effort at hospitality . . .'

'I do not feel hospitable, Alice. And I want the boy to have no illusions about his position in our household.'

'But he just got off the boat—'

'You will do what I say!' thundered her husband. Alice caved in. 'Tell him that even though you brought him over behind my back, nevertheless since he is here, I feel a responsibility for him. It is a responsibility I didn't ask for, needless to say, but one I am willing to assume.'

Alice translated. Vittorio listened, saying nothing, his eyes on Augustus.

'Tell him,' continued the banker, 'I am willing to educate him and provide for his food and shelter.'

Alice translated.

'However, there will be no question of our adopting him.'

'Augustus!'

'Tell him!'

'I will not! The whole idea was to make him our son—!'

'I told you I didn't want an Italian as an heir!' said Augustus, with soft venom. 'If you are incapable of producing children, that is a cross we must bear. But I will not accept second best!'

'You don't know him! How can you assume he's inferior—'

'Tell him.'

'I will *not!*'

'Alice, you'll do as I say, or by God, I'll kick this Wop out into the streets!'

55

She closed her eyes a moment, trying to compose herself. Then she said, in Italian, 'My husband says it will not be possible for us to adopt you for a while. But after a period of time, it will be arranged . . .'

'Are you telling him what I said?'

'Yes, Augustus.'

'Tell him he can live with us, but he is under no circumstances to think of himself as an equal.'

'Augustus, this is monstrous—!'

'*Tell* him.'

'But what will he be? A servant?'

'Yes.'

'I won't allow it! It's cruel . . .'

'*That's* the way it will be. He's not going to have a free ride on *me*, I can assure you. And if he doesn't like this arrangement, tell him I am willing to pay his passage back to Italy. *Not* first-class, I might add. Furthermore, if he at any time behaves in an improper fashion—if he exhibits any of the immoral characteristics of his race—I will personally make sure that his punishment will be commensurate with his crime. I don't intend to import a virus into my family.'

Alice was enraged, but she told herself not to exacerbate the situation. Give him time, she thought. *Time.* He's doing this now to pay me back, but in time he'll come to love Vittorio . . . I know it . . .

She turned to the boy and said, softly, 'My husband wants you to understand that for the time being it will be . . . awkward for you to be a member of the family. That until we all get to know you, and love you, it may perhaps be better if you are . . . well, more like a boarder in our house. Just for a while, of course. Will that be all right, my dear?'

Vittorio had been mesmerized by the angry face of the banker. Now he tore his eyes away and looked at Alice. He was not fooled. He knew what was being said, and he knew that his benefactress was going through agonies. The glass slipper was turning out not to be a perfect fit after all.

'I understand,' he said. 'The Signor doesn't want me, but it doesn't matter. I'm here now, in America. Nothing will make me go back to Sicily. Even your husband.'

Alice switched to English.

'He understands,' she said, coolly.

'Good. I assume he is a Roman Catholic?'

'He is.'

'While I don't approve of Catholicism, I will not try to dictate

56

his faith. However, I would prefer it if he were to become, in time, an Episcopalian. Tell him.'

Alice translated. Vittorio eyed Augustus.

'I will not,' he said, 'leave my religion.'

When this was translated, Augustus shrugged.

'So be it,' he said. 'Well then, I think we understand each other. You are taking him up to Dutchess County?'

'Yes.'

'I'll be up the day after tomorrow, as usual.'

Alice rose out of her chair.

'Don't you think,' she said, 'you could make some friendly gesture to him? At least welcome him to America?'

Once again, the banker's cold eyes riveted on the boy.

'As far as I'm concerned,' he replied, 'Vittorio will have to earn my friendship. And respect.'

'Augustus, I've never known you not to be a gentleman. The least you can do is shake the child's hand.'

Augustus stood up, came slowly around the desk and extended his hand. Vittorio rose and took it.

'I wish you no ill will . . .' Augustus began.

'Hah!'

He glared at his wife.

'That will do, Alice. In fact, I *don't* wish him ill will. This awkward situation has been caused by your precipitous and ill-advised decision. However, if the young man earns my respect, I wish him nothing but good luck in our country. Tell him that, please.'

Alice did. Vittorio looked the older man in the eye and said, quietly, 'I will do my best to please the Signor.'

They unclasped hands, and Alice led him out of the office. Augustus watched them go, thinking, the little beggar's got guts. I'll give him that. He's got guts. Didn't flinch once . . .

Twelve-year-old Lucille Elliot dived into the cool water of Lake Minnehonka in Dutchess County and called to her younger brother, Rodney, 'What do you think the Wop will look like?'

Rodney was floating on his back.

'He'll probably have spaghetti coming out of his ears. Or maybe he'll have a monkey, like an organ-grinder.'

'I'd *love* a monkey! Oh Rodney, let's ask him to get one, if he doesn't have it already.'

Lucille, the eldest child of Augustus's sister, Virginia, swam to a wooden float and climbed up on it. Virginia had moved to New York from Elmira shortly after her brother. With Augustus's help, she had met red-haired Carter Elliot, the heir to a department store fortune. Carter and Virginia had been married in 1867 and promptly started producing children, to Alice's envy and despair. The two families were close enough to share two cottages on the wooded shore of the freshwater lake, and each July and August the Elliots and Dexters fled the heat of the city for the rural pleasures of Dutchess County.

Now Lucille sat on the float, scratching a chigger bite on her right ankle. With red-gold hair inherited from her father, blue eyes and fair skin, she was good-looking, and she knew it. She lay back to bake in the hot July sun, contrary to the orders of her mother, and contemplated the impending arrival of Aunt Alice's mysterious Sicilian.

'How will we talk to him?' she said to Rodney.

'I don't know,' said her brother, 'but I've got a present for him.'

'What?'

'You'll see.'

During the train ride from New York to Pawling, Alice and Vittorio said little to each other. Alice was so embarrassed and upset by the meeting with her husband, she could do nothing but stare out the window. Just before Brewster, she felt a hand on hers. She turned to Vittorio.

'Non importa, Signora,' he said, *'Andrà tutto bene.'* Things will work out.

Alice tried to smile. She found herself intrigued by his courage.

When they reached Lake Minnehonka, the numerous Elliot children hurried to the front of the cottage to gaze with ill-concealed curiosity at 'the Sicilian.' They waited as Alice and the boy climbed out of the buggy. Then Alice led Vittorio up to the line.

'Children,' she said, 'this is Vittorio.'

His eyes wandered over the Anglo-Saxon faces of Rodney, Edward, George, Eugenia and finally Lucille. When he reached the pretty redhead, who was looking at him with the expression of a biologist examining an exotic frog, Vittorio Spada felt an odd tingle he had never experienced before.

He solemnly shook hands with the Elliots one by one.

But he could barely take his eyes off Lucille.

58

That evening, when he climbed in bed for his first night in America, he felt something squishy against his legs. Jumping out of bed, he turned on the lamp and looked at the sheets.

Rodney Elliot's present was a mess of cold and smelly spaghetti and meatballs.

CHAPTER 4

The Mediterranean sun bit mercilessly into the sweaty back of Franco Spada as he raised his sledgehammer for the thousandth time that day, then smashed it down on the rock, crushing it into rubble that would eventually end up as part of the roadbed of the new Rome-to-Naples railroad. The island of San Stefano was one huge rock that, for the past thirty years, had been slowly converted to rubble by a generation of prisoners pounding their sledgehammers under the eyes of a hundred rifle-armed guards. The island, no more than six kilometers in diameter at its widest point, jutted out of the blue Tyrrhenian Sea fifteen kilometers off the city of Gaeta. In the fourteenth century, the Knights of Malta had built a fortress on it. Five hundred years later, the Bourbon Kings of the Two Sicilies had converted the grim stone building into a prison, erecting a small commune of houses for the guards near the prison walls, the only other structures on the island. The Bourbons had unleashed their Spanish streak of cruelty in the conversion. Ninety-nine cells, each sixteen feet square, housed eight prisoners apiece, the only fenestration being a foot-square hole in the ceiling ten feet above the stone floor, the hole being open not only to the heat but the rain as well. Murderers, thieves and rapists were imprisoned with anarchists, socialists and other political prisoners with no regard to the differences in their crimes. Furthermore, in a final burst of sadism, the prisoners were permanently coupled together by leg chains, night and day, the manacles unlocked only when one prisoner was to be punished. In these hellish couplings, a murderer could be chained to a university professor who had had the temerity, or foolishness, to antagonize the local authorities. Sometimes the couplings, which could last for years, resulted in friendship, sometimes in physical love. More often it led to a hatred which frequently terminated in murder. The prison of San Stefano was the ninth ring of hell from which very few people returned with either their health or their sanity.

Franco had been relatively lucky. Upon his arrival at the island in July, he had been chained to another new arrival at San Stefano, Fillipo Pieri, the twenty-six-year-old son of a prominent physician in Florence. Fillipo had become a socialist at the University of Bologna, but it wasn't his political views that had condemned him to twenty-five years at hard labor—although they helped. He had gotten into a drunken brawl with a certain Antonio Bianchi, a classmate who had made a pass at the love of Fillipo's life, a girl named Nelda. In the fight Antonio banged his head against a stove and died within the hour. Since Antonio was the son of a prominent manufacturer, the trial was well publicized and the prosecution didn't fail to emphasize Fillipo's socialist politics. Only the fact that he was himself the son of a respected physician saved him from receiving a term of life imprisonment.

The two young men, chained together twenty-four hours a day, both convicted of violent crimes, both intensely bitter, soon overcame the gulf of their dissimilar backgrounds and, for better or for worse, tried to accommodate themselves to their situation. They were in Cell 43 with six other men: one bank robber, one embezzler, one anarchist who had unsuccessfully tried to assassinate the Mayor of Turin, one violinist who had strangled a ten-year-old girl and then raped her, a Milanese who had specialized in swindling gullible widows, and a Venetian counterfeiter whose engraving was—unluckily for him—second rate. The combined sentences of this motley crew totaled (according to Fillipo's calculation) 218 years, assuming the two life sentences, Franco's and and that of the child-killer Giovanni Fermi, to average fifty years each.

The men slept on straw mattresses on the floor. Their toilet was an open drain. They were allowed one bath a week, one new uniform every two years. They lived in filth, breathed stench, ate gruel and wormy pasta, and worked a nine-hour day on the rock pile six days a week.

The prison was considered, according to the Royal Commission on Prison Conditions which wrote a report in 1877, to be 'strict but secure.'

'Spada!' said Tullio Settembrini, one of the guards, coming over to Franco at four that afternoon. Franco stopped work and looked at Fat Tullio with the combination of respect and hatred he had quickly learned was the best way to deal with his gray-uniformed keepers. The respect flattered their egos, which

was necessary. The hatred reminded them that he was not 'soft.'
Once a prisoner was known as 'soft,' his life became unbearable. Franco, Fat Tullio knew, was anything but 'soft.' His spirit
was as hard as his muscled body, the skin of which had been
turned almost black by the August sun. 'Spada, the Captain
wants to see you.'

'Why?'

'He'll tell you. Come on. You, too, Pieri.'

Franco and Fillipo put down their sledgehammers and followed Fat Tullio. The two-foot length of chain that connected
Franco's left ankle to Fillipo's right required them to walk in
reverse step, Franco's left leg and Fillipo's right always going
forward together. This strange method of ambulation was known
by the prisoners as the San Stefano Shuffle. They reached the
line of black, horsedrawn vans which transported the men from
the prison to the rock pile at eight in the morning, then returned
them home at five in the afternoon.

'Get in,' said Fat Tullio, pointing to the first van. They
obeyed, climbing in the empty vehicle and sitting next to each
other on the plank benches. Clang! The iron doors shut. After a
moment they could feel the van rumble into motion.

'What do you think he wants?' asked Fillipo. He was a thin,
sandy-haired man with watery blue, myopic eyes and a straggly
beard.

'Who knows?' shrugged Franco. 'At least we're getting off
the pile early.'

The trip across the island took a half hour, and the two
prisoners traveled it in silence. Not only were they too exhausted
to talk after eight hours on the rock pile, but there was little to
talk about. During the four weeks they had been chained
together, they had told each other their stories, spewed forth
their bitterness and frustration, fantasized about sex and escape,
complained about the food and their animal-like living conditions, cursed the guards behind their back . . . in short, done
what all prisoners do when they first arrive. But now a certain
numbness was growing over them as the reality of the years
stretching ahead sank into their consciousness. Four weeks had
seemed forever. What would a year seem like? Five years?
Twenty? The horror of it created a desperation that plunged them
both into silence.

Fat Tullio unlocked the van doors, and the two men climbed
down to the cobbled courtyard in the center of the prison.

'This way.'

He pointed to the door of the office of Captain Gaetano

Zambelli, the commandant of the prison, and the two men hobbled toward it, Fat Tullio following. At the door Fat Tullio knocked.

'Come in.'

Fat Tullio opened the iron door, and Franco and Fillipo went into the neat, cheerful office of the commandant. Whitewashed walls, spotless, decorated with two huge portraits of King Umberto and Queen Margherita, the latter smiling regally, her long neck swathed in a diamond-and-pearl collar. On the barred windowsills, clay pots of pink geraniums. Behind a rather severe desk, Captain Zambelli, a Neapolitan with an unusually long face and a drooping black moustache. He had improbably sad eyes, rather like a puppy's, and beautifully manicured, artistic hands. The prisoners had nicknamed him *La Donna dei Dolori* —'The Lady of the Sorrows'—because he always looked as if he were about to weep as he issued Draconian punishments for minor offenses. The men laughed at him, but it was the laughter of hatred. One of the favorite games in the prison was How to Kill Zambelli by Inflicting the Most Pain.

'Ah, Spada,' sighed the commandant, wiping his long nose with a handkerchief. 'You have received a package.'

He indicated a large box before him on the desk. Franco looked at it.

'It's from Princess dell'Acqua,' continued the commandant. 'You have fancy friends.'

The sad eyes looked at the two prisoners, both filthy and shirtless.

'I was, of course, forced to read the letter and inspect the contents of the package. Prison regulations, you know.'

Zambelli pulled a large, leather-bound book out of the box.

'The Princess has sent you a beautiful Bible,' he went on. 'Quite handsome. Beautiful leather. From Florence, wouldn't you say, Pieri?'

Fillipo shifted his weight on his tired feet. He was terrified of Zambelli.

'Yes, sir,' he mumbled.

'Well now, since you are a university student—or *were* until you turned killer—and since Spada can't read, perhaps you'd be so kind as to read him what the Princess has written.'

He handed the folded note across the desk. Fillipo took it, opened it, admired the crest and the quality of the paper, then read aloud:

My dear Franco:

You may not wish to receive my correspondence, but I intend to write you anyway—even if you do not reply. It is, under the circumstances, the very least I can do.

You will, I hope, be pleased to know that Vittorio has been sent to America. He is being adopted by my friend, Mrs. Dexter, whom you must remember. The Dexters are a wealthy family, well-placed socially, and they will give Vittorio the advantages he certainly would never have had in Sicily. I personally escorted him to Liverpool to catch the ship. His last words were of you. He loves you, Franco, and is heartbroken about what has happened.

I know that you blame me for your imprisonment. I understand your feelings: I blame myself. Dear friend—and I like to think we are friends; I, at least, feel a friendship toward you—I know in my heart you are innocent. If it is any consolation during this time of despair, I will never cease doing everything I can to overturn your conviction. It is difficult, because of my husband, but I have friends and relatives in the government, and I will continue to plague them to reopen the investigation of the murder. Unhappily, things move slowly in Rome. But I will persevere.

In the meantime, I send you this Bible. I know you are not particularly religious, but perhaps the study of Divine Scripture will not only bring you some peace of mind, but also, perhaps, will improve your reading skills. I particularly recommend the first chapter of the Second Book of Machabees.

Believe me, dear friend, in my deepest expressions of sympathy and friendship,

Sylvia, Princess dell'Acqua

Captain Zambelli sniffed, wiped his nose and looked sadly at Franco.

'Well, "dear friend," perhaps the rumors about you and the Princess were true after all?'

Franco looked stony.

'She's not my friend,' he said, 'and I don't want her damned Bible.'

'Ah ah: we must not speak disrespectfully of the Holy Book. You should take it and do as the Princess recommends: improve your reading skills. Perhaps you can get Pieri to help teach you.

You're going to be here a long time: you should improve your mind.'

'Why?'

Zambelli shrugged.

'Who knows? Perhaps the Princess can get you out of here. I certainly hope so. It gives me no pleasure to see you in here. No pleasure at all.'

And the sad face smiled slightly.

'But I'm curious why she recommended Second Machabees,' he went, opening the book. 'It seems an obscure selection . . . I took the trouble of reading the first chapter—hope you don't mind. I found nothing particularly enlightening in it. Well, not *quite* nothing . . . It's the last book of the Old Testament, you know, a rather dreary account of the persecution of the Jews in the second century, B.C. But here, in verse sixteen—which the Princess has very delicately underlined in pencil—they talk about the priests of Nanea entering the Temple through a secret entrance. Now, why do you suppose the Princess underlined that particular passage?'

He looked at the two prisoners.

'I have no idea,' said Franco.

'But you're not using your imagination! Do you think the Princess is trying to tell you that there is a secret entrance to this prison? Or more to the point, a secret *exit?*'

Silence.

'Or perhaps there's a secret entrance to this book?'

He closed the Bible, then reopened the front cover. The endpapers were elegantly swirled. Zambelli ran his fingers over the inside front cover.

'Interesting,' he said. 'I think there's something under the lining. I'd hate to think the Princess was so unoriginal as to try to smuggle you something in a book lining? She must not have a very high opinion of our intelligence if she did.'

Franco watched as the commandant picked up a letter opener, inserted it under the paper and sliced it open. He pulled out five one-thousand-lire notes and held them up, fanning them. He looked at the money with mournful eyes.

'She did,' he sighed. 'She smuggled you money—probably thinking you could bribe your way out of here. Such an old trick . . . and such a lot of money.' His eyes lifted to Franco. 'Alas, "dear friend," prison regulations are very specific about attempts to smuggle money in to prisoners. The money is to be confiscated by the State, and the prisoner is to be punished. Tullio, unchain Spada.'

Franco stared incredulously at Zambelli as Fat Tullio knelt to unlock his manacle.

'But I had nothing to do with this!' he said. 'How can you punish *me* for something she did?'

'I can hardly punish the Princess, can I? Tullio, put him in solitary confinement for two weeks. A diet of bread and water.'

'NO!' roared Franco. 'You bastard, I didn't *do* anything!'

'Three weeks.'

'Son of a bitch—!'

All his rage and frustration exploded. He didn't know what he was doing. He acted instinctively, like an animal. Fat Tullio had just finished unlocking the leg chain. Now Franco smashed his two fists down on the back of the guard's head. He grunted and crumbled to the floor. Franco jumped over him and ran for the door. He had just opened it when he heard an explosion and felt something hit his left shoulder. The force of the bullet spun him off balance, and he stumbled forward into the courtyard, falling on the pavement.

Captain Zambelli stood up. He was still holding the revolver he had pulled from his desk drawer.

'Tullio,' he said, 'take him to the infirmary. After they've taken out the bullet, put him in solitary for a month.'

Fat Tullio was struggling to his feet, rubbing the back of his head.

Fillipo Pieri watched as the guard weaved uncertainly out of the office, then poked his rifle in Franco's back. Blood was oozing out of the shoulder wound.

'Get up, you bastard,' grunted Fat Tullio.

Franco slowly got to his feet. He looked back into the office, first at Zambelli, then at Fillipo.

'See you next month,' he said to his friend.

Fillipo Pieri nodded numbly. He was awake in a nightmare.

PART II

LOVE AFFAIRS

1890-1892

CHAPTER 5

On November 12, 1890, Victor Dexter, the former Vittorio Spada, knocked on the door of his adopted father's office in the Dexter Bank and went inside.

'You wanted to see me, sir?' he said in an English that ten years of night school and life in New York had made fluent and idiomatic. At twenty-two, Victor was tall, slim and startlingly good-looking. His adopted cousin, Rodney Elliot, still called him the Wop, and with his dark curly hair, Victor looked undeniably Mediterranean. But he sounded American.

Augustus, now fifty-one and seriously overweight, looked up from his papers.

'Yes, Victor. Sit down, please.'

Victor took the chair in front of the desk. If his adopted father's hostility had waned over the years, due to Alice's continuous championing of Victor's virtues and the erosion of time, Victor and Augustus were still stiffly formal to each other.

Augustus removed his pince-nez and wiped the lenses with a handkerchief.

'As you know, Victor, my wife and I are giving a Christmas dance for the Elliot children on December tenth. We are fortunate enough to have a ballroom, which the Elliots don't; and even though my wife's health is delicate, she has insisted on giving the dance. However, she informs me you aren't attending. Might I ask why?'

'I have night school . . .'

'Yes, of course. I know. You're an extremely hardworking young man, Victor, and I'm pleased with what you've done at school and here at the bank these past two years. But we have a saying in this country that all work and no play makes Jack a dull boy.'

'I know the saying, sir.'

'Oh, you do?' Augustus never ceased to be amazed at Victor's mastery of English. It had undermined the banker's assumption that no immigrant's intelligence could possibly be up to par. 'Well, both my wife and I agree that while your development has been exceptional—quite exceptional, in fact—socially, you haven't been . . .' He paused and looked at Victor directly in the eye. 'Well, dammit, Victor, you *are* our adopted son. You have to start getting out in society. You're a good-looking young man, you could be an asset to the family. Do you follow me?'

As always, Augustus's manner was gruff. But Victor felt there was something new in his tone, an almost imperceptible note of pleading.

'I follow you, sir.'

'You *are* interested in women?'

When Victor thought of the agonies his nonexistent sex life caused him, he almost laughed.

'Yes, sir. But I don't have much opportunity to meet them.'

'I realize that. And I admit that's partially my fault. My wife . . .' Again, he paused, '. . . your mother . . .' he forced it out, and it was the first time Victor had heard him say it '. . . has tried to get me to buy you proper clothes and send you to dancing school and so forth, but I, well, I resisted her. I'm prepared now to admit I was wrong. Your mother wants you to go to the dance, Victor. And . . .' he took a deep breath, as if the admission were painful to him, '. . . so do I. Will you go?'

Victor was too dazed to answer for a moment. After ten years of being something above the servants in the Dexter household, but not quite part of the family despite Augustus's reluctant adoption of him six years before, this approach was new and startling.

'I realize,' Augustus continued, 'you don't have proper dress clothes. I have informed Brooks Brothers that they are to outfit you and charge it to my account.'

Another miracle.

'I'm waiting for an answer, Victor.'

He came out of his daze.

'Yes, sir. I'd be glad to go. And thank you for the clothes.'

Augustus untensed.

'Good. That will be all, Victor.'

Victor got out of the chair, still hardly able to believe this turn of events.

'No, wait a minute—it won't be all. Sit down, Victor.'

He obeyed. Again Augustus seemed to be undergoing difficulty articulating his thoughts.

'I think I should tell you that . . . your mother is quite

seriously ill. Dr. Compton tells me her tuberculosis has taken a turn for the worse, and we may have to send her to a warmer climate soon. I don't think I have to mention that in the past, things have not been, well, what they might have been between you and me, which has caused Alice a good deal of sorrow. For her sake, and for mine, I hope our relationship can improve.' He paused. 'Frankly, you're not the son I would like to have had. But you're the son I have.' They eyed each other a moment. 'You may go now.'

Victor left the office. Augustus had dropped him a crumb of warmth, but Victor was aware that it was, at best, a half-hearted crumb.

'And would you be takin' the tea tray up to Mrs. Dexter?' said Emma Flynn, Augustus's stout Irish cook. 'That's right: a nice slice of lemon. And mind you, wake her up gentle if she's asleep. The poor woman suffers in this cold weather.'

'Yes, Mrs. Flynn,' answered Maureen O'Casey, whose brogue was as thick as the cook's. Despite Augustus's dim view of immigrants, his entire household staff of six (except Cyril, the butler, who was English) was Irish, because the Irish were cheap to hire. Now Maureen, who was twenty and just four months off the boat, picked up the silver tray and made her way out of the kitchen to the back stairs to start the long climb to the third floor. The Dexter house on Madison Avenue had undergone certain improvements in the past decade—it had been wired for electricity and telephones had been installed—but Maureen reflected that no one gave a damn about the help: They still had to puff their way up steep stairs with heavy trays. Well, it's steady work, she thought.

The second floor held the ballroom, a billiard room and a small library. On the third floor were the four bedrooms, and the servants' rooms were on top. Now as Maureen emerged from the servants' stairs on the third floor, she saw young Mr. Victor at the end of the hall, talking on the phone. Maureen was no beauty, but she was ripe and, during her three weeks on the Dexter staff, she had done her best to catch Victor's eye. Now she stepped into a shadow to eavesdrop.

'Lucille?' she heard him say, and she noticed an excitement in his voice. 'It's Victor. How are you?' Pause. 'That's good. Say, I was wondering if you had an escort to the dance here next month? Yes, I'm going, believe it or not. I'd be honored if . . . well, if I could be your escort.' A long pause. 'Oh.' Maureen stifled a giggle. The tone of that 'oh' left no doubt about what

71

Lucille had said. 'You're going with Bill Wharton. Well, I understand. I hope you'll save me a dance. Good-bye.'

He hung up. Maureen stepped out of the shadow and headed for Alice's bedroom. As she approached him, Victor looked up. He was still standing by the phone, his face expressionless.

Maureen smiled at him.

'She said "no," did she?'

Victor shrugged.

'She couldn't believe I asked.'

'Well, I don't see why. I think a lot of girls would be real happy to have you as their escort.'

'Not Miss Elliot.'

'Got a crush on her, have you?'

Victor didn't answer. Sticking his hands in his pockets, he walked down the hall to his small bedroom in the rear of the house. Maureen watched him go.

Ah, he's half daft with love, that one, poor lad! she thought. Wish he'd moon like that over *me*.

Sighing, she knocked on Alice's door, then carried the tea tray into her bedroom.

The Dexter ballroom was far from being the largest ballroom in New York, but Augustus took pride in it anyway. Fifty feet by forty, with twenty-foot ceilings, it dominated the second floor of the house, and through its four sets of French windows on that snowy December night, the sixty guests could peer out on Madison Avenue below, where their coachmen in silk hats and ankle-length coats huddled around coal fires provided by the Dexter servants for their semicomfort. The ballroom was, like the rest of the house, rather oppressive and gloomy, with its heavy paneling done in the *mauresque* style, although a number of large English landscapes added a note of cheer, and the two crystal chandeliers gave an effervescent sparkle. Huge Chinese vases, from which leafy palms sprang, squatted in the corners; gilt opera chairs lined the walls; and behind the fat black Steinway piano stood a Coromandel screeen that was the best piece in the room.

Promptly at nine o'clock, Mr. Fadely's String Ensemble struck up a lively polka, and Bill Wharton led Lucille on to the parquet floor.

'You're looking swell,' said Bill, who prided himself on being up on the latest slang. He also prided himself on his good looks, his parents' money and being captain of the Yale football team.

72

She looks fabulous, thought Victor, who was watching the couple from one of the corners of the room. Far from proving a tonic to his spirits, the Dexter ball had plunged him into a severe depression. Though he knew Alice wanted him to be there and he would never have disappointed her—especially since she had been too weak to get out of bed for her own party—still, he wished he were somewhere else—anywhere else. He had nothing in common with these guilded youth of New York society. Those that knew him thought of him as some sort of freak, the Dexter's house immigrant who went to night school on Twenty-third Street and worked as a teller in the bank. He couldn't exchange small talk with them because he didn't know any small talk. He had bought himself a book entitled *How to Learn Ballroom Dancing on Your Own*, and had been practicing in his room, but he had never actually danced with a girl. The thought of making a fool of himself in front of these people caused him to break out into a cold sweat, even though he wanted nothing more in the world than to dance with Lucille Elliot. Lucille, Lucille! How beautiful she looked in her white ballgown, her red-gold hair swept up in rich curls, the pearl necklace around her long neck, her big blue eyes looking into Bill Wharton's as they twirled around the floor! Lucille was everything he wanted. As far as Lucille was concerned, Victor could have lived on the planet Neptune.

'Hey, Victor, why are you hiding in the corner?' said Rodney Elliot, coming up to him. Rodney was a sophomore at Princeton, and Victor thought he was the most obnoxious of all the Elliot cousins. 'Pie-ing' Victor's bed with cold spaghetti his first night in America had been the first of a long line of stupid practical jokes and insults that Rodney had heaped on Victor during the past ten years.

'I'm not "hiding," ' said Victor. 'I'm watching.'

'Well, I've got someone who wants to meet you. She's a real beauty, and I told her all about you—how dashing you were and all that. Hey, you look good in that new tailcoat! Really suave! You're the best-looking Sicilian here. Come on: Maxine's dying to meet you. She's in the billiard room. Say, it's some swell party, isn't it?'

He led Victor out of the ballroom.

'Maxine who?'

'Maxine Vanderbilt. She's one of *the* Vanderbilts and a classmate of Lucille's at Vassar. 'Course, I know you'd rather have Lucille, but Maxine's not a bad second choice, and . . . .' he lowered his voice, '. . . they say she's *hot*.' He winked, then opened the door to the billiard room. 'She's waiting for you. Her mother's a dragon, but we got her some champagne so she won't bother you. Go to it. And good luck!'

Giving him another wink, he shoved him through the door, then closed it after him. The room was paneled in dark walnut, and the only illumination was a huge, curlicued brass lamp with green shades over the billiard table. He saw a girl in white standing at a window. Now she turned, and Victor, for the thousandth time in his life, cursed Rodney.

Maxine Vanderbilt was a fright, with buck teeth, a fat nose and frizzy hair. She smiled at him.

'Hello.' Her voice was like a foghorn. 'Are you the Italian cousin?'

As he wanted to strangle Rodney, at the same time he felt sorry for this ugly girl who was as much a butt of the joke as he was. They were both misfits.

'Yes,' he said, uncertainly. 'I'm Victor.'

They both stood motionless, separated by the fat-legged billiard table, immobilized by awkwardness.

'I'm *so* interested in Italy,' said Maxine. 'I'm taking a course in Italian art.' Pause. 'Of the early Renaissance.'

He was burning with rage. It was so cruel to her, as well as to him. He was used to the cruelty, the constant taunts and practical jokes, but this, somehow, was too much.

'Would you . . .' he hesitated. Oh God, why wasn't she Lucille? '. . . like to dance?'

Her smile was almost pathetically eager.

'That would be lovely.'

She came around the table, and he noticed the armpits of her white dress were stained. Poor girl, the only husband she'd ever get would be someone after her Vanderbilt name and money.

'I'd better warn you that I'm a terrible dancer,' he said. 'In fact, I've never danced at all.'

She looked surprised.

'Never?'

'Never. But if you're willing to take a chance with the biggest clod in New York . . . ?'

She looked at him rather sadly.

'No one else has asked me to dance, Mr. Dexter,' she said.

He forced a smile.

'Then, shall we show them our stuff?'

She smiled and took his arm. To hell with Rodney, he thought. To hell with all of them! I'll show the bastards; *We'll* show them!

He led her out of the billiard room back to the ballroom, where a waltz was in progress.

'If I step on your toes . . .' he began.

'Mr. Dexter, I have *very* strong toes.'

'Good. Shall we?'

And he led her on to the floor. Rodney Elliot had to go out to the hallway so his parents wouldn't hear his howls of laughter.

'Victor's dancing with Maxine!' exclaimed Lucille to Bill Wharton. They were sitting the waltz out. 'Can you believe it? Thank heaven—poor Maxine hasn't had a dance all evening.'

'They make a handsome couple: the frog and the greaseball.'

She turned on him, angrily.

'What a horrid thing to say!'

'It's true, isn't it? She looks like a frog.'

'Maxine's a very sweet girl, and just for that I'm going to make you dance with her!'

'Fat chance.'

She frowned.

'You know, Bill, you're a good-looking man, but at times you can be downright ugly.'

'What do you mean by that?'

'You're too dumb to understand.'

She took the small pencil attached to her dance card and scratched out Bill's name on the next dance.

'Hey, what are you doing? That's my dance!'

'Not anymore. I'm writing in Victor.'

'Him? But he hasn't asked you!'

'I'm asking him.'

'You mean you'd dance with that greaseball?'

'I like grease.'

She left him to walk out on the dance floor. The waltz had ended, and the overheated dancers were catching their breaths. She came up to Victor and Maxine, who were standing at the side of the room in front of a gilt console table holding two elaborate crystal candelabra and surmounted by a fancy gilt mirror.

'Maxine,' she said. 'I had no idea you waltzed so well!'

'Oh, Victor's the good dancer . . .'

'Yes, isn't he?' She turned and smiled at him. 'And I claim him for the next dance. His name's on my card.'

Victor stared at her.

'How did my name get on your card?'

'I put it there. Maxine, you won't mind if I have *one* dance with him?'

'Oh, no . . .'

'*I* mind.' Bill Wharton had come up behind her. 'My name was on the card first.'

Lucile turned to him.

'And I crossed it off!'

The music started, another waltz. Bill shoved Victor aside and put his hand on Lucille's waist.

'Sorry, *paesano*,' he said to Victor. 'But since this isn't a tarantella, I think she wants to dance with me.'

'Bill, let me go—!'

Victor grabbed his arm and jerked him around.

'She wants,' he said, softly, 'to dance with *me*.'

Bill Wharton's smile was pure, Yale-bred insolence.

'Is that so? I tell you what: why don't you go down to the kitchen and make us some pizza? I hear Neapolitans make the best pizza in the world . . . But I forgot: you're Sicilian, aren't you?'

Lucille saw Victor tense, saw his fist clench. Quickly, she took his arm.

'Come on, Victor.'

'Wait a minute . . .'

'*Victor!*' she insisted. 'Just because Bill's rude . . .'

'Yes,' said Maxine, turning on Bill, 'I think you're *extremely* rude. You might learn some manners from Mr. Dexter. Excuse me.'

She walked away, leaving Bill red in the face with anger.

'I think it was terribly nice of you to dance with Maxine,' said Lucille as Victor waltzed around the floor. 'And pay no attention to Bill. He can be a boor at times.'

'Maxine was being nice to dance with me, since I've never danced before.'

'You're doing extremely well, if you ask me. And you look very handsome in your new clothes. I've never seen you looking so good.'

'You always look beautiful to me, Lucille.'

He had blurted it out, and immediately kicked himself for telling the truth. He was leaving himself wide open for her ridicule. To his surprise, Lucille said nothing. She even looked rather pleased.

When the dance ended, he was so elated he said, 'Some punch?'

'I'd love some.'

They crossed the crowded room to the punch table, where two footmen were ladling out nonalcoholic strawberry punch.

'Uncle Augustus doesn't know this,' said Lucille, 'but Rodney tried to spike the punch.'

'I wish someone would spike Rodney.'

'Oh, he's not that bad. I know you don't like him, and I suppose I don't blame you, but he's just an immature brat. And speak of the devil.'

He turned to see Rodney and Bill Wharton coming up beside him. They both held cups of the pink punch.

'Hey, here's Victor!' grinned Rodney. 'The great dancer!'

'And ladies' man,' added Bill. 'Don't forget that.'

'Not to mention Beau Brummel,' continued Rodney. 'Would you look at that coat? The cut of the lapels? The immaculate white shirt front? Why, you'd almost think he was a real gentleman! Oh—ex-*cuse* me!'

He threw his cup of punch on Victor's shirt.

'How *clumsy* of me!' he smiled. 'Gosh, Victor, I'm really *sorry.*'

Bill Wharton lifted his cup over Victor's head and tilted it. The punch poured over his hair and streamed down his face.

'Now, look what *I've* done,' said Bill. 'Gee, Rodney, we're both so clumsy . . .'

'You're both so *drunk!*' said Lucille, angrily.

'I'll handle it,' said Victor, gently shoving her aside. By now a crowd was gathering. He turned to the two troublemakers. With the punch matting his hair, he looked a mess, but Maxine Vanderbilt thought he looked wonderfully dignified.

'Would you two "gentlemen" care to step outside?' he said quietly.

Rodney snickered.

'Hey, Bill, the Wop wants to fight. Two bits he carries a knife . . .'

Crack! Victor's right fist slammed into Rodney's jaw. The amazed Princetonian 'oofed' and fell back on to the punch table. His weight cracked one of the legs of the table, and Rodney and the two punch bowls and three dozen glass cups slid to the parquet floor with a resounding crash. The debutantes and their chaperoning mothers screamed. The men yelled with excitement. Bill Wharton grabbed Victor and turned him around.

'You Dago son of a bitch . . .'

He punched Victor in the gut, then caught his jaw with an uppercut. Now it was Victor's turn to fall backward, stumbling over Rodney and crashing into the broken glass of the punch bowls. Victor's ears were ringing from the blow, and his lip was cut and bleeding; but now his long-dormant Sicilian temper erupted like Mount Etna. Scrambling to his feet, he charged Bill Wharton. The Yalie had twenty pounds' advantage and was a trained boxer, but Victor had the advantage of outrage. He tackled him, crashing him to the floor. The two men rolled over and over, scattering the guests, hitting each other with a ferocity that made the chaperones wince, their daughters gasp. Lucille and Maxine watched with wide-eyed excitement.

Mr. Fadely's seated musicians grabbed their violins and ran as the two rolled toward them. Music racks toppled and crashed. Bill got to his feet, grabbed one of the racks with both hands, raised it over his head and smashed it down on Victor. Screams. Victor raised his arm in time to avert the blow. Again he got to his feet. Blood was running out of his mouth and nose, and his right eye was blackening. Now he charged Bill, blindly. Like a bull he rammed his head into his stomach. The Yalie flew back on to the keyboard of the Steinway grand. Cacophony shrieked from strings which moments before had sung Strauss. Now the two were on the floor again, under the piano, wrestling, bumping against the fat, fluted piano legs . . .

'Victor!'

He looked at the patent leather shoes, the sharply creased trousers. He knew the voice: Fear froze him. It was the advantage Bill needed. He grabbed Victor's throat with both hands and started whacking his head against the floor.

'VICTOR!'

The voice was a roar of rage, backed with all the pompous authority of Augustus Dexter.

Straining every muscle, Victor broke Bill's stranglehold, pushed him away, then crawled out from under the piano and wobbled to his feet. Leaning on the keyboard, panting, he looked at his adopted father. Augustus's fat face was red with rage.

'You will go to your room,' he said, his voice now soft.

Victor wiped his bloody mouth with his sleeve. He saw Bill crawl out from under the piano and stand up, looking rather uncertainly at Augustus. Then he pointed at Victor.

'He started it, Mr. Dexter,' said Bill. 'He hit me first.' And his friends around the room chorused agreement. Augustus glared at Victor.

'Is this true?'

Victor took a deep breath.

'Yes, sir,' he said. 'And what's more, I'm going to finish it.'

Grabbing Bill's shoulder, he jerked him around to confront him. Bill's fists flew up, but it was too late. Pow! Victor's right fist connected with Bill's chin, hard. Bill fell backward into the arms of a surprised Augustus. As the portly, popeyed banker supported the slumping Yalie, Victor started across the room to the doors. The assembled company watched him in silence, unable to believe this cyclone had erupted in the genteel ballroom. When Victor reached the doors, he turned and said in a loud voice:

'Si, sono Siciliano! E sono fiero! E lei é caca!'

He walked out of the room, wondering if anyone there knew that *caca* meant 'shit.'

Maxine Vanderbilt understood no Italian, but the homely girl in the sweat-stained ballgown had never met a man who excited her more than Victor. She was intelligent; she knew she would probably never get a man like him.

But she would treasure that one waltz with him the rest of her life.

He needed fresh air.

He had shattered his secure world, and for the grief this would cause his adopted mother, Alice, he felt shame. He genuinely loved Alice, as she adored him. Even so, he was glad he had fought Bill and Rodney. Ten years of resentment and inferiority had exploded, and he felt purged. He had no idea whether Augustus would kick him into the street, but at this moment he didn't care. He was kicking himself into the street.

Hatless, hugging his coat, he walked up Madison Avenue, leaning into the wind. It was a bitterly cold night and snowflakes iced his thick, punch-matted hair. Suddenly he knew where he wanted to go. It was late, almost midnight, but he didn't care.

He hurried across Fortieth Street to Fifth Avenue, then continued west to Sixth Avenue where, at Forty-second Street, he climbed the iron stairs to the El station and waited for the next downtown train.

A few other passengers were on the wind- and snow-swept platform; on one of the wooden benches, a bum dozed peacefully, apparently impervious to the cold, nestling an empty wine bottle in his arms. Soon the fifteen-ton, pea-green steam locomotive puffed into the station. Victor paid the five-cent fare and climbed up into one of the passenger cars, which were painted light green with pea-green and gold trim. Inside, the car's walls were paneled in oak and mahogany; Axminster carpeting and kerosene chandeliers further pampered the passengers. A small coal stove at the end of the car provided welcome warmth. Victor took a seat and thought about his life.

He remembered a Sicilian proverb: *Che lascia la via vecchia per la nuova, so quel che perde e non sa quel che trova* —'Whoever forsakes the old way for the new knows what he is losing, but not what he will find.' The old way, Sicily, was becoming a dim memory, reillumined briefly by occasional correspondence from Princess Sylvia and the few letters from Franco allowed by the prison authorities at San Stefano. Victor realized that almost half his life had been lived in America, the new way. Yet as he was no longer a Sicilian, he was not yet an American. After learning to read, he had devoured books on Italian history as well as American history, and when the Elliot cousins asked him why he wanted to learn Italian history, he had tried to explain that Sicily was almost as different from Italy as it was from America. This they could never understand, just as they couldn't understand why Victor didn't gesticulate with his hands when he spoke as other 'Wops' did, though he tried to explain that Sicilians rarely did.

There were so many contradictions and confusions in his life! He knew he should be grateful to Augustus, and he was. The man had paid for his night school, clothed him (in a way), fed him, housed him. Victor knew he was infinitely luckier than other immigrants. Yet Augustus had never loved him, and as he thought about it, Victor realized this had hurt him the most. He remembered that in Sicily the family was the strongest social unit, the *ordine della famiglia* being the one glue that had held Sicilians together through the centuries, enabling them to withstand the *sfruttamento*, or exploitation, of the succeeding waves of conquering *stranieri*—foreigners. Yet he had never had a real mother or a real family. Even in Sicily he had been a *scomunicato*, a pariah, just as he was here in New York. Over the years the Dexters had tried to inculcate in him their own WASP standards and morals—gently, on Alice's part, harshly on Augustus's. He had tried to conform to their strange ways because he lacked an alternative. But did he really believe in Augustus's stern Protestant work ethic? It seemed to exclude the simple joys he remembered from his childhood, the sheer delight of eating a freshly picked fig or orange, or of tramping the hills around Monreale in the hot sunshine with little thought of 'success' or 'position,' those items of such enormous importance to Augustus's world. Victor thought he probably wanted a degree of success in the new world, mainly because the alternative, failure, was so cruel in this money-dominated city. Besides, after two years of working as a teller in the Dexter Bank—another thing he owed Augustus—the world of finance fascinated him. But what kind of 'position' could he ever have? Would the world of the Dexters ever really accept him, particularly now that he had caused a near-riot in their ballroom? Would Lucille ever accept him as anything but a sort of freak, a transplanted *contadino*, or peasant? Neither servant nor family, neither Sicilian nor American. That night he had finally rebelled against the new way. His instincts were guiding him downtown to Little Italy to see if, somehow, he could fit together the broken pieces of *la via vecchia*, the old way.

He got off at the Bleecker Street station, climbed down to the snow-covered sidewalk and walked west. He was headed for a small trattoria on Thompson Street where he occasionally escaped the endless succession of roasts, veals and chops of the Dexter household to wallow in *caponatina di melanzane, pasta con sarde*, tuna almost as good as the tuna of Palermo, and, most mouth-watering of all, a divinely sweet *cassata alla Siciliana*. The tiny restaurant was owned by a middle-aged couple from Trapani named Riccione. The Ricciones were fond of Victor and intrigued by his almost unique position in the uptown world, his adoption by *gli Americani,* as all non-Sicilians were referred to by Sicilians. The Ricciones' answer to the problem of the 'new way' was, like most Sicilians in New York, to transplant the old way intact from Sicily. They barely could speak English and had almost no contact with non-Sicilians. They were happy, much happier than Victor. He wanted to pour out his troubles to the Ricciones. . . .

'Been in a fight, handsome?'

He had been so absorbed in his thoughts he hadn't noticed the whore in the dimly lighted doorway, although the street was otherwise deserted. He stopped, looked at her, then put his hand to his face. He had wiped the blood off before leaving the Dexter house, but he knew his right eye was black and his upper lip swollen.

'Cat got your tongue?'

One of the forty thousand prostitutes, or 'man-eaters,' active in New York stepped out of the doorway. The gaslight illuminated her pudgy, overly made-up face. She had once been pretty, but was now well past her prime, which probably accounted for her being in a neighborhood normally fairly free of whores. The Italians moving into the southern end of Greenwich Village tried to keep the *puttane* off their streets, chasing them back to the notorious Tenderloin district south of Times Square. Victor thought this one wouldn't survive long with the competition in the Tenderloin.

'You're a regular swell,' she smiled, admiring his tails. 'Five dollars will buy you a ticket to Paradise. Ten dollars, and I'll show you tricks you never *dreamed* of, honey.'

She was so crass he almost laughed, but not quite. Sex was Victor's guilty secret. Augustus frequently reminded him he was expected to be a 'gentleman' and 'restrain his Italian proclivities.' Though Augustus never said 'sex,' the faint leer in his eyes left no room for confusion. Victor had obeyed. Meanwhile his dreams teemed with erotic playlets. When he would wake up, sweating, he would find to his horror that his sheets were sticky. Crawling with embarrassment, he would try to wipe out the stains so that the Irish laundress wouldn't spread rumors.

Sex. His secret, and anathema to Augustus's world. He looked at the whore, so plump and dirty. Why not? If nothing else, it was a final slap in Augustus's face.

'Where can we go?' he said.

'My room's on Delancey Street. We could walk, but a swell like you would probably want a cab, wouldn't you?'

It was then he noticed she was shivering from the cold. She had a ratty fur around her neck and a heavy shawl around her shoulders, but no coat. Suddenly Victor felt sorry for her. It was hardly the emotion one should feel for a whore, but he couldn't help it. She was as lonely and lost as he, despite her bravado. He had twelve dollars on him.

'Let's walk to West Broadway,' he said. 'Maybe we can find a cab there.'

'Oh, you *are* a gent,' she purred, taking his arm. 'I'll show you a real good time. My name's Doreen. Doreen the Chorine, they call me when I'm working. I'm between engagements now, and you know how it is. The theater's a hard place to make a living, and a girl has to pay the rent . . . What's your name, honey?'

'Vittorio,' he said, after a moment. 'Vittorio Spada.'

And he hailed a cab.

Her room was on the first floor of a boardinghouse, overlooking the snow-covered privy in the backyard. When she lit the gas jet, the roaches were almost too bored to scatter.

'It ain't much, but it's home,' she said, closing the door. 'And it's all mine. The Jews in the tenements around here sleep three or four families in a room, but Doreen sleeps with no one but her customers.' She gave him a broad wink as she removed the hatpins from her black felt hat with its bedraggled feather, and let her golden hair tumble over her shoulders. Victor watched her as she put her shawl and fur into a crammed closet. Then quickly, professionally, she unbuttoned her dress and stepped out of it. Her corsetted body was plump, but the curves were voluptuously right. Her naked breasts spilled over the top of her corset, a cascade of white softness. Her legs were encased in black lisle stockings, one of which had a run. Though her thighs were fat, her legs below the knees were stunning. Victor drank in the splendor of her flesh, and his trousers began to bulge.

'Better get out of those pants, honey, before you explode out. And don't mind the roaches. They're friendly. Give me your clothes: I'll hang 'em up.'

When they were both naked, she eyed his thin, muscular body with approval. Her eyes traveled down the espaliered tree of his chest hair to the base, where the tip of his erection already glistened with drops of semen, like the spout of an overheated teakettle. When he took her in his arms, she felt the damp tip press into her soft belly, felt the hot young blood pumping through his body. He was kissing her with a passion that surprised as well as excited her.

'Honey,' she whispered, 'is this your first time?'

'Yes.'

His mouth was on her neck, his hands squeezing her plump, luscious breasts.

'Good,' she said, her eyes half-closed with pleasure. 'You'll remember me the rest of your life.'

She was right. He never forgot the fantastic pleasure as the soft, damp walls of her vagina swallowed him. Her fingers dug into his buttocks as he humped her on the sagging bed. A million teenage fantasies took on flesh as he shot into her his living link with a thousand generations, past and future. When it was over, she got up to douche herself.

'Well,' she smiled, 'what do you think of fucking?'

'It's even better than pasta.'

She laughed.

'Bet your ass, Honey, you've got a natural talent and you're hung like a bull. If you want to spend the night, the next one's on the house.'

He spent the night and Sunday morning. Then he paid his delayed call on the Ricciones.

Three blocks south, on the fourth floor of a squalid tenement on Hester Street, a five-year-old Russian Jew named Moyshe

83

Davidoff huddled in bed between his two older brothers. In a bed on the opposite side of the six-by-eight-foot room, separated by a blanket hung over a clothesline, Moyshe's parents, Arvid and Natalia Davidoff, made love, the soft squeaking of their bedsprings breaking the silence of the icy night. There was neither heat nor hot water in the ten-year-old 'dumbbell' tenement, the name referring to the architectural design that placed four apartments on each floor with only a twenty-eight-inch airshaft providing air and light to the whole building. Incredibly, the design had won an award. The landlord, a German Jew, charged twelve dollars a month rent for the Davidoffs' two rooms, and he made seventy percent on his money. One foul, excrement-heaped privy in the tiny backyard serviced four floors of immigrants, all of them, like the Davidoffs, refugees from the pogroms of the Tsar, Alexander III. Moyshe spoke Yiddish and Russian. He was trying to learn English, but, like the Sicilians, the recently arrived Davidoffs were sticking mostly to their own kind, at least until they became acclimated to the harsh new world. Arvid Davidoff had managed to land a job as a garment carrier for the Apex Suit Company on West Thirty-fifth Street. For this he earned eight dollars a week. Natalia worked as a seamstress in the same firm and earned three dollars a week. Her hours stretched yawningly from seven-thirty in the morning till nine at night, with a half hour for lunch. She worked six days a week. Saturday night, tonight, was the only night either she or Arvid had enough energy for lovemaking.

The tenement was a pesthole. Slop and garbage dribbled down the dilapidated stair, and children urinated on the walls. Rats, roaches and water bugs swarmed. The single drainpipe servicing all four floors had holes from which sewer gas leaked. In the winter the building was an igloo; in the summer, an oven.

Moyshe huddled between his brothers and tried to sleep. When sleep finally came, his dream was a variation of a familiar theme.

In his dreams Moyshe Davidoff was always rich.

CHAPTER 6

'His conduct was outrageous, and I *won't* have you defending him!'

Augustus thundered the words as he stood in front of the mantel of his library, glaring at his wife. Alice, wrapped in a peignoir and blanket, was seated in one of a pair of matching wing chairs, her face pale not only from her consumption, as she called the tuberculosis that had begun terminating her life three years before, but also from the strain of the 'battle of the ballroom,' as the servants and half New York society had already dubbed Victor's fight. She knew Augustus would blow up. Even worse, she was frantic with worry over Victor's disappearance. It was the next afternoon, and no one knew where he was.

'I certainly won't defend brawling,' she said, 'but Bill Wharton is a notorious bully and undoubtedly got what he deserved.'

'You see? You *are* defending him! He broke a valuable punch bowl, dozens of cups . . . He behaved like an animal! I've always suspected he was an animal, and, by God, last night he proved it!'

'Oh, stop it!' exclaimed Alice. 'I'm so sick of hearing you belittle him! You're always digging at him, making him feel unwanted . . . Has it occurred to you *why* he did that last night? Don't you think perhaps he wanted to get back at you—at all of us?'

'Get back for *what*, for God's sake? For giving him the world on a silver platter?'

'For not loving him!'

'I'll tell you what's more important than love: feeding him, clothing him, sending him to school . . .'

'School? That fleabag night school on Twenty-third Street? You'd think it was Harvard.'

'It was an education, and I paid for it! I've given him a position at the bank . . .'

'Augustus,' sighed his wife, 'you're a very foolish man. You think of everything in terms of money. Love is *wanting* to do things for somebody, not just doing them. And you've never wanted to do anything for Victor.'

Augustus looked at her a moment, cooling down.

'No,' he finally said, 'that's not true. Lately, I *have* wanted to do things for him. I'm not getting any younger, and Victor's all I've got as an heir.' He stiffened again. 'And that's why what he pulled last night is particularly galling! *Just* when I begin to trust him, begin to have confidence in him—even pride in him! —that's when he tears the house apart! I'm telling you, it's galling. *Galling!*'

The double doors to the library opened, and Cyril, the butler, who had been stealing claret from Augustus's wine cellar for years, intoned: 'Mr. Victor.'

Four eyes turned to the door, and Victor walked in. He had bathed, shaved and put on his best dark-blue suit. His eye was still black, but his lip was less swollen.

'Victor!' exclaimed Alice. 'Thank heavens . . . where have you been?'

'Downtown,' he said, coming over to kiss her cheek.

'But why didn't you tell us? I've been so worried . . .'

'I'm sorry, Mother, but after last night I had some thinking to do.' Then he turned to his adopted father. Pulling a check from his coat pocket, he went up to Augustus and handed it to him. 'Here, sir, is a check for a hundred dollars. I hope that will cover whatever damage I caused last night. I sincerely apologize for the brawl. I was wrong, and . . .'

Until now, Augustus's hands had been clasped behind his frock-coated back. Now, swiftly, he brought his right hand up and slapped Victor's face, hard. Victor winced. Alice cried out, 'Augustus!'

'I want none of his sniveling apologies,' said the banker. Then he eyed his adopted son. 'You disgraced this family last night. You made us the laughingstock of New York. And you have the unmitigated gall to offer me a check?' He snatched the check from Victor's hand and looked at it. Then he raised his eyes. 'Where did you get a hundred dollars? Did you steal it?'

Again Alice cried out, 'Augustus! Stop it!'

'He has nowhere near a hundred dollars!'

'I borrowed it,' said Victor, evenly, 'from some Italian friends of mine downtown. I'm repaying it ten dollars a month at four percent interest. If it's not enough, sir, I'll borrow more. Is it enough?'

'It's more than enough,' said Alice. 'Augustus, give him back the check. I'll pay for the blasted punch bowl . . .'

'You will not,' said her husband. Then he put the check in his wallet, returning it to his coat pocket.

'It's enough,' he said to Victor. 'And I accept your apology, since I have no choice. But if such a disgraceful incident is ever repeated . . .'

'It won't be,' said Victor. 'I'm leaving this house today.'

Augustus looked surprised.

'You're what?'

Victor moved back so he could address both of them.

'I've lived here too long,' he said, quietly. 'I've accepted your food and your . . . hospitality, which I deeply appreciate. But I'm twenty-two. Even if I were your real son, it's time for me to go out on my own. As it is, being your adopted son, being . . . well, the cause of a certain tension here, I think it's even more important that I get out.'

'But where will you go?' asked Alice.

'The people who loaned me the money are named Riccione. They own a trattoria on Thompson Street where I used to eat dinner sometimes before night school. They have a friend, Dr. Mario Difatta, who has a large house over in Brooklyn. Dr. Difatta emigrated from Sicily more than twenty years ago, and his practice is mostly with Italians, who have started moving over to Brooklyn in droves. Dr. Difatta has a spare room he'll rent me for twenty dollars a month, breakfast included. He was at the restaurant today, and I met him and liked him. So I'm moving in tonight. He's only a few blocks from the Brooklyn Bridge, and I can take the train over to work. That is, if you still want me at the bank?'

There was a long silence. Then Alice, who looked strained, took Victor's hand.

'Of course you're still wanted at the bank. Isn't he, Augustus?'

Her husband cleared his throat.

'Yes, of course. I have no complaints about your work, Victor. You've done a fine job.'

'You see?' Alice forced a smile. 'And you've done a fine job as our son. You know you are always welcome here, no matter what happens. But much as I'll hate to see you leave the house, I can understand how you feel, and perhaps this will be better for you. But promise me you won't forget us. Promise me you'll come see us . . . and me. You're very dear to me, you know.'

Victor's eyes were full of tears. He leaned down and hugged her.

'I'd never forget you,' he said. 'Never. Till the end of my life. And of course I'll come see you. At least once a week . . . more, if you want.'

She held his cheeks in her hands.

'Oh, my son,' she whispered. 'I love you so very much.'

She was smiling, but tears were in her eyes as well.

It was then that Augustus surprised both of them.

'Are you sure,' he said, quietly, 'that you want to leave?' Then he added, 'I'll miss you, too.'

Victor looked at him incredulously, remembering the slap and ten years of hostility.

'I'm sure,' he said.

The sun was low in a clear winter sky as Victor paid the cab and stepped out in front of Dr. Difatta's turreted white house. It was situated superbly on a hill overlooking the East River, with the tip of Manhattan beyond and, to the southwest, a sweeping view of Governors Island and the channel. The house was girdled with a wide, balustraded porch, and set in a handsome yard. As Victor walked to the front door, he was impressed by the size of the rhododendrons that surrounded the house, their leaves dropping from the cold, their branches sagging with two inches of fresh snow. He rang the bell and waited, peering curiously through the beveled glass of the door.

It was opened by a fat young man with an acned face.

'You're the new boarder?' he asked in Italian. 'I'm Gianni Difatta, the doctor's son. His *only* son—he gave up trying after looking at me.' And he giggled.

Victor shook his hand, glancing around the dark entrance hall. Even if the place hadn't reeked of spaghetti sauce, it would have been impossible not to guess the owner was Italian. A huge portrait of Victor Emmanuel II hung on the red-and-white papered wall, surmounted by two tiny crossed Italian flags. Smaller portraits of Garibaldi and Verdi touched frames with a large painting of the Bay of Naples, and in the corner beneath the stair, the i was dotted by a bust of Dante.

'The old man's expecting you,' said Gianni, leading him into a parlor crowded with heavy furniture. The large round bay in the turret was a jungle of palms, and a tall marble statue of a demure nude, her dimpled hands covering her breasts and parts, stood before the handsome lace curtains. 'What made you want to move over here?' continued Gianni, navigating past the claw-footed, lace-covered, circular wooden table which groaned with family photos and a saccharine 'Rogers Group' statue of a young boy weeping over his dead dog. 'The old man said you live on Fifth Avenue with a bunch of millionaires?'

'It's Madison Avenue. And let's say I moved here because I got homesick.'

'For a *paesano*, eh?' Gianni grinned and slapped Victor's back. 'Good! Hey—you got a girl? My girl's got a friend who's a real looker, and I'll bet she'd go for you. But she won't go all the way. Hell, she won't even kiss—she's from the convent. But if you want to get laid, I know some Sheeny girls up in Williamsburg who'll drop their drawers for a bagel. Those damned Kikes are taking over in Williamsburg.'

'Sounds like you're real fond of the Jews.'

'*Fond?* I hate their guts!' He had led Victor through the dark dining room into the big, white kitchen, where a fat woman in an apron was stirring a huge pot on the coal stove.

'Hey, Mrs. Lucarelli, meet our new boarder, Victor Dexter. This is our housekeeper. She takes care of the old man and me since Momma died. She's a fabulous cook. Treat her good, and she'll make you as fat as the rest of us.'

Mrs. Lucarelli wiped her hand on her apron, then shook Victor's, beaming him a 'Welcome!' Then Gianni led him to the rear door, where wooden steps led to the cellar. 'The old man's office is down here. Sunday's his day off, but Mrs. Giambelli's goiter's acting up. He won't make house calls on Sunday unless it's an emergency . . . You go to college?'

'I went to night school. How about you?'

'I got booted out of N.Y.U. for a semester. They caught me with a bimbo in my room. The old man about strangled me . . . watch your head, there's a low beam.'

They had scrambled down the stairs to the cement cellar. Gianni led him to a door. 'Wait here: I'll see if Mrs. Giambelli's gone.' He went in and a moment later reappeared to beckon Victor. He entered Dr. Difatta's office: A big, well-lighted room with its own private door to the outside. A skeleton dangling merrily in one corner. Tall medicine chests filled with wondrous bottles. An elaborate, Gothic-letter eye chart. A white screen. An enormous black rolltop desk. In front of it, seated in a swivel chair, Dr. Difatta.

He was fat, a mountain of a man, whose chins rolled happily

over his wing collar. Now he heaved himself out of the chair and shook Victor's hand.

'Welcome to my house,' he said, in mangled English. 'You had no trouble at home? With your father, I mean?'

'Well, *some* trouble.'

'It's good for a young man to leave the nest. You, Gianni,' he gave his son a dark look, 'you should be in college 'stead of lyin' round the house, readin' cheap magazines, thinkin' 'bout girls alla time—eh! No good . . .' He raised his hand as if to swat his son, who grinned without flinching. 'Get outta here. I want to talk to Victor. Sit down, son.'

He pulled a chair up for Victor, who sat down. Gianni, at the door, winked.

'If you want to go to Williamsburg with me tonight, let me know.'

Then he was gone.

'My son,' groaned the old man, resettling in his chair. 'He's got a good head, but he don't want to use it, you know? Alla time, girls. At his age, I thought 'bout girls—sure! But I thought 'bout other things too, like studies and work . . . Now, Victor, one reason I'm glad to have you livin' here is because of Gianni. His English is worse than mine. Alla time here we speak Italian, which is bad, you know? My patients is all Italian, my friends, Gianni's friends . . . It's wrong. Now, you a nice Sicilian boy who speak beautiful English, like an American. You got nice manners, you live with a high-class family, you work hard . . . It would be a big favor to me if you'd . . . how you say? Set an example for Gianni, you know? Make him talk English to you, maybe get him interested in something besides girls, you know? If his Momma had lived, she might have done somethin' with him. She was a sweet woman, a good woman, God rest her soul. But I don't have time, and my English is bad. Would you do that for me? In your spare time, of course.'

'I'll try, Doctor.'

The fat man smiled.

'Good. You a fine young man, I can tell I'm glad you here in my house.'

And he reached over and patted Victor's hand.

'We eat supper at six—you like the food, I guarantee. *Allora* . . . go upstairs, and Mrs. Lucarelli will show you your room. Anything you want, you just let me know—okay?'

The room was on the second floor, in the front of the house, with the spectacular view of the river and city. It was spotless, with a big brass bed covered with a white spread, a marble-topped dresser surmounted by a mirror and a framed photograph of the Colosseum in Rome. After unpacking, Victor took off his shoes and flopped on the bed, staring at the ceiling. Being an 'example' to Gianni had been an unexpected part of the deal, but it was an interesting challenge. For a while, at least, he had left the 'new way.' Now he was with his own people. Dr. Difatta, Gianni and Mrs. Lucarelli were a far cry from the elegant Dexters, and Gianni seemed to be a bigoted clod; but whatever their faults, they were friendly.

It was more than a little ironic that he, after ten years of being the Wop, was now being looked up to as a paragon.

CHAPTER 7

'Well, Victor, your tally is correct down to the last penny. If you ever locked up with a shortage, I think the world would come to an end.'

The speaker was Howard Cantrell, the genial cashier of the Dexter Bank. Victor had closed his teller's cage for the day and, as was the bank's practice, then proceeded to 'lock up,' which meant tallying the cash and checks in his drawer against the deposit and withdrawal slips for the day, then comparing this to the amount of cash he had begun the day with—in this instance, five thousand dollars. After that he carried his cash drawer down the marble stairs to the cavernous vault in the basement where Mr. Cantrell would check his tally and lock up the cash for the night. Mr. Cantrell was a genial man in his fifties with a thin face, thick glasses and sparse gray hair. He had worked for the Dexter for twenty-seven years, earned the princely salary (by banking standards) of $7,000 a year, lived in a pleasant house in the Chelsea section of Manhattan with his wife and unmarried daughter, raised orchids as a hobby and sang in the local church choir. The position of cashier normally attracted men with tight accountants' souls. Mr. Cantrell was a pleasant exception.

'I got more withdrawals than usual,' said Victor.

'Not unexpected at this time of year. Around Easter, people start feeling expansive. They buy things for the house, a new hat for the missus . . . a normal reaction after a cold winter, as this one's been. By the way, Mr. Dexter asked that you drop by his office before you leave.'

'Oh, thank you.'

Victor bade him good afternoon, then remounted the stairs to the main floor of the bank. The Dexter was a private bank, conservative, priding itself on its exclusivity, drawing its customers from the tight little world of old New York families who had banked there for years. Victor's feeling was that the bank was far too conservative for its own good, that as New York exploded with vitality and the influx of millions of immigrants, the bank was passing up huge sources of potential business. Since he was only a teller, no one was asking his opinions. But he had decided to make them known anyway.

Passing the 'platform,' the area of the banking room where the loan officers sat jealously guarding their pecking order, he went into the corridor leading to the executive offices. The Dexter might be conservative fiscally, but concerning the technological advances of the day Augustus had been surprisingly progressive. The Dexter was one of the first banks to install electricity and telephones, one of the first to buy typewriters (this no minor breakthrough, since most customers and clients considered typewritten correspondence 'infra dig,' and resistance to the abandonment of the elegant copperplate handwriting of the past had been surprisingly stiff); the bank had the latest alarm systems, and Augustus had even introduced hidden cameras which could photograph robbers, an innovation he adopted from the Bank of France, which had begun the practice eleven years before. The bank was progressive in technology, but, in Victor's opinion, its fiscal policies were still hidebound.

He was admitted to the president's office by Mr. Grimsby. He went up to the desk, where Augustus was studying some correspondence. Now he looked up and removed his pince-nez.

'Ah, Victor,' he said. 'Sit down.'

Victor did.

'I have here a loan application from a certain Salvatore Volpi,' said Augustus. 'He lives on . . .' he rechecked the paper, '. . . Garfield Place in Brooklyn. He has applied for a two-thousand-dollar loan to expand his grocery business. One of the references he put down was Dr. Mario Difatta. I assume there is no coincidence in the fact that your landlord is mentioned on the loan application?'

'No, sir. I suggested to Volpi that he apply for a loan at this bank.'

'I see. Then you know Volpi?'

'Yes, sir. Dr. Difatta is well-known in the Italian community, not only because of his medical practice but through his activity with the Unione Siciliana.'

'And what is that?'

'An organization of Italian-Americans who try to help new immigrants. Dr. Difatta has taken me to several meetings. One of the biggest problems for these people is getting capital to start up businesses—or, in the case of Volpi, expanding them.

Volpi's a good man, solid, hardworking. He was complaining to Dr. Difatta about his inability to get a loan, mainly because banks don't want to grant loans to immigrants. So I suggested he try this bank.'

Augustus tapped his pince-nez on the desk.

'You didn't seriously expect we would approve it?' he finally said.

'I thought there might be a chance. There's an enormous amount of business to be picked up by a bank which is willing to invest in these people even though, by conventional standards, they don't seem like good risks.'

'Mmm. You may be right, but I'm afraid the Dexter Bank will have to pass up this golden opportunity you envisage. The loan is disapproved.'

Victor watched as Augustus scribbled something on the paper, then placed it aside. Inwardly he was burning. You old fool, he thought. You damned blind old fool.

'Will that be all, sir?'

'That will be all. Except in the future, I will appreciate your limiting your banking activities to what you're paid for: being a teller.'

Victor's jaw tightened.

'I'm sorry you feel that any attempt to bring business to the bank is an interference.'

'The Dexter prides itself on its blue ribbon clientele, Victor. We intend to keep it that way. Good afternoon.'

Victor didn't move.

'I said, "good afternoon," Victor.'

'I'm handing in my resignation. Sir.'

Augustus blinked.

'I beg your pardon?'

'I see little future in working for a bank that is as pigheadedly blind as this one. Consequently, I quit.'

His adopted father stiffened.

'You'll do no such thing! And I resent your insulting tone . . .'

Victor came up to the desk and leaned his fists on its polished surface.

'Mr. Dexter . . . no, dammit, Father, because you *are* my father, whether you like it or not . . . You're going to listen to me, for once. In the banking courses I took at night school —which *you* paid for—they said the idea of a bank is to provide a service for the community, to provide a safe place for people to keep their money and a source of capital for legitimate loans.

94

Well, that sure as hell isn't what's happening in New York, because most of the banks—just like this one—don't want anything to do with the poor, the dirty, the Wops, the Jews . . . Oh, living in Brooklyn has been a real eye-opener for me! Do you realize not five percent of the Italians over there have bank accounts? They're terrified of banks! What little money they have they hide in their mattresses or in tin cans they bury in their backyards, just the way they used to do in Italy—and why? Because none of the banks has the imagination to go to them and try and get their business! And you can sneer at them because they *are* poor, but they have the potential to be rich, if given half a chance! That's why they came to America in the first place, to better themselves. And they're willing to work for it, and work *hard*. You think nothing of my character or intelligence, but I'll tell you one thing: I'd bet every penny I have—which isn't much —that if you granted Volpi that loan, he'd kill himself working to pay it back, and with good interest! But since you're too much of a snob and too damned mean-spirited to give a poor man a chance—which was what I thought this country was all about —then I don't see much of a future for this bank, and I don't want anything to do with it.'

Augustus was literally purple.

'How *dare* you speak to me this way?'

'I should have done it a long time ago.'

'You ungrateful . . .'

'I know: Wop, Dago, Guinea. Take your pick.'

'If you leave this bank, I'll make certain you never get another job on Wall Street!'

'Then I'll buy a pushcart. That should make fascinating gossip at your club: Augustus Dexter's adopted son is selling oranges and bananas in Little Italy.'

'Are you blackmailing me?' he thundered.

'Perhaps. Approve Volpi's loan, and I'll forget everything that's been said here. Or at least I won't repeat it outside this office.'

Augustus was forcing himself to simmer down. Victor was almost amused by the agony the pompous banker was going through. Finally the older man snatched the loan application, scratched out what he had written before, then wrote something new. He thrust the paper at Victor.

'There, damn you: it's approved. But if Volpi defaults, it will be on your head!'

Victor looked at the 'Approved. A.D.' and took his fists off the desk.

'He won't default,' he said, coolly. 'And I withdraw my resignation. Good afternoon . . . Father.'

He started out of the office.

'Victor.'

He stopped, turned.

'Come here a minute.'

He returned to the desk.

'Sir?'

Augustus was wrestling with his thoughts. Whatever he wanted to say, it was obviously killing him to say it.

'Sit down.'

Again Victor sat. There was a long silence. Then:

'Do you have any idea how I got started in business?'

'You made money on the stock exchange.'

'Yes, but you don't know how I got the money to play the market in the first place. No one knows, not even your mother. I've never told anyone because, frankly, I'm ashamed of it. During the war, when I was in Georgia, I stole some jewels which I sold later in New York for forty thousand dollars. Well, I didn't exactly "steal" them. I bought them from an old darky for thirty dollars and a gold watch, but it was tantamount to stealing. Does that surprise you?'

'A little. What surprises me more is that you're telling me.'

Augustus leaned back.

'I'm telling you because I like your guts, Victor. Even when I violently disagree with you, I like your fighting me back. You've always been at a certain disadvantage with me, but now that you know I started out as a looter, perhaps we're more evenly matched.' He smiled slightly. 'From now on, I hope we can have some really rip-roaring fights.'

Victor laughed.

'I hope so, too. I sort of like fighting with you.'

'Good.' Augustus frowned. 'The house has been awfully quiet since you left, Victor. I don't suppose there's any hope of our getting you back?'

Victor hesitated. The fact that he was missed touched him to a surprising degree.

'I don't think for a while yet, sir.'

'Well . . . at any rate, don't forget your mother's birthday next Wednesday. The family is giving her a dinner party. She'll be very hurt if you're not there.'

'Oh, I'll be there. I wouldn't miss it.' He stood up and added, 'Is Lucille coming down from Vassar?'

'Yes, I believe so. Why?'

'Just curious, sir. Good afternoon. And thanks for approving the loan.'

He left the office walking on air.

'To Victor!'

Dr. Difatta raised his glass of Chianti, and the dozen other Italians around his dining room table stood to join him in the toast.

'To our border who speak so good the English and who got Salvatore his bank loan! *Salute!*'

'*Salute!*' chorused the others, drinking. Victor, sitting between Gianni Difatta and his father, had the grace to look modest. But he was pleased.

After the others sat, he rose and looked around the table. There was Salvatore Volpi, a wiry little man who was getting pleasantly drunk from the wine and his joy at having received the loan. Next, his equally wiry wife, Teresa. Then burly Paolo Nazone, a hamfisted Neapolitan who owned a small construction firm. His wife, Annunziata, a blowsy woman who had been eyeing Victor all through dinner with something more than fraternal amiability. Padre Luigi Santore, the pastor of the small Santa Rosalia Church near the Navy Yard in the heart of Brooklyn's Little Italy. Professore Primo Gonzaga, a plumply prosperous *avvocato*, or lawyer, whose interest in improving the finances of his fellow immigrants was not entirely quixotic, since the poor couldn't afford legal fees. His wife, Carolina. And two friends of Gianni's, nineteen-year-old Marco Fosco and seventeen-year-old 'Little Vinnie' Tazzi. Everyone had eaten heavily of Mrs. Lucarelli's excellent *cucina* and drunk heavily of Dr. Difatta's Chianti.

'My friends,' said Victor, 'I'm not much at speechmaking, so let me just say to Salvatore: good luck with the grocery store!'

He raised his glass as the others chorused, '*Buona fortuna!*'

Up popped Salvatore again, this time to start weaving around the table toward Victor.

'My friends,' he shouted in Italian, 'I, Salvatore Volpi, want everyone to hear: Vittorio, I'll never forget what you've done for me! Never! And someday, when you want me to help you, you let me know what you want and I'll do it. Anything! Salvatore Volpi swears on his honor: anything!'

He reached Victor and, to the latter's embarrassment, the thirty-one-year-old grocer from Calabria leaned down, hugged him and kissed his cheek.

'He's a goddam hero,' grinned Gianni Difatta an hour later as he, Marco Fosco, Little Vinnie Tazzi and Victor walked down the gaslit street. When the dinner had broken up, Gianni insisted Victor join him and his two friends for a walk. It was a pleasantly cool early spring evening, and Victor wasn't averse to some fresh air. But Gianni Difatta wasn't addicted to aimless walks. Victor wondered what he was up to.

'Professore Gonzaga's already talking about getting you into politics,' continued Gianni in Italian. 'How about that, Marco? Our Victor a congressman—maybe even President?'

'Yeah,' said Marco, the burly son of a baker, who always looked as if he needed a shave even after he shaved. 'President Victor Dexter. He could serve salami in the White House.'

The three of them laughed, but Victor looked bored.

'In the first place,' he said, 'I'm not interested in politics. In the second place, even if I were, I could never be President since I wasn't born here.'

'Change the goddam law,' said Gianni.

'In the third place, you're supposed to be speaking English.'

'You might as well give up trying to improve me. I like Italian.'

'I just about *have* given up. And in the fourth place, I'm tired and want to go to bed. So I'm turning back.'

'Oh no you're not,' said Gianni, taking his arm. 'Me and Marco and Little Vinnie got the evening all planned out.'

Marco grabbed Victor's other arm. Though neither he nor Gianni was holding him tightly, Victor thought that if he tried to break away, there might be trouble. Gianni had often bragged about the fights he and Marco got in, usually with the 'Mockies' —Jews—in Williamsburg. Little Vinnie was only five feet two, but at a boxing match put on by the Unione Siciliana the month before, Victor had seen him slaughter a man a half-foot taller than he. As for Gianni, Victor had come to barely tolerate him. That the kind and intelligent Dr. Difatta could have such a throwback of a son seemed almost an aberration of nature. But after three months, Victor had found no redeeming feature in him except a rather lumpish good humor. His attempts at improving him had been laughed off or ignored. Gianni was interested in nothing but eating, drinking, getting laid and fights.

'All right, what's the plan?' asked Victor.

'We want to show you our clubhouse. You didn't know we had a club, did you? Sort of an offshoot of the Unione Siciliana. Come on, it's not far from here. You'll like it, I guarantee.'

98

They released Victor, and the four continued down the street.

'What sort of club is it?' asked Victor.

'Sort of like a fraternity, except only for us Italians. If you like it, maybe we'd let you join.'

'Does your father know about it?'

'What the old man doesn't know won't hurt him. And you'd better not tell him.'

His tone was light.

'What happens if I do?'

No sound but their heels clicking on the brick pavement. Then: 'You won't tell him.'

'What's the name of the club?'

'It doesn't have a name yet.'

'But why all the secrecy?'

Gianni stopped and said with exasperation, 'Look, Victor, we're giving you a chance to join it. Why do you have to ask all these dumb questions? Just shut up and go along with us. See what it's all about, then if you want to join, fine, if you don't, fine. All we ask is that you don't talk about it. Isn't that reasonable?'

'Reasonable enough, I guess.'

'All right, let's go.'

They continued in silence. Ten minutes later, they approached a warehouse on the docks.

'Little Vinnie's old man works here,' said Gianni. 'He got us a key.' He pulled a key out, unlocked and pushed open a door. He waited till Marco and Little Vinnie had gone in, then signaled Victor to follow them. Gianni entered after him and closed the door. A dirty oil lamp lighted their way through packing cases to the rear of the warehouse, where Marco opened a second door. Inside, Victor saw an office, lighted by several gas jets. Around an oval wooden table were seated six other men their age. When Victor came in the room, they eyed him curiously.

Gianni closed the door and said, 'This is Victor Dexter, the guy I told you about. He's been boarding at my father's house for three months, and he's a good man. Victor, meet the club.'

He led him around the table, introducing him. Victor shook hands in silence. Then Gianni pulled up chairs.

'Our club,' he said to Victor after they had sat down, 'is for good times, but it has other purposes.'

'Like what?'

Gianni pulled a pocketknife from his pants and set it on the table in front of him.

'You got Salvatore Volpi a loan, which is good. But how

many loans are you going to be able to talk your old man into giving? Maybe a couple of dozen, at the most. Meanwhile there's millions of us here in New York, and we're at the fucking bottom. Even the Jews treat us like shit—isn't that right?'

He looked at Victor, who shrugged.

'Unfortunately, it's right.' He pointed at the knife. 'So what are you saying? That we go out and kill all the Jews in New York?'

Gianni grinned and looked around the table.

'Not a bad idea, huh?' he said with a giggle, and the others nodded.

He turned back to Victor.

'I'm saying we've got to protect ourselves against everybody, not just the Jews. And you don't protect yourself with words. That's one thing our club does: we protect ourselves, our people and our territory. We do a lot of other things, too, but that's the *first* thing. Do you want to be part of it?'

Victor looked around the table and said, 'Why is it every time more than two Italians get together, the first thing we do is organize a secret society?'

'What does that mean?'

'Just that there must be something inside us that craves belonging to secret societies, like drunks crave booze. Back in Sicily, it was the Mafia. Is that what you're trying to do: start a Mafia in New York?'

'Maybe it's not a bad idea.'

Victor stood up.

'Gianni, I know how the Mafia works in Sicily—hell, it sent my brother to prison for the rest of his life for something he didn't do. Do you think I'm going to have anything to do with the Mafia here?'

'We're not the Mafia! We're . . .'

'Whatever you are, it's the same idea, and it's crazy.'

'Crazy?' shouted Gianni. 'When those fucking Jews in Williamsburg are pushing us out? They're taking over the whole place, and if nobody else'll stop 'em, *we* will!'

'With knives?'

'You bet your ass with knives! And guns, and whatever else it takes!'

Victor shook his head.

'That's worse than crazy. It's stupid.'

Little Vinnie Tazzi leaned forward. He had a handsome, almost angelic, face. He could have passed for a choirboy if his big, brown eyes hadn't sparkled with such hostility toward what was, to him, an oversized world.

'Maybe you're *afraid* of knives?' he said.

Victor nodded.

'Yes, I *am* afraid of knives, and anybody with brains is.'

Little Vinnie turned to Gianni.

'You didn't tell us your friend was chickenshit.' The phrase he used was *avere la fifa*.

'I didn't know he was.'

'We don't want chickenshit in our club,' said Little Vinnie to Victor. 'So maybe you'd better leave.'

'That's exactly what I intend doing.'

He started around the table toward the door. Marco Fosco stood up and blocked his way.

'Just a minute,' he said. 'Gianni warned you about telling his old man about the club. That goes for anyone else.' He pulled a knife from his pocket, opened it and held the blade up to Victor's face. 'You tell anyone, and that pretty face of yours is going to look like shit.'

'Forget it, Marco,' said Gianni. 'He won't tell. He may be chickenshit, but he's a *paesano*. Let him go.'

Marco stood aside, and Victor went to the door. He opened it, then looked around the room.

'You can call me chickenshit,' he said. 'But all of you are wrong.'

And he left the room.

CHAPTER 8

The swinging door from the pantry was opened by Cyril, the butler, who was followed by a footman holding a silver tray with a birthday cake on it. As the cake was brought to the table, eighteen assembled Dexters and Elliots sang 'Happy birthday, dear Alice' to the pale woman at the head of the table in front of whom the cake with thirty-six candles was placed. 'Make a wish!' exclaimed Lucille. 'Yes, a wish, a wish!' chorused the clan.

Alice made a wish, took a deep breath to blow out the candles and went into a coughing fit. Her family's faces froze with embarrassment, but she quickly recovered.

'Perhaps Victor will do the honors for me,' she smiled weakly.

Victor got up, came around the table, blew out the candles, then kissed her. 'Happy birthday,' he said.

Afterward, the family moved to the drawing room, where Alice began opening her presents.

'How are you liking Brooklyn?' Lucille asked Victor.

'It's interesting.'

'Are the Italians better fighters than Bill Wharton?'

'Let's say I wouldn't want to get in a fight with them.'

'But you did very well with Bill! He was hopping mad! He and some of the other Yalies wanted to go out and find you to beat you up, but you'd flown the coop. Where *did* you go?'

Victor, who was standing next to her chair, remembered Doreen the Chorine and turned slightly red.

'I, uh, went downtown.'

'Well, that's vague enough. And why are you blushing?' she smiled mischievously. 'Victor, you've turned into a genuine mystery. I find it absolutely fascinating! I bet you have a girl friend over in Brooklyn, don't you?'

'Nope.'

'I think you're lying. You're in love, aren't you? I can just tell. Is she pretty?'

'She's beautiful.'

'So there *is* someone. Is she Italian?'

'No.'

'Well, I think you should bring her around so we all can meet her. Who is she?'

He looked down at her.

'You,' he said, simply.

Her eyes widened.

Rodney Elliot, who was home from Harvard for the spring vacation, was sitting cross-legged on the floor next to his younger brother, Arthur. Now he poked him and pointed across the room.

'Look at the Wop,' he whispered. 'I think he's trying to make time with Lucille!'

'You're crazy,' growled Arthur, who was in his last year at Groton. 'Victor wouldn't have the nerve.'

'Oh yeah? The Wop's changing. I wouldn't put *anything* past him.'

'So you're in love with me,' said Lucille a half hour later. She was standing at one of the windows of the small, palm-filled conservatory at the back of the house, looking up at the stars. 'Of course you're lying.'

'No I'm not.' Victor was standing behind her, watching her, loving the line of her graceful neck, the gentle curve of her back, her narrow waist . . . 'I've been in love with you for years.'

She turned around.

'That was just a crush. I think I should be very cross with you, leading me on like this. Besides, I'm practically engaged to Bill Wharton.'

'He hasn't got a brain in his head, and you know it.'

She laughed.

'You're so complimentary to my future husband!'

He took both her hands.

'Listen, Lucille,' he whispered. 'He's not good enough for you . . .'

'And you are?' she interrupted. Her tone was rather insolent, and he caught it.

'Yes,' he said, with conviction. 'I am.'

He pulled her into his arms and kissed her. She put up no resistance. She liked the strength she felt in his hard body.

'Marry me,' he was saying. 'Oh God, Lucille, I love you so much . . . Marry me, not Bill . . . Say you will . . .'

She pushed him away.

'*Marry* you?' she exclaimed.

It had blurted out of him, but he wasn't about to retract.

'Yes, marry me!'

'Wait a minute, while I catch my breath! Are you serious?' She went to a white wrought-iron bench backed by palms and sat down.

'I've never been more serious in my life.'

'But you've hardly even *danced* with me, and now you're proposing? It's incredible. Besides, I couldn't marry you. I think Uncle Augustus would have fits.'

'Then let him.'

'But if you *are* serious, how do I know you're not just after my money?'

'Your *money?*' He sounded incredulous.

'Well, my father *is* a rich man. And while I have no idea what's in Uncle Augustus's will, I rather doubt he's going to make you his heir. So it could be to your advantage to catch me, couldn't it?'

She knew she had stung him, and she liked it.

'You know something, Lucille?' he said, softly. 'The stupidest thing I've ever done is fall in love with you.'

And he walked out of the conservatory, leaving her openmouthed with astonishment. She jumped up and ran after him, stopping him in the entrance hall.

'Victor, wait a minute . . . I didn't mean to hurt you! It's just . . . well, you've never asked me out or anything, and suddenly you're asking me to marry you . . . I mean, you've confused me . . .'

'How could I ask you out? I can't afford to take you to the places you like, and you know it.'

'Well, that's silly. You can afford to take me to some inexpensive restaurant . . . I'll be home for two weeks . . .'

He was brightening.

'How about tomorrow night?'

'Well . . .' She thought a moment. She was supposed to go to the opera with Bill Wharton and his family, but suddenly Victor seemed much more interesting than Bill or the opera. 'All right. Just the two of us. I'll lie to my parents—that way we won't have to be chaperoned, which is such a bore. And I know a new restaurant that's just opened down by Gramercy Park . . . It's called Chez Paul, and the food's supposed to be *wonderful! And* cheap . . . Why don't I meet you there at, say, eight tomorrow night?'

His anger at her had vanished, replaced by excitement.

'I'll be there.'

'And Victor, you kiss *very* well.'

He took her hand, led her back into the conservatory and kissed her again.

'This,' she whispered, 'could become a wonderful habit.'

He heard someone whistle and clap behind him. He let go of Lucille and turned to see Rodney and Arthur Elliot standing in the doorway, applauding.

'Keep it up, Victor!' called Rodney. 'I always wanted to see how Italians make love!'

'Rodney,' snapped Lucille, 'why don't you go out and drown in the Hudson?'

'But you two are really good at it! Wait till Bill Wharton hears about *this* . . . Hey, Victor, why don't you get a mandolin and serenade her? Isn't that the way they do it in Venice? 'Course, we don't have a gondola . . .'

Instead of strangling him, which was Victor's first impulse, he said, 'You're right, Rodney. I wish I had a mandolin. But since I don't, well . . . This is the way we Italians make love.'

He got on one knee on the white marble floor, opened his arms wide toward Lucille and began singing in his cracked baritone:

> Celeste Aida,
> forma divina,
> mistico serto
> di luce e fior . . .

Lucille stared at him, not sure whether to laugh, intrigued by his wonderful lunacy.

> Del mio pensiero
> tu sei regina,
> tu di mia vita
> sei lo splendor.

> Il tuo bel cielo vorrei ridarti,
> le dolci brezze del patrio suol:
> un regal serto sul crin posarti,
> ergerti un trono vicino al sol . . .

> Ah! . . . .

Hitting the climactic 'Ah!' with all his lung power, Victor gesticulated with the abandoned hamminess of a fourth-rate Italian tenor. By now, Lucille was giggling but this time she was giggling with him.

> Celeste Aida,
> forma divina,
> mistico raggio
> di luce e fior,
> del mio pensiero
> tu sei regina,
> tu di mia vita
> sei lo splendor.

He got up and made a sweeping, theatrical bow to Rodney and Arthur, who were in fits of laughter. Then, smiling pleasantly, he came up to Rodney.

'Rodney,' he said, 'you are a horse's ass.'

And he left the house, heading back to Brooklyn.

He couldn't sleep that night. He tossed and turned in his bed, swept alternately by waves of desire for Lucille, contempt for Rodney and much of his world, and agonizing self-doubt. He had no money and little prospects. His teller's salary was thirty-five dollars a week, and on this he hoped to woo the heiress to a department store fortune? Taking her to dinner the next night might eat up half a week's salary! True, someday he might be left something by Alice, but as far as getting anything from Augustus, he had discounted that years before and wasn't sure he would accept anything even if he *were* in the will. He assumed he was educated enough to earn an honest living, but anything grander than that seemed out of the question. And he knew enough about Lucille to know her vision of her future was grand indeed. So why should he get his hopes up by trying to woo her? He was merely setting himself up for a painful fall.

It was almost one when he heard Gianni Difatta come in the house. A few minutes later, he heard his door softly open.

'Victor?' It was a whisper. 'Wake up. I need help.'

He got out of bed and lit the lamp. Gianni was leaning against the door holding a blood-soaked rag against his forehead.

'Jesus, what happened?'

Victor, barefooted and in his flannel nightgown, hurried over.

'I got bashed by the Sheenies . . . Can you put a bandage on me? I don't want the old man to know . . .'

'Right . . . let's go down to his office . . .'

Victor grabbed the bedlamp. They went into the hall, then hurried to the basement office, where Victor set the lamp on the doctor's desk and turned to examine the wound.

'I got hit by a rock,' said Gianni, easing into his father's swivel chair. 'It hurts like hell.'

'Wait a minute, I'll wash it . . .'

He filled a china basin, then soaked a sponge and began cleaning the cut. A blue-black lump had formed under it.

'How did the fight start?' he asked.

'We raided their clubhouse.'

'Whose clubhouse?'

'The Williamsburg Wildcats. They're a bunch of Mockies who've got a clubhouse up on Rutledge Street. Some of them ganged up on Marco yesterday, so we got back at the bastards. It was beautiful. You should have been there.'

'No thanks. Why did they attack Marco?'

'He made a pass at one of their girls. Shit, she was a bitch in heat asking for it, but they started chasing Marco . . . fucking Jews are animals.'

'And you're not?'

'Hell no! We just taught them a lesson! Jesus, watch it . . . that hurt . . .'

Victor started cutting a bandage.

'Anyway,' Gianni continued, 'they won't give us any more trouble. Especially their leader, a big Russian Jew named Shumlin, or something like that . . . I never can pronounce their names.'

'People say that about us.'

'Anyway, that's one Jew boy who doesn't look so good anymore.'

'What happened?'

Gianni grinned up at him, the pale lamp light illuminating his fat, pimpled face.

'I got him,' he whispered, running his finger from his left temple down his cheek to his chin. 'Gkkkkk . . . all the way down his fucking Jew face. He'll have that scar the rest of his life.'

'You stupid Wop,' said Victor, softly. 'And I thought I'd never use that word! What are you trying to do, start a war? You attack them, don't you think they're going to attack you back?

107

And then how does it end? Don't you realize what you're *doing?*'

Gianni smiled condescendingly.

'Jesus, you really are chickenshit, aren't you? Little Vinnie was right.'

'We should be trying to make the Jews our friends, not our enemies! We're both on the bottom—it's *stupid* for us to be fighting each other!'

'Look, Victor: you mind your business and I'll mind mine. Okay?' He got to his feet, gingerly touching his bandage. 'Anyway, thanks for patching me up. You make a good nurse. Good night.'

Victor shook his head as Gianni left the office.

'Stupid,' he muttered. And he began cleaning up the blood.

CHAPTER 9

'Vittorio Spada!'

Startled, Victor turned to see a handsome, plump woman in a hot-red silk dress, her décolletage trimmed with white feathers, diamonds clinging defiantly to every available inch of her generous and vaguely familiar body. She had just swept into the small entrance room of Chez Paul, the restaurant on Irving Place. Now she came over to Victor, extending her opera-gloved hand, a big smile on her overpainted face.

'How are you? Honey, don't tell me you've forgotten? It's Doreen the Chorine!'

He gulped slightly as he recognized the whore he had bedded the previous December. Oh my God, he thought, if Lucille comes in *now* . . .

'You look different,' he managed to get out.

'Oh honey, *am* I!' She laughed. 'Doreen's doin' *real* well for herself!' She leaned into his ear and whispered, 'Got myself a rich boyfriend—what I've been lookin' for all my life!' She looked around the room, then into the restaurant beyond. The maître d' hurried over. She exchanged a few words with him, then returned to Victor.

'He's not here yet,' she said, 'so we can chat a few minutes. Say, you're lookin' all right yourself! Didn't we have a night of it? Remember? Honey, I'll never forget *you*! You fucked me practically into the next county! But I've moved out of that dump on Delancey Street. Got me a real nice little place on Sixth Avenue, overlookin' the el . . . Lover Boy pays the rent, buys me fancy clothes, jewels . . .' She lowered her voice and winked, pointing at the two-inch diamond bracelet over her glove. 'Well, they're paste, but what the hell . . . Anyway, it was right after New Year's. I went to the castin' call for a musical—old Doreen never says "die"!—and got a job. I about fainted! Well, the show was a turkey, but after the openin' up comes Lover Boy! He'd been in the first row and thought I was the best-lookin' thing since Lily Langtry. He's been eatin' out of my hand ever since . . . Oh, let me tell you, he throws the money around! It's every old tart's dream come true.'

And she laughed so loud, Victor winced.

'You expectin' someone, honey?' she asked, suddenly concerned.

'Well, yes . . .'

'My God, your wife! Or your girl friend . . . Listen, I won't embarrass you. I'll go in and take our booth—don't worry, I'll pretend I never saw you before in my life. Wouldn't want to get you in trouble. But it was nice runnin' into you again. You're a real sweet young man. I always liked Italians. They got a natural instinct what to do in bed, and, by God, there's not many men who do. Take it from someone who knows. Well, toodle-oo.'

Blowing him a kiss, she sashayed into the restaurant. Victor barely had time to sigh with relief when Lucille came in, looking enchanting in a pale-blue dress with a feather boa, her unpainted face looking virginal after Doreen's rouge and false eyelashes. Victor came over and kissed her hand.

'You look beautiful,' he said.

'Thank you. Are you going to sing "Celeste Aida" for me again?'

He laughed.

'Any time.'

'I *loved* it when you called Rodney a horse's ass! And he deserved it, if you ask me. He really is impossible . . . what's wrong?'

Victor was staring over her shoulder at a middle-aged man who had just come in the restaurant. When the man saw Victor, he turned pale and hurried back out without saying a word.

'Victor, what is it?' she asked. 'You look as if you've seen a ghost . . .'

'Oh, it was nothing. Come on, let's eat. I'm starving.'

He led her into the restaurant, but his face was troubled.

He hadn't seen a ghost. He had seen Howard Cantrell, the cashier of the Dexter Bank.

Lucille chattered aimlessly as she studied the menu, but Victor was thinking about embezzlement, the crime feared by bankers more than robbery. And he was watching Doreen the Chorine, who was seated across the room in a booth. She was still alone and growing obviously annoyed at being alone. Kind, friendly Mr. Cantrell, with his pleasant manners, his home in Chelsea, his orchids, his choir-singing . . . Victor knew Cantrell had dozens of ways to embezzle the bank, the simplest being to withdraw funds from dormant accounts, accounts of wealthy old ladies, for instance. The bank had many such accounts that often were unused for years. It would be easy for the cashier to debit several accounts for small amounts, forging the withdrawal slips, pocketing the money himself, confident the accounts' owners would never notice. His risks would be minimal, because Victor knew there was no effective defense against a bank officer gone crooked. But still . . . Mr. Cantrell with his unblemished record of twenty-seven years at the bank? It seemed incredible, but Victor also knew that the majority of convicted embezzlers had served at least fifteen years in the banks they embezzled, that apparently it was the long years of handling immense sums which eroded their honesty, like water dripping on rock, and that at some point they began to feel that some of the money they handled was fair game . . . Had this happened to Cantrell when he became enamored of the blowsy charms of Doreen the Chorine?

'Victor,' said Lucille, 'for someone trying to impress me, you seem more interested in that woman across the room.'

He turned back to his dinner partner.

'I'm sorry . . .'

'Do you know her?'

'Well, yes and no . . .'

'She doesn't look like a woman one would admit knowing socially.'

Victor grinned.

'She's actually Mrs. Astor.'

He saw Doreen stand up and leave her booth.

'Excuse me, Lucille, I'll be right back . . .'

He hurried to the front of the restaurant where Doreen was about to leave.

'Doreen, is Lover Boy's name Howard?'

She looked surprised.

'Yes, how did you know? And the bastard's stood me up! Do you know what's happened to him?'

'No.'

She looked understandably confused as he left her and hurried back to Lucille, who was steaming.

'*Really*, Victor! To *talk* to that woman, who looks like a common streetwalker! What *is* the matter with you?'

He was rubbing the side of his face, thoughtfully.

'I think I've just found out something that could send a man to prison for the rest of his life. But I don't know what to do.'

'Why?'

Victor spread his hands helplessly.

'I happen to like him.'

He decided the only way out of the dilemma was to give Cantrell fair warning before reporting his suspicions to Augustus. The next morning when he arrived at the bank, he started for the cashier's office only to be told by one of the other tellers that Cantrell was 'looking for him.' The middle-aged man was in his small office, and he smiled as Victor came in.

'Ah, Victor,' he said, coming around the desk to shake his hand, 'how are you this morning! I, uh, wanted to explain about last night . . . Will you take a seat?'

He waved Victor into a chair, then returned to his seat behind the desk. He seemed so affable and unruffled, Victor wondered if he thought he could bluff his way out. Suddenly the familiar things in the office had taken on a new look, as if the mere suspicion of theft gave otherwise innocuous objects a sinister air. The photograph of fat Grover Cleveland on the wall—for though Cantrell was a devout Republican, his patriotism made him 'display the President,' as he put it. The oval-framed photo of Cantrell's matronly wife on the desk, her face smiling faintly. Beside her, another photo of his homely daughter, Agnes. They all looked as bland as Cantrell, but did all of them have seamy sides to their lives—as, in fact, Grover Cleveland had?

'I imagine,' he began, 'you must have thought my behavior last night rather odd . . . I mean, not even speaking to you at the restaurant. But the fact was, just as I came in the door I realized I'd left my wallet in the cab, so I hurried out to try and catch him before he drove off. Happily, he was still there, and I retrieved it. How did you like Chez Paul, by the way? Was the food good?'

The smile was so friendly, Victor wondered if he had the right to destroy this man. But he had no choice.

'Mr. Cantrell, I know about Doreen.'

The man went even whiter than he had the night before, though he continued smiling.

'Doreen who?'

'Doreen the Chorine. At least that's what she told me her name was when I spent the night with her last December for five dollars. I gather from what she told me in the restaurant that you're spending a lot more on her than five dollars. Now the question is, Mr. Cantrell, where are you getting that kind of money?'

The man crumbled. He winced, then put his hand up, half-covering his eyes as if from some invisible glare. Then he slowly turned his chair around and doubled over, his back to

112

Victor. Victor heard the soft, gurgling sobs and realized he was witnessing a man's soul dying. After almost a minute, Cantrell pulled himself together. He straightened and turned back to Victor. His face was a battlefield of emotions, as different from his normal face as Hyde's from Jekyll's.

'I stole it,' he said, softly. 'Little bits here, little bits there . . .' He leaned across the desk and smiled almost proudly. 'Do you know, Victor, I've embezzled almost two hundred thousand dollars from this bank? And you're the first one that's even guessed. Think of it: two hundred thousand dollars! That's more than you'll earn in your whole life!'

It was bizarre. Victor was embarrassed for him, embarrassed for himself causing this ultimate crisis in the man's life. He had no alternative but to plunge on.

'Look, Mr. Cantrell,' he said, 'I don't think at this point you should be bragging. I'm not going to say anything to Mr. Dexter for a while. I want to give you a chance to try and replace the money . . .'

'Replace it?' he laughed. 'Don't be a fool, Victor. I've spent it, every damned dollar of it, and I loved doing it. I spent it on Doreen, but don't think she's the first. There was Sadie, Alice, Hilda . . . God, I've forgotten their names there've been so many of them. I spent it all on women, Victor. Not a penny on my wife or my daughter. All on women. This has been going on for three years.' He paused, then shrugged. 'Do you think the preachers are right? Do you think I'll spend eternity in the flaming pits, being pitchforked by demons because I couldn't control that thing between my legs? Or do you think what I think: that there's no payoff, no heaven or hell . . . Just a big emptiness . . .' Again he paused. Then he got to his feet. 'Well, who can answer that one? Shall we go see Mr. Dexter together? You might as well get the credit for catching me.'

'Don't you want . . . well, a few days?'

'And make you an accomplice? I appreciate what you're trying to do—it's kind of you—but there's no point in waiting. It's all over, and I know it. Frankly, it's sort of a relief.'

Victor followed him to the door. Cantrell started to open it, then he hesitated.

'No,' he said, more to himself than to Victor, 'damn it, let *them* figure out how I did it. I was really quite clever, you know . . . they'll be impressed . . .' He looked at Victor, but his mind was on something else, as if making a monumental decision. 'To hell with Dexter, that fat, pompous ass! Why should he make me cringe in front of him? I'm *glad* I stole from him!'

He opened the door and ran out of the office.

'Mr. Cantrell—!'

Victor ran after him. The cashier headed for the main banking room, running around amazed bank employees.

'Hey, what's happening?' yelled one of the tellers as Victor roared past him. When he reached the banking room, Cantrell was already at the door. The bank was not yet open, and the cashier was talking to the guard.

'Don't let him out!' yelled Victor, speeding across the polished marble floor. Cantrell turned, saw him, then pushed the guard away from the door, unlocked it and ran into crowded Pine Street.

'What's he done?' shouted the baffled guard as Victor panting, came up to him.

'He embezzled two hundred thousand bucks!'

'Jesus—Mr. *Cantrell?!*'

Victor was out the door, looking both ways to spot Cantrell. He saw him running east down the middle of the street, weaving in and out of the heavy, horse-drawn traffic. Victor started after him, shoving through angry pedestrians till he got to the curb, where he narrowly missed being run over by a wagon. He wasn't sure if Cantrell had decided to try to escape the police, or whether he was running to escape the horrible reality of discovery; certainly there had been a manic look in his eyes before he bolted. But as he neared the East River, another thought entered his mind.

He saw him standing at the edge of a pier, looking down at the water.

'Don't do it!' yelled Victor, running as fast as he could.

'Why not?' Cantrell yelled back at him. He waved, almost jauntily. Then he jumped.

By the time Victor reached the end of the pier, Cantrell was already fifty feet downstream, caught in the swirling currents of the river. He went under, then reappeared, then went under again.

He never came back up.

Well, Victor thought as he leaned against one of the pilings to catch his breath, he knows the answer now.

'Three years the man had been embezzling!' exclaimed Augustus at the head of the table as he enthusiastically carved his way through one of his favorite Southdown mutton chops.

114

'Think of it, Alice: three years! And the bank examiners didn't suspect a thing. Damned bunch of blind fools . . . Of course, they were all his friends, and they tend to get careless when they know a man for twenty-odd years. Why, if it weren't for Victor, he'd *still* be stealing from us, squandering our customers' money on his fancy women . . . Victor, how are you doing with your chops? Like some more?'

After ten years of solemn, uncomfortable dinners in the Dexter dining room, Victor was, for the first time, enjoying the role of Conquering Hero.

'No thanks.'

'Then have some more wine. Cyril, fill his glass . . . That's Romanée Conti, Victor, from the Côte d'Or, the best Burgundy in my cellar. Do you like it?'

Considering the fact that formerly Augustus had begrudged his adopted son more than one glass of Italian wine, Victor could only nod happy agreement. Alice, whose consumption had thinned her to an almost ethereal beauty, was as thrilled as Victor at this dramatic change of mood and looked happier than she had in years. Finally her judgment in bringing the young Sicilian to America had been triumphantly vindicated, and she wasn't about to let her husband forget it.

'Don't you think it remarkable,' she said, 'that out of your almost fifty employees, Victor was the only one who had the wits to suspect the man?'

'Well, it was just luck on my part . . .' Victor was trying to sound modest.

'Not luck,' said Augustus. '*Brains!* Yes, I consider it remarkable, Alice, and don't think I don't intend to reward him. Victor, I dislike nepotism, but you are, after all, my son, and in this case a little nepotism is damned well deserved. How would you like to have Cantrell's job?'

Victor almost choked on his wine.

'You mean cashier?'

'That's exactly what I mean, and I'll match his salary: seven thousand per annum.'

Victor's mind was swimming. Seven thousand was to him a fortune, but even more staggering was the leapfrogging of dozens of employees senior to him. Suddenly new vistas of power were opening to him that he had never imagined before.

Augustus wiped his mouth with his damask napkin.

'Well, young man, I hope your silence doesn't mean you're turning me down?'

'No, sir. It's just that I'm overwhelmed . . .'

'Then you accept. Good. You'll start in the morning. Mr. Pritchett was cashier at the Chase before coming over to us: he can help break you in. This way, if you decide to embezzle, at least it will be kept in the family—eh, Alice?'

Augustus's ponderous attempt at humor sent Alice into an ecstasy.

'Oh Augustus, I'm so pleased!' she enthused. Then she reached out and took Victor's hand. 'Dear Victor, congratulations! Aren't you excited?'

'Of course he's excited,' grumped her husband. 'Don't embarrass him with your gushing. Naturally, I've realized all along that Victor had brains as well as guts—eh, Victor? In due time I would have promoted him anyway, but now . . . well, the circumstances are extraordinary, and his reward should be extraordinary also. Needless to say, Victor, with your new salary and position, I assume you'll be moving back to Manhattan? There would be little point in your remaining with your . . . ah, Italian friends.'

He looked down the table at his son.

'Well, sir . . .'

'Father, Victor. Father.'

'Yes, Father . . . I'll have to consider that . . .'

'Well, well, when you think it over, I'm sure you'll see it would be to your advantage to come home. Or, if not here, some other suitable quarters . . . Which brings me to something else. Alice, I don't believe we've promoted Victor socially as we should have. I mean, he's certainly an eligible young man —more eligible than most of those nitwits your women friends are always trying to hook for their daughters. Why haven't you introduced him to more young ladies?'

Alice looked stunned.

'Augustus, your memory seems rather curious this evening. If you recall, *I* was the one who insisted he come to the dance . . .'

'Yes yes, but I'm talking about finding him a wife, which is your department. I believe there's a young Vanderbilt girl available?'

'You mean Maxine? That's out of the question.'

He glared down the long table at his wife.

'I hope you're not suggesting that a Dexter is not good enough for a Vanderbilt? My father was a schoolteacher when that rascal of a commodore was an illiterate tugboat captain!'

Victor couldn't help being amused by the way Augustus was suddenly endowing him with hereditary virtues.

116

'It was a ferryboat, dear, and no, I'm not suggesting that. But Maxine is homely as a mud fence, and Victor can do much better than that. But perhaps Victor has some ideas of his own.'

'Oh? Well, yes, of course. I didn't mean to dictate to the boy . . . Well, Victor? Is there some girl you've taken a fancy to? It's time you thought about starting a family, you know. And in light of your new position at the bank, a marriage into a prominent family would be desirable for all of us.'

'In fact,' said Victor, 'I've already proposed to someone. She hasn't accepted yet, but . . . well, I've got high hopes.'

Alice and Augustus exchanged surprised looks.

'This is news!' said Augustus. 'You're a quick worker . . . who is she?'

'Lucille Elliot.'

Augustus frowned.

'Lucille? But I thought she and Bill Wharton were practically engaged?'

'Oh, Augustus,' his wife laughed, 'you're so blind! Victor's been in love with Lucille for years . . . I think it's marvelous that finally she's getting some sense. Victor's worth ten Bill Whartons!'

'But . . .'

Augustus looked completely thrown.

'Do you have anything against Lucille?' asked Victor, who had caught his change of mood.

'No, she's a fine young girl. A bit spoiled, but . . .'

'Then do you have anything against my marrying her?'

'No.'

'Obviously *something's* bothering you,' said Alice.

'You're imagining things, Alice. I have no objections to the marriage whatsoever. There might be a problem with Victor's religion, but I suppose that could be overcome . . . No, it might be an excellent match.' He was staring at Victor as if seeing him for the first time. Then he said, with an odd mixture of tenderness and awe, 'So you're marrying my niece. My God, you really *are* a Dexter! You really *are* my son!'

It had taken ten years, but Victor finally had a father.

CHAPTER 10

The 'Williamsburg War,' as the papers quickly dubbed it, took place the same spring evening Victor was being launched into the world of power banking, but it had been festering for weeks. Gianni Difatta's gang, which, after the attack on Nathan Shumlin, had acquired the name 'Avengers,' was only one of several similar 'clubs' that were springing up all over the Italian section of Brooklyn. Unlike Gianni, who came from a relatively privileged background, most of the gang members were products of the terrible poverty endured by recent Italian immigrants. Fired by a rabid anti-Semitism, as well as by a history of southern Italian violence and exaggerated machismo, the Brooklyn gangs had been skirmishing with their Jewish counterparts in Williamsburg. As Victor predicted, incident led to incident and the violence escalated. But Gianni's scarring of Nathan Shumlin's face was the spark that set off the explosion.

Gianni had already had a fight with his father. Two afternoons following the Avengers' attack on the Wildcats' clubhouse, Gianni was summoned to his father's basement office where Dr. Difatta delivered a tirade.

'Wait a minute,' Gianni interrupted, 'who told you about the Avengers? Victor?'

'Victor? What does Victor know about it? Do you think I'm blind that I don't see that lump on your forehead? Do you think I'm deaf, that I don't hear from my friends how you and that *feccie*, that scum, Tazzi and Fosco, run around the streets picking fights with the Jews? I work hard to build a good name in the new world, and *you*—you dishonor us all! Victor? I wish to God *he* were my son, rather than you! At least Victor *works!* What do you do? Nothing except fight in the streets like a *teppista*, a hoodlum! I tell you, Gianni, either you straighten out and stop this fighting, or I'll kick you into the streets. No son of Mario Difatta is going to turn into a *delinquente!*'

118

The tirade did nothing but incite Gianni to further hooliganism. Spoiled by his father's affluence, naturally lazy, not overly bright, Gianni scorned the middle-class values of his father and took to the glamour and excitement of streetfighting like an addict to opium. He had fallen under the spell of Little Vinnie Tazzi, the tiny, angel-faced son of the warehouse worker. The Avengers had begun as a leaderless democracy, but Little Vinnie was rapidly emerging as the dominant personality. Though Gianni had scarred Nathan Shumlin's face, it had been Little Vinnie who organized the raid. He had all the negative qualities of leadership: utter ruthlessness, the determination to dominate and nerves of steel. Gianni was fascinated by the pint-sized boxer.

It was Little Vinnie who called a meeting of the Avengers early that evening in the warehouse clubhouse. But it wasn't only the eight-member Avengers gang who arrived. Little Vinnie had sent out word to two other, bigger gangs: the Warlords, also from Brooklyn, and the Five Points Raiders, a notorious gang from Manhattan under the leadership of a swaggering bully named Leo Calducci. Thirty young men squeezed into the small clubhouse room, leaving so little space that Little Vinnie had to climb on the oval table to address them.

'I got word,' he said, 'that Shumlin's boys are going to try to burn down this warehouse tonight. There's almost fifty of them coming down from Williamsburg, so we're outnumbered. But we've got a couple of hours to get ready for them, and besides, one Italian's worth two Sheenies any day—right?'

Shouts of approval. Little Vinnie proceeded to pass out baseball clubs, sticks, and knives and razors to those who didn't already carry them. He organized a hose brigade to stand by on the dock ready to put out any fire that started. Ironically, the warehouse was owned by a Polish Jew, but that meant nothing to Little Vinnie. From sunset to sunrise the warehouse was the turf of the Avengers, and they were prepared to defend it with all they had.

Gianni Difatta, overarmed with a baseball bat and a knife, was in a frenzy of excitement as the Italian gangs formed a phalanx across the front of the warehouse. The gray, paint-peeling building faced a narrow cobblestone street lined with carriage houses and several small brick factories. The area was deserted at night, so interference by the police was neither anticipated nor desired, although Little Vinnie conceded that once the Wildcats started moving, word might get to the police something was going on. The solid line of young Italians, many of them carrying garbage can covers as shields, waited, their spirits kept at the boil by Little Vinnie, who walked up and down the line making spine-bracing comments spiced with anti-Semitic jokes. His troops were ready.

Shortly after eleven, the 'enemy' arrived at the top of the street, about fifty of them, many carrying torches. The Wildcat forces, led by Nathan Shumlin, whose face was still bandaged from Gianni's knife wound, stopped to look at the Italians a block away. For a long moment, no one moved or spoke as the two 'armies,' descendants of centuries of European poverty, confronted each other. Then Shumlin yelled in Yiddish, 'Let's kill the Wops!' Roars and shouts as the gang charged down the slightly inclined street toward the warehouse. Little Vinnie, the Napoleon of the slums, held out his arms, signaling his men not to move. The Wildcats plowed into the Avengers, and the battle commenced. Bats and clubs swung, knives and razors slashed, fists pummeled in a battle as fierce in its intensity, if not its scope, as Austerlitz or Waterloo. The Wildcats flung their torches at the warehouse, but Little Vinnie's hose brigade quickly put them out, then turned the water on the enemy, drenching everyone in the process. Meanwhile the wounded were staggering away from the fight, many of them bleeding profusely from knife slashes or smashed noses. One Wildcat lost half of one ear. The miracle was, considering the number of knives, that no one was killed.

Ten minutes after the first attack, Shumlin yelled at his men to 'regroup.' The two armies separated, and Gianni Difatta was yelling, 'We won! We won!' when a police whistle shrilled and two black Marias roared around the corner at the top of the block.

The armies ran in all directions, and the Williamsburg War was over. Gianni, Little Vinnie and Marco Fosco took off down the docks.

'Where'll we go?' yelled Marco.

'My place,' said Gianni. 'We'll be safe from the cops there, and I got beer.'

He and Marco were both badly cut and bruised. But Little Vinnie was untouched except for a small cut on his right cheek.

Little Vinnie, the boxer, knew how to duck.

After the dinner with Augustus and Alice Dexter, Victor walked three blocks down Madison Avenue to pay a call on the Elliots and, in particular, on Lucille. He felt like cock of the walk, and he wanted to preen his new feathers. He paid his respects to the senior Elliots, then maneuvered Lucille into the music room, relieved that Rodney was out and Arthur and the other siblings had gone to bed. When he told Lucille of his promotion, she looked impressed.

'Then this means,' she said, 'that Uncle Augustus is planning to make you his heir.'

'He didn't say anything about that.'

'Well, he *must* be thinking it. After all, to give you such a huge promotion . . .' She eyed him with new appreciation. Then she smiled. 'Isn't it funny? After all these years of being "poor Victor," you're going to be "rich Victor." You must feel terribly excited. And if nothing else, I can't accuse you of being after my money anymore, can I?'

'I never was after your money. I've always been after *you*. And as far as my being "rich Victor," well . . . I'll believe that when it happens, and maybe not even then. But I've got a good salary now. I could rent us a nice apartment, buy you nice things . . .'

'Do you want to buy me nice things, Victor?'

'I want to give you the world.'

He took her in his arms and kissed her so hard, the ferocity of his passion frightened her as much as it excited her. But she put up no resistance. It was only when she felt his hungry hands on her lace-covered breasts that she pushed him away.

'You mustn't do that,' she whispered.

'But I *want* you! I want to make love to you . . . say you'll be my wife . . .'

'I'll have to think about it.'

'Then at least say you love me!'

She looked at him. She couldn't deny she was attracted to him, physically: He was one of the handsomest men she had ever seen. But the difference in their status had always put him in a special category. Now his status was being dramatically upgraded. As presumed heir to Augustus Dexter, Victor was not only handsome, he was downright desirable.

'Yes,' she whispered, 'I think I *do* love you.'

It was the sweetest moment of his life.

All the way back to Brooklyn, his thoughts flew. He remembered vividly that moment ten years before when he had first glimpsed Manhattan from the deck of the *Servia*. But now, after a decade of painful maturation, of wrestling with a new language and a new world, now at last the fabled Golden Door was beginning to open. He had felt himself too inferior to dream of wealth and power: the shadow cast by the hostile, disapproving Augustus had made anything more than a second-class existence seem futile. But now Augustus was no longer hostile, and if he were still disapproving, he was keeping it to himself. Now Victor had a shot at the top, and the thought exhilarated him almost as much as his apparent conquest of Lucille. The power implicit in the presidency of the Dexter Bank was, to him, mind-boggling. Not only the personal power, although that held its attractions. But the potential of the bank, as demonstrated in a small way by the loan to Salvatore Volpi . . . the power of money to help his fellow immigrants . . . this was tantalizing. He was quixotic enough to have enjoyed helping Volpi. He was clever enough to realize it was good business.

By the time he approached Dr. Difatta's house, it was almost one in the morning, and he could hear the voices on the porch. Gianni, Little Vinnie and Marco, drinking beer, were still rehashing the 'war' of a few hours before.

'Look,' said Gianni, putting his beer on a wicker table and pointing to the man on the sidewalk. 'It's Victor—that shit.'

'What'd he do now?' asked Marco, who was lying in a swing and who, like Gianni, was more than a little drunk. Little Vinnie was cold sober.

'He told my old man about the club.'

'Shit, and after we warned him . . .' Marco sat up in the swing. 'Shall I teach him a lesson?'

'Not here,' said Gianni. 'We don't want to wake up the old man.'

'Where can we go?' whispered Little Vinnie, who was always ready for action.

'Behind the buggy house. There's an alley . . . But how will we get him there?'

'Leave it to me.'

Little Vinnie got up, hurried down the porch steps and went to the sidewalk, where he met Victor.

'Hey, Victor!' he grinned, sticking out his hand. '*Paesano!* You got to congratulate us: we saved the warehouse tonight.'

Victor looked at the outstretched hand.

'Saved it from what?'

'From the Wildcats! Those fuckers came down from Williamsburg to burn the clubhouse, but we held them off. Hey, I know you don't approve of our club, but you got to be glad we stopped them from burning the place, right?'

Victor shook his hand.

'Right. Congratulations.'

'Come on up and have a beer with us . . . okay? I know you think we're a bunch of animals, but you're not too high and mighty to drink with us, I hope?'

'I'm not too "high and mighty" to refuse a beer from anyone.'

'Good.'

They started up the walk toward the porch. Little Vinnie fell a few paces behind him, then pulled a knife from his pocket, swiftly opened it and jabbed the point in his back.

'Hold it,' he said, softly.

Victor stopped. He could feel the knife biting through his dinner jacket. He tried to look behind him, but the knife pushed harder, nibbling his skin.

'I said "*hold* it." That means "don't move," you dumb shit. Where were you tonight, in your pretty dinner clothes? "Dining out" with your millionaire pals?'

'What if I was?'

'Because we could have used you, Victor. That is, if you weren't chickenshit. Now Gianni tells me you're also a fucking tattletale, that you told his old man about the clubhouse, even after we *warned* you not to!'

'That's a damned lie—!'

The knife jammed harder, cutting his skin. Victor stiffened. He saw Gianni and Marco coming down the porch steps, knives in their hands.

'Now we're going to teach you a lesson, pretty boy. We're going to give you a souvenir, so that every time you start forgetting you're Italian, you'll look in a mirror and remember. All right, *move*.'

He pointed to the left side yard, where Gianni and Marco had already started around the big house. A half moon poured silver on the budding rhododendrons, creating a dreamlike atmosphere. But Victor knew the knife in his back was no dream. He was no 'chickenshit,' as he had demonstrated by taking on Bill Wharton; but fists were one thing, knives another. He knew the three 'animals' were dangerous, and his brains told him to get the hell out.

He bolted, running to the right. He heard feet thudding the grass behind him. He looked around to see the three men chasing him. He headed for the sidewalk, then ran down the empty street. To the left of him, the East River glistened in the moonlight and gaslit Manhattan twinkled drowsily.

He turned down an alley and immediately realized he had made a mistake. It was a cul-de-sac. Stopping, panting, sweating, he turned and started back.

Little Vinnie and Marco appeared at the entrance of the blind alley. They both were holding knives. They started toward him.

Victor stopped.

'You shouldn't have run, Victor,' Little Vinnie was saying, 'because that proves you're a chickenshit.'

'Throw away the knives, and I'll take on all three of you.'

'Why should we throw away our knives, you dumb shit? How could we operate on your face without knives?'

'Then *you're* the chickenshit!'

'You hear that, Marco? He says *we're* the chickenshit. A chickenshit Jew is bad enough, but a chickenshit Italian gives us all a bad name. So we're going to have to make him at least *look* less chickenshit.'

'Yeah,' grinned Marco, 'when we get done with him, his face is going to be real *scary*.'

Gianni, who was too fat to run fast, had finally appeared, wheezing.

'Stay there, Gianni,' said Little Vinnie. 'Keep watch while we give Victor a beauty treatment.'

They were only a few feet away. Now they stopped, swinging their knives back and forth in front of them in a lazy, menacing fashion.

'You told us we were all wrong, Victor,' said Little Vinnie. 'So that means you think you're all right?'

Victor was watching the knives.

'I think my way's better than yours. And a lot less people get hurt. I also think you're trying to prove something to yourselves.'

'Yeah? Like what?'

'That you're men. But you're really nothing but kids playing tough. *You're* the reason I've been called a Wop all my life.'

'Why, you bastard . . .'

Marco lunged at him, slashing the knife at his face, roaring like an enraged bull. Victor dodged the knife, grabbed the knife arm with both hands and jerked it around behind him so fast and hard that Marco stumbled, dropping the weapon. Victor let go Marco and scooped for the knife. Just as he grabbed it, Marco leaped on his back with such force Victor was pushed to the ground, rolling him over on his back. Marco smashed his fist into his nose, crunching cartilage. Victor thrust the knife up at his throat.

'Get off or I'll kill you,' he said, softly.

Marco laughed.

'You hear that, Vinnie?' he shouted. 'Chickenshit's going to kill me! You haven't got the nerve, Victor. What would your millionaire pals say if they knew you was a killer?'

'They'd probably say you deserved being killed!'

'Oh yeah?'

He was straddling Victor, his right knee pinning Victor's left arm to the ground. But Victor's right arm was free, holding the knife at Marco's throat. Now, slowly, carefully, Marco's right hand began squeezing Victor's knife wrist. At the same time, his left hand closed over Victor's throat.

'Drop the knife, Victor,' he whispered. 'Drop it.'

'Need help?' asked Little Vinnie.

'Nah, I can handle him.'

Marco was strong: Victor was having trouble breathing. But with all his strength he kept the knife at Marco's throat.

'Drop it, Victor.'

The pressure on his throat was so great that the blood was pounding in his ears. But he kept the knife at the other man's throat.

'This is taking too fucking long,' said Little Vinnie. 'I know how to make him drop the goddam knife.'

He came up behind Vinnie, aimed his foot at Victor's exposed crotch and delivered a swift kick.

Victor gurgled with pain, his body galvanizing into a protective curl. At the same time, he heard a gasp, felt Marco's weight slump on top of him, felt Marco's hands release him, felt Marco's warm blood spurt on his face. He was in such pain from the kick, he didn't realize what had happened. Then, as the nausea flooded him, moaning with pain, he pushed Marco off and struggled to his knees.

'Shit,' whispered Little Vinnie, 'you *killed* him!'

It was then he looked at Marco, lying on his back, and saw the bloody hole in his throat, saw the bloody knife in his own hand. Dimly, he realized that as his body jerked from Little Vinnie's kick, the knife must have gone in Marco's jugular.

He was too sick to say anything. He crouched on his hands and knees, praying the pain in his crotch would abate, staring at the man he had apparently killed, wondering if the opening Golden Door had just slammed shut again.

'What'll we do?' said Gianni, who had come up beside Little Vinnie and was staring in awe at Marco's corpse. 'Get the cops?'

'Are you kidding?' Little Vinnie was watching Victor. 'We'll blame it on the Sheenies.'

Victor was slowly getting to his feet. Now he leaned weakly against a brick wall and looked at Marco, whose blood was all over Victor's face and shirtfront. He dropped the knife on the ground.

'I didn't kill him,' he said, wishing the alley would stop swirling. 'You kicked me in the balls . . .'

'Oh, you killed him, Victor,' said Little Vinnie, stooping beside Marco and rubbing two of his fingers in the blood on his throat. 'And we're not going to let you forget it.'

Straightening, he walked over to Victor, who was still too nauseous to realize fully what was happening. Little Vinnie, a grin on his angelic face, put his fingers up to his face and smeared Marco's blood on his own lips. Then, standing on tiptoe, he placed his mouth against Victor's and kissed him.

'Now you're one of us,' he whispered.

Victor pushed him away, bent over and vomited.

'So you've come home,' whispered Alice, smiling up at Victor's face. The excitement of Victor's reconciliation with Augustus had weakened her, forcing her back into bed. But no amount of coughing and pain, nor the worried looks on her doctor's face, could mar the sweetness of this moment for her.

'I've come home,' he said. Home. *Was* it his home? Certainly he could no longer stay at Dr. Difatta's after what had happened the night before. Blood. He, Victor, had killed. Accidentally, yes; but still, blood. The horror of it haunted him.

'I'm so glad,' said his mother, 'so glad you're home. I missed you so . . .'

She closed her eyes, and after a moment he realized she had drifted off to sleep. He leaned down and kissed her forehead. Then he turned and looked at Augustus.

'May I talk to you?' he said. The two men went out of the bedroom.

'You told me you started your business by stealing some jewels,' Victor said a few minutes later. He was sitting in the library of the house. Augustus was sitting opposite him, smoking a cigar, watching his son with interest. He knew something was bothering him.

'That's right,' said Augustus.

'It was good of you to tell me that. I suppose I mean it was honest of you. Now I have to be honest with you.' He had been staring at the carpet. Now he looked up into his father's eyes. How will he react? he wondered, will this ruin everything? 'I got in a fight last night,' he said quietly. 'It wasn't my fault—I was attacked. It was over in Brooklyn. At any rate . . .' he paused. God, could he say it?

'What happened, Victor?'

'I . . . killed a man. Accidentally, but I killed him.'

Augustus's face remained impassive as he sucked on the cigar. Victor watched the ash glow, then dull.

'Was this with your Italian friends?'

'Yes.'

'Are the police involved?'

'No. And they won't be. My friends don't like the police. But I wanted you to know: I killed a man.'

Augustus was silent for a long while. He's not my son, after all, he was thinking. His blood is different. Sicilians . . . It's in their blood . . . violence, murder . . .

'I'm glad you told me, Victor,' he said finally. 'And I accept your word that it was in self-defense. We'll never mention it again.'

Victor looked at him, surprised at the calm manner he was accepting it. Is it possible it doesn't make a difference? he wondered.

Something inside him told him it did.

Alice Dexter died ten days later. Victor was by her bed at the end. Her last words to him were, 'My son.' When the woman who had brought him to America died, Victor gave way to uncontrollable grief.

Augustus, watching him with dry eyes, thought, Sicilians. They're overemotional, unstable. Tears, violence, bloodshed . . . He's my son. And yet, he really isn't, is he?

CHAPTER 11

Prison Diary of Franco Spada

August 12, 1892. I begin this diary in memory of my beloved friend, Fillipo Pieri, who died two days ago of what Dr. Manturi, that incompetent idiot, called 'heat stroke.' Yes, it is damnably hot in this stinking crotch of a prison, and Fillipo did pass out on the rock pile Monday, but the stroke was only the culmination of twelve years of brutality, malnutrition, living in filth, overwork—but most of all, desperation at the crawl of time. Oh God, the agony of these endless days, months, seasons, years! I have now been here on San Stefano twelve years and nine days—how many days is that? 4,389, give or take leap years, but why count? Almost every one of those days and nights, except when I was in solitary, I have lived chained to Fillipo. I have worked with him, eaten with him, talked with him, pissed with him—I have done everything but make love to him, and sometimes we even discussed that. It is common enough here, God knows, but we both decided against it. Not only is it repugnant to me, as it was to him, but we were both afraid it would ruin our friendship, and our friendship was the only thing that has gotten me through this hellish eternity on this miserable rock. When God had a kidney stone, we say here, he passed it and it dropped into the sea to become San Stefano.

Oh Fillipo, you dear sweet man, how I miss you and mourn you, but you are at least free! If there is a God—and I have serious doubts there is—may He give you an honored place in heaven for all you have suffered! If He doesn't, then He is the fiend I suspect Him to be. Who else but a fiend could create a world like this one, so full of cruelty, filth and injustice?

It was Fillipo who taught me to read and write, so this diary is a fitting memorial to him. Slowly over the years he opened up my mind, and for that, if nothing else, I owe him everything. He

128

had a fine mind; he had been educated at the University of Bologna, he taught me everything he knew—history, politics, science, even mathematics—so in a roundabout way I, too, am a graduate of the university. More important, he gave me something to live for. Someday, somehow, I will get out of this rotten hole and then use what he taught me to better the world. I know that sounds laughable from a lifer, but there is power in my mind and in my pen. Fillipo put the power there. My mind is now in a way *his* mind. For him, as well as for me, I must *use* my mind —our mind.

Since Fillipo's death, I have not been assigned a new 'wife,' which is what we call our chain-partners whether we make love to them or not (incidentally, it's a fantastic relief not to have the damned heavy hot iron 'bracelet' to drag around, and for the first time in years I can walk like a man instead of a cripple). I traded my lunch today for this notebook and pencil with Crivelli, the ex-bank robber from Naples. He was using it to draw dirty pictures. I will use it to write.

This day I will also start figuring a way to escape from here. San Stefano is supposed to be escape-proof, but there must be a way. I vow, in memory of Fillipo Pieri, to find it.

August 14, 1892. I have been made a trusty. This morning, I was called into the office of the new commandant, Captain Gaetano Dorini. He replaced 'The Lady of the Sorrows,' Zambelli, three months ago. While all the convicts were relieved to get rid of Zambelli, who was a genuine sadist, a pervert who enjoyed inflicting pain, we were all naturally curious about his replacement. You become tough on this rock—you have to —and cynical; no one expected a benevolent papa, and we didn't get one. But in some ways, Dorini is an improvement over Zambelli. He has upgraded the food. Now it's less rotten than it used to be, and there is some variety. He has increased the lunch break on the rock pile to forty-five minutes, and the extra fifteen minutes is a blessing. Most important, he has given us more yard time on Sunday. The yard is the one place we are allowed to move about freely. It's a big area, surrounded by the seven-meter wall, without grass or trees, but at least it's outdoors, it's out of our cells. Under Zambelli, we were allowed in the yard for only two hours after Sunday lunch. Dorini has given us the whole afternoon. For that alone he's earned our grudging respect. This is no resort and we are the scum of the earth. We have so little that when we are given a little, it seems like a lot.

Dorini is a short, ugly little man with warts on his face—we call him the Toad. He's far from being friendly, but there must be some good in him. At any rate, he told me he had examined my record—what's to examine? Twelve years of pounding rock? —and decided to try me out as a trusty. This means a lot—there are only forty trusties in the whole prison out of 712 prisoners —and is, I suppose, some sort of half-assed compliment to my sterling character. 'I'm taking you off the pile,' said Dorini, 'and putting you in the kitchen. You get a new cell assignment: Cell B in the trusty wing. But remember: you're always on probation. One slipup and you go back to the pile.'

I mumbled 'Thank you, sir,' which I hated saying—why thank *anyone* in this hole?—and was led to my new home and my new cellmate. The trusty wing is the royal suite of San Stefano. It's one row of twenty cells on the ground floor of the north wing of the prison. The cells are smaller than my old one —43—but there are only two men to a cell, there are bunks, and, most precious of all, there is a *window!* After twelve years of a hole in the ceiling, there is a window. Barred, true, but I can look out at the sea, breathe the sea air . . . an indescribable luxury.

My new cellmate to whom I am *not* chained (this is another enviable luxury of my new status) is one of the 'stars' of the prison: Luigi Gangi, the Mass Murderer of Milan. He is a quiet little man, about forty-five, who so far, at least, has seemed friendly. Right now, he's sitting on his bunk opposite me, knitting a sweater. (The fact that a mass murderer is allowed potentially lethal weapons like knitting needles shows how much the guards trust this particular trusty. But then, he handles knives all day. One of the many ironies of this madhouse is that the Mass Murderer of Milan is the prison dentist!) This bland-looking fellow with the dull gray eyes and bald pate murdered seven women before the police caught him. He doesn't look like he would harm a flea. Possibly the only thing that can be said for prison life is that one meets interesting types.

I wonder if Princess Sylvia has something to do with my new status? For years she has been writing me—and telling me on her monthly visits—that she was trying to pressure the prison authorities in Rome to get me transferred to a better prison, or at least make life easier for me. Well, life is certainly easier today than yesterday, so perhaps her pressuring has finally gotten some results. On the other hand, she's been telling me for twelve years she would get me pardoned, and *that* sure as hell hasn't happened, nor will it, barring a miracle, so perhaps my 'eleva-tion' to trusty status happened despite, not because of, her pressure in Rome. When I think how I hated that woman, the fact that she continues to write me, visit me, send me books and supplies (and yes, money—she bribes the guards who look the other way as she slips me lire during her visits) is testimony to her persistence, if nothing else. God knows I haven't encouraged her. But she feels guilty about me, which she should, since it was her meddling that got me in this hole and cost me my freedom. And yet . . . well, I suppose in a way I've forgiven her, at least partially. She *has* tried to do everything she could for me, she *did* get my brother to America where he seems to be doing well, and she *is* the only person outside San Stefano (except for Vittorio) who gives a damn whether I live or die. When you're a prisoner, knowing that someone outside cares takes on an enormous importance. I suppose in a way I'm sort of a hobby to her. She tells me she's 'thrilled' by my progress, my education, and I think she really is. I don't know. I resent her enormously—why should she have been given everything at birth, and me nothing? And yet I look forward to her visits. I'd love to fuck her. That would be a laugh! The convict, the peasant, becoming the lover of Italy's richest woman! I'd better stop thinking about it, it just makes me feel rutty.

Gangi's going to bed. He used to be a dentist, which is why he's doing dental work on the prisoners—the Prison Board is too cheap to hire an outsider. I guess pulling teeth wasn't enough fun for him, so he murdered instead.

What a world.

August 17, 1892. Escape, escape, escape! It's all I think of, all I live for. So far I haven't found a way, but my new job in the kitchen offers interesting possibilities, and I watch, I wait . . . This diary is becoming a potential suicide weapon. The guards are generally too lazy to pay much attention to what goes on in the cells, but periodically they search the prison. If Dorini read this, it would be back to the rock pile for Franco. I'll find a hiding place for it in the kitchen.

After the pile, the kitchen is a lark. The work is physically easier, and we get all the food we can eat. Twelve years pounding rock on a wretched diet has left me skin, bones and muscle, so a little fat will feel good. There are twelve trusties in the kitchen, preparing food for 712 men (the guards have their own food), so there's plenty of work to be done. Today I peeled potatoes—the Toad, Dorini, has added potatoes to the menu several times a week. They are shipped in monthly from Nice. The cook, an embezzler named Pollera, is from Palermo, which is good for me: We speak the same language. He has been here eighteen years and is due for release in two years. Lucky man!

The kitchen is filthy.

Gangi told me tonight why he murdered those seven women in Milan. He claims he was 'taken over' by a demon named Carlo. Carlo murdered the women, Gangi had nothing to do with it. Needless to say, this didn't go over very well at Gangi's trial, but the poor idiot has convinced himself of the truth, and it seems to give him peace of mind.

His other pastime besides knitting is reading, and he has accumulated a fair library, which is manna to me. I borrowed a biography of Lord Byron, the English poet. An interesting man. His club foot reminds me of my chains.

August 23, 1892. I have found a hiding place for this diary in the kitchen storeroom. The prison building is centuries old—the solid stone walls are two meters thick, which is discouraging —and in places the mortar has crumbled. I noticed a loose stone under one of the potato bags and managed to pry it up. Underneath is a perfect hole for the diary, and I can write my notes between potato peeling, as I am doing now. The kitchen guard, Starace, spends most of the time outside the door, sunning.

The main impediment to escape is of course the fact that San Stefano is an island, the mainland being fifteen kilometers to the east. About six years ago, a prisoner named Bari managed to get out of the prison at night by hiding in the garbage cart—a filthy way to get out, but an effective one. He was a kitchen trusty, like myself. He had arranged for one of his cousins, a fisherman from Cefalù, to pick him up on the west side of the island. There were at that time two dog patrols that walked the island shore round the clock, but Bari figured he could dodge them—and, despite his stinking of garbage, he did. But for some reason his fisherman cousin didn't show up. Bari was caught the next day and thrown in solitary for a year, which he didn't survive—no one could. But Zambelli was so furious, he tripled the dog patrols. Thus a Bari-style escape is pretty well eliminated.

However, the supply boats offer possibilities. The guards are corrupt—they have to be, their salaries are so low—and although theoretically prisoners are supposed to have no money, of course we do, and we buy all our supplies from the guards. Zambelli knew this, as does Dorini, but there's nothing they can do to stop it except, possibly, raise the guards' salaries. The result is that prisoners from the better classes of society live better than the poor. Fillipo convinced me that the only answer to the problems of the world is socialism, but I must admit that his socialist principles never stopped him from taking all the money he could from his wealthy family. Nor, I'll admit, do my socialist principles stop me taking money from Princess Sylvia.

I say one can buy things from the guards, but no one has ever tried to buy *freedom* from the guards—mainly because the guards were as afraid of Zambelli as we were. However, with Dorini maybe things have changed. Maybe if I offered an enormous amount of money—enough to make a guard rich enough to retire for life—I could get on one of the supply boats to the mainland. I think Princess Sylvia would finance it—God knows, she wouldn't miss the money. She is coming to visit me next week: I'll suggest it to her.

Meanwhile I'll get to know Starace better.

I find Lord Byron's life an inspiration. He defied the world of his day, fucked everything in sight, and died young helping the Greeks revolt against their Ottoman oppressors. If I ever get out of here, I would like to be the Lord Byron of Italy—without the poetry. Unfortunately, I have no talent for rhymes.

August 26, 1892. Some luck with Starace. He's my age, thirty-one, and the son of a peasant, also like me. He comes from outside Gaeta, is married, has a son. Like all the guards, he lives here on the island, so in a way he is as much a prisoner as I am. He tells me his wife hates it, but this job pays him more than anything he could get on the mainland, and there's a fairly decent pension, so he's sticking it out. This much I gleaned from a couple of casual conversations over a few days. Guards aren't supposed to talk to us, but they get as bored as the prisoners, so they do. But naturally, I have to be careful. If I come out with an outright bribe, he could report me to Dorini and that would be the end of Franco. So today I sidled up to the subject. 'If you could have anything in the world,' I asked him, 'what would you want?' He has a good Italian face, like mine, and I watched him as he thought about it. 'There's a farm,' he said finally, 'not far from my father's place, but it's much better. Better soil, more land, a beautiful hill with a fine old house on it. If I could buy that, I'd go there and raise grapes and be a happy man.' 'Sounds good,' I said. 'How much would it take to buy it?' He laughed. 'More than I've got.' 'I know, but how much?' He thought a minute. 'Well, I guess I could get it for a hundred thousand lire.' 'I know someone with a hundred thousand lire,' I said. Then I smiled and went back in the kitchen, leaving him standing in the door watching me with an odd look on his face.

The next move is up to him.

Gangi is getting downright friendly. Last night he volunteered to knit me a sweater, which I accepted. Poor old fart: he's been here twenty years and all he has to live for is his knitting, his books and pulling an occasional tooth. And someday, death.

A letter from Vittorio today, which always brings me joy. He tells me he is getting married next month to a certain Lucille Elliot, a cousin of the family that adopted him. My little Vittorio, getting married! God, it's hard to believe, but I wish him happiness. Perhaps, if I'm lucky with Starace, someday soon I'll be out of here and can see my brother again. That would give me great joy. We were born into a miserable world, but at least he is managing to make something out of it for himself.

I wonder if he tells the Americans his brother is serving a life sentence for a murder, even though it's a murder I didn't commit? Probably not, and I wouldn't blame him.

August 27, 1892. Starace nibbled! Just a half hour ago, he beckoned me out of the kitchen into the sun. He lit a cigarette and looked around. The kitchen opens on to a small, walled courtyard which is normally empty, as it was then, but the guards in the towers could see us.

'Shine my boots,' he said.

I knew what he was thinking—namely, that if I were doing something menial, the guards in the towers would ignore us—so I hurried back in the kitchen, got a rag, then rejoined him. 'Over here, in the shade,' he said, walking away from the kitchen door. I followed him, my heart beating wildly—obviously he didn't want the kitchen trusties to hear us. I knelt in front of him and began shining.

'Who do you know who has a hundred thousand lire?' he said, quietly. 'That woman who comes to visit you every month? What's her name—Princess somebody?'

'Dell'Acqua,' I said, shining away. 'Her husband's very rich. To them, a hundred thousand lire is nothing. If you wanted, I could ask her to buy the farm for you.'

He didn't say anything for a moment. I could tell he was as scared as I. If he helped me and got caught, he could end up one of us.

'Why,' he finally said, 'would this Princess buy a farm for me?'

'She'd do it as a favor.'

'To you?'

'That's right.'

'And what would you get out of it?'

Shine, shine, shine . . .

'Maybe a favor from you.'

'What favor?'

I stopped shining and looked up at him.

'What's the one thing in this pisshole that's worth a hundred thousand lire?' I said, quietly.

He knew but was afraid to say it.

'You tell me.'

I swallowed hard. If he turned me in, it meant a long stretch in solitary and the end of my being a trusty. It meant going back to the stinking cells, it meant being chained again, it meant the end to the little freedom I'd been given. I took the plunge.

'The supply boats,' I whispered. 'If you could get me on one of them, the Princess would buy you your farm.'

Oh God, was he tempted!

'Let me think about it,' he finally said.

'She's coming in two days, so think fast.'

I finished shining his boots, then went back in the kitchen. I'm not a religious man—far from it!—but right now I'm praying to whatever is up there.

August 28, 1892. Starace has agreed. He told me today that if the Princess will guarantee him the farm, he'll get me on one of the boats. So now it's up to her, this forty-year-old aristo whose destiny has been so strangely tied up with mine. I suppose I should have some compunctions about asking her for the money —legally it could put her in trouble, helping a criminal escape —but I don't. She got me in here, she can get me out. That sounds brutally cold, and it omits other feelings I have about her —feelings of gratitude, for instance—but that's how I feel. Her glittering world, if not she personally, is responsible for most of the misery on this planet and responsible for twelve years of my life being spent in chains. I will ask her without a qualm.

If the escape succeeds, I'll start a new life in some other country—America, perhaps, or Australia. If it doesn't succeed, they won't bring me back here alive.

August 29, 1892. Dear God, I can't believe it: I am free! FREE! I'm laughing and crying . . . my eyes are so full of tears, I can barely see to write this . . . FREE!

135

It happened less than two hours ago . . . The Princess came over on the prison boat at ten this morning, as usual . . . At eleven I was brought to the visitors' room, as usual . . . There she was, standing on the other side of the wire, looking elegantly out of place in the crowd of mostly peasant women, who always defer to her, keep their distance . . . As usual, she looked beautiful, but I noticed something different on her face . . . an excitement?

She was escorted to the chair opposite me by the guard. Each visiting booth, or cubicle, is separated from the others by meter-deep wooden walls which provide some privacy. I took my seat and leaned forward, ready to whisper my request for the 100,000-lire loan, when she cut me off: 'Franco, I bring wonderful news,' she said. 'You have been pardoned by the King.'

I stared at her.

'Pardoned?'

'Pardoned. You'll be released tomorrow morning at nine. The government has agreed to compensate you with twenty-four thousand lire, two thousand for each year you've been here.'

It took a few moments for the reality of this phenomenon to sink in, but I listened as she explained: it was true that she had been pressuring the government for years to release me, but even though her relatives and friends are powerful, her efforts were frustrated by her husband, whose influence with the government and the court was greater than hers. But her husband, that unparalleled prick of a man, was old, and three months ago he had had a heart attack. She mounted a campaign at the same time as she nursed him. She played on his pride, his guilt, his honor, his fear of eternal damnation, and it worked! God, it worked! Ten days ago he had a second attack and literally on his deathbed she got him to sign a confession. He died the next day, and after his funeral she took the confession to the Queen. The court is reactionary and was reluctant to discredit the memory of one of its most prominent men by publicizing his confession to a crime, but the Queen and the King, to their credit, are honest. They quickly processed the pardon, and I am free!

Twelve long years of suffering are behind me. God knows I'm bitter, but I refuse to let bitterness sour the rest of my life. In memory of Fillipo, who opened my mind, I will try to do something to better the lot of my miserable countrymen. I have been given little in my life, but now I have the most precious thing of all: freedom. Tonight I sleep my last night in this hole.

The Princess is a good woman, after all. Is it possible I've been in love with her all these years and didn't even realize it?

CHAPTER 12

She had been madly in love with him for years, although it had been some time until she could admit to herself that her interest in her former gardener was more complex than guilt over his imprisonment. Now, as Princess Sylvia waited on the dock at Gaeta for the prison boat, she told herself she must treat Franco carefully. She was forty, still beautiful and, as the widow of Prince dell'Acqua, one of the richest women in Italy. That she was in love with a former convict she had not even touched for twelve years struck her as wildly improbable, but the fact remained that she was. Her relentless championing of Franco's cause had been not only to right a wrong, but also to free him so she *could* touch him. His socialism intrigued her, even though her class was part of the enemy. The strength of his mind, unlocked by Fillipo Pieri, excited her. She was determined to help him in every way.

The first thing he did after getting off the boat was kneel down and kiss the dock. The next thing was to come up to her. He was wearing the same cheap suit he had worn twelve years before at his trial, except now it was too big for him. They looked at each other. Then he said, simply, *'Grazie.'*

'You owe me no thanks,' she said. 'I owe you twelve years.'

The heat was blazing, and she was holding a parasol. He looked at her slim figure in its white dress.

'We owe each other nothing but friendship. And maybe something more. But I do have a favor to ask. There's a guard at the prison named Starace. I made a deal with him to get off the island in return for a hundred thousand lire so he could buy a farm. I was going to ask you for the money yesterday, but you had better news, and now Starace will never get his farm. Would you loan me the money so I can buy it for him anyway?'

She was amazed.

'Why?'

138

'He wants off that island as much as I did. I'm free now, and I'd like to think he could be free, too.'

It was so insane and so extravagant—although with her money —that she laughed.

'What's funny?' he asked.

'I've never heard of paying a man for something he didn't do! But the money's yours—as a gift, not a loan. Now, let's go to the hotel. We'll have lunch, then catch the train for Rome. Until you get settled, I thought you could stay with me.' She started toward the waiting cab. 'Do you have any idea what you want to do?'

He went with her to the cab, unable to take his eyes off her. His sex life had been a fantasy for so long, it didn't seem real that he was able to reach out and touch her. When they were in the cab, he said, 'Take off your glove.'

She looked at him and obeyed. Then he took her hand in his and touched its skin gently. The feel of his rough skin excited her, as she excited him. He looked at her and said, quietly, 'I'd forgotten how soft a woman's skin can be.'

He raised her hand to his mouth and ran his lips lightly over the back of it. It wasn't a kiss so much as a savoring.

She thought she had never felt anything so erotic. But she told herself not to give herself to him too quickly. She had waited twelve years for him. She could wait a little longer.

Franco stood in the entrance hall of the Palazzo dell'Acqua on the Corso in Rome and gawked. He dimly remembered the splendor of the Villa dell'Acqua back in Sicily, but then he had been a gardener looking in through windows. Tonight, he was a guest. It was an enormous difference.

The exterior of the palazzo was grimly fortress-like, its Renaissance stones dark gray from three centuries of grime. Two potted orange trees in the small courtyard were the only hint of foliage. However, the palazzo was built around a beautiful garden, unseen from the street, where tangerine trees shaded fountains and flower beds. Inside, there were seemingly endless corridors, galleries, drawing rooms, apartments, all decorated with magnificence and tended by a staff of thirty. The floor of the entrance hall was a masterpiece of colored marble scagliola work. Twenty feet above Franco and Sylvia, a beautiful fresco by a pupil of Veronese sprawled across the ceiling. The marble walls contained six niches holding statues of notable Romans taken in the eighteenth century by Cardinal Scipio dell'Acqua from the excavations at Herculaneum. At the top of the imposing staircase facing the two front doors hung an enormous Rape of Europa by Titian.

After looking around, Franco said, 'It's a bit of a change from San Stefano.'

She smiled.

'I'm sure. Daniele will show you your room. After you bathe, we'll have supper.' She nodded to the butler, who led Franco up the stairs to the second floor, then down a long, painting-hung gallery. Finally reaching a door, he opened it and led Franco into a big, handsomely furnished bedroom. 'Your room, sir,' he said. He opened an armoire, revealing three suits, some shirts, socks and underwear. 'The Princess ordered some clothes made for you. She guessed your size, but if they don't fit, the tailor will be here in the morning for alterations.' He reclosed the armoire, then crossed the room to another door. 'And here, sir, is the bathroom.'

He opened the door to reveal a large, gray marble room with an enormous tub. Franco came in and looked around with curiosity. Then he pointed at the toilet.

'What's that?'

The butler looked surprised.

'That is the water closet, sir.'

'That's what you piss in?'

'Uh . . . yes, sir. I take it you've never seen one?'

'That's right. In prison we had a hole in the floor.'

'Interesting. When you're through, you pull the chain . . . like so.'

The butler flushed the toilet. Franco watched with fascination.

'Now *that*,' he said 'is progress.'

'We live, sir, in an age of miracles.'

After his bath, he was standing, naked, at the basin about to shave when he saw in the mirror the bathroom door open. A girl came in. She was about twenty, with long black hair. She had on a black robe, tied at the waist, and she was barefoot. She was sensuously beautiful, with full lips and large, sleepy eyes.

'Good evening,' she said, eyeing his buttocks. 'My name is Gia. The Princess hired me to keep you company tonight.'

Franco put down the razor and turned around, wiping his face.

'The Princess thinks of everything,' he said, running his eyes slowly up and down her voluptuous figure.

'She told me you'd been in prison many years,' she went on, untying the robe to reveal her nakedness.

'Twelve.' He was drinking in her large breasts, her slim

140

waist, her pubic hair shaped like a small flame. 'Twelve long years.'

He crossed the marble floor as she dropped the robe. He took her in his arms and reveled in the warmth of soft flesh. Like freedom, it was intoxicating. He touched his lips to hers. But after a moment, he stepped back. 'Wait here for me,' he said, grabbing a towel off a heated rack. Wrapping the towel around his middle, he hurried out of the bathroom, leaving Gia confused, then crossed the bedroom to the door. Going out into the corridor, he hurried to the top of the stairs, where he yelled down to the footman at the front door, 'You! Where's the Princess?'

The footman stared up at the near-naked man with justifiable surprise. 'She's in her bedroom, sir.'

'Where's that?'

'To the right, at the end of the hall.'

Franco ran down the hall and barged into the bedroom without knocking. Sylvia was sitting at a vanity putting on some jet earrings. She looked at him with surprise.

'I know it's warm,' she said, 'but don't you think you could wear something besides a towel?'

He closed the door and came over to her. She looked at his broad shoulders and muscled chest, his flat belly and slim hips, and her blood raced.

'I appreciate Gia,' he said, 'but I want the first woman I love to be you.'

He took her hand and pulled her to her feet, taking her in his arms and kissing her. She felt the lust in him uncoiling like a cobra, reveled in his intense masculinity, loved the smell of his clean skin. She had never felt such passion in a kiss before. Now he picked her up in his arms and carried her to the enormous baroque bed, still kissing her.

'I love you, Sylvia,' he whispered, lowering her gently to the bed. He started unbuttoning her dress.

'Let me,' she said.

He waited impatiently as she took off her clothes. Then, dropping his towel on the floor, he climbed on top of her.

'I've been dreaming of this for a long time,' he said, softly.

'So have I,' she replied. And it was the truth.

An hour later she watched as he heaped his Limoges plate with a mountain of pasta. They were having supper in a small salon on the ground floor. Its walls were lined with emerald silk, and a magnificent Murano chandelier hung from the high

141

ceiling. Above the ornate mantel hung a Guardi. Sylvia watched her new lover with a dreamy smile as he began shoveling the pasta into his mouth.

'Delicious,' he muttered between bites. He tossed off his wine in one gulp, then returned to the attack as a footman refilled his glass. 'Delicious . . .'

'The suit looks very handsome on you,' she said. 'Do you like the material?'

'Um,' he grunted, nodding.

'I didn't know your shoe size, but tomorrow we can go shopping. I'd like to give you a wardrobe, but if you feel uncomfortable about accepting things from me, you can pay me back later.'

'Why should I feel uncomfortable? Anything you give, I'll take—gladly.'

She laughed.

'Good! Because I love to give, especially to you.'

A footman removed the empty plate while a second footman placed a new plate before him and a third presented a silver tray on which four plump squab were succulently arrayed. Franco looked at them, then grabbed two with his bare hands and plopped them on his plate. The footman looked astounded.

'Did your husband leave you everything?' he asked as he started devouring the birds.

'Nearly everything. His son was killed last year in an accident, and he had never married. He left his daughter a legacy, but everything else went to me. Giancarlo loved me in his chilly way, even though I made life miserable for him for what he did to you. At any rate, at the end we were reconciled.'

'Have you had lovers?'

'That is something one does not discuss before the servants.'

'Then send them out.'

She hesitated, then signaled. The four footmen bowed out of the room. She raised her champagne glass.

'Of course I've had lovers,' she said. 'Quite a few, over the years.'

'Did he know?'

'I was discreet, but I think he knew.'

'And he didn't mind?'

'He was older. He took a worldly attitude.'

'These lovers of yours, they weren't gardeners like I was?'

'No, but then you weren't my lover.'

'But your husband thought I was, which is why he framed me. The point is, he didn't mind your having lovers who were gentlemen, but when he thought you were sleeping with a gardener, he hired the Mafia to get rid of me. That's what I call a double standard with a vengeance.'

'I won't deny it.'

'Which is why I don't feel uncomfortable taking things from you. I'm no gentleman, and I have no genteel feelings about your class. So I write my own rules.' He finished the second squab and wiped his hands on the tablecloth. Then he smiled at her. 'You see, I hate your class, but I love you. But I'll tell you what I'm going to do with my twenty-four thousand lire—my blood money. The government thinks Franco the ex-gardener and ex-convict is so dumb he'll take the money and thank his lucky stars he's free. But they don't realize Franco got educated in prison. And Franco is not going to shut up.'

'What are you going to do?'

'Start a newspaper. A socialist paper that will wake up Italy to the corruption and rot and double standards that sent me to prison for twelve years and let you live in a palace.'

He stared at her rather defiantly, hoping she would be shocked. Instead, she smiled.

'It sounds fascinating.'

'How can you say that? Don't you realize I'll be attacking your world—you?'

'Of course. Perhaps I should be attacked. Meanwhile I'll be your first subscriber. And meanwhile I'll teach you some manners. The napkin in your lap is to wipe your fingers on, not the tablecloth. And one does not eat squab with one's fingers.'

'*I'm* talking about social injustice, and you worry about manners!'

'If all the world had good manners, then there would be no social injustice and no wars.'

He studied her beautiful face.

'I guess I can learn a lot from you, can't I?' he said.

'We can learn a lot from each other.'

'You know something?' He smiled. 'I love being your lover.'

Within a week he had rented a carriage house on the via Giulia, a block from the Tiber, bought a second-hand press, hired a hungry typesetter-printer, moved a cot for himself into the rear of the carriage house, and started making up the first edition of his weekly four-page paper which he named *Libertà!* The first edition appeared on the streets of Rome a week later to profound indifference, partly because the first press run was only 5,000 copies, but also because Rome was still half empty, asleep in the summer heat. The front page of the first edition had carried a strident attack on the government written by Franco. He was proud of it even though no one seemed interested. He dreamed of making the paper a daily.

The second and third editions fared worse, and Franco was beginning to run out of optimism as well as money, when Princess Sylvia, who had been following his efforts from the palazzo, appeared at the carriage house. 'Franco,' she said, 'you may not want to hear any criticism, but I'm going to give it to you anyway. Your paper's a bore.'

He got red in the face.

'That's *your* opinion!'

'Of course it's my opinion, but it seems to be everyone else's, too. You write well, but you're saying the same thing over and over. People don't want to read that the government's corrupt —good Lord, they already know it. You have to give them a scandal, and I think I have one for you. Are you interested?'

'Am I interested? Are you joking? Come back to my editorial office.'

He led her to the small rear room and shut the door. She looked at the unmade cot, the wooden table with the kerosene lamp and piles of paper, the single chair. 'Well,' she said, 'you can't be accused of overdecorating.'

He laughed and offered her a choice of the cot or the chair. She took the chair.

'Now, what's the scandal?'

She told him that she had heard rumors at several dinner parties that the current prime minister, Giovanni Giolitti, was receiving interest-free loans from a major Roman bank, the Bank of Rome, in return for government 'favors,' including the shifting of government funds to the bank. 'They say the loans amount to millions of lire,' she added, 'and the press is afraid to say anything for fear that Giolitti will shut them down—which he's certainly capable of doing. Are you afraid of being shut down?'

'There's not much to shut down.'

'Would you be afraid of going back to prison? That's also a possibility.'

He hesitated, remembering San Stefano.

'Needless to say, I wouldn't want to, but . . . they can't retract my pardon, can they?'

'No.'

He shrugged.

'Then what's more time in prison? I almost miss it. Anyway, it's worth the gamble. It might make the paper a success.'

'It's the chance of a lifetime. But you'll have to get some proof. I'll introduce you to Giacomo Lussu. He's the president of the Bank of Milan and would love nothing better than to destroy Giolitti. I think he can give you enough information to do the trick.'

The fourth edition of *Libertà,* which appeared on the streets of Rome the morning of September 21, 1892, literally made history. Franco had borrowed enough money from Princess Sylvia to increase the press run to 25,000 copies, and he hired ninety street urchins to hawk the paper all over the city. By ten in the morning the edition was sold out as word spread like wildfire that the prime minister had been loaned over 50,000,000 lire, interest-free, by the Banca Romana, which money he had used to speculate on the Milan stock exchange. Franco could easily have sold another 25,000 copies, but at noon two police vans descended on *Libertà*'s tiny office, its publisher was arrested, the press itself 'mysteriously' destroyed by crowbars, and Franco, a little over a month after his release from San Stefano, found himself in a four-man cell in the ancient Regina Coeli prison on the left bank of the Tiber.

But the circumstances of his new incarceration were vastly different. The other Roman papers, previously too timid to print the scandal, now took up the story with a vengeance, lambasting Giolitti for his 'tyranny' and catapulting Franco to a martyr's celebrity. Princess Sylvia, throwing herself into the brouhaha with gusto, organized a torchlight march on the royal palace, where neither the police nor the *carabinieri* were able to disperse the crowd of almost 10,000 shouting Romans. The publicity and pressure were too much for the government. Giolitti hastily resigned and fled to Paris. And three nights after his arrest, Franco found himself a free man again. He was met at the prison entrance by Princess Sylvia in one of her carriages. He climbed in beside her, his face sprouting a three days' growth of beard.

'That was some scandal you gave me!' he said, grinning, as he kissed her. 'Do you realize *I,* Franco Spada, brought down the government of Italy?'

'Now don't get *too* big a head. You had a little help from me, not to mention Signor Giolitti's passion for profits. But still, it was quite something.'

'Something? It was fantastic! The paper's a success! The next issue I'm going to print thirty thousand—no, fifty thousand

—copies. We may even get some advertisers . . . my God, do you realize we might even make a *profit?*'

She laughed.

'What a horrible idea for a socialist newspaper.'

'I'm dizzy . . . I can't believe it! I want to get drunk!'

'I've got champagne on ice.'

'I heard about your march on the palace. What a wonderful thing to do. Dammit, you're a wonderful woman!'

He took her in his arms and began kissing her.

'I'm also getting to be a notorious woman. A lot of my old friends aren't talking to me because of you.'

'Do you mind?'

She kissed him.

'I'd give up everyone in Rome for you, you crazy, bad-mannered socialist.'

'My manners are getting better. I'll have you know I insisted on having a napkin in my cell.'

She laughed.

'Oh Franco, I love it! You'll be the most stylish socialist in Rome.'

He kissed her again, with great tenderness.

'We make a wonderful pair, you and I.'

She smoothed his hair with her hand and loved him with her eyes. She had never been happier.

PART III

YEARS OF GOLD

1903-1910

CHAPTER 13

On October 14, 1903, Augustus Dexter returned from lunch at his club to his office at the Dexter Bank and collapsed from a cerebral hemorrhage. Two days later he was dead.

Victor was moved deeply by the death of his adopted father. The years of hostility were not forgotten, but in the last eleven years of his life Augustus had tried to make up for them, promoting Victor rapidly through the hierarchy of the bank to the position of executive vice-president. Family ties had been strengthened by Victor's marriage to Lucille; and when the couple started producing children, Augustus reacted warmly to his grandchildren—Lorna, born in 1895; Barbara, in 1898; and Drew, in 1900. With all his faults, Augustus had been Victor's father. The thirty-five-year-old banker mourned his passing with genuine grief.

Over 300 'floral arrangements' were sent to the funeral from friends, fellow Wall Streeters, politicians and society figures, reflecting if not Augustus's personal popularity, at least his prominence in the city. He had been a fixture in New York's power structure for a number of years, but the more astute Wall Streeters had for some time written the Dexter Bank off as the 'Rip van Winkle Bank'—sleepy, stuffy, behind the fast-moving times. Now they wondered who would take the bank over. Few doubted that if the presidency fell to Victor, Rip van Winkle would wake up with a bang. Wall Street knew that Victor was full of ideas for the bank, and that only his adopted father's resistance to change had braked the aggressive young Sicilian.

Three days after the funeral, Augustus's will was read, and Victor became a wealthy man, if a disappointed one. He was left the house on Madison Avenue, the summer cottage in Dutchess County and a portfolio of blue-chip stocks worth almost a million dollars. But the stock in the Dexter Bank—the controlling shares, worth five million—Augustus left to his daughter-in-law, Lucille. At first, Victor couldn't understand why his father would set him up as the heir apparent of the bank and then deprive him of the ultimate control. Then he began to understand. Augustus's message from the grave was that, in the last analysis, he didn't completely trust him. Victor knew why, and it was his own fault: the killing of Marco Fosco. Augustus had never mentioned it again, but the act of violence must have gnawed at him over the years, reminding him of Victor's basic 'difference,' his Sicilian blood, eroding the old man's confidence in his son's stability. If Victor could kill, what else might he do? And so Augustus had given the ultimate power to his niece—his daughter-in-law.

Presumably, Lucille's Dexter blood was 'safe.'

Lucille was as surprised as Victor at the terms of the will, but she assured her husband she would use her voting power to back him completely at the bank.

'After all,' she said as they returned to their rented house on Gramercy Park, 'everyone knows you were supposed to be the next president. You're the best, and who else is there? So I'll use my stock to vote you in. It's really *our* stock anyway, darling. Uncle Augustus must have been fonder of me than I suspected. But it is wonderful to have some real money at last, isn't it? I've gotten so bored being poor.'

'We haven't exactly been poor.'

'Well, you know what I mean. Oh Victor, we can build a house now, can't we? A proper house of our own, instead of renting like tenant farmers. I've had my eye on the corner lot at Seventy-third and Fifth Avenue. Of course, they're asking a fortune for it, but it's worth it . . . How much income will I get from the bank stock?'

'About two hundred thousand dollars a year.'

'Then we can easily afford to buy it, can't we? And maybe I'll hire Mr. White to design the house, or that Mr. Delano everyone's talking about . . . It's going to be such fun! And of course it's important for a bank president like you to live in style and have a good address. Oh Victor, aren't you excited?'

He forced a smile.

'Yes, very.'

He was, in a way. He loved Lucille and trusted her, and he told himself it didn't really matter that she owned the stock.

But in his heart, he knew it did.

Within a week, Lucille was elected to the board of directors, and Victor was voted in as the new president of the Dexter Bank.

150

The first thing he did was alter the look of the bank by ordering all officers to change out of their stiffly formal striped pants and frock coats into regular business suits. This was an innovation long overdue and was greeted with relief. Next, he set up a committee to investigate possible sites for branch banks. Five years before, the separate cities of Manhattan, Brooklyn, Queens, the Bronx and Staten Island had merged into one entity. Now, even Greater New York was spilling out of its boundaries as developers began spreading their tentacles east into rural Long Island and north into Westchester County. Augustus had resisted the idea of branch banks, for in his mind the old, small, neighborly New York was the only community he was interested in. Victor saw the opportunities in expanding and was quick to reach for them.

But most innovatively, he began to reach for a new class of depositors and customers: the urban poor, the immigrants. And now the contacts he had made in the Italian community eleven years before began to pay handsome dividends. Dr. Difatta had since died, but Salvatore Volpi, Professor Gonzaga and the others he had met in Difatta's house were still alive and prospering. Shortly after his takeover at the bank, Victor invited a dozen leaders of the Italian community to lunch. He hired an Italian caterer to serve an excellent meal in the board room, and as the group seated itself at the polished mahogany table, the portrait of Augustus on the paneled wall seemed to register a slight degree of posthumous shock at the linguine and Valpolicella being served in the hitherto WASP sanctum.

'Gentlemen,' said Victor as espresso was being served, 'I've invited you here today for several reasons, not the least of which is that I want to make money.'

'Who doesn't?' exclaimed Salvatore Volpi, who now owned five grocery stores in Brooklyn. 'But first,' continued Victor, 'I want to discuss something that's hardly a secret. We Italians aren't doing well in America, and I'm not sure I understand all the reasons. I'd appreciate it if some of you could tell me what you think are the reasons.'

'One reason,' said Ettore Lombardini, the short, bearded publisher of the Brooklyn-based Italian language newspaper, *Il Corriere*, 'is that most Italians don't come here to settle. They come here to make enough money to go back to Italy and buy a farm. Do you realize, Victor, that for every one hundred Italians who come to America, seventy-three go back to Italy?'

'Yes, I've read that statistic, though it's hard to believe.'

'Not if you compare us with the other immigrants—the Jews

and the Irish, to take the most obvious examples. The Irish fled famine, the Jews fled the ghettoes and the pogroms. Even with all the faults of Italy, it's still a beautiful country where you can lead a good life with a little money. That's why so many of us go back home. After all, the climate's better than New York.'

'But there are still millions who are staying here,' said Victor, 'and it seems to me they aren't moving up as they should. The Jews are taking over the garment center, they're becoming powerful in financial institutions, in publishing, in show business . . . Where are the Italians? Carrying bricks. Waiting on tables, cutting hair, pushing pushcarts; they're stone masons at sixty cents a day, painters for a dollar a day; they're playing in orchestras . . . Hell, the only institution in America where we Italians have truly taken over is the Metropolitan Opera! So what's wrong? I can't believe we're dumber than the others, or lazier . . .'

Now everyone began telling his reason why Italians weren't succeeding, and the lunch turned into a babble of confusion, helped by the wine. Finally Victor managed to silence them.

'All right,' he said, 'obviously there are a lot of reasons. But I think I'm now in a position to help, in a small way, because here's *one* Italian who, mostly through luck, is running a bank. Gentlemen, I want to make loans to Italians on a much larger scale than this bank has operated on before. If lack of capital has hindered us in the past, that's going to be corrected. You are all influential in the Italian community. I'd appreciate it if you'd spread word around about the bank's new policy—and of course we'll be taking large ads in your newspaper, Mr. Lombardini.' The publisher looked pleased. 'Also—and there is a selfish profit motive in this—I'm anxious to get Italians to deposit their money in this bank. I think if they get word that this is one financial institution that *wants* their deposits, that isn't going to look down its nose at them simply because they're working people, they'll overcome whatever shyness they may have. As I said, I stand to gain by this. But also I think our people will gain by it. If we Italians are going to get anywhere in America, it seems to me we have to come out of the ghettoes we're creating for ourselves and get into the mainstream of American life. Depositing money in a bank strikes me as a good way to start.' He paused, then grinned. 'Besides, we pay three percent interest.'

His speech was met with good-humored applause and promises of help. Afterward, as the guests were leaving, Lombardini took Victor aside. 'I'm very excited about what you're doing,' he said, clasping Victor's hand. 'We need men like you —leaders. You can count on my editorial support one hundred percent.'

'Good. I'm in the process of hiring an advertising agency for the bank. When I get one, which should be by next week, they'll be contacting you about the ads.'

'I'll be looking forward to meeting them. By the way . . .' he hesitated, looking rather embarrassed, 'I have a niece . . . she's a nice girl, just turned twenty-three . . . she's fluent in English and Italian, since she was raised in this country, and we put her through college. She's gone to secretarial school, and takes shorthand and types. Well, she wants to work, and we want her to work, which most of our friends disapprove of. I was hoping she'd come work for the paper, but she tells me she'd rather work in Manhattan. I don't suppose there'd be anything for her here at the bank?'

'As a matter of fact, I'm looking for a new secretary, since my father's secretary is retiring. I'd be glad to talk to her.'

Lombardini looked delighted.

'Excellent! You'll like her, I guarantee! A nice girl, a fine girl . . . well, she's my niece, I'm biased, but what the hell . . . her name is Julia. Julia Lombardini. When can she come see you?'

'As soon as possible.'

'She'll be here tomorrow.'

Lucille's upbringing should have protected her from the problems of sudden wealth, but it didn't. Her bonanza inheritance woke up her dormant bad qualities: her extravagance and her social-climbing snobbery. In her defense, she lived in a particularly extravagant and social-climbing age, but this was of little comfort to Victor, who watched his wife go on a spending spree with mounting dismay. At first, she concentrated on her house, and there was little Victor could say because since their marriage Lucille had lived in quarters that, while comfortable, were certainly inferior to those she had been used to, and her complaint over the years about lack of space and adequate servants had been, if annoying, understandable. Now she threw herself into the building project with the enthusiasm of a Louis XIV. She hired a young architect, a friend of Rodney's named Archie Winstead, who was a graduate of Yale and the Paris École des Beaux Arts. Although she explained to Victor that her preference for Archie over Stanford White or William Delano was because the younger man was cheaper, there was nothing cheap in Archie's taste, as soon became evident from his elaborate plans.

'Look!' she exclaimed to Victor one night in the first week of November. 'Archie's got the rendering of the facade. Of course, it's still rough, but it can give you an idea . . . Isn't it beautiful? It will be Indiana limestone, which has such a lovely off-white color.'

Victor studied the drawing. It was undeniably handsome, a four-story building in restrained classic French style, with extremely graceful window treatments and ornamentation. Winstead, a nice-looking young man, watched his client's husband with interest.

'Well?' said Lucille, impatiently. 'Do you like it?'

'Yes, it's very handsome,' said Victor, with little enthusiasm.

'Pay no attention to him, Archie. All he's thinking about is how much money it's going to cost. You know husbands and bankers: money, money, money, that's all they think about. Well, darling, let me tell you that when this house is finished, Victor and Lucille Dexter are going to have the best-looking town house in New York, and *everyone* is going to beat a path to our door! And wait till you see the entrance hall! It will all be in marble with a beautiful curved staircase . . . Archie's done a few studies of the wrought-iron balustrade—it's going to be like the one in the Hôtel Lambert in Paris . . .'

All through dinner she talked about the house in a near-monologue. Victor listened, said nothing. But afterward, when Winstead had gone, he lit one of his increasingly frequent cigars, exhaled, and looked across the drawing room at his wife, who was devouring the latest issue of Colonel Mann's notorious society-gossip magazine, *Town Topics*.

'Do you realize,' he said, 'you're making a fool of yourself, as well as me?'

She put down the magazine.

'A fool? How?'

'By putting up this pretentious palace. Look, Lucille: I love you—I've loved you from the moment I set eyes on you—but I know your faults. You're itching to take on society . . .'

'And what if I am? Is there something wrong with it?'

'Yes. If nothing else, it's a waste of time. These people you want to impress are nothing but empty-headed snobs.'

'Oh? And what society should I cultivate? Your Italian friends? Should I get fat and cook spaghetti?'

Victor flicked his cigar ash and smiled slightly.

'That joke's always good for a laugh at my expense. No, I

154

don't expect you to cook spaghetti, but I'm warning you: you're chasing a firefly that's not worth catching. And yes, I *do* think about the money. Do you have any idea what this house is going to cost?'

'Victor, I'm not asking you to put any of *your* money into it, and certainly I'm rich enough to build myself a house and furnish it with beautiful pieces. This strikes me as little enough to ask of life, and if you loved me as you *say* you do, I'd think you'd want me to have what I want.'

'Of course I want that, and of course I want you to be happy! But I can't understand why you're not happy with what you have? I love the children, but they seem to bore you . . .'

'Oh well *really*, Victor. I love the children too, but there's nothing particularly fascinating about watching Drew learn to walk or stopping Lorna from sucking her thumb. There are other things in life besides children. It's very easy for you to sneer at society, but what else are we women supposed to do? You men run the world and expect us to swoon with ecstasy when you come home from the office and give us a peck on the cheek. Well, I have a good head on my shoulders, and I want more out of life than that. There are a lot of brilliant men and women in this world, and I intend to meet all of them. But to do it takes a proper setting—takes money. I have the money, and I'm willing to pay the price. And I'm warning you, Victor: nothing you can do will stop me.'

Again he exhaled.

'And what if you run out of money?'

She smiled.

'But darling, how could I possibly do that? And even if I did, well . . . you're the president of a bank, aren't you? You'd just loan me more.'

He wondered if she were joking. He didn't think she could possibly be serious.

CHAPTER 14

'Hey, Paulie! Little Vinnie's been looking for you.'

Paolo Durazzo, a skinny thirty-two-year-old waiter, froze at the table he had just cleared and looked at the two men standing in the door of Tony's Bar and Grill at Forty-fifth Street and Ninth Avenue. The fat man with the pockmarked face he immediately recognized as Gianni Difatta. The muscular man in the black suit next to Gianni he knew also worked for Little Vinnie Tazzi, but he didn't know his name.

Paulie Durazzo bolted for the kitchen. It was three in the afternoon, and the restaurant's last lunch customer had left ten minutes before. Only Tony, the owner-bartender, was left in the small room, and he had ducked behind the elaborately carved bar.

'Going somewhere?'

Paulie Durazzo almost plowed into the big man who pushed through the kitchen door. He held a gun.

'Please,' whimpered Paulie, backing away from the man into the glass display case holding the *zuppa inglese* and *canoli*. 'Please . . .'

'Don't give us no trouble, and I won't have to use this thing,' said the man from the kitchen, who had a thick black moustache. He grabbed Paulie's thin arm and jerked him toward the door. As they passed the bar, Gianni Difatta said, 'Thanks, Tony. Little Vinnie'll remember this favor.'

'You?' screamed Paulie at the bartender, who had stood up again and was watching the scene with impassivity. 'How could you do this to me? I work hard for you—how could you betray me?'

'Shut up,' hissed his captor.

'I'll *haunt* you!' screamed Paulie, and only the genuine terror in his voice prevented the threat from seeming comic.

The man smashed the gun butt down on Paulie Durazzo's

156

skull, and the waiter collapsed into Gianni Difatta's arms. They hustled him into the snowy street and pushed him in the back of a wagon marked 'Sandino's Fresh Fish.'

Then they headed downtown.

Paulie Durazzo awoke to find himself tied to a wooden chair. His head throbbed with pain, and it took him a moment to focus and remember. Then the terror returned.

The chair was in the center of a cellar room. There were no windows and only one solid iron door behind Paulie, which he couldn't see. In front of him, perched on a rather rickety wooden table, was a small man in a well-tailored gray suit. A pearl stickpin was in his tie. Beside him, on the table, rested a gray fedora. The man's face was handsome, and he was smiling.

'Hello, Paulie,' said Little Vinnie Tazzi. 'You're in trouble. *Big* trouble.'

It was then Paulie Durazzo realized he was naked. He tried to move his arms, but they were tied tight behind the chair. He tried to move his legs, but his ankles were so tightly bound his bare feet were tingling. Starting to sweat despite the cold, he looked to his right to see Gianni Difatta leaning against the brick wall. He looked to his left: no one. Then he turned back to Little Vinnie.

'Please,' he said in a hoarse voice, 'I'll pay you back the money! I swear to God I'll pay you back! But you got to give me more *time* . . .'

'I gave you time, Paulie,' said Little Vinnie. 'Didn't I, Gianni?'

'Yeah, you gave him a whole month. This fucking punk ought to realize how generous you been with him, Vinnie. And then he runs away.'

'I wasn't hiding, Vinnie! I swear I wasn't hiding! I got the job at Tony's so I could make the money—and I've *got* it!'

'You got eight hundred dollars, Paulie? I don't believe you.'

'Not eight—no, not eight! But I got a hundred and fifty . . .'

'You owe me eight, Paulie,' said Little Vinnie, getting up from the table. 'You've owed me eight for months, plus interest. Didn't I give you two delays?'

'Yes, but I'm *poor*, Vinnie. I got a wife and three kids to feed —I'm poor! Jesus, give me another chance!'

'I'm tired of your excuses, Paulie,' said Little Vinnie, walking to a squat iron stove in the corner. He opened the door, then placed an iron poker in the hot coals. 'I didn't *ask* you to come to me for money, Paulie. It's not my fault you're so fucking dumb you play the horses. And don't give me a lot of speeches about your wife and kids. They haven't seen you for two months, ever since you took off with the rent money. You're no fucking good, Paulie. You're a loser. Your wife and kids aren't going to miss you.'

He had taken off his coat, folding it carefully on the table. Now he rolled up his shirt sleeves and put on an asbestos-lined glove. He went back to the stove and turned the poker. Paulie Durazzo, who had emigrated to America from Naples eight years before, was trembling, watching with fear-widened eyes.

'What you going to do, Vinnie?' he whispered.

'I'm going to do what's got to be done, Paulie. You're a cancelled loan, and I got a reputation to uphold. So you're going to be an example to my other customers. When they think about running away from Vinnie Tazzi—'

'I didn't run away!' he screamed.

'When they think of stiffing me, they'll think of Paulie Durazzo and they'll change their minds. You're not going to be a pretty corpse, Paulie.'

He pulled the poker out of the fire and held it up. Its sharp tip glowed red. Then he turned and started walking toward the chair.

Paulie was crying.

'Please, Vinnie . . . please . . .'

'I'm going to kill you, Paulie. But I'm going to kill you *slow*.'

"Oh Jesus . . .'

'First your nipples. Then maybe your ears. It may take a whole hour, Paulie, but I got time.'

'Please, Vinnie . . . please . . . Mother of God—!'

'Hold him, Gianni.'

Gianni Difatta came up behind the chair and grabbed Paulie's neck in a hammerlock. Then, as the waiter gurgled and writhed with animal panic, Little Vinnie pressed the red-hot poker against his right nipple.

As the foul stench of burning flesh and hair filled the room, Paulie Durazzo fainted.

'Give the son of a bitch five minutes,' said Little Vinnie. 'Then wake him up.'

'Right, Vinnie.'

'Hey Vinnie, look at this ad in the paper!'

It was that evening. After the brutal murder of Durazzo—who had actually died in less than an hour, Little Vennie's torture technique being mercifully inadequate—they had photographed the ghastly corpse in order to terrify future 'customers,' then tied

158

it in a weighted sack and dumped it in that ever-convenient disposal unit, the East River. From there they drove to Little Vinnie's favorite restaurant on Mulberry Street, La Isola Bella, for a hearty meal of clams, fish and pasta. Nothing stimulated Little Vinnie's appetite like murder.

'What ad?' said Little Vinnie, sipping his wine.

'Here, in *Il Corriere*. A full-page ad put in by our old buddy, Victor Dexter!'

'That shit. What's it say? Read it to me.'

'It says, "A message to all Italian-Americans from the Dexter Bank and Trust Company, Twenty-five Pine Street. The Dexter Bank welcomes all Italian-Americans living in New York and invites them to open checking accounts and/or savings accounts. We have full banking services to meet your every need, and we have hired Italian-speaking tellers for your convenience. We also extend an invitation to all Italian-Americans needing personal or business financing to come speak to us. If your needs are legitimate, we will be glad to loan you money at favorable rates of interest. We welcome your business and look forward to serving you." Then there's a lot of shit about banking hours, and it's signed "Victor Dexter, President." ' He put aside the paper. 'Can you believe that fuck, Victor, ending up president of a bank?'

'I can believe anything,' said Little Vinnie, consuming his clams posillipo by the half-dozen. 'It's interesting, though. So he wants Italian-Americans with legitimate needs to do business with him. What do you think, Gianni? Are our needs legitimate?'

'Bet your ass,' grinned Gianni, wiping a blob of marinara sauce from his shirt. 'What you thinking, Vinnie?'

'I'm thinking,' said Little Vinnie between gulps of Chianti, 'that it's our responsibility as solid Italian-Americans to expand our business, right?'

'Right.'

'And when you're running a loan outfit, you need more money to make more loans, right?'

'Right.'

'And so, when your old pal's a banker, where do you go for more money?'

Gianni grinned with delight.

'To the Dexter Bank and Trust Company!'

'Shit, Gianni, whoever said you got an olive for a brain was wrong. You're one fucking smart Guinea.'

Gianni glowed with pride.

Julia Lombardini was too Italian-looking to have ever been called a Gibson Girl. But her tall, willowy figure and the straight way she held her head was Gibsonian. And in her dark brown skirt and white blouse with the puffed sleeves at the shoulders, she was certainly strikingly attractive. As Little Vinnie examined her three days after the murder of Paolo Durazzo, he thought that if Victor wasn't laying his secretary, there was something wrong with him. As Julia examined Little Vinnie, she thought that the dapperly dressed little man with the insolent smile had a name that was vaguely familiar.

'You don't have an appointment, Mr. Tazzi?' she asked.

'Nah. Just tell Victor it's Little Vinnie. He'll remember. We practically grew up together in Brooklyn.' He leaned on the desk and flashed his white teeth. 'We was like brothers.'

'I see. Well, if you'll take a seat, I'll speak to Mr. Dexter.'

'You know something? You got a real nice figure.'

She stood up.

'Thank you.'

'I used to be a boxer. Would you like to feel my muscles?'

'Some other time.'

'Come on . . . wait a minute.' He took off his jacket, then flexed his right arm. 'Look at that: you can see it right through the shirt! Ain't that something? Like Sandow, you know? Come on: feel it.'

'Mr. Tazzi, this is a bank, not a gymnasium. Please take a seat.'

She went into Victor's office. In the three weeks she had been working for the young bank president, Julia had grown to have enormous respect for him as a businessman and admiration for him as a human being. She thought she had never met anyone who was so downright nice. It never occurred to her she might be getting a crush on him, simply because Julia had been extremely strictly brought up. But certainly she had never enjoyed anything so much in her young life as her job, and she found she actually looked forward to getting to work—something she never would have thought possible.

'Mr. Dexter,' she said, coming up to his desk, 'there's a rather . . . odd gentleman outside—and I'm not sure he's a gentleman—who says he grew up with you in Brooklyn. His name is Vincent Tazzi, and he'd like an appointment.'

She was rather surprised to see the color drain from his face.

'Is he short?' he asked.

'Very. I think I've heard his name . . . I think my uncle has mentioned him . . .'

'And he wants to see *me?*'

'Yes, sir.'

Victor remembered Marco Fosco and that night he would never get out of his memory.

'Well,' he said, 'I didn't exactly "grow up" with him, but show him in.'

'Yes, sir.'

As she left the office, Victor went to the window and looked out at Pine Street, where a few automobiles were fighting their way through the horse traffic. Blood. He had never forgotten the feel of Marco's blood, the taste of it as Little Vinnie had smeared it on his mouth and then, in the supremely obscene gesture, kissed the blood on to Victor's lips. The murder had remained officially unsolved, but Victor knew that he had, if not murdered Marco, at least caused his death. The irony had not escaped him that whereas his brother, Franco, had been jailed for a murder he didn't commit, he, Victor, had not been jailed for a death he did commit. Franco had risen to great prominence in Italy—notoriety, in fact—as the publisher of the radical newspaper *Libertà*, and his love affair with Princess Sylvia had become the scandal of half Europe. But Franco had paid for his success with twelve years in prison. Was Victor now going to pay belatedly for the death of Marco Fosco, at that point in his life where he was becoming a successful and effective human being?

'Hello, Victor.'

He turned slowly to see the dangerous little man he had had no contact with for eleven years.

'Hello, Vinnie.'

'Come on, Victor: is that any way to greet your old buddy? Aren't you going to shake my hand?'

Victor came around his desk and extended his hand. Little Vinnie took it and squeezed it hard, looking up into Victor's eyes. 'Last time we saw each other,' he whispered with a grin, 'we kissed. Remember?'

Victor said nothing, but his wince gave him away.

'What do you want?'

'I want to do business. I'm an Italian-American and I saw your ad, so here I am. I want a loan.'

Victor eyed him suspiciously.

'Take a seat.'

He went around his desk and sat down as Little Vinnie pulled up a chair.

'So here you are, the president of a bank,' said Little Vinnie, looking around. 'I like your office. Class. I guess hanging around with your millionaire friends finally paid off, huh?'

'That and a lot of hard work. What do you want, Vinnie? I'm a busy man.'

Little Vinnie's eyes flashed.

'Hey Victor, don't give me the bum's rush. I know a lot of things about you—you know what I mean?'

'If you're referring to Marco . . .'

'I am.'

'Why didn't you ever tell the police?'

'Aw Victor, I'm your pal—your buddy! We wouldn't rat on you. Besides, the police didn't give a shit who killed Marco, and they wouldn't care now. But the newspapers might.' He snickered. 'I can see the headlines now: "Prominent Banker Involved in Gang Killing!" "Victor Dexter a Thrill Killer!"' And he doubled over with laughter that struck Victor as rather manic. When he calmed down, he lighted a cigarette. 'Anyway, Victor, that's all water over the dam—or maybe blood over the dam, huh? So I'm here now to arrange a loan from you. A business loan.'

'What's your business?'

'I'm starting a garbage removal company. The Tazzi Garbage Company. It's got a nice sound to it, don't it? Class. Anyway, I figure I'll need about a hundred thousand dollars to get started.'

'A hundred thousand?' exclaimed Victor, amazed.

'I have to buy a lot of wagons, get horses, rent stable space . . . it takes a lot of money.'

'Not *that* much.'

Little Vinnie sucked on his cigarette.

'Does that mean you won't approve the loan?' he asked softly.

'It means I want to know a hell of a lot more about the Tazzi Garbage Company before I loan you that much money! Do you think I'm stupid? You could start a garbage business for five thousand—less! What do you want that much money for?'

'Let's say I'm involved in several businesses that need capital. If I pay your interest, what do you care where the money's invested?'

'Believe me, Vinnie, I *care*. I suggest you fill out our loan applications, and I'll study them . . .'

'Look, Victor,' Vinnie leaned forward, '*you* fill out the loan applications, I don't mess around with that shit. Put anything you want on them—the Tazzi Garbage Company, the Tazzi Douche-bag Company, whatever. Then put a hundred thousand dollars on it and *approve* it, understand? I'll be in tomorrow morning at ten to sign the papers and pick up the money.' He stood up, took a final drag on the cigarette, then ground it out. 'Otherwise,' he smiled, 'I'll tell the newspapers about Marco and that romantic night eleven years ago when we kissed in the alley. Think about it.'

And he walked out of the office.

When Julia Lombardini came into the office five minutes later, she found her boss lying on the black leather sofa, something she had never seen before.

'Mr. Dexter, are you all right?'

He didn't answer for a moment. Then: 'I'm all right.'

She had never heard him sound so uncertain.

'I called my uncle at *Il Corriere*,' she went on, 'and asked him about Tazzi. He said the man's a hoodlum.'

Silence.

'He said that he loans money to poor people who can't get it anywhere else and charges enormous interest—up to forty percent! And he terrorizes them into paying him back, except of course they almost never pay back completely because of the interest. My uncle says that the rumor is that he's killed people.'

Silence.

'My uncle said he pays off the police.'

Finally Victor spoke.

'Does he know that for certain?'

'No, it's just rumor.'

Victor got up.

'Get me your uncle on the phone,' he said, returning to his desk.

Julia Lombardini thought that whatever it was that had been bothering him had gone away.

CHAPTER 15

Lucille took little interest in her children. After bearing them, she had turned them over to the Irish nanny, Mrs. Moffit. Which is why Victor was surprised that evening when he came home to the Gramercy Park house to be told by Lorna, his eight-year-old firstborn, that 'Mummy is upstairs giving Drew a bath.'

Lorna was a pretty girl, with her mother's coloring and a disposition that was remarkably calm. Except tonight she seemed unusually excited as she hugged her father. 'Mummy says we're all going to England for Christmas!' she exclaimed.

'She did? That's news to me.'

'Won't it be exciting, Daddy? We can see Big Ben and the King's palace! Maybe we'll even see the King in his coach!'

Victor kissed her, then set her down, smiling at her. He adored his children and would admit he was probably an overly indulgent parent; but aware as he was of Lucille's disinterest in them, he felt a need to try to make up the love they got only rare glimpses of from their mother.

'And why did Mummy say we were going to England?'

'Oh, she and Mr. Winstead want to buy furniture for the new house. Can't people buy furniture here in New York?'

'Most people can,' replied her father, who wasn't smiling anymore. He walked into the small parlor of the house and looked at the furniture. It was homey and homely: heavy oak tables, overstuffed chairs, a few 'good' pieces Lucille had wheedled out of her parents. Victor knew she despised it, and he assumed the furniture-buying trip abroad was going to be an orgy of antique buying.

He went upstairs and looked in the children's bathroom. Drew was getting a bath, but Mrs. Moffit was doing the bathing, not Lucille.

'Where's Mrs. Dexter?' asked Victor.

Mrs. Moffit, a plump Irish woman, replied, 'Oh, she was here

164

for a while, playin' with Drew, but he got her soaked, the little scamp.'

Victor kissed his son's wet head, then went to his bedroom where Lucille was brushing her hair at her vanity. He came over and kissed her.

'Good evening, darling,' she said. 'I got soaked trying to bathe Drew—he splashed all over me.'

'What made you want to bathe him in the first place? You never have before.'

'Oh, I decided I probably should pay more attention to the children. Especially since Drew won't be with us for Christmas.'

'Yes, I heard about the trip to England. You might have let me know.'

'Well, it wasn't settled definitely till this afternoon, but Archie *can* go with us after all, so I booked us a suite on the *Krönprinzessin Cecilie*. I'll leave Drew with Mrs. Moffit, but I thought Lorna and Barbara would enjoy Christmas in London. It should be terribly Dickens-y.'

'But what about me? I can't possibly go to Europe this year. There's too much work at the bank.'

'Surely you could take a month off. Or three weeks.'

'No, I can't. Maybe next year when I'm more settled in, but not my first year.'

Lucille looked at him.

'Well,' she said finally, 'I'm terribly sorry, darling, but it looks as if you'll have to spend Christmas alone.'

The cool selfishness of her tone cracked his heart.

'Lucille, what's happening to you? What's happening to *us*? We've always done everything together, but now all you're interested in is that damned house. Don't you love me anymore?'

'Of course I love you. Don't be silly.' She stood up. 'But Archie says the best antiques are in London and Paris . . .'

'Damn the antiques!' he said, grabbing her and kissing her, hotly. 'Go to Europe later,' he whispered after a moment. 'I want you with me at Christmas.'

He ran his fingers lovingly through her red-gold hair. As always, his physical presence excited her.

'And I want to be with you . . .' she said, hesitantly.

'I'll tell you what: I've been offered sixty thousand dollars for the Madison Avenue house. I wasn't thinking of selling it, because I think in the long run it will be a good investment. But I'm willing to sell it and give you the sixty thousand dollars to

165

use furnishing the new house. After all, I want to contribute something.'

'That's very generous, darling.'

'There's only one string attached, and it's not much of a string. I want you to stay here for Christmas. I want us all to be together for the holidays. I want Lorna and Barbara to help me trim the tree . . .' He smiled rather wistfully. 'Call me sentimental, I guess. Most of all, I want to be with you.'

She looked at her handsome husband. She knew he was still in love with her, and the power this gave her over him pleased her. She knew his request was reasonable, and her heart told her to give in to him. But the temptation to flaunt her power, to hurt him, was too attractive to pass up. She smiled and said, 'That's sweet of you, Victor. And I'll gladly take the sixty thousand dollars, since the expenses on the house are higher than I thought. But the arrangements are all made for the trip. And after making Archie change all his plans so he could go with me, I can hardly tell him now that the whole thing's off.'

Victor's eyes became cool.

'I'm *asking* you to stay,' he said, softly.

'And I'm telling you I can't.'

He let go of her arms. He looked at her a moment, then turned and went to the door.

'Victor,' she said, 'what about the sixty thousand dollars?'

'It's yours,' he said, curtly, opening the door. 'It'll be my Christmas present. Merry Christmas.'

He left the room. She had never heard him sound bitter before. She wondered briefly if she were making a terrible mistake.

At noon the next day, Little Vinnie met Gianni Difatta at Il Trovatore, a Brooklyn restaurant owned by a Verdi-worshipping former baker from Messina.

'How'd it go?' asked Gianni as Little Vinnie slid into the dark wooden booth opposite him.

'We got us a bank!' smiled Little Vinnie. 'I got Victor by the balls. He's scared shitless I'll tell about Marco—you ought to have seen him! He was really sweating. He said, "Vinnie, I don't care what you do with the money . . ."'

'I thought he said he did?' interrupted Gianni.

'Sure, but that was before he thought it over. Shit, it would ruin him. And what would his family think? Those Fifth Avenue birds don't like murderers. Anyway, he's scared, and he gave me the loan, and we got him over a barrel. And don't think this is the last loan! We'll field this money out, and then in a couple of months I'll hit him up for another hundred thousand. It's like being given the keys to the bank vault!'

'Goddam, Vinnie, you've got a head on your shoulders!'

'There was only one thing he wanted: that I keep the money on deposit in his bank, which I agreed to. Why the hell not? It's safer there. There's a lot of crooks around, in case you hadn't heard.'

Gianni's fat trembled with gelatinous mirth.

'Yeah, I *have* heard, Vinnie!'

'And I've been thinking things over. It's time we started branching out. Brooklyn's all right, but why shouldn't we work Manhattan, too? Right?'

'Right, Vinnie.'

'So get the boys to pass the word around that Tuesdays and Thursdays I'll be at the Isola Bella all afternoon, open for business. And that I've got a lot of new cash for loans. You know something, Gianni? I'm going to be a fucking millionaire!'

'I always knew it, Vinnie. Always.'

'Yeah, I know. And since business is booming, tell the boys they're all getting a ten percent raise across the board. And here's a little bonus for you, Gianni.'

He pulled an envelope from his jacket and handed it across the table. Gianni opened it and quickly counted the ten hundred-dollar bills. He looked up. 'You're a real generous man to work for, Vinnie,' he said. 'Real generous.'

'Yeah, I know. Now let's get some lunch, then I'm going to see Renata. I feel like getting laid. How about you?'

Gianni grinned.

'I *always* feel like getting laid.'

'The difference between you and me is, you gotta pay for it, Gianni, because you're so fucking fat. Little Vinnie gets it free because I'm so fucking beautiful. Right?'

'Right, Vinnie.'

For the thousandth time in his life, Gianni Difatta wished he had been born Vinnie Tazzi.

The man was in his mid-thirties, well-built, his thin face with the prominent nose stamped prematurely with the wrinkles of poverty. His black suit was shining at the elbows and knees, but his cheap white shirt was clean. He stood at the door of La Isola Bella restaurant, hat in hand, waiting his turn to see Little Vinnie. Finally Gianni came up to him. 'Okay, you're next. But let me warn you: treat Mr. Tazzi with respect, or you don't get no loan. Understand?'

'Yes, sir.'

The man followed Gianni through the tables of the almost empty restaurant to a booth at the rear. It was three in the afternoon of the following Thursday. Vinnie had been at his booth an hour and a half and had already loaned out $3,700 at forty percent interest. Business in Manhattan was even better than he had expected.

'Sit down,' said Little Vinnie. The man sat opposite him, placing his crumpled hat in his lap.

'What's your name?'

'Benno Lazzaroni, sir.'

'You got a job?'

'Yes, sir.'

'Yeah, well, what is it? Don't waste my time.'

'I'm night watchman at a jewelry store.'

'Which jewelry store?'

'Gérard et fils.'

Little Vinnie looked impressed.

'The one on Thirty-fourth Street next to the Waldorf?'

'Yes, sir.'

'Huh.' Little Vinnie made some mental notes as he wrote Lazzaroni's name in his notebook. 'What's your home address?'

'Two thirty Prince Street.'

'How much you want to borrow and what for?'

'My wife's got to have an operation on her back—she fell down some stairs last week and is in bad pain. The doctor said the operation's going to cost seven hundred dollars. I haven't got seven hundred dollars, sir . . . I only make twenty-five dollars a week, and I've got three kids . . .'

'Yeah, yeah, I know. I've heard the story before, lots of times. That's why I'm in this business—to help you people. Who sent you to me?'

'A policeman named Joe Cacciati.'

'Yeah, Joe.' Vinnie wrote Cacciati's name next to Lazzaroni's. 'Why don't I loan you an even thousand? There'll be hospital expenses, you'll want to buy her flowers, a lot of things . . . a thousand okay?'

Lazzaroni smiled with relief.

'Yes, sir! Thank you!'

'You know about my interest rates?'

Lazzaroni's smile faded.

'Joe said you charge forty percent. I don't know how I'm going to pay you back, but I *got* to get the money . . .'

'You come here every Thursday with ten dollars, and we'll work it out. It's gonna take you a couple of years to pay me back, but you look like a good risk. Just don't miss a Thursday, understand? I don't like to be stood up, and Joe Cacciati can tell you I got ways of collecting what's due me. But you meet your payments, we won't have no trouble. Okay?'

He pulled a thick wallet from his coat, took out ten hundreds and handed them over to Lazzaroni, who stared at the money with awe.

'Do I sign some papers?' he asked.

'You don't sign papers with Vinnie Tazzi. I know who's got my money. See you next Thursday.'

He lighted a cigarette as Lazzaroni hurried out of the restaurant.

CHAPTER 16

Victor and Lucille stood at the corner of Fifth Avenue and Seventy-third Street and watched as the big steam shovel began scooping out the foundations of the new house.

'Isn't it exciting?' exclaimed Lucille, holding her husband's arm. It was a cold late November day, and she was wearing a Russian sable coat she had bought two weeks before for $5,000.

Victor said nothing. He had sworn to himself not to fight Lucille any more about the house, although the estimates of its cost mounted to a hair-raising $600,000. It was her money and what she wanted; he had even contributed to the 'mistake,' as he thought of it, by giving her the $60,000 he had received from the sale of the Madison Avenue house. However, Lucille was getting in over her head financially, which worried him, and on the way downtown, he brought the subject of the bank stock up.

'Lucille, would you consider selling me your stock in the bank?'

She looked surprised.

'Why should I do that?' She hesitated. 'Besides, where would you get the money?'

'I think I could raise it from other bankers I know. I'd pay you a fair price, at least two points above the market.'

'But I don't see why . . .' Then she laughed. 'Ah, I *do* see. You're worried that I'm spending so much on the house, I might start selling some of my stock to outsiders.'

'Yes, that's part of the reason. You can't pay for everything out of your income.'

'Then I'm glad you brought this up, since I was going to speak to you about it anyway. I want to arrange a loan at the bank, or a mortgage or whatever you call it, to pay for the rest of the house. As you know, I wrote a check to the contractor for a hundred and fifty thousand dollars to get started, but the rest of the money I want to borrow. How do I do it? I suppose I have to put some of my stock for collateral?'

'That's why I'd rather buy it from you. It won't look good for me to approve a mortgage that big for my wife.'

'Oh really, Victor, I'm sure it's done all the time.'

'But a mortgage *that* big isn't. It doesn't look good for the bank or me, which is why it would be a lot simpler all around for you to sell me your stock. Maybe part of it now, part of it later . . .'

'I won't sell,' she snapped. 'So you can forget that little scheme. The stock's mine, and I intend to keep it. And don't think I don't see what's going through your head: it's not only that you're afraid I might sell some of it to an outsider, you're also a little worried about me, aren't you? Afraid I might not always be so supportive of you at the bank. Well, Victor, you're just going to have to live with that worry. I like things just the way they are. And if your bank won't give me the financing I need, I'll take my stock to another bank to raise the money. Would you prefer that?'

She looked at him, saw his tight lips, knew he was burning. More and more, she found herself enjoying using her power over him. Not only the power of his love, but now the power of her bank stock. She wasn't even sure why she enjoyed it, but she did.

'No,' he said finally. 'I'll arrange the mortgage.'

Now he knew what he had suspected for a long time: that his life was going to be miserable until he got the stock. The difference was that it had suddenly occurred to him how to get it.

The basement of 230 Prince Street contained a three-room apartment for the superintendent of the building, a job Benno Lazzaroni held during the day, which paid no money but offered the apartment rent-free. On a Friday morning, Benno was seated at a table sipping coffee when there was a knock on the door. Benno got up, went to the door and opened it.

There were Little Vinnie and Gianni Difatta.

'I've missed you, Benno,' said Little Vinnie, pushing the big night watchman out of the way as he came in the room. 'I've missed you two Thursdays in a row. I'm real disappointed in you.'

He looked around the tiny, low-ceilinged room which served as living room, dining room and kitchen. The only illumination was a below-sidewalk-level window.

'Where's your wife, Benno?' said Little Vinnie, sitting down at the table.

The night watchman closed the door, watching his visitors nervously.

'She's at the grocery,' he mumbled.

'So her back's okay?'

'Yes, sir.'

'I'm glad to hear it, since I paid for the fucking operation. Benno, I told you not to miss a Thursday, but you've missed two. Want to see a picture of one of my customers who kept missing payments? Show him Paulie Durazzo, Gianni.'

Gianni pulled a photograph from his pocket and held it up. Benno looked at it and winced.

'See those two holes where his eyes was supposed to be?' said Little Vinnie, pulling out a pocket knife and cleaning his nails. 'Somebody stuck a hot poker in his eyes, 'cause he couldn't "see" his way clear to pay me what he owed. I wouldn't want that to happen to you, Benno, so you better come up with twenty bucks—*fast*.'

Lazzaroni was trembling.

'Mr. Tazzi, I haven't *got* twenty dollars—not now . . .'

'You spent all the thousand already?'

'Yes, sir. The extra money I used to get my daughter's teeth straightened, and last week my son caught flu and we almost lost him, so I had more doctor bills . . .'

'You got a real unhealthy family, Benno. So you're broke.'

'Yes, sir. But I get paid tonight . . .'

He ducked as the knifeblade flew through the air at him, burying itself into the door inches to the left of where he had been standing. Little Vinnie got up, went to the door and pulled the knife out. Then he turned to Benno.

'Next time I won't miss,' said Little Vinnie, quietly. 'I tell you what, Benno: you want to cancel the whole loan, interest and all? You want to wipe the slate clean—pfft, like that?'

Benno stared at him.

'You mean . . . I wouldn't have to pay you back?'

'That's right. 'Course, you got to do something for me in return.'

'What?'

Little Vinnie sat back down.

'This jewelry store you work at: is there an alarm system at night?'

'Yes.'

'I suppose they put all their jewels in a safe, right?'

172

'Yes. It's a big one, a Chubb.'

'Uh huh. Now, uh . . . . if Gianni and I and another fellow I know showed up tonight at, say, oh . . . one-thirty, could you turn the alarm system off long enough for us to get in?'

He looked at Lazzaroni.

'Of course,' he added, 'we'd tie you up to make it look like you was doing your job, but you was overwhelmed by superior numbers . . . you know, make up some bullshit story. Meanwhile me and Gianni and my friend will be working on the safe. How about it, Benno? You let us in and keep your mouth shut, and your loan is paid off. What do you say?'

Lazzaroni didn't say anything for a moment. Then:

'Wait till after two. The Waldorf's kitchen crew next door has gone home by two.'

Little Vinnie smiled.

'You're a smart man, Benno.'

At ten past two, Little Vinnie, Gianni and Aldo Lanza, an expert yegg, or safecracker, entered the dark alley behind Gérard et fils Jewelers. To the west loomed the imposing magnificence of the Waldorf-Astoria Hotel, fifteen floors of lavish opulence filled with some of the richest people in the world, a fact M. Gérard had not been unaware of when he opened his jewelry store next door on Thirty-fourth Street. The alley was empty. Little Vinnie led the others to the steel door marked 'Gérard et fils. Service.' He tapped three times on the door, the prearranged signal. Then they waited.

After half a minute, there was a click and the door opened. Little Vinnie hurried inside.

'You done real good, Benno,' he whispered. 'Now where's the safe?'

'It's through that door. I pulled down the blinds, but I wouldn't turn on the lights.'

'We've got a lantern. Okay, Gianni's gonna tie you up while Aldo and I start on the safe.'

Benno closed the door as Little Vinnie and Lanza hurried into the next room, an office with a large safe in the east wall. Lanza, a short, wiry man with a ferret face, lighted his lantern, set it on the floor, then walked over to examine the dial.

'What do you think?' whispered Little Vinnie.

'Give me a half hour, maybe less.'

Little Vinnie waited as Lanza went to work. Five minutes later, Gianni joined them.

'Benno's tied,' he whispered. 'I gagged him, too.'

'Good. When we leave, shoot the bastard. That way, there won't be no witnesses.'

They watched Lanza work on the safe intently. Two minutes passed. Three. Suddenly the room was filled with light and policemen. While Little Vinnie roared his surprise and outrage, he and Gianni and Lanza were handcuffed and shoved out the door. 'You!' he howled at Benno Lazzaroni, who had been untied by the cops staked out in the basement just before they arrested Little Vinnie. 'You set us up! I'll kill you for this!'

Benno Lazzaroni—which wasn't the detective's real name —laughed.

'Where you're going, you little punk, the only thing you'll kill is time.'

The police pushed the three men into the alley and locked them in a black Maria.

Victor Dexter got the news forty-five minutes later from Ettore Lombardini, the publisher of *Il Corriere*, who phoned Victor's house. 'I just got word from Captain Hendrix at Police Headquarters,' said Lombardini. 'The whole thing worked as planned, beautifully. Tazzi, Difatta and Lanza are being booked for burglary. There's a possibility of a murder charge— apparently Difatta has a photograph of a man Little Vinnie hinted he murdered—but even without the murder charge, Tazzi and Difatta shouldn't be bothering us for ten or fifteen years. It was a beautiful idea, Victor.'

'Well, I figured sending a night watchman of a jewelry store to Little Vinnie was like sending a pound of cheese to a rat. Sooner or later, he couldn't resist biting. There's no way he'll ever know I was behind it?'

'No.'

'Good. So far he's drawn out a little over ten thousand dollars from his account, which the bank will have to take as a loss, but getting rid of him's well worth ten thousand. And his customers should be happy when they hear they won't have anyone to pay back. Maybe I can get their business. Thanks for letting me know, Ettore. Good night.'

He hung up. Lucille, next to him in bed, said sleepily, 'What was that all about?'

'Oh, nothing. Sorry I woke you up.'

He started to turn out the bed light, but Lucille put her hand on his arm.

'No,' she said softly. 'Leave it on.'

He looked at his wife, once the object of all his love and lust but now, lately, slowly turning into something else, something unlovable, something faintly monstrous . . .

'Make love to me,' she whispered, running her fingers over his skin. With all their fighting, Victor still excited her physically, he was still the best-looking man she had ever seen.

He leaned over and kissed her. After a moment, he stopped.

'What's wrong?' whispered Lucille.

'I don't feel like it,' said Victor, turning on his side and reaching for the light.

Lucille was amazed.

'But you *always* feel like it!' she exclaimed.

'Those were the good old days.'

'But . . . what does this mean?'

'I have no idea.'

She leaned over him and turned the light on again.

'Don't you *dare* go to sleep!' she said, shaking him. 'I know what this is all about. This is just another way of your trying to get me to sell you my bank stock!'

Victor got out of bed, yawned, picked up his pillow and headed for the door.

'Where are you going?' she exclaimed.

'To sleep on the sofa. Frankly, Lucille, you're beginning to bore me.'

Her face turned red. As he closed the door behind him, she grabbed her pillow and threw it with all her strength. It hit the door and plopped to the floor. Lucille burst into irritable tears. For years she had thought of her husband as her mouth-gaping, adoring slave who would never rebel.

Apparently the rebellion had begun.

CHAPTER 17

'We just got this cable from London,' said Julia Lombardini, handing the piece of paper to Victor. 'It's from your wife.'

Victor read it: 'Have bought two Raeburns, one Gainsborough, two Watteaus and one magnificent Lawrence. Send picture dealer money order for $193,000. His address: Mr. S. T. Claypool, 41 Bond Street, London. Merry Christmas. Lucille.'

'Good God,' he muttered.

Julia was watching him.

'Shall I send it?' she asked.

'How much does she have in her account?'

'A little over two hundred thousand dollars.'

Victor whistled.

'She's cutting it awfully close. But send it. It's her money.'

'All right. Mr. Dexter, I . . .'

She hesitated.

'What is it, Julia?'

'Well, it's just that I thought since your family's away, you might like to have Christmas dinner with my uncle and aunt. My aunt's an awfully good cook.'

He looked at her.

'That's the best idea you've had in a month! Remind me to give you a Christmas bonus.'

'Mr. Dexter, give me a Christmas bonus.'

They both laughed. He gave her the bonus.

'I'm a subscriber to your brother's newspaper, *Libertà*,' said Ettore Lombardini the next day as he, his wife, Anna Maria, Julia and Victor sat down to the Christmas dinner. 'He writes some wild stuff!'

'Is he really a socialist?' asked Mrs. Lombardini, a pleasant-looking woman in her fifties who had prepared an oddly

176

Italian-American version of Christmas, complete with roast turkey and *vitello prosciutto e funghi al Marsala.*

'He's a very dedicated socialist,' replied Victor. 'On the other hand, he lives with one of the richest women in Italy, Princess dell'Acqua, so I think Franco is a bit of a political and philosophical hybrid. He writes me that he's thinking of running for the Italian Senate.'

'There's so much corruption in Italy,' sighed Lombardini sadly. 'Maybe socialism is the answer. Certainly your brother has caught the attention of the Italian people. From what I read, he's quite the hero.'

'Not to the Church,' said Victor. 'Franco attacks the Vatican, which is dangerous in Italy. And, of course, they love to roast him for living openly with the Princess.'

'It sounds very risqué,' smiled Julia, who was sitting opposite Victor. 'But I suppose that sort of thing is more accepted in Italy.'

'Well,' said Victor, 'yes and no. My brother has the idea that marriage is a bourgeois invention. On the other hand, he and the Princess have had twin sons, illegitimate of course, which puts the children in a sort of limbo. I don't know: there are many things about Franco I admire. But with all the razzle-dazzle, when it really comes down to it, he has things pretty well going for him.'

Ettore Lombardini laughed.

'In other words, all the comforts of marriage, but none of the responsibilities. No wonder he's popular in Italy!'

'Exactly. And I'm afraid my brother is something of a ladies' man, too.'

'He sounds fascinating,' said Julia. 'Have you ever gone back to Italy to see him?'

'No, but I intend to soon. Or at least when I can get the time. It's funny, but Italy is such a dim memory to me—or at least Sicily—that going back will be like seeing it for the first time.'

'Ah, here comes the turkey!'

A heavyset black woman carried in a tray with a huge bird on it and set it in front of Ettore, who started to carve.

The delicious meal was over at three in the afternoon, and Victor asked Julia if she'd like to 'walk off' the food with a stroll on the beach. Ettore's comfortable brick house was in a new development on Sheepshead Bay, with a wonderful view of the channel. It was a cold, gray day, with a snappy wind creating small whitecaps on the water, but the air was clean and invigorating, and both of them filled their lungs with it.

'I like your uncle and aunt very much,' said Victor. 'How are you their niece?'

'My mother was my uncle's sister. She died several years ago, and since my father was dead, Uncle Ettore took me in. They've been very kind to me.'

A seagull swooped over their heads, cawing cheerfully. In the distance a liner was heading into New York from Europe, its four tall stacks spewing coal smoke. Victor looked at it, thinking of Lucille.

'When does your wife come home?' asked Julia, reading his thoughts.

'The fifth of January.'

They walked a while in silence, Julia's skirts flapping about her ankles as she hugged her Persian lamb coat around her. Then she laughed.

'What's funny?' asked Victor.

'I was just thinking of your brother in Rome, living in sin and apparently loving it. Then I thought of the Holy Father, and the look on his face when *he* thinks of your brother!'

'It's even worse,' grinned Victor. 'Princess Sylvia's brother-in-law is one of the most powerful cardinals in the Church.'

'Your brother must be *very* popular. But if you don't mind my saying it, I just can't imagine *your* brother doing all these wild things.'

'Why? Am I so dull and conventional?'

'You're not dull at all, but you are conventional, and . . . I don't know: the president of the Dexter Bank having a brother who's a socialist . . . well, it's sort of wonderful!'

He stopped and took her hand.

'I suppose I am conventional,' he said, 'because I'm falling in love with my secretary.'

Silence for a moment as the wind blew her hair.

'What about Mrs. Dexter?' she said finally.

He looked troubled.

'I loved her more than anything else in my life. I still *do* love her, I guess, but she seems to be pushing me out of her life. She seems more in love with *things* than with me anymore. I don't have fun with her, the way we used to. I find I have a great deal of fun with you, Julia.' He hesitated. 'Am I embarrassing you?'

'A little.'

He took her in his arms and kissed her. After a moment, she pushed him gently away.

178

'I don't . . . want to become involved with you that way,' she said. 'No, that's a lie. I do. I'm . . .' she shrugged, '. . . in love with you. I have been for some time. But I don't want to become your mistress. It's too complicated, too messy. Those things never work out happily.'

'Sometimes they do.'

'In plays. I don't want to ruin your marriage and have your children hating me. So . . . ' she looked him in the eye, 'let me just be your secretary.'

Victor frowned.

'All right, at least for the time being. But maybe you'll change your mind.'

'I doubt it. I think we'd better get back to my uncle's.'

They started back down the beach.

'Well,' said Ettore, warming his hands before the fire in the library where they were all having espresso, 'our friend, Little Vinnie, is enjoying his first Christmas at Sing-Sing. Only nineteen more, and he'll be a free man.'

'Don't joke about it,' said his wife, pouring the coffee. 'I feel sorry for criminals.'

'Don't feel sorry for Tazzi,' replied Ettore. 'He's scum. He and the others like him give us Italians a bad name here in America. Victor, would you like a brandy with your coffee? Or perhaps some Amaretto?'

'No thanks.' Victor took the small cup. 'I just wanted to thank all of you for a wonderful time today. I need hardly tell you Julia's become a favorite of mine, but you're all very special people.'

'Thank you,' smiled Anna Maria. 'You're very special yourself, Victor.'

He stirred his coffee a moment.

'I have a favor I want to ask of you,' he said.

'Anything,' said Ettore. 'What is it?'

Victor began to tell.

CHAPTER 18

The Italians came on the morning of January 6, 1904. Two hundred of them lined up in front of the Dexter Bank waiting for its doors to open, defying the icy weather that turned horses' and humans' breath to steam. When passersby asked what was happening, the Italians, the vast majority of them obviously poor from their threadbare clothes, replied in broken English, 'The bank she's-a give 'way Italian-English deek-shunaries and-a pizza with five-dollar deposit.' The story swept around Wall Street, causing howls of laughter, and the Dexter Bank and Trust Company was promptly dubbed the Pizza Bank and Trust.

When the bank opened, the line moved slowly, newcomers rebuilding the tail and, by noon, actually increasing it. At one point in the morning, the president of the bank and his secretary came out to pass around mugs of hot coffee and chocolate. The chief officer delighted the crowd by talking to them in Italian. 'Hey, Signor Dexter,' shouted one man. 'You from Sicily? So am I!' For no apparent reason except excitement, this drew cheers. One cynical bystander said to a fellow stockbroker, 'It must drive these Dagos crazy to see one of their own in a suit and tie, running a bank.'

His friend nodded agreement.

The next morning, Lucille, who had returned from Europe two days before with trunks of new clothes and crates of antiques, put down the newspaper and stared across the breakfast table at her husband. 'I can't believe this article,' she said. 'Did you see it? It's on the front page of the *Times!* "Dexter Bank Draws Thousands of Italian Depositors" . . .'

'Yes, I read it,' replied Victor, cracking his three-minute egg with a deft knife slice. 'Almost five thousand, to be exact. It was quite something.'

'But . . . according to this article, it sounds like a farce!

Giving away slices of pizza and dictionaries . . . They say everyone's calling us the "Pizza Bank." '

'Let them call us anything they want: we took in almost sixty thousand dollars in new deposits yesterday.'

'But you're turning this into a sideshow—a carnival! The bank will lose its dignity . . .'

'I'd rather be successful than dignified.'

He buttered the one slice of toast he allowed himself each morning. Victor was vain enough to want to keep slim.

'But the bank has a tradition . . .'

'Lucille,' he interrupted, 'the bank stock went up two points yesterday. As you're aware, it hasn't moved over fifty for years.'

'Over fifty?' Her voice changed from accusation to interest. 'What did it close at?'

'Fifty-two.' He bit the toast. 'You see, with all this money you're spending, I decided I had to do something to *make* you some money. Now, you own about a hundred thousand shares of stock, so every time it goes up a point, you make a hundred thousand dollars. Right?'

'So yesterday I made two hundred thousand dollars?'

'Exactly.'

She reached her hand over and squeezed him.

'Oh darling,' she purred, 'I take it all back. Forget dignity and pass out the pizza!'

'I intend to.'

In the following two weeks, the Dexter Bank took in almost a million dollars in new desposits from an estimated twenty thousand new depositors, all of them Italian, most of them depositing the minimum five dollars, but some depositing as much as a thousand dollars. Even after the 10,000 dictionaries Victor had ordered ran out, the Italians kept coming. The phenomenon amazed Wall Streeters, and it was whispered that Victor was a 'miracle man.' It was also whispered the crowds were being turned out by the Mafia or the infamous Black Hand Society. Whatever the reason, no one could deny the galvanic shock this mass influx of poor people was causing, nor the publicity it was generating, because reporters took to the story with a vengeance.

The stock started climbing rapidly. Speculators, convinced the sleepy Dexter had suddenly become hot, bought in, and the stock zoomed. By the end of the second week, Lucille was almost literally doing a jig: the stock had soared from fifty to a

sizzling sixty-eight. Lucille's paper profits were $1,800,000.
'Darling, you're a genius!' she exclaimed as she hugged her
husband. 'An absolute genius!'

Victor said nothing.

The following Monday, the phenomenon continued. The long
line of Italians formed, and the bank tellers prepared themselves
for another exhausting day. Except today, the first customer at
Window A, a wrinkled lady in her sixties, slapped her passbook
on the marble counter and said, 'I want to take my money out.'

The teller, a young Italian-American hired by Victor, opened
the book and checked the one entry.

'But Madam,' he said, 'you just deposited fifteen dollars nine
days ago.'

'I know that. I want my money back. Are you going to give it
to me?'

'Of course.'

The second customer withdrew his money, as did the third and
the fourth. A half hour after the bank opened, the chief teller
closed his window and went to Victor's office. 'Something odd
is happening, Mr. Dexter. Today they're all taking their money
out.'

Victor looked unperturbed.

'Well, it's their money.'

By noon, $74,000 had been withdrawn. Wall Street, that
hypersensitive gossip pit, was buzzing that 'something at the
Pizza is wrong.'

The next evening, Lucille was wearing a new Paris gown and
a diamond necklace for which she had paid $125,000 at
Tiffany's. She was going to a ball, but she didn't look festive.

'What *is* it?' she exclaimed, her voice shrill. 'What's going
on? Why are these Italians suddenly taking their money out of
the bank? It's in all the papers—the stock dropped twelve points
today! Twelve! It cost me a fortune!'

'It's all funny money, Lucille. The stock goes up, you make
paper profits. It goes down, you take paper losses. You're still
ahead of the game.'

'Don't give me these sophomoric lessons in economics! The
point is, something's *wrong!* It makes no sense! First, thousands
of Italians flock to the bank to put their money in, then presto!
They come back to take it out! It's insane, bizarre!'

'I don't understand it either.'

'You must have *some* idea what's behind it!'

'None at all. I'm sure things will calm down tomorrow.' He turned. 'How's my tie?'

'Beautiful.' She practically spat the word. Grabbing her silk purse, she swept toward the door. 'I'm going to have a perfectly miserable time at this miserable dance.'

Victor smiled slightly.

The next day a sense of panic set in as long lines formed around the block. Except now, non-Italian depositors were lining up to withdraw their money. Rumors swept the Street that there was a run on the Dexter, and speculators who had been running the stock up the week before were now bailing out. By noon, the stock slipped below fifty. It closed the day at thirty-nine.

Victor had been besieged all day by phone calls from members of the Dexter family and directors of the bank. He calmly told them there was no cause for panic, that everything would 'work out.' But when he got home that evening, he was met by a hurricane.

'You're doing this on purpose!' roared Lucille as he walked into the drawing room overlooking Gramercy Park. 'Admit it! What they say is true!'

'I have no idea what you're talking about,' replied her husband. 'And you might say "Hello."'

'Oh yes, look as if there's nothing to worry about . . . There isn't—for *you!* You have everything to gain if the stock goes to zero. *Then* you can buy me out! What you don't seem to realize is that it will be a bit of a Pyrrhic victory for you, since the bank won't be worth a damn!'

Victor opened a newspaper.

'The bank is in solid financial shape . . .'

'Oh, *don't* talk to me like an annual report! And put down that paper!' She ripped it out of his hands and threw it on the floor. Victor stared at her.

'Are you out of your mind?'

'I'm perfectly sane, and you know it! I'm also beginning to see you clearly for the first time in years. Poor Victor, the sweet and humble immigrant . . . also the snake in the grass! You've sucked my family dry for years, and *now*—! Not content with turning a distinguished bank into a flophouse for destitute Dagos, you're willing to *destroy* the bank, just to get your hands on my stock . . . !'

'I'm not destroying the bank!'

'Do you deny you're manipulating these throngs of Italians?'

He was silent for a moment. Then, softly: 'All right, I am.'

'How in God's name do you do it? Do you stand on the roof of the bank with semaphore flags?'

'Ettore Lombardini knows every important Italian-American in New York. He asked them to pass the word to their people to take their money to the bank. Last weekend, they told them to start taking it out.'

'So you *are* manipulating the stock?'

'Yes, but I'll pay you fifty dollars a share for your stock. You won't lose a penny. In fact, you'll make money.'

She looked at him with contempt.

'You'd go to these elaborate lengths just to force me to sell?'

'How else can I do it?'

She put her hands on her slim hips and studied him a moment.

'You know what I'm going to do?' she said finally. 'I'm going to call a meeting of the board of directors. I'm going to tell them what you've just told me. I'm going to say I think your behavior is highly irresponsible and dangerous, and I'm going to insist you be fired as president. What do you think of that?'

He picked up his newspaper from the floor.

'Fine,' he said. 'That's exactly what I'd do if I were you.'

'You don't care? It doesn't bother you?'

'Not at all. I've been thinking of resigning anyway. Start my own bank—why not? All those 'destitute Dagos,' as you so charmingly call them, are a lot of customers. By the way, I was going to stop all this tomorrow anyway, since the situation *is* becoming tricky. I mean, some of our old customers are getting nervous. If a run on the bank *did* develop, it could get very ugly . . . But now you can blame everything on me and restore the public's confidence. At least, I assume you can restore their confidence. Of course, all sorts of things could happen.'

He was reading the paper. Lucille frowned.

'What do you mean?'

'Well, the bank *is* doing extremely well. And perhaps the board would think you were being unreasonable, if not downright selfish, not to sell me your stock.'

'I don't care what the board thinks.'

Victor shrugged.

'Then it's possible I might not be able to stop things tomorrow. Maybe I can't convince the Italians to keep their money in the bank. And if the run *did* start . . .'

'So you *are* willing to destroy the bank?'

'I didn't say that. I'm just saying anything can happen.'

'Do you realize what you're doing—how dangerous this is? I

can't believe you'd jeopardize the finances of a family that took you in off the street—!'

'*I'm* jeopardizing the finances?' he exclaimed, sitting up. 'How about *you?* How long do you think you can go on spending money the way you are without selling stock? Yes, you're damned right I'm acting irresponsibly, but you've backed me into a corner! I've *got* to get the stock from you, not only because I want it—which I do—but because if I don't get it from you, sooner or later you're going to sell it out of the family. *You're* the irresponsible one, Lucille! You've turned into a silly, vain, social-climbing bitch of a woman. I can't stop you from building that damned house on Fifth Avenue, but I *can* try to stop you from squandering control of the bank out of the family, which is why I called in the "destitute Dagos." I'm not going to destroy the bank—far from it! I can turn that bank into a giant —or at least I can sure as hell try—but not with you controlling me with the stock!'

She sank into a chair, starting to cry.

'How can you say such horrible things?' she sniffed. 'If you loved me, you wouldn't be acting this way.'

'If you loved me, you wouldn't try to control me. And stop crying: that won't work with me either.'

They looked at each other.

'I suppose,' she said, drying her eyes, 'our marriage is something of a farce, isn't it? All we do is fight . . . Don't we love each other anymore?'

'I don't know.'

She was silent awhile. Then she stood up.

'Perhaps you're right,' she said. 'Perhaps I have tried to "control" you, as you put it, with the stock. Perhaps I've sensed that you don't love me anymore . . . at least the way you used to love me . . . and I thought I could hold on to you with the stock. Perhaps I *am* vain and silly . . .'

She looked at him rather sadly.

'I didn't mean it when I said you've sucked the family dry. You've brought a lot to the family and to me . . .'

She squeezed her hands nervously. He watched her, trying to read her thoughts. Finally she said, rather curtly, 'I'll sell you the stock at fifty.'

And she walked out of the room. He realized he had won the bank, but the price was probably his marriage.

CHAPTER 19

On a fall day in 1910, Senator Franco Spada rose from his seat in the Italian Senate and began his address.

'As my distinguished colleagues know, I am a Sicilian. You also know that, as a young man, I was a victim of that time-honored Sicilian institution, the Mafia. It cost me twelve years of my life, something I naturally will never forget. Now, in my careers as a newspaper publisher and a senator, I have fought for many social reforms, a few of which I'm glad to say have actually been passed into law. But today I wish to launch a crusade—and I use the word advisedly—against one of the greatest evils that still plague our nation.' He paused dramatically. 'Senators, I am speaking of the Mafia.'

He returned from the Senate to the Palazzo dell'Acqua that evening and went directly to the green salon where Princess Sylvia was waiting for him.

'Well, I did it,' he said, coming up to her and kissing her. 'And it was one of the best speeches of my life.'

She smoothed his cheek affectionately. After living together eighteen years, she still thrilled at his touch, which made the fights, the partial social ostracism, the trouble with the Vatican all somehow worth it. Sylvia and Franco had settled into a routine which was in many aspects no different from that of any other long-married couple; yet—and perhaps it was because they weren't married—there was an excitement between them that reminded people of young lovers.

'Do you think the Senate will do anything?' asked Sylvia as he poured himself a whiskey then sat down in his favorite chair. Franco was twenty pounds overweight and his hair was turning gray, but he was still a commanding figure of a man.

'Probably not. I'm convinced a third of them have ties with the Mafia, and the rest don't give a damn. Or perhaps they're afraid. It's still worth a try. How can Italy become a respectable nation when the south is run by a gang of hoodlums? The American Ambassador has been after me for months to try to get the government to do something. New York's got more Mafiosi than Palermo, and the Americans don't like it—and I can't say I blame them. Anyway, I've done what I can. Now we'll have to see.'

'You think the Senate's afraid—how about me? *I'm* afraid.'

'Don't be. They wouldn't have the nerve to try anything against me.'

'How do you know?' She came over to him, taking his hand. She was now almost sixty, but she was still a remarkably attractive woman. 'I want you to hire a bodyguard.'

'That's ridiculous. Sylvia, there are at least five thousand people in Italy who'd love to see me dead, so what difference does it make if I add the Mafia to the list?'

'The difference is they're good at killing.'

'I carry a gun, which is the best bodyguard there is. Now stop worrying.' He smiled and pulled her on to his lap. 'Though I'll admit you're sexy when you worry about me.'

'Franco, be serious.'

'I am. And how is it possible after all these years when I get you on my lap I still want to run my hand up your leg?'

Which he did. She pushed his hand away.

'You madman!' she said. 'A senator's supposed to have a little dignity.'

'What's undignified about making love?'

He began kissing her neck. She put her arms around him and hugged him tightly.

'Franco, promise me you'll be careful. *Promise* me. You know you're my whole life.'

'I promise. And don't worry.'

She saw their seventeen-year-old son, Tony, come into the room and stare at them. Quickly she got off Franco's lap.

'Oh . . . excuse me, Mother . . .'

Sylvia straightened her hair and went back to her chair as her son crossed the room. He was wearing a sweater and a pair of dark-gray slacks. He was tall and extremely thin, with a handsome, serious face. He kissed his mother's cheek, then said, 'I heard about your speech today, Father. I think it's very exciting.'

Franco looked pleased.

'Thank you, Tony. How's school?'

'Oh, fine.' He hesitated. 'I got another note from Cardinal dell'Acqua. He wants me to come to lunch tomorrow.'

'That old scarecrow,' snorted his father. 'Why doesn't he stop bothering you?'

'He doesn't "bother" me, Father. He's very interesting.'

Franco sat forward on his chair and pointed his finger at his son. 'Now listen, Tony: we all know what he's up to. His Eminence wants to get you into the Church. All right, if you want to become a priest, that's your business. But don't have any illusions about what's going on. His Eminence is wooing you because the Vatican would love nothing better than to hook one of my sons! What a propaganda victory for them: the son of the atheist, socialist, anti-Vatican Franco Spada becomes a padre? They'd love it. So bear that in mind when you talk to him. They're no fools in the Vatican.'

Tony said nothing, but his mother said, 'Franco, Tony is no fool either. If he decides to enter the Church, he'll do it with his eyes open. Won't you, darling?'

She smiled at him. Her son nodded rather uncertainly.

'I hope so, Mother.'

'You *hope* so?' exclaimed his father. 'You'd better be damned certain! I'm telling you, Sylvia, I don't like this at all. His Eminence is talking Tony into this . . .'

'He's not!' interrupted his son. 'If I enter the Church, it will be because I love it. And no one can talk you into that.'

Franco sighed.

'Well, just be careful, that's all I'm asking. And *think*. His Eminence is a smooth talker, and it's your life he's talking about.'

He got up to refill his glass.

Alcide, Cardinal dell'Acqua, was now in his seventies and suffering from arthritis. But the Secretary of State to Pope Pius X had lost none of his mental energy. Now, as he sat opposite Tony in his office in the Apostolic Palace, he sipped his wine and smiled at the young man.

'Your father is a remarkable man, Tony,' he said. His voice was thin and soft. 'That speech he made yesterday against the Mafia, well, it's bound to cause trouble. But then, Franco likes to cause trouble. Did you tell him you were having lunch with me today?'

'Yes, Your Eminence.'

'And was he upset? You can be truthful.'

'He was a little upset.'

The nun waiting on them refilled the Cardinal's wineglass, then retired from the room. Their small lunch table seemed dwarfed by the enormous space of the office. Busts of former popes stared down at them from porphyry pedestals, and a huge painting of the ecstasy of St. Theresa dominated one of the walls.

'Tony,' said His Eminence, 'you have told me in our conversations that one of the reasons you are interested in the Church is that the—shall we say unusual?—relationship between your parents has made you grow up feeling like an outsider. The fact that they have lived openly together, the fact that you and your twin are illegitimate, well, it's only natural this would have an effect on you. It's only natural you would like to *belong* to something that is dignified and, indeed, sanctified, like the Church. Now, I have known your mother for many years, since she was married to my brother. I don't believe Sylvia is happy living this way.'

'Excuse me, Your Eminence, but you're wrong. Mother is very much in love with Father . . .'

'Ah, I appreciate that. She would *have* to be to have stayed with him this long. I admire your father, Tony, but I think you'll admit he's not an easy man to live with. He is, after all, extremely unconventional. He *enjoys* being unconventional. He's almost made a career out of it, if you know what I mean.'

'Yes, I know.'

'What I'm saying is, that I can't help but think your mother would be happier if she were married to your father. Because despite all the evidence to the contrary, I think Sylvia is a rather conventional woman in her heart.'

'But Father doesn't believe in marriage . . .'

'That's one of his quaint conceits which helps sell his newspapers. This doesn't mean he couldn't be talked into marrying your mother—particularly if there were a quid pro quo.'

'Like what?'

'It's very simple, Tony. You and I have discussed religion. We've discussed the Vatican, and I have told you that if you enter the Church I will do everything in my power to help you. You will have a powerful friend in court, so to speak, which is not without its advantages. Now, let's discuss the practical politics of the situation. Your father has attacked the Church frequently over the years. This has disturbed the Holy Father, naturally. The Church is undergoing many pressures in these modern times, and we need the support of prominent citizens

189

like your father, not the abuse. The Holy Father would be pleased if he could bring your father into the Church, at least through the sacrament of holy matrimony. He would also, of course, be delighted if you joined Mother Church as a priest. But whether that happens or not, if your father can be induced to marry your mother in the Church, the Holy Father will be pleased to grant dispensations legitimizing you and your brother, Fausto.'

Tony looked amazed.

'*That's* the quid pro quo?'

'Yes, and it's one that I hope will interest you.'

'It certainly does!'

'It's time we healed the wounds of the past, Tony. Will you discuss this with your parents?'

'Of course.'

'Good. Well then, perhaps we have made some progress today. I see you don't like your soup. I can't blame you. Our food here in the Vatican is not calculated to tempt us with the sin of gluttony.'

He rang for the nun.

The police photographer snapped his shutter and the flash powder exploded, illuminating the naked corpse with a momentary glare. Franco winced at the light, then turned to the police captain next to him.

'May I smoke?' he asked.

'Of course, Senator.'

They were standing by the door of a third-class hotel room in which a struggle had taken place: The bed was torn apart, a lamp had been knocked over, the threadbare carpet on which the naked girl sprawled was soaked with blood. The girl's throat had been slit.

'Any idea who she is?' asked Franco, lighting a cigarette.

'We don't know yet,' said the captain, whose name was Martino.

The police surgeon who had been examining the body, now stood up and came to the door, wiping his glasses on a handkerchief.

'It's curious,' he said. 'She had had intercourse, but I'm not sure if it was before or after she was killed.'

'After?' said Franco. 'Are you joking?'

'Not at all, Senator. Naturally, I can't be certain until we make the proper laboratory tests, but there are bruise marks on the body, particularly around the genital area, that were inflicted after death. After the blood has stopped circulating, pressure on the body causes marks that look different and are easily discernible to the trained eye. I'd say it's quite likely the murderer made love to the body, ghoulish as it may seem.'

'Good God,' said Franco, staring at the girl. 'Who would want to make love to a corpse?'

'At least,' said Captain Martino, 'she couldn't complain about his technique.'

'You have a point. It's a revolting point, but a point. Well, my friend, I can't thank you enough for calling me. This is one of the best murders you've let me in on, and don't think my article won't praise you to the skies. Of course, if you catch the murderer,' he slipped two folded thousand-lire notes into Martino's hand, 'we'll praise you even higher. Especially if you let me know his name first. Good night, gentlemen.'

He squeezed the captain's arm, then hurried down the dimly lit stairs of the hotel and out to the street to hail a cab.

'Twenty-three via Due Macelli,' he said, climbing into the back seat of the Fiat. As the cab chugged across the Tiber toward the Spanish Steps, Franco sat in the back seat smoking as he composed the article in his mind. He had quickly learned that socialist diatribe alone, while the backbone of the paper, would not get him the kind of big circulation he had envisioned for *Libertà*, that the working classes, like the rest of society, relished gossip, scandal and gore. Over the years Franco had built up a network of contacts in the Roman police force, most of them favoring him with advance word on crimes not only because they liked him and he tipped well, but because he, like they, was a socialist. He also had a flair for crime coverage. It was a long way from emulating Lord Byron, but he couldn't care less: it was exciting and he loved it. This particular murder had not only the thrilling ingredients of violence and posthumous sex, it also had snob value. For Franco, unlike the police, had recognized the girl. By the time the cab stopped at the address on via Due Macelli, Franco was in such a beamish mood, he gave the driver a hundred-lire tip.

He let himself into the building with a key, hurried up a dark, seventeenth-century stair, produced a second key and unlocked a door. He entered a softly lit room that was so overdecorated it gave the impression of a furniture warehouse or an antique shop. The walls were jammed with pictures, prints and theatrical posters; one section between two Austrian-blinded windows held a collection of framed fans. The floor was layered with Oriental rugs and pimpled with poufs and ottomans. Stretched out on an

191

overly pillowed purple divan, dressed in a kimono, was a beautiful girl in her early twenties. Sibella Montenovo, the not-so-well-known actress, was reading a racy novel by Ouida. Now she put it down and opened her arms.

'Franco, *caro*.'

'I got a call from the police—a juicy murder! Juicy! Pour me some champagne while I write the lead.'

He sat at a desk, pulled out a pad and began scribbling as Sibella opened the champagne she had been cooling.

'Who was murdered?' she asked, filling a tulip glass.

'That's what the police would like to know. But Franco knows! Franco's seen the girl at receptions. He's even seen her at the royal palace!'

'At the *palace?*' exclaimed Sibella, carrying him the glass. She had honey-colored hair.

'That's right. Her name is Countess Sant'Elia, and she's one of the Queen's ladies-in-waiting. This can be the scandal of the decade! A member of the royal household found in a grubby hotel, naked, with her throat cut. How? Why? Most important, who? Who murdered the beautiful Countess Sant'Elia, whose husband is a rich banker? It has all the elements of a first-class *roman policier*: sex, society, possibly politics, violence— delicious! Give me a kiss . . .'

Sibella wiggled into his arms, holding his champagne as he opened her kimono and buried his face in her warm cleavage.

'Ah, Sibella,' he sighed, smiling up at her after kissing her. 'You're the sweetest tart in Rome.'

'You should know: you've tried them all.'

'What would you say if I told you I was going to become an honest man?'

'What's that mean?'

'I'm going to get married.'

'To the Princess?'

He stood up.

'Yes, after eighteen years.' He lit another cigarette. 'She's the only woman I've ever loved. What worries me is whether our love will survive marriage.'

'Then why do it? Is she putting pressure on you?'

'No. She never has and never would. It's our sons. And the Church. If Sylvia and I are married in the Church, the Pope will make the twins legitimate. It's crafty of the Vatican, but I can't refuse. It's been hard on the boys, especially Tony.'

He had gone to a window and was looking out at the man on the street below. The man standing in the doorway opposite.

'People will be shocked if you get married,' said Sibella.

He laughed and turned back to her.

'I suppose they will. I hate to disappoint my public, but it's time Franco Spada became domesticated. But Sylvia's a wonderful woman. I'm a lucky man to have had her all these years.'

Sibella pouted.

'I think it's rude to talk about her in front of me.'

'Why? You're a delicious mistress, Sibella, but there's no woman in the world like Sylvia.'

He looked back out the window. The man across the street had vanished.

Franco reached in the pocket of his coat and fingered his small revolver.

'I think I was followed tonight,' he said an hour later as he came into Sylvia's sitting room. She looked up from her needlework.

'By whom?'

Franco came over and kissed her.

'I don't know. Possibly the Mafia. I wanted you to know I'm watching and being careful.' He sat down beside her. 'But maybe I should ask Captain Martino for police protection.'

She put aside her needlepoint.

'Why don't we go away for a while? Let's go to London. It could be our honeymoon.'

He smiled and took her hand.

'Don't you think we're a little old for honeymoons?'

'Not at all! And Franco, there's no point exposing yourself to needless danger.'

'Sylvia, if the Mafia is after me, there's no use running away.' He frowned. 'I don't know. Maybe I bit off more than I can chew. God knows the government's not doing anything. I might as well have saved my breath, making that damned speech. Maybe it was stupid trying to take on the Mafia. I suppose it's part of our national heritage, like spaghetti.'

They were silent for a moment. Then Sylvia said, 'Do you know why I love you so much? And I don't mean the physical side of it, though you're still the most attractive overweight man I've ever met. But I've loved you all these years because you *have* spoken the truth. You've been a thorn in the side of the government, the rich, the complacent . . . you're one of the few men in Italy who's stood up and said, "Look how rotten everything is." That takes courage, darling, and I love your spendid courage. So don't think making that speech was a waste of time. On the other hand . . . ask Captain Martino for protection. I want my hero alive, not dead.'

He looked at her.

'I sometimes wonder if everything I've done hasn't been a waste of time. Nothing seems to change.'

'No, you're wrong. Things *are* changing, slowly. And my wonderful Franco is responsible for much of it.'

He put his arm around her and kissed her.

'And where would I be if it weren't for you?' he whispered in her ear. 'I adore you, Sylvia.'

They held each other for a while. Then she kissed his cheek.

'It's time for dinner.' She stood up. 'I thought we could tell the boys the good news.' She smiled. 'That after all these years, you and I are going to be respectable.'

'It sounds sort of dreary, doesn't it?' he said, getting up.

'Not at all. Making love legitimately may be a wonderful new thrill.'

They both laughed. Then, holding hands like young lovers, they left the room.

Fausto Spada lay on his bed in the big, second-floor room of the Palazzo dell'Acqua that he shared with his twin, Tony, and lazily scratched his genitals. Fausto was, as usual, horny. He would have been at La Rosina's, Rome's leading whorehouse, if his mother hadn't made the announcement at dinner that she and his father were going to get married.

'What do you think of it?' he asked Tony, who was seated at a desk across the room studying his chemistry textbook. They had been students at a private academy in Rome for five years. Tony's grades were excellent, Fausto's passable.

'What do I think of what?' said Tony.

'Our becoming legitimate, you idiot! How can you bury your nose in that stupid chemistry book at a time like this? This is probably the biggest thing that's happened in our lives!'

'I have an exam tomorrow.'

Fausto jumped off the bed, ran across the room, grabbed the book from his twin and tossed it under the bed.

'Damn you, Fausto—!'

Tony started out of his chair, but Fausto pushed him back in, then sat on the desk. 'What a miserable grind you are,' he said. 'The only interesting thing about you is that you're a bastard, and now *that's* being taken away from you!'

'I'm sorry I'm not as endlessly fascinating as you.'

'Oh, crap. Come on, Tony: talk to me. Are you really going to be a priest?'

'I'm thinking about it.'

Fausto laughed.

'I'll tell the Holy Father all your bad habits, like how you pick your nose in bed.'

Tony glared at him.

'That's a lot better than what *you* do in bed!'

'I *used* to do. I don't anymore, not since La Rosina's.' He lowered his voice, which became sly. 'If you become a priest, you can never have a woman. Or are you going to break your vows?'

'If I take the vows, I won't break them.'

Fausto snorted.

'Big talk! Well, maybe you wouldn't, since I'm convinced you've got cocoa in your veins.'

'I've got the same blood in my veins as you. The difference is that I respect my body.'

'Oh, how lovely! How darling! He *respects* his body! It's God's temple! And tell me, Father: why did God put that thing between your legs? To wither away under a cassock? Bullshit. It was put there to be used, and you're afraid to use it. God, how did I get a brother like you?'

Tony's face was red.

'Fausto, stop goading me! You're always *goading* me!'

'But I love you, little brother,' he cooed, leaning forward and taking Tony's face between his hands. 'And I don't want you to make a big mistake in life. The pity is, you won't even know what you'll be missing, because you've never used that thing except to pee with.' He released his twin and got off the desk to wander around the room, expostulating to the ceiling. 'Oh God, I beg Thee to give my brother just *one* piece of ass before Thou takest him into Thy Church! Just *one!* Even Jesus had *one* . . .'

'He did not,' yelled Tony, 'and you're taking the Lord's name in vain!'

Fausto whirled around.

'Me? Do that? Not on your life! Listen, Tony, I'll be serious. Come with me to La Rosina's—now, tonight. Do it just once. You owe it to yourself, and I swear if you do it once, I'll never kid you about it again. I swear! Will you go?'

His brother was staring at him, and Fausto knew he was tempted. He came back to the desk and put his hand on Tony's sweatered shoulder, squeezing it softly.

'Come on, Tony,' he whispered. 'The girls will love you, and why not? You're almost as good-looking as I am, and you've got a nice, thin body . . .'

Tony shoved his hand off.

'Leave me along, Fausto. Please.'

Fausto smoothed his brother's thick brown hair seductively.

'Come on, Tony,' he whispered in his ear. 'You owe it to yourself. Come on.'

Tony closed his eyes, tight, for almost a minute as he fought the desire that raged within him. When he opened them, there were tears in them.

'All right,' he said. 'I'll go—just to shut you up.'

Fausto hugged him, then waltzed around the room.

'Whoops!' he sang. 'Tony's losing his cherry tonight—Tony's losing his cherry!'

They bicycled across the Tiber to Trastevere, the oldest part of Rome where, in a section that had once been part of the world's first Jewish ghetto, imposed in 1555 by Pope Pius IV, La Rosina's took up the top two floors of two otherwise innocent-looking houses. 'Wait till you see the place,' said Fausto as they locked their bicycles. 'It's more than just a whorehouse—La Rosina has made it a real spectacle!'

Tony, grim-faced and nervous, said nothing as he followed his brother up well-worn stairs to an unmarked door with a peephole. Fausto rang, was checked out by the bouncer, then admitted. The twins hurried down a curtained hallway and pushed through a beaded curtain to enter a surprisingly large, circular room that soared two floors to a round skylight. The room was crowded with strolling customers and whores. It was lighted by life-sized blackamoor torchères and banked with enough palms to crowd a rain forest. Directly beneath the skylight was a round, tufted banquette on which lounged three girls, dressed only in panties, corsets and stockings. One girl was draped over a second in a languorous semiembrace, the third was smoking and chatting with a white-moustached man in his seventies. In the distance an invisible pianist tinkled bad ragtime.

Tony looked toward the ceiling. Around the second floor of the room ran a gallery of which numerous numbered doors led to what he supposed were the notorious *salles privées* (for it was well known that La Rosina euphemized and presumably somehow sanitized her 'working rooms' by giving them French names). On the wrought-iron balustrade of the gallery leaned two more girls, their breasts almost spilling out of their corsets as they idly watched the perambulating couples below. Above them the ceiling around the skylight was painted with a marvelously lewd fresco which easily rivaled the worst excesses of Pompeii: Naked satyrs in a sylvan setting chased voluptuous nudes, the satyrs' thoughts being trumpeted by enormous phalluses. But even this, as eye-riveting as it was, was not what Tony was staring at. For suspended from the pornographic ceiling were four trapezes, on which swung a nubile girl entirely in the buff.

'Did I tell you it was a spectacle?' grinned Fausto, watching his gawking twin. 'La Rosina's more than a madam, she's an impresario. Well, what do you think of it?'

Tony stared at the pink buttocks swinging lazily to and fro above him.

'It's a bit ridiculous . . .'

'Of course it is. That's the fun of it.'

'And it's more than a bit disgusting . . .'

'Then life is disgusting, because this is life, no matter what the priests say.'

Tony turned from the trapezes to look at his brother.

'And you were right to bring me here,' he added, quietly.

Fausto clapped his back.

'Of course I was! Should have done it months ago . . . Look,' he pointed at a drunk in evening clothes weaving out of one of the *salles privées*, 'Senator Boncampagni! Half the damned Senate's here . . .'

'What about Father? Does he come here?'

'Probably, though I've never seen him. Come on, I'll introduce you to La Rosina . . . You'll like her. She's very grand . . . you'd think she was a damned duchess . . .'

Grabbing Tony's arm, he led him through the crowd to a small alcove off the round room. Here, a black man in a white jacket stood behind a bar in front of which a tall woman was talking to a girl in a maid's uniform.

'La Rosina!' called Fausto. 'Look who I've brought you: my brother, Tony!'

La Rosina turned. She was in fact very grand, wearing a taupe, lace-trimmed evening gown by Poiret in the height of chic, a diamond-and-pearl choker, and a black feather that soared imperiously out of her dyed gold hair. Her face was still beautiful, defying her sixth decade with well-massaged bravado, and she knew how to conceal the inevitable crow's feet with expertly applied makeup. She smiled and extended her hand.

'Welcome,' she said in a low, melodious voice. 'I've heard so much about you from dear Fausto.'

Tony, not knowing what else to do, kissed her hand.

'What a beautiful face,' she continued, putting her well-manicured hand on his cheek. 'So much like yours, Fausto, except perhaps slightly more ethereal. But, of course, one of my satyrs on the ceiling would look like Saint Francis compared to Fausto . . . Are you frightened, young man?'

'A little . . .'

'Don't be. We'll give you Yolanda. Such a charming creature! She came to us from Puglia two years ago, almost totally inexperienced except for a few *amours rustiques,* but she has developed so rapidly in all directions. *Célestine, va amener Yolande,*' she said to the maid. '*Elle se trouve dans la chambre trois.*' Célestine curtsied and hurried off. La Rosina started to say something to Tony when she was interrupted by a scream from the round room. They turned to see Senator Boncampagni stumble into a large palm springing out of a blue china jardinière. The Senator rolled on to the floor on his back and belched happily toward the ceiling. La Rosina frowned.

'The Senator, as usual, has overindulged. One would think a man related to half the Roman aristocracy could handle champagne.'

She dispatched the bartender to help the Senator to his feet, but Tony was watching the exquisite girl Célestine was leading out of Room 3.

'That's Yolanda,' whispered Fausto. 'The best lay in the house. Do you like her?'

Tony nodded, numbed by her beauty. The girl, wearing a white robe, came down and joined them.

'This is Yolanda,' said La Rosina. 'Yolanda, dear, this is Fausto's twin, Tony.'

'He's a virgin,' said Fausto. 'Make him happy.'

Fausto's blood-engorged, vein-laced penis, which was known affectionately at La Rosina's as Mont Blanc, shoved into the whore's moist vulva and began to piston. Her name was Angelina, and she squealed with pleasure as he humped her: she adored his strong young body and his young lust that seemed so wonderfully randy after the middle-aged fumblings of most of her customers. Even his sweat smelled good to her. She wrapped her legs around his waist as his shaft filled her with exquisite, torturous, aching desire.

Afterward, she said, 'It seems wrong to get paid for what's so much fun.'

Fausto laughed and got dressed. Then he went out on the gallery and walked around to Room 3. He listened at the door but heard nothing. He leaned on the balustrade and waited as the pianist downstairs segued into the Maple Leaf Rag. Ten minutes later the door opened and Tony came out. His thin face looked paler than usual.

'Well?' asked Fausto. 'Did you like it?'

Tony said nothing. He started down the stairs, Fausto behind him. When they were outside, unlocking their bicycles, Fausto persisted. 'You have to have *some* reaction!' he blurted.

'What do you want me to say?' Tony exclaimed, angrily. 'Yes, I liked it! Does that make you feel better?'

'Do you want to come back tomorrow night?'

Tony didn't answer. He climbed on his bicycle and started home.

The next morning, he told his mother he had decided to become a priest.

CHAPTER 20

Lorna and Barbara Dexter, fifteen and thirteen respectively, stood by the door of the ballroom and watched the twirling dancers with the wide-eyed excitement of the young. Lucille had been successful: the town house on Seventy-third and Fifth had become a showplace and her parties fashionable. In the process she had spent literally millions, but the money showed. Her taste was unerring, and the furnishings were first-rate. On the walls of the ballroom with its magnificent crystal chandelier, two full-length portraits by Lawrence of the Earl and Countess of Derby made the dancers feel almost on speaking terms with the venerated English aristocracy. But there were living titles on the dance floor as well, including two viscounts and a sprinkling of baronets. Lucille might have been a social climber, but she was an effective one.

'Does a father get the privilege of seeing whether the dancing lessons he's been paying for have worked?'

Lorna smiled at her father, who had just come over to her.

'I was hoping *someone* would ask me!'

'Well, you're not an official guest, you know. And you should be doing your homework.'

'Oh Daddy, I've done it.'

They waltzed on to the crowded floor, Lorna looking lovely in her white dress, Victor pencil-slim with touches of gray at his temples.

'You're looking beautiful, Lornie,' he said, using the family nickname.

'Oh thanks, Daddy! Do you think I'll be a heartbreaker?'

'Without a doubt. And you'll have a chance to try out your charms on your Roman cousins next month.'

Her eyes lit up.

'Are we going to Rome?'

'Yes. My brother and Princess Sylvia are getting married. Finally.'

Lorna giggled.

'Uncle Franco must be *terribly* wicked! I can hardly wait to meet him. I think it's just nifty to have someone wicked in the family. Are we *all* going to Rome?'

'That's right.'

'Mummy too?'

'Yes.'

She didn't say anything for a moment. Then, rather timidly: 'Will you and Mummy fight?'

Victor winced. The waltz ended and a perky foxtrot began, saving him the necessity of answering.

He left the party shortly before midnight, walked out the Seventy-third Street entrance of the house and climbed in his Great Arrow limousine, telling his chauffeur, Claude, to drive him to Fifty-fourth Street. Like all Americans, Victor had become car crazy, and this magnificent machine was one of the joys of his life. Now he settled in its leather seat as Claude drove him to a town house on Fifty-fourth between Madison and Fifth, where he got out. 'Pick me up in an hour,' he said. He walked to the front door and let himself in with a key. He went upstairs to a second-floor bedroom and turned on the lights. Julia Lombardini turned over in the bed and yawned.

'How was the party?'

He sat down on the bed, took her in his arms and started kissing her.

'It was a bore without you.'

'But you went anyway.'

'Yes, I went anyway.'

She gently pushed him away. He looked at her.

'You're mad at me,' he said.

'No I'm not. If I'm mad at anybody, it's myself.'

'Julia, don't be. It's my fault . . .'

'Oh, I don't want to talk about it. Good night.'

She lay back down and stared at the high ceiling. He took her hand.

'No,' he said, 'let's talk about it.'

'Why? What's left to say? We've gone over it a hundred times, and it's a stalemate. You won't divorce Lucille because of the children, and I've probably ruined all my chances of getting a husband by living with you . . . .'

'Listen, Julia,' he interrupted, 'I'm not a romantic fool who

201

thinks that love conquers everything. I'm fully aware of what I've done to you, and believe me I'm aware of the problems involved. But my children are growing up—in a few years I probably *will* be able to divorce Lucille and marry you, which is the dearest wish in my heart. And I know it hurts you when I go uptown to her parties, but I have to keep up *some* show—God knows, her parties bore me silly—if only for the children's sake. So it really isn't hopeless. Meanwhile, for what it's worth, you have my love.'

She squeezed his hand.

'You know your love is worth a lot to me,' she said, 'and I love you very deeply, Victor. I think I've loved you ever since I met you.'

'Don't say that! My God, I fell in love with Lucille at first sight, which was the biggest mistake of my life.'

'Well, maybe it was second sight. Anyhow, I love you, you adorable man. But it's not easy for me to be a mistress. There: I shudder even saying it! Me, Julia Lombardini, the girl everybody would have voted for as Miss Most-Strictly-Brought-Up, a mistress! It's incredible. I still can hardly believe it. I sometimes think I should be stretched out on a tigerskin rug with a rose in my mouth.'

'I'll buy a tigerskin rug and we'll try you out.'

'Besides, I want children, too. And I'm not getting any younger.'

Victor looked embarrassed. He stood up and started to undress.

'I've broken every rule in the book,' she went on, watching him, 'because I was in love with you. I suppose hearing about your brother living openly with that woman in Rome made me think I could get away with it in New York, but I can't. It's hurt my uncle and aunt terribly . . .'

'I know.' Victor's tone was grim. Losing the friendship and support of Ettore Lombardini and his newspaper had been a blow, but one that his passion for Julia forced him to accept.

'I can't wait *too* many years,' she continued, 'and Victor, I won't.'

Naked, he got in bed beside her and took her in his arms. As always, she gloried in his smell and feel and touch.

'I can't lose you,' he whispered as he kissed her.

'But you may.'

On November 18, 1910, the Cunard liner *Mauretania,* widely regarded as a marvel of the age and one of the most aristocratic liners ever to sail the North Atlantic shipping lanes, left New York Harbor for its four-and-a-half-day run to Southampton. Among its first-class passengers were Mr. and Mrs. Victor Dexter of New York and their three children, Lorna, Barbara and Drew; Mrs. Moffit to take care of the children; and Adelaide, Lucille's French-Canadian maid, whose duty it was, among other things, to take care of the wardrobe in Lucille's fourteen pieces of Louis Vuitton luggage. The first day out the ship encountered rough seas, sending a green-faced Lucille to her bed. But the second day she emerged from her suite on the boat deck determined to enjoy the considerable pleasures available to first-class passengers in this heyday of luxury liners.

For Victor his return to Italy after thirty years produced mixed emotions. He remembered the twelve-year-old boy who had sailed to New York on the *Servia,* a boy ignorant, illiterate, unable to speak English, frightened . . . His assimilation into the new world, his rise to an increasingly prominent position in the WASP world of banking, his swelling personal fortune—all this was gratifying to him, and he was proud of his accomplishments. But his family life was a shambles, and no matter how much he had assimilated into the new world, Victor retained his Italian sense of the importance of the family. The fact that New York society was becoming increasingly tolerant of divorce didn't make the idea of it any less abhorrent to him. If nothing else, the effect of divorce on his children horrified him. On the other hand, his marriage with Lucille was a charade that was becoming harder to play each day. And he loved Julia so much that the thought of keeping her in the embarrassingly compromising position she was in now was an agony. It was, as Julia had said, a stalemate. And one which was so painful to Victor that the exhilaration he should have felt returning to his native land was robbed of its sweetness.

On the second night out, he and Lucille were invited to dine at the captain's table. The event prompted Lucille to put on her most beautiful evening dress and best jewelry. At the round table, she was seated at the captain's left, the place of honor to his right being given to the Marchioness of Lansdowne. Lucille swallowed this slight without a murmur because to her left was the Marquess, and her proximity to this large dose of bored and boring nobility was, to Lucille, a social coup. Victor watched with ill-disguised distaste as his wife fawned over His Lordship. After dinner Lucille and the Marquess headed for the card room, Lucille having discovered that the one enthusiasm His Lordship had in life beside fox hunting was bridge. Victor headed for the smoking room for a cigar when he spotted Mrs. Moffit bearing down on him, her matronly bosoms swelling with indignation. 'Mr. Victor,' she said, her Irish accent becoming almost aggressive in the staid passageways of the English ship, 'I wish you'd be sayin' a few words to your eldest daughter! She's behavin' in a most in-*day*cent fashion, and she won't listen to a word I say!'

'Lornie? Indecent? Come now, Mrs. Moffit.'

'It's true! She's in the main saloon talkin' to those Harvard boys, who have only one thing on their mind . . . I told her she had no business bein' with them, but she ignored me . . . The good Lord only knows what will happen before we reach Southampton!'

Victor tried not to smile.

'I think the chances are Lornie won't become a fallen woman . . .'

'Ah, and how can you be so sure? And her only fifteen! When I was fifteen, I never so much as *looked* at a man, cruel monsters of arrogance and licentiousness that they be! No offense to *you*, to be sure . . . If you don't talk to her, I'll take no responsibility for what happens!'

Victor sighed.

'Very well, Mrs. Moffit. I'll talk to her.'

He went to the main saloon, where Lorna was seated at the grand piano playing 'Shine on, Harvest Moon' while four tuxedoed collegians leaned on the lid, bellowing the lyrics.

'I thought you said they were talking?' he asked.

'It's worse!' scowled Mrs. Moffit. 'It's like a beer hall! No *lady* would be seen in public this way.'

Victor made his way through the crowded room to the piano, reaching it just as the song climaxed to the applause of the passengers.

'Daddy!' exclaimed Lorna, 'Weren't we good? This is the Harvard debating team—they're going to debate the Oxford Union . . . Frank, Charlie . . . uh, Jerry?'

'That's right,' said a boy with thick glasses.

'And Robert. This is my father.'

Victor shook hands.

'We understand, sir,' said Jerry, 'that you're going back to Italy for the first time in thirty years.'

'That's right.'

'Is it true,' said another, 'that your brother is Italy's leading socialist?'

'Right again.'

204

'Don't you think socialism is dangerous?'

'Not as long as it's kept in the family. Now, could I buy you boys some beer?'

Which suggestion was met with enthusiasm. Mrs. Moffit looked shocked.

'I understand from Mrs. Moffit,' said Lucille at one in the morning as she climbed in her twin bed, 'that Lorna was singing songs with some Harvard boys this evening.'

'She was playing the piano for them,' said Victor, sitting in his own bed reading a ship's copy of *Bleak House*. 'Her playing's gotten quite good.'

'Don't you think you might have been a better chaperone if you hadn't bought beers for the boys?'

Victor put down the Dickens as, outside, the Atlantic swished soothingly against the ship's hull.

'There was no reason not to. And while I'm fond of Mrs. Moffit, she's a bit of a fuddy-duddy. I don't think she's been touched by a man since her husband passed out permanently in that Dublin pub twenty years ago.'

'Nevertheless, I don't think it's right for a girl Lorna's age to be flirting with college boys.'

'Flirting?! All she was doing was having a good time.'

'She's too young to be left alone with men. I realize you have a . . . well, Mediterranean standard of morality, but I expect you to raise our daughters properly. I don't want Lorna to get a bad reputation, and it can happen so easily these days.'

'Just what do you mean by my having a "Mediterranean" standard of morality?'

'Really, Victor, let's not be coy. I've been extremely sophisticated about Miss Lombardini—though I must say it's always seemed to me you could have been a little more original than to make your secretary your mistress . . .'

'I wasn't looking for originality. I was looking for a little warmth and love—qualities I sure as hell don't get out of you!'

'Oh, I know: cold, hard-bitten Lucille.' She yawned. 'Excuse me, the sea air does make one tired . . . But the point is, I haven't wanted the children to know about you and Miss Lombardini. I do think it's important they respect their father, and heaven knows it's taken a lot of fast talking to explain about their Uncle Franco living eighteen years with Princess Sylvia before getting around to marrying her! But one must make allowances for foreigners. However, because of the existing situation—with you as well as Franco—I think it becomes doubly important that we be protective with Lorna and Barbara. They're bound to hear about you sooner or later, and we must prepare them for the shock . . .'

'By being hypocritical? By lying?'

'Yes, by lying. You can't have it two ways, Victor. Apparently you can't live without Miss Lombardini . . . very well. But I'm not going to have my children's lives ruined because they have a philandering father.'

Her coolly superior manner infuriated him.

'How could their lives be ruined because I happen to have fallen in love with a warm, generous, lovable human being —unlike their mother?'

'Keep your voice down!'

'I'll shout if I damn please! You talk about morals—how about *your* morals? You flirt with anything in pants— particularly if he has a title, like that pompous ass of a marquess tonight!'

'Oh yes, I flirt, Victor. But I don't go to bed with them. That's the *big* difference between you and me.'

He turned to her slowly.

'I wish to God you'd take a lover,' he said, softly.

'But I won't, darling. Someone in the family must *try* to be respectable. And, of course, as long as I don't have a lover and you *do* . . .' she smiled, 'well, it makes it rather difficult for you to divorce me, doesn't it?'

'Do you want to hang on to me *that* much?'

'I want your money. And the bank stock you stole from me —not to mention the bank you stole from my family.'

'Stole? I paid you five million dollars for that stock, which I'm still paying off—'

'But the bank is yours, Victor. The Dexter Bank—my family's name—is yours.'

'If it's money you want, I'm willing to make you a handsome settlement.'

She studied him a moment, then said, 'No. No divorce. Not yet. You're not rich enough yet, darling.'

Her sarcastic smile returned.

'Good night, Victor,' she said, reaching for the bedlamp. 'Sweet dreams.'

And she turned off the light.

They spent three days each in London and Paris, sightseeing, then took the train to Nice and into Italy. As the train neared Rome, Victor's excitement mounted as he anticipated being reunited with the brother he wasn't even sure he could recognize, even though they had exchanged photographs. As the train pulled into the Rome station, it was Lucille who spotted him. 'That must be him!' she said, pointing to the tall man in the elegant Chesterfield and silk hat. Beside him stood Princess Sylvia, regal in a huge cartwheel hat swathed in white chiffon, which fluttered in the chilly early December breeze. 'And look at Princess Sylvia! What a stunning woman,' continued Lucille as the train squealed to a stop.

'Is that Cousin Fausto?' asked Lorna. 'Isn't he *swoony* good-looking!'

'Lorna,' said her mother, 'don't use cheap slang. Besides, that may be Antonio, his twin.'

'*He's* swoony, too!' gasped Barbara. 'They're *all* swoony! Oh, I like Italy already!'

When Victor stepped off the train, Franco headed for him, his arms open, saying in an emotion-filled voice, 'Vittorio! *Il mio fratello!*'

Victor realized he hadn't been called Vittorio in years. Time, he thought. We are all prisoners of time . . .

Then they were hugging each other, kissing, crying.

How very Italian, thought Lucille, as she watched.

'You aren't happy, are you?' asked Franco six nights later as he and Victor smoked postprandial cigars in the courtyard of the Palazzo dell'Acqua. The days since Victor's arrival had been filled with sightseeing, dinner parties, balls and receptions as all Rome vied to entertain the brother of Senator Spada. The Roman papers had heralded Victor's success story in America as a triumph of the 'Italian national character,' although *Libertà* remained modestly (and perhaps socialistically) silent on the subject. The royal family had received them in the Quirinal, Victor being amused not only by young King Victor Emmanuel's tiny stature (he had to climb a ladder to mount his horse), but by Lucille's awed expression in the presence of royalty. It had been an exciting and exhausting time, and Victor had enjoyed himself so much that his brother's question caught him off guard.

'Happy?' he said. 'Of course I'm happy, Franco.'

'Then why don't you talk to your wife?'

Victor looked up at the stars in the clear winter sky.

'Well, I suppose we don't have much to say to each other. And when we do, we shout it.'

'I thought there was trouble. Do you not love her anymore?'

'I don't know. I used to love her so much, I can't believe there's nothing left between us. When I first met her, Franco, I thought she was the most beautiful girl in the world. She was bright and fun and . . .' He sighed. 'But now all she seems interested in is money and titles. I don't know; maybe I've changed, too.'

'Is there another woman?'

'Yes. I'm very much in love with her. But divorce is difficult.'

'I can imagine. Marriage! I've always thought it was a trap. Look at Sylvia and me: we've lived together eighteen years and gotten along beautifully. Well, we've fought, but we love each other. Tomorrow we get married, and the whole relationship will probably go to hell in a bucket.'

'Not if you really love her, and from what I've seen, you do.'

Franco dropped his cigar on the ground.

'I love Sylvia,' he said, quietly, 'more than I love myself. Shall we join the ladies?'

They walked back into the palazzo.

'I don't like your sister-in-law,' said Sylvia an hour later after the Dexters had returned to their hotel. 'She's a terrible snob.'

'I know,' said Franco. 'Poor Victor. With all his success, he seems miserable. But the children are nice.'

'Oh, delightful. I think Lorna's fallen in love with Fausto.'

She climbed in her baroque bed with its four twisted posters supporting an elaborate canopy. Franco climbed in the other side.

'Fausto is doomed to have women fall in love with him,' he said. 'He got my sexiness, and Tony got your brains.'

She laughed.

'Does that mean I'm not sexy?'

'Far from it. For instance, if I were a gentleman, I'd never dream of making love to you the night before our wedding. But as you know, I'm no gentleman. And you're so sexy, I can't help myself.'

'After eighteen years, it's a little late to show restraint, wouldn't you say?'

'Definitely.'

He kissed her, running his hand through her hair.

'I love you, Sylvia,' he said. 'Now that we're about to become an old married couple, repulsively respectable, I thought I'd better remind you that I really do think you're the most remarkable woman I've ever met.'

'And I love you,' she whispered. 'I've loved you ever since that day you tried to kidnap me.'

'I was scared to death, you know.'

'I know. But I thought you were the most dashing man I'd ever met. I still do, even though you're too fat.'

'Are you going to make me go on a diet?'

'Never. I love you just the way you are, every ounce of you.'

'Fat, middle-aged and respectable. Is it the end of the world?'

'It's the beginning,' she said. He began to make love to her.

The wedding took place the following afternoon in the Church of San Giovanni in Laterano with Cardinal dell'Acqua celebrating the nuptial mass. The wedding was limited to members of the family, as Princess Sylvia wisely decided that her religious union with Franco after eighteen years of cohabitation should not be turned into a carnival. However, dozens of reporters were at the doors of the splendid church to photograph the arrival and departure of the wedding party. And that night the Palazzo dell'Acqua was the setting of one of the memorable celebrations of the day. Three hundred guests, including the royal family, crowded the huge rooms of the ancient building to drink one hundred cases of Dom Perignon and consume eighty kilos of caviar, a thousand ortolans and three dozen roasts. The long marble gallery was turned into a ballroom with a fifteen-man orchestra at one end, and as Lorna Dexter danced with Fausto, she thought the entire evening was like something out of a fairy tale.

'I can't believe anything could be more beautiful than to-night!' she enthused. 'Except maybe the wedding. That was so beautiful, I almost decided to become a Catholic.'

'I thought my father looked uncomfortable,' said Fausto in his schoolbook, but passable, English.

'I thought he looked very distinguished.'

'Well, he's taken the dive now.'

'You mean he's taken the *plunge.*'

Fausto grinned.

'Excuse me. That means he can't change his mind?'

'Yes. Well, sort of. Anyway, he couldn't possibly mind being in the Church *that* much, could he?'

'I think he could. The Church hates the socialists, so Father hates the Church.'

'Well, it's terribly confusing. Are you a socialist?'

'I'm an imperialist. I want Italy to have a great empire, like England. Then people will treat us Italians with respect.'

209

'I respect Italians. I *love* Italy! But I'm half-Italian, so I suppose it comes naturally.'

'Then you have to learn to speak Italian. I'll teach you: say *Lei è una bella ragazza.*'

'What's that mean?'

'You are a beautiful girl.'

Lorna liked that a lot.

CHAPTER 21

Julia Lombardini was nervous. Wearing her best dress and a smart new hat, she was waiting at a corner table in the small Italian restaurant in Greenwich Village. How many small Italian restaurants she and Victor had eaten at during the past six years! Julia had let him become her lover with serious misgivings, but in many ways it had worked out better than she had expected. They kept their two worlds strictly separate. At the office she was his efficient secretary, and she didn't think many people at the bank suspected they were lovers. But at night, when he wasn't with his family, their other world became fun and romance. They had eaten a thousand times at restaurants like this one, drunk wine, laughed, talked, held hands . . . and then gone back to the apartment on Fifty-fourth Street he rented for her to make love. He had been her first lover, and she adored him. Being his mistress had in reality been much less lurid than she had thought. But still, the guilt remained, the subterfuge . . .

The reason she was nervous—as well as heartsick—was that tonight she had to tell him he was her last lover.

He was ten minutes late, and she tensed when she saw him come in the restaurant. He came to her table and kissed her, then sat down and ordered some wine.

'It's good to see you,' he said, taking her hand. 'How's your cold?'

'Then you got my message?'

'Of course. I missed you at the office. You know I can't run that place without you. But you're better now?'

'I'm fine. How was Rome?'

'The wedding was fantastic. I've never drunk so much champagne in my life, and I had a helluva headache the next morning.' He reached in his pocket and pulled out a small

211

package. 'I was thinking about you all the time. I bought you this in Rome. I hope you like it.'

She opened the package as the waiter poured the wine. Inside was a black velvet box. She opened the lid and looked at the diamond bow. Victor watched her eyes widen.

'It's beautiful,' she said.

'You *do* like it?'

She closed the lid.

'Of course, but I can't take it. Give it to Lucille, or one of your daughters.'

He became suspicious.

'Julia, what is it? Why have you been avoiding me since I got back? You didn't have a cold today . . .'

'No, I didn't. I lied.'

'Then what's this all about?'

She looked at him.

'Victor, I'm getting married.'

He didn't say anything, but she saw the hurt in his eyes.

'His name is Cesare Rizzo,' she went. 'He's a wine importer in Brooklyn. I've known him casually for some time. While you were gone, he asked me for a date, and I accepted. We've been seeing each other for almost a month now. Three nights ago he asked me if I'd marry him. And I said yes.'

A long silence.

'Do you love him?' he said finally.

'No. I like him. He's a nice man, and he'll make me a good husband. I told him about you, incidentally. I've been honest with him.'

'I don't know what to say . . . I . . .' Suddenly he was angry. 'You *can't*, dammit! We love each other too much!'

'Victor, it's been six years. *Six*. I'm almost thirty. Yes, I do love you, more than I'll probably love any man in my life. But I can't wait forever for you to divorce Lucille. And you're not going to divorce her now, are you?'

'She won't divorce me! We had a big fight on the ship going over, and I told her I'd give her anything she wants! But she doesn't want divorce, at least now . . .'

'First it was you who didn't want a divorce, now it's she . . . Where does that leave me? Nowhere.'

He rubbed his hands wearily over his eyes.

'Can't you give me a few more years? I can work it out some way with Lucille . . .'

'No,' she said, quietly, 'I can't. I love you, but I've grown to hate being your mistress. I'm going to marry Cesare. I want a family of my own.'

He was beaten, and he knew it. He sank back in his seat and stared sullenly at the wineglass. She said, 'I guess the only thing left to say is thank you for six beautiful years.'

'I should thank you.'

'No hard feelings?'

He looked at her.

'No hard feelings.'

There were no feelings left at all. He felt empty.

The cable from Rome came a week later, and threw him even further into despair. It was from Sylvia. It said that Franco had been run over by a car on via Due Macelli. He had been killed instantly.

Now his grief burst out of him. His brother dead, his love gone, his wife become the enemy. He locked himself in his bedroom, sat at the window and stared out at Fifth Avenue, alternating between rage and despondent apathy. When his two daughters tried to get him to come out, he yelled at them to go away.

Lorna and Barbara had heard their father yell at their mother. But he had never yelled at them before.

Franco's funeral was attended by hundreds. Many of the rich came to gloat, but the poor came out of genuine sorrow. To them, he was what Sylvia had called him: a man who had stood up and said 'Look how rotten everything is.' Sylvia knew his faults. She knew about his mistresses. She knew that he had compromised *Libertà* to reach a wider audience, sugarcoating the socialism with society murders like the Countess Sant'Elia's. She had loved him with his faults, despite them. Now he was gone. She sat through the Mass, flanked by her two sons. Her face was hidden by the heavy black veil, but there were no tears in her eyes. She would cry in private. In public, for Franco's sake, she would be dignified.

Afterward, Tony and Fausto helped her into her limousine. The three of them sat in silence as the chauffeur started to drive them home. Then Sylvia said, 'Your father was a great man. Never forget that. And never do anything to dishonor his memory.'

'My father was murdered,' said Fausto, bitterly.

'We don't know that . . .'

'Oh Mother, we *do!* That was no "accident." The Mafia

213

arranged it. They killed him because he had the guts to stand up and say Italy ought to stamp them out. What a rotten country . . .'

His mother squeezed his arm, hard.

'Don't say that. My father died for Italy, and so did yours, in a way. Take that back.'

Fausto looked disgusted.

'All right. I'm sorry.'

Someday, he thought. Someday I'll avenge my father's death . . .

That night, she slept in the big baroque bed alone. She stared at the canopy above her and remembered half a lifetime with the man she had worshipped. She remembered his fierce lovemaking, his young body that had slowly fattened, his tenderness, his courage.

She remembered and she ached with loneliness.

'Oh Franco,' she whispered, 'my love . . .'

She hugged his pillow and wept.

PART IV

OVER HERE
AND OVER THERE

1915–1917

CHAPTER 22

He was an almost comic stereotype of an arrogant German general, complete with *Pickelhaube* pointed helmet, monocle and shiny boots. He paced back and forth in front of the fireplace in the tiny French inn, shouting at the frightened young lieutenant cowering before him. The general was so furious, his monocle kept popping out of his eye. At one point, as he jumped up and down with rage, the monocle fell on the floor and he smashed it with his boot. The lieutenant kept stealing anxious looks at the door to the inn's kitchen, from which increasingly noisy shouts of yet another fight were emanating, this one between the inn's owner and his wife. Finally the noise became so loud the general stopped shouting at the lieutenant and stomped over to the kitchen door to yell at the innkeeper instead. As he opened the door, a custard pie flew in his face.

'Beautiful!' exclaimed twenty-seven-year-old Morris David, the director-author-producer of this two-reel war comedy called *Reveille Revue*. 'Okay, everybody, we quit for the day. Joe, help Charlie get the pie off his face. We be here tomorrow at eight to finish, okay?' All this in Morris's machine-gun, Yiddish-accented English. As his four-man crew began setting up the next day's scene, Morris argued for a few minutes with the young actor playing the lieutenant, then headed downstairs to the first floor of the rented brownstone on East Fourteenth Street where, in the former kitchen of the once-elegant house, the fledgling movie mogul kept his jumbled office. It was June, 1915, almost a year after the outbreak of the calamitous war in Europe. Morris had decided a war comedy would make money and had plowed all his savings and the profits of David Productions into this, his fourth picture. Thin, tall, with curly blond hair and a rather homely face that women nevertheless responded to, the former Moyshe Davidoff had come a long way from the squalid tenement on Hester Street where, twenty-five

217

years before, he had huddled between his two brothers in bed, shivering from the cold and dreaming of riches while on the other side of the room his exhausted parents made love. Morris had sold rags, oranges, newspapers, each time inching up until, in his early twenties, with only a rudimentary education, he graduated to stockings and finally shoes. Shoes got him into the minor leagues. His energy was so fierce, his talent for wheedling unwilling buyers into purchases so extraordinary, that he landed a job as a traveling salesman for a large shoe company. For five years he covered New England and, later, the Midwest, his mangled English making him a joke to the Yankees and Hoosiers who, nevertheless, while laughing at him, bought. Morris became famous in the shoe business and, in the process, salted away the respectable sum of eight thousand dollars.

He was nearing that childhood dream of riches, but knew there was still a long way to go. Moving pictures seemed to him a short-cut. Now, his fourth production almost in the can, he was already planning his fifth film. But there were problems.

Twenty minutes later, when Ned Farber, his thirty-year-old camerman-associate producer came into the office, Morris was screaming on the phone.

'You're a *gonif*, a *shmuck*, a *chazzer*! Dustin Farnum only got five thousand to star in *The Squaw Man*, for Chrissake! What makes you think this *putz* of an actor you represent is worth ten? *Ten?!* I can't believe my eyes—*ten?!* I wouldn't pay him ten thousand if he walked on water! Go to hell with your ten!'

And he slammed down the phone.

'I take it,' said Ned, whose English was infinitely better than Morris's, 'we don't have a star for *Down for the Count?*'

'All agents are *gonifs*,' simmered Morris, 'but *this* one! To hell with him: I'll get a star nobody's heard of!'

'That's not much of a star,' said Ned, plopping into a torn sofa and sending up puffs of dust in the process. 'Morris, why don't you give up? You've been trying three weeks to get a name for five thousand, and it's just not going to happen. The agents know we're all making money, they want their actors to get a piece of the pie. So pay ten thousand.'

'How? How can I pay ten when my budget's thirty-five? Can you explain, please, when every penny's spent? You think I'm the U.S. Mint, I can print the money?'

'Did you ever hear of banks?'

'Don't talk to me from banks. Bankers are all Goyim: they hate us Jews. What bank will loan me money? Please explain?'

'I told you, Victor Dexter . . .'

'Do you think I'd trust a Wop? The Goyim are bad enough . . .'

'But Morris, he's one of *us!* He's an immigrant! Will you listen to me a minute?'

Morris sank back in his desk chair.

'I'm listening.'

'I told you my cousin's a teller at the Dexter Bank . . .'

'Why would a Wop hire a Jew? Please explain.'

'This Mr. Dexter likes everybody in his bank: Wops, Goyim, Jews . . . he wants *everybody's* money . . .'

'Sounds like a Jew.'

'But he isn't. Anyway, my cousin was trying to make time with Mr. Dexter's secretary, this girl named Miss Casati, and she told him Dexter loves the theater and invests in plays.'

'Who's producing plays? I'm making pictures.'

'Plays, pictures—it's all show business! I think Dexter will listen to you. I think you ought to go talk to him. If we have to pay ten thousand for a star, pay ten thousand and borrow the five you need from a bank.'

'I don't like banks. Bankers are all *gonifs*.'

'Morris, to you the whole world's a *gonif*.'

'You got a better explanation?' He thought a minute, then shrugged. 'Okay, I'll go to talk to him. I'll bet you a bagel he won't even let me in his office.'

'You've got a bet.'

'So you want to write a book about me?' asked Victor, eyeing the attractive brunette in the light-green dress sitting on the opposite side of his desk. 'Why?'

'Because you're a well-known man, a powerful banker, and Americans are interested in their business leaders. I hope you don't have a prejudice against women writers?'

'No indeed. One of my daughters wants to be a writer.'

'That would be Barbara,' said Elaine Fitzsimmons. 'The one at Vassar.'

'You've done your homework. But I'm not sure I want a book written about me. Will it be flattering?'

'Why shouldn't it be?'

'Bankers have been getting a lot of bad publicity lately.'

'If you're referring to Mr. Morgan, don't you think he deserved it? Don't you think he had too much economic power?'

'Speaking as a former rival of Mr. Morgan, I'd say yes, he had too much power. On the other hand, I admired him. He had integrity.'

'But you approve of the Federal Reserve System?'

'Yes. Miss Fitzsimmons, I can see you've got a lot of questions. Unfortunately, I don't have a lot of time, so I'm not sure how I can be of much use . . .'

'I realize I can't take up your business hours, Mr. Dexter, but I was hoping to be able to have at least a dozen interviews with you, perhaps on weekends?'

Victor rather liked this brash young woman who seemed so sure of herself, and he rather liked the idea of being the subject of a book. But he wished Miss Fitzsimmons weren't quite so pretty, because if he invited her to the weekend house on Sands Point he had bought three years before, might not Lucille get suspicious his motives were mixed? On the other hand, Lucille would be at the house, along with Lorna. And when school let out next week, Drew and Barbara would be there, so how suspicious could anyone be?

'All right,' he said. 'Would you like to be our houseguest for two or three weekends out at Sands Point? You can talk my ear off?'

She smiled.

'I was hoping you'd say that. I'd love it. And, frankly, getting out of town on the weekends isn't going to be a hardship. How about this weekend? I don't mean to sound pushy, but the sooner I can get started, the sooner I can write the book. And believe me, Mr. Dexter, I can use the money.'

'This weekend it is. If you take the nine-twenty train from Pennsylvania Station Saturday morning, I'll have my chauffeur pick you up at the station. And bring some sailing clothes. If it's nice weather, I'll take you out on my boat.'

'It sounds better and better. But do I have time for a few more questions?'

'Of course.'

'You're one of the country's leading Italian-Americans. You established a chair in Italian History at Harvard in the name of your late brother, Franco Spada, and you have established a Franco Spada Scholarship Fund for Italian-American students out of your own funds. You're also chairman of the Italian-American Society. Last month Italy went to war against Austria and Germany. What would your sympathies have been if Italy had gone the other way—in other words, if it had remained Germany's ally?'

'I wouldn't have liked it, naturally, but as it is I think Italy has made a mistake anyway. I think Italy should have done everything it could to stay out of the war, because it seems to me it has very little to gain and a lot to lose.'

'But since Italy *is* in the war, do you hope that America will get in it also?'

'Absolutely not. America should stay out—that war has nothing to do with us!'

'But don't you think Germany should be defeated?'

'Of course, but not by us. President Wilson may have been a good professor at Princeton, but if he gets us in that war, I hope history damns him.'

'Then you're an isolationist?'

'I'm a pacifist. War achieves nothing but death.'

She made some hasty notes in a small black notebook, then put it in her purse and stood up.

'I'll have a lot more questions to ask you Saturday,' she said.

'I hope my answers make sense,' he said, getting up to escort her to the door. 'What are the titles of your previous books? I want to read them.'

'Oh no. They were terrible! Two novels that failed totally. I'd be ashamed to have you read them.'

Victor looked confused.

'But you have a publisher for this book? I believe you said Harper Brothers?'

'Yes, but they didn't publish the novels. Well, thank you so much, Mr. Dexter. I'll see you Saturday.'

She shook his hand, gave him a radiant smile, then left the office. Victor thought a moment, then went back to his desk and flipped on his intercom. 'Miss Casati, may I see you?'

When his secretary came in, he said, 'Get me the president of Harper Brothers.'

'Yes, Mr. Dexter. And there's a Mr. Morris David to see you.'

Ten minutes later Morris was sitting in the same chair so recently warmed by Elaine Fitzsimmons's trim bottom, watching Victor suspiciously, as if the banker might bite him.

'I want to borrow five thousand dollars,' he said.

'I see. What for?'

Morris squirmed for a moment, then jumped up.

'I shouldn't have come here,' he mumbled to himself. 'It's a waste of time . . . Thank you, Mr. Dexter, nice to meet you, good-bye.' He was halfway to the door.

'Wait a minute! Don't you want to tell me—'

'It's a five-reel comedy!' exclaimed Morris, turning back.

'*Five* reels! Nobody's made a comedy that long, and you're going to tell me I'm *messhuge!* So do I need this from you?'

'What's *"messhuge"*?'

'Crazy! Do I need you to tell me I'm crazy? I'm plenty sane! I know this movie will make millions, but you're not going to believe me, I can tell. Bankers is all the same: no imagination, no *chutzpah*. All you know how to say is no.'

'I can't say no or yes until I know something about it. And if you can convince me your movie's going to make millions, I'm interested. After all, the film industry's the fifth biggest industry in America—why shouldn't I be interested? So why don't you sit down and talk?'

Morris eyed him warily.

'They tell me you're Italian. You don't sound Italian. You don't look Italian.'

'Nevertheless, I'm Italian.'

'Huh. I wish I spoke English as good as you. You don't think my real name is Morris David, do you? You think I'm a Jew, don't you?'

'I wouldn't think you were Irish, no.'

Morris laughed.

'I changed my name,' he said, going back to the chair. 'My real name's Moyshe Davidoff, and my parents came over from Russia. Did you change your name? You must have. Dexter don't sound Italian to me.'

'My real name's Vittorio Spada.'

'*That* sounds Italian. Okay, we both change our names, we got something in common, right? So maybe you think I'm *messhuge*. What's "crazy" in Italian?'

'*Pazzo*.'

'*Pazzo!* Mmm—nice. It *sounds* crazy, like *messhuge*. Okay, you won't think I'm *pazzo*.' He sat down. 'So what do you want to know?'

'Well, what's the name of this five-reel comedy?'

'*Down for the Count*. I'll tell you the plot: you'll laugh so hard you'll cry in your pants. It's about this beautiful *shiksa*—all blond, beautiful curls like Little Mary—she works in a dress factory, see? And her boss makes a pass at her, but she's a *maydele* and says no to him, so her boss, who's a *momzer*, a *teivel* and a *putz*—'

'A what? What's a *putz*?'

'A prick.'

'Oh.'

'Anyway, he accuses her of stealing from the company,

which is a *grosse ligent*, and the girl is so afraid of being taken to jail, she takes all her savings and buys a train ticket to California. On the train she meets this good-looking guy who says he's a boxer, but who's really a *shmeichler* . . .'

'Translation, please.'

'A . . .' Morris waved his hands helplessly. 'Like a three-card-monte shyster.'

'A con artist?'

'That's it! Anyway, Little Mary likes him and trusts him, but he *shmeichels* her out of the little money she has left and gets off the train in Ohio. So she has to get off, too, because she's *urem* —broke.' He paused for breath, then plunged back into the plot, which was so full of mistaken identities, pratfalls, con jobs and twists that Victor gave up trying to make any sense of it and just listened. Finally Morris reached the climax, 'Which is when Little Mary challenges the *shmeichler* to a prize fight and knocks him out! Don't you love it? But it turns out they're really in love, and he's really the son of a millionaire, so they get married and live happily ever after, fade-out, the end. How could it help but make *gelt?*'

Victor tactfully cleared his throat.

'Well, it certainly sounds . . . exuberant.'

'You don't like it? You didn't laugh.'

'It's hard for me to visualize . . . I take it you're the writer?'

'I'm everything—writer, director, producer, seller . . . I don't let nobody else screw the picture up. *My* pictures have the Morris David touch, which is genius!'

'Mmm.'

'If I have a star, I can sell the New England rights alone for twenty thousand dollars. And Ohio, Pennsylvania, Indiana and Michigan should be worth five thousand apiece . . . I know the territory, I sold shoes there.'

'Motion pictures aren't shoes.'

'It's all the same! Movies, shoes, corsets . . . you got to know how to *sell*, and I can sell.' He paused. 'But I'm not selling you, am I?'

'I'd like to see a copy of your budget, and I'd like to see one of your previous productions . . .'

'*Undressed Salad* is playing at the Fairfax on Fifth Street and Third Avenue.'

Victor made a note.

'I'd like to suggest a plot change,' he said.

'*Everybody* always wants to change the plot!'

'Instead of Little Mary and the *shmeichler* getting off the train

223

in Ohio, why don't you let them go all the way to California? That way you could shoot the picture in California. I hear the whole industry's moving out there anyway to avoid Mr. Edison's trust.'

Morris groaned.

'Wouldn't I like to move!' he said. 'But that takes more money . . .'

'How much?'

'I don't know, probably five thousand . . . I'd have to move my crew out there and all the equipment; they haven't got much out there . . . Maybe ten . . .'

'Wouldn't it be worth it?'

'Sure, if I had the money. It's better weather, too.'

'Put it in your budget and come back to see me in the morning. Meanwhile I'll become one of your paying customers.'

'You'll love it!' exclaimed Morris, standing up. 'You'll laugh so much, you'll cry in your pants!'

That afternoon Victor took a taxi to the Fairfax, sensing that a chauffeured limousine wasn't the wisest mode of transportation to the Lower East Side. He hoped the movie would be good because he liked Morris David and the idea of becoming part of the motion picture industry intrigued him. The Fairfax had been a nickelodeon until the previous year when its owner upgraded it to a Motion Picture Theater, but the price was still a nickel. *Undressed Salad* was on a double bill with a western called *The Purple Mask*. Three kids wearing dirty caps were studying the stills on the poster, trying to decide whether to invest in tickets. Victor came up to them.

'Do you boys want to see the movie?' he asked.

'We want to see the western,' said one of them.

'I'll tell you what: I'll buy your tickets for you if you'll sit through both movies and tell me after what you thought of them.'

Their faces lit up.

'Oh boy! You've got a deal!'

He bought the tickets, but he didn't need their critique. Ten minutes into *Undressed Salad*, he was laughing so hard he almost cried in his pants.

Morris David might be *messhuge*, but he made funny movies.

CHAPTER 23

The big white house standing above the rocks of Long Island Sound had been Victor's attempt to fill the void left in his life after he lost Julia Lombardini. He needed something to divert his mind from his unhappiness, and this pillared house with its eighteen airy, sun-filled rooms, its tennis court and pool, its twelve tree-filled acres and its superb view of the Sound was diversion on a grand scale. It was also something of a sop to Lucille. Victor was not without guilt about his long affair and realized that no matter what his rationalizations, Lucille had been right: in the eyes of society, he was at fault. He also was acutely aware of the effect on his children, who not only had to endure the tension between their parents but the confusion about the mysterious 'other woman' in their father's life, whom they had inevitably heard about. Victor figured buying the country home would help bring his family together again, and in this he had been right. The children loved the place, as did Lucille. It was much more convenient than the cottage in Dutchess County, and it had the added attraction of the Sound. Moreover, fashionable New Yorkers were discovering the North Shore, which pleased Lucille, who always liked to be where the social action was.

The following Saturday afternoon, Lorna was swinging in a hammock at the side of the house, sipping iced tea, when she said to her mother, 'Who's that woman sailing with Daddy?'

'A Miss Fitzsimmons,' answered Lucille. 'She's writing a book about your father.'

'Really? How exciting!'

'Yes, isn't it?'

Lucille looked out at the Sound where, some hundred feet offshore, Victor's forty-foot sloop, the *San Sebastiano*, was tacking in the summer breeze.

'Your daughter's very beautiful,' said Elaine Fitzsimmons, leaning back on the white canvas cushions as Victor manned the helm.

'Thank you.'

'How old is she?'

'She'll be twenty this August.'

'That means she's a Leo. You're a Virgo, which means you're very good with money.'

'That's convenient for a banker. Now, Miss Fitzsimmons, what's your game?'

'I beg your pardon?'

'I called Harper Brothers. They've never heard of you.'

She stared at him a moment, then laughed. He looked at her with surprise.

'I don't see what's funny,' he said.

'Well, I do. Oh dear, I'm caught. You see, I've never been published and when you haven't been published, it's impossible to get a publisher interested in a book you haven't written. But I knew that if I came to you without a publisher, you wouldn't talk to me. So I lied. I made up Harper Brothers. I suppose now you're furious with me?'

She ran her hand through her hair and smiled.

'It sounds as if you'd make a better novelist than a biographer.'

'But I've tried novels and I always get stuck. Please, Mr. Dexter: I really will write a very good book about you. Say you'll cooperate with me.'

'Well, I suppose if I don't you'll write it anyway. But I think from now on you'd better stick to the truth with me. And my name's Victor. I'm coming about.'

'What's that mean?'

'It means *duck*.'

She ducked as the mast swung over her head.

The weather was so idyllic, dinner was served on the front terrace overlooking the Sound. A table holding hurricane lamps was set for four, with Elaine opposite Lorna and Victor and Lucille at each end. As dessert was served, Lucille, who looked lovely in a white summer dress, said to Elaine, 'And what have you found out from my husband so far?'

Elaine helped herself to the sherbet and fruit.

'Oh, lots of things,' she said. 'The Dexter Bank has thirty-three branches, twenty-three hundred employees and assets of almost a billion dollars. It's the eighteenth largest bank in America and invests in everything from steel mills to a diaper company. Victor has even invested in a motion picture company.'

'Ah, the fascination of money,' said Lucille. 'Money and power. It's what life's all about, but I don't see how you can simply put a lot of statistics in a book. What fascinates people is how people *get* money and power. Has my husband told you about that?'

'Not yet.'

'You must ask him. Or will you tell her, Victor? For instance, will you tell her how you bullied me into selling you my stock?'

Silence except for the crickets and the lazy lap of the tide on the rocks.

'Probably,' Lucille continued with a smile, 'You wouldn't use the verb "bully," would you? Perhaps "tricked" is the better one. You mustn't let my husband's pleasant facade fool you, Miss Fitzsimmons. He's quite a tricky man and *very* clever. But of course he wouldn't be as rich and powerful as he is if he weren't, would he?'

Lorna was staring at her mother.

'Mother, how can you say these things in front of a stranger?' she exclaimed.

'But Miss Fitzsimmons isn't a stranger, darling, not if she's writing a book about your father. And we want the book to be truthful, don't we? I doubt if your father would tell the truth. Would you, Victor?'

Victor coolly continued eating.

'I don't need to say anything,' he replied, 'since you do the talking for me.'

Lucille turned back to Elaine.

'Bankers are supposed to be pillars of the community,' she went on, 'but of course that's a myth. We have so many myths in America, but that particular one had always amused me, being married to a banker.'

Lorna got up.

'Excuse me. I think I'm going to bed.'

She went in the house. Lucille watched her go, then said to Elaine, 'Lorna adores her father and doesn't like it when I say unflattering things about him. The wife is supposed to support the husband—another beautiful American myth—but I think it's more important to be truthful. Of course . . .' and she looked down the table at Victor, '. . . if the husband were faithful to the wife, the wife would be more inclined to be supportive. Don't you agree, dear?'

Victor put down his spoon.

'Since you seem determined to embarrass me and our guest,' he said, 'let me say that for years I've tried to be a good husband. Not a perfect one, I'll admit, but a good one. Have you been a perfect wife?'

'Perfect enough,' she said, getting up. 'Well, it's such a lovely evening, I think I'll take a stroll along the beach. Will anyone join me?'

'No thank you,' said Elaine.

'Victor? We could walk hand in hand in the moonlight. It would be terribly romantic.'

'I'm not feeling very romantic.'

Lucille laughed.

'I can't imagine why. Well, *à bientôt*.'

She walked off the terrace toward the Sound. When she was out of earshot, Elaine said quietly, 'She hates you, doesn't she?'

'Yes,' replied Victor. 'But she's usually not quite so obvious about it.'

He put down his napkin, wondering if Lucille were opening a new campaign in their long marital war.

The three boys in swimming trunks let themselves off the end of the dark pier, quietly sliding into the water. Then they swam under the doors of the boathouse, surfacing beside the sleek mahogany speedboat.

'Goddam, she's a beauty,' whispered Harry Stephens, who was sixteen.

'You sure you know how to run this?' asked Bill Layton.

'It's just like a Tin Lizzie, except it floats,' said fifteen-year-old Drew Dexter. 'Come on, let's go.'

He climbed out of the water into the rear of the boat.

'You guys get the doors,' he whispered. 'Then we'll just paddle this baby out nice and quiet.'

'If old man Chester catches us, there's going to be hell to pay,' said Harry.

'Screw him. Besides, he won't catch us. Hurry up with the doors!'

'Yeah, *we* do all the work!—

'Somebody's got to steer the boat, don't they?'

'To hell with you, Drew. You always get the easy job.'

'That's 'cause I'm smartest.'

'Says who.'

Harry and Bill climbed on the boat platform and opened the doors. Then they pushed the speedboat toward the bay, jumping in the stern as she cleared the dock. The open waters of Long Island Sound glistened enticingly beyond the bay, a full summer moon spilling silver on the scene.

'We should have picked a night when there wasn't any moon,' whispered Harry. 'If he looks out his window, we're goners.'

'He's asleep,' said Drew. 'Jesus, you worry too much. Okay, let's paddle her out, then I'll start her.'

'I suppose *we* paddle while you fiddle with the magneto?'

'That's right,' grinned Drew, who had a masculine version of his mother's good looks.

'Shit.'

The two boys pulled oars out of a compartment and started paddling as Drew climbed in the driver's seat. He examined the instrument panel.

'It was made in Michigan,' he said, looking at the manufacturer's name on the speedometer.

'So what?'

'Thought you'd want to know. I heard old man Chester paid a thousand buckeroos for it. Sure looks it.'

'How long do we have to paddle?'

Drew turned to look back at the shore where, on top of a slope, Frank Chester's pseudo-Tudor estate slumbered beneath pine trees. They were about thirty feet away from the pier.

'Five more minutes,' he said.

'Shit.'

Five minutes later, Drew started turning the crank and the powerful engine roared to life.

'Here we go!' he yelled. He pushed the gear forward, then jammed the throttle full. The boat's trim bow lifted out of the water and took off, spewing a white wake which sparkled in the moonlight.

'Ten knots, twelve . . .' called Drew, watching the needle climb. 'Fourteen knots! That's almost thirty miles an hour!'

Frank Chester, a fifty-year-old partner in one of Manhattan's most prestigious law firms, was a light sleeper and had been wakened by the noise of the engine. Now he climbed out of bed and ran to the window to see his new speedboat racing out of the bay into Long Island Sound.

Frank Chester went to the phone to call the Coast Guard.

'I can't believe you've done this!' roared Victor the next morning in the breakfast room overlooking the Sound. 'I can't believe *my* son stole a speedboat—'

'We didn't steal it!' interrupted Drew, who looked a bit shaken by his three hours in the local jail. 'We just *borrowed* it! We were going to bring it back, but he called the Coast Guard . . .'

'Tell that to Frank Chester! He's threatening to press charges, and it happens to be a felony . . .'

'Frank Chester will do no such thing,' said Lucille. 'His wife's been dying to get on my guest list for years . . .'

'Lucille, shut up! Drew has to learn respect for the law!'

'But you're treating him as if he were a common criminal! It was just a prank . . .'

'If Frank Chester's son "borrowed" your Rolls-Royce for a few hours, I doubt you'd think it a prank!'

'Frank Chester's son's too fat and lazy to borrow a cup of sugar, much less an automobile. I'm not saying you should reward Drew for what he did, but you don't have to threaten him with a jail term.'

'There was a cockroach in my cell,' said Drew. 'A big one! It was something.'

Lucille made a face.

'Drew dear, not at the breakfast table. Well, Victor, what are you going to do besides yell at him? Transport him in the hulks to Australia? Chain him up in the Château d'If?'

'Lucille, it's incredible to me that you can take this flip attitude when your son has committed a crime which could get him five years in a reformatory.'

'It's *not* a crime!' she shouted, her eyes blazing. 'And quit using that word! No son of mine would ever commit a crime!'

'Oh? Because he's got your blue blood in his veins, I suppose he's outside the criminal code? Good God, plant that idea in his head and he'll go out and rob a bank. Drew, you're a fine young man, and I'm proud of your athletic record and your grades —you've done very well at Andover. But you're a little too cocky for your own good. So this summer, instead of loafing around with your pals, you're going to get a job.'

'Oh Dad, come *on* . . .'

'And not just *any* job, but a job that'll knock you down a peg or two.'

'But summer's the only time I get to have any fun!'

'That's too bad.'

Victor got up from the table and went through the house to his office. The moment he was out of the room, Drew said to his mother, 'Don't let him do this, Mom! Is isn't fair. I don't want a crummy job . . .'

Lucille sipped her coffee, torn between her instinct to defy Victor and protect her adored son, and her common sense, which told her that after all Victor was right. For once, her common sense won out.

'I'm sorry, Drew, but I have to agree with your father.'

'Aw, shit!'

'Drew!'

'Sorry.'

When Victor returned he said, 'You start work at seven tomorrow morning.'

Drew rolled his eyes.

'Doing what?'

'Working on the road crew of the town of Sands Point for twenty-five cents an hour.'

Drew looked disgusted.

All of Victor and Lucille's children were predictably good-looking, being the offspring of handsome parents, but the middle child, Barbara, was breathtaking. She had inherited Victor's black hair, large brown eyes and narrow face; she had luminous skin, and her figure was tall and perhaps too thin. But while her classmates at Vassar agreed that Barbara Dexter was a beauty, when it came to her personality she got mixed grades. 'Moody,' 'shy' and 'sensitive' were adjectives often used to describe her, while others, less friendly, called her 'standoffish' and 'snooty.' The latter was unfair, for Barbara was no more interested in social position than her classmates. But she was introverted and introspective, much given to romantic daydreaming, the products of her vivid imagination sometimes finding their way to paper in the form of short stories. Barbara usually tore her lucubrations up after reading them, certain they were no good. But she dreamed of writing a novel some day. And certainly the world of books was to her much more real and exciting than the pleasant world she inhabited. She devoured books and haunted bookstores. And the afternoon following her brother's speedboat caper, Barbara was in Miss Simpson's Book Shoppe, Sands Point's tiny answer to Brentano's, leafing through the summer's best seller, Booth Tarkington's *The Turmoil*.

'I love Booth Tarkington,' she said to Miss Simpson, the

pincenezed proprietor. 'He and Gene Stratton Porter are my two favorite novelists.'

'Well, that's a very good book,' said Miss Simpson. 'I read it last week. Mr. Tarkington makes a splendid point, in my opinion.'

'What's that?'

'That the country's getting too big for its britches. Big cities, big businesses, big buildings . . . the whole country's going to collapse from overweight.'

'Then I'll buy it. And I'll get my father to read it. He thinks big is better.'

'Well, he's a businessman, and they all think that way, I suppose. But I remember this country when I was a child, and it was a much nicer place to live in then. Yes, sir, may I help you?'

A tall young man with a motoring cap and goggles had come in the store.

'Yes, please. I'm lost. I'm looking for the house of Victor Dexter.'

Miss Simpson's eyebrows raised slightly at his heavy accent.

'This young lady can help you. She's Mr. Dexter's daughter.'

Morris David turned to look at Barbara, and his goggled eyes liked what they saw.

'A banker could have such a looker for a daughter? It don't seem possible. My name's Morris David, and your poppa and I is in business together. The movie business.'

Miss Simpson's eyebrows went even higher. As for Barbara, she had never heard English like this before.

'Yes, my father's spoken about you,' she said. 'If you wait a minute, I'll show you the way home. Miss Simpson, I'll take the book.'

'I'll put it on your account, dear. Shall I wrap it?'

'No thanks. I'll just carry it.'

'My car's outside,' said Morris. 'It's a Model T. Did you hear the one about the man who named his Ford after his wife?'

'Why?'

'After he got it, he couldn't control it. You're not laughing. It's a lousy joke, I'll admit. Come on, I'll drive, you show me the way.'

He held the door for her, and she went out to the sidewalk, where a dusty Model T was parked.

'I bought it last year,' said Morris, holding the car door for her, 'and it's only broken down twice. Not bad. But I got to sell it.'

'Why?'

'I'm going to California next week.'

He closed the door, then went to the front of the car and started cranking. After four hard turns, the motor came to life, backfired twice, then settled down to a happy, rumbling, rattling chug. Morris jumped in the driver's seat and they were off.

'Which way?' he asked.

'The first left, then just go straight. Are you going to California to make a motion picture?'

'That's right, thanks to your poppa. He invested fifteen thousand dollars of his own money in my company, and I only asked for five! He loved my last picture so much . . . you saw it, maybe? *Undressed Salad?*'

'No, I'm afraid I don't go to movies much.'

'It's possible? You don't like movies?'

'I prefer books.'

'Books?' he snorted. 'Books is for *shmucks.*'

'I beg your pardon?'

'*Shmucks!* It's a Yiddish word for . . .' he searched his mind as he roared around the corner, '. . . you know, *shmucks!* Fools, except that's really not what it means. English is a lousy language. Am I going too fast? Everyone says I drive like Barney Oldfield.'

'Oh no,' she lied. She was hanging on to her hat with one hand and the door with the other as the car roared down the dirt road.

'Maybe I should put the top up? You'll get dust in your eyes, maybe?'

'No, really, I'm fine.'

'Okay. You got a boyfriend?'

'No, I'm not much interested in boys.'

'Why not?'

'Oh, I don't know.'

'You just haven't met the right one yet. When you do, you'll fall hard. I know your type.'

'I'm not sure I'm a "type," Mr. David.'

'*Everyone's* a type! At least women is. Are you in school?'

'Yes, Vassar.'

'What's Vassar?'

She looked surprised.

'It's a college for women.'

'I'm not so sure college is good for women. They'll start thinking they're as good as men, and then the whole world will be a mess.'

233

'I think that's the most contemptible thing I've ever heard!' she burst out. 'Women *are* as good as men, maybe even better!'

'Then why do men run the world?'

'And look at the mess they're making of it. A horrible war in Europe with thousands of people being slaughtered, and why? Because the Kaiser—a *man*—is a pigheaded bully. If women ruled the world, there wouldn't be any wars.'

Morris grinned.

'You got a temper. That's nice.'

She blushed slightly.

'I'm sorry. I didn't mean to yell.'

'So yell! It's good. It gets the poison out, like pus from a pimple. You know what I mean?'

'I'm afraid I do. Oh—here's the driveway.'

She pointed to an imposing whitewashed-brick Georgian gate, its pillars surmounted by stone jardinières spilling pink geraniums. Morris turned in and started toward the house.

'Your poppa called this a country house. It looks more like a palace to me. I like rich men. I'm going to be rich some day and have a place like this and everyone will be jealous. What's so funny?'

She was biting her lip.

'Oh, nothing.'

'You're laughing at me! Why? Because I talk bad?'

'Oh no. It's just . . . well, you're so blunt.'

'Because I tell the truth? What's the point of being rich if it's not to show off? Listen, I've been poor. I can tell you, it's not to brag about. Look at the ocean! It's beautiful.'

'That's Long Island Sound.'

'So, it's water.'

He parked the car in front of the house and jumped out, hurrying around to open the door for her.

'Did you come to see Father on business?' she said, climbing down.

'That's right. I got some papers for him to sign.'

'Well, it's been very nice meeting you, Mr. David.'

'You're leaving? You don't live here, maybe?'

She laughed.

'No, I live here. I'm going to the side yard. There's a hammock there, and I want to read my new book. You can laugh at books, Mr. David, but they make movies out of them, so they can't be all bad, can they?'

'Movies is better.'

'Read a few books and maybe you'll change your mind. Well . . . good-bye.'

She held out her hand. He took it and shook it. Then she started walking around the house. He watched her a minute, then ran after her.

'Hey!' he yelled. She stopped and turned. He came up to her and took off his goggles.

'Yes?'

'Uh . . .' His mind was racing. He looked at the book in her hand. 'If you think that book would make a good movie, let me know. Okay?'

'All right.'

'You see, I make up my own scripts, but maybe you got a point. Maybe I should read books, except they bore me. So maybe you can read them for me. You'd be reading for your poppa, too, since he's my partner.' He smiled at her. 'You can be a partner, too. Would you like that?'

She studied his face.

'Yes, I think I would.'

Rather to her surprise, she liked Morris David, too.

CHAPTER 24

Elaine Fitzsimmons sat in the tearoom of the Times Square hotel sipping cocoa and watching the people, many of whom she knew were connected in some way to the theater. Broadway fascinated this twenty-six-year-old daughter of a Yonkers policeman, even though Broadway had so far rebuffed her efforts to make a theatrical career. Elaine lived in a theatrical boarding-house on West Forty-third Street, sharing a room with another aspiring young actress. She took lessons from Mrs. Colefax-Cheyney, an aging British thespian who preached round tones and 'class, always class,' trying to convert her mostly middle-class pupils into cardboard duchesses. There was something faintly ludicrous about it all, but Elaine loved the excitement, the sheer raw energy that the theater district emanated as it churned out its dozens of annual plays, revues, musicals, operettas and spectacles. She was convinced that someday her Big Chance would come. Perhaps, she thought as she sipped her cocoa, it already had.

She spotted the woman as she came into the tearoom and reflected that Mrs. Colefax-Cheyney would have approved. Tall, reed-thin, elegantly dressed, her ensemble finished with a toque, her every move seemed to murmur 'class, always class.' She saw Elaine and came over to her table, sitting opposite her.

'I'm sorry I'm late,' said Lucille Dexter, taking off her gloves. 'Any progress?'

'I'm afraid not.'

Lucile looked surprised.

'But it's been a month! Nothing's happened?'

'Nothing. Your husband has been a perfect gentleman.'

'You've encouraged him?'

'Well, I've tried to be subtle. But I think he knows I like him. In fact, I do. Your husband's a very nice man, Mrs. Dexter. I wonder if you shouldn't reconsider this whole venture.'

'I'll thank you to do what you're paid for,' snapped Lucille, adding to the waiter who had appeared, 'Tea, please. With lemon.' The waiter moved away as she continued in a less hostile tone, 'I realize Victor can be charming. I used to be in love with him myself, before certain things happened. But as I said last month at Sands Point, beneath the pleasant facade is a very clever, self-centered man, and I've had enough of it. I should have divorced him years ago when he had a mistress, but then I wasn't ready for divorce. Now I am. Unfortunately for me, to the best of my knowledge Victor has been faithful and, as you know, the only grounds for divorce in New York is adultery.'

'I told you I won't go to bed with him.'

'I don't expect you to, and it's not needed. Just let me know when he makes the inevitable pass—and he'll make it, believe me. Victor's one great weakness is women. He'll hire a hotel room and ask you up. When he does, phone me. I have the photographer and the detective ready. Does he still believe you're writing a book about him?'

'Yes.'

Lucille chuckled.

'Well, you're a clever actress, my dear. You should do well in the theater. Here: I have something for you.' She pulled an envelope from her purse and handed it across the table. 'There's five hundred in cash in it. When we get the necessary photographs, you'll get the rest of the money.'

Elaine put the envelope in her purse.

'I asked a friend of mine about this,' she said. 'I didn't mention any names, of course, but he said the police call this "entrapment."'

'Don't worry about the police or entrapment. None of this will ever get into a court. The divorce will be settled privately, and no one will get hurt. Ah, here's my tea. Nothing like a cup of hot tea on a hot day. Did you know the Arabs drink hot tea to keep cool? Interesting, isn't it? Something about the body temperature . . .'

Elaine thought Lucille Dexter would keep cool in Death Valley.

Victor sat up in bed and lighted a cigar.

'So Lucille has added self-centeredness to my other vices,' he said, twirling the cigar slowly under the match. 'I must say, if no man's a hero to his valet, some men become outright villains to their wives. Lucille must see me as some sort of Machiavellian monster.'

237

'She's so cold,' said Elaine next to him, stretching with pleasure after making love. 'She's really an unlikeable woman. What did you ever see in her?'

'She was a charming girl, once. But time has changed her. Time changes all of us. It's probably changed me more than I like to admit. Maybe Lucille's version of me is the true one, I don't know. Maybe I am self-centered.'

'Oh no,' said Elaine, running her fingers over his naked shoulder. 'You're a very dear, sweet man, a—very unselfish man. She's just twisted you around in her mind because she's jealous of you, because you're a success and she's not.'

'She's a success. She has everything she ever wanted out of life: the social position, the beautiful home, the flattery, the sycophantic boobies that fawn on her . . .'

'Maybe that's not enough for her. You have power—*real* power—and that's very attractive to a woman. Maybe she wants to destroy you because she knows she could never have your kind of power.'

'Perhaps. I think it's more likely she just wants to wring every cent out of me she can. I'm sure her lawyer has told her that if she can get compromising photographs of me, she's got me over a barrel. Which she would. So I've got you to thank for letting me in on what was happening.'

'I didn't like it from the start,' said Elaine, sitting up next to him. They were in a room in a small hotel on upper Broadway. 'But I needed the money, so . . .' she shrugged, 'I'm not proud of myself, but I like the way it's turned out.' She smiled at him, and he put his arm around her and kissed her cheek.

'Me too,' he said. 'Besides, I'm probably the only man in America whose wife is paying his mistress.'

'Yes, isn't that lovely?' laughed Elaine.

'But we've got to stop this farce. I've put off divorce, Lucille's put it off . . . there have been the children to think of, but they're old enough to handle it—at least I hope so. It's time Lucille and I settled accounts. I just hope it can be done with a minimum of bloodletting. You see, the problem is she's spent all her own money, so . . .'

The door burst open and the flash powder exploded.

'Beautiful, Mr. Dexter! Just one more—smile!'

A second explosion. Victor was out of the bed racing toward the door, but the two men were already running down the hotel corridor toward the fire stairs. 'Better get your pants on!' yelled one of them over his shoulder. And their laughter mocked him as they ran down the stairs.

He came back in the room and closed the door. He looked terrified. Elaine was crying.

'How did it happen?' she sobbed.

'They must have followed us. Jesus Christ . . .'

He started getting dressed as fast as he could.

'You thought you were so clever, didn't you?' said Lucille, with a ring of triumph in her voice. It was an hour later. She was in the small sitting room off her bedroom on the second floor of the Fifth Avenue house. 'You and that slut of an actress. As if I didn't figure it out yesterday, when she told me nothing was happening, that you were being the "perfect gentleman." As if *you* knew anything about gentlemanly behavior.'

He sank into a chair.

'All right, Lucille. You've got me where you want me. Just spare me the gloating.'

'Why should I spare you anything? What did you ever spare me? You humiliated me with your secretary for years. You stole my bank stock—'

"God*dam* you, I never stole anything from you! I never stole anything from anyone . . .'

'Shut up. I'm doing the talking now.'

He said nothing. She got up from her chaise longue and went to the door to lock it. 'I knew you'd take her to bed sooner or later,' she said, leaning her back against the door, 'but it was only yesterday that I realized the game that little baggage was playing, taking money from me while sleeping with you. Or I should say, the little game you both were playing. Oh, it was so typical of you, Victor, and what a good laugh you must have had at my expense! Except this time, I outsmarted you. I told my detective not to wait for Miss Fitzsimmons's phone call, but to start following her instead. And voilà! We struck pay dirt—and I emphasize the dirt. Now, for obvious reasons, I don't want to use these photographs. But I'm willing to, Victor, unless you give me everything I want. Is that understood?'

He nodded. She went back to the chaise and sat down, putting her slippered feet up, arranging the folds of her lavender peignoir as she watched him.

'I want,' she said finally, 'a million dollars a year.' He stared at her. 'And don't tell me you can't afford it,' she went on. 'One advantage of that repulsive new income tax—the *only* advantage!—is that it makes it difficult for husbands to hide what they have from their wives. You've become terribly rich over the years, Victor: my congratulations.' She pulled a slip of paper from the pocket of her gown and looked at it. 'You're on the board of directors of nine major corporations, in each of which you own large amounts of stock. You've been buying real estate in Manhattan and Westchester County for a number of years . . .' She looked up. 'How easy it is when you're the president of a large bank to arrange financing! And all that inside information you hear down on Wall Street!'

'Everything I've done has been straightforward and above-board.'

'I don't doubt it. You're honest, in your way—at least with business. But the point is, you're very rich. My lawyer estimates you're worth between twenty and twenty-five million dollars. So you can afford to pay me a million a year. You see, Victor, I could go after the bank stock, but I decided not to. You've often said you work hard, while all I'm good at is spending, and you're right. So you continue working to make the money. And I'll continue spending because I do it so well. What do you say?'

He didn't answer for a moment.

'What about the children?'

'We can make an arrangement for them to spend a certain amount of time with each of us. I'm willing to be generous on that score.'

'I see.' He stood up, putting his hands in his pockets. 'All right, I agree to your terms.'

'I thought you would. Are you bitter?'

He thought about this.

'No,' he said finally. 'I think after twenty-three years of marriage, all I am is numb. And perhaps a little sad.'

He went to the door to unlock it.

"Victor.'

He turned to look at her.

'What?'

'Do you hate me?'

'Of course not. As furious as I've been at you, I could never hate you. Now that it's all over, I feel sorry for you.'

She stiffened.

'*Sorry?* Why?'

'Because I think I know what you're going to become.'

He walked out of the room for the last time, closing the door behind him. Lucille stared at the door, amazed at the fact that suddenly she wanted him to come back.

As he walked down the elegant curved stair with its beautiful wrought-iron balustrade, he thought of the children. Lorna could probably cope with the divorce: she was old enough and a level-headed girl. And Drew, though the youngest, could probably cope also. Drew was wild and a bit of a showoff, but basically he was tough. The divorce might throw him for a while, but he would quickly adjust. How proud he was of his son, despite his outrage at the speedboat caper. The greatest hope of his life was that someday Drew would succeed him at the bank, but he was wise enough not to try to push him into it. Time would mature Drew.

But Barbara worried him. This shyest of his children, who seemed so happy in her world of books, how would she react to the divorce? He decided he had to tell her immediately, and as gently as possible.

He found her in the downstairs library, reading a letter. When he came in the paneled room, she looked up and said, 'I got a letter from Morris David! He writes as funny as he talks, and his spelling!'

'This isn't your first letter, is it? ' said her father, sitting next to her on the sofa.

'Oh no, we've been writing like mad to each other. He's so interesting . . . You know, I was never particularly interested in movies, but he's made me be. It must be fascinating watching them make one.'

'Would you like to see one being made?' he asked.

'Oh yes!'

'So would I. I've been thinking about making a trip to California next month. Would you like to come with me?'

Her excitement was genuine.

'Very much!'

'Then we'll do it.'

'Oh Daddy, that's wonderful! And I've always wanted to see California. You know, it seems like the other side of the world, but it's really not *that* far away, is it? And it will be fun on the train . . .'

'Barbara,' he interrupted, 'I have something very serious to tell you.'

His tone made her apprehensive.

'You're not . . . sick or anything?'

'No, thank God. But it's something that's going to affect all of you. You know I love you very much and would never want to hurt you. However, I'm afraid this may hurt.' He paused, then took her hand. 'Your mother and I are getting divorced.'

She frowned, but otherwise didn't react.

'You know,' he went on, 'that we've had fights over the

241

years. I won't say anything about your mother, because I want you always to love her. But I want you to love me, too. And I'll admit that I'm a lot at fault in this.'

'Was it that Miss Lombardini?' she asked quietly.

'Well, that was part of it, certainly. You know, marriage is an odd institution, though the human race doesn't seem capable of dreaming up a better way of raising children. But it can't work without trust. I lost your mother's trust, and, in my defense, I'll add that she lost mine. At any rate, what was once beautiful has turned ugly, and I think that now it's really better for all of us if we leave each other. Will you forgive me for being such a bad father?'

She leaned over to hug him.

'You're a *wonderful* father,' she said. 'And there's nothing to forgive you for, at least as far as I'm concerned. No matter what you do, I'll always adore you.'

'Thank you,' he said, suddenly terribly moved by the loss of his past. 'That's the nicest thing you could have said.'

'But it's true. And you're starting to cry . . . !'

She pulled a handkerchief from his jacket pocket and wiped his eyes for him.

'We Italians always cry,' he said, trying to make a joke out of it, 'when we lose something or someone . . .' He looked at his daughter sadly. 'I loved her so much once. I don't suppose I'll ever love anyone again as much as I once loved your mother.'

'Oh Daddy,' she whispered, 'I'm so sorry . . .'

Again she hugged him. For a long time they sat on the sofa together as the sun set over Fifth Avenue.

CHAPTER 25

To Captain Count Ernst von Ritter of the Württemberg Mountain Battalion, the sight was unforgettable: the Italian lieutenant sitting on the ground weeping as his men surrounded him, weapons at their feet, hands in the air, shouting *'Eviva Germania! Eviva Germania!'* As elated as he was by the sweeping German-Austrian victory that October day in 1917, the young German officer couldn't help but feel a pang of pity for his defeated Italian opponent. The Italians had been routed. Soldiers like these were throwing down their arms, embracing their enemies, in some cases killing their own officers if they tried to stop them from surrendering. For almost two years, the Italians and Austro-German forces had been deadlocked along a thirty-mile front stretching north and south along the Isonzo River in the pre-Alpine remoteness of northeastern Italy. A total of eleven battles had been fought, the Italians gaining a few miles here, losing them there, in a struggle for territory that had become essentially meaningless to the men on both sides. Meanwhile the loss of life had been staggering, if not appalling. In the Tenth Battle alone, for instance, begun the previous May, the Italians had lost 157,000 men compared with 75,000 on the Austrian side. This wasn't war, it was slaughter. In the Eleventh Battle, fought the previous month, the Italians had driven the Austrians back some five miles, again suffering twice the casualties of the opposite side. But this, the Twelfth Battle of the Isonzo, which was to be known as the Battle of Caporetto after a village with that name on the Isonzo River, was a devastating defeat for the Italians. Captain von Ritter, sent with German reinforcements to bolster the Austrians after the Eleventh Battle, had heard that those Italians who were not giving up were fleeing east to the Piave River. If this were true, it meant the Austro-German forces might be able to capture Venice.

Von Ritter's men quickly rounded up the rain-soaked Italians as the captain sloshed through the mud toward the Italian lieutenant. In the distance the Austro-German artillery rumbled, its booms echoing through the valleys and between the hills. Occasionally the chatter of Italian machine guns answered back. Von Ritter looked down at the man, whose uniform was filthy. Now he spoke in the excellent Italian he had learned as a child when his parents took him to Capri to spend the winters.

'My name is Captain Count Ernst von Ritter. I extend my sympathy to you.'

The lieutenant looked up. He hadn't shaved in days, and his eyes were bloodshot from fatigue. The blond German officer executed a snappy salute. The Italian returned it in a half-hearted manner.

'I'm Lieutenant Fausto Spada,' he muttered as the rain ran off his nose.

'You will please come with me, Lieutenant Spada.'

Fausto slowly got to his feet. He thought his world had come to an end.

During the course of the day, von Ritter's company captured almost two thousand more prisoners, although 'captured' is hardly the word, since the Italians were stampeding into the arms of the Germans. It was an embarrassment of riches. Von Ritter didn't have the food or facilities for that many prisoners. He knew by a message from his fellow officer in the Württemberg Battalion, Captain Erwin Rommel, that Rommel's problem was even worse: he claimed to have taken in nine thousand Italians. Von Ritter decided to improvise through the night and in the morning try to march his prisoners to the battalion headquarters and turn them over to the commanding officer, Major Sprosser. Meanwhile the Italians would have to stay cold, wet and hungry, although their captors were not much better off, being too far in advance of their line to have shelter or anything more than minimal rations. Winner and loser alike sat in the endless rain, huddled against the Alpine winds and dreaming that perhaps this defeat would mean the end of the war.

'Cigarette?' asked von Ritter, coming up to Fausto who was sitting on the ground, his back against the trunk of a tree. He eyed the handsome gold case.

'Thanks.'

The two officers lit their cigarettes with difficulty, then von Ritter sat down next to him, cupping his cigarette to protect it from the rain.

'It's not been a good day for Italians,' said von Ritter.

Fausto said nothing.

'I regret I can't provide some food for your men,' the German went on, 'but as you can see, we're really not prepared to handle this kind of situation.'

'The glorious Italian Army,' said Fausto with naked bitterness. 'I've never seen my men move so fast as today, when they stumbled over themselves giving up to you.'

'I think you're being a little harsh, Lieutenant. Your army has fought bravely, considering your lack of artillery.'

'That's kind of you, Captain, but the fact is, we Italians are good soldiers only in spurts. I've seen it too often: we can be as brave as Cossacks for about fifteen minutes, then we get bored with it and want some pasta and a woman. I suppose that's why we're doomed to be a second-rate nation.'

'You were first-rate two thousand years ago.'

'We lost something along the way. Maybe it was leadership. Our politicians are cretins, and our generals belong in an asylum. In a way, I can't blame my men for quitting. What's the point of getting killed for General Numbskull? Not to mention our pint-sized king.' He flipped his cigarette in a puddle. 'You speak excellent Italian, Captain.'

'Thank you. My parents used to rent a villa on Capri in the winters. Under the present circumstances I suppose it's ridiculous to say this, but I love Italy.'

'So do I, though right now it's rather difficult to.'

'Some Cognac?' Von Ritter pulled a flask from his hip pocket and unscrewed the top. 'It's Martell. Germany may destroy France, but it's only to get our hands on her vineyards.'

'Thanks.'

Fausto took a swig, then leaned back against the tree trunk. 'I needed that,' he said, giving the flask back to von Ritter, who also took a swig.

'Are you related to the late socialist, Franco Spada?'

'He was my father.'

'I thought I recognized your name. It's too bad your father was killed. From everything I hear, the end result of this damned war is going to be socialism for all of us, if not communism. Your father had good vision—better than the Kaiser's.'

'Perhaps. I didn't agree with him politically.'

'Oh? Then you're not a socialist?'

'It's a pipe dream.'

Von Ritter studied him a moment.

'We probably have mutual friends in Rome,' he said, mentioning a few aristocratic names.

'Yes, I know them,' said Fausto.

'If anything's to be saved of Europe, it's going to be up to men like you and me to do it.'

Fausto's eyes were closed.

'Perhaps.'

'Men of our class.'

The endless drip of rain.

'I've put a light guard on the prisoners,' von Ritter continued. 'Not only do I not have the manpower to guard them properly, but they don't want to escape anyway. So it's certainly possible that if one of them *did* want to escape tonight, he'd probably have an excellent chance of getting away with it. Well, I can see you're exhausted. I'll let you sleep. Good night, Lieutenant.'

He got to his feet. Fausto had opened his eyes and was staring at him.

'They say,' said von Ritter, 'that in Moscow, Lenin's winning. They say that on the walls in Milan and Turin, they've painted posters saying "Viva Lenin." The same thing's happening in Germany. It's not only *your* political leaders, Lieutenant, who are fools. Good night.' He smiled. 'And bon voyage.'

He walked away through the rain. Fausto watched him, his heart pumping with a new excitement that erased his exhaustion. Von Ritter stopped a moment to say something to the guard stationed a few meters away. The guard saluted, and von Ritter walked on. The guard turned his back on Fausto, leaned against a tree and let his rifle go slack.

Fausto looked around. He was at the edge of the encampment, and the next nearest guard was twenty meters away. He, too, was facing the mass of prisoners who were squatting in the mud, most of them asleep. Was he dreaming, or had von Ritter invited him to escape? Or was it a trick? But that made no sense . . .

He got to his feet, watching the guard. He kept his back to him. If Fausto walked south, he would eventually reach the Adriatic, assuming he didn't encounter enemy patrols. From there he could hire a boat to take him to Venice . . .

Von Ritter had opened the cell door! Of all the ironies of this crazy war, this was the craziest. As Fausto walked away from the camp, it was all he could do to stop from laughing out loud.

Shortly after the outbreak of the war, Princess Sylvia had volunteered to the Italian Government to turn her palazzo on the Corso into a hospital for wounded soldiers. The government, hard pressed for adequate facilities to treat the swelling number of casualties, readily agreed, particularly since the Princess said she would pay for the equipment out of her own funds. One hundred and fifty beds were brought into the ancient building, one hundred of them going into the huge marble gallery. Meanwhile the Princess put out an appeal for volunteer nurses to help the professionals she hired, and the response was gratifying: Fifty Roman women, ranging in age from eighteen to sixty, signed on, and society women found themselves emptying bedpans and mopping floors alongside housewives, dental assistants and secretaries. Amid the appalling confusion, inefficiency and corruption of the Italian war effort, Princess Sylvia's hospital was an exceptional example of something that actually worked.

One afternoon early in November, she was sitting in the entrance hall rolling bandages with three other women when the front door opened and a young officer appeared.

'Fausto!' she exclaimed, dropping her bandages.

'Momma!' His arms were spread. She got up and ran across the floor to him. As they hugged and laughed and kissed, she said, 'You're not hurt? You're all right?'

'I'm fine—well, a little underweight—and the Army's given me a month's leave after my heroic escape from the Huns!'

'Then you *were* captured?'

'Yes, but they couldn't hold Fausto Spada. I killed ten of them with my bare hands, stole an airplane and flew over the lines to freedom!'

'You're lying.'

'Well, a little. It was interesting—I'll tell you later what happened. How's the hospital?'

He had smelled the disinfectant when he came in the door. Now he looked down the long gallery, where the beds lined the walls. When he remembered the many festive balls that had been held in the elegant room, the sight of the silent patients, some sitting up, others asleep, was depressing.

'Every bed is occupied,' said his mother. 'And there's a waiting list. Oh Fausto, there's so much suffering. *So* much.'

He looked at her face and saw the fatigue.

'And you?' he asked. 'Are you all right? You look tired.'

'I'm exhausted, but I manage.'

'How's Tony?'

'He's been a great help. He'll be so thrilled to know you're home.'

Fausto looked over her shoulder at the table where the three other nurses were still rolling bandages, watching the reunion of mother and son. He noticed one nurse in particular.

'Momma,' he said softly, 'who's that? The pretty one on the left?'

His mother turned to look.

'Oh, that's Nanda Montecatini, the daughter of Paolo Montecatini. You know, the jeweler. She's such a sweet girl.' She looked at her son. 'I suppose you want me to introduce you?'

'I wouldn't mind.'

'She's Jewish, you know. Or half-Jewish on her father's side. Her mother's a Catholic.'

'Well, I'm half-atheist on my father's side. We should make an interesting couple.'

His mother led him across the hall to the table.

'Nanda, dear, this is my son, Fausto. He asked to be introduced.'

Fausto took the girl's hand and kissed it as his eyes took in her dark-brown hair and large, brown eyes.

'Welcome home, Lieutenant,' she said.

'Thank you, Signorina,' was all he said, but his thoughts were written all over his face. When it came to women, subtlety was not Fausto's long suit.

His mother led him down the gallery, and the eyes of the wounded followed him. Death was in the ancient hall: Fausto could almost feel it. Amputees, victims of gassing; there was one man half of whose face had been obliterated by a mortar fragment and whose single remaining eye, an island of agonized intelligence in a sea of bandages, looked at him with envy and sadness and pain . . . Princess Sylvia said a few words to each of them as she passed their beds, but most were too numb or depressed to say much in reply. They were almost at the end of the gallery when she stopped at the foot of a bed.

'This is an American,' she whispered. 'He volunteered to drive an ambulance, and last month he got gassed. He lost his sight, but we think he has a fair chance of regaining it. Tony comes every day and talks to him and prays for him. His name is Johnson.' She came up to the side of the bed and leaned over the young man with the bandage over his eyes. 'Mr. Johnson,' she said in English, 'Tony's brother is here. Would you like to meet him?'

She signaled to Fausto, who came up beside her.

'Mr. Johnson's from New York City,' said the Princess.

'I have cousins in New York,' said Fausto, looking down at the blond young man who was holding up his hand. At first, Fausto thought he wanted to shake hands. But his mother said, 'He wants to feel your face.'

Fausto leaned down as Johnson's fingers explored his eyes, his nose, his mouth.

'You must look like Father Spada,' the young man said finally.

'We're twins,' said Fausto, straightening.

'He's a wonderful person,' said Johnson. 'A swell person.'

'And he thinks the same of you,' said Princess Sylvia. 'Can we get anything for you?'

The New Yorker forced a smile.

'How about a new set of eyes?'

'We think your old ones are going to be fine soon.'

She smoothed his hair with her hands. Then she and Fausto went to the end of the gallery and upstairs to her private apartment. When they were alone, she sat down and was silent. Then she looked at her son and said, 'Most of them are so brave. They're all frightened, and some of them are bad-tempered and complain a lot . . . But most of them are brave. What a stupid mistake this horrible war is. But at least you're home.'

He came to her. She put her arm around him and hugged him. 'I was so worried. The government's so confused, they didn't know what had happened to you.'

He pulled up a chair and sat next to her. 'This German captain —von Ritter was his name—he captured me and my men, but then he let me go! It was fantastic. He told me people like him and me were the only ones to save Europe, then he more or less invited me to escape! So I just walked away. Have you ever heard of anything so incredible? It must mean that the Germans are getting scared.'

'Oh, I think they are.' She closed her eyes a moment.

'Are you all right?' asked Fausto.

'I'm just tired. I think I'll take a nap, then we'll have dinner and you can tell me all about it.'

He helped her to a couch, and she lay down on it. He kissed her and she smoothed his cheek.

'I'm *so* glad you're home,' she said. Then she closed her eyes and added, 'It's all changing. Everything is changing . . .'

He held her hand until she fell asleep. With something of a shock, he realized his mother was getting old.

'Hello, Father,' said Eddie Johnson, the blind American ambulance driver.

'Hello, Eddie,' said Father Antonio Spada, sitting down on the wooden chair next to Eddie's bed. 'How are you feeling today?'

'Oh, about the same. Say, I met your brother an hour ago. I didn't know you had a twin. Your mother introduced him to me.'

'Yes, I'm looking forward to seeing Fausto. We were afraid he might have been killed. I'm going upstairs to see him in a minute, but I wanted to see how you are first. I've been praying for you, Eddie. Every night I pray for you.'

The American grinned.

'With the Vatican on my side, I've *got* to get my sight back, right?'

'Right,' smiled Tony, looking down the corridor at the nurse in the entrance hall and fighting back the hideous thoughts in his mind. 'I'm going to say a little prayer for you now, Eddie.'

'Make it a big one. I've got plenty of time. But are you sure Catholic prayers work for Protestants?'

'God is the father of us all, Eddie.'

'Well anyway, I don't have to close my eyes to pray.'

'Oh Father,' Tony said, 'we beseech Thee to grant our fervent wish . . .' Not *that* wish, he thought. Get her out of my mind! Oh God, do you know? Do you see into my mind, my heart? '. . . that Thy son, Edward, be granted the blessed gift of sight. He has been so brave to come to Italy to help us in this war, and it is doubly hard for us Italians to know that this good American has been wounded. So Father, listen to our prayers and give Edward back the use of his eyes. We ask it in Thy holy name. Amen.'

'Amen,' said Eddie. 'Father, thank you.'

'Eddie, I know you're going to be all right. I *know* it.'

'Thank God for you. I don't know if I could have made it this far without your help. I get awfully scared here, in the dark. But knowing you care makes all the difference.'

'I care, Eddie. Very deeply.'

Dear God, the nurse! he thought. I mustn't look at her. I *mustn't* . . . But he was looking at her with his excellent eyes.

The bronze plaque on the shop in the via Condotti read 'P. Montecatini. Gioielliere.' The portly young man in the well-cut suit glanced for a moment at the window next to the door where a diamond-and-ruby bracelet dangled from the wrist of a wax arm. Then the man went into the jewelry store. Paolo Montecatini was known to be the best jeweler in Rome, and his store reflected his status: the rock-crystal chandeliers, the rich carpet, the gilt chairs, the attendants in cutaways, all whispered 'grand luxe.' The display cases held some of the most beautiful jewelry in Italy, fashioned by craftsmen who had worked for Paolo in some instances for twenty years, ever since he went into business for himself after an apprenticeship in the diamond markets of Amsterdam and five years as a salesman for Cartier in Paris. Fluent in six languages, suave, Paolo knew how to handle the rich and, in selling to them, had become rich himself.

The young man presented his card to one of the salesmen and asked to see Signor Montecatini. A few minutes later, Paolo appeared in the main salesroom. He was medium height, comfortably overweight, impeccably dressed in a cutaway and striped pants with a blue polka-dot bowtie around his wing collar —his trademark. A balding pate, a gray Vandyke and a pince-nez polished off his lapidary urbanity. Now he shook the young man's hand, inclining his head in a slight bow.

'Signor Bassano, I'm delighted to meet you. Can I be of service?'

'It's rather confidential . . .'

'Shall we go in my office?'

He conducted Bassano into his handsomely furnished office, which was hung with autographed photos of celebrity customers, the most prominent being the Queen of Italy, who had bought a diamond necklace from him in 1910. He held a chair for Bassano, then went around his cluttered desk and sat down.

'Now, sir.'

The young man pulled an envelope from his pocket and handed it to the jeweler.

'As you can see from this letter, Signor Montecatini, I am one of the secretaries to the Minister of the Interior, Signor Picchiatelli. The Minister is interested in buying an important piece of jewelry for his wife—it's their tenth anniversary. However, during wartime, the Minister feels it would not be judicious for him to be seen entering a luxury establishment such as your own, if you understand what I mean.'

'Ah yes, of course.'

'Consequently, he sent me in his place. If you could put together a selection of stones, I could take it to the Minister —with one of your men, of course. He is prepared to make a decision this afternoon. The Minister is interested in diamonds —first quality, of course. I believe the phrase is "blue river"?'

'Yes.'

'The Minister wishes to pay in pounds sterling and is willing to go as high as twenty thousand pounds.'

'I will be only too happy to accommodate the Minister, and I believe we will be able to show him some of the finest quality stones in Europe. Did he specify any preference as to cut?'

'The Minister prefers marquise.'

'If you will excuse me a moment, Signor.'

Paolo got up and left the office. In his outer office, he said to his secretary, 'Phone the Ministry of the Interior. Check if the Minister has a secretary with this name.' He gave her Bassano's card, then went to the vault to select a tray of stones. Paolo had no doubt Bassano was the genuine article. He knew that Italy was entirely dependent on England for coal, that the government had been paying millions for adequate supplies, and that the man in charge of the purchases was Signor Picchiatelli, the Minister of the Interior. Undoubtedly Signor Picchiatelli was receiving kickbacks from the English suppliers, or perhaps he was involved in arbitrage on the sly with the huge funds at his disposal: either way, he must have a large amount of pounds sterling he was eager to convert into portable gemstones. The stone he would buy would undoubtedly end up in a safety-deposit box, perhaps in Switzerland. The chances of it ending up on his wife's finger were minimal.

Paolo Montecatini had sold to government ministers before. He knew this was the way of the Italian world. As an Italian, Paolo Montecatini thought the corruption was deplorable. But as a jeweler, he wasn't about to lose the business.

They had eaten dinner at a small restaurant on the Piazza del Popolo. Nanda Montecantini had been charmed by Fausto; certainly nothing in his conversation hinted of the terrible reputation he had around Rome. Her mother had been shocked when he asked Nanda to dinner and had insisted on chaperoning them. Nanda had staged a scene, stating that chaperones were old-fashioned. Her father, Paolo, obviously eager to nourish a possible union with a son of Princess Sylvia, had sided with Nanda, so she had been allowed to go out with Fausto unescorted. She was enormously attracted to this superb animal of a man, but she was strictly brought up. And now, as he put his arm around her in the back seat of the taxi, she began to wonder if her mother hadn't been right after all.

She let him kiss her. But when his hand slipped down her belly and began massaging her vulva, she became panicked.

'Don't,' she whispered.

'Shut up.'

'Fausto, please—!'

The taxi driver, hearing the noise, turned around.

'Hey,' he said, 'not in *my* taxi!'

'Keep driving,' said Fausto.

'But *where?* You don't give me no address?'

'Just keep driving. You'll get a good tip.'

The driver shrugged and obeyed.

Nanda realized the unthinkable was happening to her: he intended to rape her in the taxi. Both his hands were under her skirts tugging at her underwear. She started beating his head with both fists, but it did no good. He was climbing on top of her now, awkwardly straddling her. She brought her knee up hard, and he howled with pain. She watched as he collapsed on the floor of the cab, holding his groin and moaning.

'Goddam, I don't want no murders in my cab!' shouted the driver. 'You can fuck her, okay, but don't *kill* her!'

'Take me home,' said Nanda, amazed at her coolness. 'Number sixteen viale Bruno.'

Fausto was crawling back in his seat.

'You little bitch,' he whispered. 'I'll remember this.'

'You're disgusting,' she whispered back. 'You're just like they say: a pig. I never want to see you again.'

Fausto huddled in the corner of the cab, still rubbing his aching genitals, eyeing her, wanting her more than ever. He wasn't ashamed of his behavior, just furious at his miscalculation. He had been told Jewish girls loved to fuck. Obviously he had been told wrong.

'I apologize,' he said. 'It won't happen again.'

She said nothing. She was sitting straight, clutching her chinchilla wrap, staring out the window.

'Will you have dinner with me tomorrow night?' he asked.

She didn't answer.

'I'll pick you up at seven.'

Silence.

'I'll take you to the Grand, so wear your best dress.'

She turned on him furiously.

'If you have the *nerve* to come to my house, you'll have to break down the door to get in!'

'All right,' he grinned, 'I'll break the door.'

She simmered, thinking that after all there had been something terribly exciting about his attack on her. Disgusting, insulting, degrading, true; but . . .

'You won't have to break down the door,' she said finally. Then she turned back to the window, hating herself for giving in to what she knew was the most primitive part of her personality. But also, unfortunately, the most powerful . . .

'Bless me, Father, for I have sinned,' said Father Antonio Spada, sitting tensely in the dark confessional of the Sistine Chapel. Through the grill he could dimly see the hawkish profile of Cardinal dell'Acqua. After nights of feverish agony in his tiny room in the Vatican Palace, he had requested His Eminence to take his confession, which the old man had agreed to do, although with a certain confusion. As he had promised Princess Sylvia seven years before, the Cardinal had taken Tony under his wing after the slim young man had finished his seminary training and taken his holy orders. With ill-disguised favoritism, the Cardinal had brought Tony on to his staff, giving him a wide variety of tasks, all of which he had performed well, if not brilliantly. There had been no hint of trouble, at least as far as the Cardinal knew. And now, the request for him to hear confession.

The Cardinal fingered his scapular and waited.

'I have had lustful thoughts,' Tony said finally. 'I have prayed and struggled to purge them from my mind, but they are too strong for me.'

'We are all subjected to these thoughts at times,' soothed the Cardinal, wondering who in the world was tempting Tony. 'They are the temptations of the Devil. As long as we do not give in to them . . .'

'But I *have* to give in to them or I'll go crazy!'

The outburst shocked the aged prelate. He was further shocked by the sound of sobs: Tony was falling to pieces next to him in the ancient confessional. His Eminence waited until the emotional storm had passed.

'Is the girl someone close to your family?' asked the Cardinal.

'No. Well, yes, in a way . . . She's a nurse working at Mother's hospital. Her name is Nanda Montecatini. I don't know why, but . . .' There was another burst of strangled sobs. '. . . I've fallen in love with her. And the worst part is, Fausto is taking her out . . . I'm so jealous, so jealous . . .'

'Have you had these temptations before?' asked the Cardinal, treading warily through the snakepit of his protégé's libido.

'Yes, I've been attracted to women before, but it's never been like this. I can't . . . I can't handle it. Tell me what to do, please . . . Every time I see her, I want to touch her . . .'

'Then you must not see her again.'

'No! Oh no, I have to . . . I can't lose her . . .'

'Tony, pull yourself together!' said His Eminence with unusual asperity. 'You're a priest, a soldier in Christ's Army!

Don't think there haven't been other priests like you before, and there'll be more like you later. Have you told anyone else about this?'

'No, of course not . . .'

'Thank heaven! And thank heaven you had the sense to come to *me*. You know you have a brilliant career ahead of you in the Church, and after all I've done to nourish that career, I'm not going to allow you to ruin it by . . . by *that*. You would bring shame and scandal on the Mother Church, on your family, on me . . .'

'But I want her! I love her!'

'I don't want to hear about it. I'll arrange to have you sent to a retreat . . .'

'No! I won't go! I'll leave the Church!'

'You'll do no such thing. Has she given you any sign that she reciprocrates your love?'

'No. I've never even spoken to her.'

'Then there's still hope. Listen to me, Tony: you must conquer this devil inside you. It can be done: it's been done by thousands of others before you. You must pray to God to give you the strength. It may be the greatest test of character in your life . . .'

'I'm not sure I *want* to conquer it!' he interrupted. 'I may have made a horrible mistake entering the Church. You remember I told you I decided to become a priest after Fausto took me to La Rosina's. The reason was, I loved it! I loved being with the woman! I wanted to do it over and over again! It frightened me so much, I decided to become a priest the next morning before I lost the Faith, but now . . . now I'm not sure . . .'

'Don't say these things! You're embracing this devil, rather than fighting it.'

'Yes,' whispered Tony, 'I want to embrace it.'

'There's too much at stake! Too much . . . Listen, Tony: you know the Church is in trouble. It's not only this interminable, infernal fight with the Italian Government, it's the war, it's modern times . . . you know the Church is nearly bankrupt. We *need* men like you. Surely you understand the Holy Roman Church is more important than your moonstruck crush on the Montecatini girl?'

'*Is* it?' was the quiet response.

'That attitude is not worthy of you. I want you to go back to your room and stay there until I send for you. You will fast and pray for twenty-four hours. By then, I will have made the necessary arrangements. Do you agree to do this?'

A long silence. Finally: 'Yes.'

'When you have come back to your senses, I will grant you absolution. Until then, your immortal soul is in grave peril. But you *will* conquer this! Now, go.'

Tony emerged from the confessional and looked up at the glorious ceiling of the Sistine Chapel. Tears blurred his vision as he stared at Michelangelo's rendition of God. Then he looked at Eve in the Garden. He had looked at Eve many times, secretly ogling her beauty. Now he tried to concentrate on God.

But his eyes kept creeping back to Eve.

'You sold me a fake!' roared the Minister of the Interior, and when Baldo Picchiatelli roared, it was a blast from hell. 'Look at it! It's not even a good paste! My wife wore it to a dinner party last night, and when Signor Bulgari saw it, he almost laughed! I was mortified—*me*, a Minister of the Crown! Look at it!'

He threw the dimond ring on the Oriental rug covering the floor of his office in the Palazzo dei Conservatori overlooking the Piazza del Campidoglio. Paolo Montecatini, his face livid, leaned down and picked up the ten-carat marquise diamond. He looked at it, then placed it on Picchiatelli's desk.

'This is not the ring I sold you,' he said. 'This is paste. I sold you a diamond of the first quality.'

'Liar! I paid you twenty-three thousand pounds sterling for junk! I want my money back or by God, Montecatini, I'll close down your shop and run you out of Italy!'

Paolo Montecatini had nerves of steel, which was fortunate because he knew Picchiatelli's threat was no bluff.

'May I suggest to the Minister that there are several explanations to what has happened? First, that the Minister has been robbed—'

'Impossible. The ring has been in my safe at home, and my house is guarded round the clock.'

'Then possibly someone on your staff, or perhaps one of your servants, has managed to switch the ring . . .'

'I tell you, it's impossible! The only possible answer is that you swindled me, you goddam Kike!'

'There is another possibility,' said Paolo, biting his words. *'You're* swindling *me!'*

The six-foot-three, two-hundred-and-ninety-pound Minister almost visibly swelled with rage.

'You dare accuse *me?* I have half a mind to arrest you on the spot . . .'

'May I suggest that the Minister would be ill-advised to do

anything of the sort? Don't you think I see through this? Don't you think I know *why* you insisted on paying me in pounds sterling? It was odd how there was coal dust on those banknotes.'

'What are you implying?' The Minister sounded more cautious.

'That you've been taking kickbacks when you buy coal from the English.' The accusation was a gamble, but the look on Picchiatelli's face made it obvious that Paolo had gambled on a winning ticket. 'And that you want to convert your cash to jewelry. Now, Signor Picchiatelli, I do not object to greedy politicians. I'm willing to admit I'm ready to make a profit off greedy politicians by selling them jewelry as I did with you and many others. But when the politicians get so greedy that they try and swindle *me* by buying good stones and then claiming I sold them paste, then, Minister, I'm ready to take the whole story to the newspapers. One newspaper in particular: *Libertà.*'

'That piece of junk,' snorted Picchiatelli. 'It has no influence anymore.'

'It has influence *enough*. My daughter is an intimate friend of Fausto Spada, whose mother owns the paper. If you arrest me, Fausto will have the story in *Libertà* the next morning. Think about it, Minister. Of course,' and he smiled, 'if this is all a practical joke . . .'

The Minister studied him a while. Then he, too, smiled.

'You're a gutsy man, Paolo. I knew you were clever, but I didn't know you had balls as well. Yes, this was all a practical joke.'

'A not very funny one.'

Picchiatelli shrugged as he got to his feet.

'Ministers of the Crown are not known for their humor. Unfortunately, they are known for their greed. Perhaps mine got a little carried away . . .'

He came around the desk and picked up the paste-diamond ring.

'This cost me four thousand lire. I'll keep it as a souvenir. And perhaps a moral lesson . . .' He put the ring in his pocket and looked at Paolo. 'You must know a lot of interesting secrets, my friend.'

'Fortunately, discretion in my business is a necessity, not a luxury.'

'Yes, I see what you mean. If you became indiscreet, Rome might become a very dangerous place for you.'

'Is that a threat?'

'Merely an observation. So . . .' he put his hand on his shoulder to guide him to the door, '. . . your daughter is intimate with Fausto Spada? If she marries him, it would be a feather in your cap, eh?'

'It would be an interesting combination: a son of Princess Sylvia marrying, as you put it, a Kike.'

The Minister shrugged.

'My apologies. You may not believe this, but I really am not anti-Semitic.'

'Minister, may I humbly suggest that's what everyone says —until they call us Kikes. Good afternoon.'

Giving an elegant little bow, he left the office. The Minister of the Interior closed the door, then returned to his desk. He pulled the paste diamond from his pocket and looked at it. 'Shit,' he mumbled. He threw it in a wastepaper basket and went back to work.

On the northbound train to Milan, Fausto sat by the rain-streaked window and thought about love and war and his future. After a month's leave, he was rested and heavier; he had been ordered to rejoin his commanding officer, who had moved to Milan after the great retreat of the Italian Army to the Piave River. Fausto wasn't exactly burning to get back in the war, particularly after his grand disillusion at Caporetto. But orders were orders.

He thought about Nanda Montecatini, whom he had about made up his mind to propose to. Being the son of Princess Sylvia and coheir with Tony to a sizable fortune, he knew he could have the pick of the crop when it came to choosing a bride. Certainly he could do better socially than Nanda. But the beautiful Jewess excited him sensually in a way few of the pallid Roman debutantes had ever come close to. After his disastrous initial miscalculation in the taxi, which he admitted was a stupid error, he had behaved more gently with her, and in their kissing and petting he had detected an awakening sensuality in her that excited him. This was hardly the rapture of romantic love, but Fausto wasn't all that interested in love, sex being more than enough for him. In all other categories, Nanda struck him as well suited to be a wife and mother. He was no more nor less anti-Semitic than most of his contemporaries. The papacy had invented the ghetto in the sixteenth century, and anti-Semitism existed in Italy, as was evidenced by the Minister of the Interior who would probably not have tried to swindle Paolo if he hadn't been a Jew. But there was little of the virulent hatred of Jews that existed in Austria, France and Germany. Jews were 'different,' but they were accepted. In Fausto's mind Nanda's Jewishness made her rather exotic. Besides, she had been brought up a Catholic by her mother, and her father's Jewishness was limited to weekly visits to the synagogue, so for all intents and purposes, the Montecatinis were not much different from any other upper-class family.

Then there was Nanda's father, whom Fausto liked enormously. He found Paolo Montecatini one of the most interesting, cultivated and intelligent men he had ever met. Some of the most pleasant hours of his leave had been spent talking to Paolo in the library of his beautifully furnished house on the viale Bruno in the fashionable Parioli section of Rome. Fausto had described to him the rout at Caporetto and found that Paolo shared his frustrations about Italy. The older man told Fausto about some of the more grotesque examples of official venery he had encountered, in particular his experience with Signor Picchiatelli, though he was careful to name no names. He agreed with Fausto that unless some new, virile and uncorrupt political force appeared to clean out the Augean Stable of Italian politics, Italy was doomed to second-rateness, if not worse. Paolo had urged Fausto to take over the moribund *Libertà*, telling him that a newspaper publisher could wield great power. While Fausto agreed with him, he shied away from the life of a publisher. Not only did he not share the socialist ideals *Libertà* had been founded to promote, but running a newspaper struck him as drudgery. Fausto thirsted for action. Even the war, rotten as it had been, was at least exciting.

By the time the train had pulled into the Milan station, marriage to Nanda was looking better and better. He hired a cab to drive him out to Monza, where, in the old royal palace, General Benedetti, his commanding officer, had set up temporary headquarters. By now the rain had tapered off to a drizzle, but Milan still struck him as a soggy, dreary town with little of the color of his beloved Rome. Besides, the traffic was terrible. As the taxi inched through the crowded streets, Fausto thought of Tony. His sudden transfer to a monastic retreat north of Naples the week before had surprised him as well as his mother. Tony hadn't even come around to say good-bye, but had merely written his twin a note wishing him good luck. Fausto sensed something was bothering his brother, but he had no idea what it was.

Suddenly his taxi was brought to a dead stop. Fausto rolled down his window and looked out. Ahead of them, a large crowd gathered, the overflow spilling into the streets to tie up the traffic. They were listening to a stocky man addressing them from the base of a statute of Garibaldi. He gesticulated frequently with his right fist, his left fist at his waist, and though Fausto couldn't hear what he was saying, the repeated cheers of the crowd left little doubt as to his oratorical prowess.

The taxi driver got out and came around the front of the car to lean on the hood and sulk. 'We'll be here for hours,' he said, 'with *that* windbag.'

'Who is it?' asked Fausto.

'The editor of *Popolo d'Italia*. He just got out of the Army, where he was wounded in a trench. Everybody says he's a big war hero, but I say he's a pile of shit.'

'What's his name?'

'Benito Mussolini.'

Fausto got out of the taxi to walk closer and listen. What he heard first impressed him, then excited him. He wondered if he were viewing that new, virile, uncorrupt political force he and Paolo Montecatini had talked about in Rome.

PART V

THE FILMING OF *RUSSIA*

1920

CHAPTER 26

The airplane circled slowly over the Beverly Hills estate as the newsreel cameraman leaned out the open cockpit, grinding his camera to record for posterity the gala scene below. It was a warm January afternoon in 1920, and the King of Comedy, as film producer Morris David had become known in Hollywood, was hosting a reception to commemorate the opening of his enormous Spanish-style house. His wife of eighteen months, Barbara Dexter David, had named the house Casa del Mar after the distant view of the Pacific from the back terrace of the hilltop estate. Gathered around the red-tile-roofed mansion, milling about on the sodded lawn around the sixty-foot pool or going into the gaily striped marquee for champagne Morris had stockpiled to beat the legalization of Prohibition, which had occurred two days before, was the royalty of Hollywood. From the plane they looked like ants, but on the silver screens around the world they were giants, gods and goddesses to millions of people whose dollars, pounds, francs, marks, lire and rupees had in ten years transformed the sleepy, sunbaked town of Holly-wood—once known for its citrus fruit—into the world capital of fantasy. Charlie Chaplin was there, as were Buster Keaton, Nazimova, Rod La Rocque, D. W. Griffith, Mae Busch, Mack Sennett, Constance Talmadge, Barbara La Marr, and the most popular couple in the world, Douglas Fairbanks and Mary Pickford. Also present was a sprinkling of titled Europeans, former gods and goddesses who had been ousted from their ancient positions of veneration by the recent bloody war, by revolution, by public disenchantment and, most tellingly, by their fellow guests the movie stars, whose physical beauty and talent were more impressive to the public than coats of arms. But not to Barbara David's mother, Lady Pembroke, who was also at the party. The former Lucille Dexter had the year before married ('bought,' according to her family) the youngest son of a hard-up British earl. Lord Archibald Pembroke, at twenty-seven, was, to put it charitably, rather younger than his wife. To put it factually he was twenty-seven years younger than Lucille, but his father's title dated from the seventeenth century, and that was what counted with the new Lady Pembroke. Lucille was mildly interested in the movie stars around her, and she was impressed by her son-in-law's estate (though secretly she thought it was 'gaudy'); but as a member by marriage of the British aristocracy, she considered herself infinitely superior to 'movies,' as picture people were still contemptuously referred to by native Los Angelenos, no matter how famous they were. Her husband, on the other hand, was overwhelmed by the stars, in particular Barbara La Marr, whose slumberous, dark-haired beauty held his pale-blue, bloodshot eyes riveted to her. Archie, as he had been dubbed by Lucille's children, thought the whole show was 'r-r-r-ripping,' for Archie came fully equipped not only with stringy, blond aristocratic good looks but also an aristocratic stammer. Lord Pembroke was also getting as drunk as a lord.

Lorna had also come to California to see her younger sister's grand new house, but Victor had begged off, using work as his excuse. Barbara understood: her father didn't want to run into Lucille. Not that there would have been recriminations or ugliness, but simply that it would stir up painful memories. Victor would be in California later anyway, for he had a fifty percent partnership in Morris's company, David Productions. After the phenomenal success of *Down for the Count*, Morris had produced eight other comedies, all financed by Victor, all equally successful. Morris's success, of which Casa del Mar was the most visible symbol, had swollen Victor's fortune as well. It seemed zany Morris had the magic touch: the public loved his crazy comedies. What the public didn't know was that Morris David was about to announce a new departure for David Productions. But Victor Dexter knew, as did Barbara. And for the first time, Victor had declined to invest in his son-in-law's film. Morris had been furious and raged against Victor's *mishegoss*. It was crazy for him not to invest! How could he, Morris, fail?

Barbara, on the other hand, was not so sure her father was crazy.

At precisely five the orchestra under the striped tent struck a loud chord, the dancers stopped and Morris stepped up to the microphones. 'Ladies and gentlemen—and agents,' he added, getting a laugh, though his mangled English was still a dependable laugh-getter on its own. 'I want to welcome all you beautiful people to my new home. And if you think it looks like a million bucks, believe me, you're right. The bills! *Oy vay!*'

Lady Pembroke's eyebrows went up in patrician disdain, although curiously enough, after she had gotten over her initial shock at having a Jewish son-in-law, Lucille had become rather fascinated by Morris, whose whirlwind energy and ego made him an unclassifiable force of nature. Lord Pembroke giggled and burped. Barbara David sighed. She knew somehow Morris would let the cost of his house 'slip' out. Morris was un-abashedly *nouveau,* and she had given up trying to cure him of his braggadocio. It was part of him, like his mangled English, his zest, his warmth, his zaniness, and his fierce lovemaking. Barbara had grown to love him through his letters, as she had grown to love the picture business. Movies were like Morris: crazy, exciting, fun. If they were also vulgar like Morris, well, life was vulgar.

'I say *my* home,' Morris went on, 'because I'm a conceited *shmuck*. It's also my wife's home, my beautiful *shiksa* wife, Barbara . . . Barbara, darling, where are you? There she is! Come on up, darling, I want to show you off. Can you imagine a beautiful classy dame like this marrying a *klutz* like me? That's the only thing that worries me about her: she's got rotten taste in men.'

'No I don't,' laughed Barbara as she came up to hug him.

'Seriously, folks,' said Morris, 'we all work in a business where love is a product—"Make a love story, make a million," right? Well, I'm here to tell you I believe in love stories, because I'm *living* one. Barbara, darling, I love you. And if that's not enough for you, you got half the house and pool.' At which point he kissed her on the lips as the two hundred guests applauded. Most of them were used to show people's public displays of affection, even though it still embarrassed Barbara, and Lady Pembroke's eyebrows shot up again. Yet the emotion was genuine, even if it was given star billing: Morris did love his beautiful, classy wife and was continuously amazed he had won her. When he released her, he continued: 'You know something? She's smart, too. She's the best script reader in Hollywood, and she don't charge me to do it. And you know what she told me when she read the script of my new moving picture? She said, "Morris, you got a turkey." Isn't that right, darling?'

Barbara managed a game smile, though she was amazed at his bluntness.

'Well,' she said, 'let's say I told you it was a change of pace for you.'

'Sure it's a change of pace! I know it! Who wants to do the same thing all the time? You get stale! So I'm taking this festive occasion to announce to all my friends—both of them . . .' A laugh. '*And* my enemies that David Productions is taking on Goliath: *Drama*. My next movie won't be a comedy, it'll be a tragedy. The greatest tragedy in the history of moving pictures —and, according to my accountant, the greatest tragedy in the history of my pocketbook. Maybe he's right, who knows? Moving pictures is a gamble. *Life* is a gamble! But I got faith in this movie.

'Let me tell you a little story. My parents, God bless their memory, was poor. They were Russian Jews, and I don't have to tell you no one comes poorer, right? Plus, Jews wasn't so popular in Russia. They liked them so much, they killed them. Okay, my parents got out and came to the new world. They struggled hard, so hard they died young. But when I was a kid, they told me stories about Russia, stories I've never forgotten. So, and I don't have to tell you what happened in Russia three years ago, right? The greatest event of this century, maybe? The Tsar's family getting wiped out the way he used to wipe out us Jews? It's got to be one of the greatest stories in the world, right? So, in memory of my parents, and in memory of all the Russian Jews who was killed in the old country—and, I'll admit, in hope of making a buck or two—I'm making the greatest picture of all time, and it's called *Russia!* It will tell the whole thing: the suffering of the poor, the pogroms of the Jews, the corruption of the court—we'll get in a lot of racy scenes—Rasputin, the war, the revolution . . . the whole *megillah!* The budget for the production—listen to this, you won't believe it—is two million dollars! *Two!*' Predictably this brought gasps and applause. Nothing impressed Hollywood like record budgets, and this was a record. The half-dozen reporters invited by Morris's publicity man, Nat Finger, were busy taking notes. 'And,' continued Morris, who was having the time of his life, 'do I got to tell you I've signed the greatest director in moving pictures to make this epic? Do I got to tell you who he is? Who else but the German Genius, the director of that brilliant movie, *Lust* . . . Wilhelm von Gastein! Willie, where are you? Come on up . . .'

A short, paunchy man in a tight-fitting, white double-breasted suit made his way through the applauding crowd to the orchestra platform, where Morris and Barbara embraced him.

'Willie,' said Morris, 'tell them in two words what you think

266

of *Russia*. Maybe three words. Words is cheap, unless you're talking to writers.'

'*Russia*,' said the pompous little man in a leaden Teutonic accent, 'will be a work of genius.'

'There: you got it!' exclaimed Morris. 'If a genius tells you it's a genius, it's got to be a genius, right?'

Wrong, thought Barbara, who had argued fiercely with Morris about Willie von Gasbag, as he was known in picture circles. Barbara thought the German Genius was a pompous fraud. But the intellectual critics all said he was a genius, just as Willie said he was, and for the first time in his life, Morris was paying attention to the newly prestigious critics. It was, in his wife's opinion, a mistake, but Morris had recently shown signs of intellectual pretension. He told her he was tired of *just* making people laugh, he wanted to make them cry, make them think. He wanted to be respected, like D. W. Griffith.

'All right,' he went on, 'I know you're wondering, so who's he got to star? So let me tell you what holds this gigantic epic together: a love story, what else? The heroine is a beautiful Russian grand duchess who's loved by this *shmuck* footman, but of course she spurns him. Comes the revolution, the *shmuck* footman turns out to be a captain of the revolutionary army, except he's really not a Bolshie—we don't want the audience to hate him. So he's against the Tsar, and he's against the Bolshies —who's he for, you're asking? I'm telling you he's for the Grand Duchess Xenia, who he saves from a firing squad, and who will be played by one of Hollywood's loveliest young leading ladies—Laura Kaye!'

Wild cheers and applause as an exceedingly pretty blonde in a white chiffon dress hurried up to the platform and kissed the Davids. Laura Kaye, the daughter of a Nebraska judge, smiled and said into the microphone, 'I just want to say I'm tremendously thrilled to be appearing in Mr. David's epic, and I know it will be an epic success!'

More applause. Then Morris said. 'The footman-turned-revolutionary will be played by a star every American woman dreams about, a man who sums up what we like to think of when we say, "clean-cut, rugged, red-blooded American male." It gives me great pleasure to announce—Rex Armstrong! Rex, come on up . . .'

The applause greeting the former Waldo Radebaugh, the son of an Urbana, Illinois, minister, who had become the leading male sex symbol in the movies, was not quite so enthusiastic as

Laura Kaye's ovation. Morris was looking around. 'So Rex, where are you? You're hiding from me?'

'Look under the bar!' someone shouted, which brought a roar of laughter. Except Morris wasn't amused. 'Is he drunk?' he whispered to Barbara.

'Here I am!' a voice yelled from the edge of the crowd, and everyone turned to look at the Star. 'I'm talking to your sister-in-law, Morris,' Rex continued. 'I just asked her for a date, and she turned me down. *Me,* Rex Armstrong!'

'She's a smart woman,' yelled Morris. 'Lorna, watch out for him. He's worse than the fan magazines say.'

Lorna laughed as Rex left her side to go to the podium. In fact, she had been tempted to accept the actor's invitation. Lorna was not immune to the excitement and glamour of being asked out by Rex Armstrong, and she had to admit he was one of the best-looking men she had ever seen. But Lorna was engaged to a New York doctor named Thompson Randolph. Tommy, as he was called, was a jealous man, and the last thing Lorna needed was to have her fiancé read in the gossip columns that Lorna Dexter had gone out with Rex Armstrong. So, regrettably, she had declined. She told herself that some day, undoubtedly, she would kick herself for not having gone out with America's heart-throb.

'What do you think of Rex?' asked Barbara ten minutes later as she joined her sister. 'Isn't he a dreamboat?'

'Definitely,' said Lorna. 'And I gather from what your guests say he drinks like a fish.'

'Like Moby Dick. And speaking of sots, our new stepdaddy is doing all right in the booze department.'

'You mean Ar-Ar-Archie?' giggled Lorna, looking across the lawn to Lord Pembroke, who was talking to a tall young man. 'He's positively weaving! Who's he talking to?'

'That's a pianist named Carl Maria von Gersdorff. He's visiting some friends of ours, the Palmers.'

'What a funny name.'

'He's Austrian. Want to meet him?'

'I don't think so. This sun mixed with the champagne is giving me a headache. In fact, I'm going inside to lie down for a few minutes. Do you mind?'

'Of course not. Do you want an aspirin?'

'I have some. I'll be down in a while. Your party's a smash.'

'Thanks, darling.'

Lorna kissed her sister, then made her way through the crowd to the terrace and went inside. Casa del Mar's thick walls kept it comfortably cool, and while Lorna marveled at the near-constant sunshine and fabulous air in California, she was glad to get out of it for a while. She went upstairs to the bedroom she was staying in, took two aspirin, then lay down to doze away her headache.

She was awakened a half hour later by music. Not the orchestra on the lawn, though she could hear that faintly in the distance playing a foxtrot. This music was coming from downstairs: beautiful, dreamy music. She sat up and checked her watch. Her headache was gone, and she was ready to rejoin the party. She went to the bathroom to check her face, then left the bedroom and started down the stairs. The piano music seemed like an enchanted barcarolle, limpidly beautiful with an elegant melody that caressed her ears. Reaching the bottom of the stairs, she crossed the tiled entrance hall to look into the two-story living room. Lorna liked the Spanish architecture of her sister's new house—it seemed right in southern California—and the living room, with its great leaded bay window overlooking the pool, its red-velvet Spanish sofas, its big spiral painted-wood Mexican candlesticks on the tile floor, and its elaborately carved wooden balcony over the main entrance, was a reasonable facsimile of a Spanish mission—or, perhaps, a movie set of a Spanish mission. At the end of the room was a Steinway grand, draped with a fringed Spanish shawl. The tall Austrian was playing. No one else was in the room. When he saw Lorna, Carl Maria von Gersdorff stopped playing.

'Please don't stop,' she said, coming into the room. 'That was so beautiful . . . what was it?'

'The "Andante Spianato" of Chopin,' he said, standing up. He had a deep voice.

'I've never heard it before—not that I know much about music. I'm Lorna Dexter, Barbara's sister.'

She had come up to the piano. Now he took her hand and kissed it.

'I'm delighted to meet you. My name is Carl Maria von Gersdorff.'

He spoke with a Viennese accent. He wasn't a very good-looking man, having a long and rather mournful face with a dark moustache. But she liked his eyes. There was humor in them.

'My sister said you were a pianist, but I had no idea you were so good. Do you play for the movies?'

He looked surprised for a moment, then he grinned.

'Yes, that's right. I play on the sets. Mood music!' He sat back down at the piano and struck a minor chord. 'Tragedy!' he proclaimed, hammily 'The tragedy of Mother Russia!' Then he swung into the William Tell Overture. 'The chase! Excitement! The sheriff is after the bandits!' He segued to 'Liebestraume,' and his face became dreamy. 'Passion! Romance! The great love scene! The hero pours out his love to the heroine, who pretends to scorn him . . .' He stopped, looked at her and laughed. 'What trash,' he said. 'What unmitigated trash. Beethoven would get sick to his stomach. He was lucky to have died before movies were invented.'

'I take it you don't like movies?'

'They bore me. They're fairy tales for children. Why do I want to watch a shadow of a man on a screen kiss the heroine? I'd rather kiss her myself. Like Barbara La Marr. I'd give a lot to kiss Barbara La Marr.'

And he grinned.

'Don't you think it's rather hypocritical to attack the movies when you make your living from them?'

'What do you mean?'

'Well, you said you play on the sets . . .'

He sighed as he stood up.

'I see you've never heard of me. Ah well. I'm not Paderewski yet. I don't play for the movies. I'm a concert pianist. I'm out here taking a rest before I give a concert tour in Mexico next week.'

'How stupid of me!' said Lorna, feeling crawly with embarrassment at having mistaken him for a movie player. 'I *have* heard of you. Didn't you give a recital at Carnegie Hall recently?'

He smiled.

'You are a charming liar. No, I've never played Carnegie Hall, but it's nice of you to think I might have. Are you . . . *Mrs*. Dexter?'

'Miss. And I really *have* heard of you . . .'

He stuck his hands in his pockets. He was well over six feet tall, but she wished he weren't quite so stoop-shouldered. She also thought he could stand to lose twenty pounds.

'Well, Miss Dexter, whether you've heard of me or not, if you'd have dinner with me, I could tell you a lot more about myself. Of course, I assume if you wouldn't go out with Rex Armstrong, I don't have much of a chance.'

'I didn't want to go out with him because I didn't want my fiancé to read about it in the papers. Besides, he seems terribly conceited.'

His eyes went to the solitaire diamond ring on her finger.

'So you're engaged? Well, there goes dinner. Might I ask whom you're engaged to?'

He was studying her intently.

'A doctor back in New York.'

'You're very beautiful, Miss Dexter. Your doctor is a lucky man.' He paused, then took his hands from his pockets. 'Well, I must go now. It's been delightful meeting you.'

Again he took her hand and kissed it. Then he started across the room. She watched him.

'Mr. von Gersdorff,' she blurted out.

He stopped and turned.

'Yes?'

She felt rather foolish.

'I, uh . . .' Mentally she kicked herself. 'I don't think that just because a woman is engaged, she can't accept dinner invitations from other men. I mean, especially if her fiancé is three thousand miles away.' She hesitated, 'I mean, that seems so old-fashioned, don't you think?'

His face lit up.

'*Definitely* old-fashioned. There aren't any restaurants worthy of the name in this curious town, but they tell me the food at the Hollywood Hotel is passable. Of course, we won't be able to get wine.'

'We could take a bottle of my sister's champagne,' said Lorna, wondering what madness had prompted her to accept his invitation.

Carl Maria smiled.

'Excellent!'

The Hollywood Hotel was a long, Mission-style building, three stories high, with awninged windows and two perky cupolas over the central section. It was the home of newly arrived actors and actresses, who would rent rooms while waiting for parts in movies that would enable them to rent—or build—a house. Its scruffy decor and itinerant clientele gave the place an air of unreality and impermanence that was ideal for a movie-town hostelry. But, though *Photoplay* hinted at orgies in its rooms, the place was drearily respectable, managed by a beribboned dowager named Mrs. Hershey who made sure no alcohol was sneaked in even *before* Prohibition, and that no one spent the night in anyone else's room. She spotted the suspicious-looking bag Lorna was carrying the moment she and Carl Maria entered the lobby.

'Excuse me, Miss,' she said, bearing down on them like a tanker, 'what's in that bag?'

Lorna looked at Carl.

'Cough medicine,' she said.

'I have terrible laryngitis,' said Carl, going into a coughing fit to prove his point. Mrs. Hershey looked skeptical.

'Nevertheless, I'll have to check your bag. Prohibition, you know.'

Lorna handed it to her. Mrs. Hershey reached in and pulled out a bottle of cough medicine. Giving them a cool look, she unscrewed the cap and sniffed the contents.

'If that's cough medicine,' she growled, 'I'm Mary Miles Minter. No alcohol in this hotel. If you want to eat here, you'll have to check this at the desk.'

'Well, we tried,' sighed Carl. 'But can you tell me one thing, Madame? Why does America, the richest country in the world, make life so miserable for everyone?'

'I don't write the laws,' said Mrs. Hershey, grimly. 'All I do is make sure the law's obeyed at the Hollywood Hotel.'

She returned to the reception desk with the bag as Carl and Lorna went into the dining room. They were led to a table by a waiter who, in his off hours, was a stunt man for westerns. After they ordered, Carl said, 'I was named after Carl Maria von Weber. It's a wonderfully romantic story. Want to hear it?'

'Very much,' said Lorna, sipping the ice water.

'My father was a doctor in Vienna. Very respectable, married to a very respectable woman. They had four very respectable children and lived in a very respectable house. One night when he was about forty, my father went to the opera and fell in love with the soprano. I mean he *literally* fell in love with her watching her sing.'

'That only happens in the movies.'

'Ah, but you're wrong. That's why I find movies boring: life is much more exciting. Well, the soprano's name was Gabriella Rausch, and my father made her his mistress. That would have been perfectly acceptable, but my father was a little crazy and he walked out on his wife and four children and moved in with Gabriella. It was a great scandal, and my father lost most of his patients—because he walked out on his family, you see. That just wasn't done. But my father didn't care. He was crazy in love —crazy! He had some money, so he took care of charity patients for free.

'He'd been living with Gabriella for a year when I was born —that was thirty-one years ago. My mother's favorite composer

272

was Weber, so she named me after him. She died when I was twelve, and my father was so heartbroken, he moved to New York. And that's why I'm an American.'

'That's a very nice story,' said Lorna. 'And you're right, it's very romantic.'

'You don't disapprove of my father leaving his family?'

'It doesn't matter whether I approve or not. I still like the story.'

'You don't disapprove that I'm illegitimate?'

'Why should I?'

He grinned.

'I make up for it by being *very* romantic.'

The waiter served the steaks as Lorna watched Carl. He certainly wasn't handsome, she thought, but there was something extremely attractive about him. And charming. And likeable.

'How long are you going to be in California?' he asked, cutting into his steak.

'Another week.'

'How do you like it?'

'California? It's nice. It's different. And it's been fun watching the movies being made. My sister adores it out here.'

'She's very beautiful. So you'll be going back to New York? And your doctor?'

'That's right.'

'And what's his name?'

'Tommy Randolph. He's very nice.'

He made a face.

' "Nice"? What kind of adjective is that to describe the man you're engaged to? You say California is "nice," and your fiancé is "nice," too?'

'Well, he *is* nice,' she said, defensively. 'Everybody likes him.'

'Ah, but do you *love* him?'

'Of course.'

'You don't sound convinced.'

She stiffened.

'Mr. von Gersdorff . . .'

'Carl.'

'All right, Carl. If I didn't love him, I wouldn't be engaged to him.'

'That doesn't follow at all. Lots of women marry men they're not in love with. Let me guess: this Tommy is very respectable, nice-enough looking, solid, serious . . . and your parents approve of him. He plays golf badly and likes to sail, and he wants three children—two sons and a daughter.'

She stared at him.

'He plays golf very well,' she corrected. Then she laughed and said, 'But the rest is pretty good. How did you guess so well?'

'I figured that your sister married unconventionally, and your reaction would be to look for a husband no one could complain of. But you see, that's a great mistake. Marry with your heart, not your head. I think your heart's not very excited about this Tommy. This steak is terrible, isn't it?'

'I don't think you should go around giving advice to people you hardly know.'

'Why not? Advice is free. And maybe I'm right. Maybe you should do something unconventional, like my father did, and like your sister did.'

'For instance?'

He put down his knife and fork and looked at her.

'Come to Mexico with me,' he said, quietly. 'Perhaps, after we get to know each other, we'll find we're in love.'

She smiled.

'I thought you didn't like movies? That line could only happen in a movie.'

'Going to Mexico with a stranger? I'll bet it happens all the time.'

'I think you've got me all wrong, Carl. I'm not that kind of woman.'

'Aren't you?' he said, looking into her eyes. Then he shrugged. 'Now you're insulted. Well, I apologize. And anyway . . . I tried.'

He returned to the attack on his steak.

'But,' he added, 'I'd love to have you with me in Mexico.'

She said nothing. She was surprised how tempted she was to accept his offer.

CHAPTER 27

On the first day of principal photography of *Russia*, everything that could go wrong did—and more. Morris had built a new studio on Santa Monica Boulevard not far from the United Artists studio, and technically his facilities were the best in Hollywood. Already considered antediluvian were the open-air stages of the earlier flickers, which necessitated actors and stagehands grabbing furniture and props to run them indoors during rain showers: Morris's studio had six large indoor stages. *Russia*'s screenplay, written by Morris, ran to a staggering three hundred pages, and included many exteriors which would be shot on a ranch in the San Fernando Valley. But the first scene Willie von Gastein wanted to shoot was an interior 'orgy,' and Morris and Barbara were both present on Stage One as the great director began the great epic.

The scene was a depiction of one of Rasputin's infamous St. Petersburg parties at which the Svengaliesque monk reputedly seduced society women by the score, and it was one that von Gastein had been salivating to direct, his *spécialité* being aristocratic decadence. Rasputin was played by a tall, bearded English actor named Myles Pierson whose Cockney accent would mercifully not detract from his silent portrayal. The orgy took place in the palace of Prince Kropotkin, played by a White Russian emigré count whom von Gastein had paid $10,000 for a minor role simply because he was—or said he was—a count. Sprinkled among the elegantly costumed party guests were, by von Gastein's account, at least a half-dozen genuine European titles. Whether this was true or not (and Nat Finger's press releases claimed it was, needless to say), Morris David was satisfied that they all *looked* aristocratic. And the set, groaning with gilt and four—count 'em, four—crystal chandeliers, certainly *looked* like a palace. If von Gastein was spending tank

275

cars of Morris's money, at least Morris was getting his money's worth in terms of glitter.

'Now, ladies and gentlemen,' von Gastein's voice boomed through his megaphone, the 'gentlemen' coming out 'chentlemen,' 'the secret of orgies is that they start quiet and build in intensity until they explode in a ravishment of the senses.'

'Is that right?' Morris whispered to his wife.

'How do I know?' shrugged Barbara. 'I've never been to an orgy.'

'Consequently, the opening shot,' continued von Gastein, 'will be subtly elegant. You are all the highest members of Russian society. I will remind you that the footmen will be passing real caviar and real champagne—compliments of our producer, Mr. David—and, needless to say, aristocrats *sip* champagne, they don't swill it. As we rehearsed it, we will begin with a full shot of the entire company, and then the camera will dolly *slowly* in on the face of Rasputin. Mr. Pierson, of course, will be swilling the champagne, since he's a peasant, and ogling the derrière of the Grand Duchess Xenia, Miss Kaye. We are all in our places? Beautiful. Signor Guarda, music please.' He signaled to the three-man ensemble, and the violin-piano-harp trio began to play 'Pale Hands I Love, Beside the Shalimar.' 'The footmen are ready? Excellent. All right, ladies and gentlemen, we begin *Russia!* Cameras! Action!'

'Oh Morris,' whispered Barbara, taking his hand, 'it's so exciting! Good luck, darling!'

And she kissed his cheek as three tripod cameras began grinding the scene from different angles, and the main camera, on a dolly manned by the famed Swedish cameraman, Nils Svenson, began to move slowly toward Rasputin, who was sprawled on a Louis XV sofa.

'Everyone talk!' shouted von Gastein. 'Make conversation! You're talking about the war, the Tsar, the Tsarina, Rasputin . . . it's 1917 . . . Talk, that's it! Countess Golitzine, give us a laugh . . . that's it, not too much, a refined, *decadent* laugh . . . *CUT!!!*'

He screamed so loud, Barbara literally jumped. Von Gastein was out of his canvas chair, charging on to the set. 'You laughed too *much!*' he raged at the white-faced extra playing Countess Golitzine. 'I *told* you, a decadent laugh! A sophisticated, jaded laugh! Do you think it's sophisticated and jaded to throw back your head and bray like a donkey? Do you think a *countess* would laugh like this? I *showed* you in rehearsal how to laugh! Fifty times, a hundred, I showed all of you! What's your name?'

'Countess Golitzine,' said the trembling girl.

'You stupid slut, I mean your *real* name!'

'Winifred Jones.'

'Winifred Jones is a common, vulgar name! How did I get an extra with a vulgar name like Winifred Jones? Where are you from?'

'Kansas City, Missouri.'

'Kansas CITY?!' screamed von Gastein. 'A whore named Jones from Kansas City is supposed to know how to play a countess? You filthy slut, you're *fired!* Get off my set! Get OFF! *WHORE!'*

The girl burst into tears and ran off the set. Barbara was appalled.

'Morris, you can't let him treat people like that!' she said.

'What can I do? He's a genius!'

'Genius, baloney! He's a monster!'

'SILENCE!' roared von Gastein, glaring at Barbara. 'Mrs. David, I will remind you that on *my* set, no one is allowed to talk but the director!'

Barbara was simmering.

'Excuse me, Mr. von Gastein, but I will remind *you* that my husband is the producer of this motion picture. I will also remind you that these people are actors and human beings and should be treated with a little common courtesy!'

Von Gastein glared at her, eyes bulging. Then he threw down his megaphone and walked off the set. 'I quit!' he yelled. 'Quit —through! I refuse to be ordered about by a bourgeoise. Get a cowboy to direct this piece of shit.'

'Willie!' yelled Morris. 'Now you've done it!' he hissed at his wife. Then he ran after the director. 'Willie, we're all nervous —let's not go crazy yet . . . Let's talk . . .'

While Morris and Willie shouted at each other and Barbara sank into a chair, Sonny, Laura Kaye's favorite poodle, escaped from Miss Kaye's dresser's arms, ran over to a 'spider' (one of the heavy-duty multiple electric outlets on the floor of the stage), lifted his leg and peed. The resulting sizzle of sparks dimmed half the lights and threw the yelping dog halfway across the stage, where he bit Rasputin's ankle. Myles Pierson howled for a doctor to give him rabies shots, while Laura went into hysterics over her poodle and insisted a veterinarian be sent for.

By the end of the day, when Willie finally and reluctantly agreed to return to the picture, only ten feet of film had been shot. Morris's account calculated the wasted day had cost David Productions $11,478, including fees for the doctor and the vet.

But Morris's troubles were just beginning. Three nights later he was awakened by a phone call from the German Genius, who was in jail. Von Gastein's neighbors, alarmed by muffled screams emanating from Willie's basement, had called the police, who, when they raided the house, found a naked actress tied to a chair in a cellar room. The walls of the room were hung with an impressive collection of Hungarian whips, although Willie had been indulging his sadomasochistic fantasies not by whipping the girl but by tearing her hair out, strand by strand. The police also found enough pornographic photographs to start a library. Willie's reaction to his arrest was indignation at the violation of his 'civil rights.'

A groaning Morris rushed to the police station to bail out his director, and Nat Finger managed to keep the incident out of the papers and shut the girl up by offering her a minor role in Morris's next picture. Barbara tried in vain to talk her husband into replacing the German Genius, but Morris persisted in his faith in the man, telling her the dailies of the 'orgy' sequence were brilliant. The filming of *Russia* continued.

However, during the second week of production, trouble of a new and even more ominous sort loomed. Rex Armstrong had already shot a few minor scenes, but his first major scene took place in the dining room of the Grand Duchess Xenia's palace. Igor, the footman played by Rex, was to serve quail to the Grand Duchess and by the love-smitten look on his face convey to the audience the unsurprising fact that the male star of the picture was gaga over the female star. Willie had gone to his usual ludicrous lengths to achieve authenticity, in this instance hiring the chef of the Alexandria Hotel to prepare a giant peacock stuffed with quail. The dining room table sagged under the weight of rented silver candelabra and four tureens overflowing with flowers. Although it cast some legitimate doubt on his familiarity with grand-ducal eating habits, Willie had stuck a champagne fountain in the center of the table, featuring two pudgy *putti* squirting Louis Roederer Cristal out of their mouths. Behind each of the ten dining room chairs stood a liveried lackey. And outside the glassless windows, flakes of gypsum fluttered down, simulating snowy St. Petersburg in seventy-eight degree California.

Barbara and Morris were on hand to watch the first take of the scene. After the usual preliminaries, Willie shouted through his megaphone, 'Are we ready?'

'Ready, Mr. von Gastein,' replied his assistant director.

'All right. Rex, you'll come through the door with the peacock. Places, everybody.'

Laura Kaye, looking splendid in a Ruritanian white-lace evening dress trimmed with seed pearls, took her place at the head of the table. No other people were at the table except the lackeys, because it was Willie's conceit that showing the Grand Duchess Xenia dining alone with ten lackeys would dramatize her contempt for social justice, as well as her hauteur and general bitchiness. All of this grand-ducal snottiness would melt like spring ice in the Bay of Finland after Igor turned on his proletarian charm, but that was to come later. For the moment the temperature in Grand Duchess Xenia's ample bosom hovered near zero.

'Signor Guarda.'

The trio launched into the languid 'Andante Cantabile' by Tchaikovsky.

'Cameras! Action!'

The cameras whirred. Two doors were opened, and in came two footmen bearing an immense silver tray on which rested the stuffed peacock. The footman on the right was Rex, looking handsome as ever but strangely lost. The footman on the left started down the table toward Laura Kaye, as he had been instructed, but Rex walked right into the table and fell face down into the champagne fountain.

'CUT!' howled Willie over Laura Kaye's scream as the stuffed peacock flopped on to the table, spilling its quail, one of which rolled into Laura's lap. 'Cut, cut, cut, cut!' Willie was dancing a little jig of fury. 'Rex, can't you *see?* You walk right into the fucking table? Are you blind?'

Rex was standing now, champagne dripping off his face.

'He's *shikker!*' gasped Morris. And indeed, America's heart-throb was drunk. Another day's shooting was lost, and Morris's accountant figured the delay cost another $11,000.

Morris was a rich man, but by the eighteenth day of shooting on *Russia*, he knew he was in bad financial trouble. As he drove down Sunset Boulevard in his yellow Marmon for his appoint-ment at the Bank of America, he looked at the mammoth Belshazzar's Palace set built by Griffith three years before for his dinosaurian flop d'estime, *Intolerance*, and shuddered. There was no more potent symbol of the folly of megalomania than this infamous set which, with its plaster elephants and giant columns, still loomed preposterously over the humble bunga-lows of Sunset Boulevard even after it had been condemned as a fire hazard by the Los Angeles Fire Department. The last thing Morris wanted to be reminded of was *Intolerance*, which had left the audiences cold, but he knew people in the industry were already comparing *Russia* to *Intolerance*, and the huge Winter Palace set Morris had built in the San Fernando Valley to the Belshazzar's Palace set. The Winter Palace set—which was to be the backdrop for one of the climactic scenes of the film, the storming of the Tsar's palace by the revolutionaries—had been originally budgeted at a mind-boggling $150,000 but had ended up costing almost $200,000, a tenth of the total budget. Willie von Gastein's extravagances, Rex's drinking binges and plain bad luck were also wreaking havoc with the budget, but Morris knew the ultimate blame was his. The monumentality of the concept of the film had set him on fire, and he had pushed the project against everyone's advice. If *Russia* flopped, it would be no one's fault but his own.

When he reached the bank building, he took the elevator to the seventh floor, where he was ushered into the office of the senior vice-president, Elbert Dean. Dean exuded a midwestern affability, but Morris knew that behind the rimless glasses and friendly smile lay an incisive mind. Victor had given Morris the luxury of relative freedom from money worries. Now that luxury was gone. Morris felt almost as miserably uncomfortable in Dean's office as he had five years before when he had first entered the office of the man who became his father-in-law.

'Elbert, I need a million dollars,' he blurted out even before the banker could remark on the weather. 'Will you loan it to me?'

'Then the rumors are true,' said Dean. 'You're over budget.'

'They're true. But *Russia* will make millions! I know what they're saying—it's another *Intolerance*—but they haven't seen the dailies! They're brilliant . . .'

Elbert held up his hand.

'Morris, don't sell me. *All* dailies are brilliant. But why are you coming to me instead of Victor Dexter?'

Morris looked glum.

'I could lie, but I won't. Victor didn't like *Russia* from the beginning.'

'And you've put up the two million yourself?'

'Yes.'

'And you want another million.' Elbert looked at a piece of paper. 'Morris, we hold a seven-hundred-thousand-dollar first mortgage on your house and a million-dollar mortgage on your studio. Even if I believed in *Russia*, which I don't, I couldn't

280

recommend this bank loaning you more money. Frankly, I'm worried about the money we've already loaned you.' The pale-blue eyes behind the rimless glasses looked up from the paper. 'What about your wife? She's a wealthy woman. Can't she help?'

Morris rose to his feet.

'Before I'd ask my wife for a penny,' he said, 'I'd go back to selling shoes. Thanks for nothing, Elbert. I knew I was wasting my time coming here. Why don't I listen to myself?'

Lorna had returned to New York the week after her dinner with Carl Maria von Gersdorff, and Lord and Lady Pembroke had gone north at the same time, first to weekend with William Randolph Hearst at San Simeon, then for a week's vacation at a dude ranch in Nevada. Now they had returned to Los Angeles to catch the train back to New York. Lucille was reading a magazine in her suite at the Alexandria Hotel when the bell rang. Since Ar-Ar-Archie was out playing golf, Lucille got up to answer the door herself.

'Hello, darling,' she said, kissing her daughter as Barbara came into the room.

'You're looking wonderful, Mother. The dude ranch must have agreed with you.'

'Oh, it was all right. Archie kept falling off horses. He's not much of a cowboy. How's Allen?'

She referred to Barbara's one-year-old son.

'Still sucking his thumb, but he'll get over that. Mother, how much am I worth?'

She had taken a seat in the living room of the suite. Now her mother looked at her with surprise.

'What an odd question,' she said. 'Why do you want to know?'

'I know Father set up a trust fund for each of us, but I have no idea how much is in it—you know how secretive he is about money.'

'Oh yes, indeed. But you still haven't answered my question. Why do you want to know? I hope you're not thinking about loaning Morris money for his motion picture?'

'Mother, he's in trouble. He needs a million dollars quickly, and no one will loan it to him because everyone says *Russia* is going to be a flop. I *have* to help him out!'

'Because he's your husband?'

'Yes.'

'You've told me you were against his making this silly epic, and you *still* would give him the money?'

'I love him,' she said, simply.

'A million dollars is a lot of love. Has Morris asked you to invest?'

'Oh no. He'd never ask *me*. He'd ask you or anyone else, but he's too proud to ask me. And, of course, Father's already turned him down, so that's out. He really is in a corner, and even though I think . . . Well, I don't have particularly high hopes for the film, but I want to help him anyway. Is my trust fund big enough for me to raise a million on it?'

'Oh yes.'

'Then I'm going to call Father and ask him to arrange the loan. May I use your phone?'

She put through the call. Transcontinental phone service had been inaugurated five years before, in January, 1915, and was still something of a novelty. But communication was surprisingly clear, and within five minutes she was talking to Victor. Rather to her surprise, her father put up no objections and said he would arrange to have the money available for Morris's account in the Dexter's correspondent bank, the Bank of America, by the next day. The loan would be at the regular business rate, which was four percent. He sent his love and wished Morris luck. When Barbara hung up, she reflected that there were definite advantages to having a banker for a father.

During the call, Lucille had gone into her bedroom. Now Barbara went to the door to see her mother sitting in a chair by the window, tears streaming down her face.

'Mother, what's wrong?'

'Oh, nothing.'

Barbara came into the room.

'You can't be crying about nothing. What is it?'

Lucille took her hand.

'It's just . . . I was thinking how nice it must be to love someone the way you love Morris. He's such a peculiar man, but . . . well, you didn't even think twice about loaning him the money, did you?'

'No.'

'I wish I were like you.' She bit her lip, trying to stop the tears. 'All I did with your father was take from him. Take, take, take . . . Oh, I'm not pretending that if I had it all to do over, I would have done differently, but still it makes me feel ashamed. Oh God, if there's anything I hate, it's middle-aged women crying over their mistakes . . .'

'Maybe it's good to cry.'

'Perhaps. The irony is, it turns out your father was right about me.'

'What do you mean?'

'After we agreed to divorce, the last thing he said to me was that he felt sorry for me because he knew what I'd become. I've never forgotten it, and damn him, he was right. I know what everyone says about me, including you and Lorna and Drew . . . that I "bought" Archie, and it's true. He doesn't give a damn about me, and I know it. I'm just a silly, vain woman who bought a young husband and a title.'

Barbara squeezed her mother's hand.

'We all love you, just the same,' she said.

'Do you?'

'Of course.'

She leaned over and kissed her. Lucille hugged her daughter.

'At least I did one good thing in my life,' she whispered. 'I had two wonderful daughters.'

When Morris came into Casa del Mar, he said to his butler, 'Where's Mrs. David?'

'Upstairs in the nursery, sir.'

Morris ran up the stairs two at a time, hurried down the hall and barged into the pretty nursery, where Barbara was sitting in a rocking chair giving Allen his bottle.

'No!' he exclaimed, pointing an accusing finger at his wife. 'I won't take your money! It was nice of you, I appreciate it, but Morris David don't accept money from his wife! I don't care how bad things is, *NO!*'

Barbara looked unruffled.

'Is something wrong with my money?'

'You bet it's wrong! Every producer in Hollywood will say I'm a kept man!'

'You'd take my father's money, but you won't take mine? That's a curious double standard, Morris. Besides, I'm not "giving" it to you. I'm investing it in David Productions. Under certain conditions.'

He glared at her.

'Conditions, yet! What means "conditions"?'

Barbara got up, kissed Allen's forehead, and put him in his bassinet. Then she turned to confront her husband.

'Morris, you are a genius at making comedies,' she said. 'There's no one in Hollywood who can make funnier movies

283

than you. And the odd thing is, the funniest movie you've ever made is turning out to be *Russia*.'

His face turned red.

'*Funny?!*' he shouted. 'Monumental, yes! Spectacular, yes! Moving, tragic, exciting, yes! But *funny?!*'

'It's a laugh riot. Honestly, when I watch the dailies, it's all I can do to stop from howling. Laura Kaye acts about as much like a grand duchess as I do, and Rex! Well, all I'll say about Igor the footman is that with revolutionaries like him around, it's a wonder the Tsar's not still on his throne. You have to face it, Morris: your movie is just plain silly.'

He started to say something, but it fizzled out. He sank into the rocking chair. For the first time, Barbara saw fear in her husband's face.

'Silly?' he said, softly. 'Is *that* what you think?'

Barbara came over and kneeled beside him, taking his hand.

'Oh darling, I don't want to hurt you, but I have to be honest with you for your own good. Well, for mine and Allen's too. I know what you're trying to do with *Russia,* and I think it's admirable and wonderful, but you're *not* D. W. Griffith. You're Morris David, and that's wonderful enough by itself. You told me you wanted to be respected, you wanted to do more than "just" make people laugh—don't you realize there are millions of people who love you because you *can* make them laugh? Is there anything more wonderful than that—making people happy? I don't give two hoots about Grand Duchess Xenia or the Russian Revolution, and I have a sneaking suspicion the rest of America doesn't either. But make me laugh, and I'll love you forever.'

He was staring at her.

'You think it's going to be a turkey?' he whispered.

'*This* movie—yes,' she said, standing up. 'But if you'd do what I want you to do, I think you'd have one of the greatest successes of all time.'

'What? What do you want me to do?'

'Turn it into a comedy,' she said flatly. 'Get rid of that Hamburg humbug, Willie von Gasbag, direct the thing yourself and play it for laughs. You wouldn't even have to reshoot the footage you already have, since it's funny as it is. Just stick in a little slapstick and make the whole thing a parody.'

'What means "parody"? Speak English, please.'

'All right, a joke. Make a joke of the whole thing!'

His eyes bulged with disbelief.

'Make a joke of the Russian Revolution? The World War? This is your idea of a joke?'

'What else can you call it if it's not a joke? A horrible joke, admittedly, but still a joke. People are sick of the war, sick of Bolshevism—but make them laugh at it and maybe they'll understand it a little better. Oh believe me, Morris, you could *do* it! You could make it a wonderful comedy! And if you will—if you'll get rid of Willie and turn it into a comedy—I'll invest the money you need. But I won't invest in this flop you're producing now. I love you, but I'm not suicidal.'

He got out of the chair and went to the window, looking out at the swimming pool. She watched his back, waiting anxiously for him to say something. Then she saw his shoulders moving up and down. It took a few moments before she realized he was shaking with laughter. He turned, and she saw tears of merriment running down his face.

'The scene in the dining room!' he snickered. 'When Rex was *shikker* and he fell in the champagne fountain! We could keep it in! It was funny!'

She ran over and hugged him.

'It was a howl!'

'We'll make Igor a drunk! A drunk who stumbles through the Russian Revolution and manages to save the Grand Duchess Xenia!'

'Rex can play a drunk! He *is* a drunk! Oh Morris, it's wonderful!'

They started laughing and dancing around the bassinet while Allen David lay on his back, sucking his thumb, staring curiously at his odd parents.

CHAPTER 28

After his divorce from Lucille, Victor had moved into a suite on the eighth floor of the Plaza Hotel. He didn't particularly like living in a hotel, but Lucille had kept the house, Drew was at Harvard, Barbara was on the coast, Lorna had an apartment of her own and was engaged. Suddenly he didn't feel needed anymore by his family, and a hotel seemed as good a place as any to live by himself. He was fifty-two now and beginning to feel middle-aged. He was terribly lonely, and at least in a hotel there were people around. Some day he thought he would find an apartment, but somehow he never seemed to get around to doing it.

He was always delighted when Lorna came to see him, which she did often, and this April evening was no exception. When she came into the suite, she was looking particularly pretty in a pale-blue dress, and her cheeks were as pink as the tulips in Central Park below.

'I'm taking you to dinner,' she said, kissing her father. 'I'm even picking up the check. How's that for a surprise?'

'It's a nice surprise. What's the occasion?'

'Are you ready for a shock? I'm engaged!'

He looked confused.

'Yes, I know. You've been engaged for months. In fact, I'm beginning to wonder if you're ever going to marry Tommy.'

'I'm not engaged to Tommy any more. I'm totally *un*engaged to Tommy, thank God. Dr. Randolph is a pleasant bore, and it would have been a disaster if I'd married him.' She squeezed her father's hands. 'Daddy, I've met the *most* wonderful man! His name is Carl Maria von Gersdorff, he's the most brilliant pianist in the world, and we're getting married next month! Now: what do you think of that?'

Victor shook his head slowly.

'I don't know *what* I think of it. When did all this happen?'

'I met him last January out at Barbara's, and I rather liked him—no, I'll be honest: I liked him a lot. And then, a few weeks after I got back to New York, he called me up and asked me out. And I said yes.'

'But you were engaged . . .'

'I know. I don't care. Oh Daddy, I'm *mad* for him! You're going to love him, too—you'll see tonight. He's coming to dinner with us.'

'You say he's a pianist? Does he make a living at it?'

She kissed his cheek.

'No,' she smiled. 'But he will, someday. And don't say he's after my money, because he isn't. Barbara did all right with Morris, didn't she? And he was poorer than Carl.'

'Not when she married him. But I'm the last person to be against someone who's poor. I was as poor as you can get, once. I just wondered if he can support you.'

'I doubt it, at least for a while. But we'll get by.'

'Where will you live?'

'He's going to move into my place.'

'You can't live there, in two rooms. Well, we'll find you a place. Congratulations, Lorna.'

She hugged him.

'Oh Daddy, I'm so happy! Are you happy for me?'

'I'm very happy for you. Very.'

And he meant it. But now his last daughter was leaving him. He felt even lonelier than before.

Morris David's office in the studios of David Productions was impressive. Barbara had picked the furniture for it, and the room was filled with English antiques. Laura Kaye was sitting on a Regency chair in front of Morris's George III desk, looking delicately English in her smart white suit and white hat, but definitely not antique. Morris saw plenty of beautiful women in Hollywood, but this pink-faced blonde with the gorgeous mouth and the big breasts was in a luscious class by herself.

'You have to talk to Rex, Morris,' she said. 'He's going around town saying I'm sleeping with him, and it's making me furious! And it's not good for the picture, either. If that gets in the papers, it could really hurt *Russia*.'

Morris stood up to come around the desk.

'I know,' he sighed. 'Rex gets drunk and says whatever comes into his head—which happens to be you these days. I'll shut him up, don't worry. By the way . . .' He was standing next to her. Now he put his hand on her shoulder. '*Are* you sleeping with him?'

She gave him a cool look.

'No,' she finally said. 'Oh, I'll admit he's good-looking, but I don't sleep with drunks.'

'You're a smart girl, Laura. In this town, if you sleep with someone, sleep with someone who can do you some good.'

She continued to look at him. He moved his hand down her shoulder, slowly. He was aiming for her big breasts.

Laura Kaye didn't stop him.

The premiere of *Russia* took place at the Egyptian Theater on the night of May 12, 1920, and it was considered one of the most spectacular events of the year. Searchlights stabbed the sky as hundreds of fans squeezed against the police barricades to ogle the celebrities disgorging from their limousines.

'Look: Rex Armstrong!' screamed one girl, and the crowd went wild as the star stepped out of his Hispano-Suiza. The former Waldo Radebaugh looked great in his tails—he was even sober—and his date, Barbara La Marr, was a vision (she had a small gold box filled with cocaine in her silver lamé handbag). When Laura Kaye's limousine pulled up, it was the men's turn to go wild, and Laura didn't fail her fans. As light bulbs flashed, she smiled and waved, and her escort, Rod La Rocque, smiled and waved, and a legendary Hollywood night was in the making.

Morris and Barbara David got few cheers, even though Barbara looked as beautiful as any movie star in a black sequined gown and chinchilla wrap. Around her neck was a diamond necklace that Morris had given her that afternoon for her 'faith and inspiration,' as he had awkwardly put it, 'in *Russia*.' Morris didn't care if the fans didn't know who he was. Morris wasn't even nervous. He knew he had a hit. Everyone who had seen *Russia* had been ecstatic. The word of mouth was that it was the funniest movie *ever*.

And it was. The audience howled from beginning to end, after which they gave a standing ovation. 'It's the key to the Mint!' grinned Morris, as he kissed his wife. 'And it's all ours!'

Barbara smiled, but she said nothing. She was thrilled at the success of *Russia* and thrilled for her husband.

But inside she was burning.

When they returned to Casa del Mar from the opening-night party, it was three in the morning and the servants were asleep.

Barbara turned the lights on in the living room, then threw her chinchilla wrap on one of the Spanish sofas.

'What a night!' chortled Morris, following her into the big, two-story room. 'What a night! I knew they'd love it, but *so* much they loved it! What a night.' He came up to his wife and took her in his arms. 'You're beautiful,' he said, kissing her. 'And you saved it for me. When we get old and I say to you, "Barbara, darling, your husband is a great man," you say to me, "My husband is a *shmuck,* because he wanted to play *Russia* straight." Say it to me, darling, because it's true. Tonight is all thanks to you.'

He kissed her again. She stepped back and slapped him with all her strength.

'What the hell—?'

He held his stinging cheek, staring at her.

'That's for Laura Kaye!' she exclaimed. Then she walked across the room, took a cigarette from a marble box and lighted it. Morris watched her.

'You found out,' he said. 'How?'

'That's not important.' She turned on him, exhaling. 'Morris, I love you. You're my husband, the father of my son, and last but hardly least, a brilliant filmmaker. I suppose I've known all along that with all the beautiful women in this town, it was inevitable you'd cheat on me. All right, you've done it. It hurts me deeply—*very* deeply—but you've done it, and you'll do it again. I can't stop you—I won't even try. But I want you to tell me. I want you to be honest with me about your cheating—and I know that sounds crazy. The one thing I won't stand for in our marriage is lies.'

'You want a list?' he burst out. 'I should write you a list? On Monday, I slept with Laura Kaye. On Tuesday, with Mary Miles Minter . . .'

'No, I don't want a list,' she said, bitterly. 'Don't be stupid. I just want to know . . .'

She stopped, sank into a chair and started to cry.

'No, I *don't* want to know,' she sobbed. 'Sleep with whomever you want, but just keep them out of my sight . . . I don't want to know about it . . .'

Morris was crawling with guilt. He came to her and took her in his arms. 'I'm sorry,' he whispered, kissing her wet eyes. 'Oh God, I'm sorry . . .'

'Don't you see, I love you, you crazy man! And I'm afraid I'll lose you . . . Oh Morris, just *tell* me if you fall out of love with me. Please *tell* me. I can take your sleeping with them, but I couldn't *stand* thinking you were in love with them. Can you understand that?'

'I'll never love anyone but you,' he said, kissing her. 'Never. No one but you.'

'Oh God, if I could believe that . . .'

'Believe it! I swear! All right, I cheated on you. Could I *not* make a pass at Laura! Would I be normal if I didn't? Do you want a husband who's not normal? But does that mean I love her? No! I love *you*, my wife, my darling, brilliant *shiksa* Barbara, and I'll love you till the day I die! Believe me! I swear!'

She looked at his offbeat face that she had come to adore and, despite her bitterness, she started to laugh.

'Oh Morris,' she sighed, 'you could talk your way into the Vatican.'

'The Vatican? I want to see the Pope?'

'You know what I mean.' She took his face in her hands and kissed him. 'I adore you,' she smiled. 'I adore you so much, I'll let you cheat on me. Oh damn you, you're having your cake and eating it, too!' She paused. 'It was a brilliant movie, my love. I was *very* proud of you.'

They went upstairs to make love.

A week later Lorna Dexter married Carl Maria von Gersdorff in New York. Lorna knew she was pregnant at the wedding, but naturally enough she kept the news to herself. Her father, who had come to like Carl enormously, gave them as a wedding present a town house on Sixty-fourth Street between Park and Madison. Lorna's wedding present to her husband was a magnificent Steinway grand. Carl's wedding present to his wife was himself.

Lorna gave birth to a daughter eight months later. She agreed to Carl's suggestion that they name her after his mother, and the baby was christened Gabriella.

PART VI

SMART MONEY

1925

CHAPTER 29

'How would you like to triple fifty thousand dollars in three months?'

The question came from Sonny van Cleef, the scion of a family that was long on bloodlines and short on cash. Sonny had been one of Drew Dexter's roommates at Harvard, and he and Drew and their dates were drinking bootleg gin at Connie's Inn on Seventh Avenue at 132nd Street, one of the first Harlem nightclubs to become popular with whites. Louis Armstrong and his orchestra were playing a hot rendition of 'Sweet Georgia Brown' while Princess Vikana, a gorgeous beige chanteuse, sang, backed by a chorus line billed as 'Thirty Beautiful Brownskins.' The low-ceilinged club was packed with 'down-towners,' the men in tuxes or tails, the women mostly in short evening dresses that showed plenty of leg. Millicent Chapin, Drew's date whom *Vogue* had described as 'one of New York's smartest young socialites,' wore a knee-length white dress dripping with opalescent beads and paillettes. Drew, like the century, was twenty-five years old; but in this high noon of the Jazz Age, all America seemed twenty-five. Drew, three years out of Harvard and a junior executive at the Dexter Bank, knew enough to be cynical about get-rich-quick schemes, particularly if they came from Sonny van Cleef. But Drew was bored. He longed to make a killing. He was always ready to listen.

'What's it this time, Florida real estate?' he asked, lighting a Chesterfield.

Sonny, a fatuous-looking redhead, shook his head.

'Christ, Drew, you don't think I'm *that* dumb?'

'Yes I do. I haven't forgotten that chain-letter scheme you suckered me into at Harvard. That cost me a hundred bucks and two months' suspension.'

'Why don't you two shut up?' said Millie Chapin. 'I can't hear the music.'

'Yeah, shut up, Sonny,' Drew agreed.

Sonny leaned closer and lowered his voice so the women couldn't hear.

'You've heard of Serge Wittgenstein?'

Drew looked rather impressed.

'The plunger? Sure.'

'He's forming a pool in American Hotel stock. He's going to run it up and down and make a bloody bundle. It's a sure thing. He's selling units at fifty thousand each. If you're interested, I can introduce you to him.'

'Where the hell did you meet Serge Wittgenstein?'

'At the Hotcha Club. He's there practically every night. He plays poker in the back room. He's a lousy poker player—I took him for two hundred bucks the other night.'

'What's in this for you?'

'I get a two percent finder's fee for every investor I bring in.'

'That figures. So you try to sucker your old roommate? Thanks a lot, Sonny. You're a real pal. Next time I want to get my throat slit, I'll give you a call.'

'Look, Drew: Wittgenstein's a fast operator, but you've got to admit he's smart as hell and has made millions on the Street. It couldn't hurt to *meet* him.'

Drew blew a lazy smoke ring, which hovered in the blue glow cast by the spotlight on Princess Vikana. He was tall, athletically trim, good-looking, his black hair parted in the middle and slicked with brilliantine, his tight-fitting tux custom tailored by Brooks Brothers, his lapis lazuli and gold studs and cufflinks from Black, Starr and Frost. Drew looked the part of the cocky young Wall Streeter, and he knew it and gloried in it. Cocky young Wall Streeters didn't back off from meeting someone like Serge Wittgenstein.

'I'll meet him,' he said finally. 'What the hell, I've got a soft spot for crooks.'

'Serge Wittgenstein isn't a crook.'

'Says you.'

'If Sonny'd get an honest job, he wouldn't have to be hustling all the time,' said Millie as she checked her face in her mirrored compact. Millie was always checking her face, Drew thought, whether at restaurants, movies, plays—or, as now, under the streetlight. They were waiting for a red light to change. Drew was driving her home to Sutton Place in his Arabian Sand Mercedes-Benz sports car.

'Sonny's a horse's ass,' said Drew.

'I liked Connie's Inn. Will you take me there again?'

Rather than answering, Drew stepped on the gas, and the car roared through the intersection. Millie wondered at his rather surly mood, then took a last look at her reflection, checking the eye-shadow over her left eye. Everyone said the twenty-three-year-old slim blonde was a knockout, but Millie never tired of checking it out for herself.

Ten minutes later, Drew parked in front of her parents' Sutton Place town house. Millie's father was one of the most prominent surgeons in New York.

'Do you want to come in for a drink?' she asked.

'No thanks. I'm going downtown.'

He got out his side of the car, hurried around and opened the door for her. It was a warm April night, and Millie wore a light wrap. Now she got out.

'Oh, come in for a few minutes,' she persisted.

'What's the point of it? We'll neck for a while, then you'll say you have to go to bed. I've got better things to do.'

She was stung by his cool insolence.

'It's so wonderful being with you, Drew. You're so *romantic*. Strauss waltzes, candlelight, the works.'

'If you want Strauss waltzes, go to Carnegie Hall. Come on, I'll see you to the door.'

He started to take her arm, but she pushed his hand away.

'What do you *expect?*' she whispered. 'I can't go to bed with you!'

He shrugged.

'Okay, be a Vestal Virgin. I'll see you around town, Millie.'

He walked around the car again and got in.

'You go to *hell!*' she said, furiously. 'You conceited bastard.'

'Sure has been fun, Millie. Maybe Sonny van Cleef'll take you back to Connie's Inn.'

He gunned the Mercedes, leaving Millie in a cloud of exhaust.

It's a trick, she thought. One of his rotten, smart-ass tricks to make me come crawling to him. Well, I won't crawl!

The sexy *bastard*.

The Hotcha Club was in Greenwich Village, a half-block west of Washington Square near Mother Bertolotti's Italian restaurant, above which John Reed had written *Ten Days That Shook the World*. It was near three in the morning when Drew parked his car and went into the speakeasy. He spotted Sonny van Cleef and went over to him.

'Serge is in the back room,' said Sonny, escorting him

through the half-empty club to a rear door. Inside, three men were seated at a baize-covered table playing poker. One of them Drew recognized from photographs he had seen in the newspapers. He was a moon-faced man in his thirties, bald and losing the weight battle. He had what one inspired reporter had called 'basilisk' eyes, meaning that his glance, like that of the legendary dragon, was lethal. The basilisk eyes now looked at Drew and Sonny. Serge Wittgenstein blinked sleepily, then bet fifty dollars on a pair of aces. He lost to three sevens.

The winner announced he was cashing in his chips, and the second player followed suit. After they left the room, Sonny introduced Drew.

'Ah yes, the son of the eminent Mr. Victor,' said Serge in a vaguely Russian accent, using the familiar appellation used for Victor by officials of his bank. 'Care for a game? *Vingt-et-un* or five-card draw, nothing wild?'

'How much are the chips?' asked Drew.

'The blues are a dollar, reds five and whites ten.'

Drew pulled out a roll of bills and peeled off a fifty, which he tossed on the table.

'I'll take five whites.'

Serge Wittgenstein smiled.

'I like your style, Mr. Dexter.'

'My friends call me Drew.'

He took the seat opposite Serge. Sonny van Cleef took an empty chair, but he was not asked, nor did he volunteer, to play. Sonny had three dollars on him and change.

'Then I hope you will permit me to be your friend,' said Serge, who it was variously reported had been born either in Vienna, Russia, Romania or Poland. One even said he came from Transylvania, hinting darkly at family ties to Count Dracula. Actually he was the son of a Moscow art dealer who had fled the revolution with a dubious Cranach wrapped around his pudgy waist. Convincing a rich American pickle heiress in Paris that the Cranach was genuine, Serge had sold it for $50,000, which he took to New York to use as his grubstake on Wall Street. The rest had been a history of plunging, stock pools and bear raids, all executed with panache, all tainted with rumors of manipulation and underworld ties. Someone had dubbed him 'The Lizard of Wall Street.' Drew decided the name fit.

'What is your game?' said Serge.

'Five-card draw, jacks or better to open, nothing wild?'

'Excellent. Cut for deal?'

Serge won the cut and dealt. Drew picked up four low hearts and the trey of clubs.

'I can't open.'

'I'll open,' said Serge, 'with fifty dollars.'

He put out five white chips. Drew looked at his four tempting hearts.

'I'll call,' he said, shoving out his five chips.

'How many cards?'

'One.'

He threw out the club. Serge sniffed rather disdainfully and dealt him a card.

'I'll draw three.'

Drew picked up his new card slowly. He couldn't believe his luck: the ace of hearts!

'The opener bets another fifty,' said Serge with sublime confidence. Drew pulled out his bankroll and peeled off two more fifties.

'I'll see you and raise you fifty.'

Serge's bushy eyebrows went up.

'You carry a lot of cash, my friend. That doesn't make you nervous down here in the Village?'

'Should I be nervous?'

'You never know when you might be held up.'

'It's safer than Wall Street.'

'You have a point.'

'Are you in the game?'

Serge studied his cards.

'You drew one card,' he said, 'and you raised me. Either you are a superb bluffer, or you are extremely lucky. Either way, I would be a fool to see you. But, alas, when it comes to poker, I'm a fool. I'll see you.'

He pushed in the extra fifty.

'Two pair, kings on sevens,' he said, laying down his cards.

'A heart flush,' smiled Drew, laying down his and raking in the chips and cash.

Serge pulled out a gold cigarette case and tapped and lighted a black, gold-tipped Sobranie.

'Something tells me,' he said, exhaling, 'I should not play poker with you.'

'Sonny tells me you're playing another game with American Hotel stock.'

'Ah yes.' The basilisk eyes darted to van Cleef, then back to Drew. 'Mr. van Cleef assured me you are discreet. Are you?'

'Discreet enough.'

'Mmm.' He sucked on the Sobranie, studying the young man's face. Then he said, 'American Hotel Corporation is old, the management is stodgy. They own twenty-three hotels across the country . . . Buffalo, Cleveland, Indianapolis, St. Louis, et cetera. The hotels are clean, if uninspired. Most of them make a slight profit, but the real value is the real estate they sit on. Most of it is in the center of town, and these cities are expanding rapidly, as you're probably aware. The hotels could be sold to developers for spectacular profits, but the present management isn't interested. They talk about amusing things like "Service to the community," "traditional ties to their customers" . . . that sort of drivel. I'm putting together a pool of five million dollars to . . . shall we say inject some excitement into the stock? It's the old game I'm sure you're familiar with. We'll run the stock up, buying long. Then, when the suckers are scrambling to get on the elevator ride, we'll dump our stock, sell short and take our second profit as the elevator goes down. I estimate we can triple our money in a month.'

'Sonny said three months.'

'Mr. van Cleef is conservative. As you can see, I'm not. I'm putting in a half million of my own money and will, of course, handle the operation. Here's a list of the other men who have invested.' He pulled a piece of paper from his jacket and handed it across the table. 'You can see we have some very solid names. There are two fifty-thousand-dollar units still available. If your luck at poker is any indication of your luck at business, we'd certainly like to have you along for the elevator ride.'

'It's a golden opportunity, Drew,' urged Sonny.

Serge laughed.

'Ah, the anxious middleman! Mr. van Cleef, let me tell you something about extracting money from investors: *doucement*. *Dolce con amore*. Never oversell them, particularly when you're trying to get them to invest in someone like me, who has such a deliciously lurid reputation. I'm sure Mr. Dexter has many suspicions, many doubts . . . especially since his father, the inestimable Mr. Victor, is such a pillar of the financial community. I imagine Mr. Victor would not be exactly ecstatic having his son involved with the shady Serge Wittgenstein, eh, Drew?'

Drew didn't answer. He was studying the list of names, which were undeniably blue chip. Serge checked his Cartier watch.

'*Bozhe moi*, it's three-thirty! I have to get home.' He lumbered to his size-fourteen, patent-leathered feet. 'I have a breakfast date at the Plaza which I shall undoubtedly miss. I punish myself physically and shall probably die young, but it will have been such fun! Delighted to meet you, Drew. If you are insane enough to join my pool, you may reach me at this number by Monday next.' He gave him a business card. 'And may I remind you: discretion, eh? *Mais ça va sans dire, n'est-ce pas?* Good evening, gentlemen.'

He walked out of the room. When the door closed, Sonny said, 'Isn't he a character?'

'Yes, and he doesn't make any bones about his reputation. Of course, that's part of the act: instill confidence by being blunt about your shadiness.'

'But you're interested?' urged Sonny.

Drew stood up.

'Maybe. I'll have to think about it. And learn a lesson from Serge: don't be so goddam anxious. Christ, you couldn't sell life insurance on Death Row.'

He drove back uptown in his Mercedes to East Sixty-second Street, where, in a handsome town house between Second and Third Avenues, he rented the bottom two floors for $2,400 a year, rents being quoted by the year rather than the month in that age of cheap housing. He let himself in the ground-floor kitchen, then went upstairs to undress. The apartment was done in good taste—Drew had inherited his mother's eye—but the bedroom was a bachelor mess with clothes thrown everywhere. On the walls were tacked dozens of photos of movie and sports stars, Babe Ruth in juxtaposition with Clara Bow.

He undressed, got in bed, turned out the light and thought about Serge Wittgenstein and smart money. Part of Victor's divorce settlement with Lucille had been the setting up of a million-dollar trust fund for each of the three children. Drew had used his income from the trust to finance his high life, which he certainly couldn't have managed on his meager bank salary alone, but he didn't have fifty thousand dollars available from the trust to invest, nor could he borrow from the bank without letting his father know. And Drew had no illusions about what Victor would say if he learned his son were investing in one of Serge Wittgenstein's notorious pools. Drew had mixed feelings about Victor. Part of him admired the great American success story of his life, his power and wealth. Another part chafed at Victor's preachy determination that his son not become a rich brat, that he be responsible, have character. Drew remembered the incident of stealing the speedboat ten years before, and his father's outrage. He knew that working on the road gang had been 'good' for him and had probably helped his 'character,' but he had hated it just the same. Now at the bank it was the same thing all over again. Victor was making him start at the bottom and work up. If anything, he was harder on Drew than on the others. It was galling, infuriating; being the son of the president was almost a handicap. Victor was a rich man—his wealth was estimated at around thirty million—but Drew wanted to be richer, wanted to outdo him. And you didn't get rich being as stodgily conservative as his father had turned out to be.

He had about sixty thousand dollars in government bonds that he had inherited from an Elliot aunt. He decided to sell them off and have himself a little fling.

The following Monday evening, Serge Wittgenstein, who lived in and operated his business out of a luxurious five-floor Normandy-style town house in the East Fifties, made a phone call to a number in Brooklyn. The man who answered had a soft voice with an Italian accent.

'Dexter invested the money,' said Serge.

There was a long silence. Serge could hear the man's breathing. Then he said, 'Good. Keep me informed.'

The man hung up.

CHAPTER 30

The house was a nineteenth-century brownstone on St. Luke's Place in Greenwich Village. Drew rang the bell then waited, watching the kids play stickball on the pleasant block which had been the birthplace of the city's mayor, Jimmie Walker. Millie opened the door. She was wearing a blue skirt and a white blouse. Her long legs were stockingless, and she was barefoot.

'I like your new block,' he said, coming in, 'but it's a bit of a change from Sutton Place.'

'The house belongs to Ellie Saybrook's parents, but they're in Europe so Ellie said I could move in till I find a place of my own.'

He went into the living room and looked around. The high-ceilinged room was furnished in prewar style with heavy wooden chairs and tables; there was even a Tiffany lamp on one table, and a big Victorian painting of two sleeping dogs. But in the corner was a brand-new radio. The two tall windows looking out on the rear garden flooded the place with light.

Drew flopped on the big, overstuffed plush sofa and put his feet on the arm.

'Did you have a fight with your parents?' he asked.

'No. I just decided it was time to get out on my own.'

He studied her. She seemed tense, nervous. A slow grin came over his face.

'I have an idea there's more to it than that. Where's Ellie now?'

'In Philadelphia at a wedding.'

'So we've got the place to ourselves?'

She nervously lit a cigarette.

'Drew, I'm sorry I yelled at you the other night, but . . . well, you were so damned *rude!* You know you really can be awful . . . oh, *damn*.'

She turned her back to him and smoked furiously. He got off

the sofa and came to her, putting his arms around her slim waist. He kissed the back of her neck and whispered, 'Calm down.'

She turned to him, and there were angry tears in her eyes.

'Sometimes I hate you,' she said, softly, 'but other times I want you more than anything else in the world.'

He gently rubbed her back.

'Tired of being a Vestal Virgin?' he asked.

'Sick of it.'

'It's about time.'

She stubbed out the cigarette.

'You may not believe this, but I'm not quite sure what we do.'

'Well, first we find a bedroom.'

'That's easy enough. Let's go upstairs.'

She led him to the second floor, then into a medium-sized room overlooking sunny St. Luke's Place. A big walnut bed with a white chenille spread looked welcoming. She pulled the shades down over the two windows, then turned to him.

'Now what?'

He sat on the bed and started untying his shoes.

'You mean to tell me at Smith they didn't teach you *anything?*'

'They don't teach sex in college, you nitwit. All we learned is what we got out of hot novels, and in those they never *describe* anything. The hero starts "raining kisses on the heroine's upturned face," then they skip to the next chapter.'

He laughed.

'I'll see if I can fill in the blank pages. We have to take our clothes off, you know.'

She started unbuttoning her skirt.

'I figured *that* much out. Isn't there something you have to put on so we don't have a baby?'

'You're jumping ahead.'

'Oh.'

When they were both naked, he got off the bed and came to her. She stared at him with undisguised curiosity as the late afternoon sun, filtered by the window shades, filled the room with a soft glow.

'So *that's* what it looks like,' she said, quietly. 'It's sort of funny-looking.'

'I know, but it does two things awfully well.'

She reached out and put her hand on his smooth chest, feeling him. Then he took her in his arms and pulled her against him. She liked the feel of his hard body. As he began kissing her, his warmth filled her with awakening excitement.

'Drew?' she whispered.

'What?'

'I know it's supposed to be very chic just to do it and not feel anything, but . . . do you feel anything for me?'

'No.'

She pulled back and looked at his face.

'Nothing?'

'I just want to lay you. But if it'll make you feel better, I'll tell you I'm madly in love with you and every time I see you, heavenly choirs start yodeling.'

She looked hurt. She went over and sat on the bed.

'Well, I guess I asked for that,' she finally said. 'And at least you're honest.'

He came to the bed.

'Look, Millie: you're a beautiful girl, you're a sharp dresser, you come from a good family—you've got everything going for you. Why do you give a damn whether I love you or not? Love is for teenagers in a Buffalo high school. This is Manhattan.'

'You make it all sound so cold.'

'It's a cold world.'

She frowned.

'Then I don't think I want to do it after all.'

'Oh no. You ask me all the way down here to St. Luke's Place and bring me up to the bedroom . . . oh no, Millie. I don't go for that cock-tease crap.'

He pushed her back on the bed and straddled her.

'Drew—!'

'Shut up. You talk too much.'

He started kissing her, hotly, holding her wrists against the white spread. She struggled a bit, then stopped. She felt his penis becoming stiff against her, and she began to panic.

'Drew, the thing . . .'

'What thing?'

'I don't want to get pregnant!'

'Shit.'

He got off her, went to his pants and fished something out of his wallet. She watched his back as he put the rubber on. She was furious at herself for the way she had handled him—or mishandled him—and she hated his coldness. But his broad back veeing down to his tight buttocks intrigued her. She wanted him enough to crawl, and she knew she was crawling.

He came back to the bed saying, 'You won't get knocked up now.'

She put up no resistance as he climbed on her again.

'This may hurt a little,' he whispered, kissing her small breasts.

She tensed as he eased into her, but he knew what he was doing. She felt a rage in him that was tightly controlled, a fierce hunger that excited her and slightly frightened her. She moaned as he broke her hymen, and then a plum sweetness began filling her.

Afterward, he said, 'That wasn't so bad, was it?'

She fondled his thick black hair, which was the most obvious reminder of his half-Italian genes.

'I loved it,' she smiled. 'Is it as nice at night as it is in the afternoon?'

'You'll find out tonight.'

He kissed her, then got off the bed.

'Oh Christ,' he said, looking at the chenille spread. 'We'll have to send that to the laundry.'

He really is a cold-blooded son of a bitch, she thought.

The entire personal wealth of the twelve directors of the Dexter Bank had been estimated at over $500 million; the president of the bank, Victor, was by far the poorest director, though 'poor' was a relative term. By any yardstick except that of the tycoon, he was a rich man, but the divorce settlement with Lucille had drained his resources. His lawyers had come close to fainting when he told them he had agreed to give Lucille a million dollars a year. They had wrangled with Lucille's lawyers, and a three-million-dollar settlement had been agreed to, along with the establishment of million-dollar trusts for each of the three children. The payout was made over five years, so it wasn't until 1921 that Victor had any income to invest. The five lean years were made up for with a bang when he bought 25,000 shares of a small outfit called the Ajax Radio Corporation. When commercial radio took off, the shares of Ajax soared from two dollars to $110 in three years. Victor exercised options on another 25,000 shares so that when he sold out in 1924, he pocketed a profit of millions.

This was the most spectacular of his investments, but he made others almost as successful. However, Victor had a peasant's innate fiscal caution, and he didn't like the speculative fever that was sweeping the country. He began selling off all but his most bluechip stocks, reinvesting in treasury bills and Manhattan real estate. Thus, while he was still the 'poor man' on the board of directors, Victor's income enabled him to live well and support the many charities he had become involved with.

Living well for Victor meant the Sands Point house for weekends and a handsome Fifth Avenue apartment he moved into in 1921, finally tiring of the Plaza. It also meant mistresses, for Victor at fifty-seven retained his lively interest in women. They came and went, satisfying him physically but not emotionally. If he had gotten over Lucille, he had never gotten over the *idea* of Lucille. He desperately wanted a wife he could love. His many business friends tried to matchmake: he was constantly being invited to dinners where his dinner partner 'happened' to be an unattached female. Certainly he was a desirable catch, and the divorcées and widows seated at his side made an effort. Victor, always hopeful, followed up many times with invitations to a play or the opera; but, lonely as he was, the magic spark didn't seem to ignite. He told himself he was acting like an old fool. He had his children, his three grandchildren, his varied interests; his life was full, and he had much to be thankful for. He should settle into the serenity of late middle age. But serenity eluded him.

He kept remembering Julia Lombardini.

Julia had been one of the sweetest idylls of his life, but Victor was honest enough to admit his moral duplicity had soured it for both of them. He knew he was not the pillar of decency the public considered him. Many of Lucille's attacks had been justified. Thus it was always with a certain reluctance that he preached to any of his children, especially Drew. Unhappily, Drew needed periodic sermons; and on that May morning as his son was ushered into Victor's office, the venerated president of the Dexter Bank prepared himself to launch a blast.

'Good morning, Father,' said Drew.

'Good morning, Drew.'

Drew took the chair in front of the desk and waited, wondering what this was all about. Victor wasn't in the habit of summoning him to his office for idle conversation.

'Drew,' Victor finally said, 'I don't have to mention that the relationship between fathers and sons—especially successful fathers and bright sons—can be difficult. There are enough plays and films written on the subject to make it seem like a national disaster, even if it isn't. And the problem has been made worse by your modern attitudes, which to my generation are rather baffling. On the other hand, I'm aware you must think of me as an old fuddy-duddy . . .'

'Not at all,' interrupted Drew. 'I've always thought you were very hot stuff, particularly with women.'

'I'm sure you consider that a compliment. I suppose the

biggest difference between you and me is that I consider it the most devastating comment you could make on my life.'

'Oh come on, Father. There's nothing wrong with liking the ladies! You and Mother didn't get along, so it was natural you'd play around.'

'Natural, perhaps, but not particularly admirable. At any rate, I won't pretend I've been a perfect father or husband. But my life isn't that important anymore. Yours is. You're the future, Drew. I want you to be a fine, honorable man—better than I was. *Far* better. I suppose there's an element of self-justification in this—that perhaps I can make up for some of my failings through you—but selfish or not, that's what I want. I'm proud of you, Drew, terribly proud. You could have turned out a spoiled, rich brat, and I don't think that has happened. From what I can observe, you seem to enjoy your work here at the bank?'

'Well, I'd like a little more responsibility.'

'That's understandable, and I'm glad you're ambitious. I *want* you to be ambitious. But Drew, I learned something yesterday that has made me extremely upset.'

Oh oh, he thought, here it comes.

'You bear a proud old name on Wall Street,' Victor continued. 'A name I adopted, but one that you were born to, through your mother. You never knew your great-uncle Augustus, whom I had many fights with—some of them right here in this very room—but Augustus Dexter, for all his faults, was a formidably honest man who would never have dealings with anyone whose character was in the slightest degree shady. I've tried to do the same thing during my time here at the bank. I expect you to do the same thing during your time.' He paused, eyeing his son. 'Is it true,' he said finally, 'you invested money with Serge Wittgenstein?'

Drew shifted uncomfortably.

'What if it is?' he said. 'Don't I have the right to invest my own money where I want?'

'No. Not with a man like Wittgenstein.'

'I've made a fortune with him! I've tripled my money!'

'On this bear raid of American Hotel stock? Good God, I wish you'd lost every penny! Don't you realize that man represents the scum of the financial community? That he's nothing more than a common thief, suckering thousands of investors out of their savings?'

'Come on, Father: he's not the only one! The stock market's a sucker's game: anyone with any brains knows that!'

'Oh yes, smart money. And what happens when the suckers

catch on, Drew? Did you ever think of that? It's so easy to become contemptuous of those invisible people out in Ohio who buy the stocks and bonds, but they're not fools, Drew. They also happen to be the backbone of this country, and I won't have my son profiteering at their expense! Do you understand?'

Drew glared at him.

'I didn't "profiteer." I made a legitimate profit, and I see nothing wrong with it. I gambled with my own money. I could have lost, but I won. I don't see why you take it out on me, when the whole system is geared to what I've done! Isn't capitalism supposed to be a gamble?'

'Yes, but not a racket! You know the American Hotel pool was rigged from beginning to end. Don't you see that you and I can't afford to be connected with men like Wittgenstein?' Victor paused. 'I want you one day to run this bank. You know that. But Drew, even though you're my son whom I love very deeply . . . if you have anything further to do with this Serge Wittgenstein, I'll have to reconsider your future. I don't like threats, but in this instance I feel I have no alternative. I know you're probably resenting this . . .'

'Resenting?' exploded Drew. 'You're goddam right I'm resenting it!' He stood up and leaned on the desk. 'Listen Father, times have changed and you haven't changed with them. You fought for your little Italian investors, and you won. I'm fighting for *me*. And if you think I'm any less of a man than you were, then you don't know your son very well. So Father, you can take the Dexter Bank and stuff it. I quit!'

He headed for the door. Victor was stunned.

'Drew!' he cried out. It was a cry of hurt more than anger. 'What?'

'Listen to me! This is insane! There's no reason for us to be this illogical! Now come back and sit down and we'll talk this out . . .'

'Father, there's nothing to talk out. Only one person's going to control my life, and it's not going to be you. It's going to be me.'

He slammed out of the office. Damn him, thought Victor. *Damn* him! He's pulled the same blasted trick on me I pulled on Augustus . . . but my God, I can't lose my son . . .

He flipped on his intercom and said to his secretary, 'Get me Serge Wittgenstein.'

307

'Your father tried to buy me off,' said Serge late that night as he and Drew played five-card draw in the back room of the Hotcha Club. Drew looked up from his freshly dealt hand.

'What do you mean?'

'He called me this morning. It must have been just after the dramatic little scene you told me about. He was extremely agitated—quite unlike my preconception of Mr. Victor. He asked me how much money I wanted to have nothing more to do with you. I was shocked. It was very emotional.'

'He has some nerve! I hope you told him to go to hell.'

'On the contrary. I told him I would do what he asked for free.'

Drew put down his cards.

'You *what?*'

'My dear fellow, your father is absolutely right. You should have nothing to do with me, at least in market dealings. I hope we can remain friends socially.'

Drew shook his head in frustration.

'Damn it, I can't excape him! That's what the fight was all about this morning: his trying to control me! Now you, of all people, are agreeing with him!'

'Your father's a very important man. I have no wish to alienate him.'

'So *that's* it. You're protecting your own skin . . .'

'Well, that's partially it. You can hardly blame me. But he *is* right. You should stay with the bank and be a pillar of the community.'

Drew shoved his chair away from the poker table and got up to pace around the room.

'I'm *tired* of being Mr. Victor's son, I'm *tired* of the bank . . . Why should I have to spend the rest of my life being some sort of model of moral rectitude? Do you think *he's* Father Christmas? Hell no. He's had a string of mistresses a mile long . . .'

'That's different.'

'Why?'

'It just is. Don't be an ass. People don't care if bankers sleep with dogs, but one *hint* of hanky-panky about money and they go crazy. So your father's right. You shouldn't play games in the market: it's too highly visible. Go back to the bank and be a good boy. If you want a little action on the side, well . . . I have other interests beside the market. Much more lucrative and

308

invisible interests. If you want, I might let you in on some of them.'

Drew looked at him.

'Like what?'

'Oh, this club, for instance. I own it.'

'You do?'

'Well, I and a silent partner. One doesn't brag about owning speakeasies, but the profits involved are astronomical. And the people one meets are interesting.'

'You mean bootleggers?'

Serge smiled as he practiced a one-handed shuffle with an extra deck.

'Of course.'

'What's your silent partner's name?'

'He wouldn't be very silent if I told you that, would he? But sit down, Drew. Let me tell you about something we're interested in. Maybe you'll be interested, too. And perhaps you could be a help to us.'

Drew sat down.

'Cigarette?'

'No thanks.'

'As you know, there's a fortune to be made in good Scotch whiskey. Not the rotgut the mob sells, but the real article. Now there happens to be an English shipping line that is for sale. It's the Graham-Howells Line, a fine old firm, but the family has died out and it's up for grabs. It owns fourteen freighters in fairly decent shape which would be ideal for my purposes, but —because other parties are interested for the same reason I am —the price is high: they're asking fifteen million for the lot, ships, crews, goodwill and so forth. Unfortunately, fifteen million is a bit beyond my financial reach. And because I'm greedy and sniff incredible profits in this operation, I don't want to bring in a lot of partners. What I really want is financing from a bank, but alas . . .' he spread his manicured hands and smiled. '. . . few bankers are willing to talk to me. Now, perhaps you see where *you* might come in. I hasten to add that technically there would be nothing we are doing that breaks American laws . . .'

'Bootlegging?'

'Ah, but we don't bring the booze in. We offload it outside the three-mile limit, and *they* bring it in. We're merely shippers, though I grant you that the spirit of the enterprise is a bit so-so.'

'In other words, you want me to influence my father to make the loan?'

'Something like that. The bank makes its legitimate profits, we make ours. You and me. I'm willing to make a seventy-thirty split: seventy percent for me, thirty for you. And it's all legal.'

'You don't know my father. If he saw your name . . .'

'My dear Drew, my name would never appear, nor would yours. The Graham-Howells Line would be bought by a Canadian company based in Quebec. I can furnish impeccable credentials and names. Your father would suspect nothing.'

Drew thought. He saw with perfect clarity that the whole thing was fraudulent, that its success depended on milking his father's soft spot: himself. But that was not the least appealing aspect of it. This way, he, Drew, would be controlling his father instead of the other way around. Plus, it was legal—or legal *enough* —and undoubtedly profitable for the bank as well as himself . . .

'I think,' he finally said, 'the split should be sixty-forty.'

Serge Wittgenstein smiled.

'My dear Drew, you and I are very much alike. Sixty-five –thirty-five.'

Drew extended his hand across the poker table and they shook.

CHAPTER 31

Ten days later Drew presented the loan dossier to his father, adding his recommendation for approval.

'I've checked out the French-Canadian Investment Group who are buying Graham-Howells,' he said. 'They're all top-notch people in Quebec. As I told you, they were going to Barclays for financing, but I think if we can get the business it would be a feather in our cap—and mine.'

'Yes, I agree,' said Victor. 'I'll go over the papers.'

'I don't mean to rush you, Father, but they would like an answer by Friday.'

'I'll give it to you before then.'

'Thanks.'

After Drew left, Victor studied the papers for a few minutes. Then he contacted his secretary.

'Get me Frank Pritchard of the Pritchard Lines, please. Then I'd like to talk to Ellsworth Singleton at the Pinkerton Detective Agency.'

'Yes, Mr. Victor.'

If what Victor suspected was happening were true, it had a vaguely familiar ring to it.

The next afternoon at lunch at the Bankers' Club, Victor asked his guest, Frank Pritchard, a question.

'Why would anyone pay fifteen million dollars for fourteen freighters that are, from what I can gather, rustbuckets?'

The chairman of the Pritchard Steamship Lines, who had arranged loans through Victor in the past, sipped his cream-of-leek soup.

'Is this the Graham-Howells Line?'

'Yes.'

'Then the answer's simple. I hear bootleggers are trying to buy it to bring over Scotch whiskey. Apparently the bidding's so heavy they've run the price way up. The company's not worth half that.'

Victor sighed.

'I was afraid of that. Which bootleggers in particular?'

'Well, I'm no expert on the underworld. But apparently they're the big boys. Don't tell me the Dexter Bank is considering financing hoodlums?'

'Never.'

Victor's answer was so crisp, Frank Pritchard looked at him with surprise.

Ellsworth Singleton was a homely man of medium height who chain-smoked. At forty-seven he had been with the Pinkerton Detective Agency for twenty-three years and was considered one of their resident experts on the underworld. Now, after shaking Victor's hand, he sat down, lit a Camel and said, 'What can I do for you, Mr. Dexter?'

'Who's trying to buy the Graham-Howells Shipping Company?'

'There are three principal bidders, according to my sources. Two in New York, one in Chicago. In Chicago, it's Capone. Here it's Owney Madden and Vinnie Tazzi.'

A long silence.

'When did Tazzi get out of prison?' said Victor.

'Let's see: he was first sent up over twenty years ago for a jewel robbery. As I recall, he tried to knock off a jewelry shop next to the Waldorf . . .'

'Gérard et fils,' interrupted Victor. 'It was in 1903. He and another man named Gianni Difatta got twelve years. Difatta died in a prison fight several years later. Tazzi, as far as I know, served his full term.'

The detective was staring at him.

'You know a lot about Tazzi,' he said.

'More than I'd like. What happened to him then?'

'He was released from Sing-Sing in 1915, and to the best of my knowledge went straight for a while. He even tried to enlist during the war, but his prison record kept him out. I think it was then he started backsliding. He got into pimping, and then, when Prohibition started, bootlegging. That's made him big time.'

'How big is he?'

'He's right up there with Dutch Schultz and Owney Madden. He's got a big operation—almost five hundred men work for him. He's probably worth five or six million.'

'Where does he operate out of?'

'A speakeasy he owns in the Village. It's called the Hotcha Club.'

'I take it the government can't touch him?'

'Not so far. He's clever and he's careful. He operates through middlemen.'

'Like Serge Wittgenstein?'

'He's one of them.'

'Is Tazzi dangerous?'

'He's a killer.'

Not that Victor had to be told. He remembered Little Vinnie —now, apparently, Big Vinnie. The killer with the angel face, now a middle-aged angel. The man whose life and career had been a dark and bloody mirror image of his own. 'My way's better,' Victor had said to him in that Brooklyn alley so many years before. And it *was* better. But Little Vinnie continued to haunt him. 'We're going to give you a souvenir,' he had said, 'so that every time you start forgetting you're Italian, you'll look in a mirror and remember.' Victor remembered. The mirror was Vinnie Tazzi.

'Is there anything else you'd like to know about Tazzi, Mr. Dexter?'

'Nothing that I can't guess. Once, years ago, he tried to extort funds out of this bank. Then, he used blackmail. Now, he's trying to do the same thing, except his method's a little more subtle this time. If nothing else, the man's persistent.'

'Can you handle him, or do you need us?'

'I can handle him,' said Victor, quietly.

Serge Wittgenstein was playing poker in the back room of the Hotcha Club when the door opened and Vinnie Tazzi came in.

'I want to talk to you,' he said. 'Alone.'

'Game's over, my friends,' said Serge. Chips were quickly cashed in and the room cleared. When they were alone, Vinnie sat down at the table.

'So Dexter nixed the loan,' he said.

Serge Wittgenstein began tearing at a hangnail. The dapper little gangster in the black suit was one of the few men on earth who made him nervous.

'His son called me this afternoon. He was furious. He knows about you.'

'How did he know? Did you tell him?'

'Me? Of course not, Vinnie! Why would *I* tell him?'

'Then who did?'

'His father. He figured it out—how, I don't know. He gave

Drew holy hell and has forbidden him to have anything to do with me. So the whole deal's off. I'm sorry . . . I thought we had it sewn up . . .'

'You fat fuck,' said Vinnie. 'You must have tipped him off.'

'I swear I didn't! I *swear!*'

Vinnie pulled a gold toothpick from his pocket and began slowly cleaning his teeth. Serge watched him, sweat beads forming on his temples.

'Maybe Victor *did* figure it out,' he said finally, more to himself than to Serge. 'The bastard always was smart . . .' He put the toothpick away. 'So how are we gonna get the fifteen million to buy the ship company?'

Serge shrugged.

'Raise it from individual investors, the way I wanted to do in the first place. It wasn't *my* idea to waste all this time with Drew Dexter.'

'It was a good idea, and it almost worked. And if there's anything I hate, it's fat fucks telling me I made a mistake.'

Serge swelled with indignation. He stood up.

'I don't have to take this sort of abuse from you!' he exclaimed.

'Sit down,' growled Vinnie.

Serge sat down. Vinnie pointed a finger at him. 'Don't forget who bailed you out two years ago when the stock you were betting on to go down went *up*.'

'I paid you back! And whose idea was it to buy Graham-Howells?'

Vinnie lowered his finger.

'All right, we're partners. We shouldn't fight. But when I want to call you a fat fuck, I will.'

'It's not very polite . . .'

'Then lose weight.' He thought awhile. A long while. Then: 'We've only got a week. I hear Capone's almost got the fifteen million raised. And where are we? Nowhere. Okay, we'll try a more direct method.'

He stood up.

'What are you going to do?' asked Serge.

'You'd better stay out of this.'

Vinnie went to the door.

'Vinnie,' asked Serge, 'why do you hate Victor Dexter?'

The little gangster turned and looked at him.

'He owes me,' he said.
'For what?'
'Twelve long years in Sing-Sing.'
And he left the room.

CHAPTER 32

The former Lucille Dexter was now also the former Lady
Pembroke. In 1923 Lucille had caught Lord Archie *in flagrante*
with the upstairs maid in one of the guest rooms. This was the
final blow to an already rickety marriage. Lord Archie was paid
off (it cost Lucille almost $400,000), and he returned to
Perfidious Albion. One would have thought Lucille's passion for
the European aristocracy would have been sated, but less than a
year later she met, while taking the cure at Baden-Baden, a
thirty-nine-year-old French count named Honoré de Beaumont.
Count de Beaumont was a self-styled expert on beauty and
health. He lived on wheat germ, oats and bananas, shunned
sugar, salt and meat as if they were the plague, and drank a
bottle of white wine a day to 'thin the blood.' This slim and
elegant Frenchman fascinated Lucille who, as she neared sixty,
was becoming almost obsessed with diets and health. Though
formerly a passionate carnivore, she adopted Honoré's diet and
vowed never to touch meat, sugar or salt again in her life. She
and Honoré spent hours daily doing Yoga exercises, and he
introduced her to a special skin cream made by a former
courtesan in Paris that was guaranteed to remove wrinkles. He
whispered to her that one of the ingredients was sperm. Lucille
shuddered, but by now she was so under his spell she would try
anything. The skin cream seemed to work, and the diet and
exercise made her feel younger than she had in years. In June,
1924, they were married in Paris. The wedding reception was
catered by Fauchon, which was hard-pressed to maintain its
standards of *haute cuisine* and still defer to the Count's dietary
taboos.

The Count and Countess divided their time between Paris and
New York. Honoré's ascetic life-style did not preclude party-
giving and, rather to Lucille's dismay, her new husband
launched a series of spectacular entertainments that were almost

ruinously costly. Like Lord Archie, Honoré's pedigree was blue chip, but his financial resources were as slim as his waist: Lucille paid the bills. In May, 1925, Honoré conceived the notion of throwing a costume ball at the town house on Fifth Avenue. The theme of the ball would be 'A Night During the Terror,' duplicating a ball given by one of Honoré's ancestors in 1794 in the Faubourg Saint-Germain. At that party, held during the height of the Terror, aristocrats who had lost one or more relatives to the guillotine wore red ribbons around their necks to commemorate the bloody slash of the blade. Honoré proposed doing the same thing, with the women wearing the diaphanous, breast-revealing fashions of the period. When Lucille mildly remonstrated to her husband about the cost of yet another huge party, Honoré reminded her how much money they were saving with their nonexistent butcher bills.

The party was dubbed the Red Ribbon Ball by the tabloids, and the Grand Guignol aspect of the extravaganza caught the public's morbid fancy: It became *the* party of 1925, and invitations were prized like cabochon emeralds. Toy guillotines appeared in toyshop windows, and there was a brief fad of secretaries wearing red ribbons around their necks to work. The cost of the party was inaccurately reported to be over $100,000, which prompted the *Times* to write a grumpy editorial on the follies of the rich. All this did nothing but draw bigger crowds to the corner of Seventy-third Street and Fifth Avenue on the night in question, and several dozen policemen were needed to keep them from spilling into the streets, blocking the stream of limousines waiting to disgorge their red-ribboned occupants at the front door.

Drew, who escorted Millie Chapin, had the good sense to park several blocks away and walk to his mother's house. Millie looked sensational in a pale-green Directoire dress that was so gauzy her body showed through quite plainly; only cleverly sewn extra tucks of material in strategic places prevented her from being picked up by the Vice Squad. Her blond hair was curled in the style of the period, and the only decoration she wore besides the red neck ribbon was one of green silk just below her rather flat breasts. As the cool spring breeze fluttered her gauzy draperies against her body, outlining her splendid, sandaled legs, the men in the crowd hooted and clapped. Millie smiled, as if to say, 'Aren't I gorgeous?' Drew was not to be outdone in sensationalism. He had rented a blue-and-white-striped silk jacket, boots, and a pair of fawn breeches that were so tight he wore a jock strap to prevent his considerable equipment from being too publicly displayed. Even so, the bulge at his crotch elicited whistles from the girls in the crowd. Drew loved it.

Inside the town house, a ghost from the eighteenth century would have felt at home. Honoré had banned electricity for the evening, and pre-Edison candles flickered magically in the doré sconces and crystal chandeliers. Liveried servants took Directoire hats and coats as the guests slowly mounted the graceful stair to the second-floor ballroom to be greeted by their hosts. Lucille had had copied a diaphanous gown worn by Mme. de Récamier. While more modest than Millie's, it still showed her diet-slim figure to advantage. Honoré had decided his wife must show up everyone else at the party by wearing, instead of the obligatory red ribbon, a thin necklace of rubies he had designed for her at Van Cleef and Arpels. Lucille thought this was a bit much, but, as usual, she went along with his wishes. In the increasing loneliness of her essentially empty, if glittering, life, Lucille had found she needed her young husbands like addicts need heroin. And, like an addict, she was willing to pay the price.

The dance opened with a stately quadrille which few of the guests knew how to do. But Honoré wisely decided that one eighteenth-century dance was enough, and the band reentered the twentieth century by segueing into a Charleston. The dance floor quickly filled, and Drew and Millie threw themselves into the wild dance with appropriate abandon.

'Well, what do you think of it?' asked Drew as he flapped his hands back and forth across bent knees.

'Oh, it's a giggle. And so is your stepfather. Is he a fairy?'

'I don't think so. Why?'

'He's so piss-elegant he sort of reminds me of one.'

'Mother's his third wife.'

'That doesn't mean much.'

'For a girl who'd never made love till last month, you've certainly picked up a lot of exotic sexual information.'

'Oh, living in the Village has taught me a lot, and I'm a *very* quick study.'

'So I've noticed.'

'For instance, a lesbian made a pass at me the other day.'

'My God, you're going *too* fast! Where?'

'At this literary cocktail party I went to. A friend of Ellie's has opened a very intellectual bookshop in the Village, and she threw a "do" for this Brazilian novelist who's written a lesbian love story. *Very* shocking. Anyway, the novelist had a monocle

318

and Louise Brooks bangs and a tweed suit—the works—and she asked me if I'd go to bed with her.'

'I hope you didn't.'

'Of course not. Women don't interest me that way. Besides,' she smiled, 'I've got you.'

They were sipping champagne in the downstiars library. It was midnight, and the thin curtains before the open windows on Fifth Avenue fluttered lazily in the night breeze. Drew's eyes were devouring the curves of her body as Millie lazed in a sofa, smoking. The ceiling shook with the pounding of feet as the crowd danced the Black Bottom above them.

'I told you about Serge Wittgenstein,' he said, after a while. 'Well, he's gotten me in a lot of trouble with my old man.'

'What kind of trouble?'

'It turns out he's in cahoots with a bootlegger named Vinnie Tazzi, and they were using me to get a big loan from the bank.'

'You didn't know they were using you?'

Drew avoided her eyes.

'I knew.'

'You *knew* these crooks were swindling your father, and you went along with it?'

'It wasn't *exactly* a swindle . . . Oh hell, yes it was, and yes I went along with it.'

'But why?'

'I was trying to hurt the old man and everything he stands for! You don't know what it's like having him *preach* at me all the time!' He simmered down. 'Anyway, I had a hell of a row with the old man, as you can imagine. And then I began thinking about myself and life and all that, and I've come to the conclusion I want to get married. And it's you I want. How about it?'

She exhaled slowly.

'Are you serious?'

'Very.'

'But you told me you didn't feel anything for me at all. You said love was for high school kids.'

'Maybe I was wrong. Maybe I was just being a smart-ass. Anyway, how about it?'

'It's a terribly casual proposal.'

'But it's a genuine one.'

'I'd hate to think you want to marry me just because you're mad at your father.'

'That's only part of it, though I'll admit it *is* part of it. I think if I get married and have kids, it'll get him off my back a little.'

'But you don't love me?' she asked, coolly.

He looked at her.

'I think I do, Millie. I don't think there's a hell of a lot of love in me, but whatever there is, you've got it. Do you love me?'

She put the cigarette out.

'I'll have to think about it,' she said.

Let *him* sweat a while, she thought, triumphantly. Let *him* crawl!

He didn't notice the black Buick pull out of Sixtieth Street.

Drew had just turned into Sixty-second Street, having taken Millie home to St. Luke's Place, and now he headed for his garage near Second Avenue. The Buick parked and waited until he emerged from the garage. He began walking west toward his apartment. The Buick started up the empty street. The back door opened. Two men jumped out and ran up behind him. He heard their footsteps and turned. The first man grabbed his arm.

'What the hell . . .'

'Come on, fancy pants. Christ, would you look at this fucking outfit?'

He started to struggle. The second man pulled a blackjack from his pocket and smashed it on his head.

Drew slumped into unconsciousness.

Mrs. Julia Lombardini Rizzo was dusting the small living room of her house in Brooklyn when she heard the doorbell ring. She looked at the clock on the mantel: a little after ten in the morning. Wondering who could be calling at that hour, she went to the window and looked at the front stoop. A tall, slim man in a well-cut suit was at the door, a black Homburg on his gray head. For a moment she didn't recognize him. When she did, she hurried from the window to a mirror and checked her reflection. Julia was forty-six, and her hair was graying also, but she had kept her figure and was still an attractive woman. The brown housedress she was wearing wasn't the best thing in her wardrobe, but she didn't have time to change it. She went into the small entrance hall and opened the door.

'Hello, Julia,' said Victor, removing his hat.

She hadn't seen him in almost twenty years, but all she could think of to say was, 'Hello, Victor.'

'I realize this is rather awkward, but could I talk to you? Something has happened . . .'

'Of course. Come in.'

She glanced past him at the long, black Packard which was attracting a small crowd of curious kids in the middle-class neighborhood. Victor came into the hall. She closed the door and pointed to the living room. 'I was just dusting,' she said, feeling foolish.

He went into the living room and looked around at the time-payment furniture, the time-payment radio, the time-payment hooked rug . . . His life was turning out to be time-payment, too. First Vinnie Tazzi, now Julia. He looked at her and his past flooded over his present.

'May I sit down?'

'Please.'

Putting his hat on a chair, he sat in an overstuffed plush sofa with lace antimacassars. She took a wooden-armed chair. Behind her a black iron floor lamp hooked its shaded light bulb over her shoulder like a curious flamingo.

'It's been a long time,' he said.

'Twenty years, isn't it? Or almost.'

'I read about your uncle's passing away. I'm sorry. He was a fine man.'

'He was old.'

'And your husband is . . . ?'

'He passed away last year.'

He looked surprised.

'But he wasn't very old, was he?'

'He didn't die naturally. Cesare was in the wine importing business. He also drank heavily. Prohibition put him out of business, which made him drink more heavily. Except it was rotgut. Last year he bought some stuff that was literally lethal. He died in agony. So much for that great moral experiment called Prohibition.' She paused. 'You didn't see his obituary in the papers because they weren't interested in Cesare Rizzo. But they're interested in the Dexters. I read about Lucille's big party the other night—what did they call it? The Red Ribbon Ball? It doesn't sound as if she's changed much. You managed to divorce her after all, didn't you? Even though you told me you couldn't do it.'

Her tone had become hostile.

'I never knew you to sound bitter.'

'I never used to be when I was . . . shall we say . . . foolish or naïve enough to believe there'd be a happy ending to our little love story. But I've thought about you a lot over the years,

Victor. I even started to write you a letter several times, but then thought better about it.'

'What would the letter have said?'

'Oh, something to the effect that, in retrospect, you were one of the most selfish men I'd ever met. It would have sounded like sour grapes, and frankly it would have been. When we broke up, I was so in love with you I felt sorry for you. But then a few years later when you divorced Lucille, I began to feel sorry for myself. You uséd me, Victor. I was a convenience to you. No one likes to be used.'

He nodded.

'I deserve that. But you left out one thing: I loved you very deeply.'

'I'm sure you did. But that didn't do me much good. I assume you didn't come out to this rather unglamorous neighborhood to discuss old times?'

'Yes, in fact, I did, in a way. But . . .' He stood up. 'I think I made a mistake. *Another* mistake. I won't bother you anymore.'

'You can at least show me the courtesy of telling me why you came.'

He sat back down.

'All right: I came because I'm frightened and I don't know what to do. You remember Vinnie Tazzi?'

'Very well. It was his rotgut that killed my husband.'

'Did you tell that to the police?'

'Of course. What could they do? What do they care? Thousands of people die from rotgut. They can't try to prove every case is murder—which is exactly what it is. They told me to hire a lawyer, but they didn't tell me what I was supposed to pay the lawyer with. Cesare's insurance just barely paid off our debts and his funeral. Forget lawyers and the police.'

He was amazed how harsh she had become. He had forgotten how poverty kills gentleness.

'You must have *some* money,' he said.

'A little comes in from an annuity Uncle Ettore left me. I get by. Why did you mention Vinnie Tazzi?'

'He kidnapped my son.'

Now it was her turn to look surprised. And concerned.

'When?'

'Yesterday morning, after Lucille's party. The police have traced him up till about four-thirty in the morning. He left his car in his garage around that time, and then he just vanished. I haven't received a ransom note yet, but I know it was Tazzi.'

'Why?'

He explained about Serge Wittgenstein and the Graham-Howells Line.

'I wanted to talk to someone,' he went on. 'Lucille's hysterical, the police don't know what to do, *I* don't know what to do . . .' He shrugged helplessly. 'I thought of you.'

She saw something new in his eyes: desperation.

'If Tazzi hurts him . . .'

He didn't finish the sentence.

She got up, came over to him, took his hand and squeezed it a moment.

'I'll heat up the coffee,' she said. 'We'll have a cup and talk.'

She released his hand and went into the kitchen.

CHAPTER 33

Serge Wittgenstein tied the silk belt of his Japanese happy coat, then lighted a Sobranie as he waited for his Japanese houseboy to bring Victor up to his third-floor office. The banker had called him two hours before, asking to see him. Serge had a good idea what he wanted to see him about.

The office had a glass-domed stock ticker, a desk with four telephones and a black filing cabinet next to a window overlooking the back garden of the town house. Over a leather sofa hung an eighteenth-century Japanese screen, its gold surface shimmering in the afternoon sun. Above the small fireplace hung a brace of nineteenth-century dueling pistols, and the room was cluttered with other objects which Serge, a passionate collector, had bought all over the world. Flanking the fireplace were two closed doors.

The hall door opened and Victor came in. Serge put down his cigarette and crossed the room, hand extended.

'Mr. Dexter, I'm delighted to meet you. Drew has told me so much about you, I feel I already know you.'

Victor looked at the hand, but didn't shake it. He raised his eyes to stare coldly at Serge's.

'What will it cost me to get my son back?' he said.

'I beg your pardon?'

'Let's not play games. Tazzi has kidnapped Drew . . .'

'Kidnapped!?'

'Get off it, man! I'm here to negotiate! The police know nothing of this, so for God's sake, don't play games!'

Serge went back to his desk and sat down.

'I'm listening,' he said.

'That's better.' Victor sat on the sofa. 'I know Tazzi's in Cuba buying a yacht he wants to turn into a gambling ship. He's been down there five days, so that no one could pin the kidnapping on him. He let his boys do it for him. He hasn't sent me a ransom note because he knows I'll figure out who's done it and come to you. So, here I am. What's the price?'

'What do you think?'

'Approval of the loan to buy Graham-Howells?'

Serge smiled, spread his hands, said nothing.

'What sort of guarantee would I have that Drew is unharmed?'

The door to the left of the fireplace opened, and Vinnie Tazzi walked in. Serge looked surprised.

'I thought you wanted *me* to handle it—' he blurted.

'Shut up.'

Vinnie walked over to Victor and looked him over.

'So,' he said finally, 'here we are, just like old times, eh, Victor?' He turned to Serge. 'Victor and I go back a long way, you know? A long time. We was kids together in Brooklyn.'

'Was I wrong?' said Victor. 'You weren't in Cuba?'

'Oh yeah, I was there. Bought me a beauty of a yacht that belonged to some sugar king down there. Got a bargain, Victor. They're bringing it up to New York next week, but I flew up yesterday. And when Serge told me you were coming to see him, well, I couldn't resist being here. I've been wanting to see you for a long time, Victor. A *long* time.'

'Have you hurt Drew?'

'Nah. No one's touched a hair of his head. I wouldn't have much bargaining power if he were hurt, would I?'

'I'll arrange the loan,' said Victor. 'I'll deposit half of it in the Quebec branch of the Bank of Canada. When Drew is returned to me safely, I'll deposit the other half. Will you accept that?'

Vinnie thought a minute, then nodded.

'Yeah, that sounds good. I'll go for that.' He smiled slowly. 'I like to see you sweat, Victor. It makes me feel real good inside.'

Victor stood up.

'I'll have the transfer made in the morning. Where will Drew be?'

'We'll let him go somewhere safe and give him carfare home. Trust me, Victor. You really ain't got no choice *but* to trust me. You know?'

Victor knew. He started for the door.

'Wait a minute, Victor. There's one other thing. Come back here.'

Victor closed his eyes in momentary frustration, then returned.

'I ain't done with you yet, Victor. You owe me a lot. Sing-Sing's a shitty place to spend twelve years, a real shitty place. You sent me there, didn't you? You set up that robbery

325

job at the jewel store and suckered me right in. I had a long time to figure that one out, so don't deny it. Did you ever think of me during those twelve years, Victor? I bet you didn't. You were sitting fat and happy in your bank, getting richer every year, becoming a big cheese . . . You didn't think of me, Victor, but I thought of you. Oh, I thought of you a lot. I thought about this moment when I'd have you by the balls again—like I did once before, remember? You outsmarted me then, but not this time, Victor. This time, I got you *good*. And I'm gonna squeeze 'em just a little tighter, Victor. Get down on your hands and knees.'

Victor stiffened.

'Go on, get *down*. That is, if you want to see Drew again. His guards are real trigger-happy, Victor. All it takes is a phone call.'

Victor slowly got on his hands and knees.

'Look at this, Serge! The big banker, Mr. Wall Street, on his hands and knees in front of Vinnie Tazzi, the bootlegger! Ain't it beautiful? Now, Victor, you see my right shoe? I want you to crawl up and kiss my toe.'

'You filthy swine . . .'

'Don't get me mad, Victor. Don't get me mad. Kiss my toe.'

Victor didn't move.

'DO IT, YOU SON OF A BITCH!' screamed Vinnie.

Victor crawled forward and put his lips on the shiny black leather toe. It was the second time in his life Vinnie had totally degraded him. He swore it would be the last.

Vinnie looked down at him, his eyes gleaming. Then, swiftly, he pulled his foot back and kicked him as hard as he could in the face. Victor moaned and rolled over on his side, clutching his right cheek with both hands.

'Last time I kicked you, it was in the balls,' hissed Vinnie. 'But you're an old man now, Victor, so I let you off easy.'

Serge had watched this with genuine horror. Now he said, 'Christ, Vinnie, that's enough . . .'

Vinnie walked to the door, looking back at Victor, who was still on the floor, holding his face.

'If I killed the fuck, it wouldn't be enough.'

He left the room. Serge hurried over to help Victor to his feet.

'Are you all right?' he said.

Victor removed his hands. The toe had gone in below his right eye, breaking the skin. Blood was all over his cheek, and already a great blue-black lump was swelling.

'Get me some water,' he whispered, hoarsely.

'I'll get a washcloth . . .'

Serge hurried into the adjacent bedroom, then into the bath, where he rinsed a facecloth in warm water. He hurried back to the office.

Victor had gone.

The next twenty-four hours were an agony of suspense. He arranged the tranfer of half the loan to the Canadian bank, then called Julia Rizzo in Brooklyn and asked her if she would come to the Fifth Avenue apartment and be with him while he waited for Drew. She arrived at noon to find him sitting in his library, drinking. He was still in his pajamas and bathrobe and hadn't shaved. A large bandage covered his swollen right cheek. When he described the scene in Serge's office, she could hardly believe it. 'He kicked you in the *face?*' she exclaimed.

'He's done worse to me. Far worse. I didn't have any choice, Julia. He has Drew.'

'I know, but it's so vicious . . .'

'*He's* vicious!' he said, turning his bloodshot eyes on her. 'A vicious dog of a man. He always has been. And I swear to you, and I swear before God: if he hurts Drew, I'll kill him.'

'Don't even talk like that . . .'

'I will. I'm Sicilian. All my life I've fought against the violence, the killing . . . but if he kills Drew, I'll kill him. I'll be just as goddam Sicilian as the man who killed my brother. I'll *kill* him!'

She knew he meant it.

The call came at three-thirty. Victor picked up the phone. 'Hello?'

'Father, it's me. Drew.'

'Oh Jesus—are you all right?'

'Yes, they didn't hurt me. They left me off in Harlem. I'm using the phone at Connie's Inn, but I can't go out on the street.'

'Why? What's wrong?'

'I'm still in this crazy costume from Mother's party! They're all laughing at me . . .'

Victor covered the mouthpiece and started laughing himself. 'He's all right,' he said to Julia. 'He's all right . . .' He uncovered the mouthpiece. 'Listen, Drew: stay there. I'll send my car up to get you. What's the address?'

'Seventh Avenue and 132nd Street. And tell Claude to bring me a raincoat so I can cover up this goddam costume!'

'Yes, I'll tell him . . . Oh God, son, we've been so worried . . . I'll send Claude right up.'

He hung up and turned to Julia.

'He's afraid . . .' he snorted with laughter, '. . . to go on the street because . . . he's in a fancy-dress costume . . .'

He sank down in the sofa and laughed and laughed until he cried.

Although Drew was unhurt, his father knew that now that Vinnie Tazzi had struck once successfully, none of his family was safe. And the police were helpless. Drew had been blindfolded and tied to a chair during his captivity, so he had no idea who the men were or where they had taken him. Vinnie had the perfect alibi, having been in Cuba at the time of the kidnapping. Moreover, there had been no ransom note. Victor had told the police he suspected Tazzi was behind it, but he didn't tell them about the Graham-Howells loan, so, in a negative way, he was involved in the conspiracy. Yet his prime interest had been Drew's safety. Julia's advice had been to deal with Serge Wittgenstein, and he agreed with her. He had even managed to keep the idea of kidnapping out of the papers, mainly because of the absence of a ransom note. The headlines had read 'Banker's Son Disappears.' When the banker's son reappeared, the story given the papers was that Drew had suffered temporary amnesia. The reports were skeptical, but they printed it.

The day after Drew's return, Victor called a special meeting of the board of directors of the bank and announced he was taking a temporary 'leave of absence.' He explained about the Graham-Howells loan which, even though the bank's money was guaranteed, was still a loan to the underworld. Furthermore, as long as Tazzi was free, there was nothing to stop the racketeer from bringing further pressure on Victor to tap the bank's resources. Consequently Victor was removing himself, *pro tem*, recommending that his executive vice-president, Brian Hughes, take over until the situation with Tazzi could be settled. When asked by the other directors what 'settled' meant, Victor was purposely vague.

That night he took Julia to dinner at a small French restaurant on the West Side, and she asked the same question as the directors: 'What does "settled" mean? How do you "settle" a man like Vinnie Tazzi? If the police are helpless, what can you do?'

'Kill him,' said Victor, calmly. He sipped his Chablis.

'Are you serious?'

'Very.'

'But he didn't hurt Drew . . .'

'Julia, my family . . . Drew, Lorna, even Barbara out on the coast . . . my grandchildren . . . They're all walking targets for this man. *I'm* a walking target. This is a very personal thing between me and Vinnie. He has a pathological hatred for me. The only reason he let Drew go was because he wanted the fifteen million dollars, but if you think we've seen the end of Vinnie Tazzi, you don't know the man like I do. I don't believe in operating outside the law. That's frontier-style stuff, that's the Mafia. But since the law doesn't seem to be able to touch Vinnie —or any of the other big racketeers—then one has the choice of either doing nothing and having one's life destroyed, or fighting back. I've had enough of Vinnie Tazzi. He's haunted my whole life. I'm going to kill him. Not emotionally, as I would have done if he'd killed Drew. But coldly. Rationally. And, I might add, safely.'

'How are you going to do it?'

'I don't know yet. I've hired Ellsworth Singleton of the Pinkerton Agency to keep me informed on as much of his activities as he can find out. Singleton has a lot of contacts in the underworld. The opportunity will happen. And I'm going to do it.' He looked at her. 'I suppose you'll hate me for this.'

'No,' she said, quietly. 'He killed my husband. An eye for an eye.'

'An eye for an eye,' he repeated, reaching out to take her hand.

The opportunity came sooner than he had hoped. Five days later Singleton called him.

'Tazzi's boat's arriving this afternoon from Cuba,' he said.

'The yacht he bought?'

'That's right. He wants to turn it into a gambling ship and operate it outside the three-mile limit. The word is he's going to keep it at anchor three miles due east of Sandy Hook. He's chartered a fishing boat to take him out tonight at ten so he can inspect it.'

'What about the crew?'

'There's only three men aboard, plus the captain. They're Cubans.'

'What's the ship's name?'

'*Lucky Lady*. She's about a hundred feet long with a white hull and a single stack. The fantail's covered with a yellow awning. My source saw it in Havana last year. It belonged to a Senor Lobo who's a big sugar king down there'

'Thanks, Ellsworth.'

After hanging up, Victor rubbed his right cheek, which was still bruised, though the swelling had gone down. Then he called his secretary.

'Get me Frank Pritchard of the Pritchard Lines.'

Vinnie Tazzi held on to the brim of the new gray Borsalino hat he had bought to celebrate his gaining control of the Graham-Howells Line. The wind was fairly strong and the sea choppy, but the night was clear and the sky above the Hudson Canyon an astronomical spectacular.

'What's that over there?' he asked the fishing boat captain, pointing to a distant light off the port bow.

'Ambrose Lightship,' said the captain. He knew who his only passenger was. He would never have agreed to take him out if he hadn't been offered five hundred dollars cash.

'That's to guide the ships?'

'That's right.'

'I've got to learn something about the ocean. I just bought me a shipping company.'

Runty little bastard, thought the captain. He probably bought it with a gun.

Ten minutes later they spotted the *Lucky Lady*'s anchor lights. Another ten minutes and Vinnie was scrambling up the accommodation ladder on the port side to be greeted by his captain, Esteban Ramirez, who wore a black turtleneck sweater and an oil-stained cap.

'Senor Tazzi,' he said, shaking his hand. 'Welcome aboard.'

'Thanks. How was the trip?'

'Not bad.'

'You got the equipment?'

'Yes, Senor. It's in the saloon.'

'Let's see it.'

'Can my men get on the fishing boat? They're anxious to get ashore . . .'

'Yeah, sure. Tell 'em I'll make sure they get all the booze and broads they can handle.'

The captain grinned.

'*Muchas gracias*, Senor.' He turned to yell in Spainish to the three other crew members who were standing on the bridge. Then he led Vinnie aft to the main saloon. The little racketeer clung to the mahogany rail: the ship was rolling in the swells, and Vinnie didn't have his sea legs.

'Does this fucking thing roll like this all the time?' he asked.

'Well, Senor, when we're at anchor, the ship she's gonna roll.'

'How can I expect customers to pay to gamble when they can't even stand up?'

'When it's rough, we can get underway. When the ship's moving, you can keep it steady.'

'You sure?'

'*Si*, Senor.'

He opened one of the doors to the main saloon and turned on the lights. It was a big room, the bulkheads of which had been painted by a Havana artist with a mural of near-pornographic nude nymphs gamboling in stylized waves. The saloon was crammed with crap tables, slot machines, baccarat tables, roulette tables and poker tables, all covered with sheets. The lighting fixtures were smoked-glass wheels with wooden hand-holds surrounding them to simulate helms.

Vinnie grinned and pointed at the nymphs on the bulkheads.

'Ain't they beautiful? The whole fucking wall's a dirty postcard!'

He jerked a sheet off one of the roulette tables and inspected the baize and the wheel.

'This is the best equipment made,' he bragged. 'It comes from Venezuela. Look at those mahogany legs—they're solid as a brick shithouse.'

'You're going to have to clamp the tables to the deck, Senor. We tied rubber tires to them, but when we hit rough seas yesterday, they were banging around.'

'Yeah, I know. But I want to have these floors refinished first.'

'Decks, Senor.'

'Huh?'

'On ships, floors is decks.'

'Shit. Floors is floors.'

They were almost deafened by the blast of a foghorn.

'What the fuck's *that*?' asked Vinnie.

His captain looked disturbed.

'I don't know.'

'It sounded close . . .'

The captain ran to the rear door and looked out. He started screaming in Spanish.

'What happening?' yelled Vinnie.

'We're being RAMMED!'

Captain Ramirez ran out on deck. There was a tremendous crash. Vinnie screamed as the ship lurched violently to port.

Then, an incredible sight: The starboard bulkhead of the saloon was ripped open by the rusty prow of a freighter. The giant steel blade tore fifteen feet into the saloon before shuddering to a stop. Vinnie had run forward to escape the bow. Now, as he pressed fearfully against the bulkhead, he stared at the wall of steel which had wrecked half the gambling tables.

'You son of a bitch!' howled Vinnie at the prow. 'Get the hell out of here!'

Grabbing a handful of spilled poker chips, he started throwing them at the prow. They plinked off the steel and bounced back on the deck.

'Senor! Senor!' Captain Ramirez was pounding on the closed porthole behind him. Vinnie ran to the port.

'The ship is sinking!' the captain yelled through the glass. 'Get on the fishing boat! Hurry!'

He vanished. Vinnie looked around. There were perhaps five feet between the prow of the freighter and the port bulkhead of the saloon, but the space was almost blocked by the crushed gaming tables which had been jammed by the mammoth weight of the freighter almost to the ceiling.

'How do I get out?' yelled Vinnie. Frantically he started climbing up the mountain of smashed mahogany. The prow started shuddering, and the *Lucky Lady* lurched slightly to starboard. Vinnie fell back on to the deck.

'Get me out of here!' he roared.

Just then the lights dimmed and abruptly went out. Now he was totally panicked.

'I can't see! I can't see! Get me out! Help! Jesus Christ, somebody HELP ME!'

The giant prow began backing slowly out the hole. The steel screeched. Vinnie ran to the port and tried to unscrew the restraining bolts. The ship lurched even farther to starboard as the freighter, its screws reversed to try to extricate its bow from the yacht, opened the hole in the *Lucky Lady*'s side even more. Water poured into the engine room. Outside, the fishing boat had backed away from the rapidly sinking yacht. Captain Ramirez and the crew stood on the deck, babbling in excited Spanish.

'The goddam helmsman must have been asleep!' said the fishing-boat captain. 'That thing came straight at you! He *must* have seen it . . .'

Inside the saloon Vinnie lost his footing on the steeply slanting deck and slid backward into a corner. He crouched with horror as he watched the dark gaming tables start toward him like silent pachyderms.

'No,' he whimpered. 'Jesus . . .'

He ducked under a roulette table, which slammed into the bulkhead. He started crawling under the table up the deck. Now the noise of crashing furniture was increasing as the list of the ship worsened. He slid back into the corner. Water. Water was beginning to pour in.

'NO!' he cried, starting to sob as he realized it was all over. 'Somebody's got to help me . . .'

There was a savage scraping sound as the weight of the flooded engine room pulled the *Lucky Lady* off the prow of the freighter. Freed from the bigger ship, the yacht went to the bottom within a minute.

Vinnie's last thought was how cold death was.

CHAPTER 34

The candlelight in Victor's dining room illuminated Drew, Millie Chapin, Carl and Lorna von Gersdorff, and, at Victor's right, Julia Lombardini Rizzo. Lorna and Drew were staring with ill-disguised curiosity at the woman they had never seen but who had been the subject of so much whispered speculation when they were children. They had also noticed the large solitaire diamond on her finger. Julia looked nervous, though she was trying to make dinner conversation with Carl at her right.

After the soup was served, Victor said, 'You probably are wondering why I've asked you here tonight. Or perhaps you've already guessed.' He smiled at Julia and took her hand. 'I've asked Julia to be my wife, and I'm honored to announce that she's accepted my proposal. I hope you all will welcome her into our family. I know you'll find that she is a warm, intelligent, wonderful human being. I hope you come to love her as much as I do. Well, that's probably not possible.'

Lorna got up, came around the table and kissed her father.

'Congratulations,' she said.

Then she kissed Julia.

'I'm so happy for both of you.'

'Thank you,' said Julia.

Then it was Drew's turn. He shook his father's hand and kissed his future stepmother. When they had returned to their seats, Julia said, 'I was a little nervous how you'd react to the news. I guess this is rather awkward to say, but . . . well, you've probably heard a lot about me in the past.' She smiled, and the others laughed. 'At any rate, it was a wonderful thing for me when Victor came back into my life. I said to him last month —rather bitterly, I'll admit—that our love story had not had a happy ending. Well, I was wrong. It's had a very happy ending.'

And she smiled at her future husband.

'It's incredible,' said Drew as he drove Millie downtown to St. Luke's Place.

'What is?'

'I think my old man arranged to have Tazzi killed.'

She looked surprised.

'Did he tell you that?'

'God no, and I'd never ask. But the freighter that rammed Tazzi's yacht belonged to the Pritchard Lines, which has a good safety record. And Frank Pritchard is an old buddy of Father's. It's just too pat for it to be a coincidence. Can you beat that? *My* father a killer? Jesus, it's wild!'

Millie put her hand on his knee.

'Like father, like son,' she said.

'What's that mean?'

'You're a killer, Drew. You just haven't had the opportunity to kill anyone yet.'

He took his eyes off the Seventh Avenue traffic to look at her.

'That's a helluva thing to say.'

'But it's true. You're a bad lot, Drew. You're conceited, cocky, overambitious and oversexed. You're so unscrupulous you tried to swindle your father to get even with him. The only good thing I can say about you is that you've got guts. You weren't scared when they kidnapped you, were you?'

'I was a little. I suppose this means you've thought over my proposal and decided to turn me down?'

She smiled as she moved her hand up his thigh.

'Oh no. I've thought it over and decided to accept.'

Again he looked at her. He felt her hand on his genitals, massaging them gently.

'Why?' he asked.

'Because bad as you are, you excite me, Drew. You excite me like no other man I've ever known. I think it's going to be very interesting being Mrs. Drew Dexter.'

He swerved the car to miss hitting an oncoming truck.

'If you don't get your hand off my prick, we may end up getting married in a hospital bed.'

'I wouldn't mind. I'm nuts about you, Drew.' She gave him one final squeeze, then took her hand away, sighing, 'I'll probably live to regret it.'

She took out her compact to check her face in the mirror.

335

PART VII

CHURCH AND STATE

1927

CHAPTER 35

Alessandro Blassetti, the sixty-year-old author of the anti-Fascist novel entitled *Il Crepuscolo,* or *The Twilight,* was sipping hot cocoa in the second-floor bedroom of his villa outside Siena, watching the unusual snowflakes falling gently outside his window, when he heard the banging on the door downstairs. Blassetti was arthritic, and a wool blanket covered his crippled legs. His hands were so gnarled by the disease he had difficulty holding his pen to write, but he had so far resisted the pleas of his wife, his children and his doctor to go south during the winter. Blassetti loved Tuscany, where he had lived all his life, and he protested that the winters were mild enough, although the present snowfall was proving him wrong. Now he set down his cocoa to listen to the argument downstairs.

His wife started shouting: 'No! You mustn't hurt him . . . he's an old man! He hasn't hurt anyone!'

Then the sound of boots on the stairs. Alessandro Blassetti watched the door. It burst open. Three black-uniformed men entered. Blassetti recognized the striking-looking man in the middle who now strode up to the man in the chair.

'Alessandro Blassetti?' said the Fascist.

'I am he.'

'You wrote the decadent novel, *Il Crepuscolo,* in which you ridiculed the views and the person of the Duce.'

'Yes, I did.' The old man spoke slowly. 'He's very easy to ridicule, you know. Aren't you Fausto Spada?'

'I'll ask the questions.'

'I admired your father. He was a fine man, a good man. He would have laughed at your Duce, the way I do . . .'

Fausto signaled the two other Fascisti. They hurried over, grabbed Blassetti, forced his mouth open, then began pouring a quart of castor oil in it. Signora Blassetti appeared in the door and started screaming.

'You're poisoning him! Stop it, stop it!'

'It's only castor oil,' snapped Fausto.

'You'll kill him, you'll kill him—!'

'Shut up.'

She sank into a chair and started moaning and sobbing. Blassetti was gagging.

'Let him breathe,' said Fausto.

The Fascisti let the old man go. He leaned over and vomited. Fausto watched him. When Blassetti had finished retching, Fausto said, 'Give him the rest.'

The Fascisti grabbed him again and forced the remainder of the castor oil down his throat.

'The Duce is the savior of Italy,' said Fausto. 'Those who oppose him are traitors to the State and will be dealt with severely. Your filthy book has been confiscated and your publisher fined fifty thousand lire. You have one week to leave Italy forever, or you will be brought before the authorities. It is only your international reputation that saves you from something worse than castor oil.'

The old man was vomiting again.

'It stinks in here,' said Fausto. 'Let's go.'

Stepping around the spreading pool of vomit, he walked to the door. Signora Blassetti looked up at him, tears streaming down her wrinkled face.

'You pig!' she said, and she spat at him.

Fausto wiped the spittle off his coat, then walked out of the room.

The man with the full mane of gray hair and the pince-nez tilted his head back slightly, closed his eyes and intoned, 'Carlo, are you there? Are you there this afternoon, Carlo? If so, please speak to us. Send us a message, Carlo. Your mother is here, and she wants to know if you're well.'

Silence. Professor Salvatorelli, who was conducting the séance in the library of Fausto's villa in the Parioli section of Rome, held Nanda Montecatini Spada's hands across the card table. Nanda's eyes were also closed. The louvers had been shut over the windows of the room, filtering the pale winter sunlight into a spectral penumbra.

'Do you feel anything?' whispered Nanda who, in her anxiousness, forgot the Professor's rule of silence during a séance.

'Carlo, are you there?' repeated the Professor. 'Your mother is so anxious to hear from you.'

Nanda half-opened her eyes to peek, breaking yet another rule. She saw the Professor stiffen, she felt his hands clutching hers strongly. Then he threw back his head and began speaking in a soft falsetto, 'Momma, it's I, little Carlo. How are you, Momma?'

Nanda was trembling.

'Oh darling, it's so good to hear from you! I'm all right, but how are *you?*'

'It's cold here, so cold . . .'

Tears were running down her cheeks.

'Darling, if I were with you, I'd keep you warm . . . My darling, I miss you *so*. Do you miss me?'

'Yes, Momma. I miss you very much. It's very lonely here . . . I have no one to play with . . .'

'But you're not afraid, darling?'

'No, I'm not afraid. Just lonely and cold . . . I must go now, Momma. I love you very much, and I miss you.'

'I miss you, my sweet one. But can't you stay? Don't go yet.'

'No, I must go. Good-bye, until next time.'

'Good-bye, darling. Good-bye.'

Silence. She opened her eyes wide. As usual, Professor Salvatorelli began to unstiffen slowly. Then, suddenly, he sagged into his chair, releasing her hands. She pulled a handkerchief from the pocket of her chic black dress and wiped her eyes. Then she got up to open the louvers.

'Did we make contact?' asked the Professor, sitting up straight and opening his eyes.

'Yes,' she sniffed. 'It was beautiful.'

'Good. I felt we might. The vibrations were right, and of course it being the second anniversary of his death was propitious. How is he?'

She came back to the table.

'The same as last time,' she said, sadly. 'Cold and lonely. Poor Carlo, my poor darling.'

'There, there.' He patted her hand as he stood up. 'Children like to complain, you know. I'm sure he's not telling us the happy side of it yet, but he will. They always do. Dear me, it's later than I thought . . .' He checked his gold pocket watch. 'I have an appointment with Countess Sforza at three. I'm afraid I have to rush . . .'

She extended her hand, which he kissed.

'Dear Professor,' she smiled, 'how happy you make me. And how sad.'

'Ah, Signora, there's no reason to be sad. Your son lives still, only in a different form in a different world. This knowledge must make you joyful. Shall I come again next week at the same time?'

'Yes, unless you hear from me first. And remember: the bills go to my father, not my husband.'

'But of course, Signora. I would never forget such an important detail.'

He held the door for her, bowing slightly as she went out. The Professor was elegantly dressed in a dark suit. Now he followed her into the white marble central hall. The villa had been built in the nineteenth century, but after Fausto bought it in 1925, Nanda had sold or stored the antique furniture and redid the whole place in the new rage, Art Deco, so that the new mixed sleekly and slightly jarringly with the old.

She started to lead the Professor to the front door, when it opened and her husband came in. He was wearing his black Fascist uniform.

'Fausto!' she said, tensing. He closed the door and came down the hall, looking at Professor Salvatorelli. 'I didn't expect you till tomorrow . . .'

'So I see. I thought I told you I didn't want Professor Salvatorelli in this house again.'

'Darling, he was just paying a visit . . .'

'You're lying, Nanda.'

He put his cap on a chair then turned to the Professor, who looked nervous.

'Professor,' he said, 'the new Italy has no room for charlatans who prey on the superstitions of weak, silly women like my wife.'

'Fausto, stop it—'

'Shut up!' he roared, turning on her. Nanda burst into tears and ran down the hall to the stairs. Fausto watched her as she disappeared upstairs. Then he looked at the Professor.

'If I hear of you bothering my wife again,' he said, quietly, 'I'll make sure you never conduct another phony séance in Rome. Is that understood?'

The Professor was trembling.

'Yes, Signor Spada.'

'Now get out.'

'Yes, Signor Spada. *Scusi.*'

He made his exit with almost comic haste.

When he entered the bedroom, Nanda was lying facedown on the big, black-lacquered bed, crying. The room was oval, with tall windows overlooking the walled garden to the rear. Everything in it—the carpet, the curtains, the walls—was white except the furniture, which was, like the bed, all of black inlay with silver stripes. On her vanity were silver-framed photos of their two sons, Carlo and Enrico.

'You asinine woman,' he said, coming to the bed. 'Do you really think that quack can talk to Carlo? The bloody *Pope* can't talk to Carlo, but that moth-eaten professor can? Use your brains, Nanda. Christ, when I married you, I thought you had some.'

She turned over and glared at him with bloodshot eyes.

'How did he know about the red mittens? He couldn't *possibly* have known I gave Carlo red mittens on his fourth birthday, but he mentioned them to me! He said, "Momma, I miss my red mittens"! And the toy train and the almond candy he loved—the Professor *said* these things!'

'You fool, don't you think he bribes the servants? Or picks up information from friends and relatives? He's a fake but he's smart. He listens and takes notes, then feeds it back to you, and you *believe* him!'

'Yes I believe him, because he brings back my son!'

'Carlo's dead!' he almost shouted. *'Dead!* Nobody can bring back the dead! We've got Enrico. Why should you ruin your life because of Carlo? You have plenty to live for.'

'What?' she said, defiantly. 'You? My wonderful, handsome husband who goes around forcing castor oil down people's throats? I thought I married a man, but what I got was an ugly bully!'

He slapped her once, twice, three times. She cringed and screamed.

'You stupid bitch,' he said, softly.

Then he walked out of the room.

She lay on the bed for almost five minutes, sobbing. Then, slowly, she sat up, rubbing her cheeks. Getting off the bed, she weaved across the room to the black-and-silver bureau, on top of which was a silver-framed photo of Fausto in his Fascist uniform. She picked the photo up, looked at it a moment, then tenderly kissed it.

Then she threw it across the room with all her strength. It smashed against the wall and fell to the floor in a shower of broken glass.

If any one place could be considered the heart of Rome, it was the Piazza Venezia, a broad and beautiful square dominated by the white marble monument to Victor Emmanuel II. By contrast, the Palazzo Venezia was austere, considered by many to be one of the finest examples of Renaissance architecture. The palace, built in 1455, had at one time been the seat of the Venetian Ambassador; but now it had become the seat of the Fascist Government, and the already infamous balcony from which the Duce made his strident speeches was in the middle of the facade facing the piazza. Fausto knew the building well, but he had never been in Mussolini's office on the second floor; so when he was admitted by the usher, his sense of expectation was matched only by his genuine awe.

The marble hall, called Sala del Mappamondo after an ancient map of the world displayed there, was sixty-six feet long and forty-three feet wide. It was two stories high and had two rows of windows overlooking the piazza. *Trompe-l'oeil* columns soared to the ceiling, heightening the sense of grandeur. At the far end of the room, a gigantic fireplace was surmounted by a huge triangle, in the middle of which was an eight-foot *fascio* surrounded by a triumphal wreath. Cleverly, there was no furniture in the room except the Duce's desk and three chairs in the far corner. Thus the desk, and the Duce, became the focal point of the chamber. The desk was uncluttered and held a medium-sized lamp with a hemispherical, fringed shade. Behind the desk stood a fifteen-foot-high baroque candlestick. Beneath the desk, at a forty-five-degree angle to the big central rug, was a smaller Oriental, one corner of which was turned up against the wall, injecting the single note of whimsy into what otherwise was a calculated study in grandiosity and bombast. However, it worked. As Fausto strode the length of the room, he was imbued with a sense of the majestic that Mussolini sorely lacked in person.

He stopped in front of the desk and gave the Fascist salute. The Duce returned it, then came around the desk to shake Fausto's hand.

'Fausto,' he said in his undeniably musical voice, 'you know I despise the aristocracy as they despise me. But, my friend, you could make me change my attitude toward those parasites. There are few people in Italy whose loyalty and courage I value more than yours. The fact that your mother is Princess Sylvia never fails to baffle me, since I know she hates me. Sit down, my friend. I want to talk to you.'

Fausto sat.

'Blassetti has left Italy, and good riddance,' said the Duce after he had resumed his seat. 'You handled that well for me, and I appreciate it. A writer like that, with a world reputation —well, it would have been stupid to have hurt him too much. Your service to the Party has been excellent, and it is time to reward you. Fausto, I am putting you in charge of my youth organization, Opera Nazionale Balilla. I am entrusting the future of Italy to you.'

Fausto was stunned. It was a dazzling promotion.

'Duce, words fail me! I am deeply honored.'

'Good. My secretary will give you the details. Details bore me, Fausto. It's *results* that are important.'

'I swear you will get the results you want, Duce! One question?'

'Yes?'

'Duce, as you know, seventeen years ago, the Mafia murdered my father. The crime was never solved—you know the power of the Mafia in those days.'

'But I broke the back of that power for all time.'

'Just so, Duce, to your eternal glory. But I would like permission to question Don Ciccio Cuccia, who recently was sent to prison. I'm convinced Don Ciccio knows who killed my father.'

The Duce looked at him curiously.

'What do you want to know that for, after all this time? Whoever did it is probably dead of old age by now.'

Fausto was trembling. Would this request cost him the favor of the Duce, cost him his brilliant new position?

'But if he isn't, Duce, I have a debt of honor to settle with him.'

'You mean you want to bring him to trial?'

'No, Duce. I want to kill him. I swore it at my father's funeral, and now that I'm in a position to track him down, I have to do it. Do I have your permission?'

'In other words, you want immunity from the State for murder?'

His tone was ominous. Fausto trembled more.

'Yes, Duce. It is a matter of honor.'

'You idiot!' thundered Mussolini, jumping to his feet. 'What do you think I've been trying to do these past few years? I've been trying to play down the violence! We're in power now, we have to stop the murders! What will the public say if the man I appoint head of Balilla, the man who is supposed to offer moral guidance to Italy's youth, is given carte blanche to murder an aging Mafioso?'

'The people would never have to know . . .'

Mussolini came around the desk, grabbed his arm and led him to the open windows in the center of the room which gave out on to the narrow balcony. The Duce took Fausto through the doors. The day was cloudy, and the Piazza Venezia was fairly empty. 'Look,' said the Duce, spreading his arm in a wide gesture, 'all Rome lies at my feet! When I speak from this balcony and there are thousands of people down there listening to me, do you know what it's like, Fausto? It's like sex. It's like I and the Italian people are lovers. That's power, Fausto: *power,* the most thrilling thing in life. And do you know what I think when I make love to the people? What I dream? I dream of a new Rome greater than ancient Rome, a new Roman Empire mightier than the last! Isn't that a fantastic dream, Fausto?'

'Yes, Duce. It's a dream I share.'

'But to make that dream come true, we must forget petty quarrels, private feuds, vendettas—that's the past, *opera buffa.* That's why you must forget this insane idea of yours, Fausto. Do you understand?'

'Yes, Duce.'

'Bravo!'

He slapped his back, and they went back into the Sala del Mappamondo. Again Fausto executed the Fascist salute.

'Duce, you have inspired me with the magnificence of your dream! I realize now how petty my own personal honor is when compared with the honor and glory of Fascism!'

'Good.' The Duce paused a moment, then lowered his voice. 'Before you go . . .'

'Yes, Duce?'

'A man's honor must be upheld, after all. A man's father must be avenged. How long would it take you?'

Fausto was stunned by this swift reversal.

'I guess . . . a week?'

'Excellent. Give me a full report when you get back.'

And the most powerful man in Italy, if not Europe, returned to his desk.

CHAPTER 36

Two days after Fausto met with the Duce, the Bishop of Brescia, Monsignore Antonio Spada, entered the Vatican through the Arch of the Bells and walked around behind St. Peter's, leaning into the windy rain which whipped his black umbrella. Tony, who was now thirty-four, hadn't been in Rome for several years, and returning to his native city flooded him with memories. His years in the Church had given him the sense of belonging and the purpose in life he had hoped it would, and his years in the provincial town of Brescia had been particularly rewarding. Yet his love affair with the Church was not without its problems. He chafed at what he considered the Vatican's increasingly outdated policies, in particular its opposition to birth control. Working among the poor in Brescia, he had seen how constant child-bearing forced them into deeper poverty. And while he understood the Vatican's position intellectually, emotionally he felt the Church was wrong.

Yet, with all his reservations about Vatican policy, he remained in love with the Church. So that when he entered the Apostolic Palace, it was like coming home. He made his way through the ancient corridors to the office that had once belonged to his mentor, Cardinal dell'Acqua. His Eminence had died eight years before at an age that was venerable even by the standards of the College of Cardinals. His successor as Secretary of State, Cardinal Gasparri, had summoned Tony from Brescia.

Tony had no idea what the summons meant, but when he found out he was pleasantly surprised.

Princess Sylvia was now in her seventies and suffered from a weak heart. Bedridden much of the time, fragile and thin, with pure white hair, the former beauty still possessed a sharp mind and a keen interest in life. Now her eyes sparkled with delight as her son sat next to her bed and told her of his promotion.

'So you'll be moving back to Rome!' she exclaimed. 'Oh Tony, I can't tell you how glad that makes me. And you'll be holding the Vatican's purse strings! Well, I'm impressed.'

Her son, who was almost as thin as his mother, smiled.

'Signor Nogara will actually be holding the purse strings. He'll be investing the money the Church is going to receive from Mussolini. But for some reason, Cardinal Gasparri thinks I've got the magic touch with money—I suppose because I managed to balance the books in Brescia. So they want me to work with Signor Nogara. The truth is, most of the cardinals can't add up a column of figures.'

His mother laughed.

'So that's why the Church is so poor! Well, you were always good at math, so let's hope you don't misplace the Vatican's bonanza. How much is Mussolini paying to make peace with the Church?'

'I don't know exactly, but it's going to be a huge sum. The Holy Father wants to invest it so the Church will be independent financially.'

'Well,' said his mother, 'if that rascal, Mussolini, can settle the Vatican problem, I'll have to admit it will be a feather in his cap. But I still think he's the scum of the earth. How nice it's going to be, though, having you in Rome!'

She took his hand and squeezed it fondly.

'How's Fausto?' asked Tony.

His mother sighed.

'You know I sold *Libertà,* but you don't know why. It was all Fausto's fault. When he forced me to hire that idiot Fascist for an editor, the paper became an insult to everything your father stood for. So I sold it. Got a good price, too—five million lire.'

'What did Fausto say when you sold the paper?'

'Oh, he was furious. He's become impossible. I hardly talk to him anymore. And poor Nanda!'

Nanda, Nanda . . . he shuddered slightly at her name.

'How is Nanda?'

'I feel sorry for her. Ever since Carlo died of rheumatic fever, she's been a wreck, surrounding herself with quacks . . . And Fausto treats her like dirt. The poor woman, I think she's still in love with him, though I can't imagine why.'

'But I don't understand: why does Fausto treat her badly?'

'Because he enjoys it. You see, Tony, Fascism plays up to all the worst instincts in people. Fausto always had a streak of the bully in him—he used to bully you when you were boys—but now being a bully has become patriotic, chic! The meaner you

348

are, the better Italian you become. Of course, it's insane. But Fausto's caught the fever. You must go see Nanda. She's so fond of you, and maybe you can cheer her up.'

Nanda, Nanda . . .

'Yes, of course I'll go see her.'

Nanda, Nanda . . .

The next afternoon he stood in the drawing room of Fausto's villa looking at the framed photograph of Mussolini on the grand piano. The picture was autographed and showed the Duce in one of his most pompous, aggressive poses. What a buffoon, thought Tony. And yet, all Italy follows him . . .

'Tony!'

He turned to see his sister-in-law in the door. Tony hadn't seen Nanda since his last visit to Rome over two years before, and he was immediately struck by her thinness. She looked as if she were going through a bad time; and yet, as always, he was entranced by her dark-haired beauty. She was also terrifically smart, with a sure sense of style. Right now she was wearing a loose Chanel suit. She hurried across the room and embraced him. 'It's so wonderful to see you!' she exclaimed. 'Your mother phoned me about your new position, and I'm so pleased for you! And for myself. Now you'll have no excuse not to see us more often—*much* more often.'

She took his hand and led him to a sofa in front of the French doors leading out to the garden. There was something in her excitement and pleasure that was almost like a little girl's. They sat on the sofa, and she devoured his face with her eyes.

'You're so thin,' she said. 'Didn't they feed you in Brescia?'

'The food's marvelous there, but I fast two days a week. And how about you? You're a stick.'

Her smile faded.

'I don't have much appetite anymore. You heard about Fausto's promotion?'

'Yes, we both got kicked upstairs the same week. Mother says he's out of town?'

'He left yesterday on something mysterious. He never tells me anything anyway.' She took a cigarette from an amber box, and Tony lighted it for her. 'Where will you be living?'

'In the Vatican. They've given me a month's vacation before taking the new job.'

'Will you spend the vacation in Rome?'

'Yes. I thought it would give me a chance to see a lot of Mother. And you,' he added.

She exhaled, then said in a defensive tone, 'I suppose your mother told you about Professor Salvatorelli?'

'She mentioned him.'

'Fausto and I had one of our juiciest fights over him.' Suddenly all her bitterness burst out of her. She turned on Tony and said, angrily, 'Why can't I see whom I want? If the man's a quack, what difference is it if it makes me feel better? God knows, *Fausto* doesn't make me feel better! He doesn't give a damn whether I live or die.'

'That's not true, Nanda.'

'How do *you* know?' she said, sharply. Then she backed down. 'I'm sorry. I shouldn't involve you with my problems. They're probably the last things you want to hear.'

'No, I want to be involved. Maybe I can help.'

She smiled slightly.

'Tony, you're so sweet. I only wish Fausto had one tenth of your sweetness. But you're in the Church. You don't know what the real world's like.'

Now it was his turn to be angry.

'Don't I? I've spent seven years working in the slums, and you tell *me* I don't know what the real world's like? *You*, who pay for séances?'

She was surprised by his tone.

'I'm sorry, I didn't mean to . . .'

'I'm not going to defend Fausto, because I think he's acting like a fool. But you're being just as foolish. He's got Fascism as an escape, and you've taken up the supernatural. Has it ever occurred to either of you what you're trying to escape *from?*'

She stared at him.

'What?'

'An emptiness,' he said, lowering his voice, 'a spiritual emptiness, because both of you have left the Church.'

'Oh Tony, don't preach. As far as that goes, I never left the Church. I just don't go anymore.'

He took her hand, marveling at the pleasure the feel of her skin gave him. 'I know you think I'm out of touch with reality because I'm a priest, but I'd like to try and show you I have a deeper sense of reality than you have, that I have a peace neither you nor Fausto has. I want to help both of you, Nanda. Will you let me try?'

She studied his face that was so reminiscent of her husband's and yet so different. She sensed his nervous strength, his compassion . . . and she sensed something else as well.

'What do you want to do?'

'Let me come here in the afternoons and talk to you for the next few weeks. I won't preach, I'll just talk. Maybe together we can find an answer to your unhappiness.'

'That wouldn't be much of a vacation for you.'

'Yes it would. I *really* want to help, Nanda.'

Do you? he thought. Or is there something else, something unthinkable?

'Oh Tony,' she cried, softly, 'I *need* your help.'

Don Ciccio Cuccia had been the Mayor of Piana dei Greci and was a power in the Sicilian Mafia. In 1925, when Mussolini visited Sicily, Don Ciccio had been his host in Piana dei Greci. Shortly after, Don Ciccio had been arrested like a common criminal, charged with various crimes (most of which he had committed), and sent to the island-prison of San Stefano. It had all been part of Mussolini's drive to stamp out the Mafia, a drive spearheaded by Cesare Mori, the *superprefetto*, to whom the Duce had given almost dictatorial powers in Sicily.

Don Ciccio Cuccia had his own cell, good food, and women were smuggled in to satisfy his aging, but still active, sexual appetite. Mussolini might have declared war on the Mafia, but the guards at San Stefano knew the Mafia had been around a long time before the Duce, and probably would be around a long time after.

Thus, when the guards came to take Don Ciccio to the warden's office, they treated him with deference and courtesy. They also told him who Fausto Spada was. Don Ciccio, a fat man, wheezed and said, 'What the hell does he want to see me for?'

The guards didn't know.

Don Ciccio was ushered into the office where the warden politely introduced him to Fausto. Then the warden and the guards went out to give the men privacy. Don Ciccio eyed Fausto's uniform and the gun holster. Then he said, 'What's this all about?'

'My father, Franco Spada, was killed by the Mafia in 1910. He was run over by a car on the via Due Macelli. I thought you might be able to tell me who was driving that car.'

Don Ciccio perspired freely. Now, even though it was cool, he pulled out a handkerchief to wipe his upper lip.

'Even if I knew, what makes you think I'd tell you?'

'There's a possibility that if you cooperate with me, the Duce might cut short your sentence.'

'The Duce.' He almost spat the word. 'Let me tell you what I think of the Duce.' And his right forearm shot up in an obscene gesture.

Fausto shrugged.

'Still, it's to your benefit to cooperate with me.'

The fat old man studied him.

'What sort of deal are you offering?'

'Possibly two years off your sentence.'

'That's a deal? Let me out of here this afternoon, and I'll tell you what you want to know.'

'Then you *do* know?'

'Maybe.'

Fausto had been leaning on the warden's desk. Now he got up, came over to Don Ciccio, pulled his gun from his holster and pointed it at his nose.

'Listen, Grandpa,' he said, softly. 'You're in no position to bargain. I could kill you, and the warden's not going to say a word. Or I could tell him to have you tortured, and don't think I wouldn't. So give me the name of the man who killed my father. Then *maybe* I'll do something about reducing your sentence.'

Don Ciccio stared at the gun. Then he looked into Fausto's eyes.

'His name is Massimo Romano.'

Fausto put the gun back in his holster and returned to the warden's desk. Taking a sheet from a memo pad, he wrote down the name.

'Where's he live?' he asked.

'In Rome. He's always lived in Rome. That's why they hired him to do the job on your father.'

'Who's "They"?'

'What's it matter now? They're all dead.'

'What's Romano's address in Rome?'

'He used to live on the via Luigi Rizzo, west of the Vatican. I have no idea if he's still there.'

'The number?'

'I don't remember. I'm an old man.'

Fausto folded the paper and put it in his pocket.

'What are you going to do?' asked Don Ciccio. 'Kill him?'

'That's my business.'

Fausto went to the door and opened it.

'I'm finished with him,' he said to the warden as he walked out into the winter sunshine.

'Professor Salvatorelli takes some of the beliefs of the Church and twists them slightly to his own purpose.'

Tony was sitting opposite Nanda at a glass-topped garden table. It was three days later, and the sun had come out to provide a beautiful and unseasonably warm day, so Nanda had decided to have lunch in the garden behind the villa. She was eating fruit and cheese and drinking white wine. Tony was fasting.

'For instance,' he went on, 'the Professor told you there's no such thing thing as death, that we merely go to another place in another form. All right, the Church says there's no such thing as death also, but the difference is that Eternal Salvation is possible only through faith in Our Lord. Salvatorelli doesn't ask for faith, he asks for gullibility.'

Nanda bit into a juicy pear. She was looking extremely pretty in a pale-blue dress with a white sweater over her shoulders.

'So you think I've been gullible?' she said.

'Of course. You've been so anxious for peace of mind you've been grabbing at straws.'

'Do you have peace of mind, Tony?'

He frowned slightly.

'Yes.'

'Why did you hesitate?'

'I wasn't aware I had.'

'But you did.'

She cut a piece of Fontina and put it on a cracker. He was watching her. Above the brick wall of the garden, the tops of the trees in the Borghese Gardens swayed gently.

'Don't you ever get hungry, Tony?' she asked, biting the cracker.

'Of course I get hungry. Right now, I'd give anything for one of those pears. But I've learned to control my body. A priest has to.'

'But there are a lot of fat priests. People say there are a lot of priests who aren't as pure as they pretend.'

Tony waved a fly away from his nose.

'I'm not saying the clergy is perfect.'

She washed down the cheese with a sip of wine.

'I admire you so much, Tony. I wish I had your strength.' She shaded her eyes and looked up. 'The sun's really quite warm, isn't it?'

She removed her sweater. Tony stared at her bare arms.

The fly buzzed around his head.

Slowly, he reached for a pear.

CHAPTER 37

The declining years of Princess Sylvia had been fulfilling ones. Respected and loved by most Romans, she was considered a grande dame of elegance, taste, intelligence and impeccable connections. The only blight in her otherwise serene old age was Mussolini, whom she detested. And, of course, Fausto.

She was reading a novel in her bedroom late one afternoon when her butler announced that her son was at the palazzo and wished to see her. When Fausto came into the room, she could tell by the excitement in his eyes that something unusual had happened. He was wearing civilian clothes—she had told him she wouldn't admit him to the palazzo in his Fascist uniform, and now he came over and kissed her. For a moment she forgot Fascism and Mussolini and held her son in her arms.

'You're looking well, Momma,' he said as she released him. He pulled an ottoman up beside her chaise.

'Well enough, under the circumstances. How's Nanda? Tony tells me he's been giving her religious instruction in the afternoons.'

'Oh? I haven't heard. I've been out of town a few days. Why is Tony turning evangelist?'

'To wean her from that dreadful quack, Professor Salvatorelli.'

'Well, if he can succeed in that, he has my thanks. Momma, I've just done something that I hope will make you very happy.'

'Quit the Fascist party?' she asked, drily.

He looked surprised.

'Of course not.'

'It would be the best thing you could do.'

'I'm not getting into another political argument with you. This is something personal. I found out the name of the man who killed Father.'

Now she looked surprised.

'How?'

'That doesn't matter. The point is, he was a Mafia executioner, as we always suspected. And now he's dead. Father's death has been avenged. I wanted you to be the first to know. I thought . . .' he hesitated, '. . . perhaps it would make things better between you and me.'

She closed her eyes and remembered that horrible night seventeen years before when the only man she had ever loved was taken out of her life. Then she opened her eyes and looked at her son, who so hauntingly resembled Franco.

'What do you mean, "dead"? What happened to him?'

'That doesn't matter.'

'But it does. Was he given Fascist-style justice?'

'I'm telling you, it doesn't matter!'

'He was murdered, wasn't he?' she said, quietly. 'Did you do it?'

'Of course not.' He was bottling up his anger, his resentment. 'And it seems to me you ought to be more concerned that Father's death was avenged than how it was done. Nobody could have done it ten years ago. After all, Father was one of the first Italians to attack the Mafia, and who's finally *done* it? Who's stamping them out? The Duce!'

'Oh Fausto,' she sighed, 'you don't understand. What has anyone gained by stamping out the Mafia with its own methods? What kind of justice is it to murder a murderer?' She implored him with her beautiful old eyes, 'Oh please, my darling: *leave* them!'

For a moment he wondered if she might not be right. Then he steeled himself, and his face went cold. He stood up.

'I did this for you as well as Father. I thought it would please you. But it's obvious nothing I do could ever please you.'

He left the room and hurried out of the palazzo. But when he was in his car, he found himself crying, and he wasn't even sure why.

Fausto's wife and his twin brother were talking in the drawing room of the villa. They didn't see him as he came in. They were standing in front of the garden doors, their backs to him, engrossed in an almost inaudible conversation. It was twilight, and gathering darkness softened the room.

After a moment Fausto turned on the lights.

'Fausto!' said Nanda, wheeling around. 'I didn't hear you come in . . .'

'Hello, Nanda. Hello, Tony. Mother tells me you two have been talking about religion. Do you always talk in the dark?'

'I didn't realize it was so late,' said Tony. 'I'd better be going . . .'

'Don't go yet. I haven't had a chance to talk to you since you got back to Rome. Stay for dinner. Nanda, we have no engagements, do we?'

'No.'

'Then tell cook we'll be three for dinner.'

Nanda sensed something was wrong, sensed that her husband was bottling something up, but she had no objections to Tony staying for dinner. On the contrary, with Fausto in one of his dark moods, she preferred having a third person present as a buffer. She left the room as Fausto came up to his brother and embraced him.

'It's good to see you, Tony,' he said. 'We don't see enough of each other any more. It rather hurts me that the moment I come home, you want to leave.'

He took a cigarette from the amber box and lighted it.

'I didn't mean to hurt you,' said Tony, uncomfortably.

'But you did. I know you and Mother disapprove of me, but there's no reason why we can't remain on friendly terms, is there?'

'Of course not.'

'Good.' He crossed the room and pressed the electric bell. 'I'm going up to change. The butler will bring you a cocktail, if you like.'

'Thanks, Fausto.'

The twins eyed each other.

'My home is your home, Tony,' said Fausto, and he went upstairs.

Tony sat in a chair and stared at the white carpet. He wished he didn't have to stay for dinner, but he was feeling too guilty to leave.

When she came downstairs in a black cocktail dress, she looked so ravishing Tony ached to have her. The low-cut dress was held up by black spaghetti straps over her bare shoulders; the skirt was cut in inverted triangles, the tips of which dangled over her knees. Her slim legs tapered to black satin pumps with rhinestone buckles. From her ears dangled diamond drops, and two diamond and ruby bracelets, presents from her jeweler father, sparkled on one arm. Behind her Fausto was wearing a tight-fitting tux.

'Did Bernardo fix you a cocktail?' he asked Tony as he came in the room.

'I told him I'd wait.'

'Well, I'm thirsty.' He rang the bell again, then walked across the room to a Victrola. 'Do you like American music, Tony? Gershwin, for instance? I'm crazy about his songs. This one's called "I'll Build a Stairway to Paradise." Nice title, too. Almost religious, don't you think?'

He put the needle on the record, and the wonderful music bounced forth. The butler came in and took drink orders.

All through cocktails and dinner, Fausto kept up a stream of light conversation, but Tony was noticeably silent.

'More Gershwin?' asked Fausto as they returned to the drawing room after dinner.

'Why not?' said Nanda, who had drunk a good deal of wine at dinner and was showing the effects. Fausto put on 'Lady Be Good.' Nanda twirled around the room to the music as Tony watched her, and Fausto watched Tony. Then he joined his wife. The young couple danced well, their bodies close together, the slight curve of Nanda's lean belly pressed against Fausto's midsection. Tony sat on a window seat, riveted by the sight.

When the record ended, Fausto went back to the Victrola.

'Now it's your turn, Tony,' he said, looking through the records. 'Dance with Nanda. She's terrific.'

'I can't,' said Tony.

'Why? Because you're a priest? Don't be silly—it's all in the family. Here's one of my favorites: "Someone to Watch Over Me." '

He put the needle on, and the languorous melody began softly uncoiling. Nanda was in the middle of the room, looking at her brother-in-law. Now, a smile on her face, she crossed the room to him, her hands outstretched.

'Dance with me, Tony,' she coaxed.

He shook his head.

'I can't. If nothing else, I don't know how.'

'Oh, it's easy. Come on: I'll teach you.'

'I can't. Please—this is embarrassing.'

She took his hands and pulled him gently from the window seat. He saw Fausto watching them from the Victrola, his face fascinated.

'Put your left arm around my waist,' said Nanda, 'and hold my other hand. Like so. That's right. Now, follow me.'

It's incredible, he thought, I'm dancing with her!

357

He smelled her musky perfume and felt her body against his. He shuddered with desire. He was drunk with Nanda, drunk with the music. He was half-aware that Fausto was baiting him with his own wife. That was monstrous, but then he, Tony, was monstrous . . .

The music stopped, and they danced a moment longer before they stopped. Nanda looked at him strangely. She had felt his desire, and suddenly she wanted him as much as he wanted her.

Fausto had a slight smile on his face.

'You dance very well for a priest,' he said. He turned off the Victrola, went to the amber box, took out a cigarette and lighted it. Then he turned to look at them. They were both still standing in the center of the room, looking at each other. 'If I didn't know you were a man of God, Tony, I might be jealous. You two look as if you really go for each other.'

Tony forced himself to turn away from Nanda.

'I don't know what you mean,' he said, lamely.

'Remember that night I took you to La Rosina's so many years ago? You never told me how you liked it, but since you decided to become a priest the next day, I assumed you didn't like it very much. But maybe I was wrong.'

Tony ran his hand over his brow. He was sweating.

'I'd better go . . .'

Fausto laughed.

'Maybe what you need is a little more experience, Tony,' he said, tauntingly.

Nanda went back to the sofa.

'You're being disgusting, Fausto,' she said.

'Am I? You mean you wouldn't like to go to bed with Tony?'

'Why are you saying these things?' said Tony, softly. 'Why are you tormenting me?'

'Because we're twins,' he said, exhaling. 'You're just like me except you hide what's inside you. I don't hide what's inside me. Go on, Tony: take my wife to bed. You have my permission.'

'Fausto!' Nanda exclaimed.

'Shut up.' He kept his eyes on his brother. 'Don't you want to, Tony? She's good at it. Or maybe you'd like to watch us do it first? Would you like to watch us, Tony?'

He smiled. Tony's face was white. Fausto ground out his cigarette, went over to his wife, took her hand and pulled her up off the sofa.

'Watch, Tony.'

He began kissing her. She tried to push him away, but he

persisted. She was just drunk enough not to fight him too long or too hard. Her body began slowly writhing against him.

Fausto pulled the spaghetti strap off her left shoulder and began kissing her upper arm as his other hand squeezed her buttocks.

'Stop it!' yelled Tony. 'For the love of God, *stop* it!'

'But I don't love God,' said Fausto. 'At least *your* God. My god is a taker, Tony. He takes life—and sex.'

He went back to his lovemaking. Tony tried to pull his eyes away from them, but he couldn't. Fausto had slipped the other strap off her and was unbuttoning the back of her dress. Nanda stood, her head back, her eyes closed, limp with desire. Fausto unhooked the last button, and the dress slipped to the floor. Her slim body in the panties and bra was revealed with stunning concupiscence. Fausto looked across the room at Tony.

'Isn't she lovely?' he said, softly.

He reached behind her and unhooked her bra, dropping it to the floor also. Tony looked at her breasts. Then he felt his underwear fill with semen.

'Oh *JESUS!*' he cried. He ran out of the room into the central hall, then down to the entrance hall, where he flung open the front door.

The last thing he heard as he ran into the night was Fausto laughing.

The next morning Fausto was ushered into the monumental Sala del Mappamondo, and again strode the great length of the hall to the desk in the corner where the dictator was studying some papers. He raised his arm in the Fascist salute and said, 'Duce, I have come to report on my mission, as you requested!'

Musslini looked up. This time, he didn't offer a seat.

'What mission?' he asked.

Fausto looked a bit confused.

'The matter of my father's murderer.'

'Oh yes, I remember. You talked to Don Ciccio?'

'Yes, Duce. He gave me the man's name and address. He was still living, here in Rome. I should say *was* living.' He grinned slightly. 'Yesterday I staked out his house in a rented car. I used a pseudonym, naturally, and was in mufti. A little after eleven, he left his house and went to a bookstore. I followed him, waited for him. He came back out, got in his car and started out of the city. He was headed for Ostia—possibly for a lunch appointment —'

'Ostia?' interrupted the Duce. 'Wait a minute . . . did you shoot him on the way to Ostia?'

'Yes, Duce.'

'And left his body in a ditch? He was driving a gray Citroën?'

'Yes, Duce . . .'

'Then *you* killed him! My God, you CRETIN!' The dictator jumped out of his chair. He was almost hysterical with rage. 'Do you know who Massimo Romano was?'

Fausto was terrified.

'The man who murdered my father . . .'

'Don Ciccio told you *that?*'

'Yes, Duce . . .'

'You IDIOT! Massimo Romano was our best informer on the Mafia! He was the one who told us about Don Ciccio's operation! You carried out revenge not for your father, but for Don Ciccio! *CRETINO!!*'

His voice echoed around the marble walls. A white-faced Fausto stood before the dictator of Italy and watched his promising career as a Fascist begin to crumble.

PART VIII

A CHRISTMAS PRESENT FOR GABRIELLA

1929–1934

CHAPTER 38

In a family of remarkably good-looking people, she was the ugly duckling. Her mother, Lorna Dexter von Gersdorff, was a beauty. Her aunt, Barbara Dexter Morris, was a beauty. Her uncle, Drew Dexter, was handsome and his wife, Millie, was renowned for her looks. But Gabriella von Gersdorff was the ugly duckling. She knew it, and even at the age of eight, her pudgy homeliness had made her shy, sensitive, the victim of a crushing sense of inferiority, and the inhabitant of a world of fantasy.

In the genetic crapshoot she had taken after her father, Carl Maria von Gersdorff. Carl Maria was a wonderful pianist and a warm, charming man, but he was not good-looking. Gabrielle had inherited his tendency toward obesity and his height. She had also inherited his rich brown hair, his big green eyes and his intelligence. And his appetite. Carl Maria loved to cook and loved to eat. 'Good music and good food means a good life,' was his motto, and as Gabriella had grown up to the sounds of Schubert, Mozart, Beethoven, Chopin and Liszt, she had also grown up to the smells of *tafelspitz, leberknödlsuppe, zwetschenknödl, marillenknödl,* and the wonderful peasant stew, *beuschl.* Carl Maria instilled in his only child a love for things Viennese, and along the way taught her German with a Viennese accent (complete with the proper 'district' intonation, since each district, or *Bezirk,* in Vienna had its own accent). Because she had also learned Italian from her grandfather Victor, whom she adored, she was trilingual at an age when most children are struggling over their first irregular French verbs.

Lorna's wedding present to her husband of a concert grand had been followed two years later by a second one. The two were placed bow-in-bow at the end of the second-floor living room of the Sixty-fourth Street town house, and Carl Maria would practice all day and far into the night, his thunderous chords eliciting howls of protest from the neighbors. Carl Maria ignored the protests. He loved his life and his family, even though he knew in his heart that he would never be in the first rank of the pianists of his generation. Lorna also ignored the protests. She was devoting her life to her husband's career, and happily set about making their house the center of New York's music scene. All the great pianists of the day came to dinner: In later life Gabriella would boast that her earliest memory was hearing her father and Rachmaninoff playing Mozart on the two grands.

It was a happy house, but Gabriella's fat kept her miserable. When she was eight years old and five feet six and still growing, she sagged the scales at 176 pounds. All those dumplings her father lovingly cooked, all that pasta when she went to her grandfather's for dinner, all went to her hips, her stomach and her behind. Her relatives dismissed it airily as baby fat that would go away in time, but it seemed miserably permanent to Gabriella. In her third-floor bedroom, she almost blotted out her bureau mirror by sticking snapshots of her family in the frame. She had a vampire's loathing of full-length mirrors and when she would inadvertently catch her reflection in a shop window, she would burst into tears. Convinced she was doomed to a lifetime of ugliness, if not grotesqueness, she put an exaggerated value on good looks. She was to learn soon enough from a close relative how treacherous good looks could be, but this didn't shake her lifelong conviction that beautiful people were somehow superior.

She loved to read and devoured books. She loved *Alice in Wonderland* and the Oz stories, and empathized with Alice and Dorothy who, like herself, were different and lost. Unhappily, since she loved music, she had inherited none of her father's musical talent. After two years of piano lessons, she could barely manage the simplest Mozart, much less chopsticks, and her clumsiness led her to such tears of frustration and keyboard-pounding tantrums that her parents wisely gave up and stopped the lessons. She did have one talent, though. She could draw beautifully. She loved to sketch and do watercolors, and her sense of color was so vivid and imaginative that her mother framed her best efforts and hung them around the house to show off to visitors.

The house was full of visitors when Carl Maria and Lorna were home. But half the year he was away giving concerts, and since Lorna always went with him, Gabriella was left with the cook-housekeeper, Frau Grunewald, a plump and kindly Viennese widow who lived on the top floor. Gabriella loved Frau Grunewald, who added to her caloric intake by constantly baking delicious cakes and cookies (including a weekly Sacher torte that reduced Gabriella to tears of ecstasy). But she missed her parents, and when they were gone she spent even more time in her room reading, drawing, playing with her dolls and fantasizing. Her favorite was a beautiful French doll she named Adele. It had been a birthday present from her grandfather Victor, which made it all that much more precious to her. She could spend hours playing with Adele, who became a sort of alter ego. Adele, after all, never gained weight. Adele wore clothes beautifully, unlike Gabriella whose dresses had the proportions of tents.

To outfit Adele even more gorgeously, Gabriella started drawing dresses for her. Then, in a natural progression, she decided to try and make one of the dresses. She borrowed Frau Grunewald's sewing box and started looking around the house for suitable material. The dress she had designed was a sand-colored cocktail dress, and it so happened that one of the chairs in the library was covered in crushed velvet that was very close to the color Gabriella had in mind. Quaking at the thought of what would happen when her parents came home, she took one of the chair arm covers and scurried up to her room where she attacked it with a pair of scissors. The result was a doll's dress that looked awful, but the experience intrigued her. If she could learn to sew, she could make a whole wardrobe for Adele!

She asked Frau Grunewald to teach her to sew. She was an apt pupil and quickly learned the various stitches and even the fundamentals of dressmaking, since Frau Grunewald, with old-world thrift, made most of her own clothes. Then she returned to her bedroom and launched her grandest fantasy to date.

She opened an imaginary Paris boutique called Chez Gabriella and designed an entire 'collection' for Adele, complete with the obligatory wedding dress for a finale. Since Adele had only one pair of shoes, the 'showing' would lack a certain finesse; and since Gabriella also had to do her homework, the designing of the collection took several weeks. But she threw all her considerable energies into the task, and there was something pathetic about this fat, frumpy girl sitting on her bedroom floor sketching dress after glamorous dress for the eternally beautiful doll, Adele, to wear to imaginary balls and galas where she would inevitably entrance the handsome prince.

But when it came time to make the clothes, she realized she

couldn't use arm covers, and she figured she would need at least twenty dollars to buy the material. It was January, 1929, and her parents were on a concert tour of South America. Gabriella's weekly allowance was five dollars, paid out by Frau Grunewald (who in turn was paid by Carl Maria's business manager, who handled all the domestic expenses when the pianist was on tour); but Gabriella didn't feel like saving up a month's allowance. She wanted to make the clothes *now*. Consequently, on a cold Saturday morning, she walked the six blocks to her grandfather's Fifth Avenue apartment. Grandpa Victor was, she knew, a soft touch.

Victor was only sixty-one, but the previous fall he had had a heart attack that was sufficiently serious for his doctor to insist he retire. The thought had appalled Victor, but Julia had backed up the doctor and so Victor, with great reluctance and sadness, stepped down from the presidency of the bank he had run for a quarter century and stepped up to the position of chairman of the board. He had serious doubts about picking Drew as his successor—his memory of his son's involvement with Serge Wittgenstein was still fresh—and there were senior officials in the bank who deserved the presidency more. But Drew was his son, and he was a Dexter. Drew and Millie seemed to be happily married, and Millie was pregnant. Lucille, still married to the Count de Beaumont, strongly backed her son's candidacy. Victor figured he could, as chairman, control Drew. Thus at the age of twenty-eight, Drew Dexter became president of the Dexter Bank and Trust Company, and also became one of the youngest men of influence on Wall Street.

When it was announced, the bank's stock dropped four points in one day.

Gabriella was admitted to her grandfather's apartment by the butler, who told her Mr. Victor was in a conference with Mr. Drew and she could wait in the drawing room. Gabriella was surprised at this because she knew her Uncle Drew invariably went to Connecticut for the weekends, even in the winter, but she went into the drawing room to watch the snow falling on Central Park. The park and the city looked magical, and she was watching two kids throwing snowballs at each other when she heard her grandfather shouting—something also unusual.

'Damn it, Drew, you're a banker, not a stockbroker! When will you *ever* learn the difference?'

Intrigued, she went to the library door to listen. Victor's voice had returned to normal, so she couldn't hear everything; but it was obvious her grandfather and her uncle were in a battle royal.

As best as she could make out and understand, her uncle wanted to set up something called an investment trust that the bank would manage, and her grandfather was vehemently against it. Uncle Drew kept insisting the bank would make millions; Grandfather kept rebutting that it was too speculative, that no matter what everyone said, the bull market could not go on forever, and that an investment trust was dangerous. Gabriella knew nothing about banks and stocks and cared less. But her grandfather's reiteration of the words 'dangerous' and 'potential disaster' intrigued her. She wondered what a 'disaster' would be like. However, the argument soon bored her, and she went back to the window to watch the snowball fight, which was much more fun.

The meeting wasn't over for twenty minutes, and when Uncle Drew finally came out of the library, he looked angry.

'Hello, Gabriella,' he said curtly, as he put on his Chesterfield.

'Hello, Uncle Drew.'

As always around her good-looking relatives, Gabriella was reminded of her own homeliness, which made her shrink into her shell. She also sensed that, even though Uncle Drew was always polite to her, as was Aunt Millie, and though they gave her nice presents at Christmas and on her birthday, neither of them liked her. Gabriella attributed it to her fatness and 'strangeness.' With a child's perspicacity, she had guessed the truth: they *didn't* like her. Now Uncle Drew, obviously in a snit, didn't even bother to be particularly polite. Grabbing his bowler hat, he slammed out of the apartment.

Gabriella waited a moment, then went into the library where her grandfather was seated in a wing chair. She thought he looked rather pale, but as always when he saw her, Victor smiled and opened his arms.

'Gabriella! What brings you out on this snowy day?'

She came over and kissed him. Victor put his arm around her ample waist. Of all his grandchildren, he particularly adored this one, mainly because she *was* different. Gabriella reminded him of himself when he was a boy, brought over to the new world —so vastly different then—and plopped into the middle of a family, all of whom thought he was 'different.'

'Well, I wanted to see you,' said Gabriella, truthfully. 'And I also wanted to see if you'd lend me twenty dollars.'

'Twenty dollars? Now what in the world do you want all that money for?'

He smoothed her hair fondly.

'Do you remember that beautiful doll you gave me last year? The one I call Adele? Oh, Grandpa, she's my favorite doll in the whole world! Really, I just *love* her!'

'Good. I'm glad.'

'Anyway, I know you'll think this is funny, but I designed a wardrobe for her.'

'You did? Why, that's wonderful.'

'And you see, I want to make the clothes for her. But I have to buy the material, and I think it's going to cost me twenty dollars, which I don't have. But if you'd loan it to me, I'd pay it back. I could save out of my allowance. I don't know how long it would take . . .'

Again he smiled, and she thought he had the most wonderful smile in the world.

'I'll tell you what: I'll give you the twenty dollars.'

'Oh, you will? Oh, Grandpa, *thanks!*'

She kissed him, and he laughed.

'Now, be honest,' he said. 'You knew I'd give it to you, didn't you?'

She looked embarrassed.

'Well, I thought *maybe* . . .'

He got out of the chair.

'That's all right. What are grandfathers for, if not to . . .'

He suddenly lurched forward, grabbing onto a chair with one hand while his other clutched his chest. She looked at him, puzzled.

'Are you all right?' she asked.

'Get me a glass of water, please,' he whispered. 'Hurry.'

He was fumbling in his coat pocket for something. She was suddenly frightened.

'Grandpa, what's wrong?'

'Hurry . . .'

She ran out of the library and headed for the kitchen. She heard a crash behind her and turned to look. He had fallen to the floor, knocking the chair over in the process.

'Grandpa!'

She ran back into the library and knelt beside him. His face had turned extremely white, and he was gasping for breath, trying to loosen his tie. She loosened it for him and opened his collar.

'I'll get the water,' she said, starting to get up. He grabbed her hand and pulled her back down beside him. His lips were moving, trying to say something.

Like most children, Gabriella never thought of death and was hardly aware of what it meant. But she guessed her beloved grandfather was dying, and the thought almost paralyzed her. Tears running down her cheeks, she leaned close to his mouth to try and hear what he was saying. To her surprise, it was in Italian.

'Tell Lucille,' he whispered, 'she was my first love.'

'*Primo amore*,' he said.

Then time stopped for Vittorio Spada. Gabriella thought her heart would break.

The funeral was private, and Gabriella was taken to it by Frau Grunewald, since Carl Maria and Lorna were in South America. Nor could Barbara and Morris David get to New York from the coast in time for the ceremony. But Julia was there, as were Drew and Millie and the Count and Countess de Beaumont. Gabriella watched Lucille, as she couldn't bring herself to look at either Victor's bronze casket or her Uncle Drew. She remembered the argument he had had with his father just before Victor died. In her heart she was convinced the argument had brought on the fatal heart attack, and she would never forgive her Uncle Drew for that.

Her grandmother Lucille was wearing a sable coat and a black-veiled hat. To Gabriella she was a remote, if glamorous, figure, and she found it somehow incredible that her grandfather had once been in love with her. Now, after the casket slipped into the earth, Gabriella left Frau Grunewald's side and walked through the snow to the Countess de Beaumont.

'Grandmomma,' she said, 'could I whisper something to you?'

Lucille, to whom dieting was a religion, did not approve of her granddaughter's obesity and, like most of the family, thought Gabriella was 'strange.' Moreover, as a mother she had never been particularly fond of children, handing them over to nannies and governesses, as did most women of her class and generation. But as she grew older, she found that she was much fonder of her grandchildren than she had been of her own offspring. This included Gabriella, despite her fatness and shyness.

'Of course, dear,' she said, leading her away from the others. 'What is it?'

'Grandpa told me to tell you that you were his first love.'

Lucille looked confused.

'When did he say that?'

'Just before he died. He said it in Italian.'

As the winter wind flapped her black veil, she remembered the Sicilian boy who had come to the lake cottage so many years before. The 'Dago' who could never take his eyes off her. Victor, who had proposed to her so impetuously in the old house on Madison Avenue, who had been so wonderfully ridiculous when he sang 'Celeste Aida.' Victor, whom she had treated so callously in later years. And yet, his dying thought had been of her.

The Countess de Beaumont suddenly felt very old and very much alone. It occurred to her that perhaps Victor's love had been the most beautiful thing in her life.

CHAPTER 39

Gabriella didn't think much about the stock market crash. She had spent Black Tuesday at school wrestling with the War of 1812 and long division. She noticed that her mother looked nervous when she came home, but, as was her habit, she went directly to her bedroom to kiss Adele and then curl up with her current book. But the next day, the other girls in her class were talking about it—or repeating what they heard their parents saying. And in the middle of November, 1929, Carl Maria and Lorna took their daughter into the library of the house to have what Lorna called a 'family consultation.'

'I don't know if you'll understand all this,' she began, 'but your father and I have talked it over, and we think you should be told a little of what's happening.

'When your grandfather died eleven months ago, he left most of his estate to his widow, your grandmother Julia. We all knew this was what he wanted, and so there was no problem about that. A long time ago, your grandfather had set up what are called trust funds for his three children, your aunt Barbara, Uncle Drew and myself. Now, what he *didn't* leave to your grandmother Julia was his stock in the bank. Do you know what stocks are?'

'I think so.'

'Tell me.'

'They're pieces of paper everyone at school says aren't worth much anymore.'

Laura and Carl Maria exchanged looks.

'They *used* to be worth something,' said Carl Maria. 'They're shares of ownership in a company—or, in your grandfather's case, the bank.'

'Your grandfather had a lot of bank stock,' continued Lorna. 'In fact, he had the most of anyone. You could say he owned the bank. Now, when he died he left all his stock to us three

371

children: Aunt Barbara, Uncle Drew and myself. We shared it equally. But because Uncle Drew works at the bank, he wanted to buy my stock and Aunt Barbara's stock. Are you following me?'

Gabriella nodded.

'Yes, I think so.'

'Good. But this gets a little complicated. Shortly after your grandfather died, Uncle Drew set up something called the Dexter Investment Trust. What that was was a company managed by the bank. People would buy shares in the trust, and then the bank would use this money—which was millions and millions of dollars—to buy and sell stocks. The idea was that the bank knew so much more about stocks than the average investor, it would have an advantage in the stock market. Do you understand that?'

Again she nodded.

'The afternoon I was at Grandpa's—the day he died—he and Uncle Drew were fighting about that. Grandpa got real mad and told Uncle Drew it was dangerous.'

Lorna looked at her husband and said, drily, 'It's funny how Drew never mentioned that.'

'I think,' continued Gabriella, 'that Grandpa got so excited and mad that perhaps that's why he had the heart attack right after.'

'If that's true I hope Drew carries it on his conscience the rest of his life. That is, assuming he has a conscience. At any rate, Uncle Drew persuaded your aunt Barbara and me to give him our bank stock in return for the equivalent amount of shares in the Dexter Investment Trust. And we did.'

Silence, except for the ticking of a clock.

'That wasn't very smart, was it?' asked Gabriella.

Her mother sighed.

'Well, at the time it seemed all right. After all, your uncle Drew is my brother. Anyway, what's happened is that the Investment Trust has gone bankrupt, which means that my shares and your aunt Barbara's are worthless. What's even worse, my other money was in the market, and that's been pretty well wiped out, too. Of course, we have the money your father makes from his concerts, but . . . well, what all this is leading up to, darling, is that we're going to have to change a lot of things about the way we live.'

'Does that mean we're poor?' asked Gabriella.

'Not exactly poor, but we're certainly not rich anymore. We may have to sell this house . . .'

'Oh *no!*' she blurted out. 'This is *our* house! We all love it here!'

'I know, darling, but it's an awfully big place, and the taxes are high. We'll find another place almost as nice, maybe in Europe. It's so much cheaper to live in Europe, and your father and I are thinking of moving there for a while. Would you like to live in Europe?'

She was crying now.

'No!' she wailed. 'I like it *here!*'

Her father came over and hugged her.

'It's going to be all right,' he said, kissing her over and over. 'Really. You'll see. We'll have a lot of fun in Europe.'

'Oh Daddy, do we *have* to? What about Uncle Drew?' She turned to her mother. 'Is he poor, too?'

'Oh no. He's sitting very pretty. The bank's all right. It's just his Investment Trust that went under.'

'But isn't he going to give you your money back? After all, it was his idea, and it's his fault!'

Her mother looked embarrassed.

'Your uncle Drew doesn't see it that way. He says no one forced me to swap the stocks . . .'

'But you're his *sister!*'

'That doesn't seem to make much difference with Uncle Drew.'

Gabriella took a deep breath as the impact of this treachery hit her.

'Then he's a bad man!' she shouted. 'And I'll hate him the rest of my life!'

She ran out of the room to share her new fears and anxieties with her doll, Adele.

What followed was four years of rootless roaming about Europe as the world sank into devastating depression and Mussolini's brainchild, Fascism, came to power in Germany. They certainly were better off than most of their contemporaries. Julia, appalled by what Drew had done, gave Lorna an outright cash gift of $50,000 to compensate, at least partially, for her losses. Lorna was deeply touched by this, since Julia was no blood relative. They sold the town house and most of the furniture. The bottom had fallen out of the real estate market, but they still netted almost $40,000 from this transaction, so their cash position was good. But Lorna was so traumatized by the shock of her reversed fortunes that she became something of a miser. Convinced the world had gone to the dogs, that nothing

373

was secure anymore, she salted her money away in safety-deposit boxes and saving accounts. But not in the Dexter Bank. She had tried to conceal from Gabriella her personal hurt and rage at her brother's greed, but her fury was as intense as her daughter's.

She put her money in the Chase Bank, cursed her brother and sailed for Europe.

Second-class. The new penury relegated them to second-class hotels and pensions—all neat, clean and cheap. Carl Maria's concert career had never achieved first rank, so he was playing in provincial towns rather than world capitals. Gabriella was put in a convent school outside Lyons, where she learned French and ate. On holidays she traveled with her parents. It was a pleasant enough life, with the advantage of seeing almost every corner of Europe, but the rootlessness of her existence made Gabriella crawl even farther into her shell. She missed New York terribly and no longer felt she was an American. She didn't know what she was.

The phone call came to the convent in the spring of 1934. Her parents had been driving from Brussels to Ostend, where Carl Maria was to give a concert. It had been raining, and the car went into a skid, crashing into an oncoming truck. They had both been killed instantly.

Gabriella locked herself in her tiny room for two days. Now it was all gone: the music, the *tafelspitz*, the love.

Now she knew what she was.

She was alone.

CHAPTER 40

Like millions of others, the Countess de Beaumont had been knocked for a financial loop by the Depression. But Lucille, for all her faults, had guts: the loss of her fortune didn't faze her in the least. She put the beautiful Fifth Avenue house on the market. When she couldn't find a buyer, Beaux Arts town houses having become white elephants, she grandly gave it to New York University, sold off some of the furnishings at a loss, and moved with her most cherished belongings into a suite in the genteel, but definitely ungrand, Hotel Champs Elysées in the East Fifties.

This was too much for her husband. The Count de Beaumont liked his creature comforts and was in no mood for genteel hotel suites. He packed his well-cut clothes in his Louis Vuitton bags, left Lucille a three-line farewell note on his crested stationery and decamped for France.

The loss of her third husband was a much greater blow to Lucille than the loss of her money, and for several weeks she was on the verge of despair. She even went to the Automat and ate a hamburger in defiance of his vegetarian principles (the fact that she found it delicious came as a shock). But Lucille was not ready to be counted out yet. She had her health, enough money to live comfortably, and her spirits began to return.

Her problem was, she was lonely.

Thus, when she heard the news of Lorna and Carl Maria's tragic accident, she conceived the idea of taking in her strange, overweight granddaughter. They were both virtually alone in the world, and who else did the child have to turn to? She sent a cable to the convent in Lyons asking her to come stay with her. To her delight, Gabriella accepted.

She arrived in New York on May 5, 1934, and Lucille, who hadn't seen her since Victor's funeral five years before, was shocked by her appearance as she came down the gangplank.

375

She was now fourteen and had shot up to five foot eight. She had also ballooned to 245 pounds: she looked like a fat giantess. She wore a cloth coat over her tweed suit, and flat, black patent leather shoes. Her hair was clean but uncombed, and her eyebrows needed plucking. As Lucille surveyed Gabriella, the thought of overhauling her tickled her fancy. But she certainly would have her work cut out for her.

She came up and kissed her.

'My dear, dear Gabriella,' she said. 'I'm so glad to see you.'

'It was kind of you to send for me, Grandmomma,' replied the shy girl.

'Not kind at all, child! I *wanted* you. I'm all alone now. It will give me great pleasure to have you with me. Let's get a porter, then we'll taxi uptown.'

'It's good to be back in New York,' said Gabriella, looking around. 'Europe is nice, but New York is my home.'

Lucille gave her an affectionate hug.

'It's good to have you home.'

In the taxi Lucille carefully refrained from mentioning the accident in Belgium.

'You know, I never thought I'd get used to not having my own limousine and chauffeur,' she said. 'Can you imagine, I've never driven a car? In my day, ladies *never* drove themselves. Well, I've gotten used to taxis. It's amazing what one can get used to even at my age.'

'Do you miss your house, Grandmomma?'

'Not a bit. It was too big, and the bills! Heating bills, servants, fresh flowers . . . well, that was all lovely while it lasted, but I fear that way of life is gone forever, at least for me, thanks to Mr. Roosevelt. Dear me, he *does* like to tax people, doesn't he? Well, I suppose it's inevitable. We can't have people starving. Of course, all my friends *loathe* the man, but I think he's rather attractive. He has *panache*. Mr. Hoover was so dreary. I've even toyed with the idea of voting for Mr. Roosevelt in the next election. I'd do it just to irritate my son, if for no other reason.'

'I suppose,' said Gabriella, 'that Uncle Drew hates him?'

'Can't *stand* him!'

And I hate Uncle Drew, thought Gabriella.

The hotel suite, which was on the sixth floor, consisted of a good-sized living room, a small dining room, a kitchenette, and two bedrooms and baths. It was freshly painted, and Lucille's beautiful furniture gave it an elegant ambience despite the lack of space.

'Well, it's not much, but it's home,' she said. 'And the hotel cleans for me, which is nice. Here's your bedroom, my dear. The view in the front isn't much, but out the back there's a nice little garden. Now, I expect you to be neat! I won't have clothes all over the place.'

'Oh, I'm neat, Grandmomma. The nuns made sure of that.'

'Good. And here's Bien-Aimée! Come meet my granddaughter, darling.' A curious-looking black cat, with orange and white patches, one large orange patch over the left side of her face being particularly noticeable, had come into the room. Now Lucille scooped her up in her arms and smoothed her fur. 'Bien-Aimée's a dear when you get to know her,' she said, 'but she can be mean at first. Isn't she marvelous-looking? She's a tortoiseshell. Say hello to Gabriella, Bien-Aimée.' The cat looked at the girl with cool disdain. Gabriella reached out two fingers and tentatively patted her head. 'There! She didn't scratch you. That's a good sign. I think we'll all get along famously. Get unpacked, dear, then come out for some tea. We have much to talk about.'

'Why was Uncle Drew so mean to Mother?' asked Gabriella a half hour later as her grandmother poured tea from a handsome Regency silver pot.

'Ah well, he was mean to me, too,' replied Lucille, sadly. 'The whole thing's my fault, in a way. I trust you don't take sugar?'

'Yes. Two lumps, please. And milk.'

Her grandmother frowned.

'We'll cure you of *that* soon enough. Sugar is terrible for you. You shan't have any cookies or cake either because I don't approve of them. But I have two small pieces of buttered bread for you, if you'd like.'

'Thank you, Grandmomma. I'm starving.'

Lucille refrained from comment on her appetite and gave her the tea and bread.

'You were asking about Drew. Well, I'm afraid my son inherited my worst faults and none—or few—of his father's virtues. You see, my dear, when you get as old as I am, one of the few advantages you have is that you're able to look back over your life and try to figure out where you went wrong—and why. Of course, not all old people do this, but some do, and I've tried

377

to. What you told me at your grandfather's funeral touched me deeply and made me feel rather . . . guilty.'

'Guilty? Why, Grandmomma?'

'When I was young, I was very pretty. I was conceited and in many ways rather insufferable. Your grandfather Victor fell madly in love with me, poor man, and I'm afraid I took advantage of it. I was in love with him, too, but I was interested in society and money—not that they're not important, mind you, but I put too much importance on them. Which is why I feel guilty about your grandfather. I used his love, and I didn't appreciate it enough when I had it.' She sighed and sipped her tea. 'But that's all in the past now. We have to think of the future: *your* future. We have to think about a proper school for you. And pardon my saying it, dear, we have to think about your figure.'

Gabriella winced.

'What's to think about, Grandmomma? I'm fat, and I'm not pretty. I know these things, and I've accepted them, and I'd really rather not talk about them . . .'

'Nonsense! We *must* talk about them. More important, we must do something about them.'

'That's easy for you to say because you're pretty. *Everyone* in my family is pretty except me.'

She turned her face away. She was embarrassed and ashamed. Lucille reached across the table and put her hand on her arm.

'Gabriella, you're thinking all wrong. A few people are lucky: they're born beautiful. But most people have to work at it. If you worked at it, you could be a striking woman. You have your mother's beautiful skin, your eyes are lovely, your hair could be lovely if you took proper care of it. And most important, you could be thin.'

'No I can't,' she mumbled.

'Well, my dear, if you gorge yourself you can't be thin. You have to go on a strict diet. But the *one* good thing my last husband taught me was how to eat and how not to eat. I could make you thin, Gabriella, if you'd listen to me. Will you listen to me?'

She looked at her grandmother.

'Why?' she asked. 'You never particularly cared for me before.'

Lucille smiled.

'But I care for you *now*.'

Gabriella sighed.

'I'll listen to you,' she said. 'But it won't do any good. I'm just naturally fat. And I love to eat. Sometimes I think the only thing in my life is food.'

'Then we'll have to find *other* things.'

She started the diet the next day, and it was, to say the least, Spartan:

> *Breakfast.*
> ½ grapefruit. 1 banana.
>
> *Lunch.*
> 2 oz. cottage cheese.
>
> *Dinner.*
> 1 piece chicken or fish.
> 1 serving boiled vegetable.
> Small salad.
> Fresh fruit.

Gabriella was used not only to three whopping meals a day, but she was also an inveterate snacker: by eleven the first morning, she was ravenous. The cottage-cheese lunch did nothing for her except make her nauseous. By three the first afternoon, she had sneaked out of the hotel, gone to a hamburger stand and eaten three burgers, two orders of French fries and a banana split. When she finished this orgy, she burst into tears. The waitress looked at her.

'What's wrong, honey?' she said.

'I'm supposed to be on a diet!' wailed Gabriella.

'Some diet.'

She went back to the hotel and locked herself in her room, hoping to avoid her grandmother. Lucille was wily: she guessed what had happened, but said nothing until dinner. 'Well, dear,' she said as Gabriella tackled her chicken breast, 'how was the first day?'

'Not as bad as I thought it would be, Grandmomma.'

'Good. You weren't hungry?'

'Oh, a little.'

'Well, I ordered a new set of scales, which should be here in the morning. We'll weigh you tomorrow, then every day after that. It's very important to get in the habit of weighing yourself every day, by the way. I've made an appointment with my doctor on Friday. He'll give you a checkup and determine what your correct weight should be. That way we'll have a target, which is psychologically important. Do you like your string beans?'

'Yes, Grandmomma.'

'Good. We'll have a nice salad, then I'll take you to a movie. Your Uncle Morris has a new film at the Music Hall. Would you like to see that?'

'Oh yes!'

'Finish your chicken.'

When the new scales came, she weighed in at 249 pounds. The doctor told her she should weigh 135 pounds. Her grandmother whittled that down to 125 pounds. Gabriella weighed almost exactly double what she should.

In the taxi back to the hotel, she slumped gloomily in the back seat. 'A hundred and twenty-five pounds!' she moaned. 'It'll take me months to lose that much! Maybe even years! Oh Grandmomma, can't I just stay fat?'

'Of course you can. You can do anything you want. But wouldn't you like to be thin?'

She didn't answer. Her grandmother took her hand.

'Gabriella, I know it isn't easy, but I want you to *try*. And I want you to be honest with me, too. There's no point going through this charade of dieting in front of me, then sneaking off to stuff your face with hamburgers.'

She cringed.

'You *know?*'

'Yes dear, I know. You're not very subtle, telling me you're going for a walk, then coming home with catsup stains on your dress. Honestly!'

'But I get *so* hungry! I just think I'm going to die!'

'That's called "losing weight." Next time you want to sneak off, will you promise me you'll come talk to me first? You see, it's so important you lose five or ten pounds. That way, you'll feel encouraged and you'll want to stick to it. So will you promise to talk to me?'

She sighed.

'I promise.'

The taxi had stopped at a traffic light, and her eyes were glued longingly to a hot-dog stand.

CHAPTER 41

She surprised herself. She actually stuck to the diet for a month. The first week there was a dramatic weight loss of six pounds; then, for four agonizing days, nothing happened. She dreamed of food: Viennese food, Italian food, French food, French fries. She came close to breaking the diet, but she stuck to her guns. Then the pounds started melting. By the end of the first month, she had lost eighteen pounds. By the end of the long, hot, Depression summer, she had lost forty-two pounds, and for the first time in her life she began to believe she might some day look like other people.

She was enrolled in Miss Hewitt's Classes where, also for the first time in her life, she began to make friends with girls of her own generation. While she was still a 'chubby,' she didn't mind it so much anymore; in fact, name-calling only fired her determination to stick to the grueling diet. While she still dreamed of caloric goodies, months of cottage cheese and fish had dulled her interest in food. By necessity, she became interested in other things: movies, books, her studies, her friends, even her clothes. Even, to her surprise, boys.

These heretofore alien creatures began catching her eye, even if, so far, she wasn't catching theirs. Her best friend at Miss Hewitt's, Ellen Kemp, had a seventeen-year-old brother named Nick who was a fourth former at Lawrenceville. Nick broke his leg in a football game and was taken out of school for a week until his New York doctor could make sure the cast was set correctly. The Kemps' father was a corporation lawyer, and the family lived in a pleasant apartment on Park Avenue at Sixty-eighth Street. Ellen brought Gabriella home on several occasions, and it was there she met Nick. He was pleasant and good-looking, with blond hair that was almost white. He exhibited nothing more than polite interest in his younger sister's pudgy friend, but Gabriella could hardly take her eyes off him.

She began dreaming about Nick Kemp instead of French fries.

Lucille's social life had been restricted by her age and reduced circumstances, but she still went out frequently to dinner parties. At such times Gabriella either went to Ellen's apartment or stayed home: being by herself did not bother her. But although she was a loner—albeit one who was coming out of her shell —she got along well with her grandmother, and a deep bond grew between the two. The only rift was over Drew. Frequently Lucille tried to persuade her granddaughter at least to pay a call on her uncle and his wife, Millie. But Gabriella refused. However, at Christmas, 1934, the matter came to a head.

'Your uncle is having a family gathering,' Lucille said one morning, 'this Christmas Eve at his apartment. Barbara and Morris are coming from Los Angeles with their children, and Drew wants us to be there, too. Now I know what you think about Drew, dear, and I sympathize with you. But he is, after all, your uncle, and this is your family. I really hope you'll go . . .'

'No,' interrupted Gabriella. 'I never want to see him or speak to him. Ever.'

Her grandmother sighed.

'You're just being stubborn. I'm going, and you can't stay here by yourself on Christmas Eve. It's unthinkable.'

'I'd rather be by myself than with him.'

'Gabriella, I'm asking it as a favor to me. No matter what Drew has done, I don't want my family at each other's throats. Your aunt Barbara was hurt just as much by Drew as your mother, and she's going. Besides, you're not being very clever. Your sulking doesn't hurt him. He'll just think you're an impossible girl who probably deserved what happened. But if you're nice to him, perhaps he'll start feeling guilty.'

Gabriella thought about this. Grudgingly she admitted there was some truth in what her grandmother said. Besides, she was now down to an almost-svelte (by her standards) 145 pounds. It would be pleasant to show off her new figure.

'All right,' she said. 'I'll go.'

The object of her hatred stood at the living room window of his apartment at One Beekman Place and complacently surveyed the East River below. Drew had reason to feel good. The world was still suffering through the seemingly endless Depression: Communism was triumphant in Russia, Fascism in Germany and Italy; but Drew, in his luxurious aerie, was far removed from these uglinesses. He was young, healthy, good-looking and rich.

He had made many enemies in his five years as head of the Dexter Bank, but Drew wasn't interested in being liked. He was interested in being powerful.

One Beekman Place had been built by the Rockefellers a few years before, and its amenities included not only spacious apartments with river views, but a swimming pool and a health club in the basement for the exclusive use of the tenants. The Depression had soured Americans' long love affair with the rich, and such luxury was coming under increasing attack. But Drew didn't read left-wing publications. To him, the Depression's low prices had turned the world into a bargain basement for those with money, and he had bought fine antiques and paintings with zeal and a good eye inherited from his mother. Picassos, Renoirs, Pisarros, Monets and Rousseaus hung around the walls, but Drew's favorite was a superb Ingres portrait of the Duchesse de Choiseul-Praslin, the plump victim of one of the nineteenth century's most sensational murders, which hung over the rose marble mantel.

'Zip me, will you?'

He turned to see Millie in the door of the big living room. She was attaching a diamond earclip, and she looked smashing in a black-and-white-striped evening gown by Schiaparelli. Drew, who was dressed in a tux, crossed to her and zipped the back of her dress.

'I think Angela could have at least stayed around long enough to dress you,' he said, referring to his wife's maid.

'On Christmas Eve? Don't be silly. She wanted to be with her family and boyfriend. There *was* an Emancipation Proclamation, you know, so don't be a Scrooge. And fix me a drink, will you?'

'Wait till the guests get here. It would be nice on Christmas Eve if you didn't pass out in the soup.'

She started to say something, when the doorbell rang.

'The guests *are* here,' she said, heading for the bar. As she mixed herself a double martini, the hired-for-the-evening butler opened the front door to admit Barbara and Morris David and their two children, Allen, fourteen, and Gloria, twelve. The phenomenal success of *Russia* had made both Morris and Barbara financially independent for life, so that Morris, while still bitter at his brother-in-law for what Drew had done to Barbara in 1929, had not attempted to assassinate Drew as he might have if they had needed the money. Still, in Morris's book, Drew was a prime son of a bitch and a disgrace to his father's memory. Barbara agreed that her younger brother had behaved reprehensibly, costing her a fortune. But she had insisted to Morris that to carry on an endless family feud was pointless, and it was time to bury the hatchet. So they had come with their children.

But Barbara was interested in something else. She wanted to see her niece, Gabriella. Her mother had written about Gabriella's physical transformation, which delighted Barbara. But she also felt guilty about the girl. Of all the family, Gabriella had been hit the hardest, first by the loss of her parents' money, then by the loss of her parents. Barbara hadn't seen her for years. Now she wanted to show her niece that there were other members of the family beside Lucille who loved her and cared for her.

Unfortunately, Gabriella was late.

'I won't go, I won't *go!*'

She threw herself on her bed and began beating her pillows with her fists. Lucille was aghast: until ten minutes before, Gabriella had seemed calm and delighted with the beautiful new dress her grandmother had given her for Christmas. Then, just as they were about to leave the hotel suite, she became almost hysterical and ran into her room, throwing herself on her bed and bursting into sobs.

'Gabriella, I don't understand you!' exclaimed her grandmother. 'What's wrong? Why don't you want to go? You look lovely—or at least you *did*, until you started crying . . .'

'They'll laugh at me,' she sniffed. '*He* will—Uncle Drew . . .'

'He will not!' She sat on the edge of the bed and held her hand firmly. 'Now listen: you've worked hard for months. You've taken off so much of the weight, your hair looks beautiful, your eyebrows are plucked—you're a lovely young lady, Gabriella. *Lovely.* You must have confidence in yourself.'

'But I'm afraid . . .'

'I don't believe it. You? What do you have to be afraid of? Listen, my dear, I've come to know you fairly well these past months. Underneath all your insecurities you're a very tough young lady. I don't believe for a moment you're afraid.'

She sat up, looking rueful and sheepish.

'Well, I am,' she said.

'Nonsense. Now run in and wash your face. Then let's go. We're late already.'

'Do I *really* look pretty?' she whispered, nervously.

Her grandmother gave her a hug.

'You look lovely,' she smiled, smoothing her hair affectionately. 'Now, hurry.'

Gabriella went into the bathroom and washed her face. Then
she looked in the mirror. She didn't believe she looked pretty.
But she wasn't ashamed of her reflection anymore.

On the way up in the elevator at One Beekman Place, she told
herself over and over to be strong, not to let her nervousness
show, not to disgrace herself and her grandmother in front of the
Ogre, Uncle Drew. The elevator stopped, and the elevator man
opened the door. They stepped out into a small, marble-floored
foyer where, on a lovely console table, a Chinese vase held a
spray of fresh flowers. On the door to the apartment hung a holly
wreath.

'Merry Christmas,' she muttered to herself as her grandmother rang the bell.

The butler opened the door, and they entered the large
entrance hall with its eighteenth-century French lantern and
handsome stair. Beyond, in the living room, the others were
having cocktails while the two David children eyed the Christmas tree with the two sons of Drew and Millie.

Lucille took Gabriella's hand and whispered, 'Courage!' They
walked into the living room. She saw Uncle Drew coming
toward her, a smile on his face.

'Mother! Merry Christmas,' and he kissed Lucille. Then he
turned to Gabriella. 'It's true!' he exclaimed. 'You've turned
into a swan.'

He kissed her cheek. She wanted to bite him.

Millie managed to stay sober through dinner by watering her
wine. She had started drinking heavily after the birth of their
first son, George, when she discovered Drew had been sleeping
with the wife of one of his best friends during Millie's
pregnancy. She hadn't been surprised by Drew's infidelity. She
knew his character. But somehow, even though expected, it had
hurt, and Millie turned to alcohol to numb the pain. In a classic
vicious cycle, the more Millie drank, the more Drew played
around. By the birth of their second son, Andrew, in 1931, there
wasn't much left of their marriage but distrust and rancor. They
stayed together only because of the children. In her drunker
moments Millie marveled how she could have ever fallen in love
with such a son of a bitch.

After dinner the party left the dining room to return to the
beautiful Christmas tree for the opening of the presents. There

were fabulous toys for George and Andrew Dexter, a new baseball mitt for Allen David, books for Gloria David . . . Gabriella saw the envelope with her name on it, but waited till most of the other presents were opened before picking it up. 'To Gabriella from Uncle Drew and Aunt Millie.'

They saw her pick it up, and Drew came over to her.

'Gabriella,' he said, softly, 'I know things haven't been right between us. I hope this will help fix them.'

The Devil speaks softly, she thought as she opened the envelope. Inside was a check made out to her. Her eyes bulged as she saw the amount. Twenty-five thousand dollars!

Slowly she tore the check in pieces and threw them in her uncle's amazed face.

'I can't be bought,' she said.

As she walked out of the apartment, she heard her uncle roar, 'You fat *BITCH!*'

PART IX

DEATH OF A DREAM

1936

CHAPTER 42

Colonel Fausto Spada put his two-engined Caproni fighter plane into a dive and headed for the hill where an Ethiopian soldier had been firing at him. He had the Ethiopian in the sights of his machine gun. The man was tall and, like all the other Ethiopian soldiers, even the elite Imperial Guard, he was barefoot. Now he threw down his rifle and began running for a clump of trees. Fausto's finger was on the firing button: The poor bugger is dead, he thought. As dead as the hundreds of other Ethiopians he had slaughtered during the past few months. Death rained from the sky on black savages, many of whom had never seen a wheel, much less an airplane, until Mussolini's army invaded the mountainous African kingdom the previous autumn, in October, 1935.

He was about to squeeze the firing button when the Ethiopian stopped running, turned and stared up at the in-zooming plane. The bastard's defying me! thought Fausto. He's defying me, the black son of a bitch!

For a split second Fausto was judge, jury and executioner for the anonymous black man below him. He had killed so often that inflicting death had come to mean almost nothing to him, but for some reason the Ethiopian defiance of death struck him as wonderfully noble. It was far from a noble war. All the technology of the twentieth century was being hurled at a nation barely out of the Iron Age. Was it a dormant guilt that prevented Fausto from squeezing the trigger?

He didn't know, but he didn't fire. The Caproni flew over the Ethiopian's head and started for Addis Ababa to rejoin Fausto's squadron.

The Ethiopian, standing on the hilltop watching the plane dwindle in the distance, looked puzzled.

So did Lieutenant Ercole Malli, flying on patrol with Fausto.

Assuming his superior officer's gun had jammed, he flew in and shot the Ethiopian for him.

'Fausto's coming home!' exclaimed Nanda Spada as she hugged her father at the door of her villa. Paolo Montecatini had just arrived for dinner with Nanda and her son, Enrico.

'How do you know?' he asked.

'I got a telegram from Addis Ababa just an hour ago. He's sailing on the *Conte Biancamano* tomorrow, and they should dock in Naples in ten days. Isn't it wonderful news?'

Her father handed his bowler hat to the butler. Well into his seventies and now a widower, the old jeweler still dressed elegantly.

'Did he get leave?'

'No, he's coming home for good.'

'Has he been wounded?'

'No, thank God.'

'Then why is he coming home?'

Nanda's elation ebbed slightly.

'Well, he didn't say. What's wrong, Father?'

'Nothing.'

'You don't look very excited about the news.'

Paolo checked to make sure the butler had returned to the pantry.

'What surprises me is that you're so excited. When Fausto left last year, you told me you were glad to be rid of him.'

'I was. But I've missed him. I've even missed our fights.' She took her father's hand and smiled. 'Come on: Enrico's so anxious to see you. He got a very good grade in English today, so congratulate him.'

She led her father into the drawing room, where her sixteen-year-old-son stood up to embrace his grandfather.

'So your father's coming home,' smiled the old man, admiring Enrico's dark good looks, 'and you got a good grade in English, all in one day! You must be excited.'

'I am, Grandfather. But most of all about Father. Do you think the Duce will give him a medal? The papers call him a hero.'

Paolo sat down.

'Who knows what the Duce will do? I think half the time the *Duce* doesn't know what he's going to do.'

Nanda sat beside her father. Suddenly she looked rather nervous.

'You don't think Fausto's in some sort of trouble, do you?' she asked.

'Why would he be in trouble?'

'Well, just a moment ago, you wondered why he was coming home . . .'

Her father smiled.

'You know me,' he said. 'Whenever I hear good news, I get suspicious. When I hear bad news, I'm almost relieved. I'm a born pessimist.'

After dinner Enrico excused himself to go upstairs and do his homework. Alone with his daughter, Paolo said, 'I didn't want to say anything in front of Enrico, but I think you ought to know something I heard this morning.'

'What?'

'A very high-ranking member of the government was in the store, buying some jewelry for his mistress—I sold him a beautiful brooch—and he asked me if I'd heard anything from Fausto. I said no, and he told me he heard that Fausto had resigned from the Fascist Party.'

Nanda looked stunned.

'Why would he do that?'

'I don't know except I hear rumors that a lot of Fascists are quitting because they can't stomach what's happening in Ethiopia. Of course, all we get is propaganda here in Rome, but people say it's a bloodbath out there. At any rate, if Fausto *did* quit, then that would explain why he's coming home. He's too well known for them to do anything except try and sweep him under the carpet.'

Nanda remembered her husband's Fascist fervor and said, 'I can't *believe* he'd quit.'

Her father shrugged.

'We don't know what he's seen. At any rate, if he has quit things may become a bit uncomfortable for all of us.'

They looked at each other. Nanda knew what he meant.

Five days later Enrico dribbled a soccer ball down the field, then kicked it to his teammate, Tino Torelli. It was a bright, cloudless day, and the scrimmage was being held on one of the three soccer fields of Enrico's school outside Rome. His team, the Blues, were two goals behind. Now Tino Torelli passed the ball back to Enrico, who had run up to the goal. He kicked hard. The ball sailed toward the goal, but the goalie caught it and threw it to his right halfback, who started dribbling it toward the Blues' goal.

'Hey, Jew-boy!' yelled the grinning goalie. 'Not a bad shot for a Kike.'

Enrico couldn't believe what he had heard.

Two days later he entered the bedroom of his grandmother on the second floor of the Palazzo dell'Acqua. Enrico loved the room. It had a timeless elegance that was comforting and beautiful. Princess Sylvia smiled as her grandson came up to her baroque bed. For an old woman who had to spend most of her time in bed, a visit from anyone was a pleasure. But a visit from her adored Enrico was a particular pleasure.

'How are you, Grandmomma?' he asked, bending down to kiss her.

'Much better now that you're here, you darling boy,' she smiled, putting her hand on his cheek. As she had shrunk with age, her skin had taken on an almost translucent quality. Enrico never tired of looking at her. To him, his grandmother was the most beautiful old woman he had ever seen.

'And how is school?' she asked.

'Oh, fine,' he lied, pulling up a chair and sitting beside the bed.

'You must be excited that your father's coming home.'

'Yes, I am.'

'Now tell me, have you fallen in love yet?'

He looked embarrassed.

'Not yet. I don't have much time for girls.'

She smiled.

'Ah, but you will. And how the girls will love you!'

'Do you think so?'

'Take it from an old woman who's always had an eye for goodlooking men: the girls will love you. Enrico, my dear child, what wonderful things you have to look forward to! Just as I have wonderful things to look back on. Here we are, you and I, at the opposite ends of life. I suppose if I were a good grandmother, I'd give you all sorts of advice about how to cope with life. But that would do nothing but bore you. The wonderful thing about life is that everyone has to learn for himself. But that's what makes it interesting, don't you think?'

'I suppose. Except . . .' he shifted uncomfortably, '. . . there are some things you don't enjoy learning about.'

'What do you mean?'

He looked at her.

'Grandmother, do you think of me as a Jew or an Italian?'

She looked surprised.

'I think of you as my grandson,' she replied. 'But what a strange question! Why did you ask?'

'Because at school they've started calling me "Jew-boy." Word's gotten around that Father quit the Fascists and that he's a traitor . . . which he isn't! I'm certain he's no traitor!'

'Of course he isn't,' said his grandmother, sharply. 'He's just come to his senses at last! It's the best thing Fausto's ever done.'

'That isn't the way the guys at school think. He's a traitor, and suddenly I'm a Jew. I'm only a quarter Jewish! I've always thought of myself as an Italian, but now . . . well, I guess I'm also a Jew. It's confused me, and . . . it's frightened me, too. I mean, if the same thing happens here that's happening in Germany, where will I be? *What* will I be?'

She reached out and took his hand.

'You will still be Enrico Spada.'

'But that's no answer! What if they put labels on us? What if they make me wear a Star of David on my coat? This is my country, except . . . maybe it isn't? I don't know . . .'

She didn't say anything for a while. She saw how deeply troubled he was. Finally, she said, 'I don't think there's any easy answer to what you're asking. And if these things come to pass —if Mussolini passes racial laws—I wouldn't know what to tell you except to be brave, which is easy advice but hard to do. But I think you must realize that you are *both* a Jew and an Italian. That you are the heir to *two* wonderful heritages. That may cause you some difficulty in life because what we're living through now is insane. But in the end you will be a richer man because of your two heritages. And maybe even a better man.'

'I never thought of it that way.'

'When I was young there weren't even Italians, much less Italian-Jews. One was either a Roman or a Neapolitan or a Florentine. The map has been changed so drastically in my lifetime, and maybe it will be changed even more in yours. Nothing is guaranteed in life except your brains and your character. You have good brains and character, my darling boy. You'll do all right.'

'Unless I get my brains kicked out,' he said.

She tried to hide her look of fear, but he felt her grip tighten on his hand.

'Oh Enrico,' she whispered. 'Don't even *think* that.'

But he was thinking it.

CHAPTER 43

The troopship *Conte Biancamano* was a rustbucket, and as it made its slow way through the Red Sea and the Suez Canal it was also an oven. It was crammed with wounded veterans of the Ethiopian War, and in its hold were over two hundred filled coffins. Mussolini had defeated the Ethiopians, but at a terrible cost in lives. Still, the Italians had an empire, for what that was worth.

A few passengers on the ship were not wounded, and the most illustrious of them was Count Galeazzo Ciano, son-in-law of Mussolini and, until recently, head of Fausto's squadron, La Disparata. At thirty-three Ciano was returning to Italy to become Foreign Minister. The day before the ship docked at Naples, he summoned Fausto to his cabin. It was the best cabin on the ship after the captain's, but it was still small. Two open ports and an electric fan moved the hot air slightly, but Ciano's shirt was blotched with sweat. He was a good-looking man, but there was an incipient bulge around his middle. He was sipping a gin and tonic when Fausto came in, but he offered his former comrade-in-arms neither a drink nor a seat.

'Spada,' he said, 'I'm giving you one more chance. There will be reporters at the dock tomorrow, and I'd like you to tell them you're one hundred percent behind the Duce's policies.'

Fausto's face was drawn with fatigue, and he needed a shave. He shook his head.

'No,' he said. 'I told you: I'm through.'

Ciano put his drink on a rusted steel table.

'Dammit, Fausto,' he exploded, 'what do you expect us to fight these niggers with? Blow darts? Spears? We launched a modern campaign, and it's been a damned successful one! What difference is it if a nigger gets killed with a machine gun or an arrow? He's still dead! Your squeamishness is stupid—*stupid!*'

Fausto knew that Ciano had adopted his father-in-law's bullying, screaming style.

'This wasn't war, this was slaughter,' he replied, calmly. 'I love Italy as much as you or any man, but what I've seen made me sick. If that's what Fascism's about, then I *have* been stupid to believe in it.'

'Fascism's made Italy a great power!'

'So what?'

Ciano's anger iced.

'I hope,' he said, quietly, 'you don't plan to say any of this to the newspapers?'

Fausto smiled slightly.

'And would they print it if I did?'

'No. But your family's well known in Italy, and you're something of a war hero. You could make trouble for us. If you keep quiet we won't do anything to you or your family. But I hope I don't have to remind you you married a Jewess?'

Fausto had never particularly liked Ciano. Now he realized he hated him.

'You don't have to remind me.'

You cocky son of a bitch, he thought.

As he made love to her his first night home, his wife reveled in the feel and smell of his flesh. His lovemaking was as fierce and exciting as Nanda remembered, but Fausto was different. She had sensed it when he came off the ship. He was—what? Softer? Less sure of himself? Perhaps even guilty or ashamed? Whatever it was, she liked the new Fausto. She had loved the old Fausto but never liked him. As she lay in his arms after love, she realized that Italy might have gained an empire from the Ethiopian War, but she had gained a lover.

'What made you quit them?' she asked.

He stared at the ceiling for a while, then made a peculiar answer.

'A black man standing on top of a hill,' he said finally.

The ancient palazzo on the Corso was prepared for mourning. The servants talked in whispers, and the velvet portieres in the sitting room off Princess Sylvia's bedroom were closed. Enrico Spada sat by one of the tall windows, watching his father and his uncle. His uncle Tony had recently been given a cardinal's hat, and Enrico was rather in awe of the black soutane with the red sash and the red cap. Yet Tony didn't seem to have been changed much by the honor, perhaps only slightly more reserved. At forty-three he looked as if he were younger. He was still thin to the point of gauntness, and Enrico thought he exuded an almost palpable spirituality. His twin looked older than forty-three, and it pained Enrico to see his much-admired father losing his looks. His black hair was thinning, and his increased drinking since his return from Ethiopia two months before was bloating his face. Fausto had yet to find anything to replace Fascism with except alcohol.

The door to the bedroom opened, and the doctor came out.

'She wants to see her sons,' he said, quietly. 'Your Eminence first. But only a few minutes, please.

'Is there any change?' asked Tony, getting up.

'I'm afraid not. She's . . .' he shrugged helplessly, '. . . too old.'

Tony went into the darkened bedroom and closed the door softly. In a way, death and the afterlife were his profession; but the impending death of his mother was something so personal and heartbreaking that he felt less like a Prince of the Church than a little boy losing something infinitely precious. He crossed the high-ceilinged room with its old furniture, its tables cluttered with bibelots and photographs of family and friends, its silk lampshades, its ancient paintings. How tiny she looks! he thought. This fragile old woman in the huge bed . . .

She seemed to be asleep. He knelt beside the bed and began to pray. Then he felt her hand on his cheek. He took it and kissed her palm. She was looking at him now and smiling.

'A cardinal,' she whispered. 'How proud I am of you.'

He wanted to tell her that he wasn't proud of himself, that his life as a priest had been an unending struggle with his carnality, that to further his career in the Curia he had stifled his many criticisms of Vatican policy, that he dealt with lire and gold and numbered Swiss bank accounts and investments in Italian industry much more than with human souls and certainly more than with the poor. He wanted to tell her of his fears for the Church's future because of the threat of Fascism and the unending erosion of 'modernism.' But he told her none of his guilts and fears. He told her only of his love.

'Momma,' he said, softly, 'I'm proud of *you*. Everything you've done has been so good . . .'

'No, no,' she interrupted. 'I'm no saint. Far from it.'

'You are to me.'

'Pray for me, my darling. And pray for Fausto. I worry about him so . . . I think he has changed though, don't you?'

'Yes, I do. He's come to hate the Fascists.'

396

'Thank God.' She closed her eyes, and for a moment he thought she had slipped away. But then she started speaking again, almost inaudibly.

'I'm so old now. The past has gone forever, hasn't it? Things were so beautiful once, but everything seems . . . ugly now. Your father was so beautiful . . .'

She was silent again for a while. Then she said, 'I must see Fausto now.'

'Yes, Momma.'

He stood up and leaned over to kiss her. She smiled at him.

'Good-bye, my darling. I love you so very much.'

'And I love you, Momma.'

He took a final look at her, then left the bed and went to the door. He paused a moment to wipe his eyes, then went outside.

'Fausto, she wants to see you.'

His twin stood up and came to the door. The two brothers looked at each other a moment, and Tony thought Fausto looked frightened. He opened the door for him, and Fausto went into the bedroom.

Fausto looked frightened because he was. He was terrified his mother would, on her deathbed, berate him for his Fascist past. He came up to the bed and knelt. He wasn't sure why, but kneeling seemed the right thing to do. She reached out her hand and he took it.

'Two divine boys,' she whispered. 'One good and one bad, though I don't think you're bad anymore.'

'I was wrong about a lot of things, Momma.'

'It's so easy to be bad, you know. Being good is hard work. Like Tony. He doesn't tell me, but I know he suffers to be what he is. You must suffer a little too, Fausto.'

'I do, Momma. A lot.'

She smoothed his hair.

'Yes, I think you do. I came very close to disinheriting you. I almost hated you. Of course, a mother can never *really* hate her child, but I was close . . . You will get everything, Fausto, except what I'm leaving to the Church. But you must swear to me you'll not let one lira go to the Fascists. Do you understand? Not one lira.'

'I swear, Momma. They'll get nothing of mine.'

'Yes, I think you mean that, thank God.' She didn't say anything for a moment. Then she said, 'Now kiss me.'

He got up and kissed her.

'Take care of Enrico,' she whispered. 'He's frightened.'

'I know. He'll be safe.'

397

'Good.'

She closed her eyes, and he began kissing her hand, crying with shame for the sadness he had caused her. It was while he was kissing her hand that she died.

PART X

GABRIELLA IN LOVE

1940

CHAPTER 44

Nick Kemp hardly recognized Gabriella von Gersdorff, she had changed so much. He remembered a fat, tall, gawky girl who used to come to his parents' apartment in New York with his younger sister, Ellen. The twenty-year-old stunner who was smiling at him on the terrace of Morris and Barbara David's Beverly Hills estate was a far cry from the shy schoolgirl of six years before. She was still tall—five foot nine, just three inches shorter than Nick. But the fat had vanished, revealing a striking figure with full breasts. Her rich brown hair was parted in the middle, falling loosely in natural curls to her shoulders. Her face did not conform to any normal standard of beauty, but she had learned to accentuate her best features—her eyes and skin—and play down the one that was not so good—her too-big nose. Her mouth was voluptuously full and lipsticked a slashing scarlet. She was wearing a white evening dress, the thin, pink diagonal stripes of which coiled around the curves of her hips, giving her the look of some luscious peppermint-stripped candy fantasy. The skirt was slit up the side to show long, sexy legs with ankle-strapped high heels. Gabriella didn't try to play down her height for fear of dominating shorter men. She wasn't interested in shorter men. She was extremely interested in this tall, blond ensign on whom she'd had a crush since she was fourteen. When Ellen had written her that her brother had been transferred to the San Diego Naval Base after his graduation from Annapolis, Gabriella had screwed up her courage and invited him to the party her uncle and aunt were giving for the star of Morris's new picture, *Angel of Desire*, the glamorous Erica Stern. The other guests milling about on the Japanese-lantern-lighted lawn of Casa del Mar could hardly take their eyes off the Budapest-born blond beauty; but Nick Kemp's eyes were on Gabriella.

'What happened to you?' he said, shaking her hand. 'I hardly recognized you!'

'I grew up,' she smiled. 'And I went on a diet. I hope it's an improvement.'

'You look sensational! I can hardly believe it. Ellen said you'd lost weight, but *this!* Wow!'

Gabriella tried not to show how pleased she was.

'Can I get you a drink?'

'Sure, but not yet. I want to keep looking at you. What are you doing in Hollywood? Why aren't you in college? What made you think of inviting me to this party?'

'Oh well, the last one's easy enough. Ellen wrote me you were stationed in San Diego, and I thought you might enjoy meeting some movie stars. And . . .' she looked a little embarrassed, '. . . well, I wanted to see you again. As for the other two, my grandmother died last year . . .'

'I'm sorry to hear it.'

'She had cancer.' She hesitated, remembering the agony of Lucille's last months and her own agony as she watched the old woman she had come to adore cling gamely to life, never complaining even though she was in almost constant pain, until death mercifully took her away. 'I miss her very much,' she added, quietly.

"I'm sure.'

'Anyway, I was sort of left alone in the world, and so my aunt Barbara asked if I wanted to come out here and live with them. And I'd never seen California, so here I am.'

'Do you like it?'

'Not as much as New York, but it's certainly interesting. Anyway, I'd had two years of Radcliffe, which was enough for me, so Uncle Morris got me a job at his studio.'

'Let me guess: you're his new discovery, the new Judy Garland.'

She laughed.

'Me, a star? I'm the lowest of the low. I work for Jacques Delmas, who's the designer for Uncle Morris's pictures. Right now, I'm working on Erica Stern's negligée for *Angel of Desire*. It's *very* sexy.' She hesitated. 'Would you like to meet her?'

'Why not?'

'Come on, I'll introduce you.'

She led the white-uniformed ensign through the crowd of movie people to the pool, where Erica Stern was sitting at a table flanked by Morris and Barbara David. Nick was prepared to see a woman much less beautiful in real life than her carefully photographed screen image. But he was surprised to see that she was as gorgeous in the flesh as on film. She was that rarity, an almost flawless beauty. Her fluffy halo of blond hair was expertly dyed, her eyebrows were shaved and new ones penciled in to enlarge her languorous eyes; makeup was expertly applied to highlight her cheekbones. She wore a gold lamé dress with padded shoulders that gave her a slightly masculine look.

'Aunt Barbara, Uncle Morris: I want you to meet Ensign Nicholas Kemp.'

They shook hands.

'And this is Erica Stern.'

The star held out her hand and smiled.

'I'm *mad* for sailors,' she said in her middle-European accent. 'Especially good-looking blond ones. You must promise, Ensign Kemp, to make Beverly Hills safe for democracy.'

'I'll try,' grinned Nick.

'And what do you do when you're not at Hollywood parties?'

'I'm communications officer on a destroyer.'

'Dahling,' she said in a Tallulah Bankhead rasp, 'communicate with me and I'll de-*stroy* you.'

She threw back her head and laughed. Nick realized she was a bit drunk. Barbara, who was wearing a stunning yellow dress and three diamond bracelets, said, 'We're delighted to have you here, Ensign. Any friend of Gabriella's is always welcome.'

'Thank you, Mrs. David.'

'We're very proud of Gabriella,' she continued, smiling at her niece as she put her arm around her waist. 'Did she tell you what she's doing at the studio?'

'Yes, working with the costume designer.'

'She's much too modest. Jacques *swears* by her! He says he's never had such a good seamstress since he worked with Poiret in Paris.'

'It's true,' said Erica. 'She's a marvel! She has magic fingers.' And she took Gabriella's hand and kissed her fingers, smiling at her. Gabriella looked a bit flustered, as did her uncle.

'Get the Admiral a drink,' he said to Gabriella. 'Then show him around, introduce him to movie stars. Everyone wants to meet movie stars, and we got a ton of 'em here. Gary Cooper, Hedy Lamarr, Bette Davis—we got 'em all! We even got a grandson of the Emperor of Japan! Would you believe that? A Nip who's a movie fan?'

Erica released Gabriella's hand.

'Who's that, Morris? You didn't tell me about him.'

'He's that kid over there,' said Morris, pointing to a man in a white dinner jacket on the other side of the swimming pool. 'I can't pronounce his name—what is it, Barbara?'

403

'Shoichi Asaka,' said his wife. 'Prince Shoichi Asaka. And as usual, Morris has it all wrong. He's not Hirohito's grandson and he's not a "kid." '

'They all look like kids to me,' said Morris. 'Bunch of slanty-eyed fishheads.'

'Fishheads?' asked Gabriella, confused.

'That's what they eat, the *shmucks*.'

'Morris, I doubt Prince Asaka eats fishheads,' said Barbara. 'He's a great-grandson of the emperor Meiji, who was Hirohito's grandfather, and thus he's a cousin of the present emperor.'

'Cousin, grandson—they all look alike,' said Morris.

'He's twenty-nine, and he went to Harvard. Now he's taking a graduate course in electrical engineering at U.C.L.A.,' Barbara continued. 'The Japanese Consul called Morris last week to arrange a tour of the studio for the Prince, who had a wonderful time. And Morris asked him to the party. Now he's calling him a fishhead.' She turned to her husband. 'I can remember when you used to be rather sensitive about what people called foreigners.'

'I wasn't a foreigner,' huffed Morris. 'I was an immigrant. It's different.'

'I've never met a cousin of the emperor,' said Erica. 'Morris, go get him. And don't insult him.'

'Who's insulting? I asked him to the party, didn't I? I'm feeding him, giving him free booze? Who's insulting?'

As Morris started around the pool, Erica turned to Nick.

'What made you join the Navy, Mr. Kemp?' she asked.

'Well, it's sort of a family tradition, Miss Stern.'

'Erica, darling.'

'Uh . . . Erica. My mother's father was an admiral. He was part of the flotilla that took the Philippines at the turn of the century. And I like the sea, and well . . . I went to Annapolis. And here I am, talking to movie stars. So what they say about the Navy is true: you see the world.'

'Ah, but this isn't the world, Mr. Kemp. This is Hollywood. The world is real, but in Hollywood, everything is fake. Except . . .' and she smiled the famous Erica Stern smile, '. . . sex.'

She turned the famous Erica Stern eyes from Nick to Gabriella.

'Here he is!' exclaimed Morris. 'Prince Asooka, and he's dying to meet you, Erica.'

'Prince A*sa*ka,' corrected the Japanese in the well-cut white dinner jacket and wing collar, 'of the House of Fushimi.' Then he turned to Erica and bowed as he kissed her hand. 'Miss Stern,

404

I hope I speak not only for myself but for thousands of my countrymen when I say that your films have given the world great pleasure. To share your radiant beauty with humanity is a mark of your generosity of spirit.'

He spoke excellent, if stiff, English.

'Well, darling,' said Erica, 'I *do* get paid.'

'You know my wife,' said Morris. 'And this is my niece, Gabriella von Gersdorff, and Lieutenant Cramp.'

'Kemp,' corrected Nick. 'And I'm an ensign.'

The Prince kissed Garbriella's hand and shook Nick's. He was of medium height and wiry build, and had a pleasant face. Now he turned back to Erica.

'We Japanese admire your films so much,' he said, 'because in them you make love seem a thing of gentleness and beauty. That is a very Japanese characteristic.'

'Then,' said Nick, drily, 'we can assume you Japanese don't love the Chinese?'

The Prince looked at him.

'We won't talk politics!' said Morris, quickly. 'Everybody have a good time—ah, here's that *ferkokte* orchestra! At last! I pay them to play, and they take twenty-minute breaks, yet! Unions! *A putz shteyt, ober di tsayt sheyt nit!*'

He shook his head sadly as the orchestra started playing 'You're the Top.' Nick turned to Gabriella.

'Dance?'

'I'd love it.'

He led her across the lawn to the wooden floor under the big awning.

'What was that your uncle said?' he asked as they began.

'Don't ask me. It's probably dirty. Uncle Morris loves saying dirty things in Yiddish. It shocks the people who understand, and the rest of us don't know what he's talking about. What did you think of Erica Stern?'

'She's gorgeous enough, God knows. But I couldn't quite make her out. Is she a little bit fried?'

'Probably.'

'Is she a big boozer?'

'I don't think so.'

She wasn't thinking of Erica Stern. She was thinking of Nick Kemp and how nice it was to be in his arms.

'When do you have to be back in San Diego?' she asked.

'Not till Monday morning. I'll drive back tomorrow night.'

'Would you like a tour of Uncle Morris's studio tomorrow?

There won't be much going on because it's Sunday, but I could show you around.'

'That's a great idea! If Prince Asaka gets a tour, why shouldn't Nick Kemp? And afterward, I'll take you to lunch. Know any good places?'

'I know a wonderful place in Venice—right on the water.'

He whirled her around the dance floor. Gabriella might have had a crush on Nick before, but now she was experiencing what the French call a *coup de foudre*. She had been struck by lightning.

It was a spectacular January day: seventy degrees, a cloudless sky, and the Pacific was living up to its name. They sat on the deck of the restaurant over the water eating abalone and drinking good white California wine.

'Making movies must be fun,' he said as she admired the way the California sun gleamed off his golden hair.

'Actually it's pretty boring,' she said. 'Even the exciting stuff —fight scenes, things like that—seem to drag on forever.'

'Well, I enjoyed seeing your uncle's studio. What's his new movie about? *Angel of Desire?*'

'It's a dumb story. At least the script reads that way. But Uncle Morris doesn't usually pick losers. It'll probably be a hit when he gets done with it. And the public loves love stories.'

'How about you? Do you love love stories?'

'Of course. I love to cry at the end. Gabriella the Kleenex Kid, they call me.'

'Have you ever been in love?'

She hesitated.

'No, I don't think so.'

'You don't *think* so? Then you haven't been in love, because when you're in love you *know* it. It hits you like a ton of bricks.'

She stared at him as he cut his abalone.

'Are . . . *you* in love?' she asked, nervously.

'Yep. In fact, we're about to get engaged. She's a wonderful girl—you'd like her. Her name's Carol Dennison. I met her last month at an Officers' Club dance. She was the date of our operations officer. He was pretty mad at me when I started dating her, but now . . . well, the better man won.'

He grinned at her.

'Excuse me . . .'

She got up.

'Are you all right?'

'I'll be right back.'

She hurried into the restaurant and went to the ladies' room. Locking the door, she pounded her fist against the rose-wallpapered wall, then burst into tears. 'Damn, damn, damn, damn, DAMN!' she said, kicking the wastebasket in a final spasm of savage frustration. Then she washed her face, fixed her makeup and returned to the table.

'You're sure you're all right?' he asked, holding her chair.

'Never felt better in my life,' she snapped as she sat down.

'Well, you picked a good restaurant,' he said, returning to his chair. 'That was some of the best abalone I've ever eaten.'

'Mine stank. It was like rubber. And this wine is pitiful. Chateau Tiajuana.'

He looked at her.

'Is it something I said?'

'Is what something you said?'

'You look as if you're ready to strangle someone—maybe me.'

'Well, I'm not.'

'Seriously, what's wrong?'

'*Nothing!*' She looked at her watch. 'I have to be home by two.'

He signaled for the waiter.

'Sure has been fun,' he said, drily.

As he drove her back to Beverly Hills in his 1938 Ford coupe, she said, 'I'm sorry.'

'For what?'

'I was very rude to you. I shouldn't have been.'

'Want to tell me what it was all about?'

She sighed.

'Can't you guess? I'm a poor loser.'

'You got mad when I told you about Carol?'

'What else? I had this wonderful fantasy you were going to fall madly in love with me. Well, scratch *that* fantasy. I'd rather start working on a new one.'

'But you hardly know me! Why would you give a damn whether I fall in love with you or not?'

'Morris David Productions present: *True Confessions!* Teen-age Gabriella develops mad crush for brother of schoolmate. Brother ignores her, but teenage girl continues to burn flame. Years pass, calendar leaves fall. Teenage girl now grown up but still has crush on friend's brother. She invites him to party. He looks more yummy than ever. She about swoons in his strong, manly arms. He tells her he's in love with someone else.

407

Gabriella goes to ladies' room and kicks wastebasket. Fadeout, the end. It's another dumb story.'

He smiled.

'No, it's a nice story. And I'm flattered. Really. But you'll get over me.'

'Oh God, why do people always say that? You're the first man I've ever been in love with, and you *don't* get over your first love!'

'How do you know?'

'I read it in a fan magazine,' she sulked.

He pulled over to the curb and parked. Then he turned to her.

'Be serious a minute. You're not in love with me. At best, it's some sort of schoolgirl crush. You said at lunch you've never been in love.'

She looked at him sadly.

'I lied.'

'Well, you must have other boyfriends . . .'

'I don't want a boyfriend. I want a *lover*. I want you. I didn't sleep at all last night. All I thought about was you, and how I was dying to see you again, and how I wanted you to touch me, to kiss me. There—see? Now you know what kind of girl I am. I'm a female sex-fiend.'

He smiled.

'Okay, sex-fiend, how about a kiss?'

She bit her lip and looked out the window.

'No,' she said finally. 'That'll just make it worse later on.'

He saw the tear running down her cheek and was profoundly moved. He had never met anyone like her before, never encountered such intensity of wanting. He reached out and touched her arm.

'I'm sorry,' he said, softly.

She shrugged.

'Look, I'm not lucky in love. Maybe I'll be a great business-woman. You'd better get me home before I get hysterical.'

He squeezed her arm. Then he started the car and headed for Beverly Hills.

'I love you, Charmion!' sighed the British officer as he kissed the hand of the notorious German spy who was reclining on a chaise longue in the Hotel Adlon in Berlin.

'Then prove it, darling,' replied Charmion. She was wearing the negligée Gabriella had designed.

'How? How can I prove it?'

'The plans,' she whispered, kissing his forehead as the camera

408

dollied in, 'for the submarine. Give me the plans, and I'll give you . . . me.'

'Cut!' yelled the director. 'Okay, everyone—lunch break.'

Erica Stern got off the chaise longue as her dresser hurried up to her.

'How did it look?' Erica asked her.

'Very good, Miss Stern.'

'That dialogue is ghastly. Tell Gabriella to come to my dressing room. A button's loose on this negligée.'

'Yes, Miss Stern.'

Erica went to her dressing room and lighted a cigarette. The room had no frills or nonsense, no pictures of family or friends: The glamour queen didn't waste glamour on her workroom. Erica took off the negligée and hung it on a hanger. Then, wearing nothing but her panties and bra, she sat down at her dressing table, crossed her world-famous legs and picked up *The Magic Mountain*, continuing to read where she had left off.

Gabriella knocked.

'Come in,' called Erica.

'Marie said you have a loose button?' said Gabriella as she entered.

'Yes, darling. The second from the top. It's over there.'

Gabriella glanced enviously at the glorious legs, then went to the wardrobe and examined the button.

'How's your dashing sailor?' asked Erica.

'He dashed right out of my life,' said Gabriella, opening her sewing kit.

'Oh? What happened?'

'Nothing happened. He's engaged to be married—or about to be.'

'Too bad, darling. He was very good-looking.'

'He was gorgeous.'

Erica put down her book and watched her.

'Men are such brutes,' she said. 'I've never met one that I thought had half the character or sensitivity of a woman.'

'I suppose they are brutes, but I guess we're stuck with them.'

'Perhaps.' She ground out her cigarette. 'Well, I'm sorry to hear about your sailor, but a girl as attractive as you won't have any trouble finding another man. Do you have anyone special?'

'No, not really.'

'Are you a virgin, darling?'

Gabriella looked up from her sewing. Rather embarrassed, she said, 'Well . . . yes.'

'Oh dear, you Americans have such curious ideas about sex.'

She got up and went over to the bed covered with a plaid spread and sat down, close to Gabriella. Again she crossed her legs. 'For instance, you all seem to assume that sex can be done only one way. And, of course, there are so many interesting variations.'

Gabriella kept her eyes on her sewing.

'Take your sailor, for example. He was indeed very good-looking, but the male body is really rather unattractive. It's so square and hairy. Do you know what I mean? The female body, on the other hand, is a masterpiece of nature. All gentle curves and smoothness. The curve is inherently more attractive aesthetically than the straight line. It's obvious to me God made Adam first and decided he was a tryout. *Eve* was the triumph. Do you agree, darling?'

'I really haven't thought about it. There, you won't have any more trouble with that button.'

She hurriedly put her needle back in her sewing box.

'Thank you, darling. You're really so clever with a needle. And Jacques tells me you design as well, and that your designs are terribly good. Do you want to go into fashion?'

'Yes.'

'And be a designer?'

'Well, that's my dream anyway. But that's in the future.'

'Why not make the future now? I tell you what: you design me an evening gown, and if I like it I'll pay you to make it for me. And I'll wear it to parties around town and everyone will say, "Who made that stunning dress?" and I'll say Gabriella von Gersdorff and voilà! you're in business.'

She smiled at the girl, who looked stunned.

'Oh, Erica—*would* you?'

'Didn't I just say I would?'

'Oh God, I don't know what to say—how to thank you . . .'

'We'll think of ways, darling. Now run along and dream up something brilliant.'

'Oh yes, I will . . . oh *thanks!*'

She hurried out of the dressing room, conjuring up spectacular evening gowns out of the air.

She didn't want to think about what sort of thanks Erica might want.

CHAPTER 45

The U.S.S. *Darwin* was tied up at its normal berth at Dock 3 at the San Diego Naval Base. It was the Saturday following the Davids' party for Erica Stern, and Ensign Nick Kemp was officer of the deck, which meant that the other officers and two-thirds of the crew were ashore on liberty and Nick was in charge of the ship for the day. Weekend duty was the curse of junior officers, but Nick knew that one Saturday out of every four he was stuck, and he accepted his fate stoically. It was a balmy, lazy day, and he was reading *Life* magazine in the wardroom when his messenger appeared at the door.

'Mr. Kemp, there's a four-striper coming down the dock! It looks like Captain McDermott.'

'Oh, shit,' muttered Nick, jumping out of his chair and grabbing his hat. Theoretically the officer of the deck was supposed to stand on the quarterdeck, not read *Life* magazine in the wardroom. As he ran aft, he wondered what the hell Captain McDermott, the executive officer of the naval base, wanted on the U.S.S. *Darwin*, one of the most insignificant ships on the base.

He came out on the quarterdeck just as his quartermaster, Carson, was piping the captain aboard.

'Permission to come aboard, Ensign,' said the captain, following the naval custom.

'Permission granted, sir!' saluted Nick, staring with surprise at the man in the white suit who had followed the captain aboard.

'Mr. Kemp, I believe you know Prince Asaka?' said McDermott.

'Yes, of course. How are you?' said a flustered Nick, shaking the Japanese's hand.

'Very well. And you?'

'Uh . . . fine.' Nick looked slightly bewildered.

'Prince Asaka asked for an informal tour of the base,' went on

Captain McDermott. 'He particularly asked to see you and your ship. You will extend to him all courtesies.' He turned to Asaka. 'Would you care to join me for lunch at the Officers' Club after touring the *Darwin?*'

'You are very kind, Captain. But if it were possible, I would prefer having lunch with Mr. Kemp—here, on board this lovely ship. It might give me a better taste of life aboard a naval vessel.'

'I see.' He turned to Nick. 'I trust you can feed the Prince?'

'Well, uh . . . I was going to have hot dogs . . .'

'Excellent,' smiled the Prince. 'A great American institution, the hot dog. I'm very fond of them myself. However, I could hardly subject Captain McDermott to such humble fare, and also I fear I have already taken up too much of his valuable time. Why don't I lunch here with Mr. Kemp, and then I'll join you later at the Officers' Club?'

'Well, all right. Then I'll turn you over to Mr. Kemp.'

'Thank you so much, Captain.'

The Prince shook hands. Then McDermott returned Nick's salute and went down the gangway. Asaka smiled at Nick.

'I hope I am not trespassing on your hospitality, Mr. Kemp?'

'Oh no, not at all. Well: what would you like to see first?'

'I am entirely at your disposal.'

Nick took him on a tour of the ship. The *Darwin* had been built in 1927, and its equipment was ridiculously outdated, so there was little the Prince could have possibly been interested in. Yet he displayed a lively interest, mostly, Nick thought, out of politeness. He showed him the crew's quarters, the engine room, the laundry, the galley, officers' 'country' and the bridge.

'You are to be congratulated, Mr. Kemp. Your ship is in excellent condition.'

'Thank you.'

Since the *Darwin* was barely holding its own in the battle against rust, Nick thought he was either blind or a rank hypocrite. He checked his watch.

'Well: shall we have those hot dogs?'

He led him to the wardroom which, with its bilious green bulkheads, ranked low on the ambience scale, and they took places at the long, baize-covered table. As Washington, the black steward, served lunch, Asaka delivered his views on a variety of topics, including the United States from a Japanese viewpoint. The man seemed in no hurry to leave. After the steward served coffee and went back to his quarters, Asaka lighted a cigarette and settled in for more conversation.

412

'I have enjoyed myself immensely, Mr. Kemp,' he said. 'I hope I haven't bored you?'

'Not at all. It's been very interesting.'

'Our charming hostess last week, Mrs. David, told me you are an Annapolis graduate. I assume, since you are making a career of the Navy, that money is not your primary interest in life?'

Nick grinned.

'Not exactly.'

'But still, money interests you?'

'Of course it interests me. If someone sold me shares in an oil well for ten bucks and the thing struck oil, I'd be a happy man.'

Asaka flicked an ash in the tray.

'The reason I ask is that I have been entertaining an intriguing idea for a film scenario. You know I love the movies, and one of my favorite pastimes is to dream up plots. I have what I think is a good one, but I need your advice on one particular point. It's a spy movie. An agent for a foreign power—appropriately sinister —has been informed by his government that the United States Navy has installed on its ships a code machine that encodes and decodes messages by a clever system of mechanical rotors. The foreign power's cryptologists tell their government that the rotors will make the breaking of the codes almost impossible, not only because there is an almost infinite number of possible settings for the rotors, but also because the rotors—and the setting instructions—are changed every month. The cryptologists could duplicate the machine. But the only way they could break the codes would be to find some way of getting the key instructions and the monthly rotors to duplicate. Are you following me so far?'

Nick told himself to be extremely careful. Asaka had just described in a general way the new coding system installed by the Navy.

'It sounds like an interesting movie.'

'Good. Let me continue. The foreign agent meets a young American naval officer, such as yourself, who happens to be the communications officer of a small ship and is therefore in charge of the coding machine. It occurs to the agent that if he can cultivate the friendship of the officer, he might be able to persuade the officer to pass the rotors and the key instructions to the agent each month long enough for the agent to have them duplicated. There would of course be a certain risk involved, and the agent realizes he will have to pay an enormous amount of cash to, shall we say, purchase the cooperation of the officer.

413

Now, my question to you is, how much money would the agent have to offer to make the movie believable?'

Nick examined his nails. Careful, he thought. Be careful.

'Well, in the first place the officer would be a fool to try it because if he were caught he'd be court-martialed for treason and probably hanged.'

'Precisely. Therefore, the agent would have to find an officer, unlike yourself, who was a bit of a gambler in life and was willing to risk his neck for a fortune that would be deposited in, say, Mexican banks.'

'A sort of old-age pension, assuming the officer lived to an old age?'

'More than a pension. Retirement to a lively villa in Cuernavaca. Rum swizzles at sunset, the company of lovely women —the best of everything.'

'That wouldn't come cheap.'

'That's why I'm asking your advice. From your viewpoint as an American officer, what price tag would you put on it—to make the movie believable?'

Nick eyed the Japanese prince.

'One million dollars cash,' he said finally.

Prince Asaka put out his cigarette.

'That's about the figure I had in mind,' he said. 'To be paid in installments, with a down payment of fifty thousand dollars.'

'More like a hundred thousand. To make the movie believable.'

'Mmm. I see your point.'

'It's divine, darling,' said Erica Stern, examining her reflection in the full-length mirror of her bedroom on the second floor of her fake-Provincial house overlooking Sunset Boulevard. 'Absolutely divine.'

'Then you like it?' asked Gabriella, who was on her knees adjusting the hem of the evening gown she had designed and made for the star. It had been more fun and exciting than making the dresses for Adele, her French doll, when she was a fat little girl. Now she had made a dress for Erica Stern!

'Like it? I'm *bouleversée!* You have a real eye for the line, and the line is all-important. And such a perfect fit! I love the way you've done the seam down the side. It's dramatic and elegant and simple all at the same time, and that's no mean accomplishment. Even Chanel would envy you.'

'Chanel? She's my goddess. I'm in no league with Chanel.'

414

'Don't underestimate yourself. No, this is absolutely stunning. I'll wear it to the Academy Awards.'

Gabriella stared up at her.

'The Academy Awards?' she repeated, softly.

'Why not? I couldn't find a better dress.'

'You're not serious . . .'

'Gabriella, darling, you will find that when I discuss anything to do with my career, I am *dead* serious. The only problem is, now I'll have to wait till April to wear it. Well, there's a simple answer to that: you'll have to design me something else. In fact, a whole wardrobe. Now, help me out of this.'

Gabriella felt as if she were in some wonderful dream. As she helped Erica out of the dress, she barely heard the star as she listed what she wanted: beachwear for her Malibu beach house, three suits, two cocktail dresses, another evening gown . . .

'Erica Stern is a work of art,' she said as she again examined her reflection, this time wearing only her bra and panties. 'She needs an artist to dress her, and there are damned few artists out here. Jacques Delmas is all right for movie costumes, but he has no real chic, no style. You have style, plus you're young and new and different. You'll dress me, and I'll make you the most exciting young designer in America. Would you like that, darling?'

She took off her bra and draped it over the back of a chair.

'Do I even have to answer? I'd love it!'

'Good. Then we'll do it. Look, Gabriella. Look at my breasts. Aren't they beautiful?'

Gabriella was carefully hanging the dress in the closet. Now she turned to look.

'Your figure is a designer's dream, Erica.'

'Do you realize half the men in the world would give anything to see what you're seeing now?'

She squeezed her breasts tenderly for a moment. Then she turned around and looked at Gabriella.

'I had a husband, you know. In Budapest, before your uncle Morris discovered me. He's still there, as far as I know. He was a dentist. He used to beg me to let him make love to me, and it used to give me such pleasure to refuse him.' She crossed the room to Gabriella and took her hands. Smiling, she whispered, 'I would never say "no" to you, darling. Would you say "no" to me?'

Gabriella was trembling.

'You . . . frighten me,' she whispered.

'But there is nothing to fear. It would be so beautiful, you and

415

me together, side by side, while I kiss your young loveliness . . . Here, put your hand on my breast . . . like so . . .'

Gabriella felt the warm, soft skin.

'Please don't do this, Erica . . . please . . .'

Erica frowned slightly, then released her.

'I mustn't rush you, my pretty,' she said. 'But in time you'll learn there is nothing more beautiful than the love of two women. Now, run along home, And darling,' her tone became suddenly cold, 'not a word of this to your aunt and uncle. That is, if you want to design my clothes.'

She lighted a cigarette as Gabriella let herself out of the room. It was odd, but all she could think of was her grandfather Victor and how horrified he would have been if he had witnessed what had just happened.

When she got home, her aunt Barbara had exciting news for her.

'Guess what, Gabriella! Nick called you!'

'Nick?'

'Yes, about an hour ago. He's in town, and he wants to take you out to dinner tonight. Of course, I told him I didn't know if you had a date . . .'

'Oh, Aunt Barbara!' she cried, running up the stairs. 'I'm not going to play hard to get with *Nick!*'

'You're to call him! I put the number by your phone.'

'Thanks! Oh my God, *Nick!*'

Since the two David children were away at college, Gabriella had the children's wing to herself. Now she ran down the upstairs hall, burst into her bedroom and flopped on her bed. Finding the number, she quickly dialed it.

'Beverly Hills Hotel,' answered the operator.

Well, she thought, he's certainly living in style!

'Ensign Nicholas Kemp, please. I don't know which room he's in.'

'Just a moment, please.' A wait. 'He's in Bungalow Three. I'll ring for you.'

'Thank you.'

A bungalow yet! she thought. And the fanciest one! He must have won a horserace . . .

'Hello?'

'Nick, it's Gabriella! What are you doing in town?'

Don't sound so *eager*, you idiot! she thought.

'I had some extra leave, so I thought I'd take a week off. How are you?'

416

'I'm wonderful! This is a fantastic surprise . . . Aunt Barbara said you wanted to take me out to dinner tonight. What time?'

You *jerk!* Not so pushy.

He laughed.

'Can you be ready in an hour? I'll pick you up, and we'll go to the Brown Derby.'

'I'll be ready. And . . .' she hesitated, '. . . how's Carol?'

'She's engaged.'

'Oh.'

'To a Marine captain.'

'*OH!* That's wonderful! I mean . . . I'm sorry. I mean, the hell I am! See you in an hour.'

She hung up and ran into the bathroom to make herself irresistible. She had a chance!

She had tried to push Erica's lesbian advances out of her mind, but as she showered the episode returned. She had no idea how to handle it, and the thought of being branded a lesbian horrified her. But Erica's calm assurance that in time she would come to accept and even like it frightened her even more. She admired Erica's beauty—who wouldn't?—but she was not attracted to her physically. Was it possible she might be, though?

But any fears of latent homosexuality were dispelled an hour later when Nick drove up in front of the house. She hurried out to meet him. His 1938 Ford coupe had been replaced by a stunning new white Cadillac convertible, and he looked great in a well-cut blazer and light-gray slacks.

'I can't *tell* you how glad I am you're unengaged!' she said, taking his hand. 'Now I'm going to get you, come hell or high water!'

He laughed.

'You mean I haven't got a chance?'

'Not a prayer. Gabriella gets what she wants. If I could lose a hundred and twenty-five pounds, I can win you. Oh . . . where'd you get the car? It's gorgeous!'

He held the door for her, then got in himself and started off.

'Tell me what happened with Carol,' she said.

He shrugged.

'It's simple. I thought we were in love. Then the day before yesterday, she told me she was engaged to someone else. Just like that. So I thought, to hell with you, sister.'

'I'm sorry for you. Not for me, but for you. Do you feel awful about it?'

417

'I'll survive. But if I get a little tight tonight, don't be surprised.'

Four hours later, when he returned her to her aunt's house, he was in fact pleasantly tight. He parked the car and put his arm around her.

'Remember the last time we were in a car together?' he said.

'Your Ford. Of course I remember. I like this car much better.'

'Remember what you said when I asked for a kiss? You said no because it would just make it harder for you later on. I liked that a lot, Gabriella. I thought you just had a crush on me, but I was wrong, wasn't I?'

She looked into his bloodshot blue eyes.

'You were very wrong,' she whispered.

He pulled her to him and kissed her. A long and loving kiss. She had been kissed many times before and enjoyed it, but this was different.

'Will you come to Mexico with me?' he whispered.

'Yes. Aunt Barbara will faint, but yes, I'll come with you if you really want me.'

'I really want you.' Then he kissed her again.

The front light turned on.

'Oh God, Aunt Barbara!' She disentangled herself. 'Can you come in for a while?'

'No, it's late. I'd better get back to the hotel. But call me after you talk to her.'

'All right.' Impulsively she took his face in her hands and kissed him. 'I'm *mad* about you,' she smiled.

Then she got out of the car.

'Drive carefully,' she said. 'You had a lot to drink.'

'I will.'

'And Nick: thank you for the most beautiful evening of my life.'

She hurried into the house as he drove down the drive.

Her aunt Barbara was in the library reading *Town and Country* when Gabriella came into the room.

'Did you have a good time?' she asked.

'Fabulous! Oh God, he is the dreamiest man . . .' She twirled around the room, then flopped in a chair. 'Were you watching us neck?'

'Of course not. I just turned on the light so you could see.'

'Uh huh.' She thought awhile. What she was planning to do

418

was miles beyond necking. Aunt Barbara, despite her sophistication, was rather strait-laced. Gabriella decided to use a little family history to soften her up. 'Aunt Barbara,' she said, rather apprehensively, 'do you remember when my parents first met?'

She looked up from the magazine.

'Of course. It was here, at this house.'

'Mother told me that my father asked her to go to Mexico with him the first night he'd met her! Isn't that wild?' She hesitated. 'What would you have thought of Mother if she'd gone off with him?'

'Your mother wouldn't have done it.'

'She told me she was tempted.'

'She still wouldn't have done it.'

'Aunt Barbara.'

'What dear?'

'I'm going to do it.'

'Do what?'

'Nick wants me to go with him to Acapulco next weekend, and I'm going to do it.'

'You're not serious.'

'Yes I am. I was going to lie to you and say I was going by myself, but I love you and Uncle Morris and I don't want to lie to you. But I want to go. I know you'll be shocked . . .'

'I certainly am! You mean you're going to stay in a hotel with him?'

'Well, they'll be separate rooms,' she said, deciding to lie a *little*.

'Gabriella, this is very unwise. You claim to be in love with Nick, and I assume you want to marry him some day. Men don't marry girls who go to hotels in Mexico with them.'

'That's what you think! Half the girls at the studio are sleeping with men they're not married to.'

'But they're actresses. Listen, I know what you're thinking: that there's a double standard in Hollywood. I know you know my husband has a lot of girl friends. Everyone knows Morris's reputation, that he's the Casanova of Santa Monica Boulevard, for what *that's* worth. So it may seem silly to you not to sleep with a man before you marry him when they all seem to sleep with other women after marriage. But I still say, it's important for your self-respect. And if you do marry him . . . well, I'm told there's no cattier group of women in the world than officers' wives. They'd never let either of you forget.'

'I don't give a damn about them!'

'That's easy to say now. Look, Gabriella, do what you want.

419

You're twenty, and I can't forbid you doing it. But I'm certainly not going to say it's all right. And I think you'll be making a mistake as far as Nick is concerned. If you're such an easy lay, to be vulgar, why should he marry you?'

Gabriella hesitated.

'That's such an old argument,' she said.

'But such an effective one, my dear.'

Barbara picked up her magazine and began reading again. Gabriella got up and walked to the door. If nothing else, her aunt's argument was making her have second thoughts. At the door she said, 'Does it bother you that Uncle Morris plays around?'

'I don't like it, but I accept it.'

'Do you still love him?'

'Of course. But I don't love him the way I did twenty years ago. That was first love, and first love is something special. You only have it once in your life, and it's very precious. So be careful, Gabriella. And *think*.'

As she climbed the stairs to her room, she did indeed think. But her physical desire for Nick was so overwhelming, she didn't think for long. When she got to her room, she called the hotel. He hadn't gotten there yet, so she waited another ten minutes, then called again. This time, he was in.

'I talked to Aunt Barbara.'

'And she said you shouldn't do it.'

'That's right. But I'm going to do it.'

He hesitated.

'Maybe I shouldn't have asked. I'd had a lot to drink, and . . .'

'Don't you dare go back on me now!' she interrupted.

'But I don't want to get you in trouble with your family.'

'I'll handle my family. Oh Nick, I *want* to go! I'm no schoolgirl, I know what I'm doing. But I want you. Oh God, how I want you!'

He thought awhile.

'All right. We'll fly down Friday afternoon.'

CHAPTER 46

The Bella Vista Hotel was a former colonial monastery that had been converted to a posh resort on the outskirts of the little coastal town of Acapulco, which some of the Mexican rich had 'discovered' and which was currently in the throes of a boomlet. The place was charmingly decorated with sturdy Mexican furniture that blended well with the white stucco walls, the arched stone ceilings, the wrought-iron chandeliers and the fabulous views of the sea. Their room, which had once been three monastic cells, had its private terrace overlooking the ocean, and the spacious bathroom was done in bright yellow-and-blue Mexican tiles.

'*Que ustedes sean muy bienvenidos a México lindo,*' said the bellboy, smiling, and Nick tipped him a dollar, which widened his smile further. When he left Nick went out on the terrace, where Gabriella was looking at the moonlit sea. He put his arm around her and kissed her cheek.

'Like it?' he asked.

'I'd have to be crazy not to. It's so romantic, I could die.'

'Well, don't. Not at these rates. The dining room's still open, but we'd better hurry if we want dinner. And I have to get out of this uniform.'

'Kiss me first.'

He kissed her again, this time on the mouth.

'All right, let's get changed,' she said, running to the bathroom. 'Wait till you see my dress—I made it myself.' She went into the bathroom, shut the door, then opened it again to stick her head out and say, 'I've never shared a bathroom with a man before. It's sexy!' She pointed to his suitcase. 'And I'll unpack your bag.'

He had started taking off his uniform, which he had worn on the plane, but now he looked at her, rather startled.

'No, I'll do it.'

421

'But Nick, in all French novels the mistress always unpacks her lover's suitcase.'

'This isn't a French novel,' he said, rather tersely. *'I'll* unpack my bag.'

Rather puzzled by his unexpected surliness, she withdrew into the bathroom.

The dining room was banked with pink geraniums in clay pots, and the tables held small hurricane lamps. Great arched windows opened on to the main terrace of the hotel, which was lighted with lanterns, so the effect was like eating outdoors. The hotel was full, and most of the guests were Mexican or European. Gabriella's well-trained eye spotted the Schiaparellis and the Chanels as well as the incredible jewels, and she loved what she saw.

'It's beautiful,' she whispered to Nick after they were seated by the captain. They ordered rum punches, and she sighed.

'I can't believe it. Here I am in Mexico with *you!* And I'm about to be deliciously wicked, and I couldn't be happier. Have you been here before?'

'I've been in Acapulco, but never at the Bella Vista. I couldn't afford it.'

'What was this windfall you had? Did a great-aunt die or something?'

'Actually, that's pretty close to what happened. My Aunt Polly, poor old girl. She left me a hundred thousand bucks.'

She gasped.

'Then you're rich! Now I *really* have to catch you!'

He smiled.

'You're doing a pretty good job of it.'

When they got their drinks, he raised his glass and touched hers.

'To us,' he said.

'To us.'

They drank. The man in the white dinner jacket sitting alone two tables away got up and came over to them.

'Mr. Kemp!' said Prince Asaka. 'And Miss von Gersdorff. What a pleasant surprise.'

Nick got up to shake his hand.

'Nice to see you,' he said. 'Down here for a vacation?'

'Yes, and some business, too. Miss von Gersdorff, you look radiant.' He kissed her hand. 'And what a beautiful gown. Please sit down, Mr. Kemp.'

'Will you join us for a drink?'

Gabriella tried to signal Nick 'no,' but it was too late.

'I'd be delighted,' said the Prince, sitting down. 'But only a moment. I can see you two want to be *à deux*.'

He signaled the captain.

'A Cognac, please. Rémy Martin.'

'*Si*, Senor.'

'Well: you just arrived?'

'Yes, we got in about an hour ago.'

'It's a beautiful hotel, and the climate here is superb. One could almost forget there's a war on, couldn't one? Not much seems to be happening in Europe anyway, so perhaps the war will end soon. After all, why should England and France sacrifice themselves for Poland? Poland is gone—finished. It makes no sense, don't you agree?'

Gabriella resented fiercely the intrusion of the Japanese nobleman, and her mind was geared for romance rather than politics, but she couldn't help saying, 'My father was an Austrian. I don't think he would have said "forget Austria" when Hitler took it over two years ago. If Hitler took over Japan, would you say "forget Japan"? I doubt it.'

Asaka smiled.

'That hardly seems likely, but I see your point. However, you miss mine. Japan and Germany are strong nations. Poland was weak. Surely the lesson of history is that strong nations survive and weak ones die.' The waiter served the Cognac, and Asaka raised his glass. 'Shall we drink to Japanese-American friendship?'

Nick and Gabriella looked at each other. Then Nick raised his glass.

'I'll drink to that.' And he did, to Gabriella's astonishment.

'By the way,' Asaka continued, 'Baron and Baroness von Manfredi are at the hotel. He's Germany's ambassador to Mexico and an acquaintance of mine. My family had the honor of entertaining him often when he was German ambassador to Japan ten years ago, and I stayed with him when I was in Berlin during the Olympic Games. I'm joining them in the bar in a few minutes, and perhaps after your meal you would care to join us? The Baron is a fascinating man and considered something of an expert on Aztec and Mayan culture.'

'We'd be delighted,' said Nick.

Gabriella stared at him.

'I'm rather tired from the flight,' she said. 'I'd like to get to bed early.' She underlined 'bed' in her mind.

'We won't stay long,' said Nick.

'Good!' exclaimed Asaka, getting up. 'Then I'll leave you two alone and expect to see you in the bar—say, in an hour? Miss von Gersdorff'—he again took her hand—'I hope you enjoy your stay with Mr. Kemp. You make a remarkably handsome couple.'

Taking his Cognac, he left the table. Nick resumed his seat.

'Interesting fellow,' he said.

'Interesting? He's a creep! And why were you so nice to him?'

'Why shouldn't I be?'

'But Nick, he's a Jap! You yourself said it was horrible what they've done in China.'

'That doesn't mean *he's* done it himself.'

'I know, but still . . . and toasting Japanese-American friendship! I about dropped my glass when you did that!'

'Would you rather toast Japanese-American hatred? We're not at war with them, after all. And I'd very much like to meet the German Ambassador. It should be interesting.'

Gabriella sighed.

'My big romantic weekend's turning out to be the Versailles Conference.'

Nick laughed as the captain gave them the menus.

'We'll get to the romance soon enough,' he said.

Baron von Manfredi was a tall man with a considerable paunch, an elegantly trimmed white beard and a monocle, which fascinated Gabriella as she was introduced to him. His wife, far from being as stereotypically German as the Baron, was a black-haired beauty half his age who, it turned out, was Mexican.

'Dolores is my second wife,' explained the Baron as Nick and Gabriella sat down at the round table near the teakwood bar. Outside the open doors the lighted swimming pool eddied with turquoise languor as the moths and bugs dive-bombed it. 'She was my assistant at a dig at Uxmal two winters ago. We discovered some fascinating shards and love.' He ordered a round of Cognacs.

'Have you been to the Yucatan?' asked Baroness von Manfredi.

'No,' replied Gabriella, admiring her dress. 'This is my first time in Mexico.'

'You will find,' said the Baron, 'that this swimming pool is the only one in Mexico in which the water circulates. Mexicans tend to have a cavalier attitude toward cleanliness.'

His wife gave him a cool look.

'Thank you, Ulrich,' she said. 'At least Mexicans don't invade their neighbors the way Germany does.' She turned back to Gabriella. 'You must visit the Yucatan some time. It is fascinating. Except, of course, you must go in the winter. The summers are unbearably hot. You will excuse me?' she said to the others, getting up. 'I'll be back in a moment.' As the men stood, she smiled at Gabriella. 'Care to join me?'

'Yes, thank you.'

She followed the Baroness to the ladies' room.

'Your husband is very handsome,' she said to Gabriella.

'He's not my husband.'

'Oh yes, I forgot. You seem so young for a liaison.'

'It's my first time. I'm a little nervous.'

'Enjoy it, my dear. The first time is the best.'

She went into the ladies' room, Gabriella behind her. When the door closed, she checked to make sure the room was empty. Then she turned to Gabriella.

'How long have you known Prince Asaka?' she whispered.

'This is the second time I've ever seen him. Why?'

She went to the mirror to check her makeup.

'Be very careful with him,' she said finally.

'What do you mean?'

'Just that: be careful. He's a dangerous man.'

She went into the toilet, leaving Gabriella bewildered.

'Dangerous? How?' she asked.

'Ssh—keep your voice down.'

'How is he dangerous?' she whispered.

'What is your friend doing with him?'

'You mean Nick?'

'Of course.'

'Well, nothing. I mean, we just bumped into the Prince at dinner.'

The sound of the toilet flushing. Then she emerged from the stall.

'If you believe that, you're a fool.' She went back to the sink to wash her hands.

'You mean,' said Gabriella, incredulously, 'you think Nick came down here to *meet* him?'

'Of course. Just as my husband came here to meet him. Let me tell you something: I married my husband because he was rich and had a title. I didn't realize I was also marrying the representative of a man who wants to blow up the world—Herr Hitler. Take my advice: if you're smart, you'll leave here in the morning and never see your Nick again. Now let's get back to

425

the table before they suspect something. And for God's sake, don't say anything! We'll both be in danger if you do.'

She opened the door.

'Wait a minute—'

'Sshh. Come on. And smile.'

Oh my God, she thought, what *is* this? But she followed the Baroness back to the bar, where the three smiling men stood up. When she looked at Nick, for the first time her love-besotted mind began to wonder what kind of person he was.

A half hour later they went to their room. Nick locked the door and took off his jacket.

'The Baroness is lovely, isn't she?' he said, hanging it in the closet.

'Yes,' said Gabriella, sitting down on the bed. She was watching him. 'Nick,' she said finally, 'did you know that Prince Asaka was going to be here?'

'Of course not. How would I know that? The only time I've ever seen him was at your aunt's party.'

'Well, it just seemed such an odd coincidence, his being here.'

He took off his tie.

'What's odd about it? This is a popular hotel. And he must be loaded. I've read that the imperial family's fortune is one of the greatest on earth. Aren't you going to get undressed? It's sort of difficult making love to a woman with her clothes on.'

She got off the bed and went to the windows to look out at the sea.

'Nick, I made a mistake coming here,' she said. 'Aunt Barbara was right. I'd better go home tomorrow.'

He had taken his shirt off. Now he looked at her.

'What the hell does that mean?'

'Just that. I've thrown myself at you and acted like an idiot, and . . .' She turned to look at him. 'Now I've got cold feet.'

He came to her and took her in his arms.

'What's wrong, Gabriella?' he said, softly, and the nearness of his nakedness drove her almost crazy.

'I don't know what's going on here!' she burst out. 'I think you're lying to me, and I don't know why! Suddenly, I'm . . . afraid of you!'

'There's nothing to be afraid of.'

'But there is! When you were at Aunt Barbara's party, you practically insulted Prince Asaka. Now you're buddies!'

'Oh come on. Having a drink with him, I'm his buddy? You're acting like a child. I was just being normally polite.

What do you think is "going on" here, aside from my trying to make love to you?'

He pulled her more tightly against his smooth chest, and her fears began to dispel.

'The Baroness . . .' she began. She felt his muscles tense.

'What about her?'

'She told me in the ladies' room that her husband had come here to meet Prince Asaka.'

'So what?'

'She said you had come to meet him, too.'

'Then she'd had too much Cognac. Why would I want to meet Asaka?'

'I don't *know!*' she wailed. 'And she said he's dangerous! Oh Nick, you're not mixed up in some . . .' she stopped.

'Some what?'

'I don't know, some spy thing, are you?'

He laughed as he kissed her ear.

'Me? Nick Kemp, master spy? Oh boy, *you* must have had too much Cognac. Spies are for movies, like *Angel of Desire*. Be sensible.'

She relaxed.

'I guess it is a little crazy, isn't it? I mean, you don't look like a spy. But Prince Asaka sure as hell does! I'd hate to meet *him* in a dark embassy.'

He kissed his way slowly from her ear to her mouth as her hands moved up and down his muscled back. Spies, Prince Asaka, the German Ambassador and the strange Baroness von Manfredi faded from her mind as her lust for this man overwhelmed her.

'Oh Nick,' she whispered, 'I love you so much. Do you love me a little?'

'Yes, darling. And you must have heard that spies make great lovers.'

He picked her up in his arms and carried her to the bed, where he set her down. Then he kneeled before her and started taking off her shoes. She put her hands on his naked shoulders.

'I guess I'm going to have to do all the work,' he said.

'Nick,' she smiled, 'I love your hair. I just love to look at you! Is that crazy?'

'Could be. I think I'll need a little help with your stockings.'

'Oh honestly, you're so unromantic! Here, I'll do it.'

She went into the bathroom and took off her clothes. When she came out, he had turned off the lights and was in bed. She crossed the moon-splashed floor, feeling rather self-conscious naked. He said nothing as she climbed in beside him. She was more than a little frightened.

'You know,' she whispered, 'it's my first time.'

'I know.'

He turned to her and began kissing her as his hands fondled her breasts, then moved slowly down her body, caressing her skin. He was an expert lover and knew how to excite her. When she felt his hand massaging her vulva, she literally gasped with pleasure. She opened her mouth and their tongues touched. This physical intimacy with him, this exploring the nooks and crannies of his body, made her dizzy with pleasure. After a while he kicked off the sheet and climbed on top of her. She felt his stiffness pressing into her belly, felt his golden pubic hair. Her hands were exploring his muscled thighs and tight, smooth buttocks when he whispered, 'I'm going in.' She felt him ease into her and again she gasped, this time not with pleasure but shock and pain. 'Oh Nick, oh God, don't hurt me . . .'

'I'm being careful, darling.'

'Oh Nick, I love you so . . .'

She cried out in the dark as he penetrated her hymen and the blood began flowing. Then she felt him way inside her, felt his midsection begin pressing against her, slowly at first, then with increasing passion. Networks of unused nerves began waking to life as her body responded to his invasion. A massive sweetness filled her as her body pulled her inexorably to a quiet internal explosion.

After he came and pulled out, she said nothing. No word she could think of could describe how wonderful it had been.

CHAPTER 47

The next morning, after a leisurely breakfast on their terrace, they put on their bathing suits and, armed with dark glasses, suntan lotion and Gabriella's sketchpad, they started down the cliff to the beach.

'You go on without me,' Nick said, suddenly. 'I think I'm having a quick bout of *turista*.'

'Do you feel sick?'

'Just a little queasy. I always get it the first day. I'll be down in a while.'

He hurried back up to their terrace as she continued down the walk. The beach was small but beautiful and practically deserted except for the hotel beach boys, who arranged a chaise for her, gave her a towel, then brought her orange juice laced with rum. Here goes the perpetual diet, she thought as she put the straw in her mouth. One sip of the powerful, delicious drink and she forgot diets. She stretched back in the chaise, let the sun kiss her body and floated in a delicious revery as she relived his lovemaking in her memory. His sexual appetite was apparently inexhaustible, and the second time his big penis entered her she had achieved an orgasm that was even better than her first. Her body had come alive in ways she had never dreamed of. For the first time in her life, she felt like a woman. Remembering Erica's downgrading of the male body, she told herself the lesbian star didn't know what she was talking about. God had done a spectacular job on Adam and had repeated the miracle with Nick. She worshipped him.

When she finished the drink, she declined another one from the overzealous beach boy, then sat up, smeared herself with suntan oil and opened her sketchpad to begin working on Erica's wardrobe.

A half hour passed, and she began to worry about Nick.

Leaving her sketchpad and the oil, she climbed the cliff and went into the room.

It was empty. So was the bathroom. Wondering where he had gone, she started out on the terrace to wait for him when she noticed his suitcase. She remembered his strange testiness the night before when she had offered to unpack it for him. Now she went to it and tried the lock. It was unlocked, so she opened it.

It was empty.

'Looking for something?'

She jumped and turned to see him standing in the door. He had put on a Mexican shirt and a pair of slacks.

'Where did you go?'

'To buy some pills for my stomach. What are you looking for?'

He came in the room and closed the door.

'Why . . . nothing,' she shrugged. 'I just thought I'd unpack your bag, but you've obviously already done it.'

He looked at her coldly.

'I *told* you I'd unpack it. And I don't like people snooping in my suitcase.'

' "People"? I'm Gabriella, remember? And I wasn't snooping.'

'Weren't you? I suppose this is part of your stupid spy fantasy. What did you think I had in there: the secret formula for a new explosive? Or maybe a lethal gas? Christ, what a fruitcake you turn out to be.'

'Nick, I'm sorry. Really! I don't know, maybe I *was* snooping, but don't get mad at me. Please . . .'

He was taking off his shirt and slacks, which he had put on over his bathing suit.

'Well, forget it,' he said. 'Come on: let's go down to the beach.'

He started out the door.

'But what about your pills?'

He stopped abruptly, and she could almost hear his brain whirring.

'They didn't have what I was looking for,' he said, curtly. Then he went out on the terrace.

She didn't move for a moment. She knew he had lied. But then, if he hadn't gone out for pills, what had he gone out for?

And what had been in the suitcase?

When they came in the dining room for lunch, she saw the Baroness von Manfredi sitting by herself. Stopping by her table, she said, 'Good afternoon. Lovely day, isn't it?'

The Mexican woman looked at them with an expressionless face.

'Very,' she said. Her tone was icy.

'Is your husband joining you?'

'He flew to Mexico City this morning. He will be back tomorrow.'

Her eyes went to Nick a moment, then to Gabriella, who was confused by her obvious hostility.

'Well, if you'd like to join us for a cocktail this evening . . .'

'Thank you, no.'

'Gabriella tells me,' said Nick, lowering his voice, 'that you think I planned to meet Prince Asaka here. I wondered why you thought that?'

She frowned.

'But I never said any such thing!'

Nick looked at Gabriella.

'You did too!' she exclaimed. 'Last night in the powder room! You told me I was fool if I thought Nick had met Asaka by accident . . .'

'You lie!' she said, softly. 'I never said such a thing! You obviously have a wild and rather vulgar imagination.'

Gabriella was amazed. She looked at Nick helplessly.

'All right, I guess I dreamed the whole thing up. They must have put marijuana in my dessert. Excuse me.'

She walked to her table, followed by Nick. When they were seated, she said, 'Now I know you think I really am a "fruitcake," as you so winningly put it this morning. But I'm telling you, that woman lied just now. If you want to believe her, feel free. But she lied.'

Nick opened his napkin.

'Let's forget the whole thing,' he said. 'Do you want one of those rum torpedoes?'

'Why not? I might as well become a roaring alcoholic, since staying sober sure as hell doesn't make any sense.'

She couldn't forget the whole thing, as Nick so airily suggested. The culmination of odd events forced her to believe something mysterious was going on in the hotel and that Nick was involved with it; and as much as he ridiculed her spy 'fantasy,' the presence of the German Ambassador and a cousin of the Japanese emperor made it almost impossible not to infer some sort of espionage—after all, what were they doing? Smuggling dope? But she simply couldn't believe that Nick Kemp was a spy. It went against everything she instinctively felt about the man. Still, the evidence seemed to contradict her instincts, and when she thought about his mysterious 'windfall' from 'Aunt Polly,' it seemed even more suspect. A hundred thousand dollars. Nick's father was well off, but that was a lot of money. Had it been enough to buy his patriotism? And if he were a spy, then what in God's name was she doing sleeping with him and savoring every moment of it? Shouldn't she be getting the hell out?

But her desire for him cancelled her ability to act. He was so pleasant and warm during lunch and, later, back on the beach, that she told herself there was only one more day, and that to make a dramatic exit now would achieve little. So she relaxed, sunbathed, sketched and, when they returned to their room at four, made love again. It was idyllic. As he had joked, spies made great lovers.

It was only when they went to the bar for cocktails that she realized she hadn't seen Prince Asaka all day. Since the hotel was small, it was unlikely she would not have seen him unless he had spent the day in his room. Her curiosity aroused, and not wishing to engender new accusations of 'spyomania' from Nick, she excused herself, went to the lobby and asked the desk clerk if the Japanese had checked out.

'No, Senora. He has kept his room through Sunday. But he flew to Mexico City this morning with Baron von Manfredi.'

'Oh. Well, thank you.'

'*De nada,* Senora.'

She walked back to the bar, putting the scenario together in her mind. Nick had brought something—call it X—to Acapulco in his suitcase. Somewhere along the line, he had given X to Asaka and the German Ambassador—yes, that morning! As they were going to the beach. His sudden attack of Montezuma's Revenge. Had he gone back to the room, put on his pants and shirt, removed X from the suitcase and taken it to Asaka's room? Then, when he returned to their room and found her 'snooping,' had he quickly made up the excuse about trying to buy the stomach pills? Yes, that *must* be it. And then Asaka and von Manfredi had flown X to Mexico City. And that would explain why Baroness von Manfredi had gone 'cold' at lunch. While delivering X, Nick must have told them to shut her up, which

432

they did. What had she said last night in the ladies' room? 'Don't tell them what I said or we'll both be in danger'? Yes, *both* in danger.

Was *she* in danger?

'Penny for your thoughts,' said Nick as she sat down at the table.

'I was just thinking what a lovely day it's been.'

Lovely, hell! she thought as she stared at him. I'm in love with a bloody spy!

She ordered a drink, then thought about customs. Yesterday, at the Los Angeles airport, they had passed Nick's suitcase without opening it. That's why he had worn his uniform! Of course. He knew the customs men would take one look at his naval uniform and pass him through; X had been safe because it was carried by the American flag.

She realized that if she truly loved this man, she had to try her best to save him from himself before it was too late.

The problem was, it might already be too late.

'Nick,' she said that night as she lay beside him in bed, 'I have to talk to you about something very important to me.'

'What's that?'

'You. You're not going to like what I'm saying, but please listen to me. I've figured out what you've done. Oh, I don't know what was in the suitcase, but I know Asaka and von Manfredi have taken it to Mexico City. It must be important, or they wouldn't have paid you a hundred thousand dollars for it. Nick, I love you, and you are my sweet, wonderful lover. But do you realize what you've done? Do you realize you've committed treason? They could execute you! Oh God, Nick, listen to me: stop this madness before it's too late! Please!'

He didn't say anything for a while. She could hear him breathing beside her.

'I think,' he finally said, 'that when we get back to Los Angeles tomorrow, we'd better not see each other anymore.'

'Then you won't listen to me?'

'I've listened, and I've heard enough. Frankly, Gabriella, I think you're crazy.'

He turned his back to her.

'What if I go to the F.B.I.?' she said, carefully.

'Go. They'll think you're as crazy as I do.'

After a while he heard her sobs. He sat up, turned on the light and looked at her. He could see her heart was breaking. Tenderly he reached over and put his hand on her arm.

'I'm sorry,' he said, quietly.

She looked at him, tears streaming down her face.

'Don't you understand? I love you. And sooner or later, somebody's going to kill you! Oh God, Nick, stop it! Please! It will kill me if something happens to you.'

He looked at her with great compassion.

But he said nothing.

The next morning she was sick. She woke up with a bad case of the trots, and unlike Nick's, hers were genuine. After several debilitating trips to the bathroom, she was so weak she could hardly move from the bed. Nick got some medicine from the hotel manager (thus tacitly confirming her suspicions about his inability to get pills for himself the day before), and it helped a little. But she was still weak and obviously in no condition to travel. He seemed irritable and nervous. Finally, at noon he said to her, 'The plane leaves at two, and I can't miss it. I think I'd better arrange for you to stay over until you feel better. Will that be all right?'

She nodded, miserable not only from her stomach but from the terrible way the weekend had turned out. He left the room and returned a while later to tell her it was all arranged, the bill had been paid, and she could stay till tomorrow or later if necessary. Then he began packing. She watched him from the bed, realizing she would never see him again and that there was nothing left for them to say to each other.

He went in the bathroom to shave and put on his uniform. When he came out, he went to the bed and looked down at her.

'Will you be all right?' he asked.

'I suppose.'

He checked his watch.

'Well, I'd better be going. Good-bye, Gabriella.'

She didn't respond. She turned her face away, refusing to look at him.

'I'm sorry it turned out this way,' he added. 'You're a wonderful girl, but I'm afraid you let your imagination run away with you.'

'I'm creative, remember?' she said, sourly. 'I design dresses. I'll design a stunning black suit to wear to your court-martial.'

She heard him slam out of the room.

She felt miserable and alone.

At four that afternoon, she was awakened from a nap by a knock on the door. She got up, still feeling weak, but glad to realize the nausea had gone. Going to the door, she opened it.

Prince Asaka was standing in the hall.

'Mr. Kemp told me you were not feeling well,' he said, pleasantly. 'I wondered if there was anything I could do for you?'

She didn't like seeing the Japanese, but force of habit made her polite.

'No thank you. I'm feeling better.'

'My personal physician in Los Angeles gave me an excellent remedy for the Mexican Malaise. I'd be glad to give you some.'

'That's very kind of you, but I don't need any more medicine. I'll be going home tomorrow and frankly, I'll be delighted to get out of here.'

'Oh? You didn't enjoy your stay?'

'I think you're well aware it's been a disaster. I'm not completely blind, you know. I've seen what's been going on.'

His smile was exquisitely polite.

'I'm afraid I don't follow you.'

'Really, this game is a joke. Even if Baroness von Manfredi hadn't told me . . .'

'Ah, the Baroness,' he interrupted. 'Then you've heard the news?'

'What news?'

'Her husband was supposed to fly back to Acapulco with me this morning, but he decided to stay in Mexico City instead. We had chartered a small private plane in which I returned this morning. An hour ago the Baroness took the plane back to Mexico City to rejoin her husband. Unfortunately, something happened to the engine, and the plane crashed shortly after takeoff. Both the pilot and the Baroness were killed. It is a great tragedy for the Baron. She was such a beautiful woman. Like yourself, Miss von Gersdorff.' He bowed slightly. 'Then I will bid you good-bye. It's been so delightful seeing you again. And your charming Mr. Kemp.'

She was so stunned, all she could think to do was say automatically, 'Good-bye.' He walked down the corridor, and she went back in the room, closing the door and locking it.

The Baroness had talked, and the Baroness was dead. The lesson was obvious, and it had been delivered in person by Prince Asaka.

CHAPTER 48

She returned to Los Angeles the next day. She had no intention of going to the F.B.I. It was true America and Germany had broken diplomatic relations two years before as a protest against the Nazi treatment of the Jews, but Germany and America weren't at war, nor were America and Japan. She was not only too afraid for her own safety to do anything, she wasn't even sure what she could do. She had no proof of anything, only an accumulation of suspicions and assumptions. While she was ninety percent sure she was right, there was the ten percent margin of doubt. What if Nick were right and it was all in her imagination? True, the death of Baroness von Manfredi seemed too well timed for coincidence, but it *might* have been a coincidence. Plane accidents did happen. Besides, if she told the F.B.I. and they began to investigate Nick, one of two things would happen. If he were guilty he would be hanged. And if he were innocent his career would at the very least be under a cloud.

So she did nothing. She went back to work at the studio, worked on Erica's wardrobe at night, and tried to push Nick and Prince Asaka and Acapulco out of her mind.

Besides, she had something else to worry about: Erica. The shooting of *Angel of Desire* was wrapping up, and she saw her almost every day at the studio. The blond star never failed to ask her to her dressing room, or ask her to lunch or cocktails or dinner. Gabriella always had an excuse, her main one being that designing and making the clothes left her no time, which was true, but she could see Erica's patience was wearing thin, and she knew the inevitable decision on her part would have to be made. Finally, a month after returning from Acapulco, she called Erica at her Malibu beach house and told her the clothes were ready for her inspection. 'Wonderful, darling!' she said.

'Can you bring them out this afternoon? And I'll make us supper. I'm a marvelous cook. Would you like a steak?'

'Well, I've put on a few pounds, so I'm dieting . . .'

'Wonderful! I'll diet, too. We'll have a salad and some wine. See you at, say, five?'

'All right, five.'

Gabriella hung up and sighed. The inevitable was here.

Erica believed in the perquisites and privileges of stardom, and since she was making $200,000 a picture, she could afford the luxuries. She had four huge cars, including a midnight-blue Rolls-Royce Morris had bought her after the phenomenal success of *Smash-Up*, minks and sables and an enviable collection of jewels. She also had inherited a middle-class sense of the importance of capital investment from her professor father, and was buying up real estate with the avidity of a John Jacob Astor. Erica knew that success in movies was as ephemeral as physical beauty. But Los Angeles real estate was still cheap, so she had plenty left over to lavish on her beach house. She had designed it herself in an undistinguished style someone had dubbed M.G.M. Colonial, but it was pretty, and in a town where eclectic architecture was the norm, its misplaced New England charm didn't stand out like a sore thumb.

Gabriella parked her Chevrolet by the garage and carried the three big boxes to the door. Erica answered the bell in a pair of slacks and white blouse.

'Here you are,' she exclaimed. 'Let me help you with those boxes . . .'

She took the top one, and Gabriella followed her into the living room. This was not a large room, but it was tastefully done, and its views of the beach and ocean through the glass doors at the end was beautiful. The floor was bleached almost white, and chintz sofas and chairs gave a cheery ambience which was enhanced by several delightful Biedermeier chairs Erica had bought at an antique shop on La Cienega. Over the white mantel hung a portrait of Erica dressed in a cloud of white tulle.

'I can hardly wait to see what you've done,' said Erica, putting her box on a table. 'What shall I try on first?'

'Since we're at Malibu, how about the beachwear?'

'Why not?'

'It's in this box. Shall I help you?'

'Oh no, darling, I'll change in the library and give you a fashion show.'

She took the box and went into the next room, to Gabriella's relief. She had not looked forward to the intimacy of helping

437

Erica on with her clothes. What had her stomach in knots was the possibility of Erica helping her off with her own clothes. However, if Erica was in a sexually aggressive mood, so far she seemed to be concealing it. And during the ensuing show, Gabriella forgot her nervousness as she bathed in the glow of Erica's fulsome praise. The star loved the clothes, almost without reservation, and voiced her approval rhapsodically. Gabriella was particularly anxious about the finale, the evening gown, with which she had gone extremely 'daring.' It was made of black taffeta with puffy mutton-chop sleeves that gave it a neo-Victorian look from the front. But the back was practically nonexistent, swooping down almost to her buttocks.

'My God, darling,' laughed Erica as she came in the living room, 'if I back up against a refrigerator, I'll have an ass frappé!'

'Is it too much?'

'No, I love it. I've got a gorgeous back, why not show it? A touch of Shalimar on my lower spine, and every stud in Hollywood will be clawing at me. It's wonderful. The whole collection's wonderful. I love it. How much do I owe you?'

'Well, the material came to twelve hundred dollars, and my designs and labor are three hundred. So fifteen hundred, all told.'

'But you're cheating yourself! You must have worked like a dog doing this!'

'It wasn't work to me because I love doing it. And having you wear my clothes is so valuable, I probably shouldn't even charge you for the labor.'

'Don't be silly. Listen, darling, the first rule of couturier design is, charge all the traffic will bear. If a dress is priced low, most women will think it's cheap quality. However,' she added quickly, 'I'll write you a check before you take my advice. Would you like a drink?'

'No thanks.'

'Oh, come on! This is a celebration. I have a bottle of good Chablis in the refrigerator. Why don't you open it and pour us a glass while I write your check?'

Gabriella went into the immaculate kitchen and poured the wine. When she returned to the living room, Erica handed her the check.

'Voilà! The beginning of Gabriella von Gersdorff's fortune. Why don't you open a shop, darling? You must be bored silly sewing at the studio, and it's such a waste of your talent.'

She took the wine and sat down before the fireplace. Gabriella sat opposite her.

'Actually I've been toying with the idea. But I'm not sure if I have enough money. I inherited a little from my parents and my grandmother, but that's all tied up in bonds . . .'

'My God, your grandfather was a banker and you don't know how to get money? Borrow it from Morris! He's richer than the law allows.'

'Oh, I couldn't do that.'

'Don't be ridiculous. They've told me your story, how you were absolutely screwed by your uncle Drew—that turd! Morris and Barbara both adore you and would do anything to help you. It's silly not to ask them!'

'But I don't know how much I'd need to get started. I'd need a salesgirl, obviously, and a workroom to make the clothes in. And I'd have to have money to live on, since I'd have to quit my job . . .'

'Twenty-five thousand dollars,' Erica interrupted. 'That will give you a nice cushion. And I have just the place for the shop! I bought a building on Wilshire Boulevard last year that has a small florist on the corner. It's just two blocks from the Beverly Wilshire, an ideal location, but the florist died on me after Christmas, and I haven't found a new tenant yet. Why don't you rent it?'

'The rent must be awfully high on Wilshire.'

'I was getting five hundred a month from the florist. I'll give you a two-year lease for four hundred. You won't get a better deal than that.'

'No, I certainly won't. That's very generous of you.'

'But I want you to be a success, darling! And I can brag that one of my tenants is Gabriella, the chic-est new designer in Beverly Hills! Of course,' she added, slyly, 'you'll give me a nice discount on clothes.'

'Oh, certainly.'

'Well, then it's practically settled. Talk to Morris tonight. If he gives you trouble, which he won't, have him call me. I'll tell him I'll move to Paramount if he doesn't loan you the money. Why are you sitting over there, darling? Why don't you come sit next to me? That way, you can pour me more wine.'

She smiled invitingly. Oh God, thought Gabriella, here it comes!

'Erica . . .'

'Yes, darling?'

'I don't quite know how to say this, but . . . if you really like

439

my clothes and really think I have talent, then don't . . . ask me to go to bed with you.'

The smile faded.

'You couldn't possibly find me unattractive.'

'You know you're one of the most beautiful women in the world. I'd give anything to look like you. But . . .' she took a deep breath, '. . . I like men.'

Erica lighted a cigarette.

'I bet Chanel would go to bed with me,' she said, exhaling.

'I'm not Chanel. I'm Gabriella. If I start my career that way, it'll be . . . I don't know. All wrong.'

Erica glared at her for almost a full minute. Then she laughed.

'Damn! Just my luck. I discover a genius, and the little bitch is straight. All right, darling, I give up on you in the bed department. Our relationship will be pure business. But I think that discount you're going to give me on the clothes has just doubled.'

Gabriella heaved a sigh of relief and refilled both their glasses.

'I'm just realizing it,' she said. 'I'm practically in business!'

'What will you call the place?'

'Oh, I worked that out years ago when I was a child running an imaginary boutique in Paris. It'll be called Chez Gabriella.'

'Mm. Unoriginal, but to the point. Then let's toast it. To Chez Gabriella!'

'To Chez Gabriella.'

She drank the wine and felt warm and happy and relatively virtuous.

Most of the movie moguls had gone to considerable lengths to downplay their humble Jewish origins. Prompted by socially aspiring wives and living in a time of relatively unfettered anti-Semitism, they spent their millions on lavish estates and impressionist art and tried to obliterate the traces of the *shtetl* from their lives, at least when out at dinner parties. They talked movie talk, played golf at the Hillcrest Country Club, nursed their ulcers and bedded their mistresses, but talk of the Lower East Side was rare.

Morris David was an exception. He had the estate and the Impressionist painting which lifted at the press of a button to reveal apertures for film projectors. He had the classy *shiksa* wife. But Morris loved to reminisce about Hester Street. And at the glossiest Beverly Hills dinner parties, when the biggest diamonds were being displayed, he loved nothing better than to stop the show by uttering a Yiddish saying from his youth, and the cruder the better. Some of the choicer examples from his repertoire were *Er dreyt zikh arum vi a futz in bod* ('He wonders around like a fart in a bathtub'), or *Az men pisht klor, kakt men on dem dokter* ('When you piss clear, you can shit on the doctor'), or perhaps his favorite, *Nit do kayn geshmakers, vi a groyser putz un a kleyn futz'* ('There is no finer art than a large cock and a small fart'). These Delphic utterances, dropped casually in the middle of a formal dinner, would reduce even the most pompous mogul to howls of laughter, while his wife would pretend not to understand and any non-Jews present would look understandably confused. Barbara had long since given up trying to stop his anal Yiddish crudities. Whatever his shortcomings, which were many, she knew he had a warm, generous heart. Thus, when Gabriella asked her aunt whether Morris would be offended if she asked him about a loan, Barbara said, 'Of course not. Why should he be?'

Morris was immediately receptive. He loved Gabriella; he also respected the memory of her grandfather Victor, who had financed his first big movie so many years before. She told him what she wanted to do, Erica's connection with it and her dreams for Chez Gabriella. He listened attentively, puffing a cigar. Then he said, 'How much do you want?'

'It sounds like a lot of money,' she gulped.

'I'm in the movie business, what could be a lot of money? How much?'

'Twenty-five thousand dollars.'

'That's what your uncle Drew tried to give you at Christmas six years ago, and you threw it in his face.'

'And I'd do it again!' she said.

He smiled.

'Good. So would I. That man's a *putz*.' He got up and went to his desk, where he scribbled a check. Then he brought it back to her. She took it and looked at it. It was made out to her for $30,000.

'But Uncle Morris, I only asked for twenty-five . . .'

'The extra five thousand's a gift from me. Use it to make the shop pretty. *Fun drek ken men kayn koyletsh mit flekhten.*'

'What's that mean?'

'You can't roll strudel out of shit.'

She laughed and gave him a hug and a kiss.

Chez Gabriella opened on April Fool's Day, 1940. The space was small—a showroom and a workshop behind it—but that was

441

all right with Gabriella: She wanted to keep it small, exclusive and perfect. She directed the remodeling of the place herself, fought with the architect, argued with the carpenters and got what she wanted: the clean, modern New York look that was a rarity in Los Angeles. If less was more, at Chez Gabriella the least was the most: here the clothes would be the star. A few Barcelona chairs, one *ficus* tree in an exquisite Chinese pot, gray carpeting, and on the wall one large, modern painting by a Mexican artist. The windows on Wilshire Boulevard were covered with white curtains which let in a little light but filtered most of the view: She didn't want her customers looking at cars. She hired an Italian salesgirl named Lucrezia Russo. Lucrezia was twenty-five, bright, attractive, the daughter of a California wine-growing family from the Napa Valley who was trying to establish herself as an artist. Gabriella paid her fifty dollars a week, which was good money, told her she expected her to work hard and charm the customers, and quietly warned her to watch out for Erica. After trying out several seamstresses, she found a marvel in a forty-year-old Mexican woman named Rosita Guzman. It was Rosita who executed the designs under Gabriella's constant supervision. The workroom behind the boutique hummed with activity far into the night as Gabriella worked up her opening collection.

For the April first opening, there were no flashing lights, no elevated platform, no swarms of fashion reporters. With Erica and Barbara's help, Gabriella drew up a list of twenty of the most social fashionable women in Beverly Hills, only seven of whom were movie stars—Gabriella didn't want to be at the mercy of the whim of actresses exclusively. These twenty select women were invited to Chez Gabriella for a champagne showing of the collection. The press was purposely excluded. Not one of the invitees failed to appear: Barbara and Erica had spread the word around Beverly Hills and the movie colony that Gabriella was a sorceress with the needle and that Chez Gabriella was going to be *the* place to buy clothes. The guests arrived before five and were greeted and seated in small rented chairs by Lucrezia. Champagne and caviar were served by two hired waiters. Then, promptly at five, through the curtains separating the boutique from the workshop stepped Gabriella. She looked poised, but she was as nervous as a cat.

'I am Gabriella von Gersdorff,' she said, 'and welcome to Chez Gabriella.'

Then she moved to the side and announced the first design.

'To open the collection, a suit for lunch with the man you *hope* will be your lover.'

Titters from the ladies as a striking model walked through the curtains in a gray suit piped with pink. It was severely cut and had slightly exaggerated shoulders, but the only gimmick was the somewhat unusual pink piping. It was a beautiful, elegant creation. As the model passed among the women, they leaned forward to take a close look.

Gabriella could tell from the excited murmurs that she had a hit.

She had a smash hit. She sold the entire collection and was besieged with clamors for more. Jealous critics carped that Gabriella could hardly lose, being backed by Morris and Barbara David and Erica Stern, but they backed off when they began seeing her clothes at parties. There was something magical about them: she not only had flair, but a distinctive style. She worked long, hard hours to make the seemingly effortless style work. She also charged staggering prices. But as the 'sitzkrieg' in Europe heated to a blitzkrieg, as Belgium, France, Holland, Norway and Denmark fell before the apparently invincible Germans, and as America, reluctantly dragging its heels, began to gear up to a wartime economy, the ladies of Los Angeles didn't care what the price was. Perhaps more frightened by the future than they liked to admit, they wanted to buy, and they had the money to do so. Gabriella was swamped.

She rented an apartment in Brentwood, and for the first time in her life she had a place of her own. Her success thrilled her. The long years of overweight shyness, the traumas of losing her parents and her grandparents, from all of this sadness she was finally emerging into her own. The only thing lacking to make it perfect was Nick. She had thought time would heal that wound, but she was wrong. Even at her busiest, working with Rosita in the shop until well past midnight, he was never completely out of her mind. She would drive home exhausted, collapse in her bed, and he would pop into her thoughts. She told herself she was behaving like someone in a hackneyed love song, that she would never see him again and good riddance, that she should start dating other men, but it made no difference. She *was* someone in a hackneyed love song. He had gone to her head, he was the top, and she got no kick from champagne.

She wanted her man.

On the first Monday in June, a man walked into Chez Gabriella. Lucrezia Russo saw few men in the place. She certainly saw few such good-looking men in or out of Chez Gabriella.

'Good morning,' she said. 'May I help you?'

'Yes. My name is Nick Kemp, and I'd like to see Miss von Gersdorff. Is she in?'

Lucrezia, who had assumed that all-work-no-play Gabriella had a nonexistent love life, was intrigued.

'Yes, she's back in the workroom. Shall I get her?'

'Please.'

She hurried through the curtains. Gabriella and Rosita were working on a cocktail dress for Merle Oberon, who had become a recent recruit to the 'Gabriella Girls,' as her prominent clients had been dubbed by the press.

'Gabriella, there's the most dreamy-looking sailor wanting to see you. And if you don't want him, I'll take him!'

She had been squatting by the mannequin, working on the skirt. She looked up.

'A sailor?' she said.

'Well, he's an officer. His name is Kemp. Nick Kemp.'

Gabriella's face went white. She stood up, then hurried to a mirror to check her reflection. Lucrezia and Rosita exchanged looks.

'Stay in here, Lucrezia,' Gabriella said as she went to the curtains. 'I want to see him alone.'

She went through the curtains, and Rosita and Lucrezia huddled in a whispered orgy of speculation.

'Hello, Gabriella,' said Nick as she came into the boutique.

'Hello.'

They looked at each other in awkward silence.

'Did you have something you wanted to tell me?' she said finally.

'I have a lot of things. So many, I don't know where to start.' He checked his watch. 'May I take you to lunch? I know a great little seafood place in Venice. The abalone's like rubber, and they have a delicious wine called Château Tiajuana.'

'Or we could run down to Acapulco for a romantic weekend. They have interesting specialties down there. Mysterious Japanese. Wives of German ambassadors who die in plane crashes . . .'

'I had nothing to do with that!'

'Oh? Then I wasn't such a "fruitcake"? You *did* have something to do with the rest of it?'

'Look: I want to explain the whole thing, but I don't want to do it here. I need privacy.'

She hesitated.

'We won't get privacy in Venice. Let's go to my apartment.'

She went back into the workshop.

'Lucrezia, *cara*, I'll be gone for a couple of hours. Watch things for me, will you?'

'Sure. Are you going to tell us who Handsome is?'

Gabriella smiled sadly.

'The big love of my life. Or he used to be.' She started out, then added, 'Maybe he still is.'

She unlocked the door and led him into the living room of her apartment. He looked around at the Toulouse-Lautrec posters, the Mexican primitives she had become interested in, the mattress-ticking-covered daybed, and said, 'Nice. I like it.'

'It's home. Like a Coke?'

'No thanks.'

He put his cap on a table and sat down. She noticed the extra half-stripe on his shoulders.

'You've been promoted?' she said.

'That's right. I'm now Lieutenant, junior grade, Kemp.'

'Washington has an odd way of honoring spies.'

'I guess my act was more convincing than I thought.'

'Oh? It was an act?' She sat down.

'Let me begin at the beginning. Last January, a week after your uncle's party, Asaka came to my ship out of the blue. I had no idea what he was up to, but in the course of the conversation, he threw out a proposal to me. Oh, he gussied it up to sound like some cockamamie movie idea he had, but he knew what he was talking about.'

'What was he talking about?'

'He was looking for an American officer to pass him certain equipment with which, if the Japs and Germans had it, they could decode all our official messages. I can't get too technical because it's classified information. Now, why in God's name he thought *I* would be interested is still beyond me, but I sniffed something big was happening and had the wits to go along with it. The upshot was, he was offering a million dollars cash to whomever would play footsie with him.'

'A *million?* They must really want whatever it is.'

'Are you kidding? If there was a war, it would be worth a

hundred million. All right, I didn't commit myself, but I pretended to be interested. After he left, I went to Naval Intelligence and told them the whole thing. Needless to say, they were amazed—I mean, a cousin of the Emperor of Japan a *spy?* But I suggested it might pay us to play along with him . . .'

'You mean, *give* him the secret codes? Or sell them?'

'No. Sell him *phony* codes.'

'What good would that do? Wouldn't they know they were phony when they didn't work?'

'Of course. But not if we were transmitting false information in the phony codes. They couldn't decode the real stuff, but if enough phony stuff were transmitted that they *could* decode, there was a possibility we could fool them into thinking they had at least *part* of the package. And the great advantage would be that we could tell them whatever we wanted, send them off on wildgoose chases, whatever. Get it?'

She looked amazed.

'Nick, *you* thought that up?'

'That's right. It took a bit of selling, but Intelligence decided it was worth a try. So I was authorized to sell Asaka the phony codes.

'Well, I didn't do it all at once. I dragged my heels, told him I was afraid of being caught, let him work on me—but finally I gave in and agreed. He paid me a hundred thousand cash as a down payment, and the Navy let me keep enough of it to start living the high life: part of the strategy was to make Asaka think I was so gaga about getting all that dough, I couldn't resist buying the Cadillac, staying at the Beverly Hills Hotel, and so forth. I had to convince him I was *human,* you see? Mr. Weakling, otherwise why would I sell out my country? Which is where you came into it.'

'Me?'

'You. I told Asaka I wanted to make the first delivery in Mexico because I was afraid of doing it in the States. He agreed to that fast enough because I found out part of his scheme was to bring Adolf's boys into it via his old buddy, Baron von Manfredi. So we agreed to meet at the Bella Vista in Acapulco, with von Manfredi. But to keep up the act that I was Mr. Human, Mr. Weakling, I told him that I had flipped for you and insisted I wanted to bring you along for the weekend to show off my newfound wealth and, well, to have a little fun, if you see what I mean.'

Her heart sank.

'In other words, the love stuff was just a front? I was a prop?'

446

'In the beginning it was that. It didn't end up that way. But let me finish: Asaka was furious. He didn't want you around gumming up the works, but I insisted and he finally gave in. The rest you figured out. I brought the hot stuff down in the suitcase, passed it to Asaka and von Manfredi, who then flew it to Mexico City to have duplicated at the German Embassy. Meanwhile, unfortunately, they decided Baroness von Manfredi wasn't a good risk anymore and got rid of her.'

'You told them she had spoken to me in the potty?'

'No, thank God. They figured it out themselves. Apparently she had been giving them trouble for some time. She didn't like what Hitler's been doing in Europe, for good reason. So, that's about it. I had to pretend I was mad at you to keep Asaka convinced I was on his side. The unfortunate thing is, it was pretty rough on you, for which I can now apologize.'

'Why now?'

'Asaka's gone back to Japan. I asked Intelligence if I could talk to you, and they gave me permission. Unfortunately, it looks as if the Japs have caught on to our game. They refused to make the last payment and accused me of selling them rhinestones instead of diamonds. But it worked for a while, and it cost the Imperial Treasury a helluva lot of money, which they're not happy about. But we are.'

She told herself not to let him see how furious and hurt she was, but she was about to explode.

'So you're a goddam hero?'

'Well, they gave me a promotion. And they let me keep the Cadillac.'

'Congratulations. And I'm delighted I could help our grovernment in this great triumph of international intrigue. Obviously, the Department of the Navy doesn't give a damn about my feelings. Why should they? Why should you? Who am I? Gabriella, the prop.'

'Not quite. You're Gabriella, the girl I fell in love with in Acapulco.'

'Oh really? Tell me about it.' She stood up and headed for the kitchen. 'Meanwhile, I'm going to get a Coke. And a violin, so we can get the proper sound track for this love scene.'

She went into the kitchen and slammed the door. Going to the refrigerator, she pulled out a bottle of Coke, closed the door and started looking for the opener in a drawer. When she could no longer see the utensils for the tears in her eyes, she gave up looking, leaned against the wall and broke down completely.

After a while, he came into the kitchen.

447

'Gabriella . . .'

'Oh, go away!' she cried. 'You *bastard!* Haven't you hurt me enough? Are you going to force me to listen to more of your bullshit? Damn you! Damn *me* for falling in love with you! Just go *away*. Please. I've heard enough.'

He waited for a while by the door as she continued sobbing. Then he said, quietly, 'I *did* fall in love with you. When you tried to stop me that night at the hotel. When I saw how much you really cared what happened to me, I started caring what happened to you. And you can call that reflected egotism maybe, I don't know. But I love you. And I've had to wait all this time to be able to tell you. But I want you. I don't know if you'd ever consider being my wife, but if you would, that would make me the happiest man in the world.'

'Bullshit,' she sniffed.

He came across the kitchen, grabbed her, jerked her around and shook her violently.

'Damn you,' he said, 'I'm *proposing* to you! I've never proposed to any other woman in my life, and I sure as hell am not going to have *you* say "bullshit" to me when I *mean* it!'

She blinked with confusion.

'You mean . . . you really *do* mean it?'

'Jesus Christ . . .' He rolled his eyes to the ceiling with frustration, then shook her again, hard. *'Yes!'*

At which point, he kissed her. Hard. Passionately.

'Oh Nick,' she whispered as she hugged him. 'You big, beautiful, blond *bastard* . . . I accept!'

They were married July 7, 1940, and she wore a bridal gown she designed herself which everyone agreed was one of the most beautiful bridal gowns Los Angeles had ever seen. She was given away by her uncle Morris, and the gala reception was held at Casa del Mar. Her uncle Drew and aunt Millie were not invited to the wedding.

Lieutenant (j.g.) and Mrs. Nicholas Kemp honeymooned at the Bella Vista Hotel in Acapulco. On their wedding night, they make love four times. The next morning the bridegroom got a case of Montezuma's Revenge—this time real—but was cured by afternoon. They were both deliriously happy, and the bellboys agreed they had never seen two people more in love.

In August, 1940, Gabriella told Nick she was pregnant. She

448

delivered him a son the following April. She insisted on naming him Nicholas Victor Kemp, for her beloved husband and her grandfather.

In December of that year, the Japanese attacked Pearl Harbor.

PART XI

WAR

1942

CHAPTER 49

President Roosevelt was eating an apple and sorting some new specimens for his stamp collection when he was informed of the attack on Pearl Harbor. He immediately placed the Navy on a war footing. It was 1:47 P.M., White House time. At dawn the next day, Japanese time, five hundred Japanese soldiers waded ashore on the rocky beach at Basco, the chief village on Bataan Island, 140 miles north of Luzon, the northernmost island of the Philippine archipelago. It was the beginning of the Japanese conquest of the Philippines.

Letter from Lieutenant (j.g.) Nicholas Kempt to his wife.

Manila. Dec. 23, 1941

My darling Gabriella:
  I'd sure as hell like to report some good news, but unfortunately it's all bad and getting worse. The Japs attacked Luzon yesterday, which we knew was coming. They've been bombing Baguio for two weeks—that's the summer capital of the Philippines north of Manila—and they landed at Lingayen Gulf, which is just west of Baguio. I've only been in Manila ten days, and am barely learning my way around, but it doesn't look as if we're going to stay in Manila long. The Japs are already marching south and they'll probably be here in a couple of weeks—there's very little resistance being put up by our side, which is probably inevitable, considering that we're hopelessly outnumbered and most of the Filipino troops are green. Rumor has it that MacArthur wants to pull us all—Americans, Filipino troops and Quezon—back to the Bataan peninsula, which sticks out into Manila Bay west of here, there I suppose to try and make some sort of last stand until we can get reinforce-

453

ments. I don't know, maybe it will work. But there's nothing around here right now to get very optimistic about. Everyone is panicked. They say Quezon, who's the head of the Philippine Government and an old buddy of MacArthur's, tried to send a message to the Japanese to make a deal with them. So much for old buddies! MacArthur's furious with him.

'Shortie' Long may be head of Naval Intelligence here, but my boss doesn't know much more about what's going on than anyone else, including yours truly. All I've been doing is burning codes and packing up important file papers. Well, I guess I can't bitch too much. The Navy's my career, and war is what the Navy's all about.

How's Junior? Does he miss his daddy? Probably not, but his daddy sure as hell misses him. I haven't got any wet diapers to change anymore! Honest to God, I never thought I'd miss *that*, but I do. Give him an extra kiss for me. How's Chez Gabriella? Now that we're in a war, is anyone still buying clothes?

Most of all, I miss you, my darling. And I want you to keep a level head during this mess. Things aren't looking good, and the Japs seem to be a lot better at fighting than we thought. I guess we're going to have to change some of our ideas about white men being the best soldiers and everyone else not quite measuring up. But anyway, old Nick can take care of himself, and I don't want you worrying. Even if things get hairier than they are now, keep your spirits up, my sweet love. Then when we're together again after the war, I'll bore you and all our friends with my war stories.

I love you, sweetheart, and send you a big, hot kiss in this envelope.

> Ever yours, my darling,
> Nick

'Have you heard from Nick, darling?' asked Erica Stern, who had just returned from a month-long U.S.O. tour. She was standing in front of a mirror at Chez Gabriella as Gabriella and Rosita fitted a gray suit on her.

'No,' Gabriella answered, taking the pins out of her mouth. 'The last letter I got from him was dated December twenty-third.'

'My God, that's over three months ago! They can't get mail out?'

'How can they? They're holed up on Bataan.'

454

'Poor darling, I know you're worried . . .'

'He's going to be all right,' she said, quietly. 'Nick's going to be all right.'

She had said it to herself so many times during the past three months that it had become almost a prayer or litany, the constant repetition of which numbed her panic. That and hard work and her baby were all that were keeping her from falling apart. Nick's orders to be transferred to Manila had come through before Pearl Harbor, but even then there had been no question of Gabriella's going out with him. The situation in the Far East vis-à-via Japan was too tense to allow officers' wives to accompany them, even though MacArthur had refused to send the American wives and children already stationed in the Philippines home for fear of panicking the Filipinos. She had given up the small house they had shared on the San Diego Naval Base since their marriage and returned to her apartment in Brentwood. Living in San Diego and trying to run Chez Gabriella simultaneously had been awkward, but Gabriella had insisted on being with her husband and solved the logistics neatly, if expensively, by flying up to L.A. four days a week to work, returning each night in time to share dinner and bed with Nick.

And now, Bataan. Corregidor. The collapse of Malaya, Singapore, Hong Kong. The Japs in the Pacific were looking as invincible as the Germans in Europe. Los Angeles was in a tense state of panic, hardly a day passing without rumors that a Japanese submarine had been spotted off Malibu or that the Japanese Air Force was about to bomb M.G.M. It was more than a little crazy. But the worst for Gabriella was the lack of news. Keep a level head, he had written her. But how level-headed could she be when she had nightmares of Nick being captured? Or worse . . .

He's going to be all right, she repeated in her mind as she finished fitting Erica's suit. He's going to be all right.

But if only she *knew* . . . If only he could get word out . . .

The first Japanese to arrive in the town of Mariveles came in by truck at noon, April 9, 1942, and they seemed friendly enough. Mariveles was a small coastal town at the southern tip of the Bataan peninsula, from which MacArthur had embarked with as many of his Filamerican forces as he had room for to the tiny, polliwog-shaped island of Corregidor. Three weeks before, he and his wife and their four-year-old son, Arthur, had fled from Corregidor in a PT boat under cover of darkness, leaving

General Wainwright in overall command. Wainwright had ordered the forces still left on Bataan to continue fighting to the death, but Major General King, in command of the 70,000 men left on the mainland and knowing that his forces were too weak and underequipped to inflict any real damage on the Japanese, decided to disobey the order. At nine that morning—ironically, the seventy-seventh anniversary of Lee's surrender to Grant at Appomattox—King had surrendered unconditionally to the senior Japanese operations officer, Colonel Motoo Nakayama, at an experimental farm station at Lamao. When asked by King if his troops would be well treated, Nakayama curtly answered, 'We are not barbarians.' Then King, having left his saber in Manila, surrendered his pistol instead.

Nick had volunteered to remain on the mainland to help fight the Japanese. It was no act of bravery in his eyes: He assumed that it was only a matter of time before Corregidor would fall as well, and meanwhile he could be of some use rather than holing up in a cave on the small offshore island. But now, exhausted, filthy, sitting under a palm tree in Mariveles's main square watching the Japanese climb out of their trucks, he wondered what use any resistance had been. As much as he loved his country, he was as savagely bitter as the other 'Battling Bastards of Bataan' at what they considered their betrayal on the part of Washington. Where were the reinforcements, where were the planes and ships and guns and food and medical supplies they so desperately needed to stave off the hordes of Japanese who had swarmed down the island, conquering the American dependency in a matter of weeks? Did anyone in Washington give a damn whether they lived or died? Did Roosevelt give a damn whether the American flag was pulled down in front of the High Commissioner's house in Manila and replaced by the Rising Sun?

'Look at the bastards grin,' muttered Sergeant Tom Reed, a thirty-seven-year-old career Marine from Kalamazoo, Michigan, who was sitting next to Nick under the palm tree.

'They have a lot to grin about,' replied Nick. 'They won.'

'Shit. They may have won, but they're not going to win any beauty contest. Look at that one over there. He's just out of a fucking tree.'

The captain in question was indeed extremely ugly, with bowlegs, buck teeth and thick glasses—almost a caricature of a 'Nip.' Now he started shouting in bad English to the dozens of Americans sprawled in the palm tree- and frangipani-filled park

456

in the center of the town. 'You will form formation here, please. Hurry up, please. Form formation. Thank you.'

The weary, sweat-soaked Americans slowly got to their feet. It was the Thursday after the first wartime Easter, and it was blazing hot and terribly muggy. The men hadn't changed uniforms in weeks, and since at least a third of them were suffering from dysentery, the general stench was formidable. Now they limped out of the park and lined up in the street. The Japanese captain climbed on a truck to be seen. None of his troops made any hostile gesture. So far, thought Nick, not bad.

'My name is Captain Yamashita,' yelled the captain. 'You are to be advised that your General King surrendered unconditionally this morning to the Emperor of Japan. You are all now our prisoners. Our commanding officer, Lieutenant General Masaharu Homma, has ordered that all prisoners will be marched immediately northward to the town of Balanga. We will spend the night there, then tomorrow some of you will be driven by truck to San Fernando, others will march. From San Fernando you will be taken by train to Capas, then marched to Camp O'Donnell, where you will be kept until America sues for peace.'

'What if America wins?' shouted one Marine.

Captain Yamashita started giggling. Then he turned and yelled to his men in Japanese. They broke into laughter and catcalls.

'How can America win?' replied Yamashita, still grinning. 'The Japanese have taken over all the Pacific!'

The Americans looked at each other and shrugged.

'Do we get some food?' yelled another. 'Balanga's nineteen miles from here.'

'Food when you get to Balanga,' replied Yamashita. 'All right: move out, please. Let's go.'

'Ret's go,' said Nick, mimicking Yamashita's lallation.

'Move out, prease,' echoed Tom Reed.

'I hope he's not serious about marching us all the way to Balanga today. I sure as hell can't walk nineteen miles.'

'I think he's serious,' said Reed. 'The Nips are better walkers than we are. Nineteen miles is a stroll for them.'

Looking at his exhausted comrades, Nick Kemp hoped Reed was wrong. But he wasn't. The plan to march and transport the American and Filipino prisoners from Mariveles to Camp O'Donnell, a total distance of ninety miles, had been recommended to General Homma by his transportation officer, Major General Yoshikata Kawane, who had suggested the Americans

457

be fed the same rations as the Japanese troops. Furthermore, he had told Homma that field hospitals for the sick and wounded were being set up at Balanga and San Fernando, a major rail center.

Homma had approved the plan, being under the impression there were no more than 25,000 prisoners. In fact, there were 76,000 prisoners, and the Americans and Filipinos were already starving and decimated by malaria, beriberi and dysentery. Furthermore, hospital facilities were nonexistent.

Thus began the infamous Death March of Bataan.

What Nick couldn't understand at first was the apparently casual attitude of the Japanese guards. Some of the American prisoners were sent north on foot from Mariveles with no guards at all. Others, including Nick and Reed, were put under relatively heavy guard. Additionally, some of the Japanese, like Captain Yamashita, seemed friendly enough. Others burst into savage attacks against the Americans at the slightest provocation. Less than an hour after the hundred Americans in Nick's group started the long march north to Balanga, one of them spotted an artesian well by the side of the dirt road and broke ranks to get a drink. Screaming at him in furious Japanese, one of the guards swung his rifle butt and bashed his skull. The American fell to the road, unconscious.

'Shit,' said Nick, starting toward the guard. Reed grabbed his arm.

'Stay out of it,' he said.

'Fuck that! We're prisoners of war, not goddam animals!'

Jerking his arm away from Reed, he ran up to the guard, who was shouting at the unconscious American.

'Did you ever hear of the Red Cross?' yelled Nick. 'Red Cross,' he repeated, forming a cross with his fingers. 'Geneva Convention?'

The Japanese was staring at him. Now he raised his rifle and aimed it at Nick's chest. He spouted something in Japanese, obviously a warning to return to the ranks. Nick stared at the bayonet, then looked at the American. He was facedown in the dirt, the back of his head matted with blood. The other prisoners had stopped to watch. Nick looked around for Captain Yamashita, but he was nowhere in sight. He felt the bayonet jab against his chest, heard the Japanese shouting at him again. Giving up, he went back to the line of prisoners.

'They never heard of no Geneva Convention,' said Reed.

'And if they did, they've conveniently forgotten it. Oh shit
—look!'

Nick turned back to see the guard kicking the American,
apparently yelling at him to get up. When the unconscious man
failed to respond, the Japanese angrily raised his bayonet, then
plunged it into his back. As the blood spurted up, Nick winced.

He was beginning to realize he was in the middle of a
nightmare.

The march continued. To the left of the Americans soared
Mount Bataan, to the right the aquamarine waters of Manila
Bay, but the natural beauty of the setting was fouled by the dust
sent up by the trucks filled with Japanese soldiers which began
appearing, bound south for Mariveles. Quickly the line became
an almost unbroken stream of trucks, tanks and Japanese
artillery which created so much dust that the air became almost
unbreathable. The troops in the trucks jeered at the defeated
Americans, and some of them swung bamboo poles at their
heads, knocking off dirty, sweat-stained caps and occasionally
whacking skulls.

'Fucking bastards,' growled Reed. 'They think it's a game.'

'Whatever it is, we're sure as hell not going to make Balanga
tonight.'

'Which means no food. Christ, I'm starving.'

In fact, everyone was starving, and the condition of the men
was rapidly deteriorating under the grueling conditions of the
march. By nightfall they had covered less than eight miles. The
guards commandeered a rice warehouse and herded the hundred
prisoners inside, allowing them one bowl of maggoty rice each
and one drink at a well before being locked up for the night. The
warehouse was packed and fetid with the stench of the men,
many of whom were now so riddled with dysentery that they
were fouling their pants. Nick, squatting in a corner next to Tom
Reed, removed his shoes, the soles of which were half gone, and
rubbed his swollen feet. Few men were talking, but Reed
whispered, 'Want a cigarette?'

'I don't smoke.'

'Good. I only got three left, and I'll go cold turkey before I
smoke Jap weeds.'

In the morning the prisoners were released from the stifling
warehouse, and they stumbled outside, gulping the fresh air into
their lungs. Then the miserable march continued. What few
restraints the guards exhibited the first day now seemed to have
vanished, as if their cockiness was growing as the physical
condition of their prisoners degenerated. Stragglers were sum-

marily executed: Nick counted six deaths in that morning alone, and the bodies were left by the roadside to swell in the sun. Nick was outraged, but he and the others put up no further resistance to their guards, since they realized resistance merely goaded the Japanese to more brutality. But as the day progressed and the sun dehydrated the already thirsty men—most of whom were further dehydrated by the pervasive dysentery—a sort of madness gripped many of them. Passing the artesian wells that frequently bordered the road, they broke ranks to run for a drink, knowing they were courting death to do so. Most of them were shot. With an exquisite refinement of sadism, however, at eleven o'clock the guards allowed the men to run into a farm and drink from a filthy carabao wallow. Some of them even drank the overflow of a privy. Although Nick and Reed were both maddened by thirst, a sense of self-preservation restrained them from joining in this suicidal cocktail hour. Luckily so, because within a few days most of the men who did were to die from hellish intestinal infections.

At noon the guards allowed the men a half-hour's rest, forcing them to sit in the road, however, rather than allowing them to seek the shade of the trees by the side of the road. Nor were they allowed to relieve themselves in the ditches. The Americans sat numbly under the brutal sun, many of them moaning from thirst or the terrible pains of the dysentery. When the march continued, Nick said to Reed, 'Christ, they're butchers.'

They had been walking about ten minutes when a Buick appeared on the road, heading south for Mariveles.

'Must be someone important,' said Reed. 'He's got a chauffeur.'

In fact, the four-door convertible with its top down looked important. A Japanese corporal drove, while in the back seat, stiffly erect, sat a single officer, a colonel, who was watching the prisoners as he drove slowly past.

'And look!' added Reed. 'The fucking Nips are bowing to him! Do you suppose it's Hirohito?'

'No, but you're not far off,' said Nick, recognizing the young officer in the back seat.

'Where are you going?' said Reed as Nick broke ranks and ran toward the car.

'I know him!' shouted Nick. He jumped on the running board. 'Asaka!' he exclaimed. 'It's me—Nick Kemp!'

Prince Asaka stared at him, then said something to his chauffeur in Japanese. The car stopped. Asaka again turned to look at the American. He barely recognized him. His once well-muscled 175-pound body had been starved down to 150 pounds, he was filthy, he hadn't shaved in three days, and the boiling sun had bleached his hair white.

'Whatever you think of me personally,' Nick was saying, 'you've got to tell these guards to stop treating us like animals! We're prisoners of war, and there *is* a Geneva Convention. Christ, they're starving us, shooting stragglers—last night they packed us in a rice warehouse . . . You're a cousin of the emperor: you can *do* something about this! Do you want Japan to lose face in front of the whole world?'

He heard shouts from down the road and turned to see one of the Americans run into a ditch, drop his pants and start to defecate as two guards screamed at him. Asaka raised his hand and said something in Japanese. The guards immediately shut up and bowed in his direction. Asaka looked at Nick.

'We meet, Mr. Kemp, under rather different circumstances than last time,' he said, quietly. Then he barked something at the chauffeur, who jumped out of the car, ran around the hood and opened the door. Nick watched as Asaka got out of the car. An officer's sword was on the back seat. Now the chauffeur reached in and handed it to Asaka, who attached it to his belt. Then he walked down the road to the American, who was still squatting in the ditch, passing his dysentery-rotted bowels. Asaka drew the sword. The Americans, the Japanese and Nick watched as the flies buzzed around the American's head.

'The guards,' Asaka said in a loud voice, 'told you not to break ranks.'

'I don't understand Japanese, you motherfucker,' shouted the American. 'And I've got the runs. Am I supposed to shit in my pants and smell like a Jap?'

Asaka grabbed the sword with both hands, swung it at the man and decapitated him. The action had been so swift and brutal, the Americans literally moaned with shock. Then the horrors of the past twenty-four hours burst their restraint. They started yelling at Asaka, who had handed his bloody sword to his chauffeur to clean. Asaka looked at the angry, shouting prisoners, then went up to one of the bowing guards. He spoke to him for almost a minute, glancing once at Nick. Then he turned to the prisoners. The guards aimed their rifles at the men, and the shouting died down to silence.

'Mr. Kemp,' said Asaka, 'whom I knew in America before the war, has just complained to me about your treatment. He mentioned the Geneva Convention. Let me explain to you that the Japanese soldier is trained to die for his country. For the

Japanese the worst disgrace is surrender. Any loyal Japanese would kill himself before surrendering. You have surrendered. Therefore, in the eyes of these guards, you are a disgrace to yourselves and to your country. They do not consider you prisoners of war, they consider you cowardly dogs. In their opinion they are doing you a favor if they kill you.'

'Some favor,' said one Marine.

'You have been warned,' retorted Asaka. Then he walked back to the car, followed by his chauffuer, who pushed Nick off the running board, then opened the door. Before getting in, Asaka looked at Nick.

'I hope I have answered your complaint satisfactorily, Mr. Kemp.'

He got in the car. The chauffeur closed the door, hurriedly jumped in the front, started the car and drove off. Nick watched the receding Buick through the dust cloud. Then, as two guards shouted at him, he limped back into the line and the march continued.

'Who the hell was that?' asked Reed.

'His name is Prince Asaka, and he's one of Hirohito's cousins.'

'No shit?'

'Plenty of shit. He and I were involved in a little spy caper a couple of years ago in L.A.'

'What sort of spy caper?'

Nick told him.

'Then why did the F.B.I. let him go back to Japan if he was trying to buy classified material?'

'Because he was the emperor's cousin, and things were sticky enough between Japan and America then without offending the imperial family. You saw the way the guards bowed to him. He's a big deal here. These creeps think Hirohito's a genuine god, so any member of his family is one of God's relatives. Washington decided it wasn't worth it to put God's cousin on trial for espionage. So, here he is, in his Buick. And here am I, with the trots.'

'You got it bad?'

'It's getting worse.'

'Your Jap friend's got a sure cure for it.'

It soon became apparent to Nick that Asaka had instructed the guards to single him out for humiliation, if not death, because from now on they periodically shouted and jeered at him. But even worse, when the exhausted Americans were halted for the night, Nick was refused water and food. He was so weak from dysentery that he probably wouldn't have been able to retain the disgusting *lugao*, a rice mush that tasted like paste, that was the second evening's meal. But this was little compensation to a man who was starving, and when the guards pushed him away from the solitary spigot, he was so crazed with thirst he almost burst into tears. Tom Reed tried to bring him a cup of water, but one of the guards spotted him and knocked it out of his hand, spilling the precious stuff on the ground. Nick threw himself on the grass and tried to lick the moisture with his swelling tongue, but he was kicked away by shouting guards. On this night the men were locked in a barbed-wire-enclosed compound that had been used the night before by another group of prisoners and was literally a swamp of human feces. A billion mosquitoes were swarming in the air as maggots swarmed in the earth. The stench was so foul that Nick hated to breathe. Reed made his way with difficulty through the packed bodies to find Nick huddling by the barbed wire.

'Why didn't they give you any food—if you can call that crap food?' he asked, squatting by his friend.

'I think Asaka told them to starve me to get back at me for what I did to him in L.A.'

'The slanty-eyed fucks. You gonna make it?'

'Sure. Don't worry about me.'

'Don't give me any of this hero shit, Lieutenant. You don't look good.'

He didn't feel good.

That night he dreamed that he and Gabriella were walking down an empty California beach. The surf was coming in in lazy rolls, and the soft spray blew in his face. They were holding hands when they reached a large rock. Prince Asaka stepped out from behind the rock. He was holding his sword. 'You humiliated me before my family,' he said, beginning to swing the sword at Nick's neck. The blade glistened in the sun as it swung in the slow motion of dreams.

Then he woke up, trembling with fever, drenched with sweat.

The next morning the march continued, but Nick was so exhausted from hunger, thirst and dysentery, he soon began stumbling. Reed tried to hold him up, whispering, 'Keep going! You know what they do to stragglers . . .'

'Let 'em do it,' he mumbled. 'I've had it.'

'No, goddammit! They'll shoot you!'

'I can't help it. I've got to rest . . .'

With his last remaining strength, he pushed Reed away, weaved out of the line and fell to the side of the road, rolling down into a ditch. There was some stagnant water in it, but at that point he didn't care what he drank. His throat was scorched. He crawled toward the water, his tongue out.

He heard the guards running toward him, shouting, but all he could think of was the water. Then, a horrible pain as the bayonet was plunged into his lower back. He knew he was dying now, and the knowledge that his torment would soon be over gave him an odd sense of peace. They grabbed him and turned him over on his bloody back, dropping him in the water. The pain seemed far away, unreal. He watched them prepare his execution through glazed eyes, almost as if he were out of his body, an objective observer. One of them plunged his bayonet into his right side. Nick twitched, felt more pain, felt his life pouring out of him. He was aware that one of the guards had fetched shovels. Now he felt a load of dirt fall on his stomach. The Japanese were chattering excitedly as they dug. Another load of dirt fell on his face.

He realized they were burying him alive in the ditch. He tried to sit up, tried to struggle, but he could no longer control his body. He gave up, and thought of his wife and son.

It took them almost ten minutes to cover him completely. Reed watched with numb horror as one of the Japanese plunged his bayonet into the dirt one final time.

Then guards returned to the road.

As the march continued, Reed took a look back at the grave of his friend. What he saw made him go almost crazy with rage.

Nick's right hand had pushed up out of the dirt. It groped at the sun for a moment.

Then it was still.

CHAPTER 50

Happy birthday to you,
Happy birthday to you,
Happy birthday dear Nickie,
Happy birthday to you!

Nicholas Victor Kemp burped happily as his mother and Great-aunt Barbara and Great-uncle Morris finished the song. Then Gabriella hugged and kissed him and put him back in his crib. They were all in the living room of Casa del Mar. Now, leaving the child in the care of Gabriella's Mexican nanny, Clarita, they went into the dining room for lunch.

'One year old and he's so big!' enthused Barbara. 'And getting so handsome.'

'He'll be a lady-killer like his father,' said Morris, holding his wife's chair. 'Gabriella, I'll never forget that night you asked Nick here for that party we gave Erica. You took one look at him and practically drooled with your eyes.'

'It was love at first sight,' she smiled. 'That was a nice evening.'

'Not so nice when I think I actually entertained that *shmuck* of a Jap prince,' said Morris, passing the large Monet as he went to the opposite end of the table to take his seat.

'Now Morris,' said Barbara, 'let's not talk about the war.'

'No, that's all right,' said Gabriella, unfolding her napkin. 'I don't mind talking about it.'

'What's to talk about?' said Morris. 'Everything's going lousy. I'm thinking about making a wartime comedy just to cheer everybody up.'

'Maybe a musical based on Pearl Harbor?' said his wife, drily.

'Why not do a wartime love story?' said Gabriella. 'Girl

meets sailor, girl loses sailor . . .' she hesitated, then forced a smile. 'Then girl gets sailor back.'

Her aunt looked at her compassionately.

'That would be the nicest happy ending of all,' she said.

'And it's going to happen,' said Gabriella. 'I know it's going to happen.'

The butler served the chicken.

The man standing in Chez Gabriella was extremely tall and slim, and his hair was just starting to turn silver-gray. Gabriella thought he must be in his early forties as she examined the card he had just handed her. It read:

> ABRAHAM S. FELDMAN
> President
> Summit Fashions, Inc.
> New York, New York

'Perhaps you've heard of me?' asked the man, who spoke softly and precisely with no hint of an identifiable accent. He had saturnine good looks, with an extremely long and narrow nose, bushy black eyebrows over piercing brown eyes and a thin gash of a mouth; his face was heavily tanned. His elegant double-breasted dark blue suit, as well as his shirt, were custom made. She guessed his black shoes came from prewar London.

'Yes, I've heard of you, Mr. Feldman,' she replied, pocketing the card. Lucrezia came back into the boutique from the workroom. It was pouring rain in Los Angeles, and business was off; the shop was empty. 'Most people in the clothing business have heard of you. What can I do for you?'

'Come to lunch with me.'

'That's very kind of you, but I'm terribly busy right now. Besides, I hardly ever eat lunch. Being a natural fatty, I'm on a perpetual diet.'

Feldman eyed her well-governed figure with admiration.

'You can have a salad,' he said. 'I think you should accept this invitation. I have an offer which could make you several million dollars.'

This, coming from a man who had parlayed a Depression bucketshop operation into a dress company doing twenty million dollars a year's worth of business, was not to be taken lightly.

'Just a minute,' said Gabriella, heading toward the workroom. 'I'll get my hat.'

While he was waiting for Gabriella, Abe Feldman quietly propositioned Lucrezia, who quietly declined.

He was staying only two blocks away at the Beverly Wilshire, but his rented limousine had driven him to the shop. 'I hate umbrellas,' he explained, as the chauffeur held the door with one hand and the hated umbrella with the other, and they climbed into the back seat. Once ensconced, Feldman eased back in the seat as if limousines were his natural habitat. 'We'll eat at the hotel,' he said. 'It's close.'

After they were seated in the restaurant, he ordered a martini and Gabriella a glass of soda water. 'My wife,' he said, 'tells me you're the most exciting young designer in the country right now, and she's got a good eye. I've been out here a week. I've seen some of your dresses at parties, and I agree with my wife. You're good, and I hate to give out compliments. I'd like you to work for me.'

'I'm flattered, Mr. Feldman, but I'm happy the way I am. Small and independent. I sell everything I turn out, and I'm making a very handsome living at it.'

'I knew you'd say that. By the way, I'm Abe. I hope I can call you Gaby?'

'No you can't. I hate "Gaby." It sounds like that old coot of a cowboy, Gabby Hayes. I'm Gabriella.'

'All right, Gabriella. Cigarette?'

He had pulled a chased-gold case from his jacket. She estimated it cost $300 at Cartier.

'No thanks. I don't smoke. It's a filthy habit.'

'I can see you're a woman of strong opinions. Mind if I smoke?'

'No, but you ought to give it up.'

He smiled as he lit a Chesterfield.

'You're probably right. Anyway, hear me out, even if you're not interested.' He exhaled. 'America may be in a helluva mess with this war right now, but Americans have money in their pockets for the first time since '29. I mean real, spendable, blowable money. Women are working hard in the factories, and when they get off work, they're on a shopping spree. I think you'll believe me when I say we can barely supply the demand. Our big problem is not how to sell our dresses, but how to get material to make them.'

'That I can believe.'

'The point is, business if fantastic. Now, I built Summit on the working girl, the secretaries, shop assistants, the Rosie the Riveters. They'll always be the basis of my business. But I envision a continued boom after the war is over—something like the Twenties after the last war—and the secretaries and shopgirls who bought my cheap stuff in the past will be older and richer and they'll want to buy up. Okay, that's our Miss Dorothy line. Ten- to fifteen-dollar dresses, maybe as high as twenty-five or thirty. But that's still a far cry from Chanel.'

'You might say.' While she was listening intently to what he was saying, part of her mind was idly comparing him with Nick. How different the two men were. How lucky this smoothie was to be too old for the draft—or maybe he wasn't too old but had some cockamamie excuse like flat feet—while her Nick was . . . where? Half the globe away. Half the globe was in an upheaval of bloody carnage, empires were falling, and here sat Abe Feldman in a fashionable Beverly Hills restaurant, talking about his Miss Dorothy line and getting richer with each discreet tick of his Cartier wristwatch.

'Of course, Chanel is in an entirely different league from us,' he went on, sipping his martini, 'and if there's any Paris left after the war, I have no doubt that the couture houses will start booming again. But there's no reason Paris has to have a monopoly on high fashion. There's no reason America couldn't produce couture clothes, too.

'What I'm getting at is, I want to create a prestige line for Summit. I want to jump in now while the war has knocked Paris out of the picture, at least temporarily. I want to fill the high fashion gap. I'm willing to spend big money to make it work, but I don't care if it loses money because the prestige will rub off on all Summit products. I'm talking about big ad campaigns in *Vogue* and *Harper's*. The Chez Gabriella line will be everything from sportswear to evening dresses, just as you're doing here, and it will all be first-class. The best design, the most exciting ideas, the best fabrics. And once we've got them buying our clothes, we might branch into fragrances, cosmetics . . . There's no end to what we *could* do, given the financial backing, the right promotional approach, and, of course, you. Or someone like you. What do you think so far?'

She sipped her soda water.

'No one could ever accuse you of not thinking big.'

He smiled, and she admired his teeth. Caps, but a good job. Not natural, like Nick's beautiful teeth. Caps . . . That was the difference, she thought. Nick was all natural. This guy is all manufactured. But still, it's a staggering idea.

'As the ad guys say, it's a huge concept. I'm still waiting for your reaction.'

'What would I do? And how would I get paid?'

'I like you. You cut the cr . . .' he started to say 'crap' but quickly substituted '. . . superfluous. All right, what you do: you run the whole show—with me, of course. Design, promotion, quality control. I'd give you all the staff you need, and I'd give you the best. I'm a tight man with a buck, but with this I'm ready to throw the money around. How you get paid? That's simple. Once we sign a contract, I'll give you ten thousand shares of Summit Preferred, which at yesterday's close on the Amex was selling at eleven dollars. I'll give you stock options that within five years will make you a multimillionairess . . .'

'That is,' she interrupted, 'if Summit is still making money. You're Summit, Mr. Feldman . . .'

'Abe.'

'All right, Abe. What if you drop dead? I'd end up holding a lot of worthless paper.'

He shrugged.

'The Japs might win the war, too.'

'What about cash?'

'How old are you?'

'Twenty-two.'

'How did you get so tough so young?'

'I come from a tough family. How about cash?'

'You'd have a salary of thirty thousand a year . . .'

'I'm making more than that now.'

'All right, thirty-five.'

'Keep going.'

He hesitated.

'Forty?' he asked.

'That sounds better.'

The waiter handed them the enormous, California-style menus.

'So, what do you think?' asked Abe. 'Interested?'

'I'll think about it.'

'I'd like a go-ahead commitment from you by the time I leave for New York, which is Sunday. Not a final commitment, but a commitment for further discussion. I'm eager to get the ball rolling. Not to sound unpatriotic, but if the Germans collapse, which doesn't look likely soon, and Paris gets back in the haute-couture business, our advantage is shot. And gearing this up is going to take at least a year.'

'That *does* sound unpatriotic—unpatriotic as all hell—but I'll give you an answer by Sunday.'

'Good. They've got a dieter's salad on the menu . . .'

'I'll just take a dish of cottage cheese, thanks.'

'Well, at least your expense-account lunches should be cheap. Chicken salad for me, and cottage cheese for Mrs. Kemp.'

The waiter removed the menus and himself. Abe lit another cigarette and looked at her.

'I understand,' he said, 'that your husband is missing in action.'

She slowly twisted her soda glass.

'Yes. We don't know where he is, but we're assuming he's been taken prisoner. The Japanese aren't issuing prisoner lists yet. Washington knows nothing.'

'I'm sorry to hear it. I, uh, assume there would be no interference with your work if . . .'

'You mean if he didn't come back? That's not going to happen. He *is* going to come back. I don't even entertain the possibility that he won't.'

'I'm talking about investing a lot of money in you, Gabriella. So I'm going to have to ask you to think about the possibility.'

She kept her eyes on her glass. Nick, Nick . . . Here I sit talking possible million-dollar deals in this posh restaurant, and where in God's name are you? Are you suffering, my darling? Am I betraying you because I'm not suffering the way you are? What are they doing to you? Oh Jesus, where *are* you?

'If,' she said finally, 'my husband were killed, I couldn't guarantee what my emotional stability would be. I love him more than myself. And since I've got a certain amount of ego these days, that may give you some idea of what I think about him. If something happened to Nick, I'm not sure I'd want to go on living. Perhaps I would. Perhaps I'd get over it some day. But I couldn't guarantee it. So perhaps I'm not the person you're looking for after all. Do you want to retract your offer?'

She looked at him and he studied her. He liked what he saw and heard. He liked it a lot. She was a winner, there was no doubt about it. He could sniff it, and his sniffer was seldom wrong. She could make his wild dream work. He felt it in his bones.

But there was that goddam husband. He'd heard the story, how she had fallen for him like a ton of bricks, how she had never even looked at another man . . . Women, he thought. Goddam cunts with their stupid emotional hangups . . . Yet woman were his business, they had made him rich. This one could make him richer.

'Maybe I'll think about it, too,' he said. 'We'll both think. Then we'll talk Sunday.'

'Fair enough.'

'Meanwhile, will you go to bed with me this afternoon?'

She stiffened.

'If that's a joke, it's a rotten one.'

'It's no joke. Will you?'

She stood up and picked her purse off the table.

'You crude, money-grubbing, unpatriotic son of a bitch,' she said, not so softly. 'You can take your top-of-the-line business deal and shove it up your furry ass.'

As she stormed out of the restaurant, he finished his martini. She'll be back, he thought. That's one smart broad. She knows I'm offering her the deal of a lifetime.

She'll be back.

Abe Feldman had learned in the Seventh Avenue jungle that the best basis for a partnership was not mutual trust, but mutual loathing.

When Gabriella returned to the shop, dripping wet from the rain, she ran through the curtains into the workroom and burst into tears. Rosita looked up from her sewing.

'Senora, *que pasa?*' she exclaimed.

'It's nothing,' she sobbed. 'Nothing. Don't pay any attention to me.'

She wasn't crying because of Abe Feldman's insulting proposal. She was crying because of personal guilt.

As much as she missed Nick, as much as she spent anxiety-racked nights worrying about him, as much as she longed for the touch of his strong, warm body, as much as she was starved for his lovemaking, for one brief second she had been tempted to go to bed with Abe Feldman.

At nine o'clock the next Sunday morning, she was feeding Nick, Jr., in the kitchen of her Brentwood Apartment when the phone rang.

'Hello?'

'Gabriella, it's Abe Feldman. Are you still talking to me?' He sounded brusque and slightly defensive.

'My lawyer's talking to you for me,' she replied. 'His name's George Kalkbrenner of Kalkbrenner, Rice and Whitman. If you're willing to gamble on my emotional stability, talk to George Kalkbrenner.'

'I know him. He's a tough son of a bitch.'

'And what are you? If you two can work out a contract, I'll sign. Maybe. Meanwhile we have nothing to say to each other.'

He laughed.

'You're one tough broad. I like you. So we're in business?'

'Maybe. I ought to have my head examined even talking to you, you insulting creep.'

'Someday you *will* go to bed with me.'

'I'd rather go to bed with Adolf Hitler.'

She slammed down the phone. After she had finished feeding Nick, she put him in his crib and went into her bathroom to shower. As she soaped her body, again, as always, her thoughts reverted to her husband. She wanted him with every fiber of her body. It disturbed her how much her thoughts dwelt on sex recently, how she was beginning to look at men not even half as desirable as her beloved Nick, how she could even *think* of going to bed with Abe Feldman . . .

Nick, Nick, Nick . . .

She leaned against the tile wall of the shower, let the hot water cascade over her body, and pressed her hand against her vagina.

Her body sizzled with desire. She cringed with shame as she admitted to herself that she wanted a man. Not just Nick, but any man.

Oh Nick, her mind screamed, come home to me soon before I go crazy! I need you, my darling. Oh God, how I need you! Come home to me, Nick . . . soon . . .

God*dam* this stupid, rotten war!

CHAPTER 51

The negotiations between her lawyers and Abe's dragged on for weeks. Meanwhile she found out more about his private life. His wife of twelve years, Marcia, was attractive, well-dressed and, from all accounts, respectable. They had two sons in private school and a big house in Scarsdale. Abe was not respectable. He was known 'to lay everything in sight.' After his propositioning her at their first meeting, she asked herself over and over if she wanted to be in business with a man like this. Yet the attractions of the deal were so overwhelming, she kept answering, could she afford *not* to be in business with him?

One hot Sunday in July, she was spending the morning in her aunt Barbara's swimming pool. She was dunking Nick, Jr., in the water when she saw her aunt come out of the house and start for the pool. Nick was giggling and splashing his mother, who was laughing.

'Oh, you're a real bully, aren't you?' she said. 'The menace of the swimming-pool set. I'll teach you!'

And she dunked him again, bringing him back up out of the water to kiss him. He was loving it.

'Gabriella.'

'Aren't you coming for a swim?' she asked her aunt, who looked stunning in a pair of slacks and blouse Gabriella had made for her. Barbara David was one of her niece's best customers.

'A little later, darling. Could you come out of the pool? There's something I have to tell you.'

She knew then. She could tell from her aunt's face and tone. She hugged her naked baby even tighter as she waded to the pool steps and climbed out.

'Be brave, darling,' she whispered in his pink ear, but the words were meant for herself. She kissed Nick, then put him down on the grass, where he started crawling after a fat robin.

She looked at her aunt, who said, 'We just got a telegram.'

'Is it about Nick?' she asked, quietly.

'Yes, and . . . I'm afraid it's not good.' She pulled the telegram from her pocket and handed it to her. Gabriella was still dripping, but she took the piece of paper and unfolded it. 'We regret to inform you . . .'

She read it twice, then sat down on one of the pool chairs. Numbly she started drying her face. She had dreaded this moment for so long that it didn't seem real. She put down the towel and looked at her aunt again.

'There's not even a body,' she said finally. 'He was buried in a . . . ditch . . .'

'I'm so sorry, my darling,' said her aunt. 'I don't know what else to say except I'm so sorry.'

'Oh, Aunt Barbara,' she said, starting to cry. 'Oh God, oh my Nick, my love . . .'

Her aunt knelt beside her and hugged her, getting pool water all over her blouse.

'It's not fair,' she was sobbing. 'Everone I love . . . Momma and Poppa and Grandfather and Grandmother . . . and now Nick . . . Oh Jesus, it's not fair. It's not fair . . .'

'He died a hero . . .'

'Do you think I *care?* No, that's not true . . . I'm proud of him, but oh my God, to lose him! *Him!* Oh Jesus, Jesus . . .'

Barbara David could hear her niece's heart cracking, and it cracked her own as well.

Gabriella was a Catholic, albeit an admittedly lazy one of late, for which now, in her shock, she was feeling guilt. But Nick had been an Episcopalian, and his parents phoned her from New York that they wanted the memorial service to be held in their family church, St. Thomas, on Fifth Avenue. Nick had married Gabriella in the Catholic Church, which had caused a good deal of grumbling and ill-will on his parents' part, so now Gabriella felt she had no choice but to agree to her in-laws' request. He had been theirs too, after all, and besides, they had seen Nick, Jr., only once. So she packed her bag. Her aunt Barbara offered to go with her, which offer she happily accepted. She had come to love her like her own mother, and now, in this most difficult time of her life, she wanted her company. She was afraid to be alone with her grief.

They took a drawing room on the Super Chief to Chicago, and as the elegant train sped across the deserts and wheatfields of the

West and Midwest, she tried to think out her life and her future without Nick.

'I think,' she said to her aunt, 'I'll have to leave Los Angeles.'

'Because Abe Feldman wants you in New York?'

'No, I wouldn't move for him. To hell with him. And it's not the memories in Los Angeles. After all, the little time I had with Nick we were in San Diego most of the time. I just think . . . I don't know. I've always thought of New York as my home, even though I've been practically a gypsy most of my life. And right now, well, I guess when you really get hurt, you want to crawl home and lick your wounds.'

'I can understand that, but I hope you change your mind. Morris and I would miss you dreadfully.'

'And I'll miss you. You're practically my only family left anymore. I don't know . . . I'm so confused right now.'

'What about Chez Gabriella?'

She shrugged.

'I don't know.'

'And what about the deal with Abe Feldman? Isn't that almost ready to be signed?'

'Yes, but I don't know if I want anything to do with him. I'm not even sure I want to keep on designing.'

'Oh darling, you must! You're too talented to give it up! Besides, the work will keep you going.'

'Yes, I suppose. Except right now everything seems so empty. He was the excitement in my life. And now he's gone.'

She stared out the window as the train roared by a country crossing, where an old woman driving a battered, dusty Ford was watching the Super Chief. Hello, old woman, Gabriella thought. Were you ever young? Did you ever have a lover? Did you ever lose a lover?

Oh God, she thought. It hurts so, inside. It hurts so . . .

At the memorial service, they played his favorite hymn, *Jerusalem*. She mumbled the unfamiliar words and hid from the world behind her black veil. She held her baby son in her arms during the memorial address. He would never know his own father. Would he care? Ten or twenty years from now, would his dead father be nothing to him except old photos? The wives and children who had lost husbands and fathers in the First World War—did they remember now? And if not, what an insane sacrifice their men had made. And for what? A march on Memorial Day? Is that what Nick has died for?

Oh God, don't think *that*. He died a hero. Wasn't that what the minister was saying? Except what the hell does *he* know about it?

Oh Nick, sweet, beautiful Nick. My sweet love. I'll never see you again except in my memory.

She remembered how handsome he had looked in his white uniform and how warm his body felt beside her in bed, and she cursed God.

Life went on. Inevitably. She knew she had to keep on designing, if for no other reason than the grimly practical one that she needed the money. She had paid back $10,000 of the $25,000 loan from her Uncle Morris, but she still owed him, she had commitments, she had Rosita and Lucrezia depending on her, she had her customers. She had Nick, Jr.

She locked her private grief inside her, took a deep breath and rejoined the living. She found a charming apartment on Washington Mews in Greenwich Village, but kept her Brentwood apartment also, realizing she would be traveling to the coast often. She interviewed seven nannies before finding one she liked and trusted, an English refugee named Annabel Roberts. She signed the agreement with Abe Feldman and began work at his office on a blazing-hot June day in 1942.

With a cynicism born of despair, she told herself life had knocked her around enough. From now on she was going to knock life around.

She was going to make Chez Gabriella, Inc., the greatest success in America. —

PART XII

THE ETERNAL CITY

1943–1944

CHAPTER 52

On December 17, 1943, Fausto Spada parked his car in front of his father-in-law's jewelry store on the via Condotti. He had no difficulty finding a parking space because there was no gasoline available in German-occupied Rome except for official vehicles, or for people like Fausto who had connections with the Fascist hierarchy. Even bicycles had been banned because a partisan on a bicycle had tossed a bomb at some German soldiers the previous week. Rome had returned to what he remembered when he was a boy: a city of pedestrians with a few antique horse-drawn carriages.

Fausto walked into Paolo's store. Inside the elegant boutique, time also seemed to have stood still. The aging salesmen still wore striped pants and cutaways, for all the world as if the last, bloody battles of this incredibly bloody war weren't being fought a hundred kilometers south of Rome as the Germans, with surprising ferocity, stalemated the invading English and Americans. The salesmen nodded at Fausto as he went into his father-in-law's office. Paolo, now in his eighties, looked up.

'Fausto! How nice to see you . . .' he began.

'How fast can you get your important jewelry in a suitcase?' interrupted Fausto, closing the door behind him.

'Why—?'

'The Germans will be here in a half hour to arrest you and confiscate everything in the store. I was just tipped off by a friend of mine at police headquarters. So hurry! I'll take you in my car to the Vatican. You'll be safe there. Tony will take care of you.'

Paolo remained calm.

'So it's finally happened,' he said. 'Well, I knew it was coming.'

He took four leather pouches from his desk drawer, then put on his overcoat and went out of his office. Fausto followed him.

He watched as he said something to one of the salesmen. Then he followed him to the vault.

'I told them to take the jewelry in the cases and go home,' said Paolo. 'Why should the Germans have it? Besides, they'll need the jewelry to live on. I suppose I'll be in the Vatican for a long time?'

'Who knows? But hurry.'

'Yes, yes . . . don't rush me.'

He opened several steel drawers in the vault and took out necklaces, bracelets, rings, earrings, brooches. Fausto watched as the diamonds, rubies, emeralds and sapphires were slipped in the leather pouches.

'There must be a fortune there,' he commented.

'Maybe thirty million lire.'

When the bags were full, he locked the vault. The salesmen had left, having pulled down the blinds over the windows. One of them had scribbled 'Closed for Repairs' on a piece of cardboard and stuck it in the window. Paolo wrapped the bulging pouches in a newspaper. Sticking the bundle under his arm, he took one last look around at the store he had run for so many years. Then he said, 'Business has been bad anyway. Let's go.'

Five minutes after they pulled away from the curb, the Germans arrived.

His Holiness, Pope Pius XII, the former Cardinal Eugenio Pacelli, held up the diamond necklace and examined it in the light of his desk lamp in the papal office in the Apostolic Palace.

'It's magnificent,' he said to Cardinal Antonio Spada, who sat opposite him. 'How much do you think it's worth?'

Tony shifted uncomfortably in his seat. All his priestly life he had disliked the Church's quiet fascination with the material things of this world. Now was no exception.

'Signor Montecatini bought it three years ago from the Duchess of Sermoneta. He paid her then three million lire. It's probably worth more now.'

'Yes indeed, with everyone terrified of paper currency. And Signor Montecatini wishes to donate this to the Papal Treasury? How supremely generous of him! Naturally we would have offered him sanctuary anyway, but with this handsome gift, he is our honored guest. You will see to it that he is given comfortable quarters. My Lord Cardinal knows how the German racial policies against the Jews grieve us, and we will do everything in our power to protect the Italian Jews. But we can't give sanctuary to every Jew in Rome. How many do we have here now?'

'I believe it's almost a hundred, Holy Father.'

'Well, we have to be careful, or our resources will be severely strained. I think from now on we will have to be extremely selective about who we take in. The Germans, of course, are furious that we take *any*, and we must be *very* careful not to antagonize them further. But certainly any Jew as generous as Signor Montecatini will be given primary consideration. This large central diamond is particularly handsome, don't you think?'

'It is quite beautiful, Holy Father. There is something else I wish to bring to your attention, if I may.'

'Of course.'

'My brother, Fausto Spada, brought Signor Montecatini here. As you know, Fausto is out of favor with the Fascists, and he believes that by bringing his father-in-law here he has placed himself in a certain amount of jeopardy. He is afraid the Germans may confiscate our late mother's palazzo on the Corso, which there's nothing we can do about. But he has asked me if he can use the Vatican bank facilities to transfer a large sum of his cash to the Crédit Suisse in Zurich. The sum amounts to approximately sixty million lire. In return for this favor, he is prepared to offer the Church a five percent transfer fee as a gift.'

'I would gladly offer our facilities to your brother gratis—you know that. Make the transaction for him with my compliments, my Lord Cardinal.'

'The Holy Father is, as always, compassionate.'

Tony stood up. The Pope still held the diamond necklace and was still admiring the stones. After a moment, Tony said, quietly, 'Does the Holy Father wish to keep the necklace here in his office?'

'Oh . . . uh, no. Of course not. Take it to the treasury. And thank Signor Montecatini and your brother for their generosity. We will remember them both tonight in our prayers.'

'Thank you, Holy Father.'

Tony took the necklace and left.

'Tony,' said Fausto fifteen minutes later, 'it's Zio Tortelli. You know him, don't you?'

'Of course. I deal with him every day.'

Tony took the phone from his brother and began speaking with the banker. He, Fausto and Paolo were in his office on the floor below the Pope's. It was the same office that had belonged

481

at one time to Cardinal Gasparri and, even earlier, to Cardinal dell'Acqua. Fausto went to a window and looked down on the courtyard below as his brother spoke with his banker. When Tony hung up, he said, 'It's taken care of. Zio will debit your account and credit ours. I'll make the same arrangement with the Crédit Suisse. What the German's don't know won't hurt them.'

Fausto turned away from the window. 'I'm afraid the Germans *may* know, if they're checking the Bank of Rome's transactions. Well, we'll have to take that chance. Paolo, I'm leaving you in Tony's hands. I'll check your house. The Germans may confiscate it . . .'

'I know. Don't worry. I got everything valuable out a long time ago. The only thing I didn't get out was me. I appreciate what you've done, Fausto. And pray to God you don't get into trouble for it.'

'I've got a little influence left. I'll be all right.'

He embraced the old man, whose eyes were suddenly moist.

'All my life I've worked hard and kept clean,' he said. 'And now when I'm old, suddenly I'm running like a criminal. Why? Because I'm a Jew. It's crazy, isn't it?'

'The world's crazy,' said Fausto, hugging him affectionately.

'*We* were crazy,' said Paolo. 'One time we were for Mussolini. Remember?'

'It's something I find hard to forget, but I'm trying. Tony, you'll see he gets good food and not the usual Vatican bilge?'

Tony smiled.

'We'll do our best.'

Fausto embraced him.

'Thanks, brother,' he said, softly.

Then he left the office.

He had parked his car near St. Anne's Gate. Now as he emerged from the gate on to the narrow street bordering the Vatican's high wall, he saw a car parked in front of his. Pasquale Albertelli, the lean assistant to the hated Questore of Rome, Pietro Caruso, got out of the car and walked up to Fausto. As assistant to the chief of the Roman police, Albertelli held considerable power. Fausto's stomach knotted as he approached him, but he told himself to look nonchalant.

'Who gave you the tip?' asked Albertelli.

'What tip?'

'Don't play games. Someone tipped you off that we were arresting your father-in-law. We got there, and the Jew had flown the coop with all the big rocks. We tracked down one of his salesmen, and he said you'd come in the store a half hour before we did. Who tipped you off?'

'Hitler, when he started killing Jews. I thought it was time Paolo took a rest cure.'

Albertelli's narrow face didn't look amused.

'So he's in the Pope's rest home for Jews. I figured you would bring him here. All right, score one for Spada. But the Germans are going to be pissed off about this. I'd advise you to be careful from now on, my friend.' He looked at Fausto's tweed suit. 'There's another thing: you'd be smart to get out your Fascist uniform and start wearing it again.'

'I quit the Party, remember?'

'It's time you joined it again. You know goddam well you haven't done a thing for the war effort. At a time like this, we don't like lukewarm Fascists—or ex-Fascists.' He lowered his voice. 'I'm warning you, Spada: you're on our list.'

He went back to his car and got in, slamming the door. His driver turned on the ignition and the car roared down the street.

Fausto watched it go. Then he got in his own car and started for home.

Despite the fact that Nanda was getting old for childbearing, in 1938 she had given birth to a daughter whom she and Fausto named Anna. This new addition to their household brought them even closer together. For the first time in her life, Nanda felt contentment in her marriage. Tony's attempts to bring her back to the Catholic faith had resulted in some ugly moments, but ultimately Nanda had returned to the Church, which reinforced her peace of mind.

But ominous events were forging the household into an even tighter unit. As Mussolini came further under the power of Hitler, he adopted the German anti-Semitism and promulgated racial laws that made life increasingly difficult for Italian Jews. Fausto's influence had protected his wife and children and father-in-law from the worst, which was internment in the Italian concentration camps. Even so, their life was altered. Some of it was petty and annoying. Italian Jews were no longer allowed to have servants, and although Fausto argued that *he* hired the servants, not his wife, the Fascists ruled against him. Both Fausto and Nanda had grown up with many servants: they took them for granted. Now, suddenly, they had to fend for themselves. They put on a good face. Nanda bought a cookbook and began teaching herself how to prepare meals, with results that were mixed and sometimes hilarious failures. Fausto swallowed his pride and took on the housecleaning chores, also with mixed results. Helped by Enrico, he made beds, cleaned bathrooms and cursed Mussolini. However, his taking over of the gardening duties was an unexpected delight. He found he enjoyed working in the walled garden behind the house, and, as the months passed, he became good at it. It occurred to him that this was a far cry from the glories he had envisioned for himself as a young man, but that perhaps Voltaire had been right: 'Tend your own garden' was excellent advice.

However, for Enrico the racial laws produced greater hardships than the servant problem. As an official 'Jew,' he was not only barred from military service, he was forced out of the University of Bologna and denied access to any institution of learning at all. For a twenty-year-old who was a bright student, this had been an enormous blow. Enrico's young life came to a complete standstill at a time when he should have been moving with the speed and energy of youth. For two years now he had been more or less holed up in his father's villa. As being Jewish became more of a liability, more of his friends of both sexes saw less and less of him. His loneliness and inactivity turned to bitterness. Desperate for something to do to fill the endless hours, he helped his father with the household chores, prayed for Mussolini's defeat, and started secretly reading Karl Marx. As Fascism slowly rotted around him, what he read began to make good sense to him. Moreover, it was becoming increasingly obvious that the only real resistance to the German troops who were now actually controlling Rome came from the Gappisti, the members of G.A.P.: Gruppi di Azione Patriotica, the Patriotic Action Groups, or Communist partisans. Since the Germans, Italy's nominal allies, were now in reality foreign invaders who were treating Italians with the contempt they treated everyone else, the Gappisti became in Enrico's eyes heroes of resistance, imbued with the glamour of patriots. He began to scorn his father's inactivity, as well as the Fascist past. He longed to join the partisans and had broached the subject to his father, who quickly squelched the idea, much to Enrico's anger.

He was sitting at his desk in his second-floor bedroom reading, not Karl Marx, but a girlie magazine and listening to a scratched American recording of the Andrews Sisters singing 'Bei Mir Bist du Schön,' when he heard his father's car pull up in front of the villa. Stuffing the girlie magazine under his mattress, he turned off the Victrola and hurried out of his room. As he started down the stairs, he saw his parents talking in the entrance hall. Nanda turned to her son, a smile on her face.

'He's all right!' she exclaimed. 'Your father got him to the Vatican in time. He's all right!'

She turned back to Fausto, put her arms around him and kissed him.

'Thank you, darling,' she said. 'Thank you for saving an old man.'

'Don't thank me. Thank the man who tipped me off.'

'But *you* saved him. And Tony says he'll be all right in the Vatican?'

'Unless the Germans decide to invade *that*. Do we have any of that rotten coffee?'

'I'll heat it up. Come in the kitchen.'

She went into the dining room. Fausto looked at his son, who was standing on the stair, halfway down.

'Enrico,' he said, quietly, 'come here.'

He came the rest of the way down the stairs.

'Sir?'

'I don't want your mother to know this because she might get upset. But you should know it. I arranged to transfer most of my cash out of Italy. If something happens to me, go to your uncle Tony. He knows all about it. I know your Communist principles may scorn cash, but your mother and sister will need money to live on.'

'What could happen to you?'

Fausto shrugged.

'Who knows? But the Germans aren't happy about my getting your grandfather into the Vatican. We'll all have to be careful from now on. And that means your forgetting about joining the partisans. I know how you feel, and I admire you for wanting to do something, but you have to think of your mother and Anna as much as yourself. So I want you to give me your word you won't try anything foolish. Will you?'

Enrico hesitated.

'All right, I give my word. But it's unfair!'

'Everything's unfair these days.'

'But I can't do *anything!* I've been like a prisoner in this place for two years! I'm not an Italian, I'm not a Jew, I can't go out, I can't fight with Italy, I can't join the partisans, I can't go to school . . .' Seeing the look on his father's face, he simmered down. 'I'm sorry. I shouldn't say these things except I *feel* them. But I won't do anything.'

Fausto studied his son. After a moment, he said, 'Do you want a woman?'

Enrico turned red.

'That's the trouble with us Italians—or Italian Jews, if that's what I am. The world falls apart, and all we can think of is women.'

'Maybe that's the best thing about us. I repeat: do you want a woman?'

Enrico looked shamefaced.

'Yes.'

'Brush your hair. I'll take you to La Rosina's. That's one place we can go to without getting the Germans suspicious.'

Enrico scorned his father's unideological approach to the situation, but he didn't waste any time brushing his hair.

Fausto went into the kitchen where he kissed his six-year-old daughter, who was sitting at the kitchen table. Then he took a cup of coffee from Nanda.

'God, this stuff is awful,' he said, taking a sip.

'It's German,' shrugged Nanda. 'It's probably made out of old shoes.'

'I can believe it.'

'Poppa,' said Anna, 'Momma says Grandpoppa's staying with the Pope. Does he run a hotel?'

'Sort of,' smiled Fausto.

Anna's cocker spaniel ran through the kitchen after her cat, and the girl jumped out of her chair to chase him. When she was out of the room, Fausto said, 'I'm taking Enrico out for a ride. He's going stir crazy.'

'I know. I worry about him. Where are you taking him?'

'Just for a ride,' he lied.

She came up to him and put her hand on his cheek.

'Thank you again for what you did,' she said, softly. 'Are you going to be in trouble for saving Father?'

'No more than I already am.'

'You're a good man, Fausto Spada. I used to think of you as anything but that, you know. But I love what you've become. I love it very much.'

He put down his cup and took her in his arms.

'Do you still find me sexy?' he whispered, grinning.

'Wildly.'

'Then I don't mind being good.'

'You're impossible,' she smiled. 'But I love you.'

They kissed until she saw Enrico in the door.

'All right, you two: have a nice drive. And if you see some fresh eggs, buy all you can.'

'Not much chance of that,' said Fausto, following his son out of the kitchen.

There was no doubt that La Rosina's had gone downhill since its palmy apogee thirty years before. The lewd murals on the ceiling were flaking paint, sometimes in laughable places, the brass was unpolished, the rugs threadbare, and the old-fashioned gilt furniture had been partially replaced by disastrously tacky Thirties pieces of smoked-glass modernity, which someone had dubbed neo-King Farouk. But the girls were still the best in Rome, and English whiskey, French champagne and wine, American cigarettes and Turkish hashish were available in expensive profusion. The place was frequented by both Italian Fascists and high-ranking Nazis, there being a generally accepted agreement that politics and the war were off-limits topics. At night the place was jammed. But when Fausto brought his son in shortly before lunch, he knew it would be practically empty. It was. The girls were sitting around in various stages of undress, smoking, yawning or reading sex novels. Flora, the madam who had bought the place from La Rosina's estate, smiled as she saw Fausto. Flora was as different from the elegant, French-speaking La Rosina as Mae West from Ethel Barrymore. Mountainously fat, coarse, overly made up, with a big black wart on her chin, her manner was as broad as her beam. She had on a tight-fitting peach satin dress, the low-slung neck of which revealed the cleavage of her alpine breasts. Around her shoulders was a ratty boa.

'Fausto, *caro*,' she smiled as he kissed her hand. 'And your sexy son! Enrico, if my counting is right, this is your fourth time here with your father. But he doesn't know how many times you've come on your own, eh?' And she gave Fausto a wink and a grin.

'He can't afford you without me,' said Fausto. 'How's business?'

'Right now, slow. I've only got one customer, but what a customer!'

'Important?'

'Numero uno in Rome, *caro*.'

'General Mälzer, that hard-working Kraut, in a whorehouse before lunch? I'm shocked.'

'He has to come here before lunch because after lunch he's so drunk, he can't get it up.'

Fausto laughed.

'The Master Race at work and play. Well, keep him away from me. I can't stand the bastard.'

'Don't worry. You know the rule here: no politics, no war. Why do I care who wins this crappy war? I get 'em all: Monarchists, Fascists, Nazis—in a few months I'll probably be getting American G.I.s and the Gappisti. Politics change, but all men got cocks, eh? Except those filthy Communists probably won't tip . . . Enrico, *caro*, who do you want today? My beautiful Claudia, who squeezed you dry as the Sahara last time?'

'Yes, Claudia,' said Enrico, who was already stiff with anticipation.

'Look at the *ragazzo*'s pants!' chortled Flora, who knew how to gauge her customers' randiness. 'It's a good thing buttons aren't rationed, eh? Claudia! *Cara!* Here's your sweetheart, Enrico! Take him to Number four and make him happy.'

A beautiful, black-haired girl, short but ripely voluptuous, got off a bench and came over to Enrico, taking his hand.

'*Ciao*, Enrico,' she smiled.

'*Ciao*.'

'Give him a good time,' said Fausto, slipping her a wad of lire. Claudia looked at the bankroll, and her smile widened.

'For that, we can fuck all afternoon,' she said.

'Not much else to do in Rome,' said Fausto.

Enrico's fingers dug into Claudia's olive buttocks as he tried to eat her huge breasts. She writhed under his weight, biting her teeth into his shoulder. Her firm, young body smelled of sweat and cheap perfume, and the combination was infinitely erotic to him. He slavered over her breasts, her neck, then planted his open mouth on hers and sucked her tongue. Her strong legs were wrapped around his waist as he went into her. He began gently thrusting, then with increasing passion as the lust that had been swelling in him like a boil began to burst. His brain exploded as he came, the tight walls of her experienced vagina squeezing him of every drop of his semen.

'Oh God,' he said, rolling off her onto the dirty sheets. 'I needed that.'

'Feel better?' she said, getting up to douche herself.

'What do you think?'

'Your father's real nice to bring you here.'

'My father,' he said, quietly, staring at the cracked ceiling.

'You don't like him?'

488

'I love him. But my father's part of what's wrong with this country.'

'No politics at La Rosina's,' she said, rubbing some perfume into her thick, black pubic hairs.

'I know. Just fucking.'

'Something wrong with that, sweetheart?'

She came back to the bed and sat beside him, putting her hand on his smooth chest.

'I suppose not,' he sighed.

CHAPTER 53

The phone woke Fausto up. Sleepily he reached for the receiver.

'*Pronto?*' he said, not opening his eyes.

'Spada? It's Albertelli. I expect you to be at the rally today.'

'What rally?' yawned Fausto. 'And what time is it?'

'It's seven-thirty, you lazy pig! And you know what rally I mean. The one at Santa Maria della Pietà in the Piazza Colonna. Don't tell me you've forgotten what day this is?'

Fausto's eyes were opening.

'It's Thursday, isn't it?'

'It's March twenty-third, you cretin, and it's the twenty-fifth anniversary of Il Duce's founding of the Fascist Party. I want a good turnout for the rally, and I swear, Spada, if you're not there, there's going to be trouble. We've all been too lenient with you. This time, we mean business! Be there at nine—and wear your uniform. You can pick up a pass at the church.'

'I'll be there,' said Fausto, slamming the phone. He sat up, scratching his chest. Nanda, next to him, said, 'Who was that?'

'That fart, Albertelli, the Chief of Police's errand boy. Can you imagine, with Mussolini a joke, they're holding a rally to celebrate the anniversary of the founding of Fascism? The idiots. They ought to hold the rally in a graveyard.'

'Are you going?'

'I haven't got a choice.'

She put her hand on his arm as he started to get out of the bed.

'Kiss me,' she said.

He leaned over and kissed her.

'I love you, Fausto.'

'And I love you, darling.'

She watched him as he went to the bathroom. Every time he left the house, she had the sinking feeling she might never see him again.

As Fausto shaved in front of his mirror, he felt the same

unarticulated apprehension his wife did. The past three months had dragged by in ominous inactivity. Although he had retired from the Party, Albertelli had forced him to get his uniform out of mothballs and attend Fascist meetings. Though Albertelli and the other Fascist bigwigs seldom spoke to him, what little they said had become increasingly testy. But so far they had made no move. What was holding them back? Perhaps their own confusion, their own fears at the fate that awaited them when, inevitably, Rome fell. The tension in the city was becoming unbearable. People were fighting for food, and the Allied air raids were giving the ancient capital a pounding. The Pope had declared Rome an 'open city,' trying to stave off the bombers, but he had been ignored, displaying nothing but his impotence. Yet the Germans kept their hands off the Vatican, although relations between them were even more strained than before. Fausto had come close to sending Nanda and the children to Tony for sanctuary several times, but each time he held back. Since they weren't being harassed, they might as well stay at home where they were at least reasonably comfortable. Besides, if they did go to the Vatican and the Germans changed their minds and took over the Church property, then they were in real danger. So he had done nothing, playing for time, praying, like most of the Romans, that the damned Americans would break through the German lines to the south and bring an end to this painful, intolerable, dangerous stalemate.

It had been a hellish winter, and Fausto felt tired, drained, gutted. When he finished shaving, he looked in the mirror and winced. He looked old. He *was* old. He remembered when mirrors had been his best friend.

Now, mirrors were the enemy. They were death in slow motion.

At nine Fausto—shaved, bathed and in his Fascist uniform —arrived at Piazza Colonna. An armed platoon of the Fascist Republican National Guard was surrounding Santa Maria della Pietà, but they were hardly needed to keep off crowds: no one aside from a few passersby and a pushcart salesman was in the piazza, reflecting the total rejection of Fascism by the Romans and the pathetic foolishness of the rally. Fausto identified himself and picked up a pass, then entered the church. It was tiny, but even so, the aging Fascists barely filled it. He spotted Giuseppe Pizzirani, the vice-secretary of the Party; the Chief of the Province of Rome, Edoardo Salerno; and a few men who had actually been with Musolini that afternoon twenty-five years before when he and a hundred and fifty of his cohorts met in

Piazza San Sepolcro in Milan and more or less accidentally dreamed up Fascism. On the church's altar lay a large laurel wreath. It was tied with a ribbon of the colors of Rome and proclaimed: 'Il Partito Fascisto Repubblicano.'

Fausto nodded to his acquaintances as he took a seat. Then he spotted Albertelli sitting next to his boss, the Questore of Rome, Pietro Caruso. Caruso, a forty-four-year-old Neapolitan, looked like an ape and had a history of mental illness in his family. A perfect Fascist police chief, thought Fausto as he nodded to them. Caruso glowered at him, but Albertelli nodded. Then the service began.

Afterward, as Fausto was leaving the church, Albertelli grabbed his arm.

'You came,' he said. 'Good.'

'I wouldn't have missed it for the world,' said Fausto, drily. 'I was practically in tears.'

'Jokers don't live long in Rome these days. Listen: I'm invited to lunch at the Excelsior with Colonel Kappler and General Mälzer. The General wants you to join us.'

Fausto looked at him suspiciously.

'Why would General Mälzer want to lunch with the husband of a Jewess?'

'Ah well, if you'd been smart you'd have ditched her years ago.'

'I happen to be in love with her.'

'That's your mistake, not mine. Anyway, the General wants you at lunch, so be there. You don't stand up the "King of Rome." Lunch will be on the Fuehrer. Afterward, we'll walk over to the Ministry of Corporations. The Questore is going to lead us in a Party oath to the Duce. It should be quite moving.'

'It should move something, if only my bowels.'

Albertelli glared at him.

'You're a very stupid man, Spada. Be at the Excelsior at one.'

He left Fausto and hurried down the steps of the church.

The day had begun misty and cool, but as the March sun rose in the cloudless sky, it heated up. By noon, as Rosario Bentivegna seated his girl friend, Carla Capponi, at a sidewalk table at the Trattoria Dreher, the twenty-one-year-old former medical student noticed a thermometer on the wall. The temperature was already eighty. Rosario, who was known in the *macchia,* or underground, as Paolo, took a seat between Carla and a physicist named Giulio Cortini. The fourth person at the table was Cortini's wife. The Trattoria Dreher, a noisy place in

Piazza dei SS. Apostoli, was considered a relatively safe restaurant for Gappisti, and all four of the lunchers were Gappisti. Rosario was a former medical student at the University of Rome. Two months previously, the students had demonstrated against the Germans and Fascists. The schools were closed, and most of the students, like Rosario, joined the underground.

The four lunched in tense silence, fully aware it might be the last lunch of their lives. After lunch they went to 42 via Marco Aurelio, where, in a tiny room in the basement of a middle-class apartment building, they had been living in hiding from the S.S. Now, Rosario changed into a street cleaner's uniform. Cortini, the physicist, checked the bomb he and his wife had made. It consisted of forty pounds of TNT packed in pieces of iron tubing. Carefully they carried the bomb outside where stood a rubbish cart stolen from the city. They placed the bomb inside the cart. Rosario looked at the cart a moment, then turned and kissed Carla.

'Good luck, darling,' she said.

He embraced Cortini and his wife, both of whom also wished him good luck. Then Rosario, after checking his briar pipe which he was going to use to ignite the fifty-second fuse, gingerly eased the cart over the curb. The temperature was now in the low eighties, but it was not only the heat that was making him sweat as he began pushing his lethal load toward the via Rasella, near the Piazza Barberini.

The elegant Excelsior Hotel in via Veneto was a favorite hangout of high-ranking Germans and Fascists. They gathered there to drink French Cognac and bolster each other's nerves by insisting the war could be won after all. At one o'clock Fausto entered the dining room where the headwaiter, Fernando, bowed: he knew Fausto well.

'How are you, Fernando?'

'Getting by, Signor Spada. Getting by. You are lunching alone?'

'I'm ashamed to admit it, but I've been ordered to lunch with General Mälzer.'

Fernando looked across the room at a table where two Germans were sitting with Albertelli.

'I have to give him the best table,' said Fernando in a low voice. 'But he's such a drunken pig, he shouldn't be allowed in the hotel.'

He led Fausto across the dining room, which was filled with

Germans. At one end of the room, an ancient, white-haired pianist was sitting at an aging black Bechstein playing Strauss waltzes, accompanied by a Paganini-thin violinist. Fernando seated Fausto. General Mälzer, known by both Germans and Romans as 'the King of Rome,' was already well into his cups, working on his second bottle of La Tâche. The German Commandant of Rome, who liked to keep orchids in his office and wear a beret at a rakish tilt, gestured drunkenly at Fausto.

'Spada!' he said in guttural Italian. 'Glad you could join us. You know Colonel Kappler?'

He indicated the bony-faced man at his left, S.S. Obersturm-bannfuehrer (Lieutenant Colonel) Herbert Kappler, head of the Sicherheitsdienst—the S.D.—in Rome. Thirty-seven-year-old Kappler, a native of Stuttgart, loved Rome, Italian history and Etruscan vases, which he collected. He was the local representative of the Gestapo.

'Yes, of course,' said Fausto.

'Fernando, bring some more champagne for the others. And my Burgundy is vanishing with the speed of light. Better get another bottle on tap.'

Fernando bowed and left. Mälzer looked at Fausto.

'Well, my dear fellow. I haven't seen much of you lately. Albertelli here tells me you've been spending a lot of time in whorehouses. You Italians! My God, all you think of is getting laid. No wonder you lost the war.'

Fausto decided it was politic not to mention his visit to La Rosina's in December, when the only other customer had been General Mälzer. Albertelli cleared his throat.

'General, we haven't lost . . .'

'Don't give me that shit,' interrupted Mälzer, signaling the waiter to refill his glass. 'You've lost, and you know it. Or if you don't know it, you're stupid. This celebration today—the twenty-fifth anniversary of what? Lunacy. You know, Spada, these idiots wanted to put on a big show at the Teatro Adriano, but I cancelled it. Why publicize a corpse? And that's what the Fascist Party is: dead, dead, dead. The corpse is even beginning to stink a little.'

'General, I must protest—'

'Albertelli, shut up. You cretins should have soft-pedaled the whole thing instead of making a big noise. Why give the Gappisti a target? Don't think I don't know what goes on in this town. Everyone says something's going to happen today because it's Fascism's big anniversary. Well, let the bastards try. They'll find out what we Germans are made of.'

'And what *are* you made of, General?' asked Fausto, politely.

Mälzer raised his wineglass for the umpteenth time.

'Steel,' he said. He drank, then turned to glare at the pianist.

'That damned antique,' he said. 'He plays nothing but Strauss waltzes . . . he thinks that's all we Germans like to hear. Hey, YOU!' He yelled across the big room. 'Piano player!'

Everyone stared. The aged pianist turned sheet-white.

'Play something modern!' bellowed Mälzer. 'Your Strauss is very lovely, very nice, but I'm bored with it! Play . . .' He thought a moment. 'Play "Falling in Love Again." You know it?'

The pianist had gotten to his thinly soled feet. Now he bowed.

'Yes, General.'

He sat back down and signaled the violinist. They began grinding out the Dietrich song.

Mälzer was smiling.

'That's better. Shall we order?'

He signaled Fernando to bring the menus.

Rosario Bentivegna, disguised as a street clearner, was nearing the via Rasella. The streets of Rome were filled with people; even the war couldn't restrain the ancient city from coming to life in the early spring sunshine. Rosario, pushing forty pounds of TNT, was understandably tense, but his stomach twisted even further when he saw two genuine street cleaners approaching him.

'Hey!' said one of them. They were coming out of the via XX Settembre. 'What are you doing here? This isn't your district.'

'Nothing,' said Rosario, his brain grasping for a plausible excuse. 'I'm . . . carrying a load of cement.'

He could have kicked himself for the incredibly implausible excuse that he had blurted out. The two street cleaners, however, grinned knowingly.

'Oh, I get it,' said one of them. 'You're in the black market. Go on.'

Relieved, Rosario continued toward the via Rasella. Around the corner, in the Piazza Barberini, the Barberini movie house was playing 'The Lover in the Shadows,' a Swedish film about the trials of a young surgeon. In the Vatican funeral services were being conducted for a papal chauffeur who had been killed by an Allied bomb while driving a truck with Vatican City license plates. His death was being publicized by the Vatican in its ongoing campaign against Allied bombing. Elsewhere, people were reading about Mount Vesuvius, which had erupted that morning for the second time that week, belching lava forty feet deep over villages above the Bay of Naples.

Rosario turned his rubbish cart into the via Rasella. On the sunny side of the street, the ancient buildings glowed a warm sienna; on the shaded side they were gray. Rosario headed for Number 156, the Palazzo Tittoni, a building about a third of the way down from the higher end of the street. It had been the home of a pre-Mussolini Foreign Minister of Italy, Tommaso Tittoni. Ironically, considering what was about to happen, Mussolini himself had once lived in a five-room flat in the palazzo.

Now Rosario parked his cart against the curb in front of the palazzo. He began his wait. He was waiting for the approximately 150 men of the Eleventh Company of the Third Battalion, S.S. Polizeiregiment Bozen. For the past month the regiment had been in the process of being transferred from the South Tyrol to Rome, where its mission was to beef up the German police against the increasingly rebellious Romans.

At two o'clock, when the Germans were scheduled to march through the via Rasella, Rosario would light the fuse of the TNT in the rubbish cart with his pipe.

Fifty seconds later, if all went well, the Germans would be blown to Valhalla.

'Now Spada,' said General Mälzer, finishing his Charolais steak, 'I invited you to lunch for a reason. We really must work out this ridiculous situation with your father-in-law. This French beef is excellent, wouldn't you say?'

'It's very good,' replied Fausto, truthfully. It had been the best meal he had had in weeks. 'How do you mean, "work out" the situation?'

'Come now, Spada. Your father-in-law is hiding under the skirts of the Pope. Well, we know there are a lot of Jews in the Vatican, don't we? His Holiness is playing a double game, but God knows he's not the first pope to be tricky, is he? Fortunately for him, Field Marshal Kesselring, my commander, is a devout Catholic from Bavaria and has insisted we respect the Vatican's neutrality—if it can be called that. Fortunately for us, the Pope is *sehr deutschfreundlich*—what's the word in Italian? A Germanophile? As you know, he was the Papal Nuncio in Germany for twelve years, speaks fluent German, and, we believe, is not unsympathetic to our cause—at any rate, he prefers us to the Communists. So we have a standoff. Pius rails against the Americans for bombing Rome, which we like. But he hides Jews like your father-in-law, which we don't like. Consequently, I've decided it's time you and I worked out a compromise.'

'For instance?'

'Your brother, Cardinal Spada, got Signor Montecatini into the Vatican. Presumably Cardinal Spade could get him out.'

'Why would my father-in-law want to get out? The reason he went in is to avoid being deported to a concentration camp. Pardon me, General, for mentioning unpleasant subjects, but we hear you Germans have a bad habit of killing Jews.'

Mälzer shook his head drunkenly.

'Only *some*,' he said. 'Not rich Jews like your father-in-law.' He leaned across the table and lowered his voice. 'How much are the jewels worth that your father-in-law took to the Vatican?'

Fausto sipped his champagne.

'What jewels?' he said.

Mälzer glared.

'Don't give me any bullshit, Spada. You took him to the Vatican. You know damned well he took jewels with him worth millions. And, my friend, let's lay all our cards on the table. We also know that same day you arranged a transfer of your own funds from the Bank of Rome to the Vatican. It's very convenient having a twin brother who runs the Vatican's finances, isn't it? You transferred . . .' He pulled a slip of paper from his pocket and checked the figures. '59,837,422 lire on December seventeenth, 1943. That's a lot of money, Spada. Where is it now? In Switzerland?'

'Perhaps.'

Mälzer laughed.

'You know damned well that's where it is. Listen, my friend, I don't blame you. In times of international crisis such as this, the rich man with any brains uses what means he has to protect his resources. We've known you did it for several months. However, because you were once a Fascist hero popular with the people of Rome, and because your family has been popular in the past—and also because you've been smart enough to lay low and not give us any trouble—we haven't done anything so far. However, today being an anniversary for Fascism, well . . . anniversaries are good days to settle old scores. What time is it, Kappler?'

The head of the Rome Gestapo checked his watch.

'Two-thirty.'

'Then we can be assured the guards are in place?'

'Oh, certainly, General.'

'What guards?' asked Fausto, suddenly apprehensive.

'You see, my friend,' said Mälzer as Fernando decanted the new bottle of wine, 'the pawns in this little chess game between us are your wife and two children, who are Jews. So we have put them under house arrest.'

Oh Christ, thought Fausto. Oh Christ . . . but keep *cool*.

'That's why you invited me here to lunch?' he asked. 'To lay a little trap?'

'You see things very clearly. I saw no reason why we couldn't discuss this in a civilized manner. Your family, by the way, is in no danger as long as you cooperate with us. And I *know* you're going to cooperate with us.' He smiled. 'Ah, a new bottle! There's no wine like a rich Burgundy to make a man forget the unpleasantnesses of life. Your claret you can have. Give me a Burgundy any day.'

Fernando poured a small amount in a new glass. Mälzer sniffed it, tasted it and smiled.

'Perfection.'

Fausto watched the glass being filled.

'What sort of "cooperation" are you asking for, General?' he asked.

'It's very simple, my friend. You're a rich man, and it takes money to win wars. *Lots* of money. You haven't been as supportive of our side as we think you should be, but that can be easily remedied. And we're not pigs! Oh no, not at all. We're willing to be reasonable.'

'How much?' asked Fausto, and the *quanto?* came out softly.

'We want your father-in-law's jewels—*all* of them, since he's a Jew swine who's lucky to be alive. But from you we're only asking fifty percent—let's say, thirty million lire. If, within twenty-four hours, you've complied with this, then you and your family will be allowed to go to the Vatican.'

'And my father-in-law?'

'He can stay where he is.'

'How do I know you wouldn't shoot us the moment the money and jewels were transferred? Be realistic, General. You're not offering a compromise. You're asking me to play German roulette. That's the version of the game where *all* the chambers are loaded.'

'There would of course be guarantees . . .'

'German guarantees, General, are like German coffee: ersatz.'

Mälzer tapped his fingers on the white tablecloth.

'You know, it would be very easy for me to get angry with you, Spada. One doesn't speak to German generals the way you're speaking to me. But I don't want to get angry with you because I want to work this out. Would it satisfy you if the transfer were made at the Vatican? Say, in front of St. Peters? You and your family would be taken there and handed over to a Church official—your brother perhaps. Then you hand over the jewels and the money. There could be no possibility of a double cross, since we would be on Vatican territory. Would that satisfy you?'

Fausto thought about it. Yes, that seemed safe. They wouldn't dare pull guns inside the Vatican . . . Or would they?

'I'd like to think about it,' he said.

'There's not much to think about, but you have twenty-four hours. Give my office a call when you're ready to say yes. In the meanwhile, go home. I think when you see my soldiers outside your house, you'll come around to our way of thinking.'

Fausto put down his napkin and stood up.

'Well, it's certainly been an unusual lunch, General. Thank you.'

'My pleasure.'

Fausto turned to Albertelli.

'It seems I won't be able to attend the meeting at the Ministry of Corporations after all.'

'No, go home,' repeated Mälzer. 'And remember: twenty-four hours.'

Fausto looked at them, then walked away from the table. He was afraid and bitter. Leaving the dining room, he hurried to the lobby and used one of the hotel phones to call his house.

'*Pronto?*' It was Enrico's voice.

'Enrico, it's your father. Has . . . anything happened?'

A moment's silence.

'There are German soldiers all around the house. What's happening?'

It was true, then—not that he thought they'd been bluffing.

'I know all about it,' he said. 'Don't worry—they're not going to hurt you. Is your mother all right?'

'She's frightened. The soldiers say we can't leave the house —only you can come in or go out . . .'

'I know. Tell your mother everything's going to be all right. I'm going to see your uncle Tony, and I'll be home in a couple of hours. And Enrico: *don't* be frightened. All right?'

'All right, Father.'

Fausto hung up. Don't be frightened, he thought. Christ, I'm sweating like a pig . . . He hurried out of the hotel, got in his car, and started down the via Veneto toward the Vatican.

Less than a hundred yards away, Rosario Bentivegna was still waiting by his rubbish cart at 156 via Rasella. It was 2:40: The Germans were forty minutes late. Rosario was panicked. Obviously something had gone wrong, but if he had to push the TNT-loaded cart all the way back across Rome, surely he'd be stopped, the cart searched . . .

He looked down the street and listened for the boots of the Germans.

Nothing.

CHAPTER 54

It took Fausto a half hour to drive to the Vatican, because he had to wait ten minutes at a crossing while a company of German soldiers marched by on their way to the via Rasella. When he did reach the Vatican, he parked by St. Anne's Gate and hurried to his brother's office, where Tony's secretary, Father Frasseti, told him, 'His Eminence is with the Holy Father, Signor Spada. I don't expect him back for a half hour.'

'Then I'll wait,' said Fausto. 'Could you contact my father-in-law and ask him to come here? It's important.'

'Yes, of course. I'll phone his room.'

He placed the call.

'He's not answering,' the secretary said, hanging up. 'He's probably out walking in the gardens. If you'd like, I can send someone to look for him.'

'Yes, please.'

As Father Frasseti placed another call, Fausto sat down and mourned his fate. He knew there was no alternative to accepting their terms: Mälzer had him by the balls. Millions of lire in jewels, half his fortune—he didn't like it, of course, but if it got his family through the war safely, perhaps it wasn't a bad bargain.

He cursed himself for not having gotten Nanda and the children to the Vatican earlier.

The clock on the wall ticked, the minute hand jerked forward, and the clock struck a quarter past three.

At three-thirty Rosario Bentivegna heard the distant boom boom boom of the marching Germans. At last! he thought, lighting his pipe. Soon he could hear them singing. What was it? The Horst Wessel song? Stupid Krauts, keep singing, keep marching, right into my TNT . . .

He glanced down the via Rasella to where the narrow via

Boccaccio crossed it. At the corner stood another partisan, whose job was to give the signal to light the fuse.

Rosario was puffing his pipe to hot life, when the porter of the Palazzo Tittoni came out of the building into the street.

'Pss!' hissed Rosario. 'The Germans are coming! We're going to attack them! Get the hell out of here!'

The startled porter hurried away.

Just then, the Germans turned into the via Rasella from the via del Traforo. They started marching up the street, three abreast, 156 men in the battle dress, singing. Boom, boom, boom . . .

When the head of the German column passed the photo shop at Number 132, the partisan at the corner of the via Boccaccio started across the street. He raised his cap.

The signal. Rosario took a puff on his pipe, then put it to the fuse. The fuse hissed to life. Rosario put his cap on top of the rubbish cart—signal that all was going well—then crossed the street as the blond Germans came nearer, like a huge, throbbing machine, their thudding boots bringing them closer to the rubbish cart . . .

The tremendous explosion rocked the entire block and was heard throughout central Rome. Fausto and Father Frasseti heard it in the Vatican and went to a window to look out. Twenty-four Germans were instantly blown apart, parts of their bodies flying through the air, their still-living-for-an-instant blood spraying against ancient stone walls. Pieces of the iron tubing surrounding the TNT became lethal shrapnel, slicing through German flesh. The dead and the dying fell to the ground. The force of the blast caused chunks of concrete to drop from buildings. A huge hole was blasted out of a stone wall, and water burst forth, washing down the street, mixing dust with steel and blood and flesh. At the same time, a blast of compressed air roared down the street with the force of a tornado and overturned a school bus.

General Mälzer, still at the Excelsior Hotel and by now as drunk as a lord, heard the explosion, which was so near and so strong it rattled the windows.

'What's that?' he slurred to Kappler. 'An air raid?'

'I don't think so,' said Kappler, getting up. 'I'll find out.'

He hurried to the lobby. Through the front door he could see people running down the street.

'What happened?' he yelled to the doorman.

'An explosion, sir! Down by the Piazza Barberini! Must be a gas main . . .'

'Gas main, hell,' muttered Kappler. 'Get General Mälzer's car!' he ordered. Then he ran back to the dining room. Coming up to Mälzer's table, he said, 'General, I think the partisans attacked our troops. The Bozen Regiment was scheduled to march up via Rasella this afternoon, and apparently that's where the explosion happened . . .'

Mälzer's face, already red from the wine, now became crimson.

'Those BASTARDS!' he shouted, trying to get out of his chair. 'If they hurt one German, I'll blow up the whole city! Get my car . . .'

'It's here, sir.'

'I'll blow up everything! The Pope, St. Peter's, the Colosseum . . .' Mälzer was weaving across the dining room, raving like a lunatic. 'The Tiber . . . I'll shoot every fucking Wop in this city . . . If they've hurt my men, they'll be sorry! By Christ, they'll pay for this . . . they'll *PAY!*'

He raved all the way out of the hotel to his car. When he and Kappler arrived at the via Rasella, the sight of the hideous carnage drove him even wilder.

'Revenge!' he shrieked, looking at the puddles of blood. 'Revenge for my poor *kamaraden!*'

By five o'clock Fausto was becoming desperate. Tony was still closeted with the Pope. Paolo had been located and brought to Father Frasseti's office. Fausto had told him what had happened, and the old man had sadly agreed to give up his jewels. 'I'm a ruined man,' he said, sinking into a chair, 'ruined. But what's the difference? My daughter, my grandchildren, they must be saved . . .'

At three minutes past five, Tony finally arrived. He looked troubled.

'Something terrible has happened,' he told them. 'Come into my office.'

Fausto and Paolo followed him into the big office.

'The partisans attacked a company of German soldiers in via Rasella,' he said, going to his desk. 'Did you hear that explosion an hour or so ago?'

'Yes . . .'

'That was it. I've been with the Holy Father, who's been getting reports. Apparently Mälzer has gone crazy with rage . . .'

'I had lunch with him,' interrupted Fausto. 'He was drunk then.'

'Well, he's drunker now. He's threatening to blow up the whole block. The Germans are bringing in truckloads of explosives. It's terrible, terrible! The Holy Father is furious. He says the Communists are going to ruin everything for us. There are bound to be reprisals . . .'

'Tony,' said Fausto, 'everything already is ruined for us.'

The Cardinal sat down and listened in stunned silence to Fausto's story. When it was over, he asked, 'What will you do?'

Fausto spread his hands helplessly.

'What *can* we do? Nothing, except what they want. Paolo is ready to give up the jewels, and I'll pay them thirty million lire. It's blackmail on a gigantic scale, but what can you do when a gun's pointed at you? Nanda and the children's lives are the important thing.'

'I know,' said Tony. 'I'll arrange the transfer of the funds. I assume General Mälzer will accept one of the Vatican's checks?'

When Fausto arrived at his villa, he was stopped by two German soldiers stationed at his front door. He identified himself and was allowed to enter. He found his family sitting in the kitchen. He kissed Anna, whose pretty face looked frightened and who said, 'Poppa, what's happening? Why are all those soldiers out there?'

He kissed Nanda, then sat down beside her and explained the situation calmly. When he finished, no one spoke for a while. Then Nanda said, quietly, 'Poor Poppa. And poor Fausto.' She put her hand on his wrist.

That night, as they were getting in bed, Nanda said, 'Are you sorry you married a Jewess?'

He smiled at her.

'The only thing I'm sorry about is that I was such a rotten husband for so many years.'

He got in bed beside her and kissed her. Then he turned out the lights. They lay in the dark awhile, listening to the German soldiers below their open window talking.

Then they made love.

They were awakened at six the next morning by someone pounding on the front door.

'Now what?' muttered Fausto, getting out of bed and going to the window to look down. He saw one of the German soldiers at the door. A truck was parked in the street.

'What do you want?' he yelled.

The soldier looked up.

'Get dressed. You're coming with us.'

'Where?'

'No questions. Get dressed. Hurry!'

Nanda was sitting up in bed. She looked frightened.

'What do you think it means?' she asked.

'I don't know. But we'd better do what they say. I'll wake the children.'

As he hurried out of the bedroom, he was assailed by the fear of the unknown.

Fifteen minutes later, they were put into the back of the truck. It was another beautiful spring day, but Nanda had told Anna to wear a blue wool coat—'just in case,' she had said, not quite knowing what she meant. The truck pulled away from the villa and started toward the Tiber. Four of the German soldiers were sitting with them, the other two in the cab.

'Where are we going?' asked Fausto.

'No questions,' replied the German.

Anna started to whimper.

'Momma, I'm frightened,' she said. Nanda hugged her.

'Everything's going to be all right, darling.'

'But where are they taking us? And who will feed Tito and Giulio?'

They were her dog and cat.

'I put them out in the garden and left them some food and water.'

'But what if we're gone a long time?'

Nanda looked imploringly at Fausto. He got up and crossed the truck to kneel before his daughter. He took her hands.

'Has Poppa ever lied to you?' he asked.

'No. At least, I don't think so.'

'Well, Poppa is telling you we'll be home this afternoon. I told you last night I have to pay some money to the Germans, and when that's done, we're going to stay with Uncle Tony for a while. But before we go to Uncle Tony, we'll come back and pick up Tito and Giulio.'

'You promise.'

'I promise.'

And he kissed her, which seemed to calm her. As he went back to his seat opposite her, he exchanged looks with Enrico. He knew that his son knew that something had gone wrong.

Twenty minutes later, the truck pulled up in front of Regina Coeli, the old Roman prison on the left bank of the Tiber. The

505

German soldiers stood up. 'You three,' the one who spoke some Italian said, pointing to Nanda, Anna and Enrico, 'get out. You,' he pointed to Fausto, 'stay.'

'Are we under arrest?' asked Nanda.

'No questions.'

'But this is a prison!' exclaimed Enrico.

The German grabbed his arm and jerked him to his feet.

'Los, los!' he shouted angrily, pushing him to the rear of the truck. He pushed him so hard, Enrico stumbled and fell to the floor, bumping his head on the seat. Fausto jumped the soldier, smashing his fist into his jaw. The soldier 'oofed' and fell back against the rear of the cab. The other soldiers aimed their guns at Fausto. Nanda screamed, 'Don't shoot!'

By now Anna was crying with fear and panic. The soldier Fausto had hit looked at her, rubbed his jaw painfully, then started toward the back of the truck. As he passed Fausto, he suddenly turned and slammed the butt of his rifle against the back of his skull. Fausto groaned and fell to the floor of the truck, unconscious.

'Fausto!' cried Nanda, starting toward him. The soldier grabbed her.

'Get out of the truck!' he yelled. *'Los! LOS!'*

The driver had come around the truck to lower the rear gate. Now the soldier pushed Nanda off the truck. She jumped down on the cobblestones, hurting her ankle. Then Enrico was pushed off the same way. Anna, however, was handed down gently to the driver.

The child was still crying as the truck drove away.

Then they were led into the dark recesses of Regina Coeli.

Fausto came to lying on a steel bunk in a long, narrow cell. Groaning and holding the back of his head which had a sore lump, he sat up and looked around. There were six stacked bunks in the cell, three to a side, and five men were sitting on the other bunks. At the end of the cell was a basin and a seatless toilet. On the ceiling, one light bulb protected by steel mesh. On the walls, graffiti.

He recognized the man sitting on the bunk opposite him as Sabato Martelli Castaldi, a general in the Italian Air Force who had fought the German entry into Rome and then joined the Resistance. Martelli Castaldi's face was swollen, puffy and covered with ugly bruises. He was smoking a cigarette, and the cell was foul with cigarette smoke and body odor.

'Castaldi,' said Fausto, 'where the hell am I?'

'You're a guest of the Gestapo,' said the General with an elegant, mocking smile. 'Welcome to the via Tasso.'

Fausto shuddered. The Gestapo prison in the via Tasso—not far from the Villa Wolkonsky, the German Embassy—was one of the most notorious places in Rome, where torture was a commonplace. They're trying to scare me, he thought. Mälzer wants to terrify me into paying the money. The drunken fool! I'm willing to pay . . .

'What happened to your face?' he asked.

Martelli Castaldi smiled. 'Aren't I lovely?' he said, pointing to his bruises. 'Our German allies should become plastic surgeons. They do so much for one's looks.'

'Did they beat you?'

'But of course. Nothing gives them greater pleasure. Guidone here . . .' he pointed to the bunk above him where a young man of about twenty was watching. 'He was beautiful the other night. Tell Signor Spada what you did, Guidone. It's quite, quite elegant.'

The young man looked embarrassed.

'Well, they were hitting the soles of my feet with a paddle. It hurt like hell. But I let out a big fart about the twentieth time, which really shook them up.'

Fausto forced a smile, but the casual accounts of torture didn't improve his spirits.

'What did you do?' asked Martelli Castaldi, sucking on his cigarette.

'I don't know. They arrested my whole family this morning, and took them to Regina Coeli.'

'Your lovely wife, as I recall, is Jewish, is she not?'

'Yes.'

'Then there's the answer, no?' Martelli Castaldi ground the cigarette out on the floor, then leaned forward and put his hand on Fausto's shoulder. 'You heard about the reprisals?' he asked, quietly.

'For the explosion yesterday?'

'Yes. One of the guards was talking about it last night . . . I overheard him. Hitler's furious about the Gappisti attack yesterday. He's demanding ten Italians be killed for every German killed. And so far, thirty-two Germans have died.'

Fausto's eyes widened.

'But that would be three hundred and twenty Italians . . .'

Martelli Castaldi nodded.

'You multiply very well, my friend.'

The window in the steel cell door was opened, and a guard

peered through. Then it was reclosed, and the door was opened. There were two Gestapo guards outside. One of them pointed at Fausto. 'You! Colonel Kappler said to bring you to him as soon as you're awake. Hurry!'

Fausto got off the bunk.

'Good luck,' said Martelli Castaldi.

'I'll need it,' replied Fausto, heading for the door.

'We all need it, my friend.'

And the cell door was shut again.

Fausto was taken to Kappler's office in another part of the building. The office, while not large, was pleasant, and its windows looked out on a pretty *giardino alla francese*, a private garden for the S.S., with myrtle groves, tall cypresses around a pond and a marble fountain. Behind Kappler's desk hung a full-length portrait of Adolf Hitler in an open raincoat, hands on his hips in a belligerent pose, his angry eyes staring off at some glorious Teutonic triumph on the horizon. Against another wall stood a lighted vitrine filled with Etruscan vases, part of Kappler's collection. Kappler was seated at his desk, studying some papers. He looked weary. He raised his bloodshot eyes and looked at Fausto.

'I need victims,' he said, matter-of-factly. 'I have been ordered by the Fuehrer to shoot three hundred and twenty Italians and Jews as reprisals for the cowardly attack on my countrymen yesterday afternoon. The executions will be carried out by this afternoon. I have been ordered to choose people who have already been condemned to death or life imprisonment. Unfortunately, there aren't enough of these, so I have been allowed to choose people who have not yet been tried but who have committed crimes punishable by death. I have also been authorized to put Jews on my list, whether they have committed crimes or not. I have put your wife and children on my list.'

'You kill them, you bastard, and Mälzer won't get his money!'

'Calm down, Spada. I realize that. I have talked to General Mälzer about your case. Have you come to a decision about the matter we discussed yesterday at lunch?'

'Yes, of course. I was going to call Mälzer this morning, but your men arrested us . . . I agree to the deal. My brother is arranging for the transfer of the funds.'

'And the jewels?'

'Yes, the jewels also. It's all there, at the Vatican! Can we make the transfer soon? My little daughter is terrified.'

'Yes, yes, I understand. Very well. As soon as I can arrange transportation for you, I'll send you to the Vatican. And I'll call General Mälzer as soon as he gets up. You see, I've been up all night here, trying to get the list made up, but it's very difficult . . . Extremely difficult to find enough victims . . .' He said something in German on his intercom, and two guards came in the office. 'Wait with them until I can find you a truck,' he said to Fausto.

'You will get my family out of Regina Coeli soon?' insisted Fausto.

'Yes, yes, I'm working as fast as I can! Now, go!'

Fausto went out with the guards. His head was still throbbing from the blow, but he felt better. Apparently everything was going to be all right after all.

He was driven to the Vatican at eight-thirty, and he went directly to Tony's office, where he told his brother what had happened. Tony looked disgusted. 'The Germans,' he said. 'To put Anna in that prison! How could they be so heartless, so cruel?'

'We must get them out as fast as possible. You transferred the money from the Crédit Suisse?'

'Yes. Everything's ready. Except, oddly enough, I don't know whom to make the check out to. Adolf Hitler?'

'Call Mälzer. Tell him we've accepted and to get Nanda and the children over here.'

'Yes, you're right.' He flipped his intercom and said to Father Frasseti, 'Get me General Mälzer, please.'

'Yes, Your Eminence.'

'Where's Paolo?'

'I'll send for him. Poor old fellow, he had a bad night of it, saying good-bye to his jewels.'

'If this damned war ever ends, maybe he'll get them back. Maybe I'll get my money back, who knows?'

'This war,' said Tony, sadly. 'It's brought out the best in humanity and the worst. Heroism and terrible cruelty . . . But I'll tell you frankly, Fausto, what I'd tell no other man. In my opinion, the Holy Father is making a grave error not condemning Hitler. And he's ordered the Vatican newspaper to condemn the partisans as criminals for what they did yesterday.'

'Criminals?' exclaimed Fausto. 'Because they attacked the Germans? Listen, I don't like their politics, but I'll give credit where it's due. They're the only ones in Rome putting up any resistance to the damned Nazis!'

'The Holy Father wants the Romans to lay low until the

Americans come in. Perhaps it's good tactics, I don't know. But it seems to me it's wrong to condemn the Gappisti. And he told me an hour ago he's not going to lift a finger to try and stop the reprisals. That I find intolerable. Three hundred and twenty people to be murdered in cold blood, and the Holy Father remains silent?' He sighed and shook his head. 'I love the Church with all my heart, but some of its policies . . .'

Father Frasseti's voice came over the intercom: 'General Mälzer, Your Eminence.'

Tony picked up the phone.

'General, my brother, Fausto Spada, is here. He and Signor Montecatini have agreed to your terms. As soon as Signora Spada and her two children are delivered here to the Vatican, we will hand over the jewels and a check drawn on the Vatican Bank for thirty million lire. By the way, who should the check be made out to?'

He listened. Then, with a look of slightly cynical amusement.

'I see. To you, personally. Very well.'

He listened further, his look of amusement being replaced by a look of concern.

'Excuse me, General, but that is entirely out of the question . . .'

The General was evidently screaming. Tony winced, and even Fausto could hear the faint resonance on the phone.

'General,' snapped Tony, 'I obviously will have to discuss this with my brother. I'll call you back shortly.'

He slammed down the phone.

'What is it?' asked Fausto.

'The man's drunk.'

'That wouldn't surprise me. What did he say?'

Tony took a deep breath.

'Mälzer says Kappler made a mistake. No women or children are going to be executed because of what he calls the "sensibilities" of the Gestapo executioners—as if the Gestapo has ever been sensitive! Anyway, he'll release Nanda and Anna . . . but he wants to keep Enrico.'

Fausto stiffened.

'Why? I don't understand . . .'

'He says the whole picture's changed. Even he can't let Enrico off the hook because they're so desperate to fill their quota, to find enough what he calls *Todeskandidaten,* or Death Candidates. He *needs* Enrico.'

Fausto exploded out of his chair in a rage.

'NO! Goddammit, a bargain's a bargain—he *won't* have my

son! Do you think I'd allow that drunken lout to put a bullet through Enrico's head? I'll kill him first! I'll kill *all* the fucking Nazis!'

'Fausto!'

Fausto doubled over, clenching his fists to his forehead, as if someone had just kicked him in the groin. Tony hurried around his desk and grabbed hold of his brother.

'Control yourself,' Tony soothed.

Fausto straightened, tears rolling down his cheeks.

'He's just holding me up for more money,' he said.

'I don't think so. He wants blood.'

'The bastard . . . it's not only him, it's Albertelli and all those other decrepit lunatic Fascists . . . They put him up to this to get at me . . .'

'Do you think so?'

'I'm sure of it. Well, they won't have my son. Call Mälzer back. Tell him there's no deal without Enrico.'

'But you can't say that! You can't jeopardize Nanda and Anna! If you say no deal, he may kill them *all!*'

Fausto took a deep breath, trying to control himself. He nodded, as if giving into the truth of this. He sniffed, wiped his nose on his sleeve. He was sweating and trembling. Tony had never seen him like this.

'All right,' he said, softly. 'Call Mälzer back. Tell him he can have me for Enrico.'

Tony looked shocked.

'There must be some other way—'

'What? He's got me—pardon me, Your Eminence—by the balls. Tell him to send Nanda and the children here, and they can take me with them.'

His twin didn't move.

'Are you sure?' he asked.

'Do you think I *want* to do it?' Fausto exclaimed. 'Of course not! I'm not suicidal, and I'm no martyr. But I'll do it to save my family. Make the call.'

Tony hesitated. Then he returned to his desk and flipped the intercom.

'Get me General Mälzer again.'

He sat down and looked at his brother.

'Well,' said Fausto, 'I've not been a very good brother, have I? Maybe this will make up for some of the rotten things I've done in my life. Do you think it will, Tony?'

Tony didn't answer for a moment. He was thinking back thirty-four years to that night Fausto took him to La Rosina's.

Shocked as he was by Fausto's self-sacrifice, for some reason all he could think of was that faraway night, the one night in his life he had had a woman . . .

'You're not answering,' said Fausto. 'I take it that means you think it won't make any difference. Well, perhaps you're right. And I've been a rotten Catholic, too. But perhaps in the time that's left, you'll do your best to prepare me to meet . . . our parents?'

'And God,' Tony added.

'And God. I hope you don't mind doing it, Tony. For all the sins I've committed, I need a cardinal—at the very least.'

The two twins looked at each other.

'Mind?' said Tony, quietly. 'It will be an honor.'

Father Frasseti's voice came over the intercom: 'General Mälzer, Your Eminence.'

'You're sure?' Tony said to Fausto.

Fausto nodded.

'I'm sure.'

Tony went back to his desk and reluctantly reached for the phone, his eyes still on his twin.

The vast aisles of St. Peter's were almost empty as Tony led Fausto across them. Fausto had not been in St. Peter's for years, but now the solemn majesty of the basilica filled him with a certain peace, dispelling the panic that had followed his offer of himself for his son. Suddenly, horribly, this was the last day of his life. His revulsion against Fascism and himself had begun seven years before in Ethiopia; since then he had had nothing to believe in except his family. Now, in retrospect, he saw the ugliness of what he had done. To sacrifice himself for Enrico restored a sense of worth to Fausto that had been missing for too long a time. Death would be swift; but as he crossed the aisles of St. Peter's, he began to feel it might be, in a way, beautiful.

The two brothers entered a confessional, and for fifteen minutes Fausto unlocked the secrets of his heart. When they emerged Tony had tears in his eyes. He embraced his brother, then led him down the long aisle to the great altar surmounted by Bernini's dazzling baldachino. There, the two men knelt and silently prayed.

At eleven-thirty a Mercedes staff car pulled up in front of St. Peter's. Albertelli got out and walked to the right portal of the cathedral where Fausto and Tony were waiting. Albertelli knelt to kiss Tony's ring. Then he stood up and looked at Fausto.

'You rather surprise me, Spada,' he said. 'You never struck me as the martyr type.'

'You don't give me much choice,' replied Fausto. 'Was it your idea to put my family on the list of death candidates?'

Albertelli smiled slightly.

'Perhaps.'

'Does my wife know?'

'No, they know nothing.'

'Thanks for that, at least.' He turned to his brother. 'Don't say anything to them now. You can tell them later.'

'Whatever you wish, Fausto.'

'You have the check for General Mälzer?' asked Albertelli. 'And the jewels?'

Tony handed him an envelope, and pointed to a frayed attaché case beside one of the columns. Quickly Albertelli looked inside the envelope, then opened the attaché case, which sparkled with Paolo's diamonds.

'There's a fortune here,' he said in awed tones.

'How much are you getting?' asked Fausto. 'Don't tell me you're letting General Mälzer take everything?'

Albertelli looked at him, but said nothing. He closed the case, then signaled the driver of his car. Two German soldiers got out of the back seat, followed by Nanda, Anna and Enrico. They were escorted to the church.

'Fausto!' said Nanda, who looked exhausted. 'Thank God you're safe.'

He embraced and kissed her as Anna tugged his sleeve.

'Poppa, they put us in a horrible old room with a lot of women!' she said. 'It smelled awful! And Enrico said there were ten people in his room, and they smelled worse.'

Fausto picked her up to kiss her.

'It's all over now, darling,' he said. 'And we're all going to be safe with Uncle Tony.'

'But what about Tito and Giulio? You promised me you'd bring them. And I need a toothbrush and my clothes and my books and dolls . . .'

'I know, darling. Your Poppa's going to go with these gentlemen right now. We'll pack everything and bring it all back, including Tito and Giulio.'

He shot a look at Albertelli, who was watching. The Fascist had the grace to remain silent.

'You won't forget my toothbrush? I want to brush my teeth. They didn't give us anything in that horrible old place. I *hated* it!'

513

'I'll bring your toothbrush. Now give me another kiss.'

She kissed him. He hugged her tightly for a moment, telling himself not to cry, not to frighten her. Then he put her down. He went to Tony and embraced him. 'Will you get her things?' he whispered.

'Yes.'

'Thank you. For everything. I love you.'

'God be with you, Fausto. You're a brave man.'

'I'm terrified.'

He hugged him, then turned to Enrico. The young man had an odd look on his face, as if he smelled something was wrong.

'Do you want me to go with you to help pack?' he asked.

'No, I'll do it. I'll be back in a while.'

'But . . .' He looked at the German soldiers, who were watching next to Albertelli. Albertelli was holding the attaché case.

'It's time, Spada,' he said.

'Yes . . . I'll be right with you.' He came to Enrico and embraced him. 'Don't say anything,' he whispered. 'Tell your mother afterward that I love her. And I love you. Always make me proud of you. Do you understand?'

'Yes, but . . .'

'Don't *say* anything! You're a fine young man. Be a better man than I was. Good-bye. *Addio.*' He kissed his cheek, then went to Nanda. He forced a smile as he hugged her.

'I can't bring all your clothes,' he said. 'But I'll bring what I can.' And he kissed her. 'I'm glad you're free,' he added. 'I love you with all my heart.'

Then he walked over to Albertelli.

'Let's go.'

They started walking toward the car. Enrico, standing next to his mother, was trembling. Nanda looked at him and saw the tears spill out onto his cheek.

'Enrico,' she said, 'what's wrong?'

'Nothing.'

'But . . .' She looked at her husband, and suddenly she knew.

'Fausto!' she screamed.

'No,' said Enrico, taking her hand. 'He wants it this way . . .'

'*Dio, Dio*—Fausto!'

She tore away from her son and started running toward the Mercedes. The soldiers had opened the rear door, and Fausto was about to climb in. Now he looked at his wife.

514

'Nanda, go back!' he yelled.

'Fausto, where are they taking you?'

The soldier pushed him into the back seat and slammed the door. Quickly the others climbed in.

'FAUSTO!'

The car started and quickly picked up speed as it raced out of St. Peter's Square.

Nanda had been running. Now she stopped, staring disbelievingly at the car.

She saw her husband watching through the rear window. He was saying something. She couldn't hear the words, but she knew it was 'I love you.'

The Appian Way begins at the Porta San Sebastiano, south of Rome. Two thousand feet down the ancient road there is a fork, where the legend states that St. Peter saw a vision of Christ and asked, *'Domine, quo vadis?'* The right fork, leading to the old port city of Ardea, is called the via Ardeatina. Another two thousand feet down the right fork, the Ardeatine Caves lie to the right of the road. The caves were a network of tunnels that had been excavated before the First World War for a sandy volcanic dust called *pozzolana,* used in making concrete. The tunnels had been used up and abandoned.

The Ardeatine Caves had been chosen that morning by Kappler as the execution site for what now amounted to 335 Italians and Italian Jews.

At four in the afternoon, Fausto, his hands tied behind his back, was transported in a truck with thirty other prisoners from the Regina Coeli prison out of Rome to the Ardeatine Caves. When they arrived at the entrance to the caves, the Germans shouted at them to climb down. No one but Fausto had been told what was happening, but most of them had guessed; and when they saw the great crowd of prisoners standing before the caves, even those that hadn't guessed knew. Some of them were crying, some praying; most were silent. Fausto saw Martelli Castaldi, the young Guidone, General Simoni—a World War I hero who had fought the Germans the previous September —Colonel Montezemolo, the aristocratic head of the Monarchist military resistance, who was wearing a blue sweater . . . There were peddlars, sailors, businessmen, store clerks, railroad workers, film technicians. It was a true cross-section of Italian society, a sociological study caught in the amber of death.

The executions had already begun. Twenty minutes after his arrival, Fausto and ten others were marched to the second entrance of the caves. The German executioners were drinking brandy. Some of them were literally staggering: The horror of what they were doing could only be contained with the deadening relief of alcohol.

Fausto took a final look at the blue sky. Then he walked into the dark, damp tunnel.

They were marched far into the bowels of the hill until their noses told them they were approaching their destination. It was a scene of appalling horror. At least seventy-five bodies were lying on the floor of the tunnel, illuminated by flickering torches. The Germans had begun piling the bodies into a heap, since they were running out of room, and the pile, a grotesque mound of jutting arms and legs, was already ten high. Fausto winced at the macabre sight. The Germans were armed with 9 mm Maschine Pistoles, automatic pistols that fired continuously as long as the trigger was pressed, like machine guns. Now they yelled at the new batch of victims to come forward, one by one.

Fausto was filled with terror, but he was amazed how silent his companions in death were. Like him, they were putting up no resistance. There was no ringing rhetoric, no shaken fists, merely resignation, an air of 'let's get it over with.' Get life over with.

'You.'

He was beckoned. He walked to the pile of cadavers.

'Climb up,' said the German.

Fausto looked at his blond executioner.

'May you rot in hell,' he said, quietly. Then, awkwardly, his hands tied behind him, he began climbing the pile of cadavers as the prisoners before him had done. It was almost, but not quite, an amusing comment on German efficiency. Force the victim to climb to the top of the pile to be shot and spare yourself the trouble of carrying his corpse up afterward.

I am climbing over corpses, the unreal thought flashed through his mind. In a minute I will be one of them . . . Someone will be climbing over me . . . Except it won't be me. It will only be this used-up body of mine. I will be somewhere else . . .

'That's far enough. Kneel.'

Fausto's knees were in the back of a tweed-jacketed student. He felt something cold and hard press against the nape of his neck. He was thinking of his father, his mother, his son, his daughter. His last thought before death was of Nanda.

Then blackness.

PART XIII

THE QUEEN
OF SEVENTH AVENUE

1950

CHAPTER 55

The Feldman Building was eighteen floors of undistinguished Depression-style architecture at the corner of Thirty-eighth Street and Seventh Avenue. On a hot spring afternoon in 1950, with the streets of the garment center as usual jammed with horn-blowing cars and trucks, thousands of pedestrians, and rack-boys pushing their racks of dresses, all the windows of the building were open to catch whatever breeze there was except the windows on the top floor. Here, on the executive floor, Abe Feldman had installed air conditioners. Here, the windows were shut. Here, in the cool showroom, the heart of the business, Gabriella watched the buyers from the Midwest as the buyers watched the gaunt models parade on the runway.

'Number sixty-two ten,' intoned the female announcer in her fake Oyster Bay lockjaw accent. 'A lovely cocktail dress by Gabriella with marvelous treatment of the shoulders. Guaranteed to be seen at all the best cocktail parties next fall. Number sixty-two ten.'

The model twirled through the curtains and a new model appeared.

'Number forty-five seventeen,' droned the announcer, who had elevated boredom to an art form. 'A crisp suit for that important business lunch, with the unmistakable Grabriella touch in the piping and lining. What smart business girls will be wearing next fall from coast to coast. Number forty-five seventeen.'

It was a normal day at Summit Fashions. Four floors below on one of the shop floors, where the windows were open and there was no air conditioning and the whirr of seventy sewing machines almost but not quite drowned out the horns from the street below, Mrs. Rita Alvarez, a heavy, middle-aged woman who had emigrated from Puerto Rico three years before, was

519

having a fight with Artie Vogel, who had managed the shop for twelve years.

'I lose money on thees blouse!' yelled Mrs. Alvarez, standing by her sewing machine and shaking the garment in question in front of Artie's face as sweat glistened on her ham-hock arms. 'Eet's too complicated! I lose money!'

'Rita, baby,' sighed Artie, who was forty-three, skinny, and had a memorably ugly face, 'we worked out the price yesterday.'

'But I deedn't know eet was so hard!' she shouted. 'I lose money! Eet take too long!'

'Rita, baby, you don't like the work here, you're free to go someplace else.'

Smile.

Mrs. Rita Alvarez, who had six children and desperately needed the work, sat down, muttering in Spanish. Then, as Artie started down the aisle, she yelled after him, 'I'll talk to the union!'

Artie turned. The sixty-nine other workers in the hot and humid shop kept sewing, but they were watching Artie Vogel. Most of the women were, like Rita Alvarez, from Puerto Rico. They knew the 'union' was a dirty word at Summit Fashions.

Artie pulled a notebook from his hip pocket, scribbled a notation, gave Rita Alvarez a look, then turned and left the shop.

Rita Alvarez went back to her sewing.

At four-thirty Gabriella was in her office, arguing with two fabric salesmen. 'You call that quality cotton?' she said, jabbing her finger at a swatch. 'I can see holes through the weave!'

'It's Egyptian,' said the salesman, defensively.

'It's crap. Look, George, I want the best. If you keep trying to sell me crap, forget the whole thing.'

Ellen Sarne, her young secretary, stuck her head in the door.

'Numero Uno wants to see you.'

'Coming.' She hurried out of her office, shoving the fabric salesmen in front of her. Time. Everything had to go fast in the garment center, because time was literally money, late orders could be returned, late ideas could mean a disastrous season . . . Time.

She hurried down the corridor, pausing to stick her head in her private fitting room where Rosita, whom Gabriella had convinced to move to New York from Los Angeles, was working on a new dress. 'How's it going?' she asked, hurrying in to check a seam on the form. Rosita, her mouth full of pins, merely grunted. Gabriella hurried back out into the corridor. Time.

Hurry. Rush . . . She came into Abe's impressively furnished outer office. Nancy, his secretary, was on the phone. 'Go on in,' she said. Gabriella crossed to the handsome wooden doors and entered the inner sanctum. As always, he was on the phone. 'The order won't be late, dammit! We'll get it there tomorrow afternoon at the latest! Calm down, Ernie. Tomorrow.' He hung up and looked at Gabriella. 'How'd it go?'

'Marshall Field was dynamite. Almost forty thousand bucks' worth of orders. L. S. Ayres wasn't so good, but that buyer's always a bitch in hot weather. Still, she placed almost twenty thousand, and she went crazy over my checked suit.'

'She should. That's a beauty. Want to have dinner?'

'Don't you ever change your line?'

She had long since given up taking offense at his unceasing attempts to date her and bed her down. She knew his sense of macho made it imperative for him to keep trying, and it had become almost a running gag between them.

'Well, tonight's a little different,' he said. 'I'm divorcing Marcia.'

She looked surprised. This was no gag.

'Since when?'

'Since last night. We started to have another fight, but I said to hell with it, it's not worth the energy. She's as bored with me as I am with her, so why shouldn't we split? So we're going to. I'd like to talk about it with you.'

For eight years he had come on strong with her. Now he was coming on soft. It intrigued her.

'Of course, Abe. I'll have to run home to change.'

'I'll pick you up at seven. We'll go to Pavillon.'

Home for Gabriella was a charming little house on Washington Mews that had once been a coach house. It had a low-ceilinged, beamed living room on the ground floor with a big stone hearth and, behind that, a modern kitchen which opened into a tiny garden. A tortuous nineteenth-century stair led to the second floor, where there were two bedrooms and baths for her and Nick, who was now ten. When Gabriella got home from the office, Nick was in the cobblestone street in front of the house playing catch with one of the neighbors.

'Hi, Mom,' he said.

'Hi, darling.' She kissed him. 'Listen: I have to go out to dinner. I'll tell Amy to make you supper. What would you like?'

'Hamburgers.'

'Nick, you can't eat hamburgers *all* the time. Wouldn't you like some chicken?'

'Okay, but I'd rather have hamburgers. Who are you going to dinner with?'

She hesitated.

'Mr. Feldman.'

Nick looked surprised.

'Him? No kidding.'

She went into the house to talk to Amy, the cook-maid-babysitter. Gabriella knew why she had hesitated mentioning Abe's name to her son. She had kept Abe out of her private life to the extent that Nick had met him only twice. Until now, she had always had Marcia as an excuse with which to fend Abe off. But now Marcia was gone.

As she climbed the narrow stairs to take a shower and change, she wondered how a divorced Abe Feldman was going to fit into her private—and business—life.

It was part of Abe's vanity, based on the insecurity of a self-made man, to be recognized and kowtowed to by the best restaurateurs in town, and he was willing to pay for it. Henri Soulé, the proprietor of Pavillon, was not an easy man to impress, but Abe had managed to get on the great man's A list, and he was always given one of the better tables, if not the best. Now Abe lighted a cigarette, took a sip of his martini, and said to Gabriella, 'We haven't done badly in business, have we?'

'We've done very well.'

'And for two people who started off at each other's throats, we haven't done badly as people either. Or wouldn't you agree?'

'No, I agree.'

'I like you a lot, Gabriella. And I know what you're thinking: here comes Feldman again, with his line. But this isn't a line. I *do* like you a lot. I admire you, both as a businesswoman and as a woman.' He hesitated. 'Not to pry, but how's your love life these days? Still going with that ad agency jerk?'

She smiled slightly.

'No, that didn't last. You're right: he *was* a jerk.'

'You've gone with a lot of men these past eight years. Isn't it sort of odd you've never met one you really went for?'

She shrugged.

'Not particularly. I've had my work, I've had Nick . . . I'm happy. Maybe I'm that exotic creature the women's magazines are writing so much about: the Independent Woman. You know, there's no law that says a woman can't play the field—just the way you men do.'

'Perhaps.'

'You say "perhaps," but you really don't believe it. You're like all men: you think no woman's *really* happy unless she's found Mr. Right. Well, I *had* Mr. Right. And right now, I'm fine just as I am.'

'Then maybe you should try Mr. Wrong—me.'

She laughed.

'Why are you Mr. Wrong? I've grown very fond of you, Abe —with all your faults. And boy, you've got a lot of faults.'

'So do you.'

'Oh, I know.'

'Even with my faults, I'd like a chance with you. How about it?'

'Don't you think we'd be better off remaining business partners, period?'

'I'd like to try something more exciting.' He took another sip of his martini. 'I've moved into the Pierre, but I'm looking for an apartment. When I find one, will you help me furnish it? You've got great taste, and you know what I like.'

'I'd be glad to.'

'Then if that works out, maybe things will lead to things.'

'Maybe.' She smiled. 'We'll see.'

Rita Alvarez was fighting mad. The more she thought about the blouse she was losing money on, the more she wanted to spit in Artie Vogel's ugly face. Now, as she stormed into the I.L.G.W.U. offices on West Fortieth Street, she was ready to translate anger into action.

'I wanna talk to somebody eemportant,' she almost shouted at the receptionist.

'What about?'

'What you theenk? You theenk I come to union office to do laundry? I wanna complain 'bout no union at Summit Fashions, where I work!'

'Just a minute.'

Five minutes later Rita Alvarez was seated in a small office across the desk from a heavyset man named Sid Cohn.

'You know what that Mr. Feldman does!' said Rita, her anger still bubbling. 'Everyone knows! He's got the Mob on hees payroll to keep the union out! Eesn't that true?'

'I've heard that rumor,' said Sid Cohn.

'Then why don't you do something about eet? We're gettin' screwed every day at that place! We got no rights, no *nothin'*! Or . . .' she lowered her voice, giving the union organizer a suspicious glare, '. . . ees eet true what we hear? That maybe

523

Feldman buy *you* off? That he pay the union lotsa money to leave heem alone? People say that.'

'Look, Mrs. Alvarez, people say a lot of things. But I can assure you Abe Feldman isn't paying off the union. Now, exactly what is your complaint?'

She told him about the blouse.

'All right,' said Cohn, getting up, 'it's time I paid another visit to Mr. Feldman.'

'You gotta use muscle with that bastard!' exclaimed Rita. 'You gotta threaten heem with a strike!'

Sid Cohn took his checkered cap off a wall peg and put it on.

'That's exactly what I intend to do,' he said. 'Let's go.'

The view from the terrace of the fifteenth-floor duplex penthouse took in all of Central Park. As she leaned against the brick wall drinking in the view, the brisk breeze blowing her hair, Gabriella said, 'It *has* to be the most gorgeous view in New York! Oh Abe, buy it for the view, if nothing else!'

'You like it?'

'How could anyone not like it? And the layout's fantastic. But think what a beautiful garden you could have on this terrace.'

'*We* could have,' he said, taking her hands. She looked at him, then pulled her hands away and went inside the living room. The Fifth Avenue building had been put up in the Twenties, and the penthouse had belonged to a tycoon of the day who had recently died. The high ceilings, the elaborate covings, the big, leaded French doors that opened on two sides of the living room to the wide terrace which surrounded the entire penthouse, were baronial touches left over from a baronial age. The parquet floors were bare because the apartment had been emptied; light bulbs dangled on black wire where she imagined chandeliers once had hung. But still, the spaces were magnificent, and her imagination was already placing the furniture and choosing the materials.

'Would you mind leaving us alone for about twenty minutes?' Abe asked the realtor, Mrs. Stilson.

'Of course.' Mrs. Stilson was eager to please a prospective buyer for one of the most expensive apartments on the market. 'I'll wait in the lobby.'

'Thanks,' smiled Abe, all charm. 'I'd like to sort of "live" in it for a few minutes.'

'I understand. Take your time, Mr. Feldman.'

She went into the foyer. When she was gone, Abe said to Gabriella, 'So you think I should buy it?'

'It's a spectacular apartment. How much are they asking?'

'A hundred and eighty thousand.'

She whistled.

'Offer them a hundred and fifty. They'll take it. This place is a white elephant, which is why I love it.'

'I'll buy it if you'll move in with me.'

'Come on, Abe, act your age . . .'

'Is that it?' he said, grabbing her wrist. 'Is it because I'm older than you?'

'That has nothing to do with it.'

'Then why do you keep putting me off? I'm crazy about you, Gabriella . . .'

Suddenly he pulled her into his arms and kissed her. There was violence in the kiss, and passion and hunger. For the first time in eight years, she began to *feel* the man, physically. He was hard, warm, and smelled faintly of expensive after-shave lotion. She liked what she felt and smelled.

He released her and took off the jacket of his dark-blue, custom-made suit. He dropped it on the floor, then pulled down his tie.

'What are you doing?' she said.

'Getting naked,' he said, matter-of-factly. 'Take your clothes off.'

'I will not!'

'We're going to make it right here, on the living room floor. Before I pay a hundred and fifty grand for any apartment, I want a trial run first.'

Off came his shirt. He dropped it and the tie next to the coat. Then he leaned on the mantel to untie his shoes. She watched him in a state of semishock.

'You'd be surprised the places I've fucked in,' he said, 'though I generally manage some furniture—a daybed or something. The floor should be interesting. Or how about the terrace? We could give the neighbors a real show.'

Off came the shoes. He unbuckled his belt and unzipped his fly. Off came the pants. Then the gartered, dark-blue socks. She stared at his hairy legs.

'You've been invited to a party,' he said, pleasantly. 'I trust you wouldn't be so rude as not to accept?'

She hesitated. Did she want this? Did she want *him*? She was attracted to him physically, but it was nothing like the overpowering desire she had felt for Nick Kemp. But Abe had something Nick hadn't had: a razor mind, a ruthlessness that was in a way as exciting as Nick's physical beauty had been. Abe also had power and money and the ambition to be on top of the world —like this penthouse. Yes, she couldn't deny that Abe Feldman excited her. She couldn't deny she wanted him.

She began unzipping her dress. He watched as she silently took off her clothes, and she was gratified to see that the bulge in his jockey shorts grew as she stripped. When she was naked, she stood in the center of the empty living room as the sun poured through the French doors, splashing the splendor of her flesh. He pulled down his shorts, and his huge erection sprang free. Then he came across the room to her and took her in his arms, beginning to kiss her, tenderly at first. As his lips moved down her neck to her shoulders, she felt his fingers rubbing lightly over her buttocks, and she tingled with pleasure.

'I love you, Gabriella,' he whispered as his penis rubbed against her. 'I'm crazy for you . . .'

Gently he pulled her down to the floor. She lay on her back as he straddled her. Then she felt the black hair of his chest crinkling against her breasts. He was kissing her hotly now as his tenderness gave way to animal lust. There was a lot of lust in him. The energy and ambition that had made him millions on Seventh Avenue were one side of the coin; a voracious sexual appetite was the other. Now he was inside her, and she filled with his manhood. His haunches began thrusting, slowly at first, but then with increased ferocity. He was good, excellent in fact, a superb lover. She was overcome with sweet desire as she climbed to the top of the orgasm, moaning with pleasure until she finally gasped and came at the same time his warm semen flooded her.

He said nothing for a while, lying on the parquet beside her. Then he sat up, leaned over, kissed her mouth and smiled, flashing his beautiful caps.

'I'm buying the apartment,' he said. Then he reached for his socks and began putting them on.

CHAPTER 56

Gabriella paid Rosita Guzman, her seamstress, the princely salary of $25,000 a year, which made the plump Mexican one of the highest-paid women on Seventh Avenue. But Rosita was worth every penny. Hard-working, fiercely loyal to Gabriella, even-tempered during the inevitable crises and deadline meetings, Rosita was a gem and Gabriella loved her. 'I've got a wonderful idea for the new collection!' Gabriella beamed the next morning as she came in the fitting room. 'Love! That's the theme, plain, old-fashioned, corny love! I'm going to design dresses for women in love, romantic dresses, frills—God, I may even put in hoopskirts! What do you think, Rosita?'

'I think maybe you're on some kinda pill maybe?'

Gabriella laughed and hugged her.

'I *am* on a pill. A nutty pill! A crazy pill! Rosita,' she lowered her voice, 'I think I'm in love.'

Rosita's face beamed.

'Oh, that's *nice!* I'm so glad for you! Who's the lucky man?'

'Abe Feldman!'

Rosita's smile turned to a frown, like a cloud over the moon. *'Him?* That's not so nice.'

Gabriella looked genuinely surprised.

'But I thought you liked him?' she said.

'Oh, he's okay, I guess. To me and you he's okay. But to those poor people who work downstairs, he's terrible. Specially the Puerto Ricans. You don't pay much attention to what goes on down there, but *I* do, because they're my people. I mean, we all speak Spanish. I tell you, your boyfriend squeezes them dry.'

Gabriella looked sulky.

'Well, I think he's as good an employer as there is on Seventh Avenue.'

'Oh yeah? Where's the union? You know what happened yesterday? This union organizer come here to see Mr. Feldman,

527

and they had a big fight. Bet he didn't mention *that* to you, did he?'

'No . . .'

'Sure he didn't. There's a woman on the fourteenth floor named Rita Alvarez. Well, she went to the union to complain 'cause she was getting cheated on her piecework, and that's why the union guy was here yesterday. And guess what happen this morning? I just heard about it in the hall. Rita Alvarez was fired. She's got six kids to feed, and she got fired 'cause she went to the union. So tell me more about how you're in love with wonderful Mr. Feldman. If you ask me, he's a good-looking son of a bitch.'

She went back to work. Gabriella, feeling a bit deflated, returned to her office without saying anything more.

But she had plenty to think about.

'So you like Greenwich Village?' said Abe that evening as he played catch with Nick in front of Gabriella's house.

'Oh sure, it's a great place to live!' enthused Nick. 'Best place in New York! All the nuts live down here.'

Abe laughed.

'I hope you don't include yourself?'

'Yeah, I'm a nut. I'm going to be a writer when I grow up, and you've got to be nuts to be a writer.'

'Oh? And what are you going to write?'

'Movies! And I'm going out to Hollywood and write them for my great-uncle Morris, and he'll make 'em.'

'Morris David? By the time you're writing movies, he'll be a little long in the tooth for moviemaking, won't he?'

'Uncle Morris will make movies till he drops dead. He loves movies, like I do. Action movies, with a lot of gangsters and gunfights!'

'That's my kind of movie, too. Would you like to live uptown?'

'Where?'

'Oh, say on Fifth Avenue? Overlooking Central Park? You could play baseball in the park.'

Nick considered this.

'Well, that might not be so bad—I mean, the park. But I'd sure hate to leave Greenwich Village. Are there any writers on Fifth Avenue?'

'Not many.'

Gabriella came out of the house, wiping her hands on her apron.

'All right, you two: dinner.'

Nick caught the ball for the last time, then started for the house.

'Would *you* want to live uptown on Fifth Avenue?' he asked his mother.

Gabriella shot Abe a look.

'I don't know. I haven't thought about it.'

Nick looked at his mother, then at Abe, then back to his mother.

'Is there something going on between you two?' he asked.

'Nick, that's none of your business.'

'Why not? Anything you do is my business. You've worked for him eight years, and I've only seen him twice. And now in a couple of days you go out to dinner with him, and then he comes down here for dinner . . . What's going on?'

Abe, carrying his jacket over his shoulder, came to the door. 'Let's go inside, Nick,' he said, 'and I'll tell you.'

They went in the beamed living room, and Gabriella shut the door. Abe lay his coat over the back of a chair and turned to Nick. 'What's going on is that I'm in love with your mother,' he said, quietly. 'Now, I don't know if she's in love with me yet, but I'm working on her.' He looked at Gabriella. 'And with any luck, I'll get her. So that's why you and I have to become good friends.'

Nick looked dubious.

'Yeah, I suppose.'

'Do you like me?'

'You seem okay. So far.'

Abe laughed.

'That's a great recommendation. Well, I hope I improve with time. Tell you what: I'll take you to a movie Saturday afternoon. Would you like that?'

Nick's eyes widened.

'*Any* movie?' he said.

'You pick it.'

'You're looking better all the time, Mr. Feldman!'

'Abe.'

'Nick,' said his mother, pointing to his chair at the plank table, 'the idea is to play a *little* hard to get.'

'I didn't know you were a great cook,' he said after Nick had gone upstairs to do his homework. He sat on the sofa in front of the fireplace. 'But I should have guessed it. There's nothing

Gabriella can't do. Fabulous designer, fabulous cook . . . you're fabulous, period.'

She sat next to him and kissed his cheek.

'Thanks,' she said. 'And you've made a hit with Nick, which is no mean accomplishment. He doesn't like most of my boyfriends. He's *very* choosy.'

'I'm more than a "boyfriend." ' He took her in his arms. 'You are going to be the next Mrs. Feldman, whether you know it or not.'

'I think you're rushing things a bit.'

'I *always* rush things. That's why I'm numero uno.'

'Abe, why did you fire Rita Alvarez?'

A cool silence.

'Who told you about that?' he said finally.

'I heard about it. I heard about your fight with the union organizer, too. Don't you think by now it's a little late to be antiunion?'

'No!'

He said it so forcefully, she winced. He let her go and stood up.

'Listen,' he said, standing in front of her almost as if he were a prosecuting attorney. 'I built Summit Fashions up from *nothing*. I had *nothing*. My father was an immigrant Jew who was a goddam janitor all his life. Summit's *my* baby, I'm the boss, and I'm going to run it *my* way! And that means no goddam union!'

'But why? Most of the other companies are unionized . . .'

'And you know what happens the moment they unionize? They have to put one percent of the payroll into the retirement fund, one percent into health services, they've got to give paid vacations . . . Do you know why we're so big?'

'Because we're good.'

'Sure we're good, but we've got the edge! The edge is that three percent advantage we've got over the competition because we're *not* unionized and we can undersell the bastards. You know what Seventh Avenue is: it's cutthroat. It's constant war. It's survival of the smartest, and there's no one smarter than Abe Feldman. I've got the edge, and I'm going to *keep* the edge. And that means no union.'

'And what about Rita Alvarez and the six kids she had to support?'

'She'll get a job somewhere else. Look, Gabriella: I know you're thinking I'm a hard-hearted son of a bitch, and maybe I am. But the clothing business has always depended on cheap labor, and it always will. There's already a lot of talk about New York being finished as a home for the industry because the goddam union is pricing us out of the market. People are talking about moving south where labor's still cheap, and once that happens, New York *will* be finished. And where would that leave Rita Alvarez? On welfare.'

'But still . . .'

She didn't finish. He sat next to her again.

'I'm sorry,' he said, more quietly. 'I didn't mean to yell at you, but those are the facts of life. Why do you think New York's filling up with Puerto Ricans like Rita Alvarez? Because Seventh Avenue needs cheap labor, and Vito Marcantonio wants votes. Three years ago Rita Alvarez was happy because she had a better job with me than she'd ever had in her life in San Juan. Now she wants a union, and if she had the union, in five years she'd be bitching again. I don't blame her: it's human nature to look out for yourself. But you can't blame me for looking out for *me*, can you?'

'I don't know,' she said, uncertainly.

'Then forget about it. Just design your clothes, and let me run the business. We've been a good team so far, and we can be better. And the only union we need is you and me.'

He took her in his arms and started kissing her. After a moment, he took his mouth away and whispered, 'Marry me, Gabriella. Marcia's going to Mexico for a quickie divorce, and when it's over, marry me. I'll make you so goddam happy, you won't know what hit you.'

She looked up into his eyes.

'I'm already happy,' she said.

'Bullshit. I'll make you Queen of Seventh Avenue. I'll give you the fucking world. *Then* you'll know what happiness is. Say you'll marry me.'

'I'll have to think about it.'

He released her and stood up.

'All right, think about it,' he said. 'I'll go upstairs to the john. When I come down, I want an answer.'

She started to tell him to go to hell, but something kept her mouth shut. As he climbed the squeaky, ancient stairs, she thought about being Mrs. Abe Feldman. The power, the money, the influence . . . Queen of Seventh Avenue. It was tempting, so tempting. And she loved him. Who could resist the force of his energy and lust and ambition when it was unleashed, as he had unleashed it at her? Her whole life flooded back into her memory: her insecure, overweight childhood, her years of

531

wandering in Europe, the loss of her parents, the loss of her grandparents, the loss of Nick . . . Now she had tasted success, and she loved it. She was a success on her own, and to become Mrs. Abe Feldman would crown her success with his. And wouldn't Uncle Drew be jealous of *that?* And wouldn't Morris and Barbara be proud?

She thought of Rita Alvarez. She knew Abe was wrong in his antiunionism, and his callousness toward Rita Alvarez was ugly, no matter how he rationalized it. But if she were his wife, wouldn't she be able to change him? He couldn't stay antiunion forever; perhaps she could hasten the day. She heard him coming down the stairs.

'Well?' he said as he came back into the room. 'What's the answer?'

She looked at him: tall, slim, still youthfully good-looking despite the gray at his temples, beautifully dressed, so sure of himself. Abe Feldman, the ultimate winner. Damn him, she thought. He knows he's irresistible.

'When Gabriella Kemp marries Abe Feldman,' she said, 'it's got to be somewhere special. Where will we go?'

He smiled and came over to the sofa to kiss her.

'Paris. Where else?'

CHAPTER 57

Two weeks later Sid Cohn left the I.L.G.W.U. headquarters by himself and headed for his favorite bar, Paddy's. It was a few minutes before ten at night. Sid had been working late, making final arrangements for the picket line that would be thrown up the next morning around the Summit Fashions building. Sid had fought the union brass on Summit: for a variety of reasons, the brass had been reluctant to move against the company (Sid even wondered if perhaps Abe Feldman *had* slipped money under the table to the union to leave him alone). But Sid had been angered by Rita Alvarez's story, and he bulled the picket line through his superiors' objections. It promised to be a long, hot and ugly strike. Abe had shown no signs of giving in and, in fact, had sailed for Paris with his new wife, leaving Summit in the hands of his vice-president, Maury Schulman. That might be Abe Feldman's way of showing his contempt for the union, but Sid Cohn reflected that Feldman was in a weaker position than he assumed. Feldman, the self-made tycoon running roughshod over his employees, was a relic from the past. Ninety percent of Seventh Avenue was unionized. Abe Feldman's major weakness was that time was against him.

Sid turned into West Thirty-eighth Street. A few trucks were making deliveries, but otherwise the street was deserted. A blue Plymouth turned the corner and bore down on Sid, coming from behind him. The back door opened as the car went up on the sidewalk. By the time Sid realized something was happening behind him, the two burly men who had jumped out of the back seat were grabbing him, one of them clamping a handkerchief over his mouth. They pushed him into the back seat, then jumped in after him, slamming the door. The car gunned. It roared off the sidewalk back on to the street, then headed east.

The two men in the back were members of the Jerry Grossman gang, a Brooklyn-based mob that had made the garment center its territory. One of the men, whose nickname was Veal Chop, sat on Sid Cohn's chest, wedging him to the floor of the car, as the other man, whose nickname was Blade, slit Sid Cohn's throat from ear to ear.

It had all happened in less than a minute.

'*A ce moment*,' said Gabriella as she stood on the balcony of their suite at the Ritz, '*j'en ai marre de tout sauf l'amour.*'

'Subtitles, please,' said Abe, who was in his pajamas, stretched out on a sofa in the living room of the suite, reading the Paris *Herald-Tribune*. They had just finished breakfast.

Gabriella turned and came back into the luxurious, flower-filled room. Her hair was loose, and she was wearing a diaphanous beige negligée she had designed for herself which she called her 'sexpot special.' In fact, her nude body was teasingly visible through the material, with the specific details just veiled enough to create mystery and stave off charges of pornography.

'I said,' she smiled, kneeling beside him and kissing his hand, 'right now I'm bored with everything in life except love.'

'That's the way it's supposed to be on a honeymoon,' he replied. 'Do you want to go to Dior today?'

She shook her head.

'No. No fashion for at least three more days. I don't want to even *think* about seams and hemlines! I want to think about nothing but love and romance, and I've got the day all planned. We're going to be real tourists. We'll hire a car and drive out to Malmaison . . .'

'What's that?'

'Josephine's house. It's gorgeous, and there's a wonderful restaurant near there . . .'

'Josephine who?'

She stared at him.

'Napoleon's wife, dum-dum!'

'Oh. Well, what the hell, I didn't know who you meant. Why do you want to see her house?'

'Because it's beautiful, of course!'

'I'd rather go to Dior, but go on.'

'Then we'll have lunch at the restaurant, then we'll go to Versailles and spend the whole afternoon there.'

'I've seen it.'

'So have I, but it's worth seeing again. Then tonight you're going to take me to my favorite restaurant in the whole world, Grand Véfour . . .'

'Oh yeah. I'm with you there.'

'And then we'll come back here and make love ten times, nonstop.'

'Wait a minute. I'll need a backup team . . .'

There was a knock at the door.

'I'll get it,' said Gabriella, getting to her feet. She hurried across the room and opened the door.

'*Câblogramme pour Monsieur Feldman,*' said the uniformed messenger boy, ogling Gabriella's gauzy negligée.

'*Merci.*'

She tipped him, then closed the door.

'Shall I open it?'

Abe was lighting a cigarette.

'Sure.'

She opened the envelope, pulled out the cable and read it. She frowned and looked up.

'Who's Sid Cohn?' she asked.

'That son of a bitch from the union who's been trying to organize us. Why?'

'The cable's from Maury Schulman. Sid Cohn's been murdered.'

Abe sat up, staring at her.

'What?'

'I'll read the cable: "Sid Cohn murdered. Pickets called off for time being. Think you should return. Trouble. Signed, Maury." '

'That stupid asshole—why doesn't he phone me? What's "trouble" mean? Christ, put a call through to him . . .'

'But Abe, it's the middle of the night in New York!'

'Wake the son of a bitch up! His number's Eldorado 5-4728.'

While Gabriella placed the call with the operator, Abe got up and began pacing the room like a caged tiger. She had seen him angry many times before, but this wasn't anger so much as . . . what? She wasn't sure, but she thought he seemed frightened.

'Who would want to murder Sid Cohn?' she said, hanging up.

'How the hell would *I* know?'

'Well, you must have some idea. If I were a detective, I'd have an idea.'

He glared at her.

'Like what?'

'Obviously, the person I'd look for would be the person who had most to gain by getting him out of the way.'

He stopped pacing, and his face went white.

'Are you saying that *I* murdered him?'

535

'Of course not. How could you murder him? You've been here with me. Unless . . .' She hesitated, terrified to say what was growing in her mind.

'Unless what?'

'There's been talk that you pay the Mob to keep the union out. I've never believed it, but . . .'

'But what?'

'Is it true?'

He sank on to the sofa.

'All right,' he said, 'I know who murdered Sid Cohn. Jerry Grossman had him knocked off because I told him I didn't want this goddam strike! Except I didn't think he'd actually *murder* someone . . . Jesus Christ . . .'

She tensed.

'Who's Jerry Grossman?'

'He's the goddam Mob. Who do you think?'

'Then it *is* true?'

'I've been paying Grossman for four years. How the hell else do you think I keep the union out? Give me a cigarette . . .'

She brought him the cigarette and lit it for him mechanically. She was too stunned to react. He inhaled deeply, then looked at her.

'I pay Grossman two thousand a month for protection, mainly against the union. The union heads know it and respect it. They don't want trouble if they can avoid it. But this Cohn guy forced them into attacking me, so I called Grossman just before we left for Paris and told him to take care of things for me. I thought it would be the usual stuff—phone-call threats, maybe a little rough stuff—but I swear to God, Gabriella, I didn't think he'd murder the bastard!'

'But what do you *think* the Mob does?' she exclaimed, angrily, her reaction finally erupting. 'I can't believe you'd have been so stupid as to hire gangsters just to keep the union out!'

'I had to do it!'

'Why?'

'To keep the edge!'

'To hell with the edge! If you can't compete honestly, then you oughtn't to be in the business!'

'That's easy to say, but hard as hell to do!'

'Oh Abe, Abe . . .' She was so frustrated by his blindness, she wanted to scream. 'Aside from everything else, did you ever think what you're doing to the Puerto Ricans working for you? My grandfather, your father—they were immigrants who had to fight people like *you*. And now, fifty years later, you're treating these new immigrants the way your father was treated . . . I can't believe it! I just can't!'

'Well, believe it. Right or wrong, I did it.'

'Then you can undo it!'

'How?'

'Get rid of Jerry Grossman.'

'You don't "get rid" of Jerry Grossman.'

'Stop paying him! That's simple enough.'

He said nothing.

'Well? Isn't it simple?'

He had been staring at his cigarette. Now he looked up at her.

'I don't know,' he said, quietly, 'and I'm afraid to find out.'

'Abe, you've *got* to find out! You've got to get the Mob out of our business . . .'

' "Our"?'

'Yes, "our." I'm your wife, remember?' She sat next to him, cooling down. 'Look, darling, there has to be a way we can do this safely. Talk to your lawyer: he'll know how to do it. Can't Grossman be bought off?'

'I don't know. Maybe.'

'But you *do* see how important it is?'

He sighed.

'Yes, I see.'

'You'll talk to your lawyer?'

'Yes, I'll talk to Allan.'

The phone rang. Gabriella got up to answer it.

'It's Maury,' she said. She watched her husband as he came to the phone. Their eyes met. He took the phone and said, 'You're right, Gabriella. I was stupid. It was the dumbest thing I've ever done in my life.'

CHAPTER 58

The store was on Eighth Avenue and Forty-first Street, in a two-story, pale-blue building squeezed between two tenements. The sign on the window read 'New Era Novelties Co., Inc.,' and the shabby display featured a cheap lamp with a hula-dancer base whose mechanical hips slowly churned. Abe Feldman rang the bell. He was apprehensive. This wasn't going to be pleasant.

The door was unlocked and opened by an ape of a man Abe knew they called Veal Chop. Veal Chop had on a black T-shirt which his muscles stretched almost to the bursting point. Veal Chop worked out with barbells. Veal Chop was proud of his muscles.

'Yeah?' he grunted.

'I want to see Jerry.'

Veal Chop opened the door wide, and Abe walked in.

'He's in his office. You know the rules, Mr. Feldman. I got to frisk you.'

'I know.'

He held up his arms as Veal Chop quickly frisked him. Then he followed Veal Chop through the empty store front to a back room where an enormously fat man with tiny porcine eyes, bulbous lips and a huge double chin was seated at an empty desk. He had a hat on, wore a vest, and was smoking a foul-smelling cigar. Behind him stood another ape, Blade. Green window blinds were pulled down. The room was hot and foul with body odor and cigar smoke.

'Good to see you, Abe,' said Jerry Grossman, indicating a chair in front of the desk. 'Take a seat.'

Abe sat down. Grossman took the cigar out of his mouth.

'We got the union off your back again,' he said. 'Those fuckers won't mess around with Summit again, if they know what's good for them.'

538

'You're wrong, Jerry. I've talked with them. They're fighting mad. Sid Cohn was one of their own, and they're mad as hell.'

'They'll get over it.'

'What if they don't? What about the police?'

Jerry smiled slightly.

'Oh yes, the police. Have they talked to you?'

'No.'

'And they won't, either. The fix is in with the police. They'll make some noise for a while, then it'll all die down and be forgotten. We don't have anything to worry about, Abe.'

'You shouldn't have murdered him, Jerry. You went too far.'

Grossman had been leaning back in his tilt chair. Now his massive body slowly tilted upright. He leaned forward on the desk, his tiny eyes twinkling angrily. There was something chthonically evil about Grossman, as if the mephitic fumes of hell seethed in his brain.

'I never go too far,' he said in his hoarse voice. 'My problem is that sometimes I don't go far enough. I don't like complaints, Abe. I stopped the strike for you, and if the union gives you more trouble, we'll handle them. But I don't like complaints. And I think it's time we renegotiated our arrangement. My expenses are going up. This last fix cost two grand. I think our fee should be three thousand a month instead of two. You know what I mean, Abe?'

Abe pulled an envelope from his inside pocket and tossed it on the desk.

'Look at what's inside that envelope, Jerry,' he said.

Grossman opened it and pulled out five one-thousand-dollar bills and three sheets of stapled paper.

'What this?'

'The five grand is your payoff,' said Abe. 'I don't want your protection anymore. The paper is a photostat of a deposition I made to my lawyer yesterday. I told him the whole story: how I hired you, how I paid you, and what you did for me. In detail. Including the murder of Sid Cohn. Now, obviously, I don't want this to go to the D.A. any more than you do, because it would mean a prison sentence for me. On the other hand, it could mean the electric chair for you.'

'You son of a bitch, are you threatening me?' Grossman roared.

'All I'm doing is protecting myself from you. I was wrong to hire you, and I'm through with you. Incidentally, I've told the union I won't give them any more trouble, and I won't.' He stood up. 'That deposition is in my lawyer's safe, and it'll stay there. But if anything happens to me, he has instructions to take it to the D.A. So don't get any cute ideas, okay?' He looked at Blade and Veal Chop. Then he went to the door.

'So long, Jerry.'

He opened the door and started out.

'Feldman.' Grossman's voice was soft. Abe turned to look at him.

'What?'

'You've made a big mistake.'

The little eyes bored into him. Abe's skin crawled for a moment. Then he left the office, closing the door behind him.

When he got back to his office, Gabriella was waiting for him.

'Well?' she said.

She was standing by a window overlooking Seventh Avenue. He came over and kissed her.

'He wasn't happy, but after I showed him the deposition there wasn't much he could say. So we're through with the Mob, and Summit's going union.'

'Thank God. Do you regret it?'

'I guess not. I suppose I was bucking the tide. What the hell, we'll still be the best on Seventh Avenue even without the edge. Maybe *you're* my edge.' He smiled slightly. 'See? You've turned me into a goddam Boy Scout.'

'You've got a way to go yet, but you get a big merit badge for hiring Rita Alvarez back. Oh Abe, I'm glad—really glad. And I'm proud of you. It took guts to do it.'

'Guts?' He sat down at his desk. 'What about Sid Cohn's guts?'

She didn't say anything for a moment. Then she came up behind him and put her hands on his shoulders.

'I've been doing a lot of thinking since you told me about Grossman. Now that we're unionized, we're going to have to be more competitive, and I think I should design a low-priced line. I think I should get into ready-to-wear because that's where the big money is.'

'Why do that? The whole idea was to beat the Paris houses at their own game, which we've done.'

'But they're giving us a lot of competition now. It was one thing eight years ago when Paris was shut down, but it's going full blast now. I can still design my couture line, but how many dresses do I sell at the prices I charge? I'd like to design a twenty-dollar dress and sell ten thousand of them, instead of selling twenty two-hundred-dollar suits.' She leaned around him

540

and opened the sketchpad she had put on his desk. 'Look at this sketch. See? It's for a college girl. Unsophisticated, simple, very feminine and you could price it under twenty dollars.'

He studied it.

'Well?' she said.

'I like the dress. I like it a lot. But why cheapen your name? We've spent a fortune making Gabriella synonymous with quality goods . . .'

'Then don't use my name. But let me do the designs. Please, Abe. I want to do it.'

'Why?'

'Because I'm your wife and I love you and I want Summit to beat hell out of the competition—honestly. Without the edge.'

He looked at her.

'You really mean that, don't you?'

'I really mean it.'

'Then do it. That's why I married you, anyway—so no one else could hire you away. By the way, did I tell you today I'm crazy about you?'

'No, you *showed* me by getting rid of Grossman.' She put her arms around him and kissed him. 'Thanks, darling,' she said. 'You're a very special man.'

The dress was given the catalog number 23-14, and 23-14 became a classic. When it appeared in the stores in August, coming in five different colors, selling at $19.95, it vanished from the racks. Summit could barely fill the reorders: Number 23-14 had magic. Its pretty simplicity appealed to girls buying their college wardrobes, and on one memorable day, August 23, 1950, 18,743 Number 23-14s were sold from coast to coast. It was, according to Abe, the hottest-selling dress in Summit's history, and to reward his wife he bought her a diamond clip from Cartier.

He also threw a cocktail party to celebrate not only Number 23-14's success but the opening of his penthouse, which Gabriella had furnished and into which she, Abe and Nick had moved in July of that year. Abe had given her carte blanche, and she had spent a fortune on the place, but as the guests swarmed around the penthouse that September night, ogling the paintings and fabrics and antiques, everyone admitted the money was well spent.

'It's fabulous,' said Millie Dexter as she took a martini from one of the dozen hired waiters. 'But I wonder why she invited us?'

'Probably to rub her success in my face,' said Drew Dexter, who hadn't seen or spoken to his niece for sixteen years.

'She's got plenty of success to rub,' replied his wife. 'Who would have thought that fat little girl would end up *the* Gabriella? Are you jealous?'

Drew shot her a look.

'Do you think I'm *that* petty?'

'I know you are.'

'Well, you're wrong. And for Chrissake, stay sober tonight. The last thing I want is for her to see you drunk.'

'Oh, shut up.'

Gabriella looked radiant in her black-and-white cocktail dress with her new diamond clip. As she greeted the guests, she thought, am I crazy or am I the happiest woman in the world? No, I'm not crazy. I *am* the happiest woman in the world! I've got the man I love, the son I love, the work I love . . . Her mind went back ten years. Nick, her first love, was a lovely, poignant memory, but one that was fading with time. That's what living must be all about, she thought: the people who come and go in your life, each leaving something good, like Nick did, or bad, like Uncle Drew . . . and doesn't *he* look envious! Good! Let him eat crow . . . The generations living their lives and giving their heritage to their children, as Grandfather did with Mother, Mother with me, and now I with Nick . . . It rolls on and on, an ocean of time, life and death, love and hate, war and peace, success and failure . . . But the best thing is love, and how I love Abe! And how funny that I almost punched him when I first met him . . .

'What are you grinning about?' said the gentleman in question, coming up beside her and kissing her. 'You look like the Cheshire cat.'

'I was just thinking about you, and that makes me feel good and I smile. Any complaints?'

'None at all. They're going through the canapés like Grant through Richmond. Do we have enough?'

'There's plenty, but I'll go check to make sure.'

She headed for the kitchen, and he went out on the terrace. The young waiter passing the tray of crabmeat balls watched him as he had been watching him throughout the party. Not yet, he thought. Not yet.

The terrace had been turned by Gabriella into a fantasy garden in the sky, with potted trees, bushes, flowers everywhere, white wrought-iron furniture, a small fountain, and, gift-wrapping everything, the most beautiful cityscape in the world. Right now the terrace was jammed. Abe circulated, making small talk with people outside the business and shoptalk with those in. The King and Queen of Seventh Avenue, he was thinking. Me and Gabriella, the King and Queen . . .

The waiter's name was Rocco Santuzzi, and his grandfather had emigrated from Naples in 1903. Rocco had grown up in Brooklyn, and his first jail term for car theft had occurred when he was fourteen. He was now twenty-seven and had been in jail one other time since his first conviction, serving four years for armed robbery. Rocco was a Mafia hit man. He had been loaned out to Jerry Grossman for this job. Not quite yet, he thought, sensing that anticipatory thrill he always felt before committing violence. After the guests have gone . . . it's got to look like an accident . . .

The invitation had read six to eight, but the last guest didn't leave until almost eight-thirty. As the waiters finished collecting the dirty glasses and ashtrays, Gabriella collapsed in a chair.

'Thank God *that's* over,' she said.

'I just realized something,' said Abe. 'I hate big cocktail parties.'

'*Now* you tell me. But I think it went well . . . Damn, don't tell me someone spilled a drink on the rug.'

She got up to investigate the spot on the carpet. As she knelt to rub her fingers through the piling, Abe wandered out on to the terrace. There were two waiters left in the room. One of them, Rocco Santuzzi, was watching the terrace door.

'I think it's Scotch,' said Gabriella. 'I'll get some rug shampoo . . .'

She went to the kitchen. The other waiter, whose name was Bill, had filled his tray.

'Tony,' he said to Rocco, 'can you get the rest of the glasses?'

'Yeah. I'll bring 'em.'

Bill headed for the kitchen, leaving Rocco alone. He set his tray on a table and went to the terrace door to look out. It was dark now, and the city and Central Park twinkled magically. Abe was standing at the brick parapet, his back to Rocco, smoking a cigarette.

Rocco moved quietly toward him.

He was two feet behind him when Abe turned. He stared at the waiter.

'What the hell do you want?' he said.

'I'm delivering a message from Jerry Grossman.' And he charged him like a bull, pushing Abe in the chest with both hands and all his 175 pounds of muscle. Abe shouted as he fell back on the cement top of the parapet, taken completely by surprise. Rocco held him down with one hand on his stomach while he grabbed his legs with the other and lifted them up. Abe, terrified, looked down at Fifth Avenue fifteen floors below as Rocco started lifting him over the parapet. Howling, Abe managed to throw his arms around his neck. In sheer desperation he squeezed Rocco's neck as the Italian pushed him over the parapet and let go his legs. Now Abe was dangling over the street, hanging on to life by Rocco's neck, but Rocco was breaking his hold. Don't look down! he thought in panic as his feet groped for a toehold on the stone cornice he knew was just below the terrace. He felt Rocco's hands tearing at his arms. He heard a doorman's whistle blowing for a taxi below. His panicked brain thought of falling, falling . . . then the blackness of impact. His right foot felt the stone cornice, which jutted six inches from the face of the building, the architectural grace notes of the past giving him a foothold in midair. Then his other foot found the cornice, giving him some leverage, but Rocco had just about broken his hold. Despite his footing on the cornice, Abe had no balance, nor was there anything to grab on to once his grip was broken. He would fall backward and down. Fight him! he thought. Fight him . . . His face was inches below Rocco's, who was leaning over the parapet, panting heavily. Now Abe felt two hands grab his right arm just below the shoulder. Simultaneously, something smashed on Rocco's skull above him. He heard the man grunt, felt his grip go loose. He heard Gabriella saying, 'We've got you, we've got you . . .' Then he felt two more hands grab his left arm. Gabriella and Bill, the waiter, slowly pulled him up over the parapet. When he dropped to the terrace floor, he lay still, his eyes shut, his body trembling with the cold sweat of terror. He heard Gabriella telling the waiter to call the police. Then she was kneeling beside him, hugging him.

'Thank God, thank God,' she kept saying as she kissed him.

After she helped him to his feet, he looked at Rocco, who was lying on the terrace face up, still unconscious from the Scotch bottle Gabriella had smashed over his head.

'The son of a bitch pushed me,' said Abe, his teeth chattering. 'He *pushed* me! I've never been so scared in my fucking life!'

He doubled over and vomited in a bed of geraniums.

An hour later, after the police had taken Rocco Santuzzi away, Abe said, 'I need a drink *bad.*' He went to the bar and poured himself a double Scotch. He was still trembling slightly, but he felt better. 'And to think I've never been scared of heights!' he said, belting down half the drink. 'God.'

After he sat down, Gabriella said, 'Why didn't you tell the police about Grossman?'

'Because I'm going to send the deposition to the D.A. tomorrow.'

'But . . .' she looked at him. 'That means you'll go to jail.'

'Gabriella, I should have done it last spring after Cohn was murdered. Now I don't have any choice. Grossman must have thought if he had me pushed off the terrace, it would look like an accident, or maybe suicide. He's probably broken into Allan's safe tonight and destroyed the deposition. But if he has, I'll make a new one. Grossman's going to pay for this one.'

He drank more Scotch.

'If you go to jail,' she said, quietly, 'how long would it be?'

'Allan told me he might get me a suspended sentence. The worst would be a year or two. What the hell, I'll take jail over falling fifteen floors to Fifth Avenue. Jesus!' He finished his Scotch, then looked at his wife. 'Will you mind being married to a con?'

He said it lightly, but she knew he was afraid. She came to him and kissed him.

'We married for better or for worse,' she said. 'I've loved the better, and I can take the worse.'

He caressed her cheek.

'I need you,' was all he said.

'And I need you. I guess that's what love's all about.'

PART XIV

GIVE ME YOUR TIRED, YOUR POOR

1959–1960

CHAPTER 59

Morris David got up from his chair and turned off the television.

'It's crap!' he snorted. 'They call that entertainment? It's boring. And every three minutes, a commercial . . .'

'Oh Morris,' said Barbara, who was working on her needlepoint, 'stop picking on television. After all, it's free. And you like Lucy.'

'Lucy, Lucy, how many times can I watch Lucy? It's too little! Movies used to be big, but television's like a peanut. And the peanut's killing movies! I hate it! I hate television!'

He went back to his chair and sulked into it. They were in the library of Casa del Mar. The estate that forty years before had been built in a near wilderness was now surrounded by Beverly Hills as Los Angeles continued to grow and grow and grow.

'Remember how it used to be?' he went on. 'It used to be fun. It used to be exciting. What's the movie business now? Deals.'

'It always was deals, darling. And people have been saying for ten years that television is going to kill off the movies, and it hasn't happened yet. You're just restless and bored. I think we should take a trip.'

'Another cruise? Could I stand another cruise? A ship full of old dodoes playing bridge . . .'

'*We're* old dodoes.'

'Seventy-one's not old! Well, it's not young, but I don't feel old. I tell you, Barbara, I should never have sold the studio. It was a dumb mistake. Now I've got nothing to do but count my money and watch television.'

'I remember when you told me you wanted to be rich more than anything else.'

'Rich is all right, but making movies is better. You know . . .'

He stopped. She looked at him. He sank even farther down into his chair.

'Do I know what?'

'Forget it. It's crazy.'

'Morris, you've *always* been crazy. That's why I love you. If you went sane now, I don't know what I'd do with you.'

He sat up. She recognized the look in his eye. She hadn't seen it since he produced his last movie six years before, the movie that had flopped even worse than its three predecessors. Everyone said that Morris David was out of date, out of touch with the times, or just plain cornball. It had crushed his ego to the point of his selling David Productions to the enemy, a television studio. But now the look was back in his eye.

'I've been doing a lot of thinking lately,' he said. 'I haven't got much else to do. Anyway, I'm thinking about writing a movie. Oh, I know what you're going to say: Morris, you're too old, the business is run by the young, but hear me out. It's not a bad idea.'

'I'm listening.'

'The immigrants are dying out. Me, I don't even remember the old country, I was too young, but I can remember the Lower East Side, what it was like. But in ten years—who knows? Maybe twenty?—I'll be gone and we'll *all* be gone and there won't be anybody who really lived through it. It'll all just be . . . history. You know what I mean? And it shouldn't just be history because it was too important. I mean, we immigrants made this country what it is today. People like your father, my father, me . . . Am I making any sense?'

'You want to write a movie about immigrants?'

'Yes. My childhood, maybe your father's story . . . a big movie, a big funny movie.'

'Funny? You'd make it a comedy?'

'Sure. I'd have to. That's all I can write. Remember what happened to *Russia*—or what didn't happen, thanks to you.'

'I remember.'

'Well, I want to be able to sell this thing, so it'd be a comedy. But I think I could do it. I'd *like* to do it. What do you think?'

She put down her needlework and smiled at him.

'Do it,' she said.

He looked pleased.

Enrico Spada looked at the marble statue of the three men bound together at the wrists, approaching their deaths, and he remembered fifteen years before watching his father, Fausto, being driven away from St. Peter's to his death. Now the Ardeatine Caves were a national monument. Once a month

550

Enrico and his wife, Claudia, and their two sons drove out from Rome to put fresh flowers on the mausoleum inside the caves that held the remains of the 335 victims of the massacre. After Rome was liberated, it had taken a team of scientists six ghoulish months to identify the piles of rotting cadavers they had found in the caves. Enrico had identified his father's body only by the necktie Fausto had worn.

Solemnly he and his family walked past the memorial statue into the caves, Claudia carrying a vase of red roses. Fifteen years. Would the world some day forget? Perhaps. But he, Enrico, would never forget. His mother, Nanda, would never forget.

Claudia placed the roses in front of the mausoleum, then the four of them knelt to pray. Most of the men responsible for the massacre had been punished, though some of them, like Kesselring, had been pardoned, to howls of outrage from the Italians. Most of the money and some of the jewels had eventually been returned, though Paolo Montecatini never lived to see it. Enrico was now the head of the family. He ran his grandfather's jewelry business and voted the Communist Party. Life went well for Enrico.

But he would never forget. The caves had lost the horrible odor of the rotting corpses, but the stench would linger in the memory for generations.

'They're idiots!' shouted Morris David. 'How can they say my script isn't funny? What do they know from funny? Sitcoms? They're idiots!'

'Morris,' said his wife, 'calm down. Eat your lunch.'

'I'm not hungry.'

They were sitting at an umbrella table beside the pool at Casa del Mar. It was a warm day, and the smog was strangling Los Angeles.

'It's funny!' insisted Morris, returning to the attack. 'I know, and who knows comedy better than Morris David? Wasn't I the King of Comedy? I've made thirty-three movies, they're going to tell *me* about movies? They study my old movies in university film courses, and *these shmucks* are going to tell *me?*'

'Morris,' sighed Barbara, 'you're not being reasonable. Maybe you should listen to them. Maybe they're right.'

'How can slapstick not be funny? A man slips on a banana peel, it's funny. It was funny in 1915, and it's funny now.'

'Maybe it's *not* funny now.'

He glared at her.

'Why?'

'Because people today aren't innocent like we were. They've seen too much, lived through too much. People today are worried about hydrogen bombs.'

'What's hydrogen bombs got to do with banana peels?'

'All right, I wasn't going to tell you this, but I think maybe I should. Last week, I sent a copy of the script to Gabriella's son. You know Nick is crazy about movies, and I thought it would be interesting to get his opinion . . .'

'Why?'

'Because he's nineteen.'

Morris looked worried. He had a vague feeling the young were the enemy.

'And what did he say?'

'It's not black enough.'

'I'm writing a movie about *shvartzes?*'

'No, the *humor's* not black enough. But he loved the story. He loved the immigrants. He found them fascinating.'

'Of course they're fascinating! But it's funny! It's got to be funny—I wrote it!'

'Morris, did it ever occur to you that for once in your life, you might have written a drama that works?'

He looked suspicious.

'What do you mean?'

'This is what you tried to do with *Russia*. You wanted *Russia* to be a drama, remember? Well, you've made *Give Me Your Tired, Your Poor* a drama that could work, if you'd take out all the dated comedy routines. You probably made it work because it's your story.'

He thought about this.

'You mean I should tell it straight?'

'Yes. And have I ever led you wrong? Tell it straight because it's wonderful just as it is. There'll be humorous things in it, but it won't be slapstick. It will be real humor about real people. I think there'd be a big audience for it. You might have a hit.'

He took a bite of his chicken salad. Barbara knew he was hooked.

'It *is* a good story, isn't it?' he finally said, rather sheepishly.

The premiere of *Give Me Your Tired, Your Poor* took place on December 19, 1960, and old Hollywood hands reveled in nostalgia at the searchlights, the limousines, the police barricades, the crowds of fans. 'Morris David knows how to do it right,' said Laura Kaye to her fourth husband, a Texas oil man, as they climbed out of their Rolls-Royce in front of Grauman's Chinese. She remembered the premiere of *Russia,* so many years before, another world away. She wondered how many of the fans would remember *her.* Probably not many. She had never told any of her husbands she had once been Morris David's mistress . . .

Not too many of the fans recognized Laura Kaye, but they all recognized and cheered Erica Stern, who still looked stunning and incredibly young for her age. And a surprising number of them recognized Gabriella Feldman when she and Abe and Nick stepped out of their limousine. 'Look!' said one teenage girl who worshipped Elvis Presley. 'That's *the* Gabriella, the dress designer! I saw her on Jack Paar.'

'Oh, look at her dress!' squealed her female companion.

'Isn't it dreamy! That must be her husband, the one who went to jail . . .'

'Yeah,' said a boy standing next to her. 'I read about him in *Playboy.* He was mixed up with the Mafia.'

'Isn't everybody?' said an older man behind him.

'Not Morris David,' said his wife. 'Those old-timers were honest.'

'How do you know?'

'Because the country used to be honest.'

Honest, thought Abe Feldman, who had overheard the remark. Jail. Two years of my life. How humiliating and frightening it had been to go to jail, and yet the surprising thing had been that he had grown used to it. And Gabriella's loyalty and support had made it seem, if not pleasant, at least bearable. Now that it was all over, he was almost proud that he had gone to jail, proud that he had survived it. He was not a religious man, but he had paid for his sins the hard way, and now life was uncommonly sweet. He looked at his wife—so beautiful in her white satin dress, almost regal with the blood-red rubies he had given her around her throat—and he was reminded how much in love with her he was. 'You,' he whispered in her ear, 'are the best thing that ever happened to me.'

Gabriella looked surprised at the unexpected compliment, but she also looked pleased.

'We make a good team,' she smiled, taking his arm as they went into the crowded lobby. And that was what their marriage had turned out to be: teamwork. She and Abe shared everything in their lives, their work as well as their play, and in that she thought she was extremely lucky. A helluva lot luckier than poor Aunt Millie, she thought, spotting the haggard Mrs. Drew

Dexter ahead of her in the crowd. If a successful marriage was based on teamwork and sharing, then Drew and Millie's marriage was a classic example of the disastrous effects of nonsharing.

For thirty-five years Drew had shared nothing with his wife except his bed (and, lately, not even that), and the result had been predictable: alcoholism for Millie and a string of expensive mistresses for Drew. Being the wife of the president of the Dexter Bank meant seeing her husband only on social occasions, like this premiere. Drew didn't want a divorce: for such a cynical man, he had a quaintly old-fashioned belief that divorce carried a stigma, that it might damage the prestige of the bank. Millie didn't give a damn anymore whether they divorced or not. All she cared about was her martinis. Right now, all she could think was that she wished this goddam movie were over so she could get drunk. Drinking meant forgetting the broken promise that was her life.

Am I better? the voice whispered in Drew's ear as the usher led him and Millie to their reserved seats. Am I better than my father? Morris David had been amazed when Drew had called from New York and offered to finance *Give Me Your Tired, Your Poor*. Morris didn't know how Drew had heard he was having difficulty raising the nine million dollars for the movie—none of the young producers had liked the script—and the offer had been doubly startling because neither Drew nor his bank had ever shown any interest in the film business. But Drew had said he wanted to do it 'for old times' sake,' a vague expression that covered a lot of territory, and Morris, remembering Drew's treachery toward Barbara, had accepted. Drew hadn't even wanted to read the script.

Am I better than my father? The question that had nagged Drew all his life continued to nag him as he sat down. He was certainly richer than his father: Drew's fortune was three times what Victor's had been at his death. He was perhaps more influential on Wall Street. But Drew, for all his faults, wasn't stupid. In his heart he knew he wasn't better than his father. When he looked at Millie's drink-ravaged face; when he thought of his son, George, a lackluster yes-man who would some day inherit the bank and probably make a hash of it; when he thought of his second son, Andrew, who hated Drew and who had become a beatnik writing bad anti-Establishment poetry in Greenwich Village, living with a male lover; when he thought of the shambles his family had become, Drew knew that somehow he was worse than his father. Victor had been capable of loving others. Drew had never really loved anyone but himself. Which was why, at the age of sixty, he had decided to finance Morris's movie. It was a feeble step toward doing Something Good, but it was a step. He was getting more and more involved with organized charity. Maybe he might even set up a foundation some day. There were nice tax advantages in foundations, and with the Drew Dexter Foundation, perhaps that nagging question that had whispered in his mind all his life might have a more positive answer.

Nicholas Victor Kemp was thinking neither of his family nor of his past. Nick, now twenty and as good-looking as his father had been, was thinking about movies and the future and the Army. Above all other things, Nick wanted to make movies like his Uncle Morris—write them at first, then some day perhaps direct them. But in two years Nick would be out of Princeton and draft bait, and what would that mean? Might he end up a statistic like the father he had never known? Right now the world seemed peaceful enough, but there was more and more talk in the newspapers about Vietnam . . . Nick told himself to relax and enjoy the movie. Afterward, he could blot out the future with a joint. He followed his mother and Abe down the aisle of the gaudy theater and then took his seat between them.

For Gabriella, Morris's movie premiere was exciting, but in her mind another movie was unwinding in reverse. The presence of all her relatives, as well as her imminent fiftieth birthday (she now needed glasses to read, a harsh fact of middle age that had shocked her), threw her thoughts back over her life. Nick sailing off to the Philippines . . . she could still remember the hurt, although to her son the war was an unreal event, the subject of old movies seen on The Late Show. She remembered her grandmother Lucille, once so formidable and frightening to a fat little girl: how odd that Lucille, of all people, had taken over her young life and remolded her! She remembered the stock market crash—now as remote to most people as the Middle Ages—and her grandfather dying in front of her in the library of his apartment. Back, back her thoughts went through events that predated her own life but about which she had heard from relatives. Family stories, the album or scrapbook of her genes: Victor's struggle for control of the bank . . . Victor brawling in a gilded ballroom of the Nineties . . . Victor arriving in America, a frightened twelve-year-old Sicilian . . . Back even further to the Civil War and a young Gus Dexter buying jewels from an aged slave to found the family fortune. And before that, what? An America that was gone forever, a virgin, rural

America that was almost a myth, an America filled with faceless ancestors she knew nothing about and yet whose lives had contributed something to hers. She suddenly felt proud of what she had achieved in her life but also of what her whole family had achieved. Also she realized how important Morris's movie was, not only because it had given an old man something to do, but because it would recapture for millions of people a part of the precious past.

Impulsively she leaned over to give him a kiss.

'I'm so excited, Uncle Morris,' she exclaimed. 'The movie's going to be a hit!'

'You think?' said Morris, morosely. He was trying to look confident, but he was terrified. What if they don't like it? What if they laugh at it instead of with it? Was it too sentimental, too cornball? Nine million dollars! My God, he could remember when you could have bought Hollywood for nine million dollars . . . 'Who knows if it's any good?'

'*I* know,' said Gabriella. 'And my son knows. He read the final script and loved it. And if the *kids* like it . . .'

'Don't say any more. I'm superstitious.'

'All right, but don't worry. It's *got* to be a hit. It's the story of America, and America's a damned good country.'

Morris remembered Hester Street and Victor and the old days and the immigrants, and suddenly he wasn't so nervous. His niece was right: with all its faults, it was a damned good country. *Give Me Your Tired, Your Poor* had to be a hit.

And it was.

Begun in Rome, January, 1977.
Finished in New York, August, 1980.

THE END

PORTRAITS by Cynthia Freeman

The tempestuous, rags-to-riches novel of an immigrant family in America—their dreams and heartaches—their struggle to survive in an alien country . . .

JACOB   whose newfound wealth could never fill the aching void inside him.

SARA   who sacrificed everything in the name of love—even her daughter.

SHLOMO   who kept the family's disgrace a secret, and paid the price.

RACHEL   whose forbidden love for one man drove her into the arms of another.

DORIS   a Cinderella who achieved fame and happiness beyond her wildest dreams.

0 552 11730 7   Price: £1.95

A WORLD FULL OF STRANGERS by Cynthia Freeman

The story of a family you'll never forget! A rich, dramatic saga of passion and love, of sin and retribution, spanning three generations of family life—from the ghettos of New York to the glittering hills of San Francisco. . . .

DAVID   who destroyed his past to live a life of power and glory.

KATIE   who lived with her past, whose roots and memories were too deep for her ever to be able to forget.

MARK   their son, who had the courage to struggle towards the sacred heritage his father had denied him.

MAGGIE the successful and glamorous woman David wanted because she was everything Katie was not.

0 552 11775 7   Price: £1.95

JUST ABOVE MY HEAD by James Baldwin

"A novel that can overwhelm you"

SCOTSMAN

In this powerful and compassionate epic, James Baldwin returns to the New York negro revivalist scenes of his first great novel,
GO TELL IT ON THE MOUNTAIN

Tracing three decades of American history, from the violence of the South in the '60s to the civil rights rallies in the black churches, it is the story of a black gospel singer, Arthur Montana, the 'emperor of soul', evoked through the memories of his middle-aged brother Hal.

Two years after Arthur's untimely death in the basement of a London pub, Hal is still haunted by the memory of his younger brother, by the family ties that had bound them together in the face of the whirlwind hatred of the white south . . . and by the love each had felt for Julia and Jimmy Miller, brother and sister.

"This is surely Baldwin's most powerful novel for some fifteen years . . . parts of it . . . are as memorable as anything he has done".

FINANCIAL TIMES

0 552 11552 5   £1.95

A SELECTION OF CORGI TITLES

While every effort is made to keep prices low, it is sometimes necessary to increase prices at short notice. Corgi Books reserve the right to show new retail prices on covers which may differ from those previously advertised in the text or elsewhere.

All these books are available at your book shop or newsagent, or can be ordered direct from the publisher. Just tick the titles you want and fill in the form below.

CORGI BOOKS, Cash Sales Department, P.O. Box 11, Falmouth, Cornwall.

Please send cheque or postal order, no currency.

Please allow cost of book(s) plus the following for postage and packing:

U.K. Customers—Allow 45p for the first book, 20p for the second book and 14p for each additional book ordered, to a maximum charge of £1.63.

B.F.P.O. and Eire—Allow 45p for the first book, 20p for the second book plus 14p per copy for the next 7 books, thereafter 8p per book.

Overseas Customers—Allow 75p for the first book and 21p per copy for each additional book.

NAME (Block Letters) ....

ADDRESS ....

....